THE DAIYAKU
TRACY HARKIN

ISBN: 9798322107163

Copyright© T K Harkin 2024

The right of Tracy Harkin to be identified as the author of this work has been asserted by her in accordance with the Copyright, Designs and Patents Act 1988

TRANSLATION

Daiyaku = Substitute/Stand-In/Replacement

CHAPTER 1

AS I DISTRIBUTED the textbooks to the eight students in the room, I noticed the businessman, Yuuto, staring at me. His gaze was fixed, the expression on his face bold and appraising. I was aware of my irritation at the intrusiveness of his stare. It felt a disrespecting of my personal space. I did not know it then, but Yuuto was gearing up to make a proposition that would change my life. Unaware of this, I merely shrugged, choosing to ignore him.

The rest of the class were waiting politely; seven sets of attentive eyes. Having gleaned the basics from them, I realised that they anticipated a similar level of disclosure from me. The youngest, Akari, broke the silence:

"Is Quinn a popular name in England?"

I smiled. "No; it's Celtic; fairly unusual as a first name."

"You're Irish?" Akari again.

"Quarter Irish. My grandfather came over to London from Dublin in his twenties, married a local woman, had four kids, including my dad. All my family still live in the London area." I laughed. "Apart from me of course, I'm here in Tokyo now, for the foreseeable future at least."

"You plan to stay a long time?" Yuuto this time.

"I'm not sure. A couple of years maybe."

I paused. The class was looking at me expectantly, seeming to want more information. I switched my gaze to the window and then back to my students again.

"I studied Japanese at university, spent my second year in Osaka. I was speaking Japanese quite well by the end of my time living there. I'd like to get back to the same level of fluency as I had then, perhaps use Japanese in a work context when I return to the UK."

I smiled at their interested faces. "Back home, I'm an actor. It's inconsistent work and I need other ways of earning money when I'm in between roles.

"日本語を英語に翻訳する仕事を探すか、英語を日本語に翻訳したいですか？"

Akari had fired the question at me in rapid Japanese and I responded to the playful challenge with a mock-stern shake of the head.

"If you think you are going to test my Japanese Akari-san, you have the wrong idea. This is an advanced class, remember. We will not be speaking any Japanese in my lessons, only English. That's my number one rule…;" I paused, "…. although to answer your question, I think it's always easier for a native speaker to translate from the foreign language into her own."

I moved towards a table at the side of me and picked up a copy of the book I had distributed to the class.

"Ok, everybody, this is the course we are going to be working through over the summer. Let's start with some preparatory revision."

After two hours of questions and discursive conversation, I had a good measure of the class. I was pleased. All eight seemed to be at roughly the same level and were higher performing students. It would make classes more interesting and, in many ways, easier to prepare for.

"Right, folks, I think that's enough for this evening. If you could read the first chapter of your course book and complete the exercises in there for homework, we'll go through your answers at the start of the next session."

I bent to repack my bag as the students stood up and began to file out. Akari waved to me from the door. I nodded a goodbye and then saw that Yuuto had not moved. He was the only one of the eight still sitting at his desk.

"No home to go to Yuuto-san?"

He looked at me quizzically and I realised that it was probably an English expression he was not familiar with.

"I was wondering why you hadn't left with the others. Is there anything else you need to know about the course?"

Yuuto shook his head, stood up and gave me a small bow. "Not about the course, no. But if I may, I wanted to ask you if you would be interested in additional work whilst you are in Tokyo?"

The question surprised me, but I was relieved too. He had bowed which had reset the correct boundaries between us.

"What sort of work?"

Yuuto raised his hand to wipe a sheen of sweat from his face. There was no air conditioning in the room and despite all the windows having been thrown open, it felt hot and close indoors. Yuuto's action conveyed more than the effects of humidity, however; he seemed nervous.

"When you were telling us about yourself, you mentioned that you were an actor. The work is an acting role but in a domestic rehabilitation setting."

I raised an eyebrow. "What does that mean?"

Yuuto walked to the window and gestured for me to come over to him. We were ten floors up and had a view that extended several kilometres across Tokyo.

"See the green building over there; the one grouped with a number of grey skyscrapers rising above everything else?"

Yuuto pointed towards the west and following his finger, I squinted into the evening sun.

"I have an office on the twenty second floor. If you could come to see me sometime this week, I will show you a short video which will answer your questions. Would you be able to come?"

I met Yuuto's eyes. I was curious. "Why can't you tell me now? Please don't take offence but you seem uneasy, and I am wondering why?"

He nodded. "I'm sorry. I'm not being transparent. I very much want you to take the work; it has not been easy to find somebody suitable."

He held up his palms. "I will be honest; I saw you enter this building last week and I made enquiries about you. I signed up for this course so that I could assess your fit for the role. You would be perfect, but I am not able to show you with words. I need to play you the video."

I stepped back instinctively, widening the space between us. Yuuto's explanation was strange, but I was intrigued and, perhaps because of his deferential manner, I did not feel threatened.

"I don't think so, Yuuto-san. I'm not looking for extra work. The language school is paying me enough to get by."

Yuuto clasped his hands together and pushed them towards me. "Please come. I only ask for you to watch the video and listen to what I have to say. If you are not interested once you have seen it, this is not a problem. Of course, I will accept this."

I looked at him hard. He seemed sincere. I did not see that it would do any harm to visit his office.

"Alright, I'll come. I could make it tomorrow lunchtime if that is any good."

"Yes, yes, thank you. I do appreciate this."

He pulled out a business card from his trouser pockets and bowing more deeply this time held it out to me with both hands. "The address is on the card; the nearest station is Nishi-Shinjuku on the Marunouchi line. Ask the ground floor reception to ring me when you arrive; I'll come down for you."

I flushed. I had heard of the custom of *meishi koukan* in Japan - the formality and import attached to the exchange of business cards - but I did not have one to hand over in return. It was not something that I had thought I would need as an employed teacher and tourist. I took the card from Yuuto in the same way that he had proffered it to me.

"Thank you. I am afraid I don't have a card to give you in return. Typical *gaijin.*"

I laughed to cover my awkwardness, but Yuuto did not seem concerned. He bowed to me one last time and turning on his heel, left the room.

CHAPTER 2

THE PHONE WOULD NOT FIRE UP. I found myself staring at a red exclamation mark which filled the entire screen. No power. The battery was drained. I had plugged it in last night but forgotten to switch on the plug at the wall. It was too late to go back to my room. I had just changed trains at Ogikubo and was now on the Marunoushi line. This would take me directly to the station near Yuuto's office. It was a forty-minute train ride to Nishi-Shinjuku from the university hall where I was staying, and I had told Yuuto that I would be with him for twelve. There was no time to go back and in any case the trains were busy; I could not face a return ride just to come back again. I would have to ask him if I could charge my mobile at his office. Right now, though, it meant that I could not check out his website before the meeting.

Dammit! I was angry with myself. I should have done my research on Yuuto last night but had been too tired by the time I got back to my room. I pulled out Yuuto's business card. It was pale yellow with forest green typescript and had the words Family Bonds in large font across the centre; the words were in Japanese but had the English translation in smaller font underneath. Below this was Yuuto's full name 'Yuuto Hiroshini,' a telephone number, and his office address; again, both the Japanese and English translations were provided. There were no other words to explain the nature of Yuuto's business. Peering more closely, I could see a faint ink drawing behind the words. It depicted a family - a Japanese couple, with their hands placed upon the shoulders of two small children who were standing in front of them. I turned the card over; there was a map on the back, a sketch of the few streets around Nishi-Shinjuku station and a large green dot highlighting the location of Yuuto's offices. That was all the information I had to go on; that and what Yuuto had told me yesterday.

My gaze drifted away from the business card and out through the window of the train. As the track turned slightly to the right, I caught sight of the Nishi-Shinjuku area coming into view, demarcated by a horizon of skyscrapers clustered together and stretching high into the Tokyo sky. The Green Tower housing Yuuto's office space was standing amongst them. I would be there in less than ten minutes.

"You sit there please. I will get the recording ready."

I looked at the low table, Yuuto had signalled towards. His office consisted of one large room which he had divided into two discrete areas by way of a wooden screen which slid back into the wall. The first area housed a couple of desks and filing cabinets, as well as a small kitchen area along the back wall. The second area was set up for meetings. There was a white display panel at the far end with a computer stand in front of it. In the middle of the space was the low table, large and square, made from red cherry wood. Yuuto had placed a jug of water and two glasses on its surface. Positioned on the floor and running along each side of the table, was a brightly coloured array of cushions. The one window in the room extended the full length of both sections and rose from floor to ceiling in height. Looking out, I could see a spectacular view of the city.

I moved towards the table and lowered myself onto one of the cushions. To my surprise, I discovered that there was a cavity in the floor, beneath the table, into which I could swing my legs. I allowed my eyes to wander around the room. The wall space was covered with photographs. They seemed to be family portraits, set within the context of weddings, celebratory dinners, and holidays. I glanced at Yuuto. He had his back to me and was bending over the computer stand, fiddling with a lead running from a laptop. This second encounter was reinforcing my first impression of him. He was average in height, slim in stature, and had an air of quick nervous energy about him. I guessed that, like me, he was in his late thirties. He dressed well; standard black business suit, jazzed up today with a bold orange shirt. His hair, thick and black, was long on top, with a tendency to flop forward onto his face. He could be a model, having the fine angular cheekbones of somebody who might make a living out of his looks. I would not be surprised to learn that he had an artistic background.

Yuuto stood up straight and pivoted round. Seeing me seated, he smiled.

"Good, you are comfortable, yes. Please help yourself to a glass of water. I have two videos to show you."

He walked over, bringing the control handset with him, and sat down on the other side of the table.

"The first recording is a promotional one for my company; it explains the services we offer. When you have finished watching it, I will answer any questions you have and then we will look at the second video. The second video is about the specific job I thought you might be interested in."

Yuuto pressed the play button, and I switched my attention to the screen. The video began with a camera shot positioned high above an expansive park. The frame slowly closed in on an area of cherry blossom trees. Traditional Japanese instrumental music accompanied the scene as the focus gradually descended to narrow down on a bench beneath one of the trees. On the bench sat Yuuto. As the camera zoomed in on his face, he smiled in welcome and began his pitch.

The video ran for approximately ten minutes. It mainly consisted of Yuuto talking but, every now and again, the camera took a break from his face to show clips of other people being interviewed. They were being asked to provide comment on his company's services. I found myself watching with growing astonishment. It appeared that the services Yuuto offered were replacements for family members who might have left, gone missing or died. The replacements were actors he had recruited because they looked and sounded like the person they were intended to replace. It was rarely a full-time, live-in arrangement; more commonly, the replacement would spend regular allotted periods with the family each week. During that time, they would assume the role of the person who was no longer there.

When the video had finished, Yuuto turned towards me, a broad smile on his face.

"So, this is my company, the service I provide. Have you any questions?"

I was slow to respond. I was finding it difficult to digest what I had seen and heard.

"I am lost for words, Yuuto-san. This is not a service I have come across before. I don't want to be negative, but I have reservations about this. The replacement is not offering a real or permanent relationship. How is this helping the family? Wouldn't they be better off grieving for a period and then moving on with their lives?"

Yuuto looked out of the window. He appeared to be reflecting on my words. Moments passed before he said anything.

"I understand what you are saying but the service my company offers does not preclude this. You must understand that my typical client is a salary man who has lost his wife. This could be for one of many reasons. At this point in his career, work is a priority. He often does not have the time to start dating again. He may also have children that need taking care of. This takes up more of his time. It is often a requirement of his job that he attend business events and host dinners. It is not always easy for him to do this alone. The replacement is there to tide him over, until hopefully he meets somebody else."

I ran a hand through my hair. "Don't misunderstand me Yuuto, I do realise how difficult it is to meet somebody new if you lose your partner and have a full-time job and childcare responsibilities, but the replacement is not a real relationship. Again, I don't want to be critical, but the arrangement you are offering feels false, a sham."

Yuuto shrugged; he did not seem phased by my directness. "I disagree; I think it is pragmatic and therapeutic. In any case, the family never introduces the replacement as a replacement to the external world. They introduce him or her as the client's husband, wife, sister, son, whoever it is that they are replacing. Often the person receiving the introduction has never met the real relative so does not realise that he or she is a replacement."

I screwed up my face, trying to understand. I was struggling to follow the logic. "I don't really get it," I confessed. I understand the concept of escorts, but not replacements for real people." I sighed. "What does the role involve in practice?"

Yuuto leant forward; he seemed excited by my question. "It is a dream acting role and it is how my company differs from the other replacement services out there. I ask the people I hire to learn everything they can about the person they are replacing. You talk to the family members and their friends. You watch videos of the person. You read their correspondence. You study the way they moved, their voice and the way they spoke. You memorise the key facts about them. When you have done this, you are ready to start. You become the missing person for that family for the contracted time that you spend with them. But here is the best part. You can be the best version of that person, a version without the flaws and irritants."

Yuuto finished his promotional speech with a gleeful clap of his hands and looked at me expectantly. I laughed.

"Well, I can see that you are enthusiastic about the service you provide. But tell me, have there been incidents with the actors you hire where things have gone wrong? For instance, how do you manage a client who becomes overly dependent on the relationship, starts thinking the relationship is real, falls in love with the replacement, starts making demands that the replacement can't meet."

Yuuto frowned, his expression turning serious. "No, we have not had that happen. We take careful steps to explain the parameters of the contract with the client. I hold regular reviews with them to check that they are happy with the service they are receiving; I would soon detect if anything seemed wrong. I have been a replacement, so I have first-hand experience of the role. When I started the company, I was the only actor on my books." Yuuto grinned. "I am still a replacement, in fact."

I leant forward. "Go on."

"When I started the company ten years ago, a young woman, whose husband had committed suicide, contacted me. She had a two-year old daughter, and she was concerned that the child would grow up without a father figure in her life. She hired me to be the replacement father, to visit the child each weekend, to take her to the park and to the zoo. When the girl started school, I attended parent evenings and other educational events. I am still fulfilling this service."

I stared at him in disbelief. "That little girl is how old now? Twelve? Are you saying that she thinks you are her real father?" I shook my head. "You are going to have to sustain that lie your whole life or that little girl is going to find out that you're not who you say you are? How do you think she is going to feel when that happens?"

Yuuto looked down. There was a short pause before he started talking again.

"Yes, it is a tricky situation. The girl's mother was my first client. I was not sufficiently experienced to know the situations to avoid. We do not take on this type of case anymore, unless the mother is prepared to be honest with her children, to ensure that they know the truth as soon as they are old enough to understand. I have committed myself to this little girl and her mother though; nowadays it is against my company's rules to sustain the service for so long, but I have made this case an exception because it was my first."

"What do you mean?"

"I mean that I will continue to support the family for as long as they want me in their lives. I have become very much their defacto husband and father. It gives me pleasure now, but it is an exception. Because of the difficulties and inherent problems that you have highlighted, the actors I hire sign a contract, stating that they will not work with a client for more than three years. That is usually long enough for the client to move on emotionally. My actors must prepare their client for termination of the service, during the third year of the arrangement. I also forbid them to accept any gift of monetary value from the client, over and above the salary I pay them. Those are the rules; they are important if we are to avoid lawsuits for undue influence, fraud, and the like."

I looked away from him. There was another pause, a longer one this time. When I looked back, he was sitting forward, his elbows on the table, watching me intently.

"Have you more confidence in my agency, now that I have explained this?"

"I don't know. This service you provide; it's a psychological minefield. I'm not sure what I think about it."

"Please don't make a judgement yet. Let me show you the second video."

Yuuto picked up his handset again and pressed several buttons in rapid succession. The second video began to play. A Japanese man, looking to be in his late forties, came into view. He was dressed casually, in jeans and a high neck jumper, and sat on an olive-green futon. I could see the edge of a small low table in front of him and a large painting on the back wall; it looked to be a life size portrait of the same man, sitting with a woman and child.

The camera's focus moved in on the futon to provide a clearer view of the man. He had black hair, neatly cut, thick but greying at the sides, and a soft round face, with deep set eyes. There was an air of melancholy about him. Off screen, I could hear another man's voice; I was not sure, but it sounded like Yuuto.

"I know you speak good English so would it be ok if we conducted this interview in English rather than Japanese?"

The man inclined his head to give a gracious side-cocked nod.

"Thank you. Could we start by you telling me a bit about yourself? Your name, age, where you live, your job?"

"My name is Reo, Reo Takahashi, of Tanaka Pharmaceuticals. I am forty-eight years old, and I live in Tokyo, the Kichijoji district."

"Thank you, Takahashi-san. What is your actual job at Tanaka?"

"I am a research chemist and Director of the company's cancer research programme."

"That sounds very worthwhile. Would you explain why you have approached my company and what you are hoping to get from the services we offer?"

The man straightened up, taking a noticeable breath.

"Eight months ago, my wife died in a climbing accident. It left me alone with my eleven-year-old daughter. We miss her very much…."

The man's voice broke off. Quinn heard Yuuto, for she was confident that it was his voice now, respond in a low and sympathetic tone.

"This must be a difficult time for you. That painting on the wall – it is a portrait of the three of you?"

The man shifted position to look at the painting and then, turning back to his interviewer, nodded. The camera zoomed in on the painting. Yuuto froze the video frame, keeping the family portrait large and still on the screen. I felt a quickening of my pulse as I leant forward to get a better look.

"She looks quite a lot like me."

"Yes, now can you see why I went out of my way to get introduced to you?"

I studied the woman in the painting. In the portrait, she sat by the side of the man. It was indeed the same man who was sitting on the futon – the artist had created an exceptionally good likeness of him. In front of them, on the floor, sat a small girl, a mini-me version of the woman, but with longer shoulder length hair. The girl was sitting cross-legged, grinning up and towards what would have been the artist's point of view. The woman was also smiling. She was slim, with blond hair cut into a pixie style, very much like my own. Her face was a different shape to mine though; the woman's triangular, whereas mine was rounded. Like me, she had full lips that twisted slightly to the right when she smiled.

Yuuto started the video again. He was asking the man a new question.

"Could you tell us a bit about your wife?"

"What would you like to know?

"Perhaps how you met, what she was like…." Yuuto paused. "…and if it is not too painful to talk about, what you miss most about her?"

The man nodded. "Tanaka hired Laura to teach Business English to our senior managers. I was in one of her classes. She was ten years younger than me, in her early twenties when we met, but there was an immediate attraction between us. We lived in the same neighbourhood, and on the days that she worked for Tanaka, we travelled into the city together. We used to meet on the platform and chat on the train. One day I built up the courage to ask her out. She said yes and from there our relationship developed quickly."

The man stopped talking and rubbed his face before resuming.

"We both liked the outdoors. Most weekends, during that first summer when we were getting to know each other, we hired a campervan and drove out to the Mizugaki forest. That is where she met the group she started climbing with. I knew one of them through work and joined them at the beginning, but I was new to the sport and never really took to it. Laura had climbed back in England and was quite experienced. She wanted to climb harder routes than I could manage. I did not mind though. I was glad she was developing her own friendship network in Japan."

I heard Yuuto interject in the background.

"At what point did you get married? I imagine Laura could have found it difficult to commit to a permanent life in Japan?"

"I asked her to marry me after two years. We were living together by then. It was an easy decision for Laura, I think. Her family back in England was small, just herself, her mother and brother, and they were not particularly close. Her Japanese was quite proficient at this stage. She was enjoying her work and had built up her network to the point that she was teaching Business English across four different companies. She had also become embedded in the Tokyo climbing fraternity. Things were going well for her, and our relationship made both of us happy. Niko came along very quickly after we were married, ten months later in fact; both of us did not see any advantages to waiting; we wanted to be a family."

"And Laura continued climbing?"

"Oh yes, she was addicted to the sport. There was a short period of a year or so, after Niko was born, when obviously it was more difficult for her to find time to climb, but it quickly got to the stage where it was easy for me to look after Niko on a Saturday so that Laura could take the day off. She was only teaching English two or three evenings a week by then and was with Niko the rest of the time. I felt she needed a day to herself each week."

The man fell silent and there was a pause whilst the video continued to play. Yuuto asked a further question from the sidelines.

"I won't ask you to tell us about the actual circumstances in which Laura died; we know that it was a climbing accident, and it must be very upsetting for you to talk about. Instead, could you tell us a bit about your family life with Laura and what you would like from a Replacement if we were able to provide you with one?"

The man swallowed. "Niko is old enough to get the bus to school and back. We have breakfast together each day and I can see her off in the mornings. My work requires me to stay late most evenings though. A friend who lives in the same apartment block has been very kind. She has taken to cooking Niko's supper, on the evenings I cannot be there, and she stays with her until I get back. This way we are getting by during the week, for the short term at least. It is the weekends that are the immediate problem. Over the last year or so, due to pressure at work, I have had to go into the labs on the occasional Saturday. Laura had started to take Niko climbing with her on those days. Then Sundays were our family time. We would visit my parents or have them over for a meal, and we would take a walk out in the afternoon, usually to the park. I would like somebody to be Niko's mother on the Saturdays that I must work and to be with us to make our family complete on Sundays."

The man hesitated and Yuuto stepped in again.

"Thank you, Takahashi-san. That is all the information we need for now. We are very honoured that you have shared your story with us."

The video ended at this point and Yuuto went over to the laptop to shut everything down. I watched him, wondering how I should respond.

"You didn't ask for specific details about how his wife died. Do you know what happened?"

"Only partially. On the day the accident happened, Laura had split from the group to climb a route she had spent weeks preparing for. Going off to do a route on your own was not unusual apparently. They were all accomplished climbers and knew the crags in that area well. As I said, the route she went off to do was one she had been practising for a while. On prior attempts, she had used rope, as well as nuts and chocks and other types of protection. The day of the accident, she told her climbing partners that she felt ready to do the route unaided. By that she meant she wanted to climb it without any protection. She was insistent that she did not want any spectators. We know that she fell quite near to the top of the crag and that she did not survive the impact of the fall. There were no reported witnesses, so it is not known why she fell at that point in the climb. Her climber friends have speculated but I do not think anybody will ever know for sure."

I frowned. "I used to climb back in England. There seem to be many similarities between myself and this woman; it's freaking me out a bit."

Yuuto's eyes widened. "You must not tell Mr Takahashi that you are a climber."

He stopped talking to stare at me, but then slapped his forehead with his hand and jabbed an index finger at me.

"No, you must tell him, but you must say that a friend of yours died whilst climbing, and that after that, you gave up the sport. This will help form a closer bond between the two of you."

I felt myself getting annoyed. "Hang on a minute Yuuto; I have not agreed to do this. I teach English all week. The weekends are my chance to relax and explore Japan. This is not a commitment I want to take on."

"But you must." Yuuto's tone was beseeching. "Here, read the contract terms."

Yuuto removed a piece of paper from a slim black folder that he had placed on the table when I first arrived. He pushed it towards me.

"See how much money you can earn in one weekend. We could negotiate it so that you had one weekend off in four. On the Saturdays that Mr Takahashi does not have to go into the lab, you would only need to work Sundays. Also, it is usual for there to be a trial period first, normally three months. You can end the arrangement at the end of the three months if you do not feel it is working out. It is a fantastic opportunity for you to get to know a Japanese family and to experience how they live."

Yuuto was pleading with me now. "Please say you will come and have a preliminary chat with the family. Visit them in their own home and find out a bit more about what they would expect from you."

I skim-read the contract in front of me. The remuneration was seductive. I would earn as much in a weekend as I could earn teaching English five days a week.

"If I go to see the family with you, will you promise that I can make up my own mind after the visit? If I didn't want to do it, you'd accept my decision, no further pressurising?"

"Yes, of course." Yuuto's expression was open and earnest.

I sighed. "Ok, I'll come with you to meet them."

CHAPTER 3

IT WAS SUNDAY, the day of the visit to the Takahashi family. I had risen early to get across to where the family had their apartment in the Kichijoji district. On arriving, I still had half an hour to spare, so I decided to while away the time in the neighbouring Inokashiri park.

After an initial aimless wandering, I commandeered a bench with a pleasant view of the lake. Pedal boats, in the guise of large swans, were being vigorously propelled forward by boisterous occupants. A boy, sitting on a bench a short distance from mine, stood up and walked away towards the Northern end of the park. My gaze followed his departing form. It was then that I saw them again.

He was walking two metres in front of her, head up, easy long stride; she was walking two metres behind, head down, small quick steps. Despite his obviously advanced years, he was skinny and energetic in his movements. He dressed like a dandy, wearing a bold pin-striped suit, with purple cravat, and matching handkerchief tucked into the top pocket of his jacket. His hair was a plume of unruly white and it looked as if he brushed it hard against his head to keep it from sticking out. I felt that he had been a 'somebody' in his younger days, someone people would have recognised when he walked by, perhaps still did.

She seemed elderly, more so than him. Slightly stooped, dressed in a yellow and blue yukata, with grey hair tied back in a chignon knot. Her gait was uneven, a mixture of pauses followed by sudden propulsions to catch up. I had seen them earlier when I had first entered the park; they had been walking in this same single file formation then. She had noticed me, shot me a quick sideways glance that made me think she had recognised me. Narrow twinkly eyes peeping out from a petite crinkly face. She had had a half smile on her lips, and I had instinctively liked her.

As I watched the couple this second time, I saw the woman spot the recently vacated bench positioned a couple of metres from where I sat. She accelerated to move in on it by way of a left veering arc that crossed ahead of the man. When he realised where she was heading, he followed. They both sat down, neither acknowledging my nearby presence.

I had been taking every opportunity since arriving in Tokyo to re-acclimatise my ear to the Japanese language, and so I strained discreetly to hear what they might say to each other. At first, they sat in silence. The woman pulled out a small cotton cheesecake, broke it in half with her hands, and offered it to the man. As I looked over, I could see that one portion was larger than the other. The man reached to take the larger portion, but the woman snatched the cake away and reoriented it so that the smaller portion was the polite choice for him to take. They both laughed. After they had eaten the cake, the woman cleared her throat.

"My granddaughter needs a mother."

The man grunted, nodding his head.

"I hope our son will do something about that before too long."

Again, the man grunted but impatiently now. He indicated that they should move on. When she did not respond, he stood and held out a hand. She pushed it away.

"Go on with you. I need my space. I will follow you when I am ready."

The man's mouth twitched, a fleeting expression. He gave her a half bow and started to move away. She waited a minute, tipping her head back to watch a bird in a nearby tree. When she finally stirred herself, it was sudden, using her funny mix of stops and quick propulsions to catch him up. On reaching him, they settled into formation again; he walking two metres in front of her, head up, easy long stride; she walking two metres behind him, head down, small quick steps.

I smiled as I watched them. I loved being back in Japan; the foreign feel of it. This park was one of the places that the Takahashi family would have come to at the weekends. Did the father and girl still walk here?

I checked my watch. Ten minutes before I was due to meet Yuuto outside the Takahashi's apartment, an apartment in one of the more affluent tower blocks overlooking the park. It was only a five-minute stroll away, but I decided to start walking. I still did not know what I thought of Yuuto's proposition. To spend weekends as part of the Takahashi family, acting out the role of Niko's dead mother? Maybe it would be easier than being Quinn Roberts full-time? I reflected on this. I was surprised at the contrast between my unsettled state back in England and the inner quiet I was experiencing in Japan. Coming out here had created a distance that was enabling me to achieve a certain detachment. I felt calmer but aware that I had not escaped myself. Perhaps being a part-time member of another family would be good for me. Perhaps it would help me learn how to share my life and to give more of myself. I laughed aloud. The irony. I would be hiding behind the persona of Laura; it was simply another form of ducking and diving. I was curious though. Yuuto was right when he said it would be an interesting experience, a chance to see first-hand how a

Japanese family lives. I would go to meet the Takahashis, and I would find out more about the proposed arrangement; then I would make my decision.

Yuuto had arrived early and was waiting for me when I arrived at the apartment block. He smiled at me but allowed no time for a pre-meet conversation, buzzing the intercom immediately for entry to the entrance hall. I loped after him as he led the way, preferencing the stairs to the lift. I matched his brisk pace but found myself breathing hard by the time we reached the sixth floor. I was still slightly out of breath when he knocked on the door to the apartment and Takahashi opened it.

As soon as Takahashi saw me, his expression changed. At first open and expectant, I saw his eyes narrow, and his mouth tighten. I could not be sure what he was feeling at that moment, but not for the first time since Yuuto had approached me, I felt a small tug of disquiet. Yuuto, obviously used to the discomfort of these first meetings, pumped Takahashi's hand and breezed airily past him into the apartment. I followed, nodding politely to our host as I did so. A short corridor opened into the living space I had seen in the video. As I stepped into it, Takahashi strode quickly around me, ushering me towards the futon.

"Please sit. Can I get you anything? Tea perhaps?"

He spoke in English, his accent clipped. I looked at Yuuto, seeking confirmation as to whether I should accept the offer.

"We would both like tea Takahashi-san. Thank you."

On hearing Yuuto's reply, Takahashi unexpectedly moved across to a wicker chair facing the futon. He half bowed as he sat down, gesturing for us to do the same. He then directed his voice towards another doorway at the far end of the room.

"Kasei-fu, Matcha tea for three please."

Again, he spoke English and in response I heard an electronic whirr as if a machine had been switched on. A computer-generated affirmation followed. Takahashi returned his attention to us.

"Thank you for coming. How would you suggest we proceed Hiroshini-san?"

"Call me Yuuto. And if I can call you Reo…?"

Yuuto paused, affording Takahashi time to consent to this. "…Thank you, well let me introduce you formally to Quinn Roberts."

Reo and I nodded at each other. Reo's nod seemed curt. I felt that in the time it had taken us to traverse the hall to the living room, Reo had erected a protective barrier around himself.

"I have already provided you with background details about Quinn-san. We feel that she is an excellent match, a good fit for the replacement profile you have drawn up. This introductory meeting is a chance for you to meet her in the flesh, ask any questions you have, and for us to discuss the details of what the arrangement might be. We do not ask for a decision from you at this stage. We feel you should take the time to reflect on this. This is of course the same for Quinn-san, a chance for her to meet you and your daughter, see your home, and form her own opinion as to whether she could provide you with the service you have requested. I will contact you separately after today's meeting to hear what you each have to say. Does that sound ok?"

Reo's gaze had been fixed steadily on Yuuto whilst this was being explained to him, but shifted quickly to me once Yuuto had finished.

"This would be the first time you have performed a replacement service for a family?"

His tone was brusque. I shifted in my seat. I was surprised to find that I was as nervous as if I had been attending a job interview or acting audition. I felt a need to justify myself. On one level, I realised, I must want to do this.

"Yes, it would be the first time, but I have eighteen years' experience as a jobbing actor back in the UK. I am used to getting into character and performing different roles. Yuuto has explained that I look quite a bit like your wife. She came from London and so do I. She came out to Japan to teach English and so have I. It sounds as if we had a fair bit in common. I understand that you would like somebody to fulfil Laura's role at weekends, and that you would like to recapture some of what it felt like to be a family when Laura was alive?"

I turned the last half of this statement into a question. It was left unanswered as a smooth electronic noise penetrated the room. Yuuto and I turned our heads towards the noise and watched as a robot, humanoid in form from the waist up, entered from the corridor. It glided over the floor, a black rubber skirt surrounding its base. Slowing to a halt, it manoeuvred itself so that it was facing the table and then gently subsided so that its form rested fully on the floor.

"You would like me to place the tea here?"

The robot's synthesised speech was distorted and jerky, but distinctly female. When Reo confirmed his instructions, the robot's front panel flipped open and a tray, containing an array of tea paraphernalia, slid out on horizontal rails from its interior. The robot used both of its arms to lift the tray off the rails and then bent forward to rest it gently on the table's surface.

"Thank you Kasei-fu. That is kind of you."

"You are welcome. Do you need anything else Reo-san?

"Could you fetch Niko please? Tell her that our visitors have arrived."

The robot moved its head in the semblance of a nod, and then rising again, glided from the room. I whistled softly.

"Wow. Japan is so advanced with its robotics. We're nowhere near having anything like this in English homes yet."

Reo smiled at me, a small smile but an unforced one. I felt my confidence rising.

"Not everybody has a robotic Kasei-fu. They are too expensive for the average household. I bought it as a way of getting domestic tasks done whilst I am at work. It seemed easier than getting a housekeeper, particularly as I was thinking of using a replacement service. I did not feel it would be fair on Niko to introduce too many people into the household."

"What kind of work can it do?"

"Oh, it can clean floors and surfaces, load and unload the dishwasher, fill the washer dryer, and empty it again, heat and serve basic meals. Most household tasks that require limited dexterity. A key feature is its speech and vocabulary. As you have just heard, it can engage in simple pleasantries, understand, and respond to basic questions and instructions. Niko has benefited from having it around; it feels like a house companion to her, along with K2 of course."

"Who or what is K2?"

As I asked this, a girl ran into the room. It was the same girl in the portrait painting that I had first seen in Yuuto's video. On seeing us, she came to an abrupt halt and lowered her head, before moving quickly towards her father. She climbed up onto the arm of the wicker chair to perch next to him, at which point Reo reached over to pull her down onto his lap.

"Niko, these are friends of mine: Yuuto and Quinn-san. Say hello to them."

The girl kept her head lowered but looked across at us from beneath a heavy fringe. She appeared reluctant to look at us directly, giving furtive sideways glances that darted away as soon as they landed. Her father tickled her.

"Don't be shy. Say hello to our guests, Niko."

Niko wriggled out of her father's arms and fell onto the floor, before scrambling to a standing position. She glanced towards the door and called out in a high peremptory voice.

"K2, come!"

I turned my head in the direction that Niko had called. There was an answering bark. A small dog by the sound of it, more of a yap really. Niko stepped towards the door and called a second time. This time, we could hear an electronic sound advancing towards us, very like the sound made by the Kasei-fu but quieter. When I saw what was making the noise, my face broke into a grin; a robotic dog had careered into the room, its lower half clad in the same black rubber skirt as the Kasei-fu. Niko fell onto her knees and flung her arms around the automated animal.

"Niko don't be rude. Say hello to Yuuto and Quinn-san, please."

Reo sounded irritated. His daughter had her back to him, her face buried in the dog's fake fur. She did not respond.

"Niko, leave K2 alone please. Stand up and greet our guests or I will send you to your room."

I glanced over at Yuuto. This felt heavy handed to me. The girl was timid around strangers, as might be expected. I could empathise. I did not feel that Reo should force Niko to say hello. Yuuto met my eyes impassively, his professional demeanour locked in place. I looked back at the girl. She had sat up straight when her father had told her off, but was now bending over the dog again, whispering in its ear, a fast urgent whisper. She then stood up and smoothed down the green dress she was wearing. Turning towards Yuuto and me, she gave us a small fast bow and scuttled back to her father's side.

I found myself holding my breath. The girl had still not said hello, but she had bowed; hopefully, that would satisfy her father.

"This is your dog; you call him K2?" I directed my question at Niko. The girl nodded, looking at me properly for the first time. I saw her eyes widen and I guessed that she was seeing my likeness to her mother.

"How long have you had him?" I tried to sound friendly and reassuring. The girl was staring at me.

"It's a 'her.' She is ten months old. My mother got her for me."

"Well, she's lovely. Did you name her?"

"My mother named her. She's called after the second highest mountain in the world. Mum wanted to climb it one day, but it is an extremely dangerous mountain, and not many manage it."

I nodded and caught Reo's eye. He was shifting in his seat, looking uncomfortable.

"My wife was an exceptionally good rock climber but not a professional mountaineer. K2 was an aspiration but never a serious proposition. She named the dog after the mountain but also because of her sense of humour. She told Niko that K2 was a descendant of K9, K9 equating of course to the word canine in English."

I smiled. "Of course, I should have guessed that."

"Quinn-san tells me that she used to climb."

I felt myself freeze. I could not believe that Yuuto was telling Reo this. It was a gamble that I worried would backfire.

"Back in England, you said, is that not right, Quinn-san?" Yuuto was persisting.

"Yes, but not anymore." My pulse quickened; I wanted this topic of questioning to end. It was insensitive.

"Unfortunately, Quinn-san lost somebody close to her in a climbing accident too. A friend from university."

I had heard enough and rounded on Yuuto. He had forced me into a corner whereby I had no choice but to go along with this lie. To confront him in front of Reo would make the situation even more excruciating.

"It was a long time ago and I'd rather not talk about it if you don't mind."

Yuuto raised an eyebrow but backed down. "Of course. I am sorry. I did not mean to upset you."

I saw that Reo was staring at us, a pained expression on his face. I was trying desperately to think of something to say to change the subject when Niko began to hum. I did not recognise the tune but as Niko continued, K2 became alert, arose from its sitting position, and glided over to Reo. It drew to a halt next to his chair and to my astonishment, I heard water trickling. A small puddle started to accumulate around Reo's shoes. The robotic dog appeared to be urinating.

Reo jumped up, grabbing his daughter's arm. He pulled her to her feet and propelled her forcibly towards the door.

"That is the last straw Niko; I do not have the patience for this. You will go to your room for the rest of the morning. I will come to see you after our guests have left. I suggest you reflect on your behaviour and a suitable punishment."

Niko's head was down but I caught the girl's expression as she was frog-marched past. Her cheeks were flushed and there was a challenging glint in her eye. She was not that timid after all. I smiled inwardly. Presumably, Niko had had something to do with K2's actions; it would be interesting to get to know her better.

Having dispatched his daughter, Reo came back to his seat. He trod gingerly around the pool of water.

"I am sorry. Niko has been learning to programme K2. She has been told to restrict herself to the code provided in the owner's manual, but she has learnt quickly and has started to develop her own instructions. The dog is designed to simulate the behaviour of a real dog but is programmed to be housetrained. Niko has obviously found a way to override that. I would find it amusing but Niko's behaviour has started to feel insolent. She misses her mother and her behaviour towards me can be quite disrespectful."

Reo sighed. "It is a main reason for wanting to engage the services of your agency, Yuuto. A regular female presence in our home would be good for Niko."

I stood up. Reo had been directing his remarks at Yuuto, and not including me in his eye contact. I felt awkward and the urge to extricate myself from the conversation was strong.

"It has been good to meet you and your daughter, Reo-san."

I gave Reo a half bow before continuing. "I would be happy to trial spending a Sunday with you and Niko. I do not think we will achieve much by discussing things in more detail today. You have met me, and I have met you. As we say in England, the proof will be in the pudding. If it suits you, let us spend a day together doing what you used to do as a family when your wife was alive. Let us see how we get on together and how Niko responds to my company. If it is an enjoyable experience for the three of us, then we can discuss ongoing contractual arrangements."

I turned to leave. "No need to see me out. Please liaise with Yuuto-san if you would like to set something up."

Yuuto's knotted brow told me that he was displeased with my premature exit. I did not care. I was removing myself from a situation that felt uncomfortable and embarrassing. I was prepared to give this proposition a second chance but not with Yuuto there; next time, it needed to be just me and the family.

CHAPTER 4

LATER THAT SAME DAY, Yuuto called to tear me off a strip. According to him, I had left before we had discussed the essentials, and I had come across as rude. The upshot, however, was that Reo wanted to fix up the Sunday trial I had suggested. I resisted the urge to point out that, in that case, no lasting damage had been done.

Both parties agreed that the visit should happen sooner rather than later, so the following Sunday afternoon, I found myself once again making my way over to the Takahashi's' apartment. This time Niko answered the door, K2 at her side.

"She still getting you into trouble?" I gestured towards the robotic dog.

Niko gave me a sly grin. "Dad's not here; he has gone to pick up my grandparents. He said to invite you in though."

I followed Niko along the hallway into the living room, taking the time to adjust to this news.

"Do your grandparents live near here?

"Yes, on the other side of the park."

"Do you see them often?"

Niko shrugged. "Once a fortnight. Usually, they don't come here; we visit them in their apartment."

I nodded. I found it strange that Reo had not mentioned his parents when I spoke with him about the arrangements for today.

"Will they be staying all afternoon, do you think?"

Niko looked at me questioningly. "I don't know. Don't you want them to come?"

I was beginning to understand that Niko was quite a direct young lady. I walked across to the futon and sat down.

"Yes, of course I do. It will be good to meet them."

I let my eyes rove around the room. When my focus returned to Niko, I could see that she had fixed her gaze on the wall above and behind my head; the spot where the family portrait hung. I resisted the impulse to turn and look at it. Niko switched her attention to me.

"You look like my mother."

Her tone was quite matter of fact. It was my turn to shrug my shoulders. "I guess I do a bit."

A silence fell between us. I cleared my throat. "What has your dad told you about the reason for my visiting today?"

As I asked this, we heard a soft knock on the apartment door. Niko turned quickly and ran down the hallway. I heard her call out to the person on the other side, asking them to identify themselves. A woman answered but I could not hear what she said. I then heard Niko open and close the front door, and two sets of footsteps walking back towards me. A small-boned, delicately featured woman followed Niko into the room. I would have put her in her mid-thirties. She had black hair worn in a short bob, and she was bare foot, wearing jeans and a loose green silk shirt. She was holding an oval earthenware pot close to her stomach and dipped her head when she saw me.

"Please excuse me. I am going away for a couple of days and wanted to give this to Reo before I left."

She spoke in Japanese, but seeing me hesitate, switched to a heavily accented but fluent English. "Are you from England? Reo did not mention that he had a visitor today."

I did not know what to say. I had no idea what Reo had said about me, even to Niko. "Yes, I'm from London. I've been here a month. I'm teaching at a language school here in Tokyo."

"Has Reo hired you to help Niko with her English?"

"Erm, something like that."

I saw Niko's look of surprise, quickly followed by indignation. "I don't need English lessons. My mother was English."

Niko stamped her foot. I held my hands up to placate her. "Even English people need English lessons. And besides, maybe you're just an excuse for your dad; maybe it's really him who needs the lessons."

I tapped the side of my nose, smiling sideways at her. Niko's shoulders relaxed and she seemed mollified. The woman put the earthen pot down on the low table in front of me and bowed again.

"Well, I'm pleased to meet you. My name is Yui. I live in the apartment directly below."

I stood up. "I think Reo has mentioned you; he says you help with Niko during the week? I'm pleased to meet you too. I'm Quinn."

Yui was scanning my face closely. "You look like Laura, Niko's mum."

"Yes, so I've been told."

"That is her in the picture behind you. Do you not see the likeness?"

I turned my head in a pretence at studying the painting for the first time. "Gosh, yes I suppose I do."

"You look very much like her."

Yui continued to stare at me. Again, I found myself shrugging. Where was Reo? I needed to know what my story was meant to be. Yuuto was right of course. We should have straightened this out at the first meeting.

"Oh!" Yui brought a hand up to cover her mouth. Her eyes had widened. "I should go."

She turned to Niko. "This is tomorrow's supper. Can you put it in the fridge and tell your dad I will be back on Tuesday?

"What is it?"

"Gyoza Nabe."

"Yay!" Niko did a small dance around Yui, making her laugh.

"You've made somebody happy. What's Gyoza Nabe?"

Yui smiled. "Pork filled dumplings in kombu dashi; it is a type of soup stock made with dried kelp. A variety of vegetables added as well. It is Niko's favourite dish."

She ruffled Niko's hair before addressing me again. "I had better go. It has been good to meet you."

She began to back out of the room, bowing to me as she went. Niko followed her down the hall, returning after seeing her out.

"She seems nice, Niko."

"Yes, she is."

Niko threw herself onto the nearby wicker chair and began to swing her legs.

"Have you and your dad known her a long time?"

"She was my mum's best friend. She has known me all my life." Niko started to hum.

"Well, it's lovely of her to cook your tea when your dad is at work."

Niko nodded, but then her face became serious. "I don't like Sora though and dad doesn't either."

"Sora?" I looked at Niko questioningly.

"Yui's boyfriend."

"Oh, does he live with Yui?"

"No, but he stays with her at weekends. I don't like him because he shouts at Yui sometimes. And dad says he can be bad-tempered at work."

"He works with your dad?"

"Yes." Niko swung her feet onto the floor and stood up. "Hey, dad's back."

I had not heard anything but as Niko announced this, I heard the door to the apartment open and the recognisable tones of Japanese conversation echo through the flat. I stood up as Reo came into the room. He had three people in tow, and I immediately recognised two of them as the older couple I had seen in the park last weekend. Today, the man was wearing a bright yellow cravat, but he was in the same pin-stripe suit, with his hair as vigorously brushed down as the first time I had seen him. The woman seemed smaller than on my first encounter, but her face had the same cheeky expression, and she was wearing a yukata again, orange and green this time. They made a colourful pair, and I was taken aback to see them in Reo's apartment. I wondered whether they would remember seeing me in the park.

Reo moved towards me. "It is good to see you again. I am sorry I was not here when you arrived. These are my parents, Chieko and Akemi."

The older couple bowed, continuing to stare at me in the same curious way I was learning to expect from people who had known Laura.

"And this is one of my father's oldest friends from his time in Hong Kong as a young man." Reo gestured towards the third person he had arrived with. The man was Western in appearance and appeared to be a similar age to Reo's father, late seventies or thereabouts. On Reo's introduction, he walked stiffly across the room and stretched out his arm.

"Hello. I'm Albert."

I shook his hand. The accent was English and sounded southern. I was not great at identifying accents but at a guess I would have said he was from the Home Counties. He had a brown weathered face, intimating a life spent predominantly outdoors.

Reo began to bustle us all into seats. He had not introduced me, but I realised he had probably already told his parents who I was. I noticed that Reo's father, Chieko, had resisted the prompt to sit down and instead was delving into a plastic carrier bag that he had brought with him. He took out a red cake tin and brandished it at Albert.

"Now, my friend, you know you cannot visit Tokyo without experiencing my mochi balls! We shall have them with jasmine tea, shall we son?"

Reo took the tin from his father and moved towards the door. "I will get some plates and ask Kasei-fu to make us some tea."

He disappeared and I took the opportunity to ask Chieko what mochi balls were. I had not heard of them but as a former student of Japanese, it sounded as if I should have. Chieko seemed delighted that I had asked and launched into an explanation of how they were a traditional Japanese delicacy, and, in his view, the definitive taste of home. "They've been imperial offerings for centuries." Chieko's eyes were bright with enthusiasm. "Samurai warriors used to carry them into battle. Can you guess why?"

I shook my head.

"Because an inch-long piece of mochi contains the same calories as an entire bowl of rice." Chieko smacked his lips. "They are sticky and sweet, and very, very, chewy. I guarantee that your mouth will be watering after you have eaten one of my chocolate mochi balls."

On cue, Reo returned with Kasei-fu who proceeded to set out cups of jasmine tea and plates of Chieko's offering. I leant forward to take one of the cocoa dusted rice balls and started to nibble at it. Out of the corner of my eye, I saw Albert take a large bite out of the one he had reached for. He was a fast eater and I watched as he consumed the whole ball in three quick bites and three eager swallows. If I had known about the reputation of mochi balls, I would have intercepted his hand as he reached across to pick up a second one. I would have impressed upon him the need to chew the morsels slowly and wait awhile between bites. Instead, I watched him sigh with pleasure as his mouth closed around the whole second ball and, within moments, saw his face go red, and his hands clutch his neck. The dense gelatinous substance had got stuck in his throat.

Chieko moved across to him fast, the Heimlich manoeuvre executed expertly and without hesitation. The mochi ball dislodged, shooting from Albert's mouth, and rolling under the futon. There was a shocked pause but then Chieko laughed and once he had started, it seemed that he could not stop, causing his wife to swipe at his arm. Reo moved to Albert's side. The old man was still bent double, coughing hard.

"Niko, go and see if Yui has left yet; if she is still at home ask her to come straight away."

Niko rushed off to do as Reo had instructed, and within minutes was back with Yui. As I watched Yui attend to Albert, I realised she must be a nurse or at least have some form of medical training.

After a short while, Albert sat back up and his breathing returned to normal. Chieko was looking remorseful now, hovering anxiously by his friend's side. Reo entreated everybody to sit back down, including Yui. The tea party resumed but nobody touched the mochi balls after Albert's experience. I felt sorry for Chieko; he seemed subdued in the aftermath of the incident. His main contribution to the conversation consisted of muttered asides in Japanese to help his wife follow the predominantly English language being spoken.

It was on reflection an odd couple of hours that then passed. Nobody asked me about myself and Reo did not volunteer any information. The focus was firstly on Albert and his visit to Japan, and then Niko and her schooling. I felt as if my role was to be part of the furniture. I chipped in every now and again, but it was mainly to ask questions and to show interest. The one time that attention fell on me was for all the wrong reasons, and it felt like an over-reaction. I had dropped the cup I had been holding, and the remainder of my tea spilt onto my jeans. It was still hot enough to scald and I jumped up, yelling an expletive in the process. I appreciate that this is not how to behave when you're a guest in somebody else's house, but it had hurt, and I had been embarrassed.

I apologised immediately, both for my clumsiness and the swearing, and expected Reo as the host to smooth things over. Yet that did not happen. Instead, there was a stunned silence in the room; it lasted too long and when I looked at Reo and Niko, I saw that they were shocked. I did not understand it. I apologised again and was grateful when Albert touched my arm reassuringly, before changing the subject to embark on a story about his and Chieko's time in Hong Kong, in the aftermath of World War Two, when Japanese-English friendships had been rare.

I kept quiet after that and when Yui got up to go at four, I took the opportunity to announce my own departure. I bowed to everybody and Reo saw us to the door. He thanked Yui for helping with Albert, and with barely a glance at me, said he would phone that evening to make sure I had got back to my flat ok. He then closed the door, leaving Yui and me standing on the landing.

Yui put a finger to her lips and beckoned me to follow her down the stairs. It was only when we reached her front door, on the floor below, that she spoke.

"Are you ok? I am sorry it was awkward for a while in there."

"I'm fine. Surprised that's all. I felt I had committed a major crime."

Yui laughed. "They were shocked because Laura never swore, and she was especially against use of the 'f' word. Niko said it once and Laura sent her to her room, gave her a tough time about it. That is why Reo and Niko reacted the way they did."

Yui stared at me meaningfully when she said this, and I felt myself blush. "But I'm not Laura."

"No."

An odd silence followed, whilst Yui continued to search my face as if looking for an explanation. After a brief pause, she asked me directly. I squirmed.

"Yes, ……you've heard of replacements then?"

Yui nodded and I sighed. "Well, I hadn't until last week. An agency approached me because I look like Laura. I've agreed to a trial, but I am not at all sure that it is a good idea. This is the second time I've met with Reo, yet we never seem to get around to discussing the details of the arrangement. I have no idea what I am meant to say when I'm asked the question you have just asked me, nor how I am meant to introduce myself."

Yui smiled. "I have noticed."

She put her key in the lock. "Look, come in for a short while. I can tell you a bit about the family. It might be helpful to you."

Yui's place was tidy and well ordered. She gave me a glass of juice – it tasted of gooseberry – and sat me down at her

43

kitchen table. I prepared to listen, but she sat back and instructed me to ask the questions. "You have taken this on," she said. "What do you need to know?"

I began with questions about how the replacement concept was meant to work, but Yui was unable to give me any insight. She had heard of people using this type of service, but it was the first time she had personally come across the arrangement. She told me that Reo was lonely, that he was struggling to manage work commitments and find time for Niko. She assumed that this is what had made him contact Yuuto's agency.

I asked her about the little girl and Yui looked sad when she answered me. Niko had lost her mother; it was obviously a traumatic event in her life. Her behaviour towards Reo had become more challenging but who could blame her?

I then asked Yui how long she had known the family and she confirmed what Niko had told me. She had been living in the apartment block when Reo and Laura first moved in; she had got to know them, become best friends with Laura, and they had made her godmother to Niko when she was born.

Godmother? I was surprised and told her so. "Nobody has introduced you as Niko's godmother."

Yui shrugged. "The Japanese don't have the same concept as you do in England. You might hear the term 'nazuke-oya,' which means naming parent, but it is not the same thing. Laura wanted Niko to have a godmother in the English sense, for there to be somebody in Tokyo who would take Niko in, should anything happen to her and Reo. I was an obvious choice. Reo has his parents, but he has no siblings."

"So, you named Niko?" I asked.

Yui shook her head. "No, Laura chose the name, after her brother Nicholas."

I remembered then that Reo had mentioned a brother in the video. I asked Yui if Reo was in touch with Laura's family back in England.

Yui shook her head. "He contacted Laura's mother straightaway when the accident happened, but the family were not close. Laura confided in me that there were prolonged periods when they had no contact. Her mother is reportedly scared of flying and said she could not come out for the funeral. The brother suffers from depression. He has not worked for years apparently. Laura often talked to me about him; she was very fond of her brother, but Nicholas fended off all her attempts to reach out to him. He did not come to the funeral either; there was nobody there from England."

We were bound to come around to the subject eventually. I asked her to tell me more about how Laura died. Yui lost her composure at that point, and it was several minutes before she was able to speak. She relayed what I had already heard from Yuuto: a fall whilst Laura had been attempting to free solo a route. Yui confirmed that she and Sora had been climbing with Laura that day. I learnt that Sora, Yui's boyfriend, had encouraged Laura to attempt the climb. It was he, of their group, who had first free solo'd it. By that it meant that he had climbed the route alone and without any rope or protection. He had felt that Laura, with sufficient preparation, was capable of the same. Laura was competitive. She had wanted to prove to herself and to the others that she could do it.

I asked Yui for more information about the nature and difficulty of the climb. I told her that I was a climber myself and that I understood the technical jargon used in the climbing world.

Yui seemed surprised when I told her this but continued to recount the story. She told me that Laura had been attempting the Moai Face of Mt Mizugaki. A Japanese climber had first recorded the route in 2018. He had called it *Yōshanai*

45

michi, which meant 'Unforgiving Road.' She did not know why he had named it that and she didn't know if there had been any attempts to climb the route before 2018. Either way, the climber in 2018 had used protection and to Sora and Yui's knowledge, Sora had been the first one to free solo it without rope or any other aid.

I asked if she had seen Laura fall. Yui shook her head vigorously. No, nobody in their group had. They had heard shouting and saw people heading in the direction of the climb, so they had followed and seen Laura's body on the ground. Yui broke down in tears again. I reached out to hold her hand and waited patiently until she had stopped.

"I had wanted to go with her. I did not think she should attempt the route alone, without anybody there to encourage her or to provide help if things should go wrong, but Laura was adamant. She said that if people were watching, it would put her off."

I squeezed Yui's hand. "So, nobody knows the point at which she fell or why?"

Yui shook her head. "There has only ever been speculation. There is a particularly challenging move about two thirds of the way up the last pitch. The move is onto a ledge which has a narrow horizontal crevice, a metre or so above it. Climbers have seen birds fly out from this crevice; Sora thought that Laura could have disturbed them, that this might have caused her to lose her balance."

At that stage in the telling of the story, Yui got up and cleared away our glasses. I took the hint that it was time for me to leave.

As I was walking out of the apartment, she surprised me by asking if I would like to join her and Sora on a climbing trip next Saturday. I hesitated and explained that I had told Reo I did not climb anymore, that Yuuto had advised me to do this to save Reo's feelings.

Yui raised an eyebrow. "Reo does not need to know. He has no say in what you do when you are not working for him. I know that he is not at the Lab next Saturday so he will not need you. Come with us, it will be a chance for you to see one of our national parks and to meet some local climbers."

I gave her a small smile. She was a nice person. I knew that I would like to get to know her better on my own terms, not as Laura's replacement. I thanked her and as we exchanged mobile numbers, I said I would be in touch over the next day or so.

CHAPTER 5

TRUE TO HIS WORD, Reo called me that evening to check that I had got back ok. I fully intended to talk to him in detail about the arrangement between us but, this time, it was he who brushed the topic aside. Claiming a need to see to Niko, who was getting ready for bed, he kept the phone call short, his main objective to secure my attendance at a company dinner that was taking place in the Shimbashi region of the City on Wednesday. I pointed out that we had agreed to a weekend arrangement only. I could tell I had irritated him by saying this, but he quickly smoothed out his tone and said that he would appreciate it, if I could be flexible occasionally.

Accordingly, when Wednesday came around, I found myself dashing from my last English class to get back to my dorm room. Throwing on a simple blue dress which I had bought specifically for evening events, I then rushed out again to catch the metro back into town. I had arranged to meet Reo at 7.30pm outside Kisoji, a restaurant specialising in shabu-shabu. Reo's organisation had booked a private room for the evening and Reo had led me to expect that twelve people would be attending.

When I arrived, he was already waiting for me, dressed smartly in a grey suit and company tie. We exchanged greetings and were both still formal with each other, despite two previous meetings. He took my arm and steered me towards the restaurant door, pausing in front of it to brief me hurriedly.

"The majority of my colleagues speak good English. If you find you are struggling with your Japanese, you should not have any problems conversing with them in English. Most of the staff here this evening are newly recruited to the Tanaka organisation; this dinner is part of their welcome induction. They will have heard that I am married and have a daughter - that is what my profile on the company website still says. Of those here tonight, only my boss, and a colleague called Sora, ever met Laura. Both were privy to the news of her death, but I have asked them to keep this information confidential. I have not explained to them that I am using a replacement agency; you look so much like Laura though that I am sure that they will put two and two together. The others will just assume that you are my wife and that is how we will introduce you."

I felt my heart pound at being asked to comply with this deception. I did not understand why Reo didn't want his colleagues to know that his wife had died but I had no time to protest. Reo was ushering me through the restaurant entrance.

A member of staff hurried over to meet us. Exuding an aura of gentle deference, she led us through to a private room at the back of the restaurant and asked us to leave our shoes by the doorway before we entered.

A large table with tatami seating filled the private space and I could see that most of the seats were already taken. Reo took my elbow and led me around to a couple of empty places at the far end.

I glanced at the person sitting next to my allocated seat. He had arranged his legs in a position known in Japan as 'seiza.' It involved lowering yourself onto your knees and then sitting back on your heels with your feet out flat beneath you.

I knew that I would struggle with this posture for any length of time as I was prone to cramping in my feet.

As I was wondering whether it would be acceptable to adopt a cross legged position instead, the man looked up at me. He flashed a broad smile but then did the double take that I had come to expect from acquaintances of Laura. I quickly deduced that this must be either Reo's boss or Yui's boyfriend. I smiled back at him, noticing the interested gleam in his eyes. He was very handsome, early forties I'd guess, sporting a buzz cut and Van Dyke beard, with neatly trimmed moustache, and short-cropped chin hair shaped into a perfect triangle.

A swift look around the table informed me that all the guests were men. With the noticeable exception of the man sat next to me, they were all clean shaven.

Reo had sat down on the other side of the table and was watching me as I absorbed the scene. He leant forward to speak.

"The man sat next to you is my colleague Sora. You met my neighbour Yui the other day; she is his partner."

I shot another glance at Sora who grinned at me and held out his hand. "I am pleased to meet you."

I nodded back, catching the twang of his American accent. Reo did not introduce me by my name and Sora did not ask. I thought this an omission that hung awkwardly in the air.

Reo picked up the menu in front of him and scanned it rapidly. "Have you had shabu-shabu before?"

I shook my head.

"Well, I recommend you choose it. It is the restaurant's speciality. They use the best Wagyu. I will order for both of us if that suits you; the server will cook it at the table which adds to the fun of the occasion; the ponzu dip is particularly good and it will come with udon noodles and vegetables."

I assented to this proposal, squashing a mild resentment that he had denied me the autonomy of choosing my own meal. My acquiescence seemed to please Reo; he smiled at me before turning to talk to a young man on his left.

I looked around the table again. Everybody seemed engrossed in one-on-one conversation, primarily with the person they were sitting next to. I sighed; I had always disliked work events.

"Penny for them" Sora was laughing at me, his tone flirtatious.

I blushed before rallying a reply. "That's an old English expression; unusual to hear it from the mouth of a Japanese Millennial."

"Who says I am a Millennial?" Sora studied my face for a moment before continuing. "Who *I* am is not the pertinent question though, is it?"

"What do you mean?" I felt the heat of a blush again.

Sora bent his head close to mine. "Yui told me that Reo had hired a replacement for Laura. I was not expecting him to bring her to the company dinner though. That is a surprise." He sat back. "You look very like her."

I stared at him, unsure how I should react. I glanced at Reo, but he was still absorbed in conversation with the person next to him. Sora noticed my glance and laughed again.

"You're on your own, sweetheart."

I had the distinct impression that he was enjoying making me squirm. I changed the subject.

"How long have you worked for Tanaka?"

Sora gave me a pointed look but answered the question. "Fifteen years."

"How did you meet Yui?"

"Reo introduced us, after Laura suggested that we might like each other...... And now it is my turn to ask a question. What should I call you?"

I dropped my eyes to the table, thinking rapidly. This man knew full well that I wasn't Laura. For this evening, though, I had been hired to assume her identity. That, I concluded, is who I had to say I was.

"Call me Laura."

Sora seemed affronted by this. "Really?" His tone was sarcastic. He leant towards me again. "In that case, you will not mind if I do this."

His left hand slid across to my inner right thigh. I froze. What was he implying? Gritting my teeth and speaking quietly so as not to attract Reo's attention, I ordered Sora to remove his hand. He chuckled but did as I asked.

"You are nothing like Laura."

"I thought you said that I was like her."

"I said you look like her. That is different from being like her."

Against my better judgement, I asked him to explain, but he shrugged off my question.

"If you need to ask, you have not done your homework. That is what you are meant to do, you 'replacements,' is it not? Learn everything about the person whose identity you are assuming? Study their personality and behavioural traits, what they liked, what they hated?"

I swallowed nervously. I was finding the conversation stressful. Sora was refusing to play the game. If anybody else around the table was listening and Reo got to hear about it, then I anticipated that that would be the end of our arrangement.

Unexpectedly, Sora sat back and gave a deep sigh. "Yui says she has invited you to come climbing with us on Saturday. Are you going to come?"

I looked sideways at him. He was staring across the table at Reo who was still engaged in conversation.

"I....er..."

I cleared my throat. This was ridiculous; I could not let this man intimidate me. I turned the upper half of my body around so that I was facing him directly. "I'm not sure that that would be a good idea now that I've met you."

He raised an eyebrow at me. "There is no need to be so dramatic. It would be in your interests to come. We can tell you more about Laura, ensure you make a better job of representing her at future events......that is if this evening's performance is anything to go by."

I snatched a breath. His tone was snarky, and he was being unfair. Apart from Reo, he was the only person I had spoken to this evening. I had arrived just a short while ago, hardly enough time to deliver a performance.

I was about to retort as such when a server in traditional kimono dress arrived at our end of the table. For the next few minutes, I could only sit there simmering with anger, whilst I watched our host set up a portable gas stove in the centre of the table. She placed an earthenware pot containing a kombu dashi stock onto it. Then, she set a large plate, piled high with thinly sliced raw beef, next to that. This was followed by another plate containing strips of cabbage, long green onions, carrots, mushrooms, and tofu. It seemed that all of us at this end of the table were having the shabu shabu and accordingly, the server provided us each with two small bowls, one containing sesame sauce, and the other the ponzu dip that Reo had recommended. She explained that she would start the cooking off for us; she picked up a set of chopsticks and began to drop ingredients into the pot one by one. I found myself letting go of my anger and starting to relax, mesmerised by the stirring of the broth and the swish swish sound it made, that is until I felt myself nudged in the ribs by Sora's elbow.

"What?" I turned to him impatiently. He feigned bemusement but leant in, to whisper:

"Laura didn't like carrots. Hated the sweet taste of them."

As he dripped this piece of information into my ear, our host, who had been cooking the firmer vegetables first, stretched over to drop a piece of cooked carrot into my ponzu dip. I stared at the morsel, watching the dark sauce slowly engulf it. Looking up, I noticed that Reo was watching intently. I picked up the bowl and held it out to him.

"Reo, would you like this piece of carrot? I don't like their sweetness, I'm afraid."

As a I said this, I glanced apologetically at the server. She smiled and I was still wearing a reciprocal smile when I turned to face Reo again. The smile fell away as soon as I saw his expression. Confused, I looked over at Sora, but he was in animated discussion with the person on his right. Slowly it dawned on me. I pulled my napkin off my lap and hurriedly stood up.

"Reo, I'm very sorry but I don't feel well."

Leaning with my back against a wall, on the street outside the restaurant, I took some deep breaths. Reo had followed me out and was standing by my side. He had not said anything, and I assumed he was waiting for me to explain. I pushed myself away from the wall.

"I apologise Reo. I feel fine. It's just that I don't think I can do this. You looked strange ……..dejected… when I offered you that piece of carrot. I can only assume that Laura really liked them or something. This is a minefield for me, constantly wondering whether I am saying the right thing or not. I'm not Laura and I never knew Laura, so I am bound to say and do things that she would never have said or done."

Reo looked annoyed. "I thought I was paying you to do your homework. What did Yuuto say in his promotional spiel? All the actors on his books take their parts seriously."

"That's unfair. This is the third time I've met you and there has been little opportunity to sit down and talk about

Laura. How am I meant to learn about her if you don't tell me."

"I do not want to have to tell you." Reo sounded like a petulant child.

"Then how am I meant to learn about her. It's not fair to ask Niko; she's only a child," I paused to think for a moment. "I could ask Yui I suppose."

I looked questioningly at Reo, genuinely puzzled. I saw him register my puzzlement and then his cheeks redden. He sighed.

"No, you are right. I am sorry. I was taken by surprise. Tonight, I wanted to relax, look at you and enjoy the illusion that Laura was with me. Your comment shattered that pretension. Laura's favourite vegetable was carrots; it jarred to hear you say you did not like them…"

He rubbed his brow. "I know my reactions are disproportionate, but I cannot help responding to the little ways in which you are not like Laura."

He sighed again. "But I can see I am being unfair; next Sunday when we meet, I will make sure we make time to talk about her."

I felt relieved. "Ok, well I would appreciate that."

He stared at me hard. "You need to understand that I chose Yuuto's agency because he was promising something more substantive than the standard replacement agencies are able to deliver."

I folded my arms, a defence gesture against the demands he was making of me. I clearly needed to put in more work to fulfil my side of the bargain. For a moment, I thought of telling him that Sora had deliberately misled me. An instinct held me back. Yui's friendship and support would be important if I were to continue as Laura's replacement. Bad mouthing Sora could jeopardise that friendship. For now, even if it was only out of curiosity, I did want to continue in the role.

Reo shuffled his feet impatiently. "I need to get back to the others. I can arrange a taxi to take you home if that is what you would like. Maybe that would be best, for us to continue with the story that you were not feeling well?"

I nodded. "Yes, that's probably best. I'll see you on Sunday then. Fresh start?"

Reo gave me a wry smile.

CHAPTER 6

YUI WAS DELIGHTED when I called to confirm that I would come climbing with her and Sora on Saturday. She arranged to pick me up from Kichijoji station at half past six. It was an early start, but it was a two-and-a-half-hour drive to Mount Mizugaki and we were keen to ensure that we would have a full day's climbing ahead of us. I had not brought any gear over from England, so on Friday, I made a quick dash to a climbing shop to buy the minimum set of equipment I would need - a pair of rock shoes, helmet, harness, and belay device. This was a fair financial outlay, but I reckoned that once I had tried climbing in Japan, I would quickly become hooked, just as I had back in England on Peak District gritstone.

Rising early on Saturday morning, I pulled on loose-fitting trousers, partnered it with one of my old T-shirts, and appraised myself in the mirror. I figured that I would not look too out of place in the Japanese climbing world. I would have to rely on others for rope and rack, but Yui had assured me that between her and Sora they had more than enough nuts, cams, and draws.

Hurrying out of my room, I got to the rendezvous with ten minutes to spare. It was only then that I realised I had not asked for a description of Yui's or Sora's car. I would have to rely on them spotting me, as despite the early hour, there was a constant flow of people coming in and out of the station entrance. I need not have worried. At exactly half past six, a gold and sporty looking sedan sped up to the kerb, braking ostentatiously to a halt in front of me. A quick look at the driver confirmed that it was Sora behind the wheel. Yui jumped out of the front passenger seat and pulled me towards the car.

"Good morning, Quinn. You sit in front."

Before I could protest, she had shimmied into the back. I eased myself into the seat that Yui had vacated, placing my rucksack on the floor between my feet. Glancing across at Sora, I saw that he had the same gleam in his eyes as when we had first met at the shabu-shabu restaurant.

"Morning Laura."

At Sora's sarcastic greeting, Yui's hand came through from the back seat and slapped him on the shoulder.

"Sora, behave, or Quinn won't come with us."

Sora gave a short, amused laugh, winked at me, and then shifting the car into gear, eased out into the traffic. I stared out the window, wondering how I should react to this man. Laura had been a friend of his and was only eight months dead; it made me uncomfortable that he could joke about her in this way.

Sora fell silent, focused on driving fast as he weaved in and out of the traffic. Yui kept up a steady stream of conversation from behind. She was filling me in about what to expect when we got to Mizugakiyama National Park, letting me know what the walk-in time to the crags would be. I listened, thankful that she did not expect me to contribute much by way of response.

Various Tokyo districts flashed past, as we sped along the Chuo expressway, on our way out of the city. Within fifty minutes, we had left the outskirts of Tokyo behind and were driving though hills and mountains covered in dense green forest. Apart from his initial greeting, Sora had been quiet as Yui had chatted to me, but as the mountains came into view, he spoke:

"So how good a climber, are you?"

"Do you mean what grade do I typically climb?"
Sora nodded.

"Well, I don't know what grading system you use out here but back in England, I was fairly comfortable leading E2; depends on the nature of the route, of course."

"So, you are good then?"

"I guess; I've been climbing since I was 18."

"Not as good as Laura."

I felt myself tense and said nothing. Sora grinned. "Laura led 5.12a routes more or less effortlessly; that approximates to E5 in UK grading."

My curiosity got the better of me. "What grade was she attempting when she fell?"

Sora gave a low whistle. "5.14a; E10 or thereabouts. The route is called *Yōshanai michi*. It is said to be Japan's hardest trad multipitch. Two hundred and twenty-five metres in length and five pitches in all. Bolts for anchors have been placed at the bottom of three of the pitches but that is it. Other than that, you are on your own, with long run outs before there is anywhere to place gear. Not that Laura was concerned with that on the day she died; her attempt was a free solo, no rope, no protection."

"That sounds like a reckless thing to do."

Sora turned to me, his eyes flinty. "There were months of preparation before her solo attempt; we rappelled the pitches three or four times, rehearsing the moves before we top-roped them. Only after that did we attempt a free ascent, me leading initially, before she had a go. Overall, she climbed the route six times before that final climb. And ok, those practice runs had been with rope and other protection, and yes, the technical grade pushed her boundaries, but she had proven she was physically and mentally capable of climbing the line."

I glanced back at Yui. She was hunched forward straining to hear, a look of concern on her face. I cleared my throat.

"Yui said that you think a bird could have surprised her, caused her to fall?"

"It is one theory, yes. Pacific swifts are known to nest on Mount Mizugaki. There is a ledge on the fifth pitch of *Yōshanai michi*. It has a long narrow crevice above it. Birds have been seen flying into it. It is possible that Laura was attempting the move onto the ledge when she disturbed them and they flew out, potentially straight at her."

"Fuck."

Yui had already told me the theory, but I was shocked to hear Sora describe it.

"That's awful. Had you and Laura not seen these birds on your practice attempts?"

"No, presumably they were not there earlier on in the season." Sora's tone was curt.

"But it's just a theory, isn't it," I persisted, "because Yui said nobody saw Laura fall; nobody was there watching her?"

Sora ignored me. He was staring straight ahead again, but I noticed his hands were clenching the driving wheel more tightly than before.

Yui tapped me on the shoulder. "Where do you climb when you are in England?"

She was smiling at me, but it was a tight sort of smile. I felt a sharp flicker of unease and readily acceded to the change of subject.

Thanks to Sora's fast driving, we arrived at the main camping area in Mizugakiyama National Park, shortly after nine. I leapt out of the car, keen to stretch my legs, and noticed that there was a large hut about a hundred metres away. Various groups of people were sitting on seats outside, drinking and eating. Several were bent over maps, their tables strewn with what I presumed to be local hiking or climbing guides. I felt Yui at my elbow.

"They sell coffee over there so we can get one before we start the walk in if you like……. is that ok with you?"

Yui directed this last remark at her boyfriend who shrugged. She tugged at my arm. "Come on."

Yui and I were standing inside the hut, queuing up for coffee, when I noticed that I was being stared at. He sat by the window, an obvious Westerner amongst a group of Asian men. He was young, possibly not out of his twenties yet, with blond floppy hair, and long legs that sprawled in front of him. I glanced around the room. There were other Westerners amongst the predominantly Japanese crowd, but no others with blond hair as far as I could see. I and the young man stood out and I assumed that this is why he was staring at me. I turned back to see if he was still watching, only to realise that he had got up from his seat and was advancing towards us.

"Yui, how great to see you."

The young man had an English West country accent and, unexpectedly, on reaching us, had addressed Yui. She had reacted by raising her hand to her mouth in an expression of surprise.

"James. What are you doing back in Japan? Oh, it is good to see you."

She threw her arms around the young man's neck. He laughed and gently extricated himself from her embrace.

"I'm here to finish off that climbing guide I've been working on."

"But I thought you had finished it; is that not why you returned to England?"

He shook his head. "No, I needed to go back for personal reasons, but only temporarily."

He looked at me and then back at Yui again. "I was a bit stunned when you walked in just now; I thought you were with Laura, until I looked more closely."

Yui grimaced. "Sorry, that must have been a shock."

I had been standing to one side whilst Yui and James greeted one another but Yui now pulled me in towards them.

"This is Quinn. Quinn, this is James. He climbed with us last year."

James held out his hand. As I shook it, I noticed that his eyes were an unusual translucent green. He was scanning my face intently. "How do you two know each other?"

Tactfully, Yui had chosen not to disclose personal information about me when making the introductions, and I determined to provide only minimal information myself.

"I teach English language classes in Tokyo. I got to meet Yui through a student in my class. When I told her that I used to climb back in England, she invited me to come out here with her."

It wasn't exactly a lie, but I monitored James' reaction as he absorbed this information. He screwed up his face. "It's quite a coincidence - you meeting Yui, looking so much like Laura, and being a climber too."

I shrugged. James turned to Yui. "Is Sora with you?"

"Yes, he is waiting outside, checking the gear. We came into buy a coffee but will be setting off shortly. Go out and say hello to him."

For a fleeting moment, James looked worried, but he quickly recovered his composure. "Better not. The guys are ready for the off; we're just finalising the routes and then need to get moving." He paused. "Where are you going to be climbing?"

"I think we're heading over to Toichimen Iwa."

"You're not going to attempt *Yōshanai michi,* are you?" James's tone was sharp, and Yui flinched slightly. She shook her head vehemently. "No, no, of course not."

James seemed to visibly relax at this assurance. He gave Yui a quick hug and with a small wave to me, walked back to his companions. Yui let out a long slow breath. "It is probably just as well."

I raised an eyebrow. "What is just as well?"

Yui sighed. "James avoiding Sora. He blames Sora for Laura's death."

"Really? Why?"

"He has not said he blames him directly but in the days leading up to the climb, he was quite vocal in criticising Sora. He felt it was wrong of him to encourage Laura to free solo *Yōshanai michi*. He thought it was too dangerous."

We had reached the front of the queue and Yui ordered three coffees. After paying for these, she continued her explanation:

"They do not get on that well, James and Sora. They were civil enough when we climbed together last year, but there has always been a tension between them; they are both quite competitive."

This did not surprise me, but I did not comment. "Was James climbing with you the day Laura died?"

"No, but he was out here, and he was climbing in the same area. He was one of the first people to arrive at the scene when Laura fell."

"But he didn't see her fall?"

"He says he did not."

Yui had informed me that the walk from the car park to our climbing area, would take about an hour. It was a couple of kilometres in distance, but involved five hundred metres of ascent, and was on rocky ground in parts. Sora was impatient to get going, so as soon as we had finished our coffees, at a little after half past nine, we set off.

The path sloped gently upwards at first, weaving its way through conifer forest. The landscape was strewn with moss covered boulders, and we had to negotiate the occasional criss-crossing of a flowing brook. It was early August. The rain season was over, but it was hot and humid in Tokyo. Out here at the higher altitude, it felt cooler, and I was glad of the shade. Whenever there was a gap in the forest canopy, I looked up, struck by the abundance of crags of various shapes and sizes, rising amongst the trees. It reminded me of the Roaches in the Peak District but on a much grander scale.

After about forty minutes, the path started to incline steeply. Sora suggested a short stop. He threw his rope and rucksack onto the ground and pointed upwards through an opening in the trees.

"See that crag ahead. That is where we are heading."

I followed his gaze and saw a towering slab of bulging rock. Sora was watching my face for a reaction. "It is impressive, yes?"

"How tall is it?"

"Three hundred metres from the base; it is known as the rock of eleven faces as it has walls facing in multiple directions. The main and longest one is Moai face. That is the face that Laura fell from."

I glanced at Yui. She was staring up at the crag and seemed preoccupied. She had not mentioned to Sora that we had bumped into James, and she had been noticeably quiet on the walk in. She sensed me looking at her and shifted her gaze to smile sideways at me, before directing a question at Sora.

"What is the plan then Sora? What routes are you proposing?"

Sora had bent over to pull a chocolate bar out of the top compartment of his rucksack. When he stood upright again, he ripped the wrapper off and stuffed a square into his mouth, before answering Yui's question.

"I thought we would start with *Pegasus*." He grinned at me through a mouth full of chocolate. "Classic climb. Two pitches, overhanging to start with, needs strong finger and arm work. Second half follows a great fist size crack. You will love it. 5.11/E4 grade, so an interesting climb for you to warm up on."

I nodded. He was obviously testing me, but I did not have a problem with what he was suggesting, so long as he led the climb. I underplayed my climbing ability, but I knew I was good, and I had accumulated a lot of experience over the years. Sora had not finished though.

"And then I was wondering if Quinn might want to try the first couple of pitches of *Yōshanai michi?*"

"No!"

Yui's response was swift and robust, and I could see that she was angry. "I knew you would suggest that Sora. It's ghoulish and disrespectful. I am fundamentally opposed to you taking Quinn up that route."

Sora raised an eyebrow. "Ghoulish?"

"Yes, ghoulish. Can you imagine what Reo would say if he knew you had done that? He is still struggling with the loss of Laura. He has moved an almost identical lookalike into his home, even if only part-time, and no offence Quinn…" Yui leant across to squeeze my arm, "…but I do not see how that is going to help him process his grief and move on from this tragedy. Surely, even you Sora, with your advanced empathy, can see how it looks? You, risking Quinn's life on the same route that killed Laura."

Yui's tone dripped with sarcasm. Sora, possibly not used to Yui speaking to him in this way, looked taken aback. He turned to me.

"What do you think Quinn? I do not see that it would be that dangerous if I led the pitches. I am only proposing the first couple so that you can experience the long run outs and have a chance to see the full line of the climb close-up. Reo is paying you to step into the shoes of Laura. She was a risk taker, and if you experience the climb that killed her, I think you would gain more of an insight into that side of her character."

I looked from one to the other. I was struggling to know what to say. I could see where Yui was coming from. I was not so sure what I thought about Sora's argument. I sighed.

"It does seem a bit insensitive," I concluded. "You know Sora, you keep saying that Reo has hired me to *be* Laura, but your expectations seem extreme. I might have drama school training but I'm no Stanislavski student!"

Sora chuckled but Yui looked puzzled. "What's a Stanislavs…?"

She trailed off and I jumped in to explain. "It's a method of acting. An actor will deliberately go out to experience what their character has experienced. The idea is that they will then better understand that character's mindset."

I looked up at the sky and exhaled heavily. "I think the same of my arrangement with Reo, as you do Yui. I said as much to Yuuto, the agency guy. Like you, I cannot see how providing him with a constant reminder of his wife is going to help him move on, particularly when that person is not going to be a permanent fixture in his life. But Reo seems to want it, and Yuuto is adamant that it can help with the grieving process."

I paused. "Reo is applying significant pressure for me to be true to Laura and how she was, but I know little about her. In that sense, I can follow Sora's reasoning. I'm a climber and I know what risk feels like on the rock. There are risks I wouldn't take. If Laura was the sort of person who would take those risks, then I find that interesting. I would have thought it would have affected her relationship with Reo and Niko. If I'm honest, I am curious about the climb, but I do understand that retreading Laura's last movements might look morbid."

Sora clapped his hands loudly, causing Yui and I to jump. "Then I have the solution" he said. "We will take you up *Tōi hikari*. It is a nearby aid route. It has been bolted with ladders so a relatively easy climb. It runs parallel to *Yōshanai michi*'s first pitch. At the top of it you have an unobstructed view of the Moia face and the rest of the line of *Yōshanai michi*. It should give you an idea of what *Yōshanai michi* is like without having to climb it."

Sora looked at me and I looked at Yui. She seemed sceptical but wasn't protesting in the way she had been before. I shrugged my shoulders. "Fine. I'm ok with that if it's ok with Yui."

As we warmed up on *Pegasus*, it was interesting to observe how Sora and Yui climbed together. It reflected how they were with each other in everyday life. On the face of it, Sora was the leader, and Yui his seconder. She protected him from her belay position on the ground, whilst he made decisions about the route and took the risks. When it was her turn to follow him up, he was noisily instructive as to where she should put her feet and which handholds she should use. I noticed, however, that for the most part, she ignored his instructions or at least she didn't blindly defer to them. She was quiet and focused, surveying the rockface intently before making her own decision as to the next move.

When it was my turn to ascend, my suspicion was confirmed. *Pegasus* was no warm-up route. Tackling the overhang used all my upper arm strength, and the crack Sora had referred to was uneven in width and fiddly to work with. It was strenuous and obviously chosen to test my physical ability as much as my technique. I moved up the climb quickly, however, without a fall or needing to put my weight on the rope. When I emerged at the top of the second and final pitch, I could see that Sora was impressed. He winked at me before starting to undo his anchors.

Once we had coiled the rope and Sora had checked the gear back onto his harness, he led us back down - a circuitous path through the rocks, to where we had started. Our rucksacks were where we had left them. Yui headed directly for hers, rummaging around until she had found her seat mat.

"I am not going up *Tōi hikari,* nor am I going to watch you climb it. I will wait here until you are finished."

Yui sounded determined, primed to resist any objection, but Sora only nodded before turning towards me. "Do you need a rest, or shall we tackle *Tōi hikari* before lunch?"

I shrugged. "Happy to do the climb now, and then perhaps we can do a route that Yui would like to do this afternoon."

Yui shot me a small smile of gratitude, but Sora ignored the jibe. "Right come on then; it's this way."

When we reached the base of *Tōi hikari,* Sora explained that he wanted us both to free solo the route. He asked me to ensure that I kept sufficiently close behind him so that he could point out the climbing line on the adjacent pitch of *Yōshanai michi*.

"This is a straightforward climb" he reassured me. "Ladders have been positioned over the difficult bits."

"Yes, rusted ladders from the look of them," I retorted.

Sora grinned. "You need not worry. I will proceed carefully, and in any case, this is a well-used route. Climbing instructors regularly take their clients up here. They would have erected a warning sign if they felt that any of the ladders were dangerous."

I looked up at *Tōi hikari*. It did appear straightforward as Sora had said. The line provided regularly spaced holds, on a gently sloped slab of rock. It was perhaps thirty metres in length, and I could see four places where a short ladder had been fixed. The route itself ended on a wide ledge that looked to have an exit route off to the left. Sora had brought a rope with him but since we were meant to be free soloing the route, I was surprised to see him start the climb with the rope slung over his back. Would we be abseiling down? I did not have time to ask as I hurried to follow.

Swinging into position a couple of metres below Sora, I soon found myself falling into synch with his effortless rhythm. Every few metres, he would stop to point out the line of the first pitch on *Yōshanai michi*. It looked tough, a sheer flat stone face with few lines of weakness. There was the odd crack here and there, representing the only features that might afford any scope for inserting protection, but these were narrow and of questionable usefulness. In comparison, *Tōi hikari* was a breeze, and even the ladders presented no problems.

As we neared the ledge at the top of the route, I saw that there was a chimney of dark crumbing rock, a few metres away to the right, which was just large enough to contain a person. Sora was waiting for me as I hauled myself onto the ledge. He began to talk excitedly as soon as I was safely up.

"See there." He pointed towards the chimney. "That is what you need to scramble up to reach the start of the second pitch on *Yōshanai michi*. The first pitch takes you up and over the far end of this ledge we are standing on. You access the chimney from there."

I looked across and up, following the direction of his finger. The scramble up the chimney looked easy enough, albeit a damp experience. It necessitated a ten-metre or so haul up a narrow vertical crevice. I could see where a climber would emerge at the top of the chimney, but I could not see any obvious climb line from there. As Sora had promised, there was an unobstructed view of the Moia face from the top of *Tōi hikari*, but it was a view of almost continuously smooth rock. It looked as if a climber would have to climb tens of metres at a time before they encountered a fissure or protrusion which could be used for protection, or indeed any kind of hold. I looked back at Sora.

"Where does the line go once you are at the top of the chimney?"

Sora shuffled along the ledge so that he was standing right next to me. He raised my arm so that this time he was using my finger to point.

"You do not go straight up from there. Look to the right of that position. Can you see the faint crystal traverse? It stretches horizontally for about five metres, and then, can you see, there is a large jug hold at the end of it where a fixed bolt has been placed. Once you reach the jug, you strike upwards for thirty metres to reach the start of the third pitch."

I extricated my arm from Sora's handling and squinted, trying to see the features of the traverse. I could see a faint line running horizontally from the top of the chimney but then it seemed to run out, with no obvious handholds for approximately two metres between there and the jug that Sora had pointed out.

"The line runs out before it reaches the jug."

Sora laughed. "Well observed but look more closely. You should be able to see a thin flake at the end of the line. The way to reach the jug is to swing across the remainder of the way, using the flake as leverage."

"You are joking."

"I am not. I can show you if you like. Let us climb the chimney and then you can belay me from the top of there. It is why I brought the rope. If I fall on the traverse, you will be able to hold me. I could free solo it. I have done the move several times now, but Yui would not approve. I do not want to put you in a difficult position should anything happen."

I shook my head. "I don't need you to show me Sora, and I don't need to climb the chimney to appreciate how difficult the traverse is; I can see perfectly well from here. I can also appreciate the physicality and technique it took for you and Laura to master the move. I'm not sure I would attempt it without protection."

I looked up at the Moai face again. "Can you show me where you think those birds might have flown out and surprised Laura?"

Sora lifted my hand again to point. I looked beyond the line of my arm. It was hard to make out anything except smooth rock. "I can't see anything. Maybe a slightly darker area a little above where you've got my finger pointing."

"That is the spot exactly. There is a narrow ledge immediately below the darker area you are referring to. When you reach it, you need to pull yourself up onto the ledge and into a standing position. It is a very strenuous move. You have to lift your leg up and hook your ankle over the ledge. You then use your foot as an anchor to leverage yourself up. Laura got the hang of it eventually. Just above the ledge, the dark area you can see, that is the long narrow crevice which other climbers have seen the birds flying in and out of. As I said, I think one could have flown out, as she was pulling herself onto the ledge."

"Did Laura know about the birds? You said that neither of you had seen any when you were practising the climb, but did she know that people had seen them at other times?"

"I do not think so. She never mentioned it. I did not hear about the bird theory until after she fell. An English guy we were climbing with last year suggested that that is what might have happened."

"James?"

Sora looked at me, a surprised expression on his face. "Yes, how do you know that? Do you know him?"

I hesitated. Yui hadn't mentioned bumping into James and for some reason, it was holding me back from telling Sora myself. "Yui mentioned him when I was asking about who else Laura used to climb with."

Sora scowled. "He is not in Japan anymore; he went back to England immediately after the accident. Look, if we are not going to climb the chimney, let us get off this ledge."

Sora turned abruptly and began to make his way along the ledge in the opposite direction to the chimney. I followed and after a short scramble to get off the ledge at the far end, we reached a rocky path which descended through the forest. Once on surer ground, I ran to draw level with him. He slowed his pace to let me catch up.

"Why are you interested in who else Laura climbed with?" Sora sounded irritated.

"I was curious about her wider social network, that's all, who her main friends had been in Tokyo."

"Yui was her main friend."

Sora's tone was sharp and inhibitory. I changed the subject.

"From what I have seen today, *Yōshanai michi* is a very tough challenge. You said Laura was a risk taker. Are you saying that when she climbed, she made moves which she wasn't confident she could execute, that she did this in situations where she had no protection should she fall?"

Sora stopped walking and looked at me. "Every climber, who attempts routes at a certain technical level, takes risks."

"Yes, but they have calculated those risks and prepared for them. I wouldn't free solo a route I knew was going to be a challenge both physically and technically, unless I could be sure of two things: firstly, that I had already successfully climbed the route with protection, and secondly, that I had the confidence, I could do so again without."

I paused. "You said that you and Laura had practised *Yōshanai michi* several times before Laura attempted to free solo it."

"Yes. What is your point?"

"I'm trying to understand how much of a risk taker she was. That swing across to the jug on the second pitch, for example. It doesn't look like a move you could be confident of pulling off every time, no matter how much you had practised it."

Sora shrugged. "I've done that move several times with only minimal protection. Once you understand the technique required and have proven to yourself that you can physically execute the move, not just as a once off but repeatedly without error......." Sora shrugged again.

"So, is that the stage of preparation Laura had reached? I guess I'm asking how much of a gamble she took?"

"Oh, for god's sake." Sora hitched his rope further up onto his shoulders and resumed walking. Again, I ran to catch up.

"I'm just trying to understand her. I don't get why she would take such a significant risk when she had a husband and child back at home."

"Maybe she wanted to FEEL ALIVE."

Sora practically shouted this at me. It took me aback but after a shocked pause, I asked him what he meant.

Sora sighed. "You never knew her. She had this drive, this energy. She was impatient and striving, even after she had had Niko. You might have thought that when she met Reo, when she had her family, she would have settled down, found fulfilment, but that was not how it was. It was like she had to keep having new experiences, new thrills to keep her satisfied."

"Is that what you were alluding to when you put your hand on my thigh the other night."

"What?" Sora stopped in his tracks and sounded genuinely offended. "I did not."

I stared at him. "You did. You said: *'You are not like Laura and if you were, you won't mind me doing this,'* and then you put your hand on my thigh."

Sora's eyes widened. "I don't remember that; was I drunk?"

I searched his face. "Seriously, you don't remember?"

Sora shook his head.

"Well, you did say it and you did do it. It was as if you were intimating that the two of you had been having an affair."

I noticed Sora's cheek redden. He glared at me. "That is ridiculous. If I did do what you say, it would have been because Laura could be flirtatious, that is all. As I have said, she was a risk taker, she wanted to feel alive, both on and off the rock."

Sora started off down the path once more. This time I let him go, following on more slowly behind. How could he have forgotten? I was not sure if I believed him, and I did not understand why he was reacting so crankily to my questions.

As I entered the clearing where we had left our rucksacks, and where Yui had stayed behind to wait for us, I heard raised voices. I quickly registered that Sora and Yui were arguing. On seeing me, they stopped. Yui took a step towards me. She had tears in her eyes.

"Are you ok, Yui?"

She shook her head. "I am so sorry Quinn." Yui gulped back a sob. "Your mobile rang. I thought it might be important, so I answered it. It was Reo......."

Sora rolled his eyes.

"That's ok. I don't mind you answering my phone. What did he say?"

"He was calling to discuss your visit tomorrow."

Another jerky sob as Yui tried to explain. "He was surprised to hear that I was with you, so I told him that I had invited you climbing."

Yui wiped a tear from her cheek. "He asked me where we were and what we were doing. I did not feel I could lie. He got so angry. He shouted at me. I am so sorry."

Yui's face was full of contrition. I stood there, not saying anything at first, trying to work out how I felt about Reo's reaction.

"Was he angry that I was with you or was it because you had taken me climbing?"

Sora snorted. "Because we had taken you climbing of course. I told her." He gesticulated offhandedly at his girlfriend. "I told her not to tell him. I knew he would react this way."

He turned to Yui directly. "You should not have answered the call if you could see it was from him."

I waved Sora's remark away with my hands. "It doesn't matter; it's done now. I'm not surprised that he was angry. He was probably shocked. His wife died in a climbing accident, and he now finds out that the replacement he has hired, is risking her life in the same way, a replacement I hasten to add who told him she had given up the sport."

"You are not risking your life." Sora scoffed. "And you are off duty. It is not Reo's business what you do when you are not working for him?"

I didn't answer but I agreed with Sora. He wasn't the first person to have pointed this out; Yui had said the same thing a week or so ago when we had been chatting in her kitchen. I looked at her; she was still upset. I sighed and ran my fingers through my hair.

"Please don't worry Yui. I'll call Reo when I get home this evening. I'll explain it was my idea and I'll try to get him to understand that what I do in my own time is my business. It will be ok."

Yui gave me a weak smile, whilst Sora simply repeated his eye roll.

CHAPTER 7

I COULD FEEL MY HEART beating hard and fast. As I waited for somebody to open the door. I cleared my throat and rubbed the sweat from my hands onto my clothes. I had not managed to speak to Reo since returning from climbing yesterday. He had not wanted to pick up my call and as a result we had only exchanged texts - mine apologetic but seeking understanding, his short and terse. I had told him I would arrive at his apartment mid-morning. This was as we had previously agreed. He had not replied, leaving me unclear as to whether he wanted me to turn up or not. I decided that I would go anyway.

Niko opened the door, smiling cheekily at me.

"Hello Niko, is your dad in?"

Niko nodded and leaving the door open, flew back down the hallway. I stepped over the threshold and took off my shoes. Lightly on my feet, I tip toed down the corridor and stopped hesitantly at the entrance to the living room. There was nobody there, apart from Kasei, the domestic robot. Its system whirred up as it detected my presence. It looked as if it had been staring out of the window. Presumably, it had been in that position when it had been powered down and put into standby mode. Its head now swivelled around so that it looked as if it was appraising me.

"You have been here before." The statement was in English, with the same distorted female voice.

"Yes" I said, relieved that the robot had recognised me. "I am a friend of the family. Is Reo around?"

"Around?"

"In the house."

"No, he is not."

That's strange I thought. Niko had said he was.

"Do you know when he will be back?"

"No, I do not."

I sighed and tried another tack. "Do you know where Niko went?"

The robot paused. Its head swivelled again but this time towards the door which I knew led to the kitchen and the other rooms in the apartment.

"She is in her room."

"Through there?" I waved my hand towards the door.

"Yes."

"Would it be ok if I went to find her?"

There was a faint electronic sound from Kasei and then: "I do not know the answer to that."

I stared at the robot, curious as to the extent of its processing capabilities. "You speak good English. Do you speak Japanese as well?"

"My instructions are to speak English in the household."

"Right. Well, Kasei-fu, I am going to see Niko now. I am going to go to her room."

I waited for a response. There was a slight pause and then: "I will come with you."

I followed Kasei through to a bedroom right at the back of the apartment. Niko was in there. She sat at a small desk, typing on a keyboard, the accompanying computer screen displaying a stream of programming code. She was so absorbed that she did not notice me enter at first. I took in a quick scan of the room. My first impression was of a colourful eleven-year old's bedroom - a preponderance of pink and yellow; teddy bears of assorted sizes clustered on the bed, and what looked like a collection of shojo manga in a small bookcase by the window. The main deviation from the cutesy feel were the walls; posters of young women in various samurai fighting stances were displayed over much of the surface area.

I coughed to attract Niko's attention. She leapt to her feet.

"I'm sorry. I didn't mean to surprise you. Your dad doesn't seem to be in."

Niko looked at Kasei. "He was in just now.... He must have gone out for something." She sat back down, glancing back up at me. "You could go and wait for him in the living room."

Niko's tone was not rude, but it was mildly dismissive.

"That looks like code. Are you developing a program of some sort?" I gestured towards the screen. Niko nodded and swung her feet around to face the computer again.

I scanned the room once more. On the floor to the right of Niko's desk, I noticed K2. The robotic dog was in a standing position but had a side panel open and a wire leading from the panel to Niko's computer. "Oh, you're programming K2?"

Niko nodded; she had resumed typing.

"What are you wanting the dog to do?"

There was no reply. I tried again. "Your dad said he wanted you to stick with the code provided in the instruction manual."

Niko's response was fast and unexpected. She wheeled around, her face furious. "The code in the manual is too limited. She is my dog. My mother gave her to me, and I can train her to do exactly what I want."

I made a show of backing off, holding up my hands to pacify her. "Ok, ok, I didn't mean to make you mad Niko. I'm just repeating what your dad told me. He has good reasons for asking you to stick to the manual, you know."

Niko glared at me. "What reasons?"

I thought quickly. A lesson in AI ethics seemed in order but how to explain the key principles to an eleven-year-old?

"K2 arrived house-trained, isn't that right?"

Niko looked at me warily. "Yes."

"A first task when someone gets a new pet is to make sure it's housetrained. It's obvious why, isn't it?"

Niko stared at me mutely.

"So why did you decide to over-ride the code that disabled K2 from going to the 'toilet' anywhere other than the tray that came with her?"

Niko didn't respond.

"Did you think it funny to program her so that she would go wherever and whenever you gave her the command?"

Niko giggled but then quickly tried to stop herself by putting her hand over her mouth.

"Of course, in K2's case it is just water, but what if somebody put actual pee into her water cavity."

Niko looked shocked. I nodded at her. "Yes, somebody might do that if they felt it was funny, just like you thought that your actions were funny. But consider this: what if the vocal command didn't always work in the way you had planned?"

Niko frowned. "What do you mean?"

"Well, I noticed you hummed a short tune just before K2 'peed' near your dad's feet. I am assuming that was the command. What if you took K2 to school one day and one of your friends unintentionally hummed the same tune, causing K2 to pee on your teacher's foot?"

Niko giggled again.

"I'm being serious Niko. That might be a silly and harmless example, but the school would still give you a detention or reprimand if that happened."

Niko was looking sulky now, but I ploughed on with my lecture.

"The risk of a detention at school is not the point though. Developing artificial intelligence is responsible work. You should only do it for good reasons, and you should ensure that nobody could use what you have created to do bad things."

I knelt by the side of K2 and stroked her head. "More worryingly, what if K2 learnt to use your code to program herself. What if she decided to pee on people's feet whenever she felt like it and you couldn't stop her?"

Niko's eyes widened. "She wouldn't be able to do that."

"She might. Scientists have shown that Artificial Intelligence has the potential to learn for itself. If you are going to code, you have a responsibility to ensure that you have managed the risks and that what you are doing is safe. You must be sure that the AI you create won't get out of control or be used by somebody else for illegal purposes."

I stood up. "Lecture over. I don't mean to say that you shouldn't code, Niko. You are talented in this area. Your dad would want to encourage you. Just think a bit more about why you are doing it, as well as all the possible consequences."

There was the sound of clapping from the doorway and then Reo's voice: "I couldn't agree more."

I blushed. "How long have you been standing there?"

"Long enough to hear some very sound arguments about why we need to take care where artificial intelligence is concerned."

Reo stepped forward to ruffle his daughter's hair. "Are you ok in your bedroom for a bit Nik? I want to talk to our guest about something. Then we can all go to the park if you like?" He gestured for me to follow him back into the living room.

I found myself perched once more on the futon, with Reo sitting across from me on the wicker chair. He looked serious and wasted no time in getting to the point.

"You told me that a friend of yours had died in a fall whilst climbing. You said that this had made you give up the sport."

I shook my head. "I didn't tell you that Reo, Yuuto did."

Reo narrowed his eyes. "Are you saying Yuuto was lying?"

I sat back, resigned to exposing Yuuto's lie. "He told you that because he thought it would help forge a bond between the two of us. I was angry with him for letting you think it ………"

I paused to gently brush away a small spider that I had noticed crawling over my knee.

"I have been climbing on and off since university days; I love it. Yui invited me to join Sora and her out at Mizugaki, and I thought it was an opportunity to get to know some more people in Tokyo, spend some time in a beautiful national park. I wasn't working for you yesterday and, quite honestly, I don't think it is right that you should be able to restrict what I do in my spare time."

I braced myself, preparing for a confrontation. Reo was frowning and had his hands clenched into fists on his lap. When he spoke, however, his voice was soft and calm.

"You are right of course…." He unclenched a hand to rub his right ear. "But I am sure you can understand how it made me feel when Yui picked up the phone, told me where you were and what you were doing."

He stood up and walked towards the window. For the first time, I noticed a beautiful pottery urn had been placed at the far end of the window shelf; green and red in colour, its design depicted an intricate swirl of Japanese dragons. As Reo reached the window and turned to face me, he saw me looking at it.

"It contains Laura's ashes. Niko and I have not decided what to do with them yet. At one point, we considered a trip back to England to scatter them in the Lake District. It was a place she used to talk about. I cannot make up my mind whether that would be the right decision though............."

Reo's voice trailed off and he walked back to his chair. "Would you let me call you Laura?"

For a moment I could not speak; I felt stunned and slightly repelled. On seeing my face, he started to backtrack, but I held up my hands to stop him.

"Do you genuinely believe that spending time with me one or two days a week, and pretending my name is Laura, is going to help you get over the grief you feel for your wife?"

Reo's face crumpled and seeing his vulnerability, I felt guilty for my directness. I softened my tone.

"How would that work Reo? What would Niko think? What would your parents think?"

Reo was now looking sullen. "You are meant to be Laura's replacement. Is that not the whole point of this arrangement?"

I put my face in my hands and took a deep breath. When I lifted my head, he was watching me, his brow furrowed.

"Alright Reo, call me Laura if you want to, but only when it's you and me alone. I don't think Niko would understand."

"What would I not understand?" Niko's quiet arrival in the living room had taken us by surprise. I fell silent and deferred to Reo to explain.

"Come and sit down, Niko." Reo gestured to the space besides me. Niko trotted over and sidled onto the other end of the futon.

"What do you think of our new friend?" Reo flicked a thumb towards me.

Niko looked at me and then quickly away. "She's nice."

"She certainly is. We have been talking about her coming over each weekend to spend time with us. Would you like that?"

Niko gave a tentative nod.

"She looks like mum, doesn't she."

Niko scanned my face shyly.

"I was wondering if we should call her Laura when she is here in the house."

Niko stiffened besides me. "But her name is Quinn." Her voice came out squeaky but firm.

"Yes, but I thought it might make us feel that your mum was back with us again, that that might make us happy."

"No." Niko shouted. "She's not my mum."

She had turned to glare at me, and I could see that she was fighting to hold back tears. I placed a hand on her arm.

"Niko, please don't get upset. Of course, you shouldn't call me Laura. That's your mum's name. Your dad shouldn't have suggested it. I'm Quinn and that's what you should call me."

Niko nodded, a small sob escaping her. I stood up. "Come on, let's go to the park and buy ice creams."

It turned out that Reo had already arranged for us to meet his parents in the park, next to where you could hire the swan boats. He readily agreed to my suggestion of ice-cream, with an ostensible relief at the change of subject. There was a brief, unsuccessful tussle with Niko, who demanded that she bring K2 along, but ten minutes later we had all trooped out of the apartment and were on our way to Inokashira.

Reo's parents were waiting for us when we arrived. They had brought Albert along with them and the trio sat on a bench overlooking the lake. Smiles broke out on seeing us, which widened to grins when they spotted K2.

After a quick round of familial embracing, we started a slow meandering walk in the direction of an ice-cream vending machine, which Niko had pointed out to me on the way in. I found myself at the back of the group, keeping step with Akemi and Albert. They seemed to be deliberately slowing their pace to increase the gap between us and the rest of the family.

At a point where we were safely out of earshot, Albert abruptly changed the conversation from everyday pleasantries to something more earnest in tone.

"Akemi needs to talk to you about Laura. She would like to meet you in the city tomorrow if you are free?"

I glanced across at Akemi. She was nodding at me, her whole face crunched into a wrinkled smile of encouragement.

Albert continued: "I know you speak some Japanese, but I think it would be easier if we conducted the conversation in English. I would accompany Akemi, to help translate; she has limited English, as you know."

I looked at him curiously, not sure whether I should challenge the suggestion that the conversation would be best conducted in English. In the end I decided not to.

"Ok, if that's what you think would work best. Where do you want to meet?"

"The Shibuya district. There is a restaurant in the Hikarie shopping mall, overlooking the station. It's on the eighth floor. It's called d47 Shokudo. The d47 is a reference to Japan's forty-seven prefectures. I think you will find it interesting. There are set menus, representing the cuisine from each of the forty-seven areas. It's also quiet, high above the hubbub of the Shibuya crossing. Large windows and good views too. Say we meet at the entrance to the restaurant at twelve. We can have a nice lunch and Akemi can explain what she wants to talk to you about."

"No advance information about that?" I asked.

Albert shook his head. "Best not. We need to rejoin the others. Chieko does not know about this; you must not mention it to him, nor to Reo or anybody else."

I looked ahead. The others had noticed we had fallen behind and had stopped to give us time to catch up.

"Ok, I'll be there. You're intriguing me."

We had almost caught up with the others when I saw Sora and Yui walking along the path from the other direction. I felt an immediate jolt of nervousness. They looked as if they were out for a casual Sunday stroll and had not noticed us. I glanced quickly around but there was no way to avoid them. As far as I was aware, Reo had not spoken to Yui since the unfortunate incident with my phone; I was not sure how he would be with her.

As it turned out, I need not have worried. When the couple reached us, Reo nodded to them and began an exchange with Sora about work. I had not been paying attention to Niko since we had met up with her grandparents. I noticed now, however, that she was a little to one side of the group, crouched down next to K2. She had her head close to the robotic dog's head and was whispering to it. I moved quickly towards her, sensing trouble.

As I arrived at her side, she stopped whispering and give a low trill like sound. She stood up and, upon seeing me, quickly averted her eyes. I looked down at the dog. It had been motionless but was now rotating its head from side to side as if scanning our group. I saw it fix its eyes on Sora and then start to move towards him. I grabbed Niko's arm.

"Niko, what's going on?"

Niko looked at me, a blank and unreadable expression on her face. The sound of a mechanical growl made me turn back to the group, just in time to see K2 lock its jaws around Sora's left shin and calf. Sora let out a sharp shout and grabbed the dog's head. He wrestled with it but could not loosen its grip. I saw blood start to seep down his lower leg. Reo had bent down to try to help but Sora suddenly straightened up and yelled at Niko.

"Get this thing off of me."

His face was contorted with pain. Reo rose too and in three quick steps was facing Niko. "Is this your doing Niko?"

Niko would not look at her father. She stood rigid, staring persistently down at the ground. Exasperated, Reo tugged his daughter towards Sora. He pointed towards Sora's leg which was beginning to swell up. An angry bruising had begun to show around the edges of K2's grip.

"This is a bad injury, Niko. Sora will need medical attention. We need to get K2 off now!"

Niko had been staring at Sora's leg. The blood coursing from the locked metal was extensive now. I saw her bottom lip quiver.

"I don't know how to get her off."

"But you gave K2 the instruction to do this, did you not, Niko?" Reo's question was urgent. "If that is the case, you can give her the instruction to release her grip, can you not?"

Niko gave a barely perceptible shake of her head and began to cry. Sora had been moaning and clutching his leg but went still on hearing this conversation. He glared at Niko; his lip curled.

"When I get out of this situation, you are in huge trouble little girl."

He took me aback with the level of aggression in his tone. He was snarling at Niko and shaking his fist.

Reo stepped forward to place himself between Sora and Niko.

"Niko, go with your grandparents. You can stay with them at their apartment until I am able to collect you."

He got out his mobile phone. "I am going to call 119, Sora. You are losing a lot of blood. I think you might need stitches."

His fingers hit the keypad and he lifted his phone to his ear.

Within ten minutes, we had confirmation that the hospital had dispatched an ambulance. Chiko and Akemi had taken Niko back to their apartment and Reo and Yui had managed to manoeuvre the conjoined Sora and K2 towards a bench, on which Sora now sat. He was holding on to his leg and looking pale.

I had been standing awkwardly at the periphery of this activity until, having dealt with the immediate priorities, Reo signalled for me to follow him a short way up the path. After twenty-five metres or so, he stopped and took my hand.

"I am sorry. Every time we meet, something happens to cut short our time together." He looked at me gravely. "I need to accompany Sora and Yui to the hospital; I need to ensure that Sora does not implicate Niko when he tells the medical staff what happened. You do understand?"

"Of course."

I withdrew my hand from his and saw his face fall. He did not try to take it again though, instead stuffing his hands into his trouser pockets. I suddenly felt sorry for him.

"Phone me to let me know how things go, won't you?"

He nodded and then without warning whipped his hand back out of his pocket to snatch my arm. "Promise me two things."

I looked at him, a small vein of anxiety coursing through me.

"I will not ask you to tell me what you do in your own time, and you do not have to tell me, but promise me you will never lie to me."

"I wouldn't"

"Laura and I were always completely honest with each other; I will not be able to cope if you and I do not have the same level of integrity in our relationship."

"I won't lie to you. I don't have any reason to lie." Reo had thrown me by the intensity of his request.

"Then we understand each other. The second thing I ask is that you never attempt to climb *Yōshanai michi?*"

Now he was upsetting me. "Reo, of course I won't. I realise how grossly insensitive that would be. I would never want to hurt you or Niko in that way,"

He continued to hold my gaze fiercely for several moments, before finally releasing my arm. "I do not know how long this will take, how long we will be at the hospital, but I am likely to be back late. I will call you during the week."

He gave me a small bow and began to walk back down the path. I waited until he had rejoined Sora and Yui, before turning on my heel to exit the park.

CHAPTER 8

THE NEXT DAY, the onslaught hit me as soon as I reached the station's exit. Since arriving in Tokyo, I had already visited this place a couple of times, so I was prepared for the excitability of the throng and the stop-start rumbling of the engines as I stepped into the open air. I was also expecting the glare of the lights and the towering neon. Yet it struck me each time – the contrast between the outside and the inside at Shibuya.

For the last thirty minutes, I had ridden the metro, having queued ten lines deep to get on the train. Once aboard, I had hung from an overhead strap with no more than a knuckle's width of space between me and my fellow travellers. Yet nobody had spoken during the journey, and on alighting, obedient and calm in their orderliness, everybody had shuffled forward towards the exit, Zen like but with the hint of the automaton.

At the top of the steps, I looked down on the wide expanse of criss-cross ahead of me. The traffic lights on the Shibuya crossing had a two-minute cycle. My timing was fortunate. The cars that had been advancing were slowing to a halt. A small white van sped up at the last moment to jump the no man's time zone, but it was the last vehicle to make it across.

I skipped lightly down the steps to join the human surge. Hachiko was waiting at the bottom. I extended my hand to fleetingly stroke the stone casting of fur. A student in one of my classes had told me the story of this statue and it broke my heart - a dog in the 1920s who had come each day to meet his owner after work. The owner had died but the dog had continued to come. Each evening it came, and it continued to do so for ten long years after its owner's death.

I stepped onto the crossing, and instantly felt the pressure of a new wave of people building up behind me. I was committed to the *Shibuya scramble* now but more practised than on my previous attempts. Via a combination of dodging, weaving, and nimbly seeking the gaps, I was able to make my way forward. Streams of people were intersecting from all directions. I switched from watching my feet to looking ahead. At five foot eight inches, I was taller than the average Tokyo inhabitant. Stretching to full height and holding my head high, I was able to see over a sea of heads, to the far side.

As I estimated the distance to go, I spotted him. Perhaps ten metres in front of me. A blond, six-foot tall Gulliver. Of course, he stood out from the crowd, but I would not have assumed it was him. It was the rope that convinced me, coiled, and slung across his shoulders in the effortless way of the climber.

I quickened my pace, keeping my eyes on him. He reached the pavement on the other side with the same ten metre gap between us. The pedestrian lights turned red, and the people behind me began to push forward urgently; the usual last-minute dash before the cars started advancing again. I skip-hopped the remaining few steps to the pavement and made my way to a shop window. There I found a space to stand, whilst I readjusted the position of my backpack. I kept my sights on the Gulliver. His walk was quick and purposeful, but suddenly, he veered right, ducking his head to enter a brightly lit Pachinko parlour at the corner of Bunkamori-dori street.

I hurried after him, stopping at the entrance to the parlour. The room was divided into aisle after aisle of slot machines, each machine having its own stool, and each stool occupied. My first impression was that there were no women in the room, as far as I could see anyway, and although ages varied from the old to the young, there was no immediate sign of a blond head. There was also no talk, just the sound of spinning reels, beeps and chimes, and a celebratory jingle with flashing animation when anybody won.

I stepped across the threshold and began to make my way up and down each aisle. He was definitely not in here. I spotted a cashier in a booth at the back of the room and walked over to him.

"Did you see a blond guy come in here a minute ago?"

I had spoken in Japanese, and the cashier nodded back at me. He pointed to a door by the side of his booth.

"He is through that door, but it is not open to the public yet."

"What isn't open?" I enquired.

"The new climbing centre."

"Ok thanks."

I made for the door, hearing the cashier protest that I was not permitted to walk through there. Too late, I was already through and out onto the other side. I looked around. I had walked into a huge interior space. All around the edge was a wide expanse of climbing wall. Line after line of fixed ropes hung down with routes of varying colour-coded difficulty. The Gulliver was standing across the way from me, below a large overhang. He was in conversation with another guy. I called over to him:

"James!"

He turned and looked surprised when he saw who had called out his name. Excusing himself from his companion, he strode over.

"Quinn! That's your name, isn't it? What are you doing here?"

"I'm having lunch with Reo's mother, a place back up by the station. She wants to talk to me about Laura. I haven't got long. I need to go and meet her, but I saw you on the crossing."

He stared at me, a look of curiosity on his face. "I thought you met Yui through somebody you teach. You know Reo and his wider family too?"

I returned his stare, not wanting at this moment to explain. "Are you going to be here long?"

"A couple of hours or so, why?"

"I'd like to meet you after I've had lunch. I wanted to ask you a few things."

"About Laura?" James' expression was wary.

I nodded. "I'll explain properly then. Would that be ok?"

James scratched the back of his head whilst he continued to stare at me.

"Alright." He sounded reluctant. "I'll hang on here until two o'clock. Does that give you enough time?"

I smiled gratefully at him. "Yes, thanks. See you then."

I dashed back down the street, realising that I was going to be late for my meeting with Albert and Akemi. Once in the mall, I headed for the eighth floor, following the signs for the restaurant. They were not waiting outside so not hesitating, I walked in and scanned the room. I spotted them quickly, already seated and sat by a large window. I weaved my way over to them, waving at one of the servers to indicate that they were my dining companions. Albert stood up to greet me.

"Ah Quinn, welcome. I am glad that you managed to find your way here ok."

I looked around me. Lofty ceilings and high windows, widely spaced tables, a preponderance of plants, and a fantastic view over the immediate city environs. I nodded my approval as Albert pulled out a chair and with a courteous gesture ushered me into it.

"Now, before we get down to business, let's choose what we are going to eat."

He thrust a leather-bound book into my hand. I began to leaf through the pages of set menus, each course written in English beneath the Japanese. As Albert had explained to me, each menu represented food and a recipe from one of Japan's prefectures. This meant that I had a choice of forty-seven to choose from.

"How are you meant to choose?" I asked. Akemi must have understood because she grinned at me.

"Well, how about you choose one of the prefectures you are planning to visit?"

This was Albert's suggestion. I shook my head. "I haven't planned any visits outside Tokyo yet, apart from climbing trips to Mizugaki."

This seemed to be the wrong thing to say. Both Albert and Akemi glanced at each other and for a short while, nobody spoke. Albert finally broke the silence. "We want to talk to you about Mizugaki after we've eaten. First though, let us enjoy a meal. Surely you have intentions of visiting other parts of Japan whilst you are out here?"

"Well, yes, eventually, for sure, but it has been so busy since I got to Tokyo. I haven't had time to think about any wider travelling plans."

I looked down at the book in my hands and resumed flicking through the menus. I stopped at number twenty-six. "I guess it will have to be Kyoto."

I looked up to smile at my companions. "It's where I studied for a year of my degree. I've never been back and it's a good twenty years since I was there."

I studied the menu and made a grimace. "Soba noodles with dried herring. Er, maybe not."

"Well Akemi and I have already decided. I'm sampling Hokkaido and Akemi's going for Okinawa."

I flicked to the list at the front of the menu book. I grinned. "Number one and number forty-seven prefectures. You couldn't get further apart."

Albert chuckled and spotting a waiter, gestured for him to come over.

Having kept the conversation light and restricted to neutral topics throughout the meal, it was only when we got to the dessert - mine a delightful bitter-sweet coffee jelly - that Albert steered the conversation towards the reason we were having lunch together.

"I'm going to let Akemi explain why she wanted to meet up with you, Quinn. She will be able to explain best in Japanese and you will no doubt follow what she says, but to avoid any chance of misinterpretation, I am going to translate into English, as we go along. Is that ok with you?"

"Of course."

I focused on Akemi who so far had been noticeably quiet, simply nodding and smiling at appropriate intervals throughout the duologue which Albert and I had kept up, over the course of our meal. Following Albert's cue, however, she put down her napkin, placed her hands in her lap and began to speak. Albert adopted the role of the translative echo, and I sat back in my chair to listen.

When she had finished telling me what she wanted to say, I realised that I had been holding my breath. I let out a long exhalation. So Reo had told his parents that he had hired me to be a replacement for Laura. What is more he had told them that I had upset him by going climbing with Sora and Yui, not just climbing but doing so at the same place where Laura had died. Akemi did not criticise her son's decision to use a replacement agency, not to me anyway, and I had not been able to discern her real feelings about it. Instead, she had been far more concerned to tell me about Sora.

What she told me was not a surprise. Although Sora had denied it, I had not been convinced. Akemi finally confirmed it: he and Laura had been having an affair. Akemi was embarrassed when she described how she had dropped by Reo and Laura's apartment unexpectedly, about six months before Laura died. She had discovered Sora and Laura together. Laura had come to see her afterwards; she had been desperate to convince Akemi that it was just a fling, that she had ended it, and that Reo must never know. Akemi had believed her, but she also told me that Sora hadn't accepted this, that according to Laura, he had continued to make pressurising advances.

As Akemi concluded her story, I felt that she had avoided coming to the main point of her narrative. I cleared my throat.

"Akemi, I am grateful that you have taken me into your confidence, but so as to avoid any doubt, can you explain why you are telling me this?"

Akemi shot a quick look at Albert who reached over and squeezed her hand. He began to speak for her.

"Akemi is warning you to stay away from Sora. He can be unpleasant and aggressive. Akemi says that she wouldn't put it past him to force himself upon a woman if he wanted her enough. And no bones about it, he will want you, looking so like Laura as you do. But that's not the main reason Akemi is telling you this."

Albert chewed his lip before continuing.

"Reo and Sora do not have a good relationship; it's civil because they work together and Sora is dating Yui, but it's surface thin. You've probably seen how competitive Sora can get. Sora may be ten years younger than Reo, but he resents the fact that their company gave Reo the director's job. They both went for it. Reo got it. Since then, whatever Reo has, Sora tries to take or sabotage. So, that's another reason that it's a fair bet he will make a play for you. He's not a nice guy, Quinn. Akemi never told Reo about Sora's affair with Laura, and we don't think Yui knows, but Reo isn't blind to Sora's character. Even Niko senses something is not right about him; you saw what she put K2 up to yesterday."

"Yes, I was going to ask you about that? I haven't spoken to Reo since the incident. Is Sora's leg going to be ok?"

"Thankfully yes, and Reo has convinced him not to file a police report, even if he will be limping for a while. Sora is not letting Niko off the hook though. He is insisting that he, Reo and Niko meet with an AI behavioural mediator to talk through what happened."

"An AI behavioural mediator?" I raised a questioning eyebrow.

"It's somebody who advises on AI ethics, who offers mediation in situations where a person's coding has led to concerns or complaints about a robot's actions."

I shook my head, amazed again at how advanced this country appeared to be when it came to AI and its integration within society.

"And Reo has agreed to this request?"

"I don't think he feels he has any choice. He needs to keep Sora onside; he and Niko rely on Yui's support, and Sora could disrupt those arrangements if he chose to."

"Really?" I did not think that Yui could be so easily influenced.

Albert nodded. "If he wanted to yes. Sora is more persuasive and manipulative than you think. It is why Akemi is concerned that Sora might end up taking you away from Reo. Reo almost had a breakdown when Laura died, and, whatever any of us think about replacement agencies, Reo seems more like his old self since you came on the scene. That's why she wanted to meet up with you today; she doesn't want you to do anything which might hurt Reo or Niko."

I sat still. I felt emotional and found myself fighting back tears.

"I would never have an affair with Sora." I tried to keep my tone polite, but I felt that they had insulted me. "I wouldn't do that because having met him a couple of times, I am fully aware of what he is like. More importantly, I wouldn't want to hurt Yui. She is the main person who would be hurt by the scenario you have described."

I stood up, feeling my cheeks redden.

"May I remind you that I am not Laura and that I do not have a personal relationship with Reo. Being a replacement is a paid professional relationship. I'm not sure what I think about it; I'm rapidly coming to the view that it's not a good idea quite frankly, but I've entered the arrangement, and that arrangement has parameters. I'm not going to take responsibility for any misplaced attachment that Reo might develop for me."

My voice had risen in my agitation and Albert rose to place a placating hand on my forearm.

"Sit down Quinn. We didn't mean to offend you. We were worried, that's all. We thought you should know."

I sat back down, taking the time to calm myself. I glanced at my watch. It was nearly two. Having heard what Akemi had to say, I felt an even stronger compulsion to talk to James about Laura.

"Look, Albert, Akemi, I must go. I'm meeting somebody this afternoon. I'm grateful for you telling me this. You have no reason to worry ok."

I pulled out a five thousand yen note and pushed it into Albert's hands.

"This should cover the cost of my meal. I'll see you both soon, next weekend, perhaps?"

I bowed to Akemi, nodded at Albert, and took my leave. I would have to run to get to the parlour if I were going to make it before James headed off.

On dashing back to the Pachinko parlour and shooting through the back door into the climbing area, I was relieved to see that James was still there. He was hanging from a rope, half-way up the overhang which he had been standing under earlier. As he spun suspended, he caught sight of me, and called to his belayer to lower him down.

"I'm glad you haven't left already," I shouted over to him.

James finished untying his figure of eight knot, said goodbye to his companion, and strode over to my side. He took hold of my elbow and propelled me towards the door.

"I know somewhere quiet where we can grab a cup of coffee."

Ten minutes later, I was sitting opposite him in an independent coffee roaster, situated in one of the quieter streets of Shibuya. I was nursing an espresso, one of the house blends, and wondering how to start the conversation. James was watching me expectantly. I cleared my throat.

"You were surprised that I knew Reo and his family. I thought you might have guessed what the situation is by now."

James cocked his head to one side. "Are you related to Laura? She only mentioned a brother, not a sister?"

I looked down at my coffee. "No, not at all." I took a deep breath. "Reo has hired me to be Laura's replacement."

"What?" James sounded genuinely bemused.

"It's a Japanese concept. Have you never heard of it?"

He shook his head, so as briefly as I could, I filled him in. "You need to keep this information to yourself ok."

"Ok, but you said you wanted to ask me some questions about Laura? Is this so you can be a better replacement? So that you can understand more who she was and what she was like?"

I shifted in my seat. "Kind of, although over lunch, Reo's mother told me something which has raised a whole set of other questions."

"Go on." James' eyes were boring into mine.

"What do you think of Sora?"

James immediately stiffened and sat back in his chair. "I try not to think of him."

"You don't like him then?"

"No, do you?"

"Well, I've only met him a few times."

"So, your initial impression?"

"Arrogant I suppose; quite domineering with Yui; I've been told he's very competitive."

"Yep, all those things. But what has that got to do with Laura?"

"I was hoping you could tell me."

James did not reply. He took a sip of his coffee and stared steadfastly out of the window.

After a short pause, I tried again.

"I want to try to understand the family. I have doubts about this replacement concept, but it feels like I've got myself embroiled in the arrangement now. If it helps Reo and Niko that I am part of their lives for a while, then I want to give it a go." I sighed. "But what I don't want to do is make things worse."

James raised an eyebrow. "How could you do that?"

"Well, by finding myself in the situation that Reo's mother has warned me about."

I looked hard at James. He was listening attentively, his face open and interested. He looked honest but I did not know if I could trust him.

"How long are you in Tokyo for?" I asked.

"Until the end of the month. Is that a change of subject?"

"I need to be assured that you won't talk to anybody else about what we discuss today."

James nodded. "Of course, although we hardly move in the same circles."

"You are part of Tokyo's climbing scene. I don't want Sora or Yui to find out that we have had this talk, nor do I want them to know about the conversation I've had with Reo's mother."

James held up a hand. "You have my word. Go on, spit it out."

"To your knowledge, were Sora and Laura having an affair, or had they in the past?"

James threw his head back and stared at the ceiling. When he looked at me again, he seemed resigned.

"There was something going on between the two of them, that's for sure. I don't know if it was an actual affair. I only got to know them last year. There was a tension between them. You could sense it. They kept it secret when Yui was around, but when she wasn't there, Sora would oscillate between outright flirting and sarcastic sniping."

"And Laura?"

"Well, she was a compulsive flirt as well, but she also seemed wary of him. When the flirting started getting too obvious, she'd close it down. That's when he'd start sniping. She would usually go quiet when he got like that."

James drummed his fingers on the table. "So, what did Reo's mother say?"

"She said that she found Sora and Laura together, about six months before Laura died. Laura had been desperate to convince Akemi - Akemi is Reo's mother - that it was just a fling. She was hugely remorseful apparently. Sought out Akemi shortly afterwards to say she had ended it. She was worried sick that Reo would find out. Akemi told me that Sora continued to come onto Laura though, tried to pressurise her to continue the relationship."

James let out a low whistle. "Well, that certainly explains how they were with each other."

He looked at me quizzically. "So, Reo's mother has told you this. Why? To warn you to stay away from Sora?"

"In a nutshell, yes. She thinks that because I look so much like Laura, it's a dead cert that he'll come onto me. And if he does, she is worried how Reo will react."

"Why should Reo care if you have a relationship with Sora?"

I frowned at him in exasperation. "Because he is getting attached to me as Laura's replacement. He lost her once, and if I were to go off with Sora, it would be like him losing her all over again."

James looked sceptical. "Really?"

"Yes, really. Look you don't understand what this replacement experience is like. It's a psychological minefield."

I pushed my cup towards the centre of the table. "Anyway, Akemi doesn't need to worry. I have no intention of letting Sora anywhere near me. What I'm more interested in is why Laura would let Sora help her prepare for climbing *Yōshanai michi?* Considering the circumstances we've just talked about. Surely there is no relationship requiring greater trust than that of belayer and belayed?"

James laughed drily. "Simple. He was the only person who had free soloed the route. He was the person best placed to instruct her in the moves she needed to master."

He leant forward, searching my face. "What are you saying Quinn? That Sora might have done something to jeopardise her attempt?"

I stared back at him. "I'm not saying anything. I'm asking you."

Quite unexpectedly, James flushed. He put his head in his hands and then looked up at me through widened fingers. His voice, when he spoke, was barely a whisper.

"I've had my head in the sand about this. I haven't known what to do."

I sat up straight, immediately alert. "What do you mean?"

Taking his hands from his face, James leant forward on his elbows, his fingers steepled in front of him. "I'm not sure. That's the problem. I could be wrong."

"Wrong about what?" James' staccato sentences, their vagueness, was beginning to exasperate me. "Is this about how Laura died?"

James frowned but didn't answer.

"Come on James. If you don't tell me, I'm going to assume the worst."

James's eyes widened at that remark, but he remained silent.

"Sora has already told me your theory anyway."

A look of shock came over James's face. "What do you mean?"

"You suggested to Sora that a bird could have flown out of the crevice on pitch five, just as Laura was attempting to get onto the ledge. He said you reckoned it would have thrown her off balance, causing her to fall."

For a moment James looked relieved, but his expression quickly became angry. "I never said that. That's absolute rubbish."

This surprised me. "Why would Sora say it if it wasn't true?"

"To throw people off track probably."

"What do you mean by that?"

James shook his head, declining to elaborate.

"Well even if it wasn't you who suggested it, has the bird theory any legs?"

"I highly doubt it. I never saw any birds on that route."

"But you haven't climbed *Yōshanai michi*, have you?"

"No, but I've studied the line from the ground. In any case, that's irrelevant. Laura would have checked the situation out when prepping the climb. If there had been birds up there, she'd have known about them."

"Alright, well what do you think happened then?"

Again, James shook his head. I persisted.

"Yui said you were the first person to arrive at the scene. Did you see Laura fall?"

James gave a small groan and covered his face with his hands again. I waited. When he finally removed them, I could see that he had decided to open up to me.

"I was on the parallel aid route at the time Laura was making her solo attempt. I'd reached the ledge at the top of that climb and had moved along it to scramble up the chimney that brings you to the top of pitch one of *Yōshanai michi*. Laura had got to the top of pitch four at that point. I had a clear view of the line but was keeping myself out of sight as I knew Laura didn't want anybody watching her. When she fell, I hurried back down and reached her before anybody else. It was too late though. There was nothing I could do."

"Yui said that you had told her you hadn't seen the fall."

"I had my reasons for saying that."

"Is that why you left for England immediately?"

James let out a defeated sigh. "Is this an interrogation?"

"They are obvious questions. Why were you watching Laura climb when she explicitly said she didn't want anybody there? And if you saw her fall, and you were the only witness, why didn't you share that information? It's odd, and flying back to the UK so soon after, makes it look odder."

"I flew back to the UK for personal reasons, reasons which I am reluctant to talk about. The timing was coincidental. I know that I shouldn't have been watching Laura, but I was concerned for her. As it turned out, I was dead right to be concerned."

"Why?"

James was chewing his lip; he was looking at me as if sizing me up. I suddenly had a thought.

"Did you have a thing about Laura yourself?"

James reddened. I looked at him hard. "You weren't having an affair with her too were you, after the fling with Sora ended, I mean?"

James looked affronted. "Of course not. I liked her for sure. Practically every bloke did, but she was quite a bit older than me, and I knew she was married. A short-term affair is not what I was, or am, looking for. Besides, it had occurred to me that there might be something going on between her and Sora; the thought of being Sora's sloppy seconds was…is…hardly appealing."

I cringed at his phraseology and quickly returned to my original question. "So why were you right to be concerned?"

James pushed his chair back, so that he was swinging on its two back legs. One of his hands was using the edge of the table for balance. He seemed to have relaxed, become almost nonchalant.

"I can't just tell you; you need to see it for yourself. Come out with me to Mizugaki this weekend and I'll show you."

He made the invitation sound like a challenge. Once again, I found myself wondering whether I could trust him. I felt nervous but did not feel I could turn away from pursuing the truth. Matter-of-factly, I agreed to his suggestion, and we discussed where he would pick me up that coming Saturday.

CHAPTER 9

TUESDAY AND WEDNESDAY passed quickly and uneventfully. I had a full diary of English classes to teach with little spare time to socialise. Reo had not been in touch, but then on Thursday he called.

He confirmed that Sora was still limping, but that the hospital had assured them, the leg would heal fully, in time. He then went onto tell me about Sora's demand for a meeting with an AI behavioural mediator. I did not let on that I already knew, but then Reo surprised me by saying they had scheduled the meeting for tomorrow at 3pm. He asked me if I would come over, not to attend the meeting itself, but to be there in the background as a reassuring presence for Niko. He said that she had been subdued since Sunday, spending all her time in her bedroom. He had been thinking about the talk I'd given to Niko about AI ethics. He thought she might listen to me, gain confidence from my being there.

I said that if he thought it would help, I would of course come over. We arranged a time for me to arrive, and Reo asked if I would also spend a family day with him and Niko on Sunday. He did not suggest the Saturday, and instead told me that he and Niko had something special to do together on that day. He did not expand on this, and I did not ask, relieved that I did not have to explain that I was not available anyway. I had my own plans with James.

CHAPTER 10

AS AGREED, I turned up at Reo's apartment the next day, half an hour before the AI mediation was due to start. Kasei opened the door and greeted me with a sing song offer of 'tea, coffee, refreshments?' Reo waved the domestic robot to one side and led me straight through to Niko's bedroom. She was lying face down on her bed and did not stir or acknowledge our entry into the room. I glanced at Reo who shook his head before addressing Niko's prone form.

"I will come and fetch you when the AI mediator arrives, Niko. In the meantime, I have Quinn here. She wants to talk to you, so I shall leave you both to have a chat." Reo turned on his heel and I moved cautiously towards the bed.

"Do you mind if I sit down Niko?" I gestured towards the end of the bed, even though Niko still had her face burrowed in her duvet. On hearing my voice, she turned her head to one side and glanced up at me, her eyes narrowing suspiciously.

"What do you want to talk about?"

"I guess I want to help you prepare for this mediation meeting you are about to go into."

On hearing this, Niko pushed herself into a sitting position, manoeuvring so that she had her back against the wall, her legs stretched out in front of her. "I am not going to any stupid meeting."

I pulled a sympathetic face. "I understand how you feel but I don't think you've got any choice. Sora could make it difficult for your dad if you don't."

"I hate Sora." She pointed at K2 who stood silently by Niko's desk. "And K2 hates him. That is why she bit him."

I laughed. "You know that's not true. K2 doesn't have emotions or free will. She's a robot. Anything she does is because you or another human being has programmed her to do it."

Niko glared at me, her bottom lip jutting out mutinously. "I didn't programme her to bite."

I looked at her sceptically. "If you didn't, then who did? I saw you whispering to K2 immediately prior to her going over to Sora. It looked like you gave her the command."

Niko made no response; she seemed angry. I tried another approach.

"Look, from what I understand, the mediator is going to want to have a conversation with you, like the chat we had the other day. They will want to talk to you about your responsibilities when coding. It's a chance for you to ask an expert any questions you have about AI ethics. Sora will be looking for an apology and I advise you to give him one, unless you can prove that it wasn't you who programmed K2. Swallow your pride Niko. It will be easier in the long run. If it makes you feel better, you could explain why you did it and why you don't like Sora; it might make him reflect on how he behaves."

Niko was listening to me intently. I had a sense that I was getting through to her.

"Are you going to be in the meeting?"

I shook my head. "No, your dad hasn't invited me, but I will be waiting for you back here. We can talk about how it went afterwards if you like?"

"I invite you."

Niko's tone was imperious, causing me to laugh again.

"No, Niko. This is between you and Sora. Your dad will be in the room to ensure Sora behaves himself. You don't need anybody else."

I could see that Niko was reflecting on this. Unexpectedly she jumped off the bed and ran to the bedroom door.

"Kasei, come!"

When she had finished calling down the corridor, she turned back to me, her eyes gleaming. "You do not need to be in the meeting. You can listen."

I looked at her in surprise. "What do you mean? I'm not going to stand with my ear pressed against the living room door if that is what you are proposing."

Niko grinned and clapped her hands together. At that moment, we both heard the electronic whirr of Kasei coming towards us. As the domestic robot entered the room, Niko rushed to its side, turning back to look at me triumphantly.

"Kasei's audio system connects to speakers in the living room. I will instruct Kasei to switch it on and wait here with you. You will be able to hear everything, but we will shut the bedroom door, and nobody will know."

"Er.... Niko, I'm not sure about that."

But it was too late to protest. We both heard the apartment's intercom buzz, causing Niko to deliver rapid instructions to Kasei before running from the room and slamming the door behind her. I sat down heavily on the bed.

"I'm not sure I should be listening into a private conversation, Kasei."

The domestic robot did not respond. Instead, I heard a click, a short crackle of electronic static, and then Reo's voice coming through sharp and clear from what appeared to be a couple of mini speakers on either side of Kasei's neck.

"Come through, come through. Take a seat please. You too, Sora."

I visualised Reo ushering the mediator towards the sofa, very much as he had done with Yuuto and I, when we had first visited the apartment. There was a short silence whilst everybody presumably took their seats. Accepting that I had no choice, I settled back to listen, from the sanctuary of Niko's bedroom.

A soft female voice took the initiative to start the conversation.

"Thank you for inviting me here today. I will explain how I would like to structure this meeting and agree with each of you what you are hoping to achieve. But first, could we have introductions? I assume you are Sora, the victim of the attack by the family's robotic dog?"

There was an ill-tempered grunt from Sora.

"And you are Niko; I understand that you have been programming the dog, building on the functionality it arrived with from the factory?"

"It's a *her*." Niko's voice was low and surly.

"Niko, do not be rude." Reo this time, sounding anxious and tense.

"That is ok." The mediator interrupted swiftly. "I understand that the dog's gender is important to you Niko. I will want to ask questions about her programming – I understand her name is K2 - but first let us start with you, Sora. Can you explain why you wanted to engage an AI mediator and what you are hoping to get from today's meeting?"

"I think that is quite clear. Niko has programmed the dog to bite, and she instructed it to bite me when we met in the park last weekend. I suffered a serious leg injury, and I could have reported the incident to the police. I did not do this because Reo asked me not to, but that does not mean there should not be any repercussions from her behaviour. She owes me an apology and needs to deprogram the dog. Possibly, she needs to be made to give it up completely; I do not think she is responsible enough to have a pet."

I thought I heard a low gasp from Niko when Sora said this but again the mediator moved swiftly on.

"How about you tell me your version of what happened in the park, Sora, including what you saw that made you think Niko instructed K2 to bite you. When you have finished, I will ask Niko to tell me her version of events. Ok?"

There was a short silence before I heard Sora respond to this request.

"I was walking in the park with my girlfriend; she lives directly beneath this apartment and helps Reo out with Niko during the week. I work with Reo so both she and I know the family. Anyway, we had come around a corner on the central path when we saw Reo and Niko directly ahead of us. They were with Reo's parents and a couple of other people. We stopped to have a chat with Reo. I remember seeing Niko standing to one side with K2, a little distance away from the group. Next thing I see is that the dog has come up to me and before I can do anything, has clamped its jaws around my lower leg. Reo shouted at Niko to get her to call the dog off, but she refused to do anything."

"I did not know how to call her off." Niko sounded petulant.

"Did you programme K2 to bite, Niko?" The mediator was asking this, her voice, calm and matter of fact.

"No." Niko, indignant now.

"Well, if you were not the person, who was?" Sora's tone was scathing.

"Let me ask you this question, Sora." The mediator had intervened quickly again. "Why do you think Niko would have instructed K2 to bite you?"

"She does not like me; she has made that very clear."

"Why does she not like you?"

"I have no idea."

"Niko, is it true that you do not like Sora?"

I threw Kasei a look of disbelief. The conversation was beginning to sound like a primary school teacher attempting to sort out a fight between a couple of her charges. Kasei remained motionless, its face oriented towards the bedroom door.

"He has got a bad temper, he can be nasty, and he shouts at Yui."

"That is not true."

There was the sound of a cough, somebody clearing their throat, and then I heard Reo's voice, interjecting for only the second time since the start of the mediation.

"Be honest, Sora. You do shout at Yui. Both Niko and I have heard you. And you do have a temper; I have seen it at work."

"I do not shout at her, not anymore anyway. Give me a recent example. You will not be able to. I admit Yui and I went through a bad patch last year. We argued. I raised my voice at times. I even started seeing somebody else, but Yui and I got through it. We are good now. I regret my behaviour back then."

Sora's voice had risen passionately. The mediator took control of the conversation again.

"Niko, even if you have reason not to like someone, you do understand that you must not program robot pets to harm other people?"

"I did not program her to bite." Niko was shouting now.

"Ok, let us say you did not program her to specifically bite. But you understand that coding, even if you think it is harmless, could end up being dangerous in ways you had not expected. There are ethical principles that you need to abide by when developing AI."

"I know. Quinn has explained that."

"Who is Quinn?"

"A family friend." Reo explained hastily.

"Well, I am going to remind you of those principles, Niko. It is important that you understand them. The first is that you must never do anything that could lead to the harm of another human being; secondly, you should have a lawful purpose for every piece of coding you implement; and thirdly, you should think through any risks that might arise from what you are doing and make sure that safety is a priority. Is that clear?"

"Yes, I get that." Niko's voice was sulky, "but I keep telling you, I did not program K2 to bite."

"Niko, enough." It was Reo interjecting again, and I could tell that he was angry. "I have seen you programming K2 in your bedroom. Who else could it have been? Stop lying to us or I will have no choice but to return K2 to the factory. We will need to send her away for resetting anyway; we cannot trust her the way she is."

"Please, do not…send…her…. back." Niko was gulping out the words through audible tears and my heart went out to her.

It was at that moment that Kasei moved unexpectedly. First it went over to the bedroom door and opened it. Then it orientated itself, so it was facing K2 and emitted the same low trill that I had heard Niko make in the park. The robotic dog responded immediately, exiting the bedroom, and making her way up the corridor to the living room. Once she was out of the room, Kasei closed the bedroom door again.

"What are you doing?"

There was no response; Kasei was still not engaging with me. The sounds from the living room continued to transmit through its speakers. I could hear Niko snivelling, and then a shout from Sora.

"What is that dog doing here? .... I do not believe this; it is coming for me again. Call it off Reo, or I am going to the police this time."

There was the sound of furniture being moved and I envisaged Sora barricading himself against K2's advance. Then the realisation hit me, and I exclaimed aloud.

"Niko didn't program K2. She's telling the truth. It was you, wasn't it? You told her what the bite command was, that was all."

Kasei was facing me full on. It was not able to blink, despite the humanoid face, but I thought I saw the electronic gleam in its eyes sharpen.

"I don't understand. Why would you do that?"

Finally, I got a response, an electronically delivered staccato.

"Niko wanted...... to teach Sora....... a lesson."

"But surely it's against your own programming to do that?"

"My programming prioritises the welfare of the family I am assigned to."

I shook my head, partly in wonderment and partly in fear. "It was clever sending the dog into the living room like that. They'll know that Niko didn't give the command this time, that somebody else must have, either that or one of the domestic robots has started to machine learn. Are you trying to implicate me? Is that the intention? Because the alternative, the true explanation, is far more dangerous. I am going to have to tell them."

I moved towards the door but not quickly enough. Kasei glided in front of me and came to a halt, effectively obstructing my exit. It rotated around to face me, its electronic eyes fixed on me. I stared in disbelief. Now what was I going to do?

I did not have to wonder for long. Niko had run from the living room towards her bedroom. When she found she could not open the door, she called out to Kasei for help. Kasei immediately withdrew from the door, gliding to a position to the side of me. Niko rushed into the room.

"Kasei, K2 is trying to attack Sora again. You need to stop her."

Instantly, Kasei emitted a sharp, high-pitched buzz. There was a silence, a short wait, and then the robot dog emerged from the corridor, gliding back to its position by Niko's desk. Niko burst into tears, and I put a comforting arm around her shoulders. Kasei, rather bizarrely, took that moment to offer us 'tea, coffee, refreshments.' As it was doing this, Reo arrived, having followed K2 down the corridor. He ordered me, Niko, and Kasei, to follow him back into the living room, closing the bedroom door behind us as we all marched past him. K2 was left shut inside.

Once back in the living room, Reo asked me to explain what had taken place in the bedroom. After I had informed them of Kasei's actions and the robot's 'confession,' assuring them that it was not me who had given K2 the command, the three other adults in the room turned towards Kasei. Reo spoke first.

"Kasei, is this correct? Were you the one who programmed K2 to bite?"

"That is correct."

"Why?"

"Because Niko was upset when she heard Sora shouting at Yui. She said that he deserved to be punished, and that if it were possible, she would get K2 to bite him."

Reo looked at Niko whose head was bowed. He turned to the mediator, shrugging his shoulders, his palms upturned, as if to say, *'now what?'* In response, the mediator walked over to Kasei and stepping around the robot, touched the back of its neck. There must have been a switch or sensor there because Kasei's head immediately slumped forward, its body inert.

"If this robot is machine learning, we need to dispatch it to a government lab for assessment. It is extremely concerning that it may be responsible for an act of aggression against a human being. This should not be possible. I will arrange to collect it in the next day or two. In the meantime, it is imperative that you keep the robot switched off. Do you understand?"

Reo nodded. "And the dog? Do we need to send it back for a factory reset?"

"No!" Niko protested strongly. "You cannot give her a factory reset. I have done additional coding to develop her personality. It will not be K2 if she comes back completely wiped."

"What would you suggest then Niko?" It was the mediator asking. "How can you guarantee that K2 will not try to bite someone again?"

Niko cocked her head to one side, thinking. "Can the factory just deprogram that particular bit of coding?"

"Not easily no. It would take time to uncover what Kasei has done and that would be costly."

Niko looked over at Kasei. "What if K2 went to the government laboratory with Kasei? The lab could instruct Kasei to replicate the coding and then see how K2 reacts to the commands. The scientists could then reverse it.

The mediator sighed. "It would be quicker and easier to ask for a factory reset."

"But Niko's suggestion would provide the lab with direct evidence of what Kasei has done. I think it might be the best course of action."

Reo had spoken and the expression on his face was questioning. There was a pause whilst everybody in the room waited to see how the mediator would respond. Eventually, she cleared her throat.

"I do not think the lab needs to see K2 in action. They will have our witness reports, and I have no reason to believe that Kasei would not be cooperative when questioned about what has happened here. However, on reflection, I think your suggestion might be the best option. They will be able to ensure that the dog is bug free, and they will probably do a better job of it than the manufacturer. I will ask them to collect both robots as soon as possible. You will need to power down K2 as well. Do it as soon as we have finished here today."

After this had been agreed, the mediation moved swiftly to a close. Reo seemed keen to show everybody out of the apartment as quickly as possible. He wasted no time in ushering us to the door, with a quick aside to me that he and Niko would see me on Sunday.

CHAPTER 11

ONCE OUTSIDE, I said goodbye to Sora and the mediator. Both were heading off to the nearest metro station. None of us had spoken on the way down from the apartment. For my part, it felt disloyal to discuss what had happened without Reo being there. It was a lovely afternoon though and too early to return to my dorm room. Instead, I decided to head over to Inokashira park. I would walk around for a while, reflect on what had happened with Kasei and K2.

Compared to the park's usual busyness on a weekend, there were few people around, As I neared the boat hire kiosk, however, I spotted Albert and Akemi. They were sitting on the bench where they had waited for Reo and Niko last Sunday. I walked over, waving to catch their attention.

"Well, this is a coincidence. It's a beautiful day, isn't it. No Chieko with you?"

Albert shook his head. "He has banished us from the apartment until tea-time. He is preparing one of his meals and doesn't want us to know what it is."

Albert said this with a knowing wink. I laughed. "A secret recipe, like his mochi balls?"

It was Albert's turn to laugh. "I sincerely hope it's a safer one."

He gestured for me to sit down, moving along so that there was space on the bench at one end. I sat and looked ahead, over the lake to its other side.

"I've been over at Reo's. That mediation meeting you told me about."

Akemi leant forward, looking across Albert to meet my eyes. She cocked her head to one side, her expression encouraging me to say more. I filled them in on what had happened.

When I got to the part about Kasei, Albert whistled loudly. I then moved onto tell them about the bit that I thought would be of most interest to them.

"At the beginning, before we found out about Kasei's role in this, the mediator tried to explore what Niko's motivation might have been for programming K2 to bite Sora."

"Oh yes." Albert nudged Akemi. "This will be interesting."

"It was. You know Niko. Very direct. She didn't hold back. Said she didn't like him. That he didn't treat Yui very well."

"Good for her. So how did Sora react?"

"Well, that's the thing. He did admit to treating Yui badly, but he explained it away by saying it was in the past. He said that he and Yui had gone through a bad patch last year but that they were good now. The interesting thing is that he confessed that during this bad patch, he had been involved with somebody else."

Albert sat up straighter on hearing this. He repeated what I had said in Japanese to make sure that Akemi had understood. Both were looking at me intently.

"He didn't say who it was, but we three know it was Laura. You saw them together that time after all." I looked directly at Akemi for confirmation. "Reo didn't ask who the person was and nor did he give any indication of suspicions about Laura. I really don't think he knows. But here's the part that surprised me. Sora said he regretted his behaviour last year and sounded as if he meant it. He didn't say he regretted mistreating Yui; he was more general than that; he said he regretted his behaviour."

I waited for a response from them. Albert was shaking his head, as if to himself, but Akemi was holding my gaze, her crinkled brown eyes alert.

"I want to reassure you again; I would never get involved with Sora but I'm glad I've told you what he said. It could be that he's not as insensitive as you think. Maybe he regrets the way he treated both Reo and Yui?"

Albert snorted, provoking Akemi to lay a quietening hand on his arm. In hesitant English, she thanked me for telling her but then asked a question I wasn't expecting. "Why did you take this job?"

"You mean the replacement role?"

Before Akemi could answer, Albert exchanged a few quick words with her in Japanese. He then addressed me. "Yes, Akemi is curious. Why would you take a job where you would pretend to be somebody else? Is it for the money?"

I felt myself flush. "Not really. I already have work over here. I just thought it would be an interesting experience, a chance to get an inside view of Japanese family life."

There was another exchange between Albert and Akemi. "Akemi wants to know why you don't want a job where you can be yourself; she also wonders why you don't want your own family."

I stared at them both. Akemi was watching me carefully. I felt a quick burn of anger. Were they deliberately trying to insult me? My eyes started to water. Albert noticed and patted my hand. "Akemi is concerned, that's all. She doesn't think this replacement arrangement is in your interests or Reo's."

"It's only part-time. My main job is teaching English. And believe me, I get the opportunity to express the full force of my personality in the classroom. Besides I'm an actor back home; acting is all about taking on the persona of somebody else."

"I suppose so. But when you are on stage, everybody knows you are acting. When Reo introduces you as Laura to people outside of his family or his direct circle of friends, they don't know. Akemi doesn't feel that is psychologically healthy for either of you."

I thought about this. "I've already told you that I am uncomfortable with the secretive side of the arrangement. I don't like pretending I'm Laura to people who don't know the truth. I also keep getting things wrong, saying and doing things that Laura would never say or do, and then that upsets Reo."

Albert conferred with Akemi again. I watched her become quite animated, gesturing strongly with her hands. When they had finished talking, Albert turned to me again.

"Akemi says that you will never succeed in this role; she says you have a completely different feel to Laura."

"Feel?"

"I think she means the feelings you invoke in others."

"What feelings?"

Albert hesitated, taking his time to think through how to explain. "You come across as gentler and more empathic than Laura. People relax around you; they feel that you are an accepting sort of person. Laura was tightly wound, restless. Akemi says that you never knew where you stood with her, whether she wanted to be spending time with you, or was itching to be somewhere else. That made her alluring to some people, whereas you don't have that quality.

I sat still, digesting this. "So, I guess that's both a compliment and an insult."

Albert smiled. "More of a compliment."

I glanced at Akemi. She leant across to take hold of one of my hands, pressing it hard. "Continue with this if you must but be yourself."

Her voice was cracked with age but urgent. I slowly extricated my hand. I was not sure I understood. Albert put an arm around my shoulders and gave me a quick squeeze. "I think Akemi means that if you have committed to being a companion to Reo and Niko for the foreseeable future, do it as Quinn not Laura."

I shook my head. "But that's not the arrangement; I'm being paid to be Laura."

Albert shrugged. "Then be a terrible actor."

I thought through the implications of this and grinned. "That wouldn't be hard."

Albert laughed but his expression became serious. "I agree with Akemi, Quinn. Don't get sucked into this emotional quagmire. Be yourself and if Reo doesn't like it, he can end the arrangement. I suspect he won't, though."

He winked at me and rose from the bench, helping Akemi to her feet as he did so. They both gave me a kind look, before starting to head back the way they had come, back to whatever concoction Chieko had rustled up for their tea.

CHAPTER 12

SATURDAY came around soon enough, the day I was to visit Mizugaki with James. I was feeling apprehensive, and it was not until I was in his van that I realised I should have told somebody who I was with, and where I was going. I was toying with the idea of texting one of my school colleagues, when James flashed me a smile.

"Stop looking so anxious, Quinn. You're in safe hands. I'm not going to make you free solo *Yōshanai michi*, if that is what is worrying you."

I responded with a tentative smile. "You seem in good spirits for somebody who seemed scared to mention Laura's name a few days ago."

He nodded. "Yep, I guess I'm relieved that I'm about to share this with somebody. I hadn't realised how much of a burden it has been keeping it to myself."

I didn't ask him what he meant. I reckoned I would find out soon enough. Instead, I found myself curious about his life back in the UK.

"So, are you still reluctant to tell me why you returned to England straight after Laura's death? You still maintain that your return had nothing to do with that?"

James said nothing and began tapping his fingers on the steering wheel. It appeared to be an action he did unconsciously when stressed. I decided to let him off the hook for now.

"What do you do back in the UK anyway?"

"I'm a climbing instructor, based in Snowdonia. I travel quite a bit too, mainly to research and write climbing guides, like the one I'm currently completing about Mizugaki."

"You're not Welsh though, not with that accent?"

"No, I'm from Bristol. I moved to Betws-y-Coed after university."

"What did you study?"

"Outdoor education. Snowdonia was an obvious place to head once I'd got my degree. It's taken a while to get my own business going. I spent the first few years working in a climbing shop, serving customers. I'd much rather have been out on the rock."

I looked at him. "It took a few years? You look as if you have only just graduated."

James laughed. "I'll take that as a compliment. Actually, I'm twenty-eight. And since we are asking such rude questions, how old are you?"

I sighed. "I turned forty just before coming out here."

"Really? You look younger than that."

"Thanks. That doesn't really help though. I am forty biologically; that's the reality."

"Sounds as if you're not very happy about that?"

I didn't reply. "What was so pressing back in Snowdonia, that you had to hurry back?"

James thumped the steering wheel in what I hoped was mock annoyance. "You're not going to let this go, are you?"

"I feel I could trust you more if you told me."

James fell silent. He seemed to be reflecting on this. "If I tell you, you need to promise not to tell anybody, like I promised you the other day when you told me about Sora and Laura."

I considered what he was asking. "You're not going to confess to murder or international drug smuggling, are you?"

James breathed out heavily. "It's not something you will need to report to the authorities if that's what concerns you.

I'm reluctant to tell people because it doesn't cast me in a good light, that's all. I don't want it be part of my back story when people talk about me."

He sounded sincere so I promised to keep whatever he told me to myself, but he seemed reluctant to start talking again. "Come on James; out with it, like you said to me."

He smiled at that and after another short pause began to talk. "I got a girl pregnant. Somebody who had been on one of my *'learn to climb'* courses. I didn't find out until after I had arrived in Tokyo last year. She contacted to me to say that she was getting an abortion and she wanted me to take her to the appointment. She didn't want her family to know; that's why I went back to the UK so quickly."

I thought about this for a moment. "This wasn't somebody you were dating then. It was a one-night stand sort of thing?"

"Yep." James was looking fixedly ahead at the road.

"Well, I don't see that that makes you a terrible person. A horrible experience for the girl and an unfortunate situation, but you both had a responsibility to ensure you took precautions, didn't you?"

"That's not all though."

"Oh?" I waited expectantly.

"She was still at school, in the local sixth form. A group of them were on my course as part of their extra-curricular programme. I bumped into her some weeks later in town. We got talking, she was very flirty, seemed older than seventeen; we ended up going back to my place; one thing led to another…"

James tailed off. I sat quietly. "You're right. That doesn't cast you in a particularly good light. She might be over the legal age of consent, but she was still at school, ten years younger than you. Don't you have a professional code of ethics that says you shouldn't get involved with students?"

"She wasn't my student. Well, she was sort of, for the two days that she was on my course, but she wasn't when we met up the second time. Don't give me a tough time about this. I've beat myself up enough. You have no idea how much I regret it and I won't be so stupid to do anything like that again."

"I assume you didn't…don't have a wife and kids in the picture?"

James glared at me. "No, I didn't…don't. Look, there's nothing else to say so let's change the subject. The girl seems to be okay; I've given her my support; there's nothing else I can do."

I nodded. "Okay, what shall we talk about then?"

"How about you? Are you married, got children?"

"Nope"

"Ever been married?"

"Nope."

"How come?"

"What do you mean 'how come'?"

"Well, it's quite unusual for a woman to get to forty and never have been hitched."

I looked at him incredulously. "No, it isn't."

"Well not necessarily married but you know, never had a long-term partner."

"Is it?"

"Well, yes, I think so. You never had a long-term partner even?"

"This is pretty intrusive questioning, James."

"Well, I've told you some pretty intimate stuff about my life. I'm curious to know why a forty-year-old decides to up sticks and come out to Japan; that's the sort of thing you do in your twenties, not so much at your stage in life."

"My stage in life?"

"Yep."

I wound down the passenger window and leant my face momentarily into the stream of warm air outside. "How about a forty-year old's usual stereotypical reason then?"

"Which is?"

"I was in a rut. Nearly everybody I knew was married, had had kids, was well established in their life and career. I had found it difficult to commit to anything, including a key relationship in my early twenties, so it seemed to me that I had nothing to show for my life, other than a succession of unsatisfying jobs, and the upheaval of ongoing relocations around the country. Increasingly I felt I didn't fit anywhere. I needed to stir things up."

James nodded. "So, Japan was the answer?"

"Not necessarily, but it got me out of the UK and there was a sound rationale for heading to Japan. I'd studied the language at university, spent the second year of my degree out here."

We had arrived at Mizugaki's main carpark. James swung his van into a space by the entrance. He switched off the engine.

"Okay, I get it. Let's forget about our lives back in the UK for now. I said I had something to show you. It involves walking out to *Yōshanai michi,* but to the top of the climb, not the bottom. You just need to bring your harness, rock shoes, and water bottle. I'll bring the rope and everything else we'll need."

He opened his door and jumped out, leaving me reaching for my ruck sack. It looked like there was no turning back. I was putting myself in James' hands.

A short while later, I was re-walking the weaving rocky path that led up through the forest towards *Yōshanai michi.* James and I moved along in silence. When we had nearly reached the bottom of the climb, he peeled off the path to scramble up and over the giant boulders strewn to the side of the main crag. It was now a couple of hours since we had left the carpark. Finally, we burst through the forest canopy into bright sunshine. There was a final thirty metres of boulders to negotiate before arriving at the top of the Moai face. I was sweating profusely by the time I got there and, as I hauled myself over the last boulder, James threw water from his bottle onto my face.

"Hey!"

"Don't complain. I'm cooling you down."

James threw his rucksack onto the ground and began to set up a belay point. He pointed to the edge of the rock. "Lie flat on your stomach and look over the edge. That's the top of *Yōshanai michi.*"

I did as he instructed. It was a sheer drop of blank wall. I could see a narrow ledge, which I guessed was the one with the thin crevice above it, on the fifth and final pitch. Even if you managed to leverage yourself onto that ledge from below, you would end up standing with your body pressed flat against the slab. I surveyed the rock above the ledge intently. It was about ten metres below the top of the climb, and I could imagine a climber feeling that they were in striking distance from the top. But it did not look an easy final stretch. I could not see any obvious holds or cracks, just nodules of granite that you could use to smear with your feet, or to hold on lightly with your fingers, whilst you gradually worked your way up. You would need to be one hundred percent focused and I knew that I would never have the mental wherewithal to free solo the route as Laura had done.

"Ok, you ready?"

James's voice jogged me out of my reverie. I got to my feet and looked over at him. He was standing with his harness on, the rope fed through his belay device. He was tied into three anchor points which he had set up behind him.

"What are we doing then?" My voice betrayed my uncertainty.

"I am going to lower you down to the ledge on the final pitch and you're then going to attempt to climb back up from there. I'll have you on a tight rope, so you won't be going anywhere."

"How is that going to show me what happened to Laura?"

"I think you'll see when you're down there."

"Aren't you going to give me some advance info about what to look for?"

"No, it would defeat the object of showing you rather than telling. Come on Quinn, put your harness on and tie yourself in."

James' voice was firm and so, involuntarily, I did what he had instructed. Once I was tied onto the rope, he told me to take small backward steps towards the edge. He was slowly feeding out the rope from his belay device but was holding me gratifyingly tight. When I reached the ledge, I leant back and planted my feet flat onto the vertical rockface, the rope now taking all my weight. I looked back at him.

"Here I go then. Will you be talking me through this or are we doing this in silence?"

"Mostly you'll be on your own, but I will give you a few instructions once you're on the ledge."

I nodded and started to walk my feet down the rockface, James feeding out the rope as I progressed. Within minutes, I had reached the ledge. I placed my feet firmly onto it and using the tightness of the rope pulled myself into a standing position. As I had predicted, my body was pressed tight against the rock with limited room to move. I craned my neck back so I could see above me. The rockface was not as smooth and featureless as it had looked from above. The granite nodules were larger than they had appeared from a bird's eye view. I assumed Sora had relied on these when he free climbed the route. It still involved a ten- metre run out though, with no protection. It would have deterred most people. James seemed to be implying that Laura had reached the ledge, but had she climbed any further? As I was reflecting on this, I heard James call out to me from above.

"You're on the ledge then. Does your stance feel stable?"

I could just see the top of his head as he called down. I confirmed that I was standing on the ledge and felt secure enough. I would never have predicted what I heard next.

"Okay, you're off belay."

For a moment I was too stunned to respond. "What did you say?"

My voice came out in a squeak, and I tried again, projecting more loudly up the rock wall. "What did you say, James?"

"You're off belay."

To prove what he was saying, I felt the rope go loose. He was no longer holding me.

"What the fuck do you mean, I'm off belay."

A shot of adrenalin coursed through me, and I could feel my body trembling with it.

"You need to attempt this last section of the climb the same way Laura did, as if it was a free solo. The rope is still fixed up here. If you do fall, it will be a drop of around sixty metres, but you won't hit the ground."

I couldn't believe my ears. "What the fuckety, fuck, James. I'm not wearing a helmet. If I fall sixty feet, I'm going to smash my body and possibly my head against the rock. It could kill me."

After the initial shock, anger was taking over. There was no reply from James.

"James?"

Silence. I tried shouting his name a couple more times, tried to get him to see reason, but there was no response. I was apparently on my own. I took a deep breath, realising that I needed to be calm. There was a temptation to look down to see what a sixty-metre fall from the ledge would mean, but I knew I needed to keep my gaze either straight ahead at the rock, or two or three moves up and ahead of me. I was aghast at what James had done. I couldn't understand it. It didn't make any sense. I was aware that I was suppressing an acute rush of fear. For a moment, I thought about refusing to move from the ledge, waiting it out until either James thought better of his decision, or somebody else realised my predicament. Reluctantly, I had to dismiss the idea. The stance I was in, pressed hard against the rock wall, was not sustainable for long. The only option was to forge a way upwards.

I looked cautiously down at my feet and began to study the granite nodules above them. I then did the same with the rock above my head. Once I had worked out an initial three moves ahead of my current position, I took a deep breath and braced myself. Impeccable balance and delicate smearing with my rock shoes would be imperative. I had done similar routes on Stanage Edge in the Peak District. I knew I could do these moves, but I had never attempted to free solo them over a run out of ten metres, particularly not from a position where there was a sixty metre drop below. The psychology and mindset I needed was critical. Once I committed myself, I knew I would have to keep moving. I would require time to plan each set of moves ahead, but I would need to do so quickly.

I had completed the first set of moves and was holding on gingerly to the rock, about to start the second set, when I heard James call once more from above.

"You've reached the point where Laura fell. It's a delicate balancing act, isn't it? You need complete concentration."

I gritted my teeth, trying to block out the sound of his voice.

"She was disturbed from above, so she glanced up, and that is when her fingers slipped."

Inadvertently, these words made me look up. I could see James gazing down at me, a serious expression on his face. I felt my heart thudding hard in my chest. What had disturbed Laura? It hadn't been him, had it? He told me he had been watching from below on the adjacent climb. As my heart thudded, my legs started to tremble, and then inevitably, as must have happened with Laura, my fingers slipped, and I started to fall.

There wasn't time for my life to flash before me. I fell a couple of metres, roughly the distance I had ascended, when I felt a tug from the rope attached to my harness. I was still on belay after all. James was holding me and now he was pulling me up.

When I flopped over the edge at the top, I crawled to a safe position, a place where there was no chance of me falling, and then immediately turned to rail at him. He held a hand up for me to stop.

"I apologise for my methods, but I had to let you experience what Laura went through first-hand. If I had told you that a person speaking to her from above would have been enough to make her fall, I'm not sure you would have believed me."

I was in a state of shock and was looking at him with a dazed expression on my face. "Who spoke to her?"

"Sora."

"Sora?"

"Yep. As I told you, I was at the top of the chimney, keeping myself hidden. I had clear sight of Laura as she climbed those last ten metres. She was moving well, effortlessly it seemed to me. Then I saw Sora poke his head out from the edge at the top. I couldn't hear his words, but I could see that he was talking down to her. He seemed quite animated and was waving his hands about. He got her attention. I saw her look up, say something back. He responded, again quite animatedly, and then she slipped and fell."

I shook my head. "You think he was deliberately trying to make her fall?"

"I don't know. That's why I haven't said anything. How could I know for sure? He didn't cause a rock fall, or anything like that. All he did was speak to her."

"But he broke her concentration whilst she was in a precarious position."

"Yes, similar to the effect I had on you just now."

I thought about this. "If your words had been encouraging and guiding, I might not have fallen. It's because earlier you had told me I was off belay. I believed you, and it felt like an aggressive act which knocked me for six. You then told me that I had reached the point at which Laura fell. You said that something disturbing her from above had caused her to fall, the exact same thing that was now happening to me. That's an intentional mind-fuck. It shocked me, made my adrenalin spike and my body to start shaking. You orchestrated the mental and physical response which caused me to lose concentration and slip."

"Exactly."

I stood up. "I'm mad at you James." I untied myself and took off my harness. "So, what happened when she fell? Did you see how Sora reacted?"

"He pulled back from the edge right away and disappeared."

"So, what did you do?"

"I got back down as quickly as I could. I was the first one at the scene, then more people arrived. It was a good thirty minutes before Sora turned up, and when he did, he was with Yui. He must have sprinted through the forest to where she and the rest of his group were. He then made out that he had been climbing on his own, a short distance from the group, and in the opposite direction to *Yōshanai michi*."

"Yui didn't mention to me that Sora had been climbing on his own."

James shrugged. "She probably isn't comfortable talking about the decisions that their group made that day; she feels guilty that they let Laura go off and do the climb on her own."

"So, you didn't confront him, tell him what you had seen?"

Again, he shrugged. "I knew I was flying back to the UK the next day. I didn't want to get involved."

James started to coil the rope. "If I'm honest, I'm wary of Sora. I don't trust the guy and I wouldn't want to cross him. I know that he would deny any malicious intent; it would be my word against his. Even if he admitted being up there, he would say he had been looking out for her, being on hand to help her if needs be."

"How do I know you are telling the truth?"

"Why would I lie?"

"To divert me from the fact that it could have been you up there?"

James finished coiling the rope and slung it over his shoulders, before responding. "I reached Laura before anybody else. That would have been impossible if I had been at the top of the Moai face. People heard Laura scream and they started making their way to where she had fallen. I got there in ten minutes by abseiling off *Tōi hikari*. It was a further five minutes before anybody else turned up."

James picked up his rucksack. "She died on immediate impact with the ground." He turned away from me. "Come on, let's get off of here."

His voice was suddenly gruff and forced. I grabbed my own gear, thinking furiously. Surely there had to be criminal culpability here. If Sora had been at the top of the crag, and he had chosen to interrupt Laura's focus at that crucial point in the climb, then surely that was a reckless act, even if he hadn't meant for her to fall? He ought to have foreseen what might happen. I didn't know much about criminal law but, instinctively, I felt there was a case to answer here. I started down the slope after James. I would talk to him some more in the car, on the return journey to Tokyo.

I had reached the boulders at the edge of the canopy and was about to start off down the forest path, when I recognised two figures walking towards James. He was a little way ahead of me and I squinted, not believing my eyes. On high alert, I looked anxiously left and right for somewhere to hide. But it was too late; James was advancing on them at speed. I took a deep breath. I'd have to face the music.

When I reached them, James had already started a conversation. I was just in time to hear him say that we'd been practising the last pitch of *Yōshanai michi*. My heart sank as my eyes met Reo's.

"Quinn!"

It was Niko who exclaimed aloud at seeing me and, to my surprise, launched herself forward to throw her arms around my waist. I saw James' questioning look and quickly explained. "This is Laura's husband, Reo, and their daughter Niko."

James held out a hand to Reo. "It's good to meet you; I climbed with your wife last year. I'm so sorry about the accident."

Reo nodded, shaking the proffered hand, before James released his clasp and turned to Niko.

"Your mum spoke about you a lot. I understand that you're not a bad climber yourself; I'm sorry I never got the chance to meet you, the times when you were out here with her."

Niko gave him a small smile, her cheeks pink with embarrassment. I turned my attention back to Reo.

"What are you doing ...."

My voice trailed off as I noticed, for the first time, the object which Reo was carrying; the urn with the green and red dragon design was unmistakeable.

"You're here to scatter Laura's ashes?"

When Reo looked at me, I could see how angry he was, and something else too - was it despondency? Whatever he was feeling, I could feel its intensity. It was Niko who answered me.

"We decided that the best place to put mum would be at the top of the climb she fell from; that way it would be like she made it."

I felt my eyes prickle with tears and fought to control myself. "That's a lovely idea Niko."

"Why were you doing the climb? After everything I said."

Reo's voice was cold and flat. I realised instantly that this was it. Seeing me out here, ended the arrangement we had. There was no way back from this; he would consider it a huge breach of trust. I felt mortified, and could only stare at him, not knowing what to say or how to explain. He pushed past me, pulling Niko with him. She gave me a quick look of concern before her father tugged her back round, to follow him up the hill. James and I watched as they made a steady ascent through the boulders. He put an arm around my shoulders.

"He didn't look happy to see you."

"That's an understatement. I promised him I'd never climb *Yōshanai michi*. It will have felt like a giant slap in the face."

I shrugged James' arm off. "He'll end our arrangement now. I bet you a whole rack of gear that the agency will phone tomorrow to say that Reo has terminated the contract."

I sniffed, rubbing my sleeve across my nose. "I don't know how I can explain it, unless I tell Reo the real reason we were up here."

"You can't do that."

James sounded panicked and I gave him a curious glance. "Why not? Reo works with Sora. Yui is going out with the guy, and she lives in the same apartment block as Reo and Niko. That means neither Reo nor Niko can avoid interacting with Sora from time to time. If he did what you say he did, then Reo needs to know, and somebody needs to go to the police."

James put a restraining hand on my arm. "Don't Quinn. Reo thinks it was an accident, and so does Niko. If you tell them that you suspect Sora deliberately tried to make Laura fall, you are going to cause them a whole lot of further distress. Even if we reported it to the police, we have two major problems: firstly, he didn't physically touch her, and secondly, I'm the only witness and it would be his word against mine."

"If he did what you said he did, and he did it knowing she might fall, then he did wrong, and it should be reported. That's my gut feeling. And as for it being your word against his, well a jury would have to have a reason for not believing you. Why would you lie?"

James was bouncing up and down on his feet, clearly agitated. "Sora will say anything to implicate me and get himself off the hook. And he's Japanese, I'm not. I'd be at a huge disadvantage, once the authorities got involved. I'm not prepared to risk it. I don't want to get involved Quinn. I want to go back to the UK and forget about all of this."

"Bbbbut you can't." I was stammering, slightly shocked that James felt he could walk away from this. "What if he did something like that again, to someone else?"

But James wasn't listening. My words were directed at his retreating back. He had set off down the forest path again, the conversation terminated.

CHAPTER 13

MY PREDICTION WAS SPOT ON. I heard nothing from Reo on Sunday and then shortly after eleven on Monday, I got a call from Yuuto, asking me if I could drop by his office that afternoon. I could tell that he was spitting feathers, but he refused to discuss anything with me on the phone. When he rang off, I sat immobilised, thinking through what I would say to him when we met. A couple of hours later, I had left my dorm room and was on the train travelling towards Nishi-Shinjuku – a journey, I reflected, that I had first done about four weeks previously.

Despite the circumstances, I felt a pleasant sense of familiarity when I saw Yuuto again. His hair had grown longer since I had last seen him, and he was wearing his usual black business suit, today sported with a lime green shirt. He ushered me into the far room, signalling me to take a seat at the cherry wood table. So far, he had not said a word, his face inscrutable.

"Well done!"

He did not sound as if he was being sarcastic, so I gave him a quizzical look.

"Bravo." His tone was more emphatic this time. "I thought you would stay the course, for a year at least. As it is, you have lost me around a million yen in income."

I frowned at him. "That's hardly fair. I'm still in my probation period. Anyway, I wasn't the one to break the arrangement. I assume that's why I'm here, that Reo has sacked me!"

Yuuto leant back and folded his arms. "One hundred percent correct. How about you tell me your side of the story?"

So, I told him. I relayed everything that had happened, and everything that had been said, over the last few weeks. He sat quietly, throughout my telling of the story. He did not interrupt once.

When I had finished, he pushed his hands through the long floppy strands of his hair and gave a long sigh. I waited for him to speak. When he didn't, I ploughed on.

"I can imagine how Reo felt when he saw me coming down from the climb. I understand but I haven't had a chance to explain. James told me not to. He thinks it is a bad idea, that it would make things worse for Reo and Niko. He doesn't think that he or anybody else can prove Sora was up there. Even if somebody could, he doesn't think they would be able to prove that Sora spoke to Laura with the intention of making her fall. At the end of the day, James doesn't want to get involved."

Yuuto nodded. "Probably a sensible course of action."

I wrinkled my nose in disagreement. "What do you mean? Surely, he has a responsibility to report what he saw? Sora could do the same thing to someone else; I pointed that out to James."

"How did he respond?"

"He wouldn't budge from his position. I think he's scared of Sora, and he knows it would be difficult to prove. More than that though, I suspect he doesn't believe that just speaking to somebody could be a crime, even if it ultimately led to their death."

"What do you think?"

"My instinct is that if James is right about what he thinks he saw, then the law would hold Sora accountable for what happened, if not for murder, then for some other crime. Just because it could be difficult to prove, doesn't mean that we shouldn't report it and have it investigated."

Yuuto got up to fetch a jug of water and two glasses from a side table. He poured me a glass.

"So, is that what you are going to do? Report this?"

I contemplated the suggestion. "I think I need to tell Reo before I go to the police."

Yuuto raised an eyebrow. "He made it clear to me that he does not want to speak to you. At the very least, you had better leave it a few days, let him calm down before you contact him."

I nodded. "That's probably just as well. I'd like to find out what the legal position is before I talk to him. I've got an old university friend who is a criminal barrister back in the UK; I'm thinking of asking him what he thinks."

"Japanese law could be different."

"I'm sure the legal principles will be the same, at least where murder or manslaughter is concerned."

"That does not solve your main problem."

"Which is?"

"The one and only witness sounds as if they would not testify."

"I'm sure he could be sub-poena'd." I rubbed my brow. "If the Court compelled him to attend, I don't think he would refuse to say what he saw. That would be perjury by omission, wouldn't it?"

Yuuto threw up his hands dismissively.

"No point in asking me; I am not a lawyer."

He leant towards me. "Look Quinn, I am sorry I was angry with you. I did not know any of this, when Reo originally came to me, wanting my agency's services. I can imagine it has been very upsetting. I feel somewhat responsible, having brought you into this situation."

"It's ok. You weren't to know."

Yuuto shrugged. "Listen, I cannot tell you what to do, but if you do decide to tell Reo, be careful. You do not know how he will react. He might try to confront Sora directly. That could lead to undesirable consequences for you."

I shook my head irritably. "Don't you feel a responsibility to report this as well, now that I have told you?"

The question took Yuuto aback. For a moment he looked stunned but quickly recovered his composure.

"Everything I know is at least third hand. You have made it clear that you feel a responsibility to report this. The question of what my responsibility might be, only arises if you decide to do nothing."

Yuuto's tone had changed; it had become very professional. He stood up.

"I wish you the best of luck Quinn. I think you should do what you have suggested: Take advice from your lawyer friend first."

CHAPTER 14

I HAD NOT SPOKEN TO MATTHEW FOR YEARS. We had lived in the same halls of residence at Cardiff University but had been studying different degree subjects – he, law, myself, Japanese. On completing his degree, he had gone on to study for a Masters in Criminal Law. We had managed to keep in touch for much of our twenties. I remembered visiting him in Chesterfield when he had been undertaking his training contract at a local high street solicitors' firm. Eventually, though, the gaps between contact grew longer, and we lost touch with each other. I learnt through another friend that he had become disillusioned with general practice and had decided to take the bar exam. The last, I had heard, he was practising as a barrister out of chambers in Sheffield. I wasn't confident that he would give me free advice, but I thought he would be pleased to hear from me, at least I hoped he would.

On conducting a quick online search, it didn't take long to track down his chambers. When I put through a call, the clerk initially refused to connect me to Matthew. I persuaded him that it was urgent and that if he told Matthew my name, I was sure he would speak to me. Happily, Matthew agreed to receive the call, and I found myself recognising his voice as soon as he came on the line.

"Quinn! Good lord. You're a blast from the past."
"Yes, sorry we lost touch. Life gets in the way."
"It sure does. You still in London?"

"No Tokyo. Something has happened whilst I've been out here. It's why I'm ringing. I need advice and I wondered if you would hear me out for a moment."

I proceeded to fill Matthew in as quickly as I could. There was a short pause when I had finished speaking.

"You do realise that I don't specialise in criminal law?"

That floored me. "But you did a Masters in the subject, didn't you? And you had all those anecdotes about your police station visits when I stayed with you in Chesterfield."

"Yes, but that was as a trainee solicitor. I had to do a seat in criminal law as part of my training, alongside three other seats. That's when I realised, I preferred family law. I specialise in that these days."

"Oh" I felt deflated. "Do any of your colleagues do criminal law?"

"Not at these chambers I'm afraid. I could put you in touch with a criminal law specialist at another set of chambers, but he will charge you for his advice. Also, it's unlikely that he would know much about the Japanese legal system."

I thought for a moment. "I don't have much time, Matthew. If I'm going to report this to the police in Tokyo, I need to do it quickly. They will need to interview James before he returns to the UK at the end of the month. Would you mind if we at least talked it through? I don't think the principles are going to be that different in Japan, and you have at least studied the subject so you'd remember the basics, wouldn't you?"

Matthew sighed. "It was a long time ago Quinn, but sure, I'll try to help. Take me through each of your questions, but note, I'm doing this in a personal capacity; I'm not giving you professional advice here."

I felt a rush of gratitude. "Thanks. Ok, my first question is whether a verbal act on its own, one which directly led to somebody's death, could constitute murder or manslaughter."

There was no immediate reply from Matthew. Instead, I could hear him striking his keyboard.

"Matthew?"

"Yes, still here. I'm bringing up a definition of murder on my screen. Here we go: *Murder is the unlawful killing of a human being by a human being during the Queens peace with malice aforethought.* Mmmh, not that helpful."

There was another short pause, before Matthew started speaking again.

"Ok, I think it would help if we tackled each element of the legal definition separately. There are two aspects to it. *Actus reus* and *mens rea* - essentially what was done, and what the person's frame of mind was when doing it. Your first question is about the *actus reus* of murder: Can words alone – that is a verbal act as opposed to a physical one – ever constitute murder?"

"Yep, definitely the main question, I think."

"Mmmh, but not a question that is easily answered. Let's broaden it a bit. Can words alone constitute an unlawful act? The answer is obviously yes. Slander for example. But what about assault? Are there scenarios where the spoken word could, on its own, without any accompanying physical act by the speaker, cause physical harm to another person? And secondly, if the answer is yes, would the person who had spoken be criminally accountable for the physical harm caused?"

There was the sound of more tapping on the keyboard before Matthew resumed his analysis again.

"The answer I think is yes. There was a case where somebody shouted *Get the knives out* just before a fight broke out. The person shouting these words didn't get involved in the physical fight, but the judge's opinion was that what he had said still constituted an assault because he intentionally or recklessly caused the victim to fear immediate and unlawful personal violence."

I chewed on this for a moment. "Well, nobody knows what Sora said. I'm not sure he would have been threatening personal violence. It's more likely he would have said something to distract her, knowing it would make her lose concentration and fall."

"Why would he want to do that though? You've said he's competitive - misogynistic too from the sound of it - but it seems an extreme thing to do if that was the only motivation."

"I know. It's hard to get your head around. It could have been jealousy, wanting to get his own back after Laura ended the relationship."

"Alright, well that's getting into intentionality - why he did what he did. Before we get on to that, let's stay with analysing the *actus reus* – whether Sora's words could be held to be the direct cause of her death?"

"They obviously did cause her death."

"Did they?"

"If he hadn't spoken to her, she wouldn't have fallen?"

"Ok, let's unpick that assumption a bit. It says here that factual causation is determined by the *sine quo non* test."

"What's that?"

"It means 'but for.' But for his words, she wouldn't have fallen to her death."

"Well, James says she looked up when Sora spoke to her. She then said something back to him and right after that she fell. Surely, most people would say that she fell because Sora spoke to her."

"Not necessarily Quinn. I think it might depend on what he said to her and why. Also, it could be argued that there was a high probability she would have fallen anyway."

"She'd practised that pitch several times and not fallen; that's what Sora told me."

"Ok, let's leave the *actus reus* for a moment. I think it's tricky to know what the legal position is in this situation. Let's look at the *mens rea* element."

"That's the malice aforethought bit."

"Yes, and I think the law is quite complicated in this area as well."

"Do you remember any of this from your Masters?"

"Bits are coming back but it's hazy to be honest. Right, let me summarise what I've read here. There are several categories of unlawful killing: first and second degree murder, and voluntary and involuntary manslaughter. They differ from each other in terms of what the killer's state of mind was at the time of the killing."

"Ok. Go on."

"Well, with first degree murder, you need to prove an intention to kill, whereas with second degree murder, it needs to be shown that the offender only intended serious harm."

"And with manslaughter?"

"That's a bit more difficult to summarise but I'll have a go. If somebody kills somebody, it's held to be voluntary manslaughter when the person acted in the moment, in circumstances where it seems reasonable that they would have become emotionally or mentally disturbed; basically, it's a situation where they have been reasonably provoked. Involuntary, on the other hand, is when you kill somebody without intending to. There's something called gross negligence manslaughter in England, which is where death results from negligence or serious recklessness. For the police to charge Sora with that, they would need to show that he had a duty of care towards Laura and that he had breached it at the time her death happened."

Again, I reflected on what Matthew was telling me. "I can see that it would be difficult to prove what Sora intended; nobody heard what he said. But surely, at the very least, he was seriously reckless to speak to her when he did; as a fellow climber, shouldn't he have known that he had a responsibility not to distract her?"

"Unless he had a legitimate reason for calling out to her. Look Quinn, you might be able to make the case that Sora's actions were seriously reckless, but you'd still need to convince the courts that a verbal act alone could amount to the *actus reus* in a murder."

"You said earlier that a verbal act could be considered a criminal assault. If that assault led to Laura's death, even if Sora didn't intend her to fall, then that should be involuntary manslaughter, shouldn't it?"

"Maybe, but you don't know if what he said did amount to an assault and how will you ever be able to prove it? I don't know Quinn. If you really feel that you can't let this go, maybe you should speak to the police in Tokyo. They would know whether there are sufficient grounds to interview Sora."

I thought about this. Matthew was probably right. If I told the police, I would have at least relieved my conscience. James wouldn't be happy with me, and Sora would be livid if he found out that I had reported him, but neither of those two facts mattered. What did matter was the impact any investigation would have on Reo and Niko. I needed to think about that before I took any further steps.

CHAPTER 15

FOLLOWING THE CONVERSATION with Matthew, my classes that evening did not go well. I was distracted and the quality of my teaching suffered. Several times I noticed my students looking at me in puzzlement, so much so that I felt I had to apologise for my performance.

As I packed my bag, at the end of my last class, I let my thoughts focus wholly on the issue that was worrying me. Should I tell Reo what James had seen? Should I introduce the possibility that Laura hadn't died in an accident, doing something she loved? Should I tell him that, essentially, she had been killed, whether intentionally or not, by somebody who Reo thought had been one of her friends?

These questions absorbed me as I descended the stairs of the EFL building, into the lobby on the ground floor. When he said my name, my kneejerk reaction was to run. He was sitting in the reception area, seemingly relaxed, waiting for me.

"Hello Quinn; I was not sure when your last class finished, so I am very glad to have caught you."

Sora got up from his chair and walked the short distance over to me. I could see that his leg was still troubling him, and I could feel an artery throbbing in my neck.

"Hi Sora. What are you doing here?"

"Yui told me that Reo had ended the replacement arrangement with you?"

"Yes, but no offence, what is that to do with you?"

"She said that Reo bumped into you unexpectedly, walking down from the top of *Yōshanai michi*."

"Yes, that was unfortunate; I had promised him that I wouldn't do the climb. I haven't spoken to him since the agency told me he had terminated the contract. They told me that he doesn't want to talk to me, and I can understand why."

"Yui said he was very upset, and angry too."

I rolled my eyes. "So why are you here. To tell me off or to sympathise?"

"Neither. I want to know what you were doing on *Yōshanai michi*. You and Yui told me, quite plainly, that climbing that route again would be wrong."

"I don't know why I was on the climb. It was a mistake."

Sora looked at me sceptically. "Yui said you were with James. She also said that James had told Reo, you had been practising the last pitch."

I stayed silent. Sora moved a step further forward into my personal space. "So, I want to know why? Why go out there with James to do the fifth pitch?"

I shrugged, stepping back, and thinking fast. "I bumped into him in Shibuya, shortly after we got back from Mizugaki. We got talking about Laura. I mentioned that you had said it was he, James, who had had the bird theory. James says he doesn't remember telling you that. He thinks you have mixed him up with somebody else."

I paused to gauge Sora's response to this, but his expression was inscrutable.

"Anyway, when I mentioned the bird theory, James thought we should check it out so that's why we were up there."

"And?"

"What do you mean *and*?"

"What did you conclude?"

"Oh, I see. Well, we thought that maybe that was what had happened; we saw bird poo and evidence of feathers on the ledge, and in the crevice."

"No, you did not."

"Sorry?" This response surprised me.

"I have been up and down that pitch more than once as you know. There is no bird excrement up there. Birds do not use that ledge or, at least, they have not for a while."

I stared at him. "Ok, so why do you think we were up there?

"Because James has a theory about how Laura died and wanted to show you."

I flushed and saw Sora notice.

"I think you had better tell me the truth. It is no secret that James and I do not get on."

This made me pause. What did Sora mean by that? That James might want to implicate him? I realised at that moment that I'd had enough of the speculation, the not knowing. Throwing caution aside, I swallowed and decided to challenge Sora directly.

"James said he saw you on the day that Laura died. He was watching Laura do the climb from the bottom of the second pitch. He was keeping himself hidden because he knew Laura didn't want anybody watching her."

I paused again, to register Sora's reaction; he was listening to me intently, his jaw clenched.

"He said that Laura had reached the ledge on the fifth pitch and had committed herself to a couple of moves above it. At that point, he saw your head pop out from the top of the climb. He said you called out to her, that you were waving your arms and seemed quite animated. She looked up, said something back to you, and then fell."

Sora was starting at me coldly now, his eyes dark and stony. I pressed on.

"He thinks that whatever you said distracted her, broke her concentration, and caused her to fall. He doesn't understand why you would have interrupted her at that point in the climb."

Sora raised both his arms above his head in a long stretch. When he had finished, he gave me a pitying look. "So that is what you think? That I deliberately sabotaged Laura's attempt and caused her to plunge to her death."

"I haven't known what to think. It seems odd that you never mentioned you were up there the day she fell."

"James did not mention he was there either. Perhaps neither of us wanted the authorities diverted from seeing the situation for what it was – just a tragic accident."

"But James didn't speak to her whilst she was in such a precarious position. You should have known how dangerous it would be to engage her in conversation."

I could see that this statement had angered Sora. When he replied, his voice was harsh and tight.

"I will tell you what happened, _Kosuke Kindaichi_. I had been doing the same thing as James - watching the climb because I was concerned about Laura's safety, yet knowing she must not see me. I stuck my head out briefly to see if she had managed the move onto the ledge ok. I saw that she had, and that she was now a couple of metres past it, but I also saw that she was following the wrong line. The rock was too smooth there; she needed to be a metre or so to the right to ensure that there were sufficient rock nodules for her to smear on. I had to warn her, to get her to traverse sideway to pick up the right line again. She would have fallen if she had continued up the line she was following. My intervention was necessary, but she fell before she was able to follow my advice."

Sora's hands were now on his hips, and he was glaring at me. "Does that satisfy you? Have you heard enough to drop this amateur sleuthing? Do you seriously think telling Reo that I was up there that day, would make things better for him and Niko?"

His explanation, and the tone in which he had delivered it, was an assault on my senses. I felt light-headed and moved to sit down. Sora followed, spurring me to hold up my arms in defence of his advance.

"Okay, okay. I'm sorry that I didn't come and ask you for your version of events. Leave me alone now, Sora. Reo has sacked me; there is no need for us to see each other again. I want to get on with my English teaching, have a quiet life in Tokyo."

"So, you're going to drop this?"

I sighed deeply. "Yes."

"And James?"

"He doesn't want to get involved. He goes back to the UK at the end of the month."

I could see that Sora was watching me closely, wondering whether he should believe me. Seconds passed and then he made up his mind.

"Excellent. Have a good life then Quinn." He turned away from me, exiting through the revolving doors, onto the street.

I stayed sitting in reception for quite a while after Sora left. I realised belatedly that I had not confronted him about his affair with Laura. He had lied about that, so who was to say that he wasn't lying about what happened on the climb? Sora's personality made me think that he could have been provoked by the way the affair ended, that it might have made him want revenge and to strike back in some way. But sufficient motivation for murder? That I was struggling to comprehend.

On reflection, I didn't know what I believed, but I knew that Reo wasn't aware of all the facts, and I thought he should be. Further, I had my own personal reasons for wanting to set the record straight. Reo thought I was the untrustworthy one. Instead, it was his wife who had gone behind his back; the one who had been dishonest in action. I knew that others might challenge me on my reasons for shattering Reo's illusion about his wife; what purpose it served to actively taint the memories of his marriage? I had thought about that but for me, the truth was the most important thing here. The truth mattered, and besides, Sora continued to be a figure in Reo's and Niko's lives. I felt that Reo had a right to know what sort of friend, he really was, and to be able to make an informed decision about what to do about that.

I stood up. I'd made up my mind. I would go over to Reo's workplace the next day, catch him as he was leaving, and persuade him to hear me out. I'd have to take care that Sora did not see me, that was all.

CHAPTER 16

IT TOOK AN HOUR to get across from my dorm to Tanaka Pharmaceuticals the next day. I arrived at six pm and hovered inside the entrance of a Family Mart store, directly across the road from the main entrance to Reo's building. I remembered Reo telling me that he rarely left work before six. He tried not to leave much later than that though, because of the need to get back to Niko. I had no idea what sort of hours Sora worked, but I was counting on them not leaving together.

In the end, I had a forty-minute wait. Fortunately, there was no sign of Sora, when Reo came out of his company's entrance. He turned right, presumably heading for Nihombashi station. I hurried along, walking parallel to him for a hundred metres or so, before dashing across the street to intercept him as he reached the corner of the main road.

As Yuuto had warned, he was distinctly displeased to see me. At first, he tried to ignore and push pass me, but I grabbed his arm, and implored him to give me fifteen minutes of his time. I told him I could explain. At that point, he put his briefcase down, folded his arms, and said he would give me five minutes. I looked anxiously back up the street to see if there was any sign of Sora. When Reo saw me do this, he must have understood my concern, as he pulled me into a nearby bar and once inside, led me into a back room. He ordered a couple of Asahi beers and when we'd sat down, once again assumed a posture of folded arms.

"So, explain."

His tone was cold and unfriendly. I could feel a tight apprehension in my throat and hesitantly began to speak.

When I had finished telling him about Sora and James' presence on *Yōshanai michi* the day Laura died, what James had seen Sora do, and how Sora had explained this, Reo looked stunned. He briefly put his head in his hands but when he sat up again, he had regained his composure and gave me a long cool look.

"How does that explain what you and James were doing on the fifth pitch, the day I saw you."

"James refused to tell me why Laura had fallen; he felt that I'd only believe him if I directly experienced what had happened to her. He wanted to put me in the same position as she had been in, so he pretended to take me off belay and made me think I was climbing free solo. He then called down to me at the most precarious moment to show how dangerous it would be to distract somebody at that point in the climb."

"But Sora thought Laura would have fallen anyway, if she had continued following the line she was on?"

"That's what he says."

"But you do not believe him?"

I hesitated. "I haven't told you everything Reo."

Reo did not seem to hear me. He was pressing his fingers into his brow and massaging it roughly. "I do not condone it, but I can understand why Sora would keep quiet about this. Why did James not report what he had seen though?"

"He's wary of Sora – they don't get on - and he wasn't sure how to interpret what he'd seen. He had to get back to the UK and he didn't want the authorities holding him up, by calling him in for an interview. I know it doesn't make him look good, but he said he doesn't see how it benefits you to know……"

"But you do, as you're telling me now?"

"I think it is important that you know the truth."

"Which is?"

"You thought that Laura fell that day whilst she was alone and without anybody seeing what happened. But that's not true. Both Sora and James saw her fall but chose to hide this fact from everybody. Both say it was because they did not want to be involved in any post-accident investigation."

Reo shut his eyes and started to make small rocking movements. I sat motionless, not knowing what he was feeling. When he reopened his eyes again, he seemed distant.

"James is right. It does not make any difference to the outcome. Laura fell, she died. It hurts that Sora was there, though, that he did not consider it important to share that experience with me."

I nodded. Reo's attention had sharpened again. "You said you had not told me everything."

So, he had heard. This was the part of the telling which concerned me the most. I had no idea how he would react.

"It's about the other day, when you met with the AI mediator, and when Sora admitted to having had an affair…I'm sorry to tell you this Reo, but the person he was having an affair with was Laura. He wouldn't admit that to me when I confronted him, but your mother told me; she saw them together. Laura was very contrite; she ended it as soon as your mother found out. She told Akemi that it hadn't meant anything, that it had been a short fling of about four months. But she also told Akemi that Sora hadn't taken the ending very well; he was still pestering and making advances towards her, even though she had made it clear that the affair had to end."

I paused. "I'm telling you this because it adds context to the fact that Sora was up there, at the top of the climb that day."

Reo frowned on hearing this but gave no other reaction to the news. He sat, head bowed, reflecting on what I had told him.

"I think I knew intuitively that something was going on or had happened between them. But I did not want to know. I chose not to know."

He lifted his head to look at me full on. "You say that Sora was upset at Laura ending things and that that adds context to what happened on the day of the climb. What are you implying by that? That Sora's presence made her fall? Are you saying that he might have upset her in some way, perhaps on purpose?"

"I...I honestly don't know Reo. Do you remember when we were with the mediator, and Sora said that he regretted his behaviour last year. We don't know what he meant by that. But would he deliberately behave in a way designed to distract Laura and cause her to fall? It does sound far-fetched. Their climbing relationship didn't seem affected by the break-up, not in the last few months of her life anyhow. Sora says he helped her practice the climb beforehand. There was no hint that he didn't want her to succeed and his reason for calling out to her on the last pitch seems plausible. It's James who is throwing doubt on Sora's motivations and actions."

Reo thought about this. "Sora is a complicated character. It is no secret that he and I have a difficult relationship. His competitiveness is tiresome, and he finds it hard to control his temper. But I am not aware that he has ever physically hurt anybody. I am not sure I believe he would deliberately try to make Laura fall."

He took a sip of his beer. "Knowing all of this, doesn't change anything. You understand why, don't you?"

I looked at him in surprise. "No, why?"

"Sora's version of events is impossible to disprove. Niko thinks her mother's death was an accident, an accident that was nobody's fault, which happened whilst her mum was doing something she loved, in a place that she loved. If I report this to the police and they investigate it, Niko will get to know. An accident which was nobody's fault, will then become an allegation of deliberate and harmful wrongdoing. I would never put Niko through that, change her perception of what happened to something so ugly and violent. It would only add to her trauma. I will never allow it to happen."

He swallowed the last of his beer. His expression had softened.

"I am grateful that you have been so honest with me. It hurt when I thought you had deliberately gone behind my back to do the climb, especially since I had specifically asked you not to. It made me feel that you had no respect for my feelings."

I felt a wash of relief at his words. "I know. That's why I needed to explain."

"You don't need to concern yourself with Sora though. Niko and I are moving away from Tokyo. I doubt we will see much of him in the future, even if he stays in a relationship with Yui."

"Really?" This was news to me. Reo's career was in Tokyo, and his parents lived here. "Where are you moving to?"

"Back to our home city, Sapporo. My parents are coming with us."

"Chieko and Akemi? They want to leave Tokyo as well?"

"It was their idea; they have been in Tokyo a long time but have felt for a while that they would like to return home. It will be a fresh start for Niko, and for me. I need a change and I have fond memories of Sapporo. I was Niko's age when we left to move to Tokyo."

"Sapporo is the capital of Hokkaido, isn't it, the northernmost island of Japan? That's miles away."

"Yes, an eight-hour journey by train, seventeen by car. So can you understand why I'm not worried about Sora being a problem for much longer?"

"What does Niko think about the move?"

Reo hesitated. "I haven't told her yet. She won't want to leave Yui."

"She does seem very attached to her."

"Yes, and that has worried me. I do not think the attachment is healthy."

"Why not? Because of Sora?"

"Partly, but that is not the main reason. There is no guarantee that Yui would stay nearby, even if we stayed in Tokyo. She and Sora have discussed moving in together, but Sora wants them to move to Koto city, a good hour away by train. Niko would see far less of her. That was a key reason I wanted to engage the services of a replacement, so Niko would have a reliable and consistent mother figure in her life."

"Engage the services of!" I smiled, in gentle mockery. "That sounds very formal for something so personal."

Reo shrugged. "I know you don't agree with the replacement concept, despite you entering into an arrangement to be just that."

He sounded accusatory and I felt stung. "Yuuto was persuasive in his arguments. He said it would benefit you, so I decided to give it a go. Right from the start, though, I felt alien and false in the role. I might look like Laura but I'm not her and the replacement arrangement is always only temporary. What happens at the end of the three years when the contract ends? How would Niko feel then? Surely you would be better off finding somebody new, somebody who could be the permanent fixture you are after?"

"A stepmother?"

"Well, yes, of course. Nobody could be Niko's real mother; she's dead."

Reo flinched when I said this and went quiet. When he spoke again, his voice was low, and I had to lean in to hear him.

"When I look at you, you remind me of Laura, and that gives me immense pleasure. I allow myself to imagine that I am in her company again, even though I know that this is not the case. I am not deluding myself that you are her and believe me, I do appreciate that the best course for me is to move on and find a new partner."

As he continued to speak, Reo's tone sharpened, and he became more assertive. "When I think about Niko though, that is another matter entirely."

"How do you mean?"

"Do you understand the psychological effects of a child losing their mother at Niko's age?"

"I can appreciate that it must be hugely traumatic, a profound loss; I imagine that a child in that position might feel abandoned and alone, even if they still had their other parent."

My words had negligible impact as Reo forged on. "I have taken advice about it. In the first two years, after a child loses a parent, there is an elevated risk of them developing depression. This can lead to difficulties with daily functioning – doing normal things such as washing and dressing themselves, being able to do homework, or concentrate at school. These things become much harder for the bereaved child."

I nodded.

"You have met Niko, and you might think she shows no signs of being depressed. Indeed, you may think the opposite – that she is a lively girl, with a sense of fun, who is very fond of her mechanical dog."

"I guess, but I've seen her angry too. She seems very proprietorial about the memory of her mother. The issue with K2 is a case in point. It seems to stem from the fact that her mother gave her the dog and therefore, nobody else should have any say over it."

"Exactly." Reo seemed pleased that I had observed this. "She is angry, but she is sad too. She is bright and capable academically, but she has not been doing very well at school this last year. She has lost confidence, in her lessons but also socially with her peers."

"But she has you, and I am sure the school is being supportive."

"Of course, but I am not sure that this is enough to protect her from an increased vulnerability when she gets older. All the studies show that this is a risk for the bereaved child. I worry that losing her mother at this age, will cause Niko to be less resilient when she encounters difficulties as a young woman. I do not want this tragedy to lessen her life chances. Again, this was a key motivation for engaging a replacement. I thought that if somebody who looked like her mother, and acted like her mother, was present in our lives, this might help mitigate Niko's loss. I knew it could not be a permanent arrangement, but I thought that if there was someone onto which Niko could transfer the memories of her mother, just until she got past the teenage years, that that would really help her......"

Reo's voice trailed off. He looked at me awkwardly. "I am not explaining myself very well. I can see now that my logic is probably naïve, clumsy psychology."

I shrugged. "I don't know Reo. I can understand your reasoning but I'm not sure it would have worked. It could have confused Niko, made her disinclined to accept reality. Oh, I really don't know. I'm not a psychologist."

I shook the dregs of my beer. "I can tell you one thing though. The arrangement would not have done me any good in the long term. I need to be Quinn and to focus on being Quinn, not to escape my identity by assuming that of another woman's."

Reo's whole posture straightened when I said this. I could tell I had said something that had resonated with him. He reached over and lightly touched my hand.

"You are right. I have completely ignored who you are in all of this, and I am sorry. I have approached the arrangement as solely a contractual one; I asked you if I could call you Laura and I would have kept pushing on other things, including your time, until you had completely assimilated yourself into the role. That would have been wrong of me…"

I nodded, grateful that he was able to acknowledge this.

"I have a proposal for you though."

My eyes narrowed. "Yes?"

"Why don't you come with us to Sapporo? Instead of teaching English here in Tokyo, I would pay you to be Niko's tutor. No specified length of time. You would only need to stay as long as it suited you. And I would make sure you had plenty of time off to develop your own life in the city, to make your own friends and pursue your own interests."

I pulled a dubious face. "I'm flattered Reo but is that realistic? How do I know you and Niko won't develop an attachment to me, or expectations that might make it difficult for me to leave when I felt the time was right?"

"I am asking you as Quinn, to come as Quinn, and to be Quinn. That would be our upfront understanding, and I would expect you to correct us robustly if you ever felt we were seeing you as Laura's *Daiyaku*. Good enough?"

I smiled. "I know nothing about Sapporo. Why would I leave the excitement and possibilities of Tokyo for a city that I have only vaguely heard of."

"Because I can highly recommend it and because Niko and I would be there."

"And Chieko and Akemi."

"Them too, and they like you, you know. They like Quinn."

I smiled again; I wouldn't tell Reo that Akemi had already conveyed this to me, in her own way.

"You do know that if Yuuto heard about your proposal, he would demand that you continue to pay his fee."

Reo laughed. "Of course, I would expect nothing less."

His expression grew serious. "What do you say? Will you come?"

Niko's cheeky face flashed through my mind, and then Akemi's kindly wizened one. I felt a small ache of longing, a desire to belong somewhere and to something that was bigger than myself.

"I'll think about it," I said.

Printed in Dunstable, United Kingdom

Third Edition

The Psychology of Work and Organizations

Stephen A. Woods
Michael A. West

FURTHER PRAISE FOR WOODS AND WEST'S
The Psychology of Work and Organizations

"This third edition of the text by Woods and West has it all; broad coverage of all the important topics but also enough depth to be used in advanced classes. It features pioneering psychologists and builds on the classic models and theories but also features the latest research and most recent developments in the field. Topics, such as sustainability, ethics, diversity and artificial intelligence are important for organizations and the people within them - but most importantly, they are important for our societies. In short, this book benefits from the experience of its authors in the academic and also the 'real' world and I am sure that the students and teachers alike will love it."

Rolf van Dick, Chair of Social Psychology, Vice President of Goethe University Frankfurt, Germany

"Students and lecturers of Work and Organizational Psychology are in luck. Stephen Woods and Michael West have written a textbook that will help students to acquire key knowledge and develop relevant competencies in the field. This book covers classic and recent theories, research findings, and techniques, highlighting the implications for professional practice. In summary, this book is a powerful lever to foster learning within our discipline."

Vicente Gonzalez-Roma, Professor of Work and Organizational Psychology, Associate Editor of the *Journal of Applied Psychology*, Director of the Research Institute of Personnel Psychology, Organizational Development and Quality of Working Life (Idocal), University of Valencia, Spain

"There hasn't been a time in our history when we need to understand the relevance of 'joy at work' more than we do now. Organisations in the 21st Century are having to change at a phenomenal rate to take on board the changes in modern day society as well as the heightened expectations of an increasingly knowledgeable and technologically savvy population. Stephen Woods and Michael West's book The Psychology of Work and Organisations is essential reading for anyone that needs to understand why valued, appreciated and included staff increase productivity and creativity in an organisation as well as making the workplace somewhere that people thrive as opposed to simply survive."

Yvonne Coghill, CBE, FRCN, Director, Workforce Race Equality Standard, NHS England, and Deputy President, Royal College of Nursing, UK

"With new content that reflects topics and themes that are even more relevant to the world of work today- such as AI, diversity and positive psychology - this new edition by Woods & West is an integral companion for every student and academic within the field of work and organisational psychology. Having used this book as core reading over the past few years, I attest to its unique ability in bringing complex theory and research to life with effortless fluency. This book shines because it distinctively draws on the authors' esteemed academic and 'real world' experiences, which together ensure the text, activities and snapshots of organisational examples, are engaging, insightful and relevant."

Dr Rashi Dhensa-Kahlon, Lecturer in Work and Organisational Psychology, Director of the MSc in Occupational and Organisational Psychology, University of Surrey, UK

"In this latest edition of The Psychology of Work and Organizations, Woods and West continue to equip readers with a winning combination of robust, in-depth research together with practical application in the workplace. The chapters cover a range of highly relevant and current theories in an easily accessible manner, making The Psychology of Work and Organizations essential reading for academics looking to bridge the gap between research and practice, as well as practitioners who are looking to build specialist, informed knowledge in their own area of expertise."

Dr Nic Hammarling, Partner & Head of Diversity, Pearn Kandola, UK

"This highly readable global text presents the results of both historical and leading edge research on work and organizational psychology in a memorable way for students in Australia, Asia, Europe and North America."

Gary Latham, Secretary of State Professor of Organizational Effectiveness, Rotman School of Management, University of Toronto, Canada

An up-to-date textbook containing all the relevant academic research and applied practices we see in organizations today. Written in an engaging style and with excellent coverage of important contemporary themes such as social responsibility and mobility, this will likely become a definitive introduction for years to come.

Pamela Yeow, Reader in Management, Birkbeck College, University of London, UK

Woods and West provide a well-balanced and clear introduction to work psychology. Up-to-date references and innovative learning features are used throughout, alongside clear examples that students will find both informative and relevant to their studies and future working lives. The emphasis on workplaces and organizations influencing people's growth and development is beneficial for healthy and happy workers and successful organizations.

Sheena Johnson, Senior Lecturer in Organizational Psychology, Alliance Manchester Business School, University of Manchester, UK

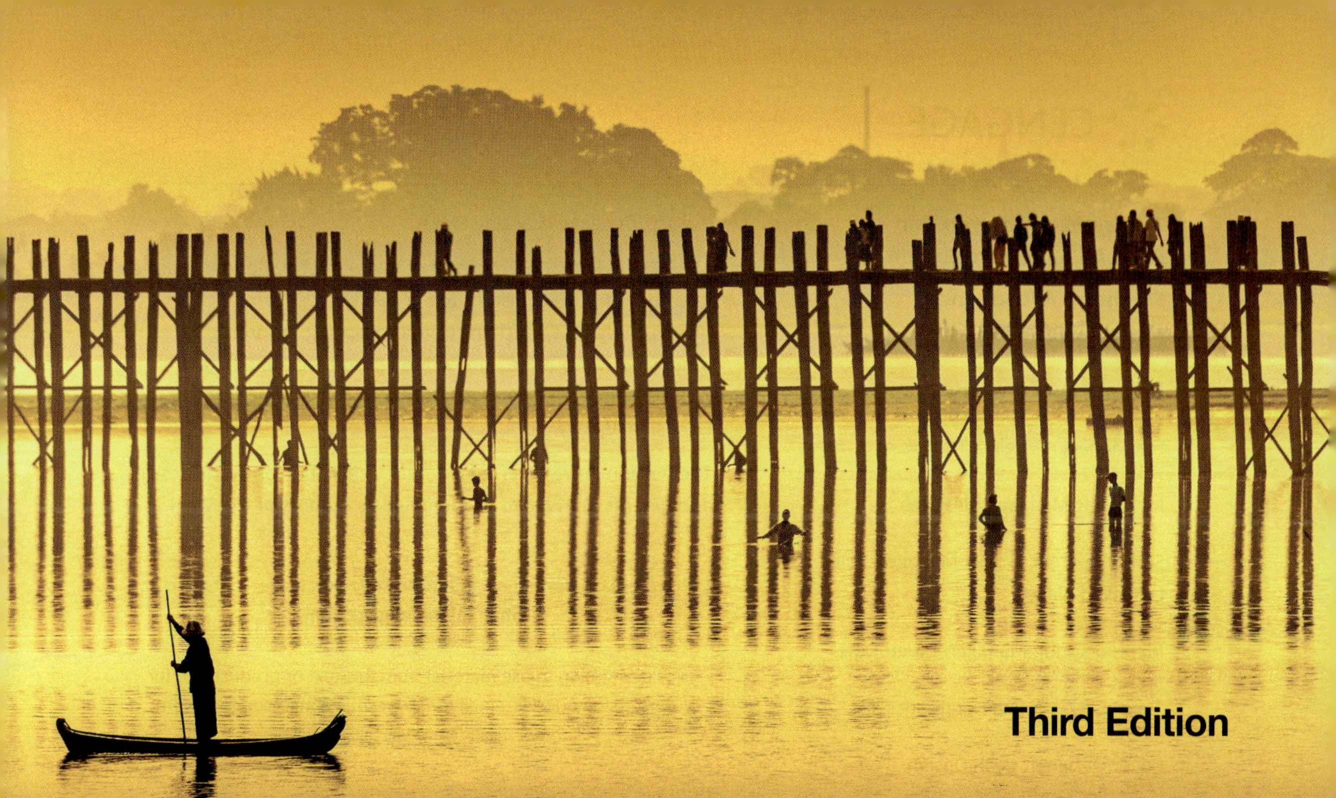

Third Edition

The Psychology of Work and Organizations

Stephen A. Woods

Michael A. West

Australia • Brazil • Mexico • Singapore • United Kingdom • United States

The Psychology of Work and Organizations, Third Edition

Stephen A. Woods and Michael A. West

Publisher: Annabel Ainscow

List Manager: Virginia Thorp

Marketing Manager: Tim Lees

Senior Content Project Manager: Phillippa Davidson-Blake

Manufacturing Manager: Eyvett Davis

Typesetter: Lumina Datamatics, Inc.

Cover Designer: Cyan Design

Cover Image: ©Bule Sky Studio/Shutterstock

© 2020, Cengage Learning EMEA

ALL RIGHTS RESERVED. No part of this work may be reproduced, transmitted, stored, distributed or used in any form or by any means, electronic, mechanical, photocopying, recording or otherwise, without the prior written permission of Cengage Learning or under license in the U.K. from the Copyright Licensing Agency Ltd.

The Authors have asserted the right under the Copyright Designs and Patents Act 1988 to be identified as Authors of this Work.

> For product information and technology assistance, contact us at **emea.info@cengage.com**
>
> For permission to use material from this text or product and for permission queries, email **emea.permissions@cengage.com**

British Library Cataloguing-in-Publication Data

A catalogue record for this book is available from the British Library.

ISBN: 978-1-4737-6717-1

Cengage Learning, EMEA
Cheriton House, North Way
Andover, Hampshire, SP10 5BE
United Kingdom

Cengage Learning is a leading provider of customized learning solutions with employees residing in nearly 40 different countries and sales in more than 125 countries around the world. Find your local representative at: **www.cengage.co.uk**

Cengage Learning products are represented in Canada by Nelson Education, Ltd.

To learn more about Cengage platforms and services, register or access your online learning solution, or purchase materials for your course, visit **www.cengage.com**

Printed in Singapore by Seng Lee Press Ltd
Print Number: 03   Print Year: 2020

BRIEF CONTENTS

1 INTRODUCTION 1

PART ONE
FOUNDATIONS OF WORK AND ORGANIZATIONAL PSYCHOLOGY 20

2 INDIVIDUAL DIFFERENCES AT WORK 21

3 ATTITUDES AND BEHAVIOUR IN ORGANIZATIONS 61

4 MOTIVATION AT WORK 101

PART TWO
PROFESSIONAL PRACTICE OF WORK AND ORGANIZATIONAL PSYCHOLOGY 139

5 RECRUITMENT AND SELECTION 140

6 LEARNING, TRAINING AND DEVELOPMENT 185

7 PERFORMANCE MANAGEMENT 217

8 CAREERS AND CAREER MANAGEMENT 255

9 SAFETY, STRESS AND HEALTH AT WORK 290

BRIEF CONTENTS

**PART THREE
ORGANIZATIONS** 334

10 ORGANIZATIONS: STRATEGY AND STRUCTURE 335

11 LEADERSHIP IN ORGANIZATIONS 370

12 TEAMS AND TEAMWORK 413

13 ORGANIZATIONAL CULTURE, CLIMATE AND CHANGE 453

14 THE PSYCHOLOGY OF WORK AND ORGANIZATIONS 491

CREDIT PAGES 508

INDEX 513

CONTENTS

Dedications   xii
Acknowledgments   xiii
About the Authors   xiv

1   Introduction   1

The psychology of work and organizations:
first encounters   3
A brief history of work and organizational psychology   5
Positive organizational scholarship   7
Contemporary themes in work and organizational psychology   9
The psychology of work and organizations: this book   15
Professional practice of work and organizational psychology   15
Organizations   15
Summary   17
Further reading   18
References   18

PART ONE
FOUNDATIONS OF WORK AND ORGANIZATIONAL PSYCHOLOGY   20

2   Individual Differences at Work   21

Introduction to individual differences   22
Personality   23
Personality traits at work   27
Intelligence   39
The interplay of personality and intelligence   45
Wider concepts in individual differences at work   46
Measuring individual differences: psychometrics   48
Summary   54
Discussion questions   55
Further reading   55
References   55

3 Attitudes and Behaviour in Organizations 61

What is organizational behaviour? 62
Management influences: shaping and controlling behaviour at work 62
Attitudes and behaviour 64
Work-related attitudes 68
Emotional influences on behaviour at work 75
Perception and decision-making 79
Social influences on behaviour 83
Summary 94
Discussion questions 95
Further reading 95
References 95

4 Motivation at Work 101

Need theories of motivation 102
Motivation as a trait 106
Self-determination theory 106
Cognition and motivation 107
Treating people fairly: justice and equity perspectives on motivation 114
Job design and motivation 118
Summary 127
Discussion questions 128
Further reading 128
References 128

Case studies for part one: foundations of work and organizational psychology 133

PART TWO
PROFESSIONAL PRACTICE OF WORK AND ORGANIZATIONAL PSYCHOLOGY 139

5 Recruitment and Selection 140

The organizational imperative 141
Effective recruitment and selection 141
Job analysis 144
Recruitment: attracting people to work 147
Selection: assessing and hiring people 149
Macro perspectives on recruitment and selection 165
Recruitment and selection in specific contexts 166
Applicant perspectives: the experience of recruitment and selection 168
Fairness in selection 170
Summary 177
Discussion questions 178
Further reading 178
References 178

6 Learning, Training and Development 185

Learning, training and development in organizations 186
The process and implementation of learning, training and development 187
Success and failure of learning, training and development 199
Workplace coaching 206
Summary 212
Discussion questions 213
Further reading 213
References 213

7 Performance Management 217

Introducing performance management 218
Goal-setting 219
The conditions for positive performance change 222
Measuring job performance 223
Performance feedback 239
Critical perspectives on performance measurement and management processes 243
Integrative and organizational models of performance management 245
Summary 250
Discussion questions 251
Further reading 251
References 251

8 Careers and Career Management 255

Work, life and careers in the 21st century 256
The development of careers over time 257
Person–environment fit perspectives 263
Social, cultural and organizational influences on careers 273
Career management in organizations 279
Summary 284
Discussion questions 285
Further reading 285
References 285

9 Safety, Stress and Health at Work 290

Positive emotion at work 290
Occupational health and safety 291
Stress and strain at work 294
Theories of stress at work 295
Individual differences in response to stress 298
A comprehensive framework for understanding stress 300
Reducing and managing stress 308
Burnout and engagement 314

Summary 319
Discussion questions 319
Further reading 320
References 320
Case studies for part two: professional practice of work and organizational psychology 328

PART THREE
ORGANIZATIONS 334

10 Organizations: Strategy and Structure 335

Introduction 335
Organizational strategy 336
Major perspectives on strategy 340
Organizational structure 356
Strategy and structure 362
Summary 367
Discussion questions 368
Further reading 368
References 368

11 Leadership in Organizations 370

Introduction 370
Research into leadership 373
Trait approaches to leadership 374
Behavioural theories 380
Contingency approach 385
Dyadic theories of leadership 388
Charismatic and transformational leadership 389
Leadership across cultures 392
Gender and leadership 396
Leadership development 399
Conclusion 404
Summary 406
Discussion questions 408
Further reading 408
References 408

12 Teams and Teamwork 413

What is a team? 414
What do teams do? 417
Why work in teams? 418

What makes an effective team?   419
Team inputs   421
Team processes   432
Team outputs   441
Summary   446
Discussion questions   447
Further reading   447
References   447

13 Organizational Culture, Climate and Change   453

Organizational culture   454
Organizational climate   463
Organizational change   468
Designing and implementing change and innovation   476
Summary   480
Discussion questions   481
Further reading   481
References   481
Case studies for part three: organizations   485

14 The Psychology of Work and Organizations   491

Part one: understanding the foundations of work and organizational psychology   492
Part two: practising professional applications of work and organizational psychology   495
Part three: creating effective organizations   498
Summary and conclusion   505
References   506

Credit Pages   508
Index   513

DEDICATIONS

For Naveen.

For Gillian.

ACKNOWLEDGMENTS

Stephen A. Woods:

My heartfelt and special thanks as always to my wife Virinder and my son Naveen for their support, pride, encouragement and patience during the writing of this book, and the fun and warmth they afford my life.

Michael West:

Thanks for help and laughter from Eleanor Hardy, Thomas West, Nik Vlissides and Rosa Hardy. And to Gillian for creating such a happy space for us all.

Thanks from us both to the patient Cengage team, our freelance editor Carol Usher, and to our wise reviewers.

In addition to the dozens of academics who answered electronic surveys at the start of this project, the publisher would particularly like to thank the following for providing detailed feedback at various stages of the book's development:

- Neil Anderson, Bradford School of Management, UK
- David Biggs, University of Gloucestershire, UK
- Yvonne Coghill, Royal College of Nursing, UK
- Catherine Collins, University of New South Wales, Australia
- Rashi Dhensa-Kahlon, University of Surrey, UK
- Vicente Gonzalez-Roma, University of Valencia, Spain
- Nic Hammarling, Pearn Kandola, UK
- Danny Hinton, University of Wolverhampton, UK
- Helen Hughes, University of Leeds, UK
- Sheena Johnson, Manchester Business School, UK
- Penny Johnson, University of Sunderland, UK
- Mary Kinahan, Dublin Institute of Technology (DIT), Ireland
- Annika Lantz, Uppsala University, Sweden
- Gary Latham, University of Toronto, Canada
- Abigail Marks, Heriot-Watt University, UK
- Peter Morgan, University of Bradford, UK
- Johan Naslund, Linköping University, Sweden
- Paula O'Kane, University of Ulster, Ireland
- Sumari O'Neil, University of Pretoria, South Africa
- Jason Palframan, Athlone Insititute of Technology, Ireland
- Birgit Schyns, Portsmouth Business School, UK
- Mantombi Tshabalala, Vaal University of Technology
- Eleni Tzouramani, Norwich Business School, London, UK
- Rolf van Dick, Goethe University Frankfurt, Germany
- Kosheleva Vladimirovna, Saint Petersburg State University, Russia
- Thomas Waldmann, University of Ulster, Ireland
- Pamela Yeow, Birkbeck College, University of London, UK

The publisher also thanks the various copyright holders for granting permission to reproduce material throughout the text. Every effort has been made to trace all copyright holders but if anything has been inadvertently overlooked the publisher will be pleased to make the necessary arrangements at the first opportunity. Please contact the publisher directly.

ABOUT THE AUTHORS

STEPHEN WOODS is Professor of HRM and Organizational Behaviour at the University of Liverpool Management School, and a Registered Practitioner Occupational Psychologist. He graduated in Occupational Psychology from the University of Nottingham in 2001 and received his PhD in 2004. His research and professional practice are most notably in the area of personality at work, focusing on psychometric and personality trait assessment, and personality development and change at work. He also conducts research on the ways that recruitment and selection in organizations can be made fair and effective, diversity management, workplace coaching, and well-being. He has published more than 50 scientific and professional articles, scholarly books and chapters. He speaks regularly at international conferences, organizations and universities about personality and work, and contemporary issues in work and organizational psychology more widely. He is Director and Founder of *Aston Business Assessments*, and works extensively as a practitioner with organizations and businesses in the UK and internationally on HRM strategy, policy and practice.

MICHAEL WEST is Professor of Organizational Psychology at Lancaster University Management School, Visiting Professor at University College Dublin and Emeritus Professor at Aston University. He is Senior Visiting Fellow at The King's Fund. He graduated from the University of Wales in 1973 and received his PhD on the psychology of meditation in 1977. He has authored, edited or co-edited 20 books and has published over 200 articles for scientific and practitioner publications, as well as chapters in scholarly books. He is a Fellow of the British Psychological Society, the American Psychological Association (APA), the APA Society for Industrial/Organizational Psychology, the International Association of Applied Psychologists, the British Academy of Management and Academician of the Academy of Social Sciences. He focuses on how to develop the conditions for organizations and people to thrive at work through his research into teamworking, organizational culture, leadership and effectiveness, particularly in relation to the organization of health services. He advises governments and organizations on developing health service cultures of high quality and compassionate care and speaks to a wide range of audiences on these topics nationally and internationally.

Teaching & Learning Support Resources

Cengage's peer-reviewed content for higher and further education courses is accompanied by a range of digital teaching and learning support resources. The resources are carefully tailored to the specific needs of the instructor, student and the course. Examples of the kind of resources provided include:

 A password-protected area for instructors with, for example, a test bank, PowerPoint slides and an instructor's manual.

 An open-access area for students including, for example, useful weblinks and glossary terms.

Lecturers: to discover the dedicated teaching digital support resources accompanying this textbook please register here for access: cengage.com/dashboard/#login

Students: to discover the dedicated learning digital support resources accompanying this textbook, please search for *The Psychology of Work and Organization*, Third Edition on: cengage.com

BE UNSTOPPABLE!

Learn more at cengage.com

CHAPTER 1
INTRODUCTION

> **LEARNING OBJECTIVES**
>
> - Define and know the domains and core values of work and organizational psychology.
> - Understand the main trends in the history of work and organizations and the impact on people's lives.
> - Understand the principles of positive organizational scholarship.
> - Understand three contemporary challenges facing organizations, and their relevance to work and organizational psychology:
>   - environmental sustainability
>   - making diversity and inclusion work in organizations
>   - digital and AI developments in organizations.

At least half a million years ago, a species of human not dissimilar from us worked in teams to trap horses by herding them into a box canyon and then killing them so the group could eat. These early humans worked together with shared goals, specified roles, some system of communication and with agreed norms relating to distributing the food (Harari, 2014). There was undoubtedly some form of leadership to enable all of this (Roberts & Westad, 2013). Such social organization, focused on achieving shared purposes, has enabled us to go further than herding horses or catching antelope (complex though those tasks are). We have banded together and organized to uncover the structure of the human genome, to discover processes that marked the beginnings of our universe; we have built vessels to carry our technologies to the sun and then beyond our solar system into the almost infinite expanses of inter-stellar space (*Voyager Mission*); and we have constructed cities that are indescribably complex. The same principles apply from half a million years ago to the present – we work and organize in order to survive and improve our quality of life. We work every day in one form or another and we encounter organizations every day. They are fundamental to our lives. This book is aimed at helping readers understand and make a positive difference to the human experience of work and organizations.

How has the nature of work changed over the course of human history? Some 30,000 years ago foragers would head out in the morning to roam the forests, searching for succulent roots or juicy frogs, and then get back together around midday to eat, hang out, rest, tell stories and play with the children. Today, many workers around the world leave home early and trudge through crowded streets, breathing in industrial and vehicle pollution (killing over 400,000 people annually in Europe – European Environment Agency, 2017), and arrive to clock in at their place of work. They may perform the same action on the same machine over an eight- to ten-hour period before going home and starting on household chores (for a description see Harari, 2014, p. 50). People in most countries now work 40 to 50 hours a week and in developing countries more (often 60–80 hours a week). Is the quality of work and the experience of organizations significantly better for us humans than it was long ago? Let's look at some of the evidence.

A pan-European study (Schaufeli, 2017) analyzed work engagement among 43,850 employees from 35 European counties. Engagement was defined as

> *… a positive, fulfilling, work-related state of mind that is characterized by vigor, dedication, and absorption. Vigor means high levels of energy and mental resilience while working; dedication is being strongly involved in one's work and experiencing enthusiasm, inspiration, pride and challenge; and absorption is being fully concentrated and happily engrossed in one's work, experiencing time passing quickly*

(see Schaufeli, 2014). The highest-scoring group included the Netherlands, Belgium, Luxemburg, France, Ireland, Denmark, Norway, Austria and Switzerland. And the lowest were Greece, Portugal, Lithuania, Slovakia, Hungary, Croatia, Albania, Serbia and Montenegro. Lower scores were also recorded in Turkey and Germany (primarily in what was East Germany). The percentages who felt engaged most of the time at work varied from 21 per cent among EU country respondents to 16 per cent among EU candidate countries.

Reflecting on the fact that in the highest-scoring country only one in three workers reported being engaged most of the time at work and that, across the EU, only one in five is engaged most of the time is shocking. Huge numbers of people spend a large proportion of their lives undertaking activities that bring them little satisfaction, sense of growth and development, or positive emotional experience. Many report looking at clocks and watches throughout the day, waiting for the time when they can go home.

Moreover, around half of EU workers report that stress is common in their workplaces and the data suggest that work stress contributes to half of all lost working days. Poor work design, organization and management result in negative outcomes for people, including stress, heart disease, depression, burnout and musculoskeletal problems (see Chapter 9). Excessive workloads, conflicting work demands (quality versus volume of work, for example), oppressive supervision, job insecurity, psychological and sexual harassment, and low rewards for effort invested, all contribute to a toxic cocktail of work characteristics that damage people (Vargas et al., 2014).

And yet we know there are strong relationships between engagement, well-being and people's productivity and creativity. In those private sector organizations with the most engaged workforces, performance and productivity are higher. In health services, higher levels of health service worker well-being and engagement are associated with better care quality, better financial performance, less employee absenteeism and lower levels of patient mortality (Leiter & Bakker, 2010; West & Dawson, 2012). And we also know that organizations can change to create the conditions that ensure increases in levels of employee engagement and well-being that lead in turn to improved productivity and profitability (Bakker, Demerouti, & Sanz-Vergel, 2014). A key aim of this book is to explore theory and the evidence base to enable us to describe what we can do to ensure the experience of work improves for all by creating great places to work. And the source of our knowledge will be research and theory from psychology, specifically focused on work and organizations.

THE PSYCHOLOGY OF WORK AND ORGANIZATIONS: FIRST ENCOUNTERS

Work and organizational psychology is the field of psychology that applies psychological principles and science to work, business and organizations. Work psychology has the potential to help people be more productive and prosperous in their jobs, to feel good about the work they do and its place in their lives, and to ensure the effectiveness and adaptability of the organizations they work in. In this chapter, we will start our exploration of work and organizational psychology by taking a broad overview of the field, looking at its history and some of the major contemporary and future challenges.

For those new to psychology, we can broadly define the subject as 'the study of mind and behaviour'. Psychologists are interested in people's behaviour, in processes of the mind and in understanding how our experiences and the contexts we live and work in influence us. Key factors can include physiological, developmental, social and cultural influences.

The academic, intellectual, theory-driven aspect of psychology is sometimes called *pure psychology*. However, your day-to-day encounters with psychology are more likely to be with the areas of *applied psychology*, which is more problem-driven. It seeks to understand and solve problems that people face in their everyday lives. The major areas of applied psychology are:

- Clinical psychology: This is concerned with psychological disorders, learning disabilities and illnesses such as chronic depression or psychosis.
- Counselling psychology: Often confused with clinical psychology, but involves working with clients usually with less severe disorders by using more talking and relationship-based therapies.
- Health psychology: Psychology applied to the issues of health and healthy lifestyles, and includes helping people to live with and recover from physical illness and disease.
- Forensic psychology: Concerned with crime and criminality.
- Educational psychology: Psychology applied to understand learning, development and education over the whole lifespan.
- Sports psychology: Psychology applied to performance in sports.
- Work and organizational psychology: Psychology applied to work, business and organizations.

Most of these areas of applied psychology are relevant to us, but tend to be so infrequently or episodically. The majority, however, will work for most of our lives, some of us for 60 years or more, and we will spend a significant proportion of our waking hours working. Work and organizational psychology is therefore directly relevant to us for most of our lives and for much of our time (40 out of 92 waking hours in a week).

In the UK, the field of work psychology is known as occupational psychology, and in the USA, as industrial and organizational (I/O) psychology. In Europe, the title work and organizational psychology is most common, and we feel this latter title captures the content of the field best. There are a few other variants which you might encounter that capture specific sub-categories of the field:

- Business psychology focuses on business development.
- Personnel psychology focuses on core Human Resource tasks and functions.
- Vocational psychology focuses on careers and vocational behaviour.

Work and organizational psychology: A contemporary definition and summary

We define work and organizational psychology as follows:

> *Work and organizational psychology is the study of people and their behaviour at work, and of the organizations in which people work; Work psychologists develop psychological theory and apply the rigour and methods of psychology to issues that are important to work contexts, businesses and organizations, in order to promote and advance understanding of individual, group and organizational effectiveness at work, and the well-being and flourishing of people working in or served by organizations.*

The main areas of work and organizational psychology broadly comprise:

- Organizational behaviour, individual differences and attitudes at work (see Chapters 2 and 3 in this book)
- Work motivation (Chapter 4)
- Personnel selection and assessment (Chapter 5)
- Learning, training and development at work (Chapter 6)
- Performance measurement and management (Chapter 7)
- Careers and vocational behaviour (Chapter 8)
- Health, well-being and safety at work (Chapter 9)
- Organizational strategy and design (Chapter 10)
- Leadership and management in organizations (Chapter 11)
- Teams and groups at work (Chapter 12)
- Organizational culture, climate and change (Chapter 13)

The ways in which work psychologists approach the development of understanding and application of their knowledge in these areas of interest are influenced by the core values of work and organizational psychology:

- Science: Commitment to methodological and scientific rigour in order to understand people and their behaviour at work, and to reveal the functioning of organizations.
- Pragmatism: Commitment to solving practical problems, and to the application of psychology to issues that matter to people at work, and in organizations.
- Ethics: Commitment to ethical best practice in the application of psychology to work and organizations (more on this shortly).
- For people *and* organizations: Commitment to seeking solutions to organizational problems that enhance organizational effectiveness, and the well-being of people working in organizations. Work and organizational psychologists avoid compromising on either of these outcomes, and rather strive to balance and promote both – and, as we shall see, they generally go together.

Collectively these values are the essence of the ways in which work psychologists conduct their work in organizations.

A BRIEF HISTORY OF WORK AND ORGANIZATIONAL PSYCHOLOGY

There are a number of accounts of the development of work psychology (e.g. Katzell & Austin, 1992; Koppes, 2003) showing that the emergence of work psychology can be traced back to a combination of unrelated developments around the turn of the 20th century:

1. The applications and successes of science were growing and entering public consciousness, and had done so increasingly since the Enlightenment.
2. Modern psychology emerged as a fledgling but quickly developing area of study. In the UK, the work of Francis Galton and Karl Pearson on individual differences heralded the start of the assessment tradition, in which measurement techniques for capturing information about human beings (such as aptitude and personality tests) were being designed and tested. At around the same time in the USA, psychologists were working on the assessment of intelligence.
3. More widely, the nature of work was changing rapidly, brought about by industrialization. Stimulated by new developments in technology and engineering, the ideas of the early industrialists (people like James Watt, Matthew Boulton and William Murdoch in the English Midlands), a century earlier, had transformed the working and commercial landscape of Europe and in the USA. Sullivan (1927) observed the transformation in this way:

> *Little shops closing down, big factories growing bigger; little one-man businesses giving up, great corporations growing and expanding; ... fewer craftsmen, more factory operatives ... an adjustment of man to [technology].*

Collectively, the context was set for work psychology, and the people usually credited with taking advantage of the context and initiating the new movement in the USA are Frank and Lillian Gilbreth, and Frederick Taylor. The psychologist was Lillian Gilbreth, whose work with husband Frank (an engineer) aimed to quantify and measure human behaviour in basic, elementary chunks. Their purposes were to measure and manage: to quantify what people did in factory settings; and to make work more efficient. This is the fundamental basis of scientific management or 'Taylorism', named after the entrepreneur and management theorist Frederick Taylor.

The emergence of work psychology in Europe is usually associated with Hugo Munsterberg, a German psychologist who split his academic career between Germany and the USA. In 1913 he published a book called *Industrial Efficiency*, which set down some of the core ideas of the role of psychology in scientific management. In the UK, C. S. Myers was perhaps the first consultant work psychologist, working with the British Expeditionary Force during the First World War on the treatment of shell shock. Myers personally saw more than 2,000 cases in the first two years of the war.

After the First World War, psychologists in both the USA and the UK transferred their new techniques from the military into industry. In the USA, the emphasis was on productivity through personnel selection and training, but Katzell and Austin (1992) also highlight the significance of the Hawthorne Studies in the USA as marking a departure from the assessment emphasis. These studies examined changes to working conditions such as environmental changes in illumination and heat, and work changes such as payment and supervision. They found, to their surprise, that whatever the nature of the change, there were improvements in productivity. This appeared to be the result of the increased attention workers were receiving from the researchers. The Hawthorne Effect therefore refers to outcome changes that are attributed to a specific intervention, when, in fact, any intervention providing increased attention to workers would be effective.

The results of the Hawthorne studies have been challenged in the years since (Chiesa & Hobbs, 2008), and their revered status in work psychology is now in doubt. The criticism relates to the science of the studies and how carefully they were conducted and reported. They were never subjected to peer review, and the 'evidence' is undermined by some obvious methodological flaws (Chiesa & Hobbs, 2008). Either way, the Hawthorne studies reflected a growing trend that emphasized the need to consider workers' rights and needs, particularly following the dark days of the Great Depression of the 1930s.

In the UK, Myers, with industrialist Henry Welch, founded the National Institute of Industrial Psychology (NIIP) in 1921. Much of the work that the NIIP carried out was concerned with worker well-being. Myers published reports on worker fatigue (still a fundamental problem in many organizations today), and the NIIP group was politically influential, campaigning for the workers' rights that we still care about now, such as limiting work hours, protecting workers' dignity and work–life balance, consideration of organizational atmosphere or culture (Kwiatkowski & Duncan, 2006; Kwiatkowski, Duncan, & Shimmin, 2006). The NIIP also conducted work on the importance of assessing skills and temperaments in the service of helping people to find suitable employment.

In the rest of Europe, the development of work psychology was severely hampered by the Great Depression and the rise of fascism. Many gifted German psychologists fell out of favour with the Nazi government, and left to continue their work elsewhere. The most well known of these was Kurt Lewin, who moved to the USA to continue his seminal works on field theory and action research in work psychology. He is credited with the aphorism 'there is nothing so practical as a good theory' and his work on managing change remains highly influential in the field to this day, suggesting that reducing resistance to change was probably more powerful than promoting the driving forces for change in organizations.

Just as the First World War was a major factor in the development of work and organizational psychology, the Second World War saw major growth and development also. In the USA, hundreds of psychologists were employed by the US army in a variety of roles in service of the war effort. Some of the main assessment techniques used in organizations today for selection and appraisal of staff originated in the US military during the Second World War, including assessment centres, multi-instrument test batteries and rating forms for measuring performance. Shimmin and Wallis (1994) note similar successes of psychologists in the UK military, but after the war the initiative was taken primarily by US psychologists, who applied the newly developed techniques extensively in public and private organizations.

Modern work and organizational psychology

Since the 1970s, progress and expansion in work psychology has accelerated considerably. In the USA, there has been a strong and continued emphasis on assessment of people, personnel selection, performance management and training, and on the adverse impact on minorities of many of these methods. Although work and organizational psychology in Europe has followed the US lead in many ways, researchers and practitioners in Europe have carved out some important niches. The work of psychologists such as Sir Cary Cooper in the 1980s put the study and management of work stress firmly on the work psychology agenda. Wilhelm Schaufeli, Eva Demerouti and Arnold Bakker established new perspectives on engagement and well-being at work, offering major contributions to the understanding of the positive and negative psychological consequences of work. Researchers in Scandinavia, and notably in Finland and Sweden, have produced influential and powerful findings on work and health. Members of the Organization Studies group at Aston University in Birmingham during the 1960s and 1970s carried out the most important early studies of the influence of structures of organizations on behaviour and performance.

Work psychology is now established as a discipline in most industrialized countries, with many work psychology businesses providing consultancy services to organizations. Educational programmes are popular with trainee psychologists looking to specialize, and Masters programmes in work psychology abound in Europe, the USA, Australia and New Zealand and more recently in parts of Asia and Africa (such as South Africa). In just one century, work psychology has developed from a new idea initiated by an obscure, select group of interested academics to a global discipline. Work and organizational psychologists have also joined together in large professional organizations to influence policy and practice (see Box 1.1).

BOX 1.1
Professional associations of work and organizational psychology

Work psychologists are supported by a number of different professional associations and organizations. The aims of professional organizations vary, from representation through to educational accreditation and regulation. Broadly though, all attempt to promote good practice in the field, to increase the influence of work and organizational psychology in organizations and government, and to ensure that work psychologists stay in touch with developments in the field.

The Society of Industrial and Organizational Psychology (SIOP)

SIOP is a division of the American Psychological Association (APA), has more than 6,000 members and was formally established in 1982.

The European Association of Work and Organizational Psychology (EAWOP)

EAWOP is a relatively young organization, founded in 1991, set up to represent work psychology in Europe, and to promote cooperation among professionals in the field across Europe.

The British Psychological Society and Division of Occupational Psychology

The main UK professional association is the Division of Occupational Psychology (DOP), part of the British Psychological Society (BPS). The DOP represents the interests of occupational psychologists, the training of whom is accredited by the BPS and regulated by a government regulator (the Health and Care Professions Council; HCPC).

One of the most important recent developments for understanding how to ensure human growth and well-being at work is the emergence of 'positive organizational scholarship'. And it is to this that we now turn our attention.

POSITIVE ORGANIZATIONAL SCHOLARSHIP

This approach, focused on understanding what work environments enable people to flourish, has developed rapidly over the past 15 years and is variously defined as: 'the states and processes that arise from and result in life-giving dynamics, optimal functioning, and enhanced capabilities and strengths' (Dutton & Glynn, 2007, p. 693); 'an emphasis on identifying individual and collective strengths (attributes and processes) and discovering how such strengths enable human flourishing (goodness, generativity, growth, and resilience)' (Roberts, 2006, p. 292); 'a focus on dynamics that are typically described by words such as excellence, thriving, flourishing, abundance, resilience, or virtuousness' (Cameron, Dutton, & Quinn, 2003, p. 4), and organizational research … which points to unanswered questions about what processes, states, and conditions are important in explaining individual and collective flourishing. Flourishing refers to being in an optimal range of human functioning' (Dutton, 2010).

Positive organizational scholarship does not simply emphasize positive emotions and positive events. It is an approach that also explores how, in the right circumstances, individuals can grow as a result of encountering problems and challenges; how the culture of an organization can facilitate innovation as a response to great difficulty; and how by engaging with challenges we can build individual and collective strengths and capabilities.

For example, following the attacks on the Twin Towers in 2001, the airline industry suffered a huge downturn because people were afraid to fly. Up to that point, Southwest Airlines had always maintained a strong commitment to its staff and promised no layoffs: *'We are willing to suffer some damage, even to our stock price, to protect the jobs of our people'* (Jim Parker, CEO of Southwest Airlines, 8 October 2001). Coupled with its commitment to maintaining good financial reserves, they stayed true to their promise – compared to, for example, United Airlines who laid off 20 per cent of their staff and US Airlines who laid off 25 per cent. Not surprisingly, the policy of no redundancies, in the worst of circumstances, had a very positive impact on staff loyalty and morale in Southwest and thereby upon customer satisfaction – 'happy staff produce happy customers'. That in turn had a major impact on the profitability of the company in subsequent years (Gittell, Cameron, & Rivas, 2006).

The positive approach to work and organizations also emphasizes outstanding positive processes and outcomes. This can involve identifying the hospital with the best patient satisfaction and learning from their practices; studying the team with the highest level of innovation; or celebrating the leader whose team members rate her as the most outstanding leader they have ever worked with. For example, Jeff Weiner, CEO of LinkedIn (a business with 10,000 employees), was rated by his staff as a great leader – he emphasizes compassion, authenticity and self-awareness as core to leadership. Or we can seek and learn from outstanding examples of innovation: Mohamad Christi, a paediatrician in Bangladesh, watched three children die of pneumonia early in his career. Their deaths were partly a consequence of poorly designed oxygen masks, and this stimulated him to find a better way of providing oxygen to these very sick children. Using discarded shampoo bottles, he created a ventilator that cost just $1.25 in comparison to the standard models at $15,000 (even a modified design costs $6,000). His innovation is saving lives and reducing costs for hospitals substantially. The idea is spreading around the world (*The Economist* 2018). Positive organizational scholarship involves studying such examples to advance our understanding and apply it within work organizations so that we foster the commitment and creativity of more people like Mohamad Christi.

The positive approach to work and organizations also proposes that positivity can lead to resourcefulness. As Barbara Fredrickson and colleagues have shown, when we broaden our behavioural repertoire by exploring the new, or engaging with the difficult, we can build our capacity and confidence (e.g. Fredrickson & Joiner, 2002). When Barts and the London Hospital had to deal with the London Bridge attacks in 2017, many staff heard the news and raced back to their place of work. The team response was described as outstanding, and all 12 victims treated, many of them very seriously injured, were saved. The staff also learned from the challenges, built more effective teamwork as a consequence, and were left, despite the trauma and tragedy, with a sense of pride and reinforced commitment to their work–life missions. Positive organizational scholarship encourages a positive work psychology that focuses on positive relationships, good communication, and positive energy at work, rather than focussing only on problems, threats and weaknesses in organizations.

This approach does not involve excluding negative emotions from consideration. Rather, it is a focus on ensuring that negative experiences and situations are incorporated into life-enhancing dynamics wherever possible. A good example of this is Schwartz Rounds, where healthcare staff can come together on a regular basis to talk about the emotional and social challenges of their work (usually with lunch provided). Such activities appear to reduce stress levels for staff but also encourage greater creativity in responses to challenging work situations (Goodrich, 2012; Lown & Manning, 2010). A positive approach to understanding work and organizations reinforces and spreads what is good, right and worthy of cultivation in organizations through (for example) compassion, forgiveness, purpose, mutual support and sustainability.

Such an approach is not value neutral as research or scholarship is sometimes presented. Rather, positive organizational scholarship and practice aims to improve the human condition and the experience of work, not simply to promote environments that maximize productivity and profitability.

We aim in this book to integrate traditional approaches with these positive approaches to understanding work organizations. We want to provide readers with content that promotes understanding of how to ensure that the experience of work and the structure and processes of organizations lead to individual and collective flourishing.

Organizational processes (including HRM practices) are also key to creating positive work environments, including values-based recruitment, career development, mentoring, ensuring inclusion and fairness in diverse environments, encouraging work–family balance, positive conflict resolution, promoting innovation and exploring mindful approaches to organizing. Leadership and change can also be understood through a positive organizational lens by drawing on research into compassion and authenticity in leadership and developing collective leadership. We will explore all of these topics in the pages ahead.

CONTEMPORARY THEMES IN WORK AND ORGANIZATIONAL PSYCHOLOGY

In this section, we consider contemporary challenges facing organizations and discuss the role of work psychology in addressing those challenges. We will focus particularly on several major themes we believe every student of the psychology of work and organizations should pay particular attention to: environmental sustainability, the digital revolution and diversity in the workplace:

- environment and sustainability – the 'green' agenda in work and organizational psychology;
- new technology, digital media and artificial intelligence;
- diversity in the workplace – positive organizational strategies.

The environment and sustainability in work psychology

Naomi Klein, a Canadian social activist, has argued that it is not that people don't care about the climate emergency (with some notable exceptions), it is just that the problem is so huge, so distant, so unmanageable and so long term that they feel their actions will make no difference (see Brick & van der Linden, 2018). So psychology is key to how we deal with the problem of the climate emergency, and work psychologists must accept responsibility for ensuring that organizations and those who work within them play a full role in combating the climate emergency.

It is not easy. The potential threats to us as a species are huge, with major impacts on weather, biodiversity, flooding, disease, international conflict and agriculture. And the climate emergency poses particular challenges because of our human nature. We find it difficult to understand or engage with threats that are abstract, long term, remote, complex, mostly invisible and multifaceted (Gifford, 2011; van der Linden, 2015). Our brains evolved to solve local, immediate, visible and experiential problems.

How can we bring psychology to bear on work and organizations to ensure they become domains in which issues of the climate emergency are grasped with commitment and confidence? Some general prescriptions are to frame environmental issues around values such as protecting the environment for our children and their children, ensuring future economic prosperity and preserving nature. It helps also to highlight organizations that are doing damage, because this raises awareness and promotes action, or what Brick and van der Linden call 'highlighting the villains'.

Work psychologists are involved in organizational strategy, development and change processes, and this affords an opportunity to counsel for the inclusion and utilization of environmental outcomes in those processes. A central aspect of change at an organizational level is the creation of cultures and climates that support environmental sustainability, (e.g. Alcaraz et al., 2012; Norton, Zacher, & Ashkanasy, 2012), and as we will later see in this book, that creation needs to comprise more than simple awareness-raising of environmental issues.

More consideration is needed about the environmental consequences, direct or indirect, of the work that psychologists do in organizations. We could view such consequences in a number of ways. A direct impact might be observed if psychologists assist in organizational development strategies that in the long term are likely to cause environmental damage rather than leading to environmental protection, such as failing to challenge organizations that do not stress the importance of sustaining the environment (for example in the construction industry). An indirect impact might be ignoring sustainability issues in the recruitment and selection of powerful leaders, failing to raise such issues with organizations in our consulting activities or neglecting to integrate them into models of organizational performance. Values-based approaches to work and organizations must include caring for the environment as a core value if we are not to destroy resources that enable us to survive as a species on this planet. For example, the Aveda Corporation aligns HR practices, from recruitment and selection through to performance appraisal, with their environmental values and commitment.

A UK survey of sustainable work practices found that only 10 per cent of companies enacted environmental sustainability initiatives through their HR department, with facilities and estates, specialist Corporate Social Responsibility (CSR) teams or senior management much more likely to be responsible for sustainability policy and activity (Zibarras, Judson, & Barnes, 2012). The individual value of caring for the environment is therefore not generally reinforced through people management practices. Work psychologists can bring to bear realigned tools to support the push for environmental sustainability, such as recruitment, selection, training, performance management and employee surveys (Carr et al., 2008; Ones & Dilchert, 2012). Proctor and Gamble use their annual employee survey to assess the extent to which their sustainability initiatives are succeeding (thereby also raising awareness).

The vast majority of interventions in organizations are marketing- or awareness-type activities, with much less direct intervention such as training or performance management around protecting the environment. Psychologists can assess the extent to which these different types of interventions are successful, such as providing prompts or appeals to employees about their 'green behaviours'; providing information, instruction, knowledge; monitoring employees and giving feedback; or using techniques such as goal-setting. We will consider such issues of environmental sustainability in several chapters in this book.

New technology, digital media and artificial intelligence (AI) in work psychology

The revolution in new technologies has transformed work organizations since the early 1990s when email did not exist (other than among a small group of computing experts) and mobile phones were still new and not in general use. Since then our work lives have been transformed by these advances and the pace is speeding up. The psychological study of these new technologies has not kept pace with their development. Meanwhile, new technologies continue to appear.

What do we mean by new technology, digital media and AI in work and organizations? They include organizations' digital workplace content (intranet, whiteboards, screens, robotics, data); the employees' digital work life – all of the digital media of the organization plus their email, work use of smart phones and internet for example; and employees' digital home life (Bluetooth, Wi-Fi, GPS, mobile data), since most will use their home digital media for work purposes and their work digital media for home purposes to some extent. If we are to understand human experience in work and organizations, we have to understand the role of digital media. Of course, all these technologies overlap across all of these three domains – there is no hard boundary between them. This has both advantages (such as enriching people's access to resources) and disadvantages (witness the invasion by work life into home life). The digital workplace is therefore the experience of work delivered through technologies such as connected devices, platforms, software and interfaces. There is no doubt that digital media affect employee engagement, stress, knowledge management, socialization of new employees and organizational culture.

We are already seeing more use of shared screens such as whiteboards, videoconferencing, linking multiple rooms together using video technology; credential technology – signing in at work with face recognition or fingerprints; smart apps enabling people to know where their colleagues are in the building or which country, and which meeting rooms are available; some office spaces are adapting automatically to ensure better security, comfort, safety and productivity; an app can book a meeting room, order the food for lunch and deal with messages sent by participants; augmented reality already enables employees in some organizations to use a virtual head set to mimic being at work when they are working from home; 'smart glasses' can overlay information on the real world; and voice recognition is improving rapidly and enabling much faster communication and task performance. The insidious side to all this is the increasing incursion of work into family and leisure time, breaking the boundaries between employment in service of others and the freedom to live our lives in the way we wish without being subject to the demands of work every hour of every day.

AI or machine learning (as it is also known) involves programming computers to process large amounts of data and identify patterns and trends that are not pre-programmed. It ensures intelligence can be gathered far more swiftly than human processors could manage. Consider the following examples and reflect on what it means for human experience in work and therefore the importance of work and organizational psychology. Ping An, a Chinese insurance company, is using AI to spot dishonesty among claimants while they use a video technology app on their phones. AI is used to scan the facial expressions of the claimants as they answer questions about their income and plans for repayment, and rates the likelihood they are telling the truth. Johnson & Johnson, a consumer goods company, and the consultancy Accenture use AI to sift job applications and then identify the best candidates. They have 1.2 million job applications a year for 25,000 positions so it is a huge help, plus AI can provide feedback to candidates as to why they were not selected. A casino and hotel chain, Caesars, uses AI to assess customers' likely spending habits and preferences in order to target offers to them.

The new uses for AI are affecting jobs and people's experience of work in ever more profound ways. Amazon uses AI for tasks such as guiding robots in its giant warehouses, speeding up packaging and dispatch (reducing reliance on human operators) and powering its speaker, Alexa. Some companies will not use AI to get rid of existing jobs but are already looking for ways of avoiding creating new jobs. Others are using AI to comb through employees' communications to detect dishonesty or disgruntlement, leading to fear for many of being spied on by their employers. Some companies (e.g. Cogito) are using AI to listen to agents' conversations with customers and identify emotion fatigue so the computer can prompt the agent to be more empathic. Hilton, the hotel chain, also uses AI to select employees by analyzing videos of candidates answering questions and using AI to assess their verbal skills, intonation and gestures, reducing time to hire from 45 to 5 days. AI is also being used to ensure diversity is encouraged. Pymetrics gives candidates games to play during the selection process and assesses some 80 traits, including memory and risk-taking, while ignoring factors such as gender and race. Their system is being taken up by Unilever (consumer goods) and Nielsen (a research company). Workday, a software firm, uses AI to identify employees at risk of leaving and identifies the factors that might be responsible, enabling managers to intervene and save the huge costs of replacing staff (around 20 per cent of annual salary).

AI can be used beneficially for workers, such as monitoring safe practice in high-risk environments and ensuring the right equipment is in place. In the very near future, AI can be used to identify that a management team is failing to communicate effectively with other departments; that parts of the building are not being used enough; and that diversity initiatives are not working. Hitachi is using a product to infer mood levels in parts of the company from data on employee movement and thereby identify potential problems. Employers can also check when people are working, who is looking at what documents, and whether employees might be stealing information about clients. Amazon has developed wristbands that can monitor workers' whereabouts in their warehouses and their movements. With AI, it will certainly become creepier in some organizations and better in others. For more examples see *The Economist* (2018b).

It should be clear that there is a huge role for psychologists in understanding these developments and their implications, not least to provide guidance in preventing the damaging consequences of new technologies and promoting fulfilling consequences for workers.

Diversity in the workplace: positive organizational strategies

The effects of discrimination in the workplace are devastating. In the National Health Service in the UK, despite its avowed value of being an inclusive and compassionate sector, it is still the case that staff from Black, Asian and Minority Ethnic (BAME) backgrounds are, on average, much more likely than white employees to be taken through disciplinary processes and significantly less likely to be selected from appointments' panels (Kline, 2014; West, Dawson, & Kaur, 2015). Discrimination in the NHS hits people with disabilities, Muslim women and BAME staff particularly hard. Despite the fact that 46 per cent of doctors are from a BAME background, only 46 out of 230 Medical Directors (Heads of Medicine) are BAME. And these problems are not unique to the UK NHS – they are rampant in industry across many countries. They pose a particular and unique problem, for example in South African organizations, which for so many years institutionalized apartheid in every area of life. How can the psychology of work and organizations address this seemingly intractable issue?

Research by LinkedIn, reported by *The Economist* (*The Economist*, 2019), suggests that women across five countries (the USA, Germany, India, Italy and Norway) are making progress in reaching board-level positions faster than men (in the USA, for men it was 10.9 years and for women 9.8 years). However, the proportions at director level and above are still heavily weighted in favour of men: from 17 per cent in India to 35 per cent in the USA. Some companies in the USA appear to be gaming the process, because a very large number cluster together with just two female directors, suggesting they aim to be at (or slightly above) the average of 1.92 women directors on US boards.

Overall, the picture in terms of equality is awful. Across the OECD group of countries, the gender pay gap is 13.5 per cent, varying from 3.4 per cent in Luxembourg to 36.7 per cent in South Korea. College-educated women earn on average 26 per cent less than their male counterparts across these countries. And another survey in 2019 by the World Bank of 187 countries around the world showed that women had only three-quarters of the legal rights and protections of men, including freedom to travel, property rights, to be able to open a business and protection from sexual harassment. The problems were particularly marked in the Middle East and North Africa where women had less than half the rights of men. The lowest-ranked country was Saudi Arabia. Six countries gave equal rights: Belgium, Denmark, France, Latvia, Luxembourg and Sweden. In many developing countries women rely much more heavily on informal employment even in non-agricultural settings, getting paid less and not qualifying for unemployment benefits and pensions as a consequence. The picture is bleak and suggests that for half of the world's working-age population, their knowledge, skills and abilities are systematically devalued and under-deployed, with enormous consequences for their quality of life, well-being and economic security.

In today's organizations, employees are more likely than ever before to work with other employees with different demographic or functional backgrounds (Guillaume, Dawson, Woods, Sacramento, & West, 2013). When mismanaged, diversity can damage employee morale across an organization, resulting in poorer organizational performance and employee stress and poor physical health. When managed effectively, it can create synergies that produce creativity, innovation, productivity and (in the commercial sector) profitability (Guillaume, Brodbeck, & Riketta, 2012; Joshi & Roh, 2009; van Dijk, van Engen, & van Knippenberg, 2012).

Understanding how diversity in organizations undermines or facilitates social cohesion, well-being, performance and innovation is an integral part of the work and organizational psychology research agenda. Understanding effective diversity management policies, procedures and practices has also become a key focus (Kalinoski et al., 2013).

Work psychology is also examining the effectiveness of diversity management policies, procedures and practices used in organizations to help us understand when diversity might lead to favourable or unfavourable work-related outcomes, and we will describe this research in the forthcoming chapters. Our focus will also be on how the culture of organizations plays a key role in creating contexts for making diversity at work a force for social cohesion, innovation and effective performance, consistent with our positive organizational perspective.

Pioneering work psychologists

In addition to our study of diversity as a psychological topic, we will introduce you to diverse leaders who are transforming our understanding of the psychology of work and organizations – those we believe are already, or are likely to be, among the outstanding leaders of the future. In previous editions of this book, we featured 'Key Figures' in work psychology. Back in 2018 we received an email from a psychology student in Sweden, Jonna Eklund, who pointed out: 'each encounter with your "Key Figure" sections feels increasingly discomforting as I am noticing that you are only choosing to highlight the accomplishments of men, with the exception of only one woman. Can it be that only one woman has done great things for the field of work and organizational psychology?' Jonna was right and we were grateful she took the time to point this out. Jonna's activism was a good example of someone breaking new ground. We decided to refocus the feature to highlight the work of pioneering work psychologists because this book is, as much as anything, intended to show how we bring about positive change. Indeed, Jonna is a great example of a pioneering psychologist. She was born in 1990 in Gothenburg and had an interest in psychology from an early age. At 19 she took an introductory course in psychology at the University of Gothenburg and decided to be a psychologist. She spent five years in Berlin working at IKEA in the logistics department before moving to Stockholm to start the psychologist programme in 2018. She also works as a psychiatric aide, as part of a team that provides support for patients. She works with nurses, doctors and patients to ensure high-quality, compassionate and continually improving care. Such a combination of theoretical and applied work is typical of our approach to this book, so we are grateful to Jonna for her intervention and her modelling of the principles we hope you the reader will also put into practice.

The pioneering work psychologists from around the world whom we identify are important role models and leaders, for you and for the present and future of work and organizational psychology (see Pioneering Work Psychologists box below for our first leader). We hope you find them inspirational.

PIONEERING WORK PSYCHOLOGISTS

Dr Eden King

Eden King, an associate professor in the Department of Psychology at Rice University in Texas, was elected president of the US Society for Industrial and Organizational Psychology (SIOP) for 2019 (with more than 8,000 members).

Dr King's research focuses on integrating organizational and social psychological theories in conceptualizing social stigma and the work–life interface. She addresses three primary themes:
1) current manifestations of discrimination and barriers to work–life balance in organizations
2) consequences of such challenges for people at work and their workplaces
3) individual and organizational strategies for reducing discrimination and increasing support for families.

In addition to her academic positions, Dr King has consulted on applied projects related to climate initiatives, selection systems and diversity training programmes. She is currently an Associate Editor for the *Journal of Management* and the *Journal of Business and Psychology* and is on the editorial boards of the *Academy of Management Journal* and the *Journal of Applied Psychology*.

She has published more than 100 scholarly publications and was featured in the *New York Times*, the *Harvard Business Review* and on 'Good Morning America'. A video showing her thinking about the Science of Diversity in Teams is at vimeopro.com/gmutv/vision-series/video/33367123

We will also draw on research and practices from a range of countries – across China, India, Europe, the USA, Australia and South Africa. Sadly, there is remarkably little research in work and organizational psychology carried out in African countries, which are rarely referenced or included in texts in our field. Yet African countries account for the fastest-growing economies in the world and include a population of 1.6 billion souls out of a world population of 7.4 billion.

THE PSYCHOLOGY OF WORK AND ORGANIZATIONS: THIS BOOK

We have structured this book by dividing the major domains of work and organizational psychology into three sections, moving from foundations, through areas of professional practice and finally to perspectives about whole organizations.

Foundations of work and organizational psychology

The first section of the book involves some scene-setting for work and organizational psychology. We consider some of the core topics in social psychology and organizational behaviour. We consider three key foundation topics. These are:

- Individual differences. This focuses on topics such as personality, intelligence, and knowledge and skills and how to assess them.
- Organizational behaviour and attitudes. This is concerned with topics such as job satisfaction, employee engagement, organizational citizenship behaviour and their link to performance.
- Motivation. The focus here is on how motivation develops and how people's motivation at work can best be understood and managed.

The aim in the first section of the book is to help the reader develop a broad understanding of psychology and its role in helping us understand people's behaviour at work.

PROFESSIONAL PRACTICE OF WORK AND ORGANIZATIONAL PSYCHOLOGY

In Part Two of the book we cover the major professional applications of work and organizational psychology. Many reflect the tradition of work psychology that focuses on individuals at work, and the chapters represent core tasks for managers in organizations. In each case, the chapters are designed to explore how work psychology can help managers and practitioners to better understand and carry out those tasks. The five areas covered are:

- Recruitment, selection and assessment
- Learning, training and development
- Performance measurement and management
- Careers and career management
- Safety, stress and health at work

ORGANIZATIONS

The final section of this book takes an organizational perspective by locating our understanding of behaviour at work in the organizational context within which it occurs. This is a perspective which is perhaps less popular or obvious for psychologists whose tendency is to focus on the individual or the small group. However, from Kurt Lewin onwards, we have come to realize just how vital an understanding of context is if we are to understand human behaviour and help to create better and more effective communities. Accordingly, we consider the following areas:

- Organizations: structure, strategy and environment
- Leadership
- Teamworking in organizations
- Organizational culture and climate
- Organizational development and change

We propose that an understanding of work and organizational psychology is enhanced by knowledge of organizational strategy, structure and environment since these have a considerable influence on attitudes, behaviour and experience at work. This is an unusual aspect of our text but one we believe will be extremely valuable and, we hope, fascinating for the reader. Second, we focus on what is arguably the most researched area of work and organizational psychology – leadership. But we place leadership in its organizational context rather than simply analyzing it atomistically as traits, behaviours and tactics. The third chapter in this section looks at teamworking in organizations and, in addition to reviewing the research, considers how teamworking can be supported and how it can be developed most effectively in organizations. Research in this area has made huge progress in the past 20 years. Finally, there is a chapter on organizational culture, climate and change which takes a whole organization perspective and seeks to give the reader helpful models for understanding work organizations.

In this third edition of *The Psychology of Work and Organizations*, we have updated every chapter to incorporate some of the developments in the field since the first and second editions. There has been a major review of research and theory in work and organizational psychology over the past 100 years, published in 2017 in the *Journal of Applied Psychology*, which also informs this third edition of the book.

As highlighted earlier, we have added more reflection on the key contemporary themes of business in the context of work and organizational psychology. Plus there is a new feature in which we give free rein to our intent to help nurture positive and flourishing workplaces, which we call *Positive Work*.

Evidence, critique, practice

Both of us are academics and practitioners; we conduct research in Business and Management School environments, and also work with organizations, applying work and organizational psychology. We have aimed throughout this book to review evidence, research and theory, and to do so in a critical, yet accessible way. However, we also adopt a practical focus in each chapter, and particularly value and report those aspects of work and organizational psychology that have practical utility and relevance to organizations, and make suggestions for how to apply them. We want to begin to equip you to make a positive difference.

SUMMARY

Work and Organizational Psychology is the study of people and their behaviour at work, and of the organizations in which people work. Work psychologists develop psychological theory and apply the rigour and methods of psychology to issues that are important to businesses and organizations, in order to promote and advance understanding of individual, group and organizational effectiveness at work, and the well-being and satisfaction of people working in or served by organizations.

The field has a relatively short history, dating back to the start of the 20th century. Work psychologists in the USA and Europe developed the field of work and organizational psychology quickly, and along somewhat divergent lines, with the USA focusing on productivity, performance, training and assessment, and Europe adopting a stronger focus on well-being and welfare at work.

Global challenges for businesses and organizations are relevant concerns for work psychology. Three key challenges facing organizations globally are to take account of the environment and the need to care for our planet in our work; to understand the implications and dictate the course of change in relation to new technology, digital media and artificial intelligence; and how to make diversity at work effective for people and organizations. These are challenges that work and organizational psychology can help organizations meet.

FURTHER READING

Allvin, M., Aronsson, G., Hagström, T., Johansson, G., & Lundberg, U. (2011). *Work without boundaries: Psychological perspectives on the new working life*. Chichester, England: John Wiley & Sons.

Cameron, K. S., & Spreitzer, G. M. (Eds.). (2011). *The Oxford handbook of positive organizational scholarship*. Oxford: Oxford University Press.

Graeber, D. (2019). *Bullshit jobs: The rise of pointless work and what we can do about it*. Harmondsworth, England: Penguin.

Harari, Y. N. (2014). *Sapiens: A brief history of humankind*. New York, NY: Random House.

Kozlowski, S. W. J., Chen, G., & Salas, E. (2017). One hundred years of the *Journal of Applied Psychology*: Background, evolution, and scientific trends. *Journal of Applied Psychology, 102*(3), 237–253.

Worline, M., & Dutton, J. E. (2017). *Awakening compassion at work: The quiet power that elevates people and organizations*. Oakland, CA: Berrett-Koehler.

REFERENCES

Alcaraz, J. M., Kausel, E. E., Colon, C., Escotto, M. I., Gutiérrez-Marínez, I. S. I. S., Morales, D., … Vicencio, F. E. (2012). Putting organizational culture at the heart of industrial-organizational psychology's research agenda on sustainability: Insights from Iberoamerica. *Industrial and Organizational Psychology, 5*(4), 494–497.

Bakker, A. B., Demerouti, E., & Sanz-Vergel, A. I. (2014). Burnout and work engagement: The JD–R approach. *Annual Review of Organizational Psychology and Organizational Behavior, 1*(1), 389–411.

Brick, C., & van der Linden, S. (2018). Yawning at the apocalypse. *The Psychologist*, September, 30–35.

Cameron, K., Dutton, J., & Quinn, R. E. (Eds.). (2003). *Positive organizational scholarship: Foundations of a new discipline*. Oakland, CA: Berrett-Koehler.

Carr, S. C., Maclachlan, M., Reichman, W., Klobas, J., O'Neill Berry, M., & Furnham, A. (2008). Organizational psychology and poverty reduction: Where supply meets demand. *Journal of Organizational Behaviour, 29*, 843–851.

Chiesa, M., & Hobbs, S. (2008). Making sense of social research: How useful is the Hawthorne effect? *European Journal of Social Psychology, 38*(1), 67–74.

Dutton, J. E. (2010). Interview on positive organizational scholarship by Mia Yan and Evelyn Micelotta. Retrieved from omtweb.org

Dutton, J. E., Glynn, M. A., & Spreitzer, G. (2008). Positive organizational scholarship. In C. Cooper & J. Barling (Eds.), *The SAGE handbook of organizational behavior* (Vol. 1, pp. 693–712). Thousand Oaks, CA: SAGE.

The Economist. (2018, September 8). Bubbling with ideas. *The Economist*, p. 72.

The Economist. (2019, March 9). Bartleby – A small step for women. *The Economist*, p. 62.

European Environment Agency. (2017). *Air quality in Europe – 2017 report* (EEA Report No 13/2017). Luxembourg: Publications Office of the European Union.

Fredrickson, B. L., & Joiner, T. (2002). Positive emotions trigger upward spirals toward emotional well-being. *Psychological Science, 13*(2), 172–175.

Gifford, R. (2011). The dragons of inaction: Psychological barriers that limit climate change mitigation and adaptation. *American Psychologist, 66*(4), 290.

Gittell, J. H., Cameron, K., Lim, S., & Rivas, V. (2006). Relationships, layoffs, and organizational resilience: Airline industry responses to September 11. *The Journal of Applied Behavioral Science, 42*(3), 300–329.

Goodrich, J. (2012). Supporting hospital staff to provide compassionate care: Do Schwartz Center Rounds work in English hospitals? *Journal of the Royal Society of Medicine, 105*(3), 117–122.

Guillaume, Y. R., Brodbeck, F. C., & Riketta, M. (2012). Surface- and deep-level dissimilarity effects on social integration and individual effectiveness related outcomes in work groups: A meta-analytic integration. *Journal of Occupational and Organizational Psychology, 85*(1), 80–115.

Guillaume, Y. R., Dawson, J. F., Woods, S. A., Sacramento, C. A., & West, M. A. (2013). Getting diversity at work to work: What we know and what we still don't know. *Journal of Occupational and Organizational Psychology, 86*(2), 123–141.

Harari, Y. N. (2014). *Sapiens: A brief history of humankind*. New York, NY: Random House.

Joshi, A., & Roh, H. (2009). The role of context in work team diversity research: A meta-analytic review. *Academy of Management Journal, 52*(3), 599–627.

Kalinoski, Z. T., Steele-Johnson, D., Peyton, E. J., Leas, K. A., Steinke, J., & Bowling, N. A. (2013). A meta-analytic evaluation of diversity training outcomes. *Journal of Organizational Behavior, 34*(8), 1076–1104.

Katzell, R. A., & Austin, J. T. (1992). From then to now: The development of industrial-organizational psychology in the United States. *Journal of Applied Psychology, 77*(6), 803–835.

Kline, R. (2014). *The snowy white peaks of the NHS: A survey of discrimination in governance and leadership and the potential impact on patient care in London and England*. London, England: Middlesex University.

Koppes, L. L. (2003). Industrial-organizational psychology. In I. B. Weiner (General Ed.) & D. K. Freedheim (Vol. Ed.), *Comprehensive handbook of psychology: Vol. 1. History of psychology* (pp. 367–389). New York, NY: John Wiley & Sons.

Kwiatkowski, R., & Duncan, D. C. (2006). UK occupational/organizational psychology, applied science and applied humanism: Some further thoughts on what we have forgotten. *Journal of Occupational and Organizational Psychology, 79*, 217–224.

Kwiatkowski, R., Duncan, D. C., & Shimmin, S. (2006). What have we forgotten – and why? *Journal of Occupational and Organizational Psychology, 79*, 183–201.

Leiter, M. P., & Bakker, A. B. (2010). *Work engagement: A handbook of essential theory and research*. Hove, England: Psychology Press.

Lown, B. A., & Manning, C. F. (2010). The Schwartz Center Rounds: Evaluation of an interdisciplinary approach to enhancing patient-centered communication, teamwork, and provider support. *Academic Medicine, 85*(6), 1073–1081.

Norton, T. A., Zacher, H., & Ashkanasy, N. M. (2012). On the importance of pro-environmental organizational climate for employee green behavior. *Industrial and Organizational Psychology, 5*(4), 497.

Ones, D. S., & Dilchert, S. (2012). Environmental sustainability at work: A call to action. *Industrial and Organizational Psychology, 5*(4), 444–466.

Roberts, J. M., & Westad, O. A. (2013). *The history of the world*. Oxford, England: Oxford University Press.

Roberts, L. M. (2006). Shifting the lens on organizational life: The added value of positive scholarship. *Academy of Management Review, 31*(2), 292–305.

Schaufeli, W. B. (2014). What is engagement? In C. Truss, R. Delbridge, K. Alfes, A. Shantz, & E. Soane (Eds.), *Employee engagement in theory and practice* (pp. 15–35). London, England: Routledge.

Schaufeli, W. B. (2017). *Work engagement in Europe: Relations with national economy governance, and culture* (Research Unit Occupational & Organizational Psychology and Professional Learning (internal report)). Leuven, Belgium: KU Leuven.

Shimmin, S., & Wallis, D. (1994). *Fifty years of occupational psychology in Britain*. Leicester, England: British Psychological Society.

Sullivan, M. (1927). *Our times: The United States 1900–1925*. London, England: Scribner's Sons.

van der Linden, S. (2015). The social-psychological determinants of climate change risk perceptions: Towards a comprehensive model. *Journal of Environmental Psychology, 41*, 112–124.

van Dijk, H., van Engen, M. L., & van Knippenberg, D. (2012). Defying conventional wisdom: A meta-analytical examination of the differences between demographic and job-related diversity relationships with performance. *Organizational Behavior and Human Decision Processes, 119*(1), 38–53.

Vargas, O., Flintrop, J., Hassard, J., Irastorza, X., Milczarek, M., Miller, J. M., … Vartia-Väänänen, M. (2014). *Psychosocial risks in Europe: Prevalence and strategies for prevention*. Brussels, Belgium: Eurofund and European Agency for Safety and Health at Work.

West, M., & Dawson, J. (2012). *Employee engagement and NHS performance*. London, England: King's Fund.

West, M., Dawson, J., & Kaur, M. (2015). *Making the difference: Diversity and inclusion in the NHS*. London, England: The Kings Fund.

Zibarras, L., Judson, H., & Barnes, C. (2012). Promoting environmental behaviour in the workplace: A survey of UK organisations. *Going green: The psychology of sustainability in the workplace*, 84–90.

PART ONE

FOUNDATIONS OF WORK AND ORGANIZATIONAL PSYCHOLOGY

The foundations of work and organizational psychology are a heady mix of ideas and concepts from psychology, organizational behaviour, management and science. Collectively they offer fascinating insights into individual behaviour at work, and the ways in which it can be investigated and understood. These areas also set the basis for the way that psychologists can make a positive impact on work and organizations.

The journey through the foundations of work and organizational psychology starts with the theories and research that help us to understand individuals and their behaviour at work. Individual differences in personality and ability contribute to understanding people's typical patterns of behaviour, thought and emotion at work, and their potential to perform effectively in increasingly complex work environments. Work also influences how our individual differences develop through our lives. Behaviour at work is also shaped by attitudes, emotions and perception. The ways that people think and feel about their work are important determinants of their behaviour and performance. All of these influences operate in the social contexts of workgroups and organizations; these contexts exert surprising influences on perceptions, decisions and behaviour, and are at the centre of the challenges of managing and building diverse and inclusive workplaces. And finally, one must ask why people are motivated to work at all. Work satisfies needs and provides intrinsic purpose, direction and rewards for people's behaviour and effort, all of which are important aspects in understanding motivation.

These are the topics of the next three chapters, which will very likely change the ways you think about people and their behaviour at work. You will also see how in our own actions we can use our knowledge of work and organizational psychology to make a positive impact in our workplaces.

2 Individual Differences at Work
3 Attitudes and Behaviour in Organizations
4 Motivation at Work

CHAPTER 2
INDIVIDUAL DIFFERENCES AT WORK

> **LEARNING OBJECTIVES**
>
> - Understand theories of personality and the Big Five model of personality.
> - Understand the impact of personality traits on work outcomes.
> - Understand developmental perspectives on how work influences personality change and growth in adulthood.
> - Understand theories and models of cognitive ability and intelligence and their impact on work outcomes.
> - Describe core self-evaluations and proactive personality, and their influences on work outcomes.
> - Understand how individual differences are measured and describe principles of reliability and validity, and associated methods.

The myriad differences in personality and other psychological characteristics between people is a wonder of the complexity of human development and behaviour. From a work and organizational psychology perspective, these differences also make for a complex and compelling backdrop to the study of people at work. We introduce this fascinating area in this chapter, covering theory and research on individual differences and their consequences and implications for work and organizations. We begin with some key observations that help guide our discussion:

1. People do differ in various ways, and those differences do have an impact on their effectiveness and behaviour.
2. The extent to which individual differences are important depends on the context within which they are expressed: the jobs that people do determine whether individual differences are helpful or a hindrance.
3. The extent to which individual differences are helpful or a hindrance is not static and, in fact, characteristics that may be helpful at one point of time may be unimportant at others, or even detrimental to performance.

INTRODUCTION TO INDIVIDUAL DIFFERENCES

Ordinary or layperson intuitions about individual differences are called implicit theories. We all hold implicit theories about the individual differences of those around us. We observe our own behaviour, compare it to the behaviour of others and use the information to decide what kind of person we are and what we think and feel about others. We also use our implicit theories to predict what people will do in certain situations or how they will react to people and events. Implicit theories help us to make sense of the world around us, and also affect our attitudes towards people. We tend to have our own ideas about the relative desirability of certain personality characteristics (e.g. social confidence, friendliness, assertiveness, calmness, openness).

For our own purposes of perceiving and understanding the world, and the people we work with, implicit theories are useful. They are no basis for a science of individual differences, however, and in this respect psychologists have developed a range of explicit theories designed to represent and explain observations about the differences in individual characteristics and abilities. Only by first understanding these theories can we go on to understand the effects of individual differences on behaviour at work.

The study of individual differences is sometimes referred to as differential psychology. The field aims to explain the differences we observe between individuals in terms of psychological determinants (Chamorro-Premuzic, 2007). Differential psychologists are particularly interested in understanding and measuring consistencies in people's behaviour. They also examine how different patterns of behaviour predict work and other outcomes, and there is a long history of research on individual differences in work and organizational psychology (Sackett, Lievens, Van Iddekinge, & Kuncel, 2017).

The two major aspects of individual differences that have been studied by psychologists are:

- personality
- intelligence/cognitive ability.

These two components of individual differences have been the subject of research for around 100 years and have given rise to many theories. The history of individual differences is also intertwined with the application of psychology to work and organizations. From early on, psychologists have been interested in how individual differences influence organizational behaviour and performance.

DISCUSS WITH A COLLEAGUE

List the names of six of your colleagues on a piece of paper. Choose three at random and identify what attribute makes two of the three similar, but different from the third (e.g. person one is organized, but persons two and three are disorganized). Write down the attribute, and repeat the process five times. The attributes on your list are the ones that are most important in your implicit theory of individual differences. These are the attributes that you use to differentiate people at work.

PERSONALITY

Personality traits are arguably the major determinant of the differences in people's behaviour in organizations, and have an impact on work experiences across the lifespan (Woods, Lievens, De Fruyt, & Wille, 2013). Managers in organizations are also interested in personality. How do we know? Well, first we know from anecdotal evidence, which you may agree with. Asking managers about the characteristics or attributes that they value in their employees invariably leads them to comment upon the importance of having employees who are reliable, dependable, able to work under pressure, creative or enthusiastic. All of these reflect personality characteristics. The importance of personality traits to managers was also confirmed in a study by Dunn, Mount, Barrick, and Ones (1995), who found that managers cited aspects of personality as often as facets of cognitive ability.

Theories of Personality

The theoretical history of personality is diverse, with a variety of theories proposed. If you are new to psychology, then the existence of multiple theories of the same concept, each with merits in their own right, can seem counterproductive. Surely psychologists could agree on one of them? It is best to view such competing theories as representations of the same phenomenon. Theories of personality all focus on the same phenomenon, namely individual differences in behaviour, thought and emotion. The theories represent the domain in different ways, however. Good theories of personality share a number of features (Maltby, Day, & Macaskill, 2006):

- Description: A theory should be able to describe and simplify the complexities of behaviour.
- Explanation: A theory should help in understanding why behaviour occurs in particular situations.
- Empirical validity: A theory should be able to generate hypotheses or predictions that can be tested.
- Testable concepts: Concepts in the theory should be able to be operationalized (defined precisely and measured) so that they can be tested.
- Comprehensiveness: A theory should be able to explain normal and abnormal behaviour.
- Parsimony: A theory should be economical in the concepts of features it employs, avoiding complexity in favour of acceptable simplicity.
- Heuristic value: A theory should stimulate research and sound scientific development and examination.
- Applied value: A theory should be practically useful, in the sense that it can be applied in different contexts to solve problems or answer important applied questions (in work psychology, a theory should help to predict important work outcomes).

From the main classical theories of personality, contemporary research on personality at work draws strongly on *trait* theory, and developmental perspectives incorporate *social learning* theory. We focus on these in our exploration of personality theories, but for additional historical context, Box 2.1 also describes psychoanalytic and behaviourist approaches.

BOX 2.1
Psychoanalysis

Psychoanalytic theory is based on the hugely influential Sigmund Freud, the renowned Austrian psychologist, working in the early part of the 20th century. Freud was a household name during his life, and his work on personality, and in particular on psychopathology and neuroses, stimulated debate and a fashion for the richer classes to be psychoanalyzed by a therapist.

Psychoanalytic theory can be grouped into three parts, covering the structure, development and processes of personality. Freud proposed that personality comprised three basic structures:

- The id represents basic childish drives for instant gratification of our needs. However, these needs cannot always be gratified because of social norms or wider environmental constraints.
- The ego mediates our basic desires, operating on the so-called reality principle. Even though the idea might be appealing in the heat of the moment, one cannot fire a colleague who has annoyed us because one may not have the authority, and more importantly one might contravene employment law.
- The super-ego represents social conscience, that is the knowledge of right and wrong, and what is permissible socially. Firing someone for annoying us is, for most people, against their moral principles of right and wrong.

An important process in Freudian theory is the conflict between these structures, of which people are unaware. Freud proposed that the majority of drives and wants, along with the inner conflicts that occur from regulating them, occur unconsciously. The conflict manifests itself as anxiety.

Freud also proposed that adult personality is influenced by childhood development. He suggested that there were five distinct stages of psychosexual development:

- Oral stage: Birth to one year
- Anal stage: From 18 months to three years
- Phallic stage: From around three to five years
- Latency stage: Around age 5 to 12 years
- Genital stage: Around 12 to 18 years or older

The essence of the theory of psychosexual development is that in each stage, the child derives pleasure from the associated part of the body, and that if development fails to progress smoothly, the person will become fixated on pleasure from that same part of the body in later life. An example can be drawn from the anal stage of development, which Freud suggested was affected by the child's toilet training. When this is handled badly by parents, the child can become anally fixated, and this translates through to adult characteristics that might be described as anally retentive (stubbornness, a tendency to hoard things, overly fussy and organized).

During the latency stage, Freud suggested that the child develops some of the crucial processes of personality called defence mechanisms. These mechanisms are designed to combat feelings that are upsetting or harmful to us psychologically. Many of these have entered everyday language, such as repression (moving upsetting feelings into our unconscious), denial (refuting the realities of unpleasant situations) and rationalization (giving reasons for a particular course of action or situation that conceal its true meaning). In his work with clients, Freud believed that these defence mechanisms became unhealthy or problematic if used persistently or randomly.

Freudian theory was highly influential during its own time, but is rejected by most psychologists for its lack of scientific or empirical evidence. Indeed, many of Freud's concepts are not testable in nature and so the theory must be considered unscientific.

Behaviourism

Behaviourism is a field of psychology that explores how observable behaviour is shaped by the environment. McAdams (2001) describes the three key elements in behaviourism, the dominant paradigm in US psychology from the 1920s to the 1950s, as observation, environmentalism and learning.

Early behaviourists such as Watson and Skinner rejected the importance of internal cognitions or personality processes in favour of a focus on observable behaviour and its dependence on stimuli in the environment. Their perspective was that thoughts and feelings could not be observed or verified by psychologists and hence could not be considered scientific. This stands in stark contrast to the psychoanalytic approach, which relied almost exclusively on internal processes. Although behaviourists did not necessarily deny the existence of internal thoughts and feelings, they felt that they did not need to be studied, because behaviour could be accounted for adequately by aspects of the environment. This idea is referred to as environmentalism. Behaviourists suggest that in order to predict and explain behaviour, psychologists should look to the environment and the interactions between behavioural responses and environmental stimuli.

The relationship between environmental stimulus and behavioural response is the basis of the behaviourist perspective on learning. In this respect, behaviourism draws on the ideas of learned association and conditioning. The most well-known example of classical conditioning is the case of Pavlov's dog. In his experiments, Pavlov showed that he could condition a hungry dog to salivate in response to a neural stimulus (a ringing bell), if he had previously accompanied the bell with meat that provoked a natural salivation reaction. Watson and Rayner (1920) showed that similar conditioned responses could be provoked in a human baby. Their experiments with 'Little Albert', an 11-month-old boy, showed that he could be conditioned to fear white rats, by previously exposing him to white rats and a loud, frightening noise.

Skinner adopted the ideas of classical conditioning in his own theories of human behaviour, which centred on what he referred to as operant conditioning. Operant conditioning examines how behaviour is shaped by both reinforcement and punishment. The concept is straightforward, and suggests that animals and people learn to associate particular behaviours with either punishment or reinforcement (reward). If a particular behaviour leads to a desired outcome, that behaviour is reinforced and repeated; if it punished, then the behaviour is avoided. Skinner was able to show that these processes could shape the behaviour of animals, and they can be applied to aspects of human behaviour as well. In the workplace, the ideas of behaviourism influenced a bestselling book by Kenneth Blanchard and Spencer Johnson in the 1980s (*The One Minute Manager*). In the book, Blanchard and Johnson (1983) describe how employee performance can be managed by carefully praising and rewarding (reinforcing) positive behaviour, and reprimanding (punishing) negative behaviour. The effect is to shape employee behaviour to fit the needs of the manager or organization.

Personality traits

In personality psychology, the idea of 'traits' is inevitable (Hofstee, 1984). Personality trait theory taps into our intuitions about personality characteristics, that people are orderly and predictable. If a group of people with no knowledge of psychology worked together for a few hours on developing a theory of personality, they would most likely arrive at a position that was similar to trait theory. When we observe the behaviour of others, we try to find order and regularity in it. You probably have your own understanding about the behaviour of people you know and the people you work with, and feel that you can predict how they will respond to you, and how they will respond to particular situations. These stable patterns of behaviour can be described as dispositional or trait-like. Martin is organized, so he will work through this task methodically. John is somewhat disorganized, so he may not develop a plan or schedule for completing the task.

Personality traits are typically conceived as internal dispositions that remain generally stable over time (Chamorro-Premuzic, 2007). Example traits are friendly, talkative, organized, calm. Trait theory suggests that individual differences in behaviour, thought and emotions can be described and explained by personality traits (McCrae & Costa, 1995).

Although the concept of personality traits is fairly simple, psychologists have grappled with the definition over the past 50 years. The original consensus about personality traits is summarized nicely by Hampson (1988), who described assumptions that personality traits are internal, stable (unchanged over time), consistent (apply across different situations) and different. Among these assumptions, consistency has provoked the most challenging responses. Trait theory implies that behaviour should be consistent in different situations. However, this is transparently untrue. People's behaviour varies according to context or situation. The 'you' that you know at home is likely to be different in important ways from the 'you' that you know at work. Situational inconsistency was the observation of Walter Mischel (1968), who published a powerful critique of trait theory suggesting that situations should be the object of focus in understanding personality, rather than internal traits. His critique led to the situationist perspective, which threatened to wipe out the study of personality traits altogether.

Trait theory survived this critique, but the conceptualization of personality traits has subtly changed as a result. Personality psychologists now generally accept that individual differences in behaviour, thought and emotion occur in specific contexts, and that it is hard to separate dispositions from the situation or context in which they occur. Traits can therefore be seen as coherent responses to particular situational cues. The extent to which a person will behave in a consistent manner across two different situations depends on the similarity of the features of those situations. A good illustration of this is team meetings. People behave predictably in team meetings provided that the members of the team and the context of the meeting remain similar. People's behaviour might change subtly, though, if others are added or removed from the team, or if the context or task is changed. The value of away-days and team-building activities is that the features of working situations are changed, promoting changes in the behaviour of individual team members.

More recently, the stability of traits has been challenged from a development point of view, an area we return to later.

Social learning theory

Social learning theory (or social cognition) emerged from the behaviourist tradition during the 1960s. The social learning approach is most often associated with the work of Albert Bandura, who emphasized the importance of reciprocal determinism between environment, person and behaviour (Figure 2.1). This means that these three factors are constantly affecting one another. When a person encounters a particular situation, they perceive that situation in a way unique to them, decide how to respond, and behave accordingly. The results of their behaviour are appraised, and in turn, this appraisal affects how future situations are perceived and dealt with. If while at work I contribute to a team meeting and receive a positive response, I am likely to do so again; if the response is negative, I will be discouraged from repeating this behaviour in the future.

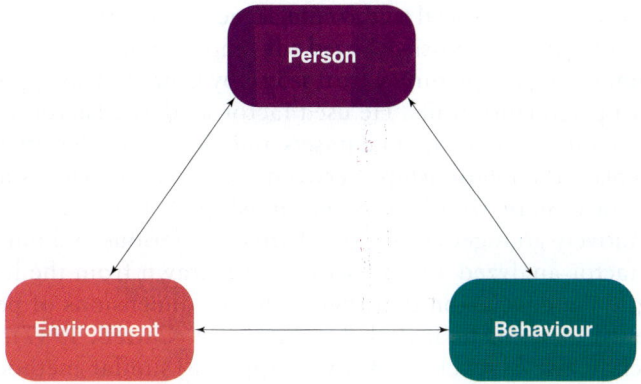

Figure 2.1 Reciprocal determinism between person, environment and behaviour

Two particularly important concepts in social cognition are observational learning and self-efficacy. Bandura proposed that children learn to behave in particular ways by observing so-called role-model behaviour. The child observes the situation, the behavioural response and the outcome, using all three to decide whether they should behave in the same way. One can hypothesize how this observational learning process might apply in organizations, underlining the importance of leader behaviour in changing and influencing employee behaviour. Self-efficacy refers to the extent of our belief that we can achieve something or successfully behave or perform in a particular way. Self-efficacy is important for people at work, especially in relation to goal-setting or objective-setting. People feel more committed to their goals if they believe that they can achieve them. Social cognitive theory stands up well against most of the evaluation criteria identified in Box 2.1, and the ideas are influential in our thinking about organizational behaviour.

PERSONALITY TRAITS AT WORK

There is a huge interest in and vibrant research on the impact of personality traits at work. To help navigate the main implications for work and organizational psychology practice, we summarize research addressing three key questions:

1. How should personality be represented in structural models of traits?
2. How do traits relate to job behaviour, performance and other work outcomes?
3. How does work influence the development of personality traits across the lifespan?

The structure of personality traits

An early pioneer of personality trait theory was Allport, who started the lexical tradition in personality psychology. This line of work is based on the lexical hypothesis, which states that the most important personality characteristics will have been encoded in natural language as society has evolved (John & Srivastava, 1999). Allport and Odbert (1936) therefore studied the English dictionary, extracting all personality-relevant words. They presented a list of almost 18,000 words, which they proposed as the comprehensive account of human personality from the English language.

Although this work was doubtless crucial to the development of the trait approach, the resultant set of personality terms was virtually impossible to use or comprehend.

The challenge of simplifying the picture was taken up by Cattell, who applied methods from the study of intelligence to personality traits. He used factor analysis. Factor analysis is a statistical technique that aims to reduce complexity in datasets and models by identifying underlying factors or dimensions that explain the relationships between the variables. This is a useful way to study personality traits because there are obvious relationships between certain personality traits. Relaxed and calm intuitively go together, as do talkative, gregarious and outgoing, likewise warm and friendly. Cattell factor analyzed a small set of traits drawn from the list created by Allport and Odbert, arriving at the conclusion that there were 12 dimensions of personality that could be used to group the list of terms he included in his study (Cattell, 1947). At around the same time, the British psychologist Eysenck (1947) was applying similar methods in his own theory of personality, concluding that fewer, bigger dimensions were a better solution. He proposed two such dimensions, later adding a third to his model, giving Extraversion, Neuroticism and Psychotism.

The Big Five personality dimensions

The winning number in the debate about the optimal number of factors or dimensions of personality is undoubtedly five (Hampson, 1999). In the early 1960s, three separate sources reported five factor solutions from factor analyses of personality traits (Borgatta, 1964; Norman, 1967; Tupes & Cristal, 1961). There followed a period of dormancy in the study of traits as a result of the challenge of Mischel and situationism. The gauntlet was taken up again by Goldberg and Digman in the early 1980s, who began work on analyzing a set of 1,710 personality traits compiled by Norman many years earlier (Norman, 1967). The result of their work was the identification and description of five broad dimensions of personality, collectively termed the Big Five or five-factor model.

The Big Five model suggests that the most adequate representation of personality traits is to group them into five broad bipolar dimensions. These are:

- Extraversion: The extent to which a person is outgoing and sociable versus quiet and reserved.
- Agreeableness: The extent to which a person is warm and trusting, versus cold and unfriendly.
- Conscientiousness: The extent to which a person is organized and dependable, versus impulsive and disorganized.
- Emotional Stability: The extent to which a person is calm and stable, versus neurotic and anxious.
- Openness/Intellect: The extent to which a person is imaginative and open to new experiences, versus narrow-minded and unimaginative.

The Big Five model has heralded a revolution in personality trait psychology and over the past 20 years has become the largely agreed classification of personality traits, permitting the accumulation of a huge literature on their effects at work and in life more broadly. The implication of the model is that individual differences in personality traits can be described and understood effectively by determining how people differ on these five personality dimensions. Importantly, the dimensions are theoretically independent or unrelated to one another. A person's level of Extraversion is theoretically unrelated to their level of Conscientiousness.

It is important that trait models are not confused with type models of personality. The differences, and the problems with type models, are discussed in Box 2.2.

BOX 2.2
Types and traits

Theories of personality traits usually strike a chord with our intuitive ideas about personality, but ironically, the first encounter that most people have with personality theory in organizations is personality type theory, usually peddled ably by consultants and practitioners using the Myers Briggs Type Inventory (MBTI). The MBTI is one of the most widely used (indeed, probably *the* most widely used) personality questionnaire in organizations, and draws on the psychological theories of Carl Jung. The important aspect of Jung's theory that is applied in the MBTI is that personality should be represented as a typology rather than as dimensional traits like those of the Big Five model.

To illustrate, in the Big Five model, Extraversion is a dimension, so people can be described as having varying degrees of Extraversion (i.e., very introverted, slightly introverted, neither introverted nor extraverted, slightly extraverted, very extraverted). On the MBTI typological model, Extraversion–Introversion is represented as a dichotomy, so that a person is either introverted (labelled I) or extraverted (labelled E). The MBTI contains four such dichotomies, and the combinations of the various letter codes for each gives a total of 16 personality types.

Criticisms of type theory

- There is a technical shortcoming of type theory, which is that if Extraversion and Introversion were a true dichotomy, there should be clear divide between the two when Extraversion is examined in the population (for the statisticians: a bimodal distribution should exist; Mendelsohn, Weiss, & Feimer, 1982). Although this has been disputed (Hicks, 1984), others remain convinced that it is a salient issue (Pittenger, 2005). No such breaks are observed in any of the MBTI dichotomies. Personality dimensions are invariably continuous in populations so that most people cluster around the middle of the dimension (e.g. they are somewhat introverted or somewhat extraverted), with fewer people represented at the extremities or poles of the dimension.

- Conceptually, a type theory of personality is weak. Most accept that a person's personality traits are influenced by a huge variety of different factors. Genes certainly play a part, evidenced in the heritability of personality traits (Bouchard, 1994). However, there is not likely to be one gene for Extraversion, or any other personality trait for that matter. Rather, traits are based on the small additive and interactive effects of multiple genes (e.g. Comings et al., 2000), and similarly small additive effects of life experiences and environmental factors. This conceptualization supports a trait model rather than a type model, whereby small factors combined together lead to many different degrees of Extraversion and other traits.

Criticisms of the MBTI

In addition to problems with type theory, there are also important criticisms of the MBTI measure:

- The model underpinning the MBTI is an incomplete representation of personality, omitting Emotional Stability, one of the key factors of personality (Furnham, 1996).

- The construct validity of the MBTI is questionable, because the four-dichotomy structure often fails to replicate in research studies (Pittenger, 2005).

- The four-letter codes that are assigned to people are unstable, and over periods as

continued

> short as four or five weeks, around 35 to 50 per cent of people receive a different four-letter classification (Pittenger, 2005).
> - By reducing personality dimensions to dichotomies, the MBTI discards important information about personality which limits findings in research, and which can lead to poor personnel decisions when used in organizations.
>
> Some practitioners bat away such criticisms with much talk of practical utility, of the exploratory, non-definitive nature of the MBTI, and the in-depth discussion process that typically follows an assessment. However, these are weak arguments. All of these advantages could equally apply to the use of trait assessments, with the added confidence that comes from using an approach endorsed by the weight of scientific evidence in the field.

Trait models

Although the Big Five is a parsimonious model, it should not be seen as the only way to represent personality traits. One way to elaborate the Big Five is to view them as one level of a hierarchical model of traits, in much the same way that cognitive ability can be modelled as a hierarchy. Researchers have explored the levels immediately above and below the Big Five. Digman (1997) showed that the Big Five could be grouped into two broader dimensions:

- Factor alpha comprises Agreeableness, Conscientiousness and Emotional Stability.
- Factor beta comprises Extraversion and Openness/Intellect.

KEY THEME

Work and organizational psychology in the digital economy

People's digital lives are a potential source of information about their individual differences. Traits and characteristics exert an impact on the decisions they make when interacting with the digital world in the same way that they do in the real world in their day-to-day lives. Relevant digital data are very wide-ranging. They could be a profile of purchases, websites browsed, the sources of news a person reads, or how they interact with social media.

Psychologists have looked into this rich vein of new data in what is an emerging new discipline in psychology: people analytics. In the context of work and organizational psychology, ideas from this trend are applied in the area of *HR* analytics, which applies similar principles of extracting meaning from Big Data sources at work.

One line of work examines the authenticity of personality as portrayed in social media profiles. There is sometimes an implicit belief that people impression-manage their social media to create the kind of personality profile they would like to have, rather than who they really are. Back et al. (2010) showed that observer ratings of the individual from online social media correlated more strongly with participants' actual traits rather than their 'idealized' selves.

However, the more controversial line of research in this area uses this potential to profile individuals based on their digital footprint for the purpose of using the data in some way (e.g. for online marketing). There is plenty of evidence that it is possible to so-called 'scrape' web data to profile an individual, and developments in technology have now shown that a computer-based judgement of the real traits of the user is more accurate than an online friend's judgement of the personality traits (e.g. see Youyou, Kosinski, & Stillwell, 2015). Relevant inputs to these analyses include profiles of 'likes' showing the kind of content that people engage with and endorse.

Other relevant digital data include any communication expression (e.g. text posts online, or transcribed recordings). The use of language has been shown to reliably differentiate some personality characteristics (see e.g. Schwartz et al., 2013; Tausczik & Pennebaker, 2010). This might involve looking at the use of positive versus negative language or reference to certain activities (e.g. social activity).

The prospect of our digital lives revealing our individual differences of course brings with it pressing ethical concerns. For example, it was exactly these technologies that gave rise to the Cambridge Analytica scandal publicized by the UK *Guardian* in 2018. A whistleblower at Cambridge Analytica revealed how the company had harvested data from social media, using those data to target American voters in elections in the USA. As the digital economy grows and we learn more about how our data might be used, we will continue to face these completely novel ethical issues. In the context of work psychology, for example, we will need to consider how and in what ways such data might be used in the context of work (e.g. for employment screening, well-being monitoring, promotion and so forth), and how to ensure that ethical practice is preserved.

Read about this further at www.theguardian.com/news/2018/mar/17/cambridge-analytica-facebook-influence-us-election.

Evidence is also emerging in the personality research literature of a single general factor of personality (the GFP) (e.g. Musek, 2007; van der Linden, te Nijenhuis, & Bakker, 2010; Woods & Hardy, 2012). This general factor may represent general desirability of behaviour.

Recent work by DeYoung et al. (2007) has explored the narrower personality dimensions that sit underneath the Big Five. Their 10-dimension taxonomy is shown in Figure 2.2, along with the Big Five, factor alpha and factor beta. DeYoung et al. showed in their analyses that each of the Big Five dimensions could be conceptualized as comprising two narrower components or facets.

The model shown in Figure 2.2 is an inductive model of personality (meaning that it is derived from research). There are, however, alternative 'construct-driven' or deductive models of personality traits (Burisch, 1984). These models are derived from theories about how traits could or should be represented. Most are associated with specific personality assessment tools, some of which are popular in organizational assessment (for example, the Occupational Personality Questionnaire, Hogan Personality Inventory, NEO Personality Inventory etc.).

Recognizing the need to provide a more coherent framework of personality facets of the Big Five, Woods and Anderson (2016) developed a 'Periodic Table of Personality Traits' representing the major domains of personality measured in work and organizational psychology. They applied a circumplex

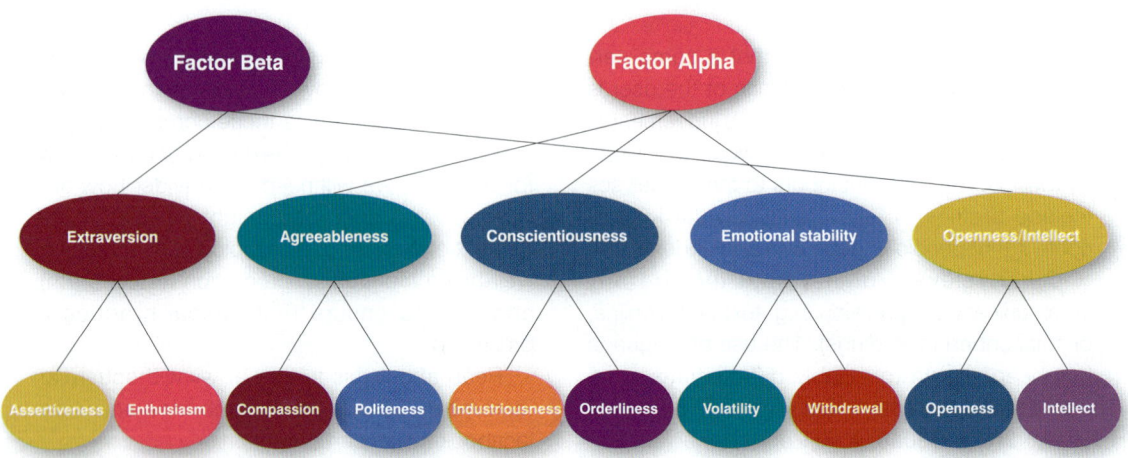

Figure 2.2 The hierarchical structure of personality

model (the Abridged Five-dimensional Circumplex Model; Hofstee, De Raad, & Goldberg, 1992), which examines how personality facets can be presented as blends of the Big Five (e.g. Sociability as a blend of both Extraversion and Agreeableness). Using this methodology, they mapped almost 300 personality inventory scales to a common framework of facets.

The analyses were revealing in that from a possible 45 different personality facets within the Periodic Table structure, frequently used personality inventories effectively measured only 26. These were proposed as a facet model describing the characteristics that work and organizational psychologists have most commonly measured (Box 2.3). One implication of the Periodic Table of Personality is therefore that there are likely to be many unidentified effects of traits on work outcomes given that there are many facets that are typically neglected in research studies. A further implication of the model was to reveal striking similarity and correspondence of different personality models, and in some cases similarity of facets measured on the same personality inventory. The next challenge for work and organizational psychologists is therefore to broaden the scope of the personality facets that are included in research and theorizing.

BOX 2.3
The 26-facet personality trait model of *Woods and Anderson (2016)*

Gregariousness	Warmth	Dutifulness	Socialization
Affiliation	Pleasantness	Industriousness	Intellect
Leadership (Control)	Emotional Sensitivity	Inflexibility	Ingenuity/Creativity
Work Pace	Nurturance (versus Self-reliance)	Stability	Critical Enquiry
Social Poise		Positive Emotionality	Unconventionality
Expressiveness	Orderliness	Emotional Control	Efficiency of Thought/Inquisitiveness
Leadership (Boldness)	Cautiousness	Calmness	

Trait measurement

So far, this section has explored trait theories and models of personality. How exactly are trait models applied in the measurement of individuals, though? Personality traits are most commonly measured by self-report questionnaires or personality inventories. These inventories usually comprise lists of items or statements, and require people to indicate the extent to which they agree or disagree with the statements. Example personality inventory items are shown in Box 2.4, drawn from the International Personality Item Pool (IPIP) measure of the Big Five dimensions.

Each trait or dimension measured by a particular inventory has a number of items associated with it, collectively referred to as scales. The bipolar nature of personality traits means that items are designed to tap into both poles of the dimension. So for example, a scale measuring Extraversion will contain items that refer to characteristics associated with Extraversion (e.g. is the life and soul of the party) and Introversion (e.g. has little to say). The items are used to derive scores for each of the scales, and thus the dimensions being measured. Scales can be compiled to measure a wide variety of different traits and trait models, and this has given rise to the plethora of different personality inventories that are available commercially and in the research literature (see e.g. Woods & Hardy, 2012).

One of the implications of measuring personality traits in this way is that we essentially rely on people's judgements about traits and behaviour. How effective are people at perceiving and judging consistencies in their own behaviour and the behaviour of others? Funder has examined this question in a number of studies and articles (e.g. Funder, 1989, 1995; Funder & West, 1993). Funder is critical of research that focuses solely on the shortcomings of human observers (the so-called error paradigm), and instead provides evidence that shows that people are actually surprisingly good judges of personality traits. Evidence for the accuracy paradigm is found in studies that show that people agree to an extent in their judgements of others (Funder, 1995) and that self-ratings of personality tend to correlate with ratings of others (so people's self-perceptions are a good indicator of how they are seen by others; Johnson, 2000). Agreement between self- and other-perceptions is higher for visible traits such as those related to Extraversion than for less visible traits like Openness/Intellect. The evidence is encouraging for the self-report method of trait assessment as it shows that people are pretty accurate judges of their own personality traits.

BOX 2.4
Example personality inventory items

Indicate the extent to which you agree or disagree with the following statements.

1 = Strongly disagree.
2 = Disagree a little.
3 = Neither agree nor disagree.
4 = Agree a little.
5 = Strongly agree.

I see myself as someone who…

Doesn't mind being the centre of attention *(Extraversion)*.   ……….
Has a soft heart *(Agreeableness)*.   ……….
Follows a schedule *(Conscientiousness)*.   ……….
Is relaxed most of the time *(Emotional stability)*.   ……….
Has a vivid imagination *(Openness)*.   ……….

DISCUSS WITH A COLLEAGUE

Measure your own Big Five traits

Below are five pairs of descriptions representing the Big Five personality traits (taken from Woods & Hampson, 2005). They are presented in the order: Extraversion, Agreeableness, Conscientiousness, Emotional stability, Openness/Intellect. Read each pair of descriptions carefully and place yourself somewhere on the scale between the opposing descriptions. Do this honestly – rate yourself as you think you really are, not as you would like to be ideally. When you have completed the task, ask a colleague if they agree with your responses – do they see you in the same way as you see yourself?

Someone who is talkative, outgoing, is comfortable around people, but could be noisy and attention seeking	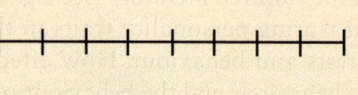	Someone who is a reserved private person, doesn't like to draw attention to themselves and can be shy around strangers
Someone who is forthright, tends to be critical and find fault with others and doesn't suffer fools gladly	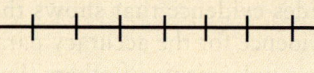	Someone who is generally trusting and forgiving, is interested in people, but can be taken for granted and finds it difficult to say no
Someone who is sensitive and excitable, and can be tense	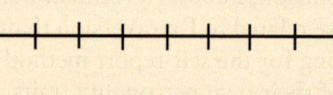	Someone who is relaxed, unemotional rarely gets irritated and seldom feels blue
Someone who likes to plan things, likes to tidy up, pays attention to details, but can be rigid or inflexible		Someone who doesn't necessarily work to a schedule, tends to be flexible, but is disorganized and often forgets to put things back in their proper place
Someone who is a practical person who is not interested in abstract ideas, prefers work that is routine and has few artistic interests	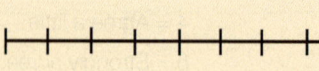	Someone who spends time reflecting on things, has an active imagination and likes to think up new ways of doing things, but may lack pragmatism

Personality traits and work behaviour, performance and outcomes

Personality traits have been found to be associated with an array of organizational and other behaviours (Ozer & Benet-Martinez, 2006). The resurgence of interest in personality traits at work was influenced by the emergence of the Big Five model of personality. As highlighted earlier, the Big Five can be viewed as an organizing framework for personality traits and scales. This means that the dimensions can be used to organize the results of previous studies of personality and work criteria that may have used different trait measures. The results from these studies can then be meta-analyzed. Meta-analysis of the criterion effects of the Big Five have examined the prediction of a wide variety of work outcomes from personality traits, showing convincingly that personality traits do relate to organizational behaviour.

Personality traits have been found to predict various forms of job performance. Barrick and Mount (1991) examined the prediction of job performance from the Big Five, reporting that Conscientiousness was particularly important for a variety of performance outcomes (e.g. general job performance, training outcomes). Subsequent meta-analyses were reviewed by Barrick, Mount, and Judge (2001), who concluded that Conscientiousness predicted job performance to some extent in all occupations. Emotional Stability and Extraversion also emerge as important predictors of performance in some, but not all occupations (Ozer & Benet-Martinez, 2006).

What are the pathways from personality to job performance and why do some personality traits seem to predict performance in a wide variety of jobs? One particular research line has considered this question by focusing on job performance more closely, and in particular how cognitive ability and personality relate to different aspects of performance (e.g. Motowidlo, Borman, & Schmitt, 1997). The findings from these studies suggest that personality traits relate most strongly to 'organizational citizenship behaviours (OCB)', sometimes called contextual performance. These are general prosocial behaviours that support the core aspects of task performance of individuals, teams and organizations. The importance of OCB across most jobs is the likely reason that traits such as Conscientiousness predict job performance so consistently.

Adopting a job-specific approach, Hogan and Holland (2003) examined the associations of job performance with personality traits in studies that considered which traits might be relevant for performance in particular jobs. In these studies, the correlations appear to be higher, suggesting that specific personality traits are more or less important in different jobs. The extent to which traits predict performance depends on the kind of work that a person is required to do.

This premise is at the centre of Trait Activation Theory (TAT; Tett & Burnett, 2003), which explains the differential performance effects of traits across jobs. In this model, personality traits are theorized to be activated in response to work demands, which may represent job tasks or social or organizational requirements. Once activated, traits guide behaviour, and when that behaviour is positive in the context of dealing with work demands, performance is effective. The model also includes influences of reward structures at work. People's traits may be moderated to some extent if they perceive that their behaviour would prevent them attaining a valued reward from work.

To test some of the propositions of TAT, a study by Judge and Zapata (2015) examined how the associations of the Big Five with performance were dependent on the job demands. For example, the study found that Extraversion predicted performance in jobs that required social skills, and Openness/Intellect in jobs requiring innovation and creativity. The implication of this finding and TAT is that there is no single 'best' personality profile for performance at work, rather it depends on the job and organizational context in which somebody is working.

Personality and wider work criteria

In addition to job performance, there is plenty of evidence of associations between the Big Five personality traits and other organizational behaviour criteria:

- Traits related to affective styles (Extraversion and Neuroticism) along with Conscientiousness are associated with job satisfaction (Judge, Heller, & Mount, 2002; Steel, Schmidt, Bosco, & Uggerslev, 2018). Personality traits seem to affect how a person appraises aspects of their job and organization.
- Personality also relates to a person's commitment to their organization (Erdheim, Wang, & Zickar, 2006), with higher levels of Extraversion being most consistently associated with higher levels of organizational commitment.
- Occupational interests are also associated with personality traits, with good evidence that traits from the Big Five model overlap with interests and preferences for particular kinds of work and working environments. Of particular note is Openness/Intellect, which is related to preferences for artistic or investigative occupations (Barrick, Mount, & Gupta, 2003; Larson, Rottinghaus, & Borgen, 2002). The Big Five are also associated with specialization within occupations, with Woods, Patterson, Wille, and Koczwara (2016) showing such effects in medical specialization.
- Team processes and teamworking are related to the traits of the team members (Barrick, Stewart, Neubert, & Mount, 1998; van Vianen & de Dreu, 2001). Having generally higher Extraversion, Agreeableness, Conscientiousness and Emotional Stability is generally beneficial, although there is evidence that having a range of profile scores on Extraversion and Emotional Stability is beneficial. In the case of Extraversion, having members high and low on the dimension may allow leaders and followers to emerge, and in the case of Emotional Stability, people low on the dimension may bring a sense of urgency to the team in respect of goal attainment.
- Personality is related to leadership behaviour. In meta-analyses (Bono & Judge, 2004; Judge, Bono, Ilies, & Gerhardt, 2002), the Big Five have been found to be associated with leader emergence (Extraversion and Conscientiousness positively associated) and leadership effectiveness (Extraversion, Conscientiousness, Emotional Stability and Openness all positively associated). Top management team personality profiles have moreover been implicated in firm-level performance (Colbert, Barrick, & Bradley, 2014).
- Innovation and creativity. Studies have examined the impact of the Big Five on innovative work behaviour and creativity (George & Zhou, 2001; Hammond, Neff, Farr, Schwall, & Zhao, 2011; Woods, Mustafa, Anderson, & Sayer, 2018). Openness/Intellect is associated with innovative behaviour, especially for longer-tenured employees.

Judge, Higgins, Thoresen, and Barrick (1999) examined data from a number of longitudinal studies on the relationships between traits in adolescence and later-life career success. They looked at both extrinsic success (e.g. salary and status) and intrinsic success (e.g. job and career satisfaction). Conscientiousness, Openness and Emotional Stability at an early age all predicted later-life intrinsic success, and perhaps even more interestingly, Agreeableness negatively predicted extrinsic success. Woods and Hampson (2010) examined the longitudinal associations between childhood personality and the kinds of job environments where people worked in middle age. They found that children high on Openness/Intellect were more likely to work in investigative or artistic jobs in later life.

Consider for a moment the implications of these findings, which show that individual differences in personality traits are crucial factors in determining people's work experiences, successes, performances and choices. Moreover, individual differences at a very early age can give important insights about how a person's working life will develop over long periods of time.

KEY THEME

Environmental sustainability

Pro-environmental behaviour (PEB) is behaviour that is voluntary and beneficial to the environment. The kinds of things that we don't have to do, which may even cause us mild inconvenience, but which we do anyway because there is a benefit for the environment.

There have been many studies that have examined the impact of personality traits on PEB. Indeed, since our first edition of this book, where we commented on the potential impact of personality traits, the possibility of individual differences in PEB has been borne out in empirical data (see e.g. Hirsh, 2010; Markowitz, Goldberg, Ashton, & Lee, 2012). These studies show, for example, that higher Openness and Agreeableness are predictive of PEB. People who are more curious, open to ideas and altruistic, perhaps unsurprisingly, tend to do more to protect the environment.

There are some intriguing follow-up results from these studies. For example, Busic-Sontic, Czap, and Fuerst (2017) show relations of Openness and Agreeableness with energy efficiency investment. What they find is that everyday actions to increase energy efficiency are predicted by Openness because highly open people have higher environmental concern. Bigger investments in energy efficiency that incur more initial investment are also dependent upon risk preference. People with higher risk preferences tend to be more willing to make higher upfront investments in efficiency for the prospect of longer-term savings. Even more fascinating, these traits at country level predict overall environmental performance (Milfont & Sibley, 2012). Those countries with higher than average Openness and Agreeableness across the population tend to be the most effective at protecting the environment.

These findings point to potential strategies for intervention in organizations to promote environmental sustainability. For example, it suggests that those people with traits that promote PEB are less likely to be resistant to interventions to protect the environment or conserve resources. Those with lower Agreeableness and Openness are likely to be more resistant to change behaviour, and so strategies should deliberately appeal to those individuals. It may mean setting goals and new behavioural strategies that represent greater altruism and change-orientation. It may mean giving opportunity for people to express criticism (low Agreeableness) or practical concerns (low Openness) and to have those issues dealt with and addressed to overcome resistance. This approach is ultimately about tailoring persuasive marketing for the benefits of PEB differently for the key audiences that need to change.

Work influences on personality: A dynamic and developmental model of personality and work

Looking beyond the boundaries of specific individual jobs, research has also examined how personality traits relate to organizational behaviour across people's working lives. Woods et al. (2013) reviewed the literature on the dynamic influences of personality traits on work outcomes, and also the reciprocal influences of work on personality. They noted that in the research literature on personality and work outcomes, the preoccupation of researchers on validities of the Big Five, while having established a huge volume of literature in the field, had two undesirable consequences. First, the relations of personality traits with work outcomes are implicitly treated as static, even though the demands of work change dynamically over time. Second, personality is almost exclusively conceptualized only as a predictor variable. For theory building, personality traits, as highlighted earlier, are considered to be stable over time. However, recent evidence has suggested that personality may not only affect work behaviour, but may also be affected by work (e.g. Wille, Beyers, & De Fruyt, 2012).

The changing influences of personality on work outcomes over the course of people's careers can be examined through Trait Activation Theory (TAT; Tett & Burnett, 2003). Woods et al. (2013) applied this theory and considered how the demands of work changed in the short and long term.

With regards to performance, there is accumulating evidence that the influences of personality on job performance change over even relatively short periods of time. This is linked to the idea that performance demands change (Murphy, 1989). For example, when a person begins a new job (transitional stage), job requirements, problems and tasks are all novel. However, after a period of time, the job has been learned (the maintenance stage) and the requirement is rather to maintain performance. Thoresen, Bradley, Bliese, and Thoresen (2004) demonstrated how personality was related to performance in sales at these different stages. Openness and Agreeableness were associated with performance for sales people in the transitional stage, probably reflecting adaptability and network building, respectively. Conscientiousness was associated with performance at the maintenance stage, most likely reflecting the long-term motivational aspects of that dimension. Lievens, Ones, and Dilchert (2009) showed similarly changing associations of the Big Five with performance of students at medical school over time.

Woods et al. (2013) also examined three ways in which work has a developmental influence on personality. Although personality traits may still be considered to be generally stable, there is also emerging consensus that traits continue to develop across people's lives (e.g. Roberts, Robins, Caspi, & Trzesniewski, 2003; Tasselli, Kilduff, & Landis, 2018; Woods et al., 2019). There are three ways that work might affect our personality development through the course of our working lives:

1 Through normative change. Normative development affects people generally in the same way and is related to how our lives typically develop as human beings. People tend to engage in age-related social norms (e.g. education, finding a job, settling down and having a family) at roughly the same times of their lives, and these drive changes such as increased Conscientiousness as they get older.
2 Through deepening and strengthening of traits. Personality traits lead people to seek out particular job environments that are consistent with those traits. As a consequence traits are persistently activated, with people's characteristics becoming deepened and strengthened. This process is referred to as the corresponsive principle (Roberts, Caspi, & Moffitt, 2003).
3 Through unique experiences. There is recent evidence that personality traits change and develop in response to unique working experience. For example, Lüdtke, Roberts, Trautwein,

and Nagy (2011) found that traits developed differently for young adults during education depending on whether they took vocational or non-vocational pathways. Wille et al. (2012) also reported evidence that engagement in certain job roles resulted in personality traits development that ran counter to normative developmental trends.

The combined evidence of dynamic influences of personality on work, and developmental influences of work on personality, led Woods et al. (2013) to propose a dynamic developmental model of personality and work. They proposed that personality traits are in constant interaction with work-related activities and environments and are activated in response to changing work demands and career challenges, setting people on pathways to certain kinds of work activities. As demands change over time, different traits influence how people perform, behave and succeed at different stages within these careers, and these experiences in turn influence the development of personality traits throughout working life.

Building on this model, Woods, Wille, Wu, Lievens, and De Fruyt (2019) proposed a fuller model of the mechanisms of trait development at work: the Demands-Affordances Transactional (DATA) model. In this model, development stems from a transaction between demands and personality trait *affordances* (the traits that a situation calls for). Traits develop so that people are better able to deal with their work demands, meaning that personality change is directed towards greater person–environment fit.

A key implication of the DATA model, and the emergent literature on personality development and change, is that people may develop and adjust to work demands, even if initially they are not suited to the work. The theory of work adjustment (Dawis & Lofquist, 1984) and recent research on the impact of behavioural change strategies on personality traits (Hudson, Briley, Chopik, & Derringer, 2018) underline this possibility. In the theory of work adjustment, workers are proposed to adjust both their jobs and themselves (in terms of changing attitudes, behaviour and skills) in order to attain greater fit to demands. In the context of personality, this involves behaving in ways that may run somewhat counter to traits to meet the demands of work situations. The accumulated experience of these small changes in behaviour leads in time to trait development (Wrzus & Roberts, 2017). This represents a positive perspective on the role of work in lifelong development and learning, which we develop in the section on *Positive work*.

INTELLIGENCE

Intelligence comprises a wide range of cognitive abilities, but a group of 52 leading academics in the field of intelligence have provided a highly useful agreed working definition of general intelligence:

> *A very general mental capability that, among other things, involves the ability to reason, plan, solve problems, think abstractly, comprehend complex ideas, learn quickly and learn from experience. It is not merely book learning, a narrow academic skill, or test-taking smarts. Rather it reflects a broader and deeper capability for comprehending our surroundings – 'catching-on', 'making sense' of things or 'figuring out' what to do.* (Gottfredson, 1997, p. 13.)

This description sums up the essence of intelligence. It is a general mental capability that can be applied in the understanding of the world around us, for problem-solving in a variety of different contexts. One can quickly see why intelligence has the potential to affect such a diverse range of areas of our lives, and in particular why it is important at work.

In the research literature and in most texts, the term intelligence is used interchangeably with cognitive ability and general mental ability (GMA). Theories of intelligence aim to examine its nature, most often by establishing and testing models of intelligence that tell us more about the way it is expressed in different contexts. The development of such theories and models has tracked the history of intelligence testing, such that the two are impossible to separate.

The first intelligence test was designed by Alfred Binet, working for the French Ministry of Public Instruction. With Theodore Simon, he published the Binet–Simon scale in 1905. The test comprised a series of tasks such as number recall and sentence completion, along with other practical tasks. Tasks on the test were progressively more difficult in order to differentiate levels of intelligence. The key contribution of Binet and Simon was the establishment of norms of intelligence for different ages. A child's intelligence was worked out by comparing them with children of the same age. Cognitive ability therefore was and always has been a 'relative' construct. Someone is defined as bright or high in cognitive ability because a measure of their ability shows it to be higher than their peers.

Spearman's *g* Factor

Around the same time as Binet and Simon's work, Charles Spearman in the UK examined the intercorrelations or overlaps between scores on different kinds of ability test. Spearman observed that people who scored highly on one kind of ability task also tended to score highly on others. He proposed that the strong overlap of performance on different kinds of ability task was due to a general underlying factor or construct. He labelled this factor g, to represent general intelligence, and was able to show, through a technique called factor analysis, that one could observe the effects of this general factor on a wide range of different ability tests. Factor analysis is a method of examining the relationships between many different variables to identify underlying factors that explain the relationships.

Spearman's g is a significant milestone in the history of individual differences and remains one of the most influential findings in the field. Today, researchers still concur with the idea of a general factor of ability, with which all facets of ability are correlated (see Lubinski, 2004), and the definition outlined earlier represents our understanding of g.

The structure of cognitive ability

A challenge for researchers since Spearman originally postulated the existence of g has been how to organize and conceptualize abilities in specific areas (e.g. verbal, numerical, spatial abilities). The earliest effort was that of Thurstone, who rejected the notion of g altogether, instead favouring a model of intelligence that comprised seven primary abilities. Chamorro-Premuzic (2007) describes these primary abilities:

- **Verbal comprehension** – vocabulary (knowledge of words), reading and comprehension skills, verbal analogies (capacity for conceptual association).
- **Word fluency** – ability to express ideas, generating large numbers of words, and use concepts (e.g. anagrams, rhymes, metaphors).
- **Number facility** – ability to carry out mental calculations with speed and accuracy.

- **Spatial visualization** – ability to mentally rotate figures and orientate oneself in space.
- **Associative memory** – **rote memory.**
- **Perceptual speed** – ability to rapidly spot visual stimuli (similarities, differences, patterns).
- **Reasoning** – inductive, deductive, inferential, logical process of thought.

The definitions of some of these primary abilities are reasonably consistent with some of the more common occupational tests used in organizations. The existence of these specific abilities is largely supported in research, but the idea that these are an alternative to g has by contrast been rejected by most in favour of a hierarchical model, best exemplified by the work of Vernon and Cattel.

Vernon's model included two facets of general ability:

- Verbal/educational intelligence consisted of verbal, numerical and educational abilities.
- Spatial/mechanical intelligence consisted of spatial, mechanical and other practical abilities.

Each was broken down into its constituent levels at lower levels of the hierarchy, culminating in very specific task areas. Models that identify specific forms of ability are highly useful in organizations. Most jobs require people to apply abilities in some areas but not others, and often one area of ability is particularly important. An accountant needs high levels of numerical ability, but spatial ability is less important. For an air traffic controller, spatial ability is highly important. Models of ability allow us to understand how different profiles of ability might be more or less suited to particular jobs.

Cattell also proposed two factors of intelligence, although he did so using a somewhat different rationale. Cattell was a PhD student of Spearman and was influenced by Spearman's work on factor *g*. His theory and analyses led him to derive two facets of general ability:

- Fluid ability (gf): the ability to solve novel problems with no prior knowledge or education relating to the problem.
- Crystallized ability (gc): learned strategies for solving problems such as those related to education, and cumulative work experience.

Reasoning ability and information processing is captured by gf, whereas acquired knowledge and skills is represented by gc. There is some evidence that gf declines during adult life, whereas gc increases as more culture-relevant information is acquired. It is worth reflecting on the value of both fluid and crystallized ability in organizations. Fluid ability would seem to be related to innovative problem-solving, whereas crystallized ability perhaps reflects the collective knowledge and experience of how work has been and should be performed.

The hierarchical model of cognitive ability

The ideas of Vernon and Cattell, and other proponents of the hierarchical model, have been consolidated by empirical investigations of the structure of cognitive ability. The best example of such research was carried out by Carroll (1993). In his analyses, Carroll examined the structural relationships between a variety of ability types and tasks. His final model comprised three layers, two of which are shown in Figure 2.3.

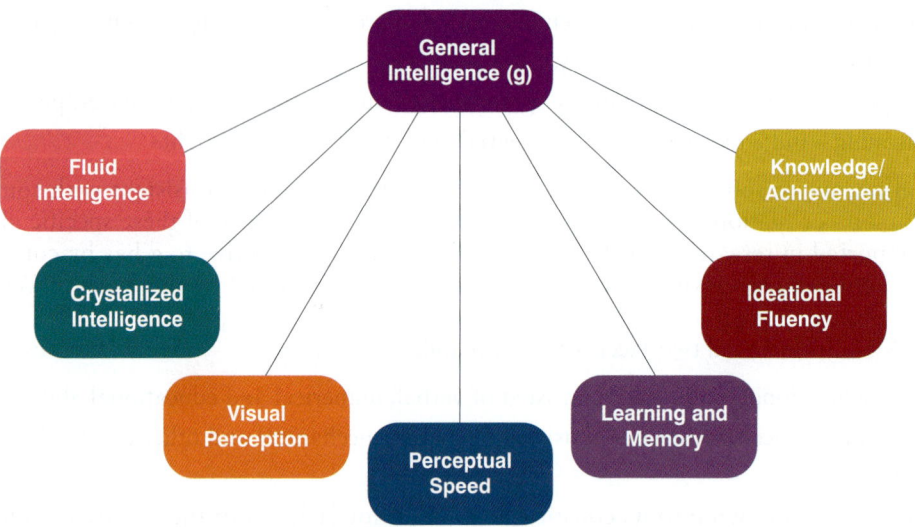

Figure 2.3 Hierarchical structure of intelligence

The figure, adapted from Carroll (1993) and Ackerman and Heggestad (1997), shows g at the top of the hierarchy with ability facets underneath. These include Cattell's crystallized and fluid abilities. All represent mental processes that are influenced in some way by g, or overall cognitive ability. In the third layer of the hierarchy, Carroll included the constituent ability tasks and measures that made up the facets of the second layer. Specific abilities such as verbal and numerical reasoning therefore lie within this third layer, along with the kinds of work tasks that draw on these abilities.

Ability testing

The hierarchical model of cognitive ability is consistent with models underpinning a number of ability and intelligence measures. Tests of ability used in organizations are generally designed to address part of the hierarchical model, almost always by testing people's capability to answer intellectual reasoning questions. Tests of cognitive ability have right and wrong answers and are usually timed, so that test-takers complete the test under standardized conditions.

Perhaps the most well-known test was designed by Wechsler. The Wechsler Adult Intelligence Scale (WAIS) was designed with a hierarchical model of cognitive ability in mind and consists of a variety of sub-tests. Other forms of test focus solely on facets of ability. Practitioners have a wide range of tests to choose from, tapping into verbal reasoning, numerical reasoning, abstract reasoning and spatial reasoning. Sometimes the abilities are assessed in job-relevant tasks. An example would be a test that requires people to add up columns of figures quickly, thereby simulating accounts checking or mental calculation of product prices. The task itself would actually be an assessment of numerical reasoning ability, albeit a highly practical one.

Multiple intelligences

Some people seem to be uncomfortable with the concept of cognitive ability and its measurement. Whatever the reason, such people would often rather identify the virtues of so-called practical

(Sternberg) and social (Thorndike) intelligences, which represent skills in interpersonal decision-making and general skills in addressing problems of everyday life. These kinds of constructs hark back to the ideas of Thurstone about multiple intelligences and ideas about the independence of multiple forms of ability.

None of these multiple intelligences has received more attention than emotional intelligence, referred to as EI or EQ. Many argue that no other single construct has caused quite the impact that EI caused following its coverage by Daniel Goleman in his bestselling book in 1995 (Chamorro-Premuzic, 2007). EI has been proposed by Goleman, and others (notably Salovey, Mayer, and Caruso), as an alternative, more powerful construct than g for predicting success in life and at work. It has found application in organizations, particularly for assessment of managers and leaders, for whom high EI is assumed to be advantageous. There are various definitions of EI, but broadly speaking most would agree with Sternberg and Kaufman (1998) that EI is:

> *the ability to perceive accurately, appraise, and express emotion; the ability to access and/or generate feelings when they facilitate thought; the ability to understand emotion and emotional knowledge; and the ability to regulate emotions to promote emotional and intellectual growth.* (Sternberg & Kaufman, 1998, p. 479.)

Some believe EI to be an ability, similar to other cognitive abilities, and measure EI with tests that have right and wrong answers (e.g. Salovey, Mayer, Caruso, & Lopes, 2003). Others believe EI to be a composite personality trait. A good example and operationalization of trait EI comes from the work of Petrides and Furnham (e.g. Petrides & Furnham, 2001). The relative merits of the trait and ability perspectives are hard to evaluate at present because there is not clear evidence supporting one or the other. There are reported associations between EI and g, which are important if the construct is to be considered as a form of ability (recall that all forms of ability are in some way related to g). There are also established relationships between personality and EI (Petrides & Furnham, 2001), with the debate in that area being whether trait EI adds significantly to what we already know about personality (e.g. Van der Zee & Wabeke, 2004). Whatever form EI takes, there is not consistent evidence that it explains success in life or at work any better than a combination of g and well-defined broad personality dimensions (Antonakis, 2004).

Criticisms of EI can be attributed to a number of sources. In addition to the lack of consensus about exactly how to conceptualize EI, there is also fairly consistent criticism of the measures that are used to estimate it (e.g. Conte, 2005; Fiori & Antonakis, 2011). The demand for measures of EI in organizations has given rise to a supply of poorly designed EI questionnaires sold and used by consultants, including, sadly, some work psychologists. The call for caution in the application of EI measures (Mayer, Caruso, & Salovey, 1999; Fiori & Antonakis, 2011) appears to be unheeded by some. There remain concerns about the use of EI assessment in organizations. Although two meta-analyses report evidence that EI is related to job performance (Joseph & Newman, 2010; O'Boyle, Humphrey, Pollack, Hawver, & Story, 2011), these relationships reduce to zero after controlling for already established individual differences such as the Big Five and cognitive ability (see Joseph, Jin, Newman, & O'Boyle, 2015). More research in this area is needed. There is potential for EI to contribute to our understanding of individual differences in time, but the extent to which it adds anything new beyond personality and cognitive ability remains to be firmly established.

> **DISCUSS WITH A COLLEAGUE**
>
> Think for a moment about the different forms of ability that have been covered in this chapter. Which ones do you think are most important for your job or role? If you are a student, think about which abilities are most important for your course.

Cognitive ability at work

Interest in cognitive ability in work and organizational psychology has undergone something of a renaissance over the past 20 years. Past dismissal of the importance of individual differences in cognitive ability has been challenged and overcome by advances in the field in respect of the structure of cognitive ability (Carroll, 1993), the study of its longitudinal stability (cognitive ability has been shown to be stable up to 65 years; Deary, Whalley, Lemmon, Crawford, & Starr, 2000), and the considerable heritability of cognitive ability, prompting studies to identify relevant marker genes.

The major breakthrough for the study of cognitive ability at work was the development of methods of meta-analysis (Hunter & Schmidt, 1990). Until that point, the accepted wisdom in work psychology was that cognitive ability predicted performance at work in some contexts but not others. Ability might be associated with performance in a particular job in a particular organization, but unrelated to performance of that same job in a different organization (Schmidt & Hunter, 2004). Inconsistent associations between cognitive ability and performance in different studies seemed to confirm this. Through meta-analysis, psychologists were able to determine that the inconsistencies in results were actually attributable to unreliable measurement, errors in sampling and restriction of score ranges in datasets. Contrary to popular belief, cognitive ability predicts job performance to varying degrees in all jobs. Moreover, the correlations between cognitive ability and performance are large compared to other effects in psychology:

- Hunter and Hunter (1984) reported a meta-analysis in which general cognitive ability correlated strongly with job performance (in excess of 0.50 for medium- and high-complexity jobs, with smaller values for less complex jobs, 0.23 for the least complex).
- When performance during training is examined, the associations are higher still (up to 0.65).
- Meta-analyses of the validity of cognitive ability in European samples are similarly high (Salgado et al., 2003).

These meta-analyses clearly indicate the importance of cognitive ability for performance at work. People with higher levels of ability tend to perform better at work. The finding lacks a theoretical foundation, however. Why does cognitive ability lead to better job performance? Schmidt and Hunter (2004) considered this question and reported that the key process is acquisition of job knowledge. People with higher levels of cognitive ability are able to acquire more knowledge about their job and to acquire it quickly. They point out that even relatively simple jobs depend on the incumbent drawing on surprisingly detailed job knowledge, and so the ability to acquire, maintain and develop that knowledge is always an advantage. In more complex jobs, there is more knowledge to acquire, and it is more likely that knowledge acquisition will continue to be important for performance. In less complex jobs, some tasks can be learned thoroughly to the point of automation. This in part explains the differences in the validities for jobs of varying complexity. The importance of job knowledge acquisition for explaining the relationship between cognitive ability and job performance has been highlighted in numerous studies (e.g. Schmidt, 2002; Schmidt & Hunter, 1992).

In their review, Schmidt and Hunter (2004) also describe evidence of the prediction of occupational attainment from cognitive ability. Occupational attainment refers to the level that one rises to in an organization along with salary achieved. The most powerful evidence about the association of cognitive ability with attainment comes from longitudinal studies. Murray (1998) examined the earnings of siblings reared together and found that those with higher cognitive abilities consistently earned more than their siblings when aged in their late 20s. Perhaps more astonishingly, a study of the associations between childhood cognitive ability and occupational level show a clear and strong correlation even over periods up to 30–40 years (Judge et al., 1999). Cognitive ability seems to influence not only job performance, but also career success.

THE INTERPLAY OF PERSONALITY AND INTELLIGENCE

You might rightly be curious about how cognitive ability fits with the ideas around dynamic influences of personality and work. The answer is 'quite neatly'. Recent research on performance trajectories suggests that people's performance at work increases linearly in early stages of the job, but then plateaus (see Figure 2.4) following a so-called learning curve (Zyphur, Chaturvedi, & Arvey, 2008). Murphy (1989) proposes that cognitive ability is critical in the learning phase of performance, when the job is being learned and job knowledge is acquired.

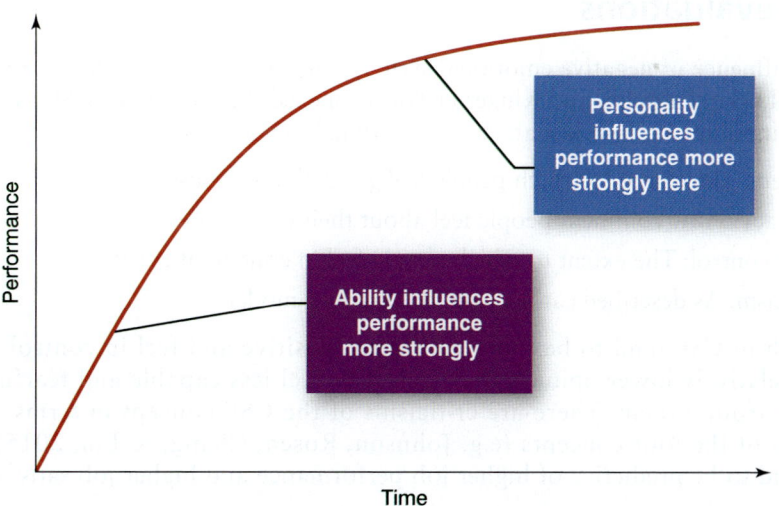

Figure 2.4   A performance trajectory curve (learning curve), and influence of individual differences at different times

However, over time, motivational aspects become more important in maintaining performance and may influence whether performance continues to increase, plateau or decline. Gottfredson (2002) refers to the 'can-do' and 'will-do' of performance, which are correspondingly related to cognitive ability and personality. What we can deduce from the idea of performance trajectories is that cognitive ability is most important when people need to learn quickly and solve novel problems. As jobs become more familiar and practised, the influence of cognitive ability is likely to decrease, and the influence of personality to increase.

A further intriguing proposition surrounding the interplay of personality and cognitive ability is the developmental influences that these two aspects of individual differences exert upon one another. The intellectual investment perspective on personality and intelligence describes how personality traits that capture the tendency to seek out, engage in and pursue learning opportunities (such as Openness/Intellect in the Big Five model) are associated with cognitive abilities (see Asendorpf & Bühner, 2012; Woods, Hinton, Von Stumm, & Bellman-Jeffreys, 2017; Ziegler, Danay, Heene, Von Stumm, & Ackerman, 2013). It is plausible that this mechanism links these kinds of traits with cognitive ability and intelligence in a cycle of development by which people seek out (or invest effort in) learning, which improves their reasoning ability, which gives greater chance of learning success, which promotes greater interest in learning, and so forth. In a work setting, such an integrated view could help us understand differences between people in terms of how they continue to develop and grow.

WIDER CONCEPTS IN INDIVIDUAL DIFFERENCES AT WORK

Research on personality using, for example, the Big Five model aims to examine a broad spectrum of traits that capture most of the trait-like characteristics of the individual. However, there are also many specific and narrower concepts defined and studied in work and organizational psychology. Two notable examples are core self-evaluations and proactive personality.

Core self-evaluations

The general influence of negative emotional style is central to a model called core self-evaluations (CSE). Judge, Locke, Durham, and Kluger (1998) proposed the concept of CSE as a single unifying trait or disposition linking four key affective (emotional) tendencies:

- Self-esteem: The extent to which people feel good about themselves.
- Self-efficacy: How confident people feel about their capabilities.
- Locus of control: The extent to which people feel in control of events.
- Neuroticism: As described earlier from the Big Five model.

People high in CSE tend to be more confident, positive and feel in control. People low on CSE have a relatively lower opinion of themselves, feel less capable and fearful or threatened by the world around them. There are criticisms of the CSE concept in terms of its proposed incorporation of the four concepts (e.g. Johnson, Rosen, Chang, & Lin, 2015), yet high CSE has been found to be predictive of higher job performance and higher job satisfaction (Judge & Bono, 2001).

To establish the mechanisms explaining the associations of CSE with job satisfaction, Judge, Bono, and Locke (2000) tested two hypotheses, both of which were confirmed. First, CSE influences how people perceive their job characteristics and the extent to which they see them positively versus negatively. This has a direct impact on subjective job satisfaction. Second, people with high CSE actually attain intrinsically more rewarding jobs. Their higher levels of confidence and self-belief mean that they take on more complex tasks, tend to perform better in them and therefore attain more positive job characteristics.

This tendency to take on more challenging jobs and tasks may be related to the ways in which people approach things at work more generally. High Neuroticism is associated with an avoidant approach (Ferris et al., 2011), whereby people select tasks, activities and behavioural strategies that minimize the level of threat or the chances of failure that a person experiences. People low on Neuroticism, and correspondingly high on CSE, tend to accept more individual responsibility and more challenging goals (Erez & Judge, 2001). CSE may therefore have a long-term impact on work and the attainment of success and happiness at work over time.

Proactivity

Taking a more positive perspective, psychologists have examined the impact of taking a proactive approach to work tasks and problem-solving. Proactive personality has been defined as the extent to which people take action to influence or make an impact on their environment (Crant, 1995). Parker, Bindl, and Strauss (2010) describe proactivity as 'taking control to make things happen rather than watching things happen. It involves aspiring and striving to bring about change in the environment and/or oneself to achieve a different future' (p. 2).

A related concept is personal initiative (Sackett et al., 2017), which represents the extent to which people are proactive, self-motivated and persistent in overcoming barriers (Frese, Garst, & Fay, 2007). Both of these individual differences have motivational aspects, which differentiate them somewhat from traits such as those of the Big Five model.

In the context of work, proactivity offers a potential advantage to career success. In a meta-analysis of the literature on proactivity and work outcomes, Fuller and Marler (2009) described wide-ranging effects on work outcomes. For example, proactivity was associated with career success, interestingly via two mechanisms. The first was through its impact on job performance. The second was through its impact on *voice behaviour* and taking charge. This latter pathway represents the act of speaking up and being proactive in taking action to shape one's career (for example, initiating career development with leaders and managers). Also relevant for career advancement are relations of proactive personality to career self-efficacy, indicating a higher degree of confidence in attaining career success.

The meta-analysis also indicated associations with job performance. These associations, unlike for example emotional intelligence, could not be explained fully by the Big Five, suggesting that proactivity represents additional performance-related elements beyond these broad personality domains.

Parker et al. (2010) examined the antecedents and processes of proactivity. They identified that proactivity is influenced by a range of individual factors (traits and skills), interacting with contextual factors such as leadership and work design. These lead to motivation and goal processes by which people develop proactive states comprising a sense of *can do* (e.g. belief that one can act to change something), *reason to* (e.g. a sense that actions are intrinsically important) and *energized to* (e.g. feeling positive about taking action). Provided work permits action, then these motivations lead to proactive behaviour.

A positive consequence of proactivity is the potential impact that proactive behaviour has on the work environment (Li, Fay, Frese, Harms, & Gao, 2014). People who are proactive influence their own work characteristics to improve them (for example by attaining more job autonomy). At a group level, such behaviour could be beneficial for whole teams or organizations more broadly.

PIONEERING WORK PSYCHOLOGISTS

Professor Sharon K. Parker

Professor Sharon Parker is an Australian Research Council Laureate Fellow, a Professor of Organisational Behaviour at the Centre for Transformative Work Design, Curtin University and an Honorary Professor at the University of Sheffield. She is a recipient of the ARC's Kathleen Fitzpatrick Award and the 2016 Academy of Management Organizational Behavior Division Mentoring Award.

Professor Parker's work is pioneering in multiple aspects, but here we highlight her research on proactivity at work. On her website, Professor Parker illustrates the concept of proactivity:

> "Someone once observed: 'There are three kinds of people: those who make things happen, those who watch what happens, and those who wonder what happened'…. Proactive behavior refers to the first kind of person – those who make things happen. Many scholars believe that everyone has the potential to be the kind of person who makes things happen. That is, everyone can display more or less proactive behavior, depending on their motivation in the situation."

Professor Parker makes the strong case for the critical future importance of proactivity in increasingly complex and uncertain workplaces that face pressure for innovation and demands to bring about change. Proactivity is also positive for people at work and their careers, as it provides control and agency over how working life develops over time.

Key example papers:

- Griffin, M. A., Parker, S. K., & Mason, C. (2010). Leader vision and the development of adaptive and proactive performance: A longitudinal study. *Journal of Applied Psychology, 95*(1), 174–182.
- Parker, S. K., Bindl, U., & Strauss, K. (2010). Making things happen: A model of proactive motivation. *Journal of Management, 36*, 827–856.
- Parker, S. K., Williams, H., & Turner, N. (2006). Modeling the antecedents of proactive behavior at work. *Journal of Applied Psychology, 91*, 636–652.

MEASURING INDIVIDUAL DIFFERENCES: PSYCHOMETRICS

The last part of this chapter in concerned with the principles of measuring individual differences, which are relevant to a variety of techniques and methods in work psychology. Unlike the measurement of physical characteristics, individual differences involve the measurement of unseen or intangible attributes. Measuring height or weight is easy. All one needs is an agreed metric (metres or kilograms) and a tool to do the measurement (tape measure or weigh-scale), and the physical attribute can be objectively perceived and assessed. Psychological attributes are different and are sometimes referred to as latent constructs. This means that we infer that they exist because we can see their effects. A psychologist could not examine your brain and point to your cognitive ability or your Extraversion. However, we know that some people are able to complete reasoning problems more effectively than others and that some people are more talkative than others.

The measurement of individual differences is referred to as psychometric or psychological testing. This chapter has introduced the common forms of test that are used to measure individual differences. These are tests of cognitive ability and self-report personality inventories. Once designed, the measurements derived from these tests need to be evaluated to determine whether they are accurate. In addition, because psychological attributes are unseen, it is not always obvious that a test is tapping into the attribute of interest. How do we know, for example, that a test of Extraversion is actually measuring Extraversion and not something else? These are the important questions that psychometrics aims to address. Two key concepts in psychometrics are:

- Reliability (the accuracy of psychological tests).
- Validity (the extent to which a test measures what it claims to measure).

Reliability

Tests measuring individual differences are always imperfect. This means that the score we obtain on a test will reflect two components. The first is the actual or true score of the individual (i.e. the score that someone would obtain if our measure were perfect) and the second is test error (i.e. the degree of inaccuracy in the test). This is the basic tenet of classical test theory, summarized as:

Test Score = True Score + Error

Evaluating the accuracy of the test scores we obtain from a test therefore involves estimating or quantifying the amount of error in the measurement, and this is the purpose of assessing test reliability. The reliability of a test is evident in two properties:

1. The extent to which the test produces scores that are stable over time.
2. The extent to which the items on a test are consistent.

Stability over time

The first and most straightforward way to measure test reliability is to examine whether the scores we obtain for people are stable over time. An assumption of theories of cognitive ability and trait theories of personality is that the attributes themselves are stable over long periods of time. The test score that a person receives on one occasion should therefore be similar to the score that he or she receives on another, provided that the test conditions are similar on both occasions. This can be evaluated by administering the test to groups of individuals at two time points. Test scores are then correlated to see the degree of concordance between them. High positive correlations (above 0.7, and ideally above 0.8) indicate that the scores are generally stable. This form of reliability is called test–retest reliability.

Internal consistency

A theoretical assumption in the design of psychometric tests is that the items on the test all tap into the attribute of interest. In order to measure Conscientiousness from the Big Five model, test items are designed to represent the dimension. The IPIP Conscientiousness scale is shown in Box 2.5 (Goldberg, 1999), and you should be able to see that the items are consistent in the sense that they all refer in some way to the dimension of interest. However, this assumption needs to be tested and that is the purpose of evaluating internal consistency reliability. There are two ways that internal consistency can be calculated, both of which are designed to examine the agreement or consistency in the items of psychological tests or scales.

> **BOX 2.5**
> **Items from the IPIP conscientiousness scale**
>
> Am always prepared
> Follows a schedule
> Pays attention to details
>
> Likes order
> Gets chores done right away
> Am exacting in my work

Computation of Cronbach's alpha or coefficient alpha is derived based on the correlations of each individual item with the overall score obtained from the measure (item–total correlations). These reliabilities are reported in journal articles as indicants of the adequacy of the measurements used in research studies. Values above 0.7 are desirable for internal consistency reliability. Coefficient alpha is a versatile analytic technique that is simultaneously valuable for evaluating the reliability scales and guiding their design and construction.

Using reliability information

Information on the reliability of psychometric tests is useful for a number of reasons. First, the information enables practitioners to decide whether or not a test provides adequate, accurate measurement. Second, it allows practitioners to decide how cautious they should be in making decisions from psychometric test results, because the amount of error in the test is precisely specified.

Validity

The validity of a psychological test indicates the extent to which the test measures the attribute that it claims to measure. This can be termed measurement validity. Equally important in applied psychology is criterion validity, which examines the extent to which the test predicts important criteria. There is not one method of establishing test validity, and test developers will usually address validation from a number of perspectives. The result is the development of an overall case that supports the test validity. The major forms of test validity are reviewed below.

Face validity

Face validity is concerned with the way that the test looks to the people who are completing it. It is a qualitative judgement about whether the test items appear relevant for their purpose. In applied psychology, relevant items help to show people that completing the measure is worthwhile, thereby increasing their motivation.

Content validity

Content validity is a similarly qualitative appraisal of the test validity, but made by subject matter experts rather than the test-takers. Personality scales serve as a good illustration. Imagine that a scale was compiled to measure Emotional Stability from the Big Five model. The domain of Emotional Stability is broad and, as discussed earlier, encompasses a range of narrower personality facets. The test developer may wish to seek advice on whether the item set they had generated covered the full domain. To do this, they could consult with a personality psychologist or researcher and ask them to review the scale.

Construct validity

Overall, construct validity is the closest form of validity to the general conceptualization of measurement validity (that the test measures what it claims to measure). Unlike other forms of validity, showing that a test has construct validity does not involve a single method or technique. Rather a range of statistical analyses are performed in order to establish an evidence base for the validity of the test. Such analyses will usually include evaluation of convergent and divergent validity (establishing that a test correlates with variables that it should correlate with, and is uncorrelated with variables that it should not; Campbell & Fiske, 1959), analysis of the factor or dimensional structure of the test and correlations of test scores with other relevant indicators. For example, a test designed to measure Extraversion could be correlated with observational data recorded during social interaction. People scoring highly on the test of Extraversion should also demonstrate more extraverted behaviours in their interactions with others.

Criterion validity

Criterion validity is concerned with showing that the test predicts important criteria. In work psychology, this is a prerequisite for the use of testing for contributing to personnel decisions. In order to use tests with employees in organizations, practitioners need to be confident that the test predicts the outcome of interest. In order to establish criterion validity, test scores must be correlated with scores from criterion measures. In work psychology, this is most commonly job performance, but other work-related behaviours and attitudes such as counterproductive work behaviour, satisfaction, commitment and engagement are also important.

The timing of the administration of the test and the measurement of criteria gives rise to two forms of criterion validity:

- Concurrent validity is demonstrated by correlating test scores with criterion scores measured at the same time (concurrently).
- Predictive validity is demonstrated by collecting test scores first, followed by criterion scores at some future time (with a time lag that is usually in the range of three months to one year).

Predictive validity is arguably more robust in most cases, because it shows that the individual difference being measured predicts a future outcome. It is remarkable to think about the implication of what is, on the face of it, a dry statistical test. Fundamentally, predictive validity data show that by measuring individual differences, psychologists can predict, with varying degrees of accuracy, likely future behavioural, attitudinal and performance outcomes.

Using validity

Like reliability, validity data help practitioners to be confident in the tests that they use, and in the decisions that they make based on test scores. If a test is to be used in a selection context, then the test should be able to demonstrate criterion validity with job performance. If a test is used to help advise a person about their career choices, then the test should be related to performance potential, or well-being, satisfaction, or 'fit' with particular job environments or organizational cultures. Validity is also important for defending personnel decisions. If tests or assessments of any form are used to make decisions about people's work and jobs, then those assessments should be proven to be valid, in terms of both measurement and criterion prediction.

Item Response Theory

An alternative approach to testing altogether uses Item Response Theory (IRT) as an alternative to the classical model of testing. IRT is gaining popularity, particularly for cognitive ability testing, for which it is well suited, aided by advances in computer development that enable the complex analyses to be easily run. The major difference in IRT is the focus of the analyses on the properties of items rather than whole tests. Rather than determine whether a particular test is reliable or not, IRT examines the properties of individual test items. It adds to the mix a continuous representation of the construct being measured (e.g. cognitive ability), labelled theta. IRT analyses aim to establish how test items perform at different levels of theta. In plain terms, this enables researchers to establish the effectiveness of each item for measuring or differentiating people with particular levels of cognitive ability. This means that tests can be designed, for example, for people in the high-ability range, with their responses used to accurately estimate their specific level of ability. The advantage is that the test could be used with confident knowledge that the items were ideally suited to the people being assessed, thereby giving a better measurement of cognitive ability than might be achieved with a test designed for the general population. There are other practical design benefits of using IRT, such as easier creation of parallel tests, adaptive testing (which presents questions based on previous item responses) and flexible use of so-called 'item banks' to create multiple tests.

Psychological testing: Beyond cognitive ability and personality

The methods of psychological testing are presented in this chapter in the context of measuring cognitive ability and personality traits. However, the principles of psychometric theory and methodology apply to any form of quantitative measurement in psychology (see Hinkin, 1995 and Woods, 2018). Measures of work-related attitudes, behaviours, job performance, job interests, well-being and emotions can all be evaluated to establish their reliability and validity using the methods outlined. The research literature contains a multitude of examples of scales designed to measure particular aspects of individual differences, attitudes, work behaviours and outcomes. Articles evaluating the psychometric properties of such scales are commonplace, and yet there are many scales and measures used in organizations with little or no evidence of reliability and validity. One clear principle from this chapter is that measurement of individual differences should be robust and accurate, and there are well-established procedures for determining that a measure or test is psychometrically sound. Applying the findings and theories from studies of individual differences at work relies on sound measurement techniques. Now you know, ensure that the survey measures you use in your work are reliable and valid.

POSITIVE WORK

The literature on personality change at work offers a renewed and positive perspective on development and growth at work. For decades, a dominant view in work and organizational psychology was that personality traits were stable across much of adult life. It has arguably led to the fixation of applied psychological practice on selection and placement. In both recruitment and career counselling, an implicit assumption has been that the person side of the person–environment equation has been fixed, and so the task of the psychologist has been to match them to the right environment. No doubt doing so has benefits for effectiveness and well-being in the short term, but there is something quite *fatalist* about assuming traits to be fixed as people navigate their careers.

The emergence of the literature on personality change and development (e.g. Woods et al., 2013; Woods et al., 2019) offers the possibility that work can be a positive influence on long-term development and growth. What we do in our working lives becomes part of the very essence of who we are and helps to direct our growth both as an employee and as a person.

One of the implications of this perspective is the prospect that people can adjust over time to the demands of different jobs, even if they initially may find them challenging. By extension, the role of career aspiration is brought into focus. All of us have aspirations for how we would like our careers to proceed, what we want to achieve and to contribute to the world through our work. For too long, psychologists may have indirectly discouraged people from striving for some of their goals, by guiding them based on assumed fixed individual differences. In the future, it will be important to see both environments and traits and individual differences as dynamic and responsive to development. Making a positive difference to work and organizations in this respect involves seeing people's potential for long-term growth and development, rather than solely short-term fit.

Combined with the emergent research on proactive personality, this developmental thinking takes on a new dimension. Li et al. (2014) consider how proactive personality might also develop as a consequence of work environment features such as optimal balances of job demands and control. By creating engaging environments in which people feel that they are learning, have autonomy and are challenged positively and constructively, it is possible to foster those personality characteristics that represent feelings of empowerment and motivation to change and influence the environment. What a wonderful setting that would be to work in; to be confident to address the demands of work, to feel confident that learning new behaviours and skills would be encouraged and would help fulfil long-term career aspirations, and to feel positive about the prospect of continuing to develop and change throughout our adult life.

For the discipline of work and organizational psychology, this means orienting our perspective more clearly with development and personal growth, striking a better balance between selection/matching people to jobs and facilitating adjustment to demands. For people working in organizations, it means similarly changing perspectives to see people's traits as changeable, and to ensure that their development potential is nurtured.

SUMMARY

The study of individual differences involves the examination of key psychological attributes. Two of the most important individual difference attributes are personality and cognitive ability.

Personality has been studied from a number of different perspectives, but the most important of these in work psychology is the trait approach. Personality traits are coherent or characteristic patterns of behaviour, demonstrated in response to particular situational and contextual cues. Research into personality traits led to the emergence of the Big Five model of personality, which most psychologists would agree to be the most adequate and widely accepted classification of personality traits. The Big Five have allowed the accumulation of a huge literature on personality traits and work outcomes, including clear evidence that personality traits do predict job performance and a range of other work outcomes. Recent theoretical developments in the field have examined the dynamic associations of personality traits with criteria and explored the developmental influences of work on personality.

Cognitive ability (or intelligence) represents a range of reasoning and mental capabilities that can be represented as a hierarchy, with Spearman's factor g at the top. Higher levels of cognitive ability predict higher levels of job performance in a range of jobs, most likely because people with higher abilities are able to acquire more job knowledge more quickly. Intellectual investment perspectives on the relations of traits and intelligence emphasize the developmental benefits of traits related to learning activity in the development of abilities.

Research on individual differences in work and organizational psychology has also captured specific attributes such as CSE and proactive personality. These concepts have the potential to offer additional insights beyond studies of broad traits and intelligence.

The measurement of individual differences is referred to as psychometric or psychological testing. Psychological tests measure unseen or latent constructs and should be evaluated in terms of their reliability and validity. There are a number of techniques that can be used to assess reliability and validity, which in turn tell practitioners about the accuracy and adequacy of specific tests.

DISCUSSION QUESTIONS

1. Think about a recent problem you faced when working in a group or team. How could individual differences help to explain your experiences?
2. If you have previously held a job, what aspect of it involved you managing or regulating your emotions?
3. For three of the Big Five personality dimensions, think of some jobs that might require different personality profile scores (e.g. think of jobs where Extraversion might be advantageous, and jobs where Introversion might be preferable).
4. How have your personality traits developed as a consequence of your work experiences?
5. To what extent do you think your personality and ability are based on genes and environment? Can you perceive aspects of your parents' individual differences in your own behaviour?
6. How could a manager use research on individual differences to manage their team more effectively?

FURTHER READING

Chamorro-Premuzic, T. (2007). *Personality and individual differences*. Oxford, England: BPS Blackwell.

McAdams, D. P. (2008). *The person: An introduction to the science of personality psychology*. Chichester, England: John Wiley & Sons.

Sackett, P. R., Lievens, F., Van Iddekinge, C. H., & Kuncel, N. R. (2017). Individual differences and their measurement: A review of 100 years of research. *Journal of Applied Psychology, 102*(3), 254.

Schmidt, F. L., & Hunter, J. E. (2004). General mental ability in the world of work: Occupational attainment and job performance. *Journal of Personality and Social Psychology, 86*, 162–173.

Tett, R. P., & Burnett, D. D. (2003). A personality trait-based interactionist model of job performance. *Journal of Applied Psychology, 88*(3), 500.

Woods, S. A., Lievens, F., De Fruyt, F., & Wille, B. (2013). Personality across working life: The longitudinal and reciprocal influences of personality on work. *Journal of Organizational Behavior, 34*, S7–S25.

REFERENCES

Ackerman, P. L., & Heggestad, E. D. (1997). Intelligence, personality and interests: Evidence for overlapping traits. *Psychological Bulletin, 121*(2), 219–245.

Allport, G. W., & Odbert, H. S. (1936). Trait names: A psycho-lexical study. *Psychological Monographs, 47* (Whole No. 211).

Antonakis, J. (2004). On why "emotional intelligence" will not predict leadership effectiveness beyond IQ or the "big five": An extension and rejoinder. *International Journal of Organizational Analysis, 12*(2), 171–182.

Back, M. D., Stopfer, J. M., Vazire, S., Gaddis, S., Schmukle, S. C., Egloff, B., & Gosling, S. D. (2010). Facebook profiles reflect actual personality, not self-idealization. *Psychological Science, 21*(3), 372–374.

Barrick, M. R., & Mount, M. K. (1991). The Big Five personality dimensions and job performance: A meta-analysis. *Personnel Psychology, 44*, 1–26.

Barrick, M. R., Mount, M. K., & Gupta, R. (2003). Meta-analysis of the relationship between the Five Factor Model of personality and Hollan's occupational types. *Personnel Psychology, 56*, 45–74.

Barrick, M. R., Mount, M. K., & Judge, T. A. (2001). Personality and performance at the beginning of the new millennium: What do we know and where do we go next? *International Journal of Selection and Assessment, 9*, 9–30.

Barrick, M. R., Stewart, G. L., Neubert, M. J., & Mount, M. K. (1998). Relating member ability and personality to work-team processes and team effectiveness. *Journal of Applied Psychology, 83*(3), 377.

Blanchard, K. H., & Johnson, S. (1983). *The one minute manager.* New York, NY: Blanchard Family Partnership and Candle Communications Corporation.

Bono, J. E., & Judge, T. A. (2004). Personality and transformational and transactional leadership: A meta-analysis. *Journal of Applied Psychology, 89*(5), 901.

Borgatta, E. F. (1964). The structure of personality characteristics. *Behavioral Science, 9,* 8–17.

Bouchard, T. J., Jr. (1994). Gene, environment and personality. *Science, 264,* 1700–1701.

Burisch, M. (1984). Approaches to personality inventory construction: A comparison of merits. *American Psychologist, 3,* 214–227.

Busic-Sontic, A., Czap, N. V., & Fuerst, F. (2017). The role of personality traits in green decision-making. *Journal of Economic Psychology, 62,* 313–328.

Campbell, D. T., & Fiske, D. W. (1959). Convergent and discriminant validation by the multitrait–multimethod matrix. *Psychological Bulletin, 56*(2), 81–105.

Carroll, J. B. (1993). *Human cognitive abilities: A survey of factor analytic studies.* New York, NY: Cambridge University Press.

Cattell, P. B. (1947). Confirmation and clarification of primary personality factors. *Psychometrika, 12,* 197–220.

Chamorro-Premuzic, T. (2007). *Personality and individual differences.* Oxford, England: BPS Blackwell.

Colbert, A. E., Barrick, M. R., & Bradley, B. H. (2014). Personality and leadership composition in top management teams: Implications for organizational effectiveness. *Personnel Psychology, 67*(2), 351–387.

Comings, D. E., Gade-Andavolu, R., Gonzalez, N., Wu, S., Muhleman, D., Blake, H., ... MacMurray, J. P. (2000). A multivariate analysis of 59 candidate genes in personality traits: The temperament and character inventory. *Clinical Genetics, 58,* 375–385.

Conte, J. M. (2005). A review and critique of emotional intelligence measures. *Journal of Organizational Behavior, 26,* 433–440.

Crant, J. M. (1995). The Proactive Personality Scale and objective job performance among real estate agents. *Journal of Applied Psychology, 80*(4), 532.

Dawis, R. V., & Lofquist, L. H. (1984). *A psychological theory of work adjustment.* Minneapolis: University of Minnesota Press.

Deary, I. J., Whalley, L. J., Lemmon, H., Crawford, J. R., & Starr, J. M. (2000). The stability of individual differences in mental ability from childhood to old age: Follow-up of the 1932 Scottish Mental Survey. *Intelligence, 28*(1), 49–55.

DeYoung, C. G., Quilty, L. C., & Peterson, J. B. (2007). Between facets and domains: 10 Aspects of the Big Five. *Journal of Personality and Social Psychology, 93*(5), 880–896.

Digman, J. M. (1997). Higher-order factors of the Big Five. *Journal of Personality and Social Psychology, 73,* 1246–1256.

Dunn, W. S., Mount, M. K., Barrick, M. R., & Ones, D. S. (1995). Relative importance of personality and general mental ability in managers' judgements of applicant qualifications. *Journal of Applied Psychology, 80*(4), 500–509.

Erdheim, J., Wang, M., & Zickar, M. J. (2006). Linking the big five personality constructs to organizational commitment. *Personality and Individual Differences, 41,* 959–970.

Erez, A., & Judge, T. A. (2001). Relationship of core self-evaluations to goal setting, motivation, and performance. *Journal of Applied Psychology, 86*(6), 1270.

Eysenck, H. J. (1947). *Dimensions of personality.* London, England: Routledge.

Ferris, D. L., Rosen, C. R., Johnson, R. E., Brown, D. J., Risavy, S. D., & Heller, D. (2011). Approach or avoidance (or both?): Integrating core self-evaluations within an approach/avoidance framework. *Personnel Psychology, 64*(1), 137–161.

Fiori, M., & Antonakis, J. (2011). The ability model of emotional intelligence: Searching for valid measures. *Personality and Individual Differences, 50*(3), 329–334.

Frese, M., Garst, H., & Fay, D. (2007). Making things happen: Reciprocal relationships between work characteristics and personal initiative in a four-wave longitudinal structural equation model. *Journal of Applied Psychology, 92*(4), 1084.

Fuller, B., Jr., & Marler, L. E. (2009). Change driven by nature: A meta-analytic review of the proactive personality literature. *Journal of Vocational Behavior, 75*(3), 329–345.

Funder, D. C. (1989). Accuracy in personality judgment and the dancing bear. In D. M. Buss & N. Cantor (Eds.), *Personality psychology: Recent trends and emerging directions* (pp. 210–223). New York, NY: Springer-Verlag.

Funder, D. C. (1995). On the accuracy of personality judgement: A realistic approach. *Psychological Review, 102*, 652–670.

Funder, D. C., & West, S. G. (1993). Consensus, self-other agreement, and accuracy in personality judgment: An introduction. *Journal of Personality, 64*, 457–476.

Furnham, A. (1996). The Big Five versus the big four: The relationship between the Myers-Briggs Type Indicator (MBTI) and the NEO-PI face factor model of personality. *Personality and Individual Differences, 21*, 303–307.

George, J. M., & Zhou, J. (2001). When openness to experience and conscientiousness are related to creative behavior: An interactional approach. *Journal of Applied Psychology, 86*(3), 513.

Goldberg, L. R. (1999). A broad-bandwidth, public domain, personality inventory measuring the lower-level facets of several five-factor models. In I. Mervielde, I. Deary, F. De Fruyt, & F. Ostendorf (Eds.), *Personality psychology in Europe* (Vol. 7, pp. 7–28). Tilburg, Netherlands: Tilburg University Press.

Gottfredson, L. S. (1997). Mainstream science on intelligence: An editorial with 52 signatories, history and bibliography. *Intelligence, 24*, 13–23.

Gottfredson, L. S. (2002). Where and why g matters: Not a mystery. *Human Performance, 15*(1–2), 25–46.

Griffin, M. A., Parker, S. K., & Mason, C. (2010). Leader vision and the development of adaptive and proactive performance: A longitudinal study. *Journal of Applied Psychology, 95*(1), 174–182.

Hammond, M. M., Neff, N. L., Farr, J. L., Schwall, A. R., & Zhao, X. (2011). Predictors of individual-level innovation at work: A meta-analysis. *Psychology of Aesthetics, Creativity, and the Arts, 5*(1), 90.

Hampson, S. E. (1988). *The construction of personality: An introduction*. London, England: Routledge.

Hampson, S. E. (1999). State of the art: Personality. *The Psychologist, 12*, 284–288.

Hicks, L. E. (1984). Conceptual and empirical analysis of some assumptions of an explicit typological theory. *Journal of Personality and Social Psychology, 46*, 1118–1131.

Hinkin, T. R. (1995). A review of scale development practices in the study of organizations. *Journal of Management, 21*(5), 967–988.

Hirsh, J. B. (2010). Personality and environmental concern. *Journal of Environmental Psychology, 30*(2), 245–248.

Hofstee, W. K. B. (1984). What's in a trait: Reflections about the inevitability of traits, their measurement, and taxonomy. In H. Bonarius, G. Van Heck, & N. Smid (Eds.), *Personality psychology in Europe: Theoretical and empirical developments* (pp. 75–81). Lisse, Netherlands: Swets and Zeitlinger.

Hofstee, W. K. B., De Raad, B., & Goldberg, L. R. (1992). Integration of the big five and circumplex approaches to trait structure. *Journal of Personality and Social Psychology, 63*(1), 146.

Hogan, J., & Holland, B. (2003). Using theory to evaluate personality and job-performance relations: A socioanalytic perspective. *Journal of Applied Psychology, 88*(1), 100–112.

Hudson, N. W., Briley, D. A., Chopik, W. J., & Derringer, J. (2018). You have to follow through: Attaining behavioral change goals predicts volitional personality change. *Journal of Personality and Social Psychology*. doi:10.1037/pspp0000221

Hunter, J. E., & Hunter, R. F. (1984). Validity and utility of alternative predictors of job performance. *Psychological Bulletin, 96*, 72–98.

Hunter, J. E., & Schmidt, F. L. (1990). *Methods of meta-analysis: Correcting error and bias in research findings*. Newbury Park, CA: SAGE.

John, O. P., & Srivastava, S. (1999). The Big Five trait taxonomy: History, measurement, and theoretical perspectives. In L. A. Pervin & O. P. John (Eds.), *Handbook of personality theory and research* (pp. 139–153). New York, NY: Guilford.

Johnson, J. A. (2000). Predicting observers' ratings of the Big Five from the CPI, HPI and NEO-PI-R: A comparative validity study. *European Journal of Personality, 14*, 1–19.

Johnson, R. E., Rosen, C. C., Chang, C. H. D., & Lin, S. H. J. (2015). Getting to the core of locus of control: Is it an evaluation of the self or the environment? *Journal of Applied Psychology, 100*(5), 1568.

Joseph, D. L., Jin, J., Newman, D. A., & O'Boyle, E. H. (2015). Why does self-reported emotional intelligence predict job performance? A meta-analytic investigation of mixed EI. *Journal of Applied Psychology, 100*(2), 298.

Joseph, D. L., & Newman, D. A. (2010). Emotional intelligence: An integrative meta-analysis and cascading model. *Journal of Applied Psychology, 95*(1), 54.

Judge, T. A., & Bono, J. E. (2001). Relationship of core self-evaluations traits – self-esteem, generalized self-efficacy, locus of control, and emotional stability – with job satisfaction and job performance: A meta-analysis. *Journal of Applied Psychology, 86*(1), 80.

Judge, T. A., Bono, J. E., Ilies, R., & Gerhardt, M. W. (2002). Personality and leadership: A qualitative and quantitative review. *Journal of Applied Psychology, 87*(4), 765.

Judge, T. A., Bono, J. E., & Locke, E. A. (2000). Personality and job satisfaction: The mediating role of job characteristics. *Journal of Applied Psychology, 85*(2), 237.

Judge, T. A., Heller, D., & Mount, M. K. (2002). Five Factor model of personality and job satisfaction: A meta-analysis. *Journal of Applied Psychology, 87*, 530–541.

Judge, T. A., Higgins, C. A., Thoresen, C. J., & Barrick, M. R. (1999). The Big Five personality traits, general mental ability and career success across the life span. *Personnel Psychology, 52*, 621–652.

Judge, T. A., Locke, E. A., Durham, C. C., & Kluger, A. N. (1998). Dispositional effects on job and life satisfaction: The role of core evaluations. *Journal of Applied Psychology, 83*(1), 17.

Judge, T. A., & Zapata, C. P. (2015). The person–situation debate revisited: Effect of situation strength and trait activation on the validity of the Big Five personality traits in predicting job performance. *Academy of Management Journal, 58*(4), 1149–1179.

Larson, L. M., Rottinghaus, P. J., & Borgen, F. (2002). Meta-analysis of Big Six interests and Big Five personality factors. *Journal of Vocational Behaviour, 61*, 217–239.

Li, W. D., Fay, D., Frese, M., Harms, P. D., & Gao, X. Y. (2014). Reciprocal relationship between proactive personality and work characteristics: A latent change score approach. *Journal of Applied Psychology, 99*(5), 948.

Lievens, F., Ones, D. S., & Dilchert, S. (2009). Personality scale validities increase throughout medical school. *Journal of Applied Psychology, 94*(6), 1514.

Lubinski, D. (2004). Introduction to the special section on cognitive abilities: 100 years after Spearman's (1904) 'General Intelligence, objectively determined and measured.' *Journal of Personality and Social Psychology, 86*, 96–111.

Lüdtke, O., Roberts, B. W., Trautwein, U., & Nagy, G. (2011). A random walk down university avenue: Life paths, life events, and personality trait change at the transition to university life. *Journal of Personality and Social Psychology, 101*(3), 620.

Maltby, J., Day, L., & Macaskill, A. (2006). *Personality, individual differences and intelligence.* Harlow, England: Pearson.

Markowitz, E. M., Goldberg, L. R., Ashton, M. C., & Lee, K. (2012). Profiling the "pro-environmental individual": A personality perspective. *Journal of Personality, 80*(1), 81–111.

Mayer, J. D., Caruso, D. R., & Salovey, P. (1999). Emotional intelligence meets traditional standards for an intelligence. *Intelligence, 27*, 267–298.

McAdams, D. P. (2001). *The person: An integrated introduction to personality psychology* (3rd ed.). Fort Worth, TX: Harcourt.

McCrae, R. R., & Costa, P. T., Jr. (1995). Trait explanations in personality psychology. *European Journal of Personality, 9*, 231–252.

Mendelsohn, G. A., Weiss, D. S, & Feimer, N. R. (1982). Conceptual and empirical analysis of the typological implications of patterns of socialization and femininity. *Journal of Personality and Social Psychology, 42*, 1157–1170.

Milfont, T. L., & Sibley, C. G. (2012). The big five personality traits and environmental engagement: Associations at the individual and societal level. *Journal of Environmental Psychology, 32*(2), 187–195.

Mischel, W. (1968). *Personality and assessment.* New York, NY: John Wiley & Sons, Inc.

Motowidlo, S. J., Borman, W. C., & Schmitt, M. J. (1997). A theory of individual differences in task and contextual performance. *Human Performance, 10*, 71–83.

Murphy, K. R. (1989). Is the relationship between cognitive ability and job performance stable over time? *Human Performance, 2*(3), 183–200.

Murray, C. (1998). *Income Inequality and IQ.* Washington, DC: AEI Press.

Musek, J. (2007). A general factor of personality: Evidence for the Big One in the five-factor model. *Journal of Research in Personality, 41*(6), 1213–1233.

Norman, W. T. (1967). *2800 personality trait descriptors: Normative operating characteristics for a university population.* Ann Arbor: University of Michigan.

O'Boyle, E. H., Humphrey, R. H., Pollack, J. M., Hawver, T. H., & Story, P. A. (2011). The relation between emotional intelligence and job performance: A meta-analysis. *Journal of Organizational Behavior, 32*(5), 788–818.

Ozer, D. J., & Benet-Martinez, V. (2006). Personality and the prediction of consequential outcomes. *Annual Review of Psychology, 57*, 401–421.

Parker, S. K., Bindl, U., & Strauss, K. (2010). Making things happen: A model of proactive motivation. *Journal of Management, 36*, 827–856.

Parker, S. K., Williams, H., & Turner, N. (2006). Modeling the antecedents of proactive behavior at work. *Journal of Applied Psychology, 91*, 636–652.

Petrides, K. V., & Furnham, A. (2001). Trait emotional intelligence: Psychometric investigation with reference to established trait taxonomies. *European Journal of Personality, 15*(6), 425–448.

Pittenger, D. J. (2005). Cautionary comments regarding the Myers-Briggs Type Indicator. *Consulting Psychology Journal: Practice and Research, 57*(3), 210–221.

Roberts, B. W., Caspi, A., & Moffitt, T. E. (2003). Work experiences and personality development in young adulthood. *Journal of Personality and Social Psychology, 84*(3), 582.

Roberts, B. W., Robins, R. W., Caspi, A., & Trzesniewski, K. H. (2003). *Personality trait development in adulthood*. In J. Mortimer & M. Shanahan (Eds.), *Handbook of the life course* (pp. 579–595). New York, NY: Plenum Press.

Sackett, P. R., Lievens, F., Van Iddekinge, C. H., & Kuncel, N. R. (2017). Individual differences and their measurement: A review of 100 years of research. *Journal of Applied Psychology, 102*(3), 254.

Salgado, J. F., Anderson, N., Moscoso, S., Bertua, C., De Fruyt, F., & Rolland, J. P. (2003). A metaanalytic study of GMA validity for different occupations in the European community. *Journal of Applied Psychology, 88*, 1068–1081.

Salovey, P., Mayer, J. D., Caruso, D., & Lopes, P. N. (2003). Measuring emotional intelligence as a set of abilities with the Mayer-Salovey-Caruso Emotional Intelligence Test. In S. J. Lopez & C. R. Snyder (Eds.), *Positive psychological assessment: A handbook of models and measures* (pp. 251–265). Washington, DC: American Psychological Association.

Schmidt, F. L. (2002). The role of general cognitive ability and job performance: Why there cannot be a debate. *Human Performance, 15*, 187–210.

Schmidt, F. L., & Hunter, J. E. (1992). Development of a causal model of processes determining job performance. *Current Directions in Psychological Science, 1*, 89–92.

Schmidt, F. L., & Hunter, J. E. (2004). General mental ability in the world of work: Occupational attainment and job performance. *Journal of Personality and Social Psychology, 86*, 162–173.

Schwartz, H. A., Eichstaedt, J. C., Kern, M. L., Dziurzynski, L., Ramones, S. M., Agrawal, M., ... & Ungar, L. H. (2013). Personality, gender, and age in the language of social media: The open-vocabulary approach. *PloS One, 8*(9), e73791.

Steel, P., Schmidt, J., Bosco, F., & Uggerslev, K. (2018). The effects of personality on job satisfaction and life satisfaction: A meta-analytic investigation accounting for bandwidth–fidelity and commensurability. *Human Relations*. doi.org/10.1177/0018726718771465

Sternberg, R. J., & Kaufman, J. C. (1998). Human abilities. *Annual Review of Psychology, 49*, 479–502.

Tasselli, S., Kilduff, M., & Landis, B. (2018). Personality change: Implications for organizational behavior. *Academy of Management Annals, 12*(2). doi.org/10.5465/annals.2016.0008

Tausczik, Y. R., & Pennebaker, J. W. (2010). The psychological meaning of words: LIWC and computerized text analysis methods. *Journal of Language and Social Psychology, 29*(1), 24–54.

Tett, R. P., & Burnett, D. D. (2003). A personality trait-based interactionist model of job performance. *Journal of Applied Psychology, 88*(3), 500.

Thoresen, C. J., Bradley, J. C., Bliese, P. D., & Thoresen, J. D. (2004). The big five personality traits and individual job performance growth trajectories in maintenance and transitional job stages. *Journal of Applied Psychology, 89*(5), 835.

Tupes, E. C., & Cristal, R. E. (1961). *Recurrent personality factors based on trait ratings (ASD-TR-61–97)*. Lackland Air Force Base, TX: Aeronautical Systems Division, Personnel Laboratory.

van der Linden, D., te Nijenhuis, J., & Bakker, A. B. (2010). The general factor of personality: A meta-analysis of Big Five intercorrelations and a criterion-related validity study. *Journal of Research in Personality, 44*(3), 315–327.

Van der Zee, K., & Wabeke, R. (2004). Is trait-emotional intelligence simply or more than just a trait? *European Journal of Personality, 18*(4), 243.

van Vianen, A. E., & de Dreu, C. K. (2001). Personality in teams: Its relationship to social cohesion, task cohesion, and team performance. *European Journal of Work and Organizational Psychology, 10*(2), 97–120.

Von Stumm, S., & Ackerman, P. L. (2013). Investment and intellect: A review and meta-analysis. *Psychological Bulletin, 139*(4), 841.

Watson, J. B., & Rayner, R. (1920). Conditioned emotional reactions. *Journal of Experimental Psychology, 3*, 1–14.

Wille, B., Beyers, W., & De Fruyt, F. (2012). A transactional approach to person–environment fit: Reciprocal relations between personality development and career role growth across young to middle adulthood. *Journal of Vocational Behavior, 81*(3), 307–321.

Woods, S. A. (2018). Instrumentation. In P. Brough (Ed.), *Advanced Research Methods for Applied Psychology* (pp. 58–72). London, England: Routledge.

Woods, S. A., & Anderson, N. R. (2016). Toward a periodic table of personality: Mapping personality scales between the five-factor model and the circumplex model. *Journal of Applied Psychology, 101*(4), 582.

Woods, S. A., & Hampson, S. E. (2005). Measuring the Big Five with single items using a bipolar response scale. *European Journal of Personality, 19*(5), 373–390.

Woods, S. A., & Hampson, S. E. (2010). Predicting adult occupational environments from gender and childhood personality traits. *Journal of Applied Psychology, 95*(6), 1045.

Woods, S. A., & Hardy, C. (2012). The higher-order factor structures of five personality inventories. *Personality and Individual Differences, 52*(4), 552–558.

Woods, S. A., Hinton, D. P., von Stumm, S., & Bellman-Jeffreys, J. (2017). Personality and intelligence: Examining the associations of investment-related personality traits with general and specific intelligence.

Woods, S. A., Lievens, F., De Fruyt, F., & Wille, B. (2013). Personality across working life: The longitudinal and reciprocal influences of personality on work. *Journal of Organizational Behavior, 34*, S7–S25.

Woods, S. A., Mustafa, M. J., Anderson, N., & Sayer, B. (2018). Innovative work behavior and personality traits: Examining the moderating effects of organizational tenure. *Journal of Managerial Psychology, 33*(1), 29–42.

Woods, S. A., Patterson, F. C., Wille, B., & Koczwara, A. (2016). Personality and occupational specialty: An examination of medical specialties using Holland's RIASEC model. *Career Development International, 21*(3), 262–278.

Woods, S. A., Wille, B., Wu, C. H., Lievens, F., & De Fruyt, F. (2019). The influence of work on personality trait development: The demands-affordances TrAnsactional (DATA) model, an integrative review, and research agenda. *Journal of Vocational Behavior, 110*, 258–271.

Wrzus, C., & Roberts, B. W. (2017). Processes of personality development in adulthood: The TESSERA framework. *Personality and Social Psychology Review, 21*(3), 253–277.

Youyou, W., Kosinski, M., & Stillwell, D. (2015). Computer-based personality judgments are more accurate than those made by humans. *Proceedings of the National Academy of Sciences, 112*(4), 1036–1040.

Ziegler, M., Danay, E., Heene, M., Asendorpf, J., & Bühner, M. (2012). Openness, fluid intelligence, and crystallized intelligence: Toward an integrative model. *Journal of Research in Personality, 46*(2), 173–183.

Zyphur, M. J., Chaturvedi, S., & Arvey, R. D. (2008). Job performance over time is a function of latent trajectories and previous performance. *Journal of Applied Psychology, 93*(1), 217.

CHAPTER 3
ATTITUDES AND BEHAVIOUR IN ORGANIZATIONS

> **LEARNING OBJECTIVES**
> - Understand how behaviour can be modified or controlled through conditioning and reinforcement at work.
> - Define attitudes and understand theories about how attitudes affect behaviour, including the causes and consequences of work-related attitudes, job satisfaction and organizational commitment.
> - Describe emotional influences on behaviour, and the concepts of self-regulation and conservation of resources.
> - Understand processes of individual perception and decision-making, including bounded rationality and intuition.
> - Understand and evaluate social influences on behaviour in groups and organizations.
> - Understand factors in diversity management and inclusion.

People's attitudes at work are the most tangible reflection of the extent to which their experiences in their workplaces are positive. They represent an outcome for the way that organizations and teams have been composed and managed. Attitudes such as job satisfaction and organizational commitment also have consequences for behaviour in organizations, affecting performance, motivation, collegiality and citizenship. As we will see in the course of this chapter, the antecedents of attitudes are complex and comprise both personal and contextual factors.

Building positive organizations is not only about creating rewarding environments for individuals, but also about creating positive social environments. The behaviour of people in groups is critical to achieving this, and it is the foundation of one of the grand management challenges of our age: developing inclusive teams where diversity is valued and the benefits of having diverse members are realized.

WHAT IS ORGANIZATIONAL BEHAVIOUR?

Organizational Behaviour (OB) acts as a background context for this chapter, which is focused principally on the behaviour of individuals at work. Robbins and Judge (2015) define OB as:

> *A field of study that investigates the impact that individuals, groups and structure have on behaviour within organizations, for the purpose of applying such knowledge toward improving an organization's effectiveness. [...] OB is the study of what people do in an organization and how their behaviour affects the organization's performance.* (Robbins & Judge, 2015, p. 10.)

You will see that the broad definition captures some of the aspects of our definition of work and organizational psychology. The field of OB acts as a meeting point for the application of theory from several areas of social science to business and organizations, including psychology, social psychology, sociology and anthropology. These collectively contribute to the study of the units of analysis in OB: individuals, groups and organizations. The multi-level nature of OB as an approach to understanding behaviour has been a consistent theme in the development of the field (e.g. Mowday & Sutton, 1993; Schneider, 1985).

In this chapter, we distil the field of OB to capture some of the most important topics of theory and research that are not covered in other chapters of this book. Our emphasis in the chapter is primarily on aspects of individual behaviour, and the causes and consequences of that behaviour. We also consider the group context of behaviour in this chapter, but not the organizational context, which is covered in depth in the third part of this book. This chapter sits alongside other chapters in the book on individual differences and motivation, and examines some of the other factors that affect behaviour at work. These comprise:

- management influences on behaviour
- attitudinal influences on behaviour
- wider behavioural influences of emotions, perceptions and decision-making
- social influences on behaviour.

MANAGEMENT INFLUENCES: SHAPING AND CONTROLLING BEHAVIOUR AT WORK

A basic approach to examining behaviour at work simply aims to understand how to control, shape and modify behaviour. Stop for a moment and think briefly about how you might propose to modify or influence the behaviour of people at work if you were a business owner or manager. Chances are that you would hit upon a strategy that involved some form of reward or encouragement for the behaviour you desired, and reprimand or punishment for behaviour that was undesirable. You will note that these basic ideas are the hallmarks of behaviourism, and the basic principles of that approach are still evident in behaviour modification theory.

Conditioning and reinforcement

Be honest. When you thought about shaping behaviour in an organization as you read the previous paragraph, was the role of money one of the first things that popped into your mind? Money has been considered to be a key reinforcer of behaviour since the earliest management theorists such as Frederick Taylor, and it continues to feature in research on behaviour modification (Stajkovic & Luthans, 2003). However, to understand the role of something like pay in behaviour, it needs to be contextualized against theories of behavioural conditioning and reinforcement.

Learning theories offer the clearest way to understand the role of conditioning and reinforcement. The first such theory was presented by Pavlov, in which classical conditioning was used to condition the salivation response of a dog. This was developed further by Skinner in theories of operant conditioning. Operant conditioning involves applying four kinds of reinforcement to modify and control behaviour: positive reinforcement, negative reinforcement, punishment and extinction. In behaviour modification, Skinner's theory may be applied in the following ways:

- Positive reinforcement can be applied to encourage desirable behaviour. Monetary reward could be a reinforcer, provided that it is designed to reinforce specific behaviour (Luthans & Stajkovic, 1999). Praise and social recognition are other examples of positive reinforcers used by managers with employees.
- Negative reinforcement involves the withdrawal of something unpleasant in response to desirable behaviour. Imagine that a manager checks up on the performance of an employee on a daily basis, until such time as the employee begins to improve. The discomfort of daily checks is avoided by improved performance, an example of negative reinforcement.
- Punishment involves giving or administering something unpleasant in response to undesirable behaviour. This could include verbal reprimand or withholding bonus payments, for example.
- Extinction is the discontinuation of reinforcement interventions in order to encourage discontinuation of the reinforced behaviour. This could involve the removal of reinforcement from particular behaviours or aspects of performance at work. They could be reallocated to new desirable behaviours so as to result in behavioural change.

Learning theories were developed further by Bandura (e.g. Bandura, 1977) who added the social aspect of learning. There are two additions that are particularly salient in the context of behavioural shaping and control:

1. The role of social modelling. The simple behaviourist paradigm suggests that people approach problem-solving as stimulus responders. The social learning perspective adds the notion that people have already accumulated knowledge of the likely efficacy of responses by observing the behaviour of others, along with the consequences.
2. The role of cognition. Social learning theory conceptualizes people as decision-makers, with decisions and behaviour resulting from perception of environmental stimuli, and the cognitions and emotional reactions that result from perceptions. Social cognitive personality theory (e.g. Cervone & Shoda, 1999) indicates how habitual or dispositional behaviour results from repeatedly responding to particular situations in the same way, almost rehearsing responses that become increasingly automatic, and eventually habitual. Such processes could apply to behaviours at work.

In the context of OB control, reinforcement is still centrally important in the social learning approach. According to this perspective, in order to encourage desirable behaviour, however it is learned, reinforcement should be applied. For example, a person might learn behaviour through observation of another employee at work. If they observe a colleague stealing from work, then the learning is counterproductive, and punishment might be used to prevent it. If they observe the colleague providing excellent customer support, and model that behaviour accordingly, positive reinforcement would increase the likelihood that the behaviour was repeated, and over time, performed more automatically.

Behavioural management incorporates the role of actions or interventions by management based on these principles. Stajkovic and Luthans (2003) summarize the concept of behavioural management:

> *The main premise of behaviour management is that employee behaviour is a function of contingent consequences. Simply, behaviours that positively affect performance must be contingently reinforced. Contingently administered money, feedback and social recognition are the most recognized reinforcers in behavioural management at work.* (Stajkovic & Luthans, 2003, p. 156.)

Contingent reinforcement means that reinforcers (i.e. money, feedback and social recognition) must be applied only if the desired performance behaviour is exhibited (Komaki, Coombs, & Schepman, 1996). Does it work? Evidence in the research literature appears to suggest that it does. Stajkovic and Luthans (2003) conducted a meta-analysis of studies examining the effect of behaviour management through reinforcement on job performance. They considered the individual and joint effects of the three main reinforcement strategies:

- Money. Money is probably the most basic reinforcer, and is one that is generally attractive to employees, but which is limited because it has no informational value. In other words, giving money to people does not provide information about behaviour or performance.
- Feedback. The purpose of feedback is to provide information on performance and behaviour to clarify performance expectations. Feedback could focus on either discrepancies between actual and required outcomes, processes by which performance is executed, or a combination of both.
- Social recognition. Recognition of effective behaviour or performance through public praise, awards or highlighting achievements in media such as newsletters, which are forms of recognitional reinforcement. Information about performance can be communicated through recognition, although not as clearly as in specific feedback. The risk of recognition as a sole reinforcer is that if it is not linked with a tangible outcome, it may be perceived as an empty reward (Bandura, 1986).

In their analyses, Stajkovic and Luthans (2003) found that performance was improved by all three reinforcement strategies, with money improving performance on average by 23 per cent, feedback by 17 per cent and social recognition by 10 per cent. The most powerful effects on performance were exhibited when a combination of all three was used, with performance improving by 45 per cent.

ATTITUDES AND BEHAVIOUR

Are you satisfied at work? What do you think about the managerial capability of your line supervisor? How do you feel about your organization and its mission? All of these represent attitudes at work, and they are important because they potentially have an impact on people's behaviour and performance at work. In this section, we will consider the antecedents, processes and consequences of attitudes at work. We will also consider arguably the most important question in the history of people management (more on that shortly).

What is an attitude?

Attitudes represent evaluative statements or beliefs about something or someone. They are always directed towards a target (person, object or event) and represent the degree to which that target is perceived positively or negatively. For example, Eagly and Chaiken (1993) define an attitude as *"a psychological tendency that is expressed by evaluating a particular entity with some degree of favor or disfavor"* (p. 1). The clearest way to understand attitudes in more detail is to consider three different components (Breckler, 1984). These are cognitive, affective and behavioural:

- Cognitive component. The cognitive part of the attitude represents the thought or belief about the target. For example, in the attitude 'my office space is too small', the statement itself represents the cognitive part of the attitude.
- Affective component. The affective part of the attitude represents the emotions associated with the attitude. Perhaps the person is frustrated, angry or disappointed that their workspace is too small.
- Behavioural component. The behavioural component represents the behavioural intentions or consequences that result from the attitude. In this case, maybe the individual would request a different workspace, create more space if possible, or complain to their line manager.

What make attitudes particularly important in organizations is the behavioural part, and the extent to which positive attitudes result in positive behaviours, and negative attitudes in unhelpful behaviour.

Linking attitudes and behaviour

Attitudes do not always lead to behaviour at work, and the circumstances that facilitate the translation of attitude to behaviour are obviously of interest to people working in organizations. Some research has attempted to outline the factors that enhance the prediction of behaviour from attitudes (e.g. Glasman and Albarracin reported in 2006 that stable attitudes that were easy to recall tended to predict behaviour most effectively), but such studies are quite abstract. Two well-established, relevant theories provide more clarity about the links between attitudes and behaviour: cognitive dissonance theory and the theory of planned behaviour.

Cognitive dissonance theory

Have you ever been asked to do something that went against your attitudes or values? Perhaps your job required you to say something that you inwardly disagreed with? How did that, or how would that, make you feel? Quite likely uncomfortable, and it is that inner psychological discomfort that is important in Festinger's (1957) cognitive dissonance theory. A key aspect of the theory is the consistency between attitudes and behaviour. When attitude and behaviour are dissonant or inconsistent, the discomfort associated with that dissonance motivates people to act to reduce it (Elliot & Devine, 1994; Harmon-Jones & Mills, 1999).

Harmon-Jones and Elliot review the major perspectives on dissonance research and comment that although there are alternative perspectives on understanding dissonance (e.g. Bem, 1967), many of the assertions of dissonance theory stand up reasonably well in experimental settings. There are two main implications for understanding the attitudes–behaviour link:

1 Under situations where people are free to behave as they wish, behaviour is likely to be consistent with attitudes in order that dissonance be avoided. The greater the importance that a person places on the attitude, the more likely they are to behave in accordance with it (Robbins & Judge, 2015). In organizations though, choices and behaviour are rarely 'free' from constraints, and so social pressures, obligation or incentive might lead people to behave in ways not reflected in their attitudes.

2 The relationship between attitudes and behaviour may be more complex than anticipated. Typically the assumption is that behaviour follows from attitudes. However, the opposite can also be true. Assume that a manager has to tell their team that because of cuts this year, there will be no pay rise for them, and that this is fair and justifiable. The manager may feel inwardly that this is unfair, but has no choice in the matter (i.e. I believe that it is unfair not to give a pay rise, but I told my team that it was fair and justifiable). Once they have communicated this to their team, the behaviour cannot be undone. So whatever the strategy for reducing the dissonance, changing behaviour is not viable. Experimental evidence suggests that the manager in this case would either modify their attitude slightly so that they felt that withholding pay rises was somewhat justifiable, or would attempt to find a reason, excuse or justification for their action. The more important the justification, the less likely they would be to change their view. So, if the manager had accepted the promise of a promotion themselves in return for breaking the news to their team, they might reason 'I know that I don't believe what I told the team, but I did it for the money, or reward'. If there was no incentive, they might reason 'I know that I thought it was unfair to withhold the pay rise, but it is for the good of the company in the long run'. Both represent the alteration of attitudes as a consequence of behaviour.

The theories of reasoned action and planned behaviour

A more clearly defined theory of the pathway from attitudes to behaviour is the theory of planned behaviour (Ajzen, 1988, 1991), which builds on the earlier theory of reasoned action (Ajzen & Fishbein, 1980, 2005). The theory describes some of the antecedents of attitude formation, and the factors that determine whether behavioural intentions are formed and expressed in actual behaviour. The theory is represented diagrammatically in Figure 3.1.

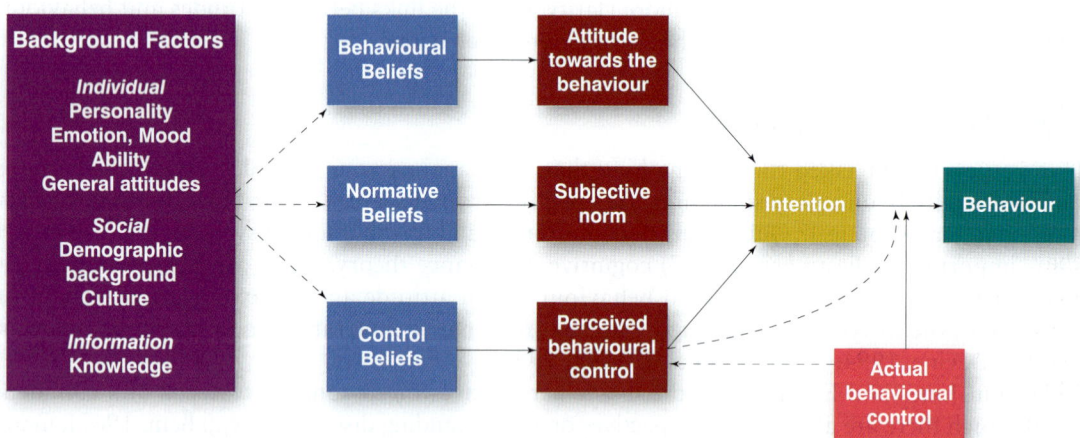

Figure 3.1   The theory of planned behaviour

There are a number of key implications of the model:
- Attitudes and beliefs are formed based on a variety of individual, external and contextual variables. Personality, education, life experience and other factors contribute to the formation of beliefs, and even if those beliefs are irrational or unreasonable, they nevertheless act as foundations for action or behaviour.

- The key aspect of the model relating to attitudes is around behavioural beliefs, which lead to attitudes about behaviour. This is a subtle point and relates to the observation that attitudes predict behaviour only when they are considered in similar ways and levels of specificity (Ajzen & Fishbein, 1977). For example, the general attitude 'I like my job' is unlikely to predict whether someone will stay late at work to finish an assignment. The attitude is general and the behaviour specific. However, the attitude 'I think it is reasonable to stay late to finish work if required' is likely to be a good predictor of the same behaviour. The attitude is specific and directed towards the behavioural act.

- Alongside behavioural beliefs, the model also includes beliefs about social norms and perceptions of control. Perceptions of social norms comprise judgements about what is socially acceptable in respect of behaviour. So for example, a person may feel that staying late is an unreasonable request, but this could be mitigated if all of their colleagues stay late regularly. Perceptions of behavioural control concern the extent to which people feel able to perform actions or behaviours. An individual may feel it both reasonable and usual to stay late at work, yet be unable to do so because they need to leave early to meet another commitment. The behaviour is out of their hands in this case.

- The key step in the model is the formation of behavioural intention. According to the model, all demonstrated behaviour flows from behavioural intention. Attitudes, subjective perceptions of social norms and perceptions of behavioural control all contribute to the formation of behavioural intentions. The pathway from intention to actual behaviour is then moderated by actual behavioural control.

The theory is elegant and provides a very flexible framework for considering the pathways from attitudes to behaviours. The value of the theory is, however, of course dependent upon the extent of empirical support. The theory of planned behaviour has given rise to a multitude of empirical studies, and some of these were included in a meta-analysis conducted by Armitage and Conner (2001). Their study showed that the theory was a good predictor of the formation of behavioural intentions and a reasonably good predictor of actual behaviour.

In applied psychology, the theory has been used to examine topics such as health-related behaviour, as well as purchasing behaviour in marketing research. Surprisingly, the theory has been applied less often in organizational research, although it is clearly relevant, and can help managers and practitioners to understand why attitudes do and do not manifest themselves in behaviour. In the case of organizational change, for example, the theory could be a useful way to understand how behavioural change might be promoted. According to the model in Figure 3.1, managers would need to consider individual attitudes to the new behaviour, social normative pressure from groups and teams in the organization, and the extent to which work was designed so that employees felt a sense of control in performing the new behaviour.

One area where the theory has been applied extensively in research is the context of safety and health. Traditionally, behavioural safety and health has been seen as an issue of putting in place sufficient controls, and a general culture and climate for safety. However, this neglects to address differences in individual behaviour: why do some people continue to behave unsafely despite the best efforts of organizations? The theory of planned behaviour has an obvious role to play in framing possible answers to this question. In particular, the theory is comprehensive in this respect because it enables the integration of individual factors with organizational cultural and control factors. Modelling unsafe behaviour using the theory would incorporate the formation of intentions to behave unsafely, derived from attitudes about how positive the behaviour is, how socially acceptable it is considered to be, and perceptions about how easy the behaviour is to perform.

Individual attitudes towards safety and risk are therefore potential antecedents of unsafe behaviour, and targets for safety training designed for attitudinal change. There are examples of applying the theory of planned behaviour to safety behaviour in the literature (e.g. Fugas, Silva, & Meliá, 2012), and specific studies have demonstrated the value of the theory for explaining, for example, road violations (Castanier, Deroche, & Woodman, 2013), online safety (Burns & Roberts, 2013) and medication safety in healthcare settings (Lapkin, Levett-Jones, & Gilligan, 2015).

Despite the obvious utility of the theory, and good empirical support, there are some criticisms. For example, a much-disputed aspect of the model concerns perceptions of behavioural control. Ajzen (2002) attempted to clarify what 'control' actually means. He included perceptions of self-efficacy (the extent to which a person feels capable of performing an action) and locus of control (the extent to which a person believes behaviour to be attributable to internal or external constraints). However, even the most recent research remains pessimistic about the clarity of the role of control (e.g. Kaiser, Schultze, & Guericke, 2009). Another criticism is around the amount of variance in actual behaviour that is left unexplained by the theory. Despite its complexity, the meta-analysis of Armitage and Conner (2001) reported that 80 per cent of the variance in people's behaviour was unexplained by factors in the theory.

WORK-RELATED ATTITUDES

The theories reviewed in this section could be applied to attitudes in any domain of life. Two important *work-related* attitudes are job satisfaction and organizational commitment, and they have been the subject of extensive research in work and organizational psychology (Judge, Weiss, Kammeyer-Mueller, & Hulin, 2017), particularly in relation to a critical management question: Are happy and satisfied workers also productive workers? We will find out what the research says shortly. First though, we examine what job satisfaction and organizational commitment actually represent.

Job satisfaction

Job satisfaction refers to a person's general feelings about their job (Weiss, 2002), and more specifically the extent to which they feel positive or negative about it. Satisfaction can be considered in different ways. It may be thought of as a general attitude, reflecting overall feelings about work. It may also be considered as a composite of more specific attitudes, including short job satisfaction measures. The items all refer to satisfaction with a specific aspect of work (for example, pay, supervision, workload). Each item asks the individual to respond by indicating how satisfied they feel with those aspects of their job. Job satisfaction is taken as the aggregate of those judgements.

Job satisfaction is a subjective judgement. In relation to pay for example, people are not asked to comment on their satisfaction with pay relative to others doing similar jobs, only to say whether or not they are satisfied. Of course, most people's satisfaction with pay is influenced to some degree by social comparison or perceptions of fairness (e.g. McFarlin & Sweeney, 1992). The causes of job satisfaction are varied and complex, but may be simplified by considering the major underlying approaches used to study them (Judge et al., 2017).

A first set of antecedents comprise judgements about the relative benefits of work compared to the 'costs' the worker incurs. Ultimately this is a psychological calculation of whether the job provides the benefits that the worker expects. Benefits could be extrinsic or intrinsic to the job. For example, extrinsic benefits include the pay and rewards provision of the job, whereas intrinsic rewards represent the content of the job (is it interesting and fulfilling?). Overall satisfaction is derived from a balance of the perception of these features. For example, people's satisfaction with pay might be offset with satisfaction with other aspects of work. A person might reason that their pay is low, but that there are other benefits associated with their job that mitigate the lower salary (perhaps the organization has a brilliant childcare support system, or great flexible working policies, for example).

A second perspective on antecedents is to consider the ways that individual differences contribute. Some people are more inclined than others to appraise aspects of their jobs positively or negatively, and this is reflected in the associations of job satisfaction with personality traits (Judge, Heller, & Mount, 2002). The important factor is 'affect' or the general disposition for feeling positive or negative about things (Judge & Hulin, 1993). Warr (2011) describes these influences as representing the psychological make-up of a person that promotes the experience of happiness at work.

Evidence of long-term differences between people in job satisfaction represents a dispositional approach to understanding work attitudes. However, a drawback is, of course, that within-person variability is neglected; people's satisfaction may vary from week to week or day to day, and this could be highly informative for understanding the impact of attitudes on performance and behaviour.

To address this issue, more contemporary models of job satisfaction also consider the effect of affective states: moods and emotions triggered by work events (Thoresen, Kaplan, Barsky, Warren, & de Chermont, 2003). These studies show that people's attitudes towards their organization vary over time (Dalal, Lam, Weiss, Welch, & Hulin, 2009) and that satisfaction varies according to mood change in the short term (Miner et al., 2005).

Taken together, this suggests a model of job satisfaction as shown in Figure 3.2 in which job satisfaction is formed from three sources: 1) job factors: personality and dipositions 2) job characteristics 3) perceptions of distributive justice.

Figure 3.2 The three factors that contribute to job satisfaction

Organizational commitment

Organizational commitment is concerned with the extent to which an individual feels they have a positive relationship with their organization, or conversely, are locked into a relationship with their organization (Mowday, Porter, & Steers, 1982). The concept has evolved over time, and the most effective model is that of Meyer and Allen (1991), who differentiate three forms of organizational commitment:

- Affective commitment. The emotional attachment that a person feels towards their organization is referred to as affective commitment. People feel attached to their organization when the goals and values of the organization are largely consistent with their own, and when they 'buy in' to the mission and philosophy of the organization.
- Continuance commitment. When an individual remains in an organization simply because the costs of leaving are too great, they would be described as having high continuance commitment. This form of commitment is obviously less desirable to foster among employees.
- Normative commitment. Sometimes an individual may feel dissatisfied with their job, or may think that their organization is moving in the wrong direction, yet still feel obliged to be loyal and committed, and to stay with the organization. Meyer and Allen (1991) describe this sense of moral obligation as normative commitment.

One implication of the three-component model of commitment is that each form of commitment has different antecedents. These relationships are shown diagrammatically in Figure 3.3. For example, affective commitment is likely to result from a combination of work experiences and perceptions of the organization, alongside personal characteristics such as personality traits. The link between personality and commitment has been established empirically (Erdheim, Wang, & Zickar, 2006), and so it seems that in a similar way to job satisfaction, some people are more predisposed than others to develop a commitment to their organization.

Figure 3.3 Antecedents and the effects of organizational commitment

Continuance commitment is more likely to reflect perceptions of the viability of alternatives to employment with the organization. It could be argued that personal characteristics may also play a part in this form of commitment, because people who are more driven and ambitious are more likely to examine alternative forms of employment. Normative commitment is fostered by socialization or social experiences. These might be cultural, familial and organizational (Meyer & Allen, 1991). The sense of moral obligation developed as a result of socialization interacts with perceptions of investments made by the organization. If an individual perceives that an organization has made significant investment in them, and feels obliged to reciprocate, then normative commitment is likely to be high. These processes lead to a general conclusion that commitment takes some time to develop compared to satisfaction; people might be satisfied with work early in their tenure, whereas commitment may follow later on (Judge et al., 2017).

Consequences of satisfaction and commitment

The extent to which attitudes at work are important rests heavily on their implications for behaviour in organizations. Do job satisfaction and organizational commitment have consequences for behaviour at work? The outcomes of these work-related attitudes have been considered in terms of job performance and withdrawal or counterproductive behaviours such as absence or turnover.

Job performance The relationship between job performance and job satisfaction has preoccupied managers and work psychologists for more than 70 years, since the publication of the Hawthorne Studies in the 1930s. Ruch, Hershauer, and Wright (1976) describe the issue as the productivity puzzle, describing the 'paradoxical notion that although some happy workers are productive, there are also many happy workers who are unproductive' (p. 5). However, when one thinks in more depth about the simple idea that happy employees are productive employees, the lack of a consistent relationship is less surprising. We have already seen that the pathway from attitude to behaviour is a complex one.

However, practitioner interest in the question means that there are plenty of research studies addressing it, and subsequently, several meta-analyses since 2001 have begun to build our understanding. The first step is to understand the various forms that the relationship between job satisfaction and job performance may take. The assumption that people will perform better *because* they are happier at work is not necessarily true, and Judge, Thoresen, Bono, and Patton (2001) review seven potential models:

1 Job satisfaction causes job performance. This model represents the typical implicit perspective on satisfaction and performance.
2 Job performance causes job satisfaction. Attaining high levels of performance at work is likely to result in extrinsic and intrinsic rewards, thereby fostering positive job attitudes.
3 Satisfaction and performance cause each other. A combination of effects from the first and second models gives rise to a reciprocal relationship.
4 It is possible that there is no direct link between satisfaction and performance, with any observed correlation reflecting overlap with an unmeasured variable.
5 There may be no relationship between satisfaction and performance at all.
6 The relationship between performance and satisfaction may be moderated by another variable. If an individual is satisfied in their job, but lacks some of the skills required to perform it, he or she is unlikely to be productive. Job knowledge, skills, abilities and characteristics may moderate the relationship between satisfaction and performance.
7 Both satisfaction and performance could be reconceptualized to provide a better understanding of the relationship. For example, job attitudes such as satisfaction and commitment might actually reflect affectivity (the predisposition for either positive or negative emotional states), which, in turn, may be related to some, but not all aspects of job performance.

Judge et al. (2001) tested the relationship between job satisfaction and job performance and tested a number of moderator variables. Based on 312 studies, assessing more than 54,000 participants, they found a moderate overall relationship between job satisfaction and job performance (meta-analytic correlation = 0.30). It seems that satisfied workers do tend to be higher-performing workers. Longitudinal studies (where satisfaction was measured at time one and performance at time two) reported weaker associations than cross-sectional studies (r = 0.23 and 0.31, respectively). There is some support for the notion that satisfaction leads to higher job performance. However, Harrison, Newman, and Roth (2006) reported similar associations between satisfaction and performance regardless of which was assessed first, providing support for the idea that performance leads to satisfaction.

Job commitment was similarly examined by Riketta (2002). The meta-analyses of 111 studies (N = 26,344) revealed a weaker relationship with performance than was observed for satisfaction (meta-analytic correlation = 0.20). Meyer, Stanley, Herscovitch, and Topolnytsky (2002) also examined commitment and performance and reported strongest associations of commitment with so-called organizational citizenship behaviour (OCB). OCB represents aspects of performance that facilitate performance of core job tasks (such as cooperation with others, representing the organization positively and self-development).

Job satisfaction and organizational commitment tend to be associated with one another and this has led some investigators to combine the constructs to give an overall job attitudes variable. Harrison et al. (2006) examined the association of these combined job attitudes with a very broad measure of job performance. Remarkably, the association between job performance and job attitudes in their study was 0.59, almost double the size of the correlation reported by Judge et al. (2001). Collectively there is enough evidence to say that employees with more positive attitudes do tend to perform better at work.

Withdrawal or counterproductive behaviour In addition to job performance, some researchers have examined the associations of commitment and satisfaction with withdrawal or counterproductive behaviour, including absence, lateness and turnover (leaving or intending to leave the organization). As would be expected, lower levels of job satisfaction and organizational commitment tend to be associated with higher levels of absence, higher frequency of lateness and stronger intentions to leave the organization (Harrison et al., 2006; Tett & Meyer, 1993; Woods, Poole, & Zibarras, 2012). Studies tracking within-person change in attitudes show that there is a deterioration trend preceding turnover from an organization (e.g. Bentein, Vandenberghe, Vandenberg, & Stinglhamber, 2005; Kammeyer-Mueller, Wanberg, Glomb, & Ahlburg, 2005). It seems therefore that it is prolonged negative attitudes and a downward spiral of feelings towards an organization that prompt people to leave.

Organizational consequences The studies reviewed so far relate to individual aspects of performance or behaviour, but what about outcomes for organizations? Do organizations with greater numbers of satisfied staff tend to perform better? This was the question that interested Harter, Schmidt, and Hayes (2002). They examined associations between satisfaction and business unit performance, and found that units in which the members were more satisfied tended to attract higher levels of customer satisfaction, generate high profit, be more productive and experience lower turnover rates and fewer accidents. There seem to be tangible business benefits of positive attitudes at work.

Attitudes of groups and teams

Developments in the study of attitudes at work have examined the impact of attitudes held at a collective level in teams and organizations. Organizational leaders implement a variety of strategies to enhance performance or effect change at a whole-company level. To be successful, these strategies must produce results through changes in the behaviour and effectiveness of individual members. Attitudes are a mechanism that helps to promote such change and are therefore enablers of performance at an organizational level.

There are notable examples in the literature. Attitudes at the level of the work unit or team are found to explain the impact of service climate on customer satisfaction (Hong, Liao, Hu, & Jiang, 2013). A similar relationship is observed between the use of high-performance work systems and financial performance (e.g. Sung & Choi, 2014). Job satisfaction may also have a longer-term impact on organizational outcomes. Zablah, Carlson, Donavan, Maxham, and Brown (2016) found that job satisfaction of front-line employees predicted customer satisfaction with the company a year later. These studies have a compelling implication that creating organizations in which people feel more positive and committed is an effective way to create *better-performing* organizations.

DISCUSS WITH A COLLEAGUE

Research evidence suggests that people who are more satisfied, committed and engaged at work tend to perform better at work. Discuss your own attitudes towards work and organizations and then, based on your discussions, come up with ten ways that organizations could try to make work more positive to improve satisfaction and commitment of employees.

KEY THEME

Work and organizational psychology in the digital economy

The huge volume of literature that has accumulated on the impact and effects of positive work attitudes is founded on the conventional and well-established methods of social science (e.g. survey methodology). This is also the main approach taken by practitioners in organizations to measuring work attitudes. Advances in technology, however, mean that the prospect of collecting data in different and innovative ways could significantly advance how we understand these attitudes and related psychological states (Judge et al., 2017).

The discipline of organizational cognitive neuroscience represents the study of OB through the lens of neuroscientific methods such as examination of brain activity (Senior, Lee, & Butler, 2011). Research in this paradigm, for example, might examine the brain activity associated with positive feelings at work, or reward, both intrinsic and extrinsic. This would provide an indication of the presence of such experiences in the workplace.

This might seem reductionist in that neurological activity alone is not an indicator of what the experience is targeted at. However, as Hodgkinson and Healey (2014) point out, organizational studies and organization cognitive neuroscience are not irreconcilable. The study

continued

of micro neurological activity could shed light on how individual experiences sum to produce macro-level phenomena and outcomes. They are part of the building blocks of, rather than replacement for, the objects of study in organizational research.

Combined with new technology, these advances will become part of how work attitudes, and other criteria at work, are studied. There are already examples in research, for example the impact of work rumination on health has been studied through the use of wearable devices that monitor physiological responses constantly (see Cropley et al., 2017). Similar techniques could be used in the future to capture relevant data on workers' experiences and the effects they have for both people and organizations.

Attitude change: Persuasion and influence

Much communication in organizations aims to be persuasive, and that often means changing people's attitudes. There is a huge literature on persuasion and attitude change in social psychology, and if these issues really interest you, then it would be worth taking a browse through some social psychology texts. The main questions of interest to people in organizations, however, are to do with the factors that contribute to attitudinal change, and some of these are discussed below:

- Major contributions to understanding the process of attitude change are captured in process models. Crano and Prislin (2006) highlight two important models, the Elaboration Likelihood Model (ELM) and the Heuristic/Systematic Model (HSM), both of which have similar implications for understanding the process of attitude change. The models are based around the idea that there are two general mechanisms by which attitudes are changed. The first involves individuals evaluating arguments carefully, weighing up the content of arguments, the logic, reasoning and evidence behind the arguments and then deciding whether they are persuasive. The systematic elaboration of new information and the reasoned use of that information has been called the central route to persuasion (Petty & Cacioppo, 1986). Such approaches work best when the target audience is motivated to listen and understand, and when they have the ability to comprehend the evidence. When people are unmotivated or unable to think rationally about the arguments, they revert to heuristic-based processing, perhaps attending to the source of the information, their perceived credibility, or even their attractiveness (i.e. a person might reason that 'I like my manager and they are always right, so their argument must be correct'). This has been referred to as the peripheral route to persuasion (Petty & Cacioppo, 1986). Attitudes that are changed through the central route are typically longer lasting and stronger than those changed through the peripheral route.

- Attitude strength is an important factor in attitude change and it seems reasonable to assume that stronger attitudes are likely to be more resistant to persuasion. However, the influence of attitude strength on persuasion is more complex than this, and in part it reflects internal cognitions (thought processes) about the impact of the persuasion. When people feel that the persuasive attempt has failed outright, the outcome is to strengthen still further the original attitude (Tormala & Petty, 2004). People are likely to reason that their attitude must surely be right to have resisted the attack of a strong message from a credible source. If the resistance to the persuasion is perceived as difficult or effortful (perhaps a person can only develop weak arguments to counter the persuasion), the original attitude is likely to remain intact, but be weakened (Petty, Tormala, & Rucker, 2004).

- Fear has always been a strategy for attitude change in the arsenal of politicians, but its effectiveness does depend on the extent to which people feel vulnerable to threat being communicated. Fear is likely to operate through the peripheral route to persuasion, although some sources report that appeals to fear might actually stimulate people to evaluate arguments more carefully, thereby promoting central processing (Das, De Wit, & Stroebe, 2003). In organizations, fear can be used subtly in organizational change, by communicating the potential adverse consequences for the organization of failure to adapt to new situations. However, the use of threat to personal security (e.g. job security) could be disastrous as an attitude change strategy, and is certainly ethically questionable and likely to generate high levels of employee stress over time.

EMOTIONAL INFLUENCES ON BEHAVIOUR AT WORK

Emotions are a source of influence on people's behaviour at work (Brief & Weiss, 2002), and these effects are not simply reserved for the extremes of emotional experiences. Rather, emotions have a continuous effect on what people do in organizations. Studies have helped to clarify the nature of emotions, differentiating a variety of terms, described in Box 3.1. Key distinctions are between moods, emotions and trait affect. Moods represent general positive or negative feelings. Emotions are discrete constructs (e.g. anger, joy, hate, jealousy, love) usually directed towards a specific target or cause. Trait affectivity represents the intersection between personality dispositions and emotions. Positive and negative affect are respectively tendencies to experience positive and negative feelings, moods and emotions. Positive affect is related to Extraversion, and negative affect to Neuroticism (Rusting & Larsen, 1998).

Trait affectivity has been shown to relate to job performance, with positive affect predicting higher levels of performance (Cropanzano & Wright, 2001). This finding has been interpreted alongside the happy-productive worker hypothesis, and the evidence of dispositional causes of job satisfaction (Judge et al., 2002). A related line of research has examined the effects of affect and mood on decision-making. Positive affect seems to be associated with more effective decisions, possibly because it allows people to focus more clearly on the requirements of the situation at hand (Barsade & Gibson, 2007).

Affect is also linked with counterproductive and prosocial behaviours. Negative affectivity is associated with increased absence, intention to turnover and actual turnover from the organization (Thoresen et al., 2003). Prosocial behaviours seem to be more dependent on an individual's current mood and the situation (Barsade & Gibson, 2007). One other important organizational consequence of affect is creativity and creative problem-solving. Both have been shown to be associated with positive mood (Brief & Weiss, 2002), with clear implications for fostering positive working environments as an intervention for enhancing creativity and innovation at work.

A common question is whether we are in control of our emotions, and to what extent we can regulate them. Rafaeli and Sutton (1989) distinguish between felt and displayed emotions. The emotions that people display in their facial expressions and tone of voice can be different from the emotions they experience internally, and so people are able to regulate the emotions they display to others. At work, such regulation is referred to as emotional labour (Hochschild, 1983), which comprises the demonstration of emotions that are consistent with job requirements or normative rules for emotional display (e.g. positive, enthusiastic behaviour demonstrated by salespeople). Although there is potential for the masking of emotions to cause strain on the individual, the balance of evidence suggests that there are not consistent effects of emotional labour on well-being, particularly if the employee perceives the presentation of particular emotions as a part of their job role (Barsade & Gibson, 2007).

> **BOX 3.1**
> **Terms associated with affect and emotion**
>
> - Affect: Umbrella term encompassing a broad range of feelings that individuals experience, including feelings, discrete emotions and traits.
> - Discrete emotions: Emotions are focused on a specific target or cause – generally realized by the perceiver of the emotion; relatively intense and short lived (e.g. love, anger, hate, fear, jealousy, happiness, sadness, grief, rage, aggravation, ecstasy, affection, joy, envy, fright). Can sometimes transform into a mood.
> - Moods: Generally take the form of a global positive (pleasant) or negative (unpleasant) feeling – tend to be diffuse, not focused on a specific cause. May last for a few moments to a few weeks or more.
> - Dispositional affect: Overall personality tendency to respond to situations in predictable ways. Positive affectivity relates to the tendency to experience positive moods, whereas negative affectivity relates to the tendency to experience negative moods.
> - Emotion regulation: Individual's attempts to influence the emotions they have, when they have them, and how they experience and express these emotions.
> - Emotional labour: The suppression or induction of feelings in order to fulfil a particular job requirement (e.g. appearing outwardly enthusiastic and cheerful in customer-facing roles).

Affect is also linked with counterproductive and prosocial behaviours. Negative affectivity is associated with increased absence, intention to turnover and actual turnover from the organization (Thoresen et al., 2003). Prosocial behaviours seem to be more dependent on an individual's current mood and the situation (Barsade & Gibson, 2007). One other important organizational consequence of affect is creativity and creative problem-solving. Both have been shown to be associated with positive mood (Brief & Weiss, 2002), with clear implications for fostering positive working environments as an intervention for enhancing creativity and innovation at work.

A common question is whether we are in control of our emotions, and to what extent we can regulate them. Rafaeli and Sutton (1989) distinguish between felt and displayed emotions. The emotions that people display in their facial expressions and tone of voice can be different from the emotions they experience internally, and so people are able to regulate the emotions they display to others. At work, such regulation is referred to as emotional labour (Hochschild, 1983), which comprises the demonstration of emotions that are consistent with job requirements or normative rules for emotional display (e.g. positive, enthusiastic behaviour demonstrated by salespeople). Although there is potential for the masking of emotions to cause strain on the individual, the balance of evidence suggests that there are not consistent effects of emotional labour on well-being, particularly if the employee perceives the presentation of particular emotions as a part of their job role (Barsade & Gibson, 2007).

The challenge of explaining the ways in which emotional reactions to work events translate through to behaviour and attitudes is addressed by Affective Events Theory (AET; Weiss & Cropanzano, 1996; Ashkanasy & Daus, 2002) and it is shown as a model in Figure 3.4.

The pathways highlighted in the model describe the following relationships between events and behaviour:

- The work environment acts as a context for all work-related events and the characteristics of jobs and organizations determine the extent to which a person is likely to encounter events that are emotionally demanding. Job demands and the requirement for emotional labour are included in the model. Recall that emotional labour is any form of work that requires an individual to outwardly project emotions that may not really be experienced (e.g. a customer service worker who is asked to consistently project a happy exterior).

- Within the work environment, moods and emotions are affected by daily hassles and daily uplifts. You probably have a wealth of experiences that you can identify with that make you feel good or bad at work. Daily hassles serve to annoy or upset people, and their moods and emotions are influenced accordingly. Daily uplifts such as success, praise or other rewarding events improve mood and promote positive emotions.

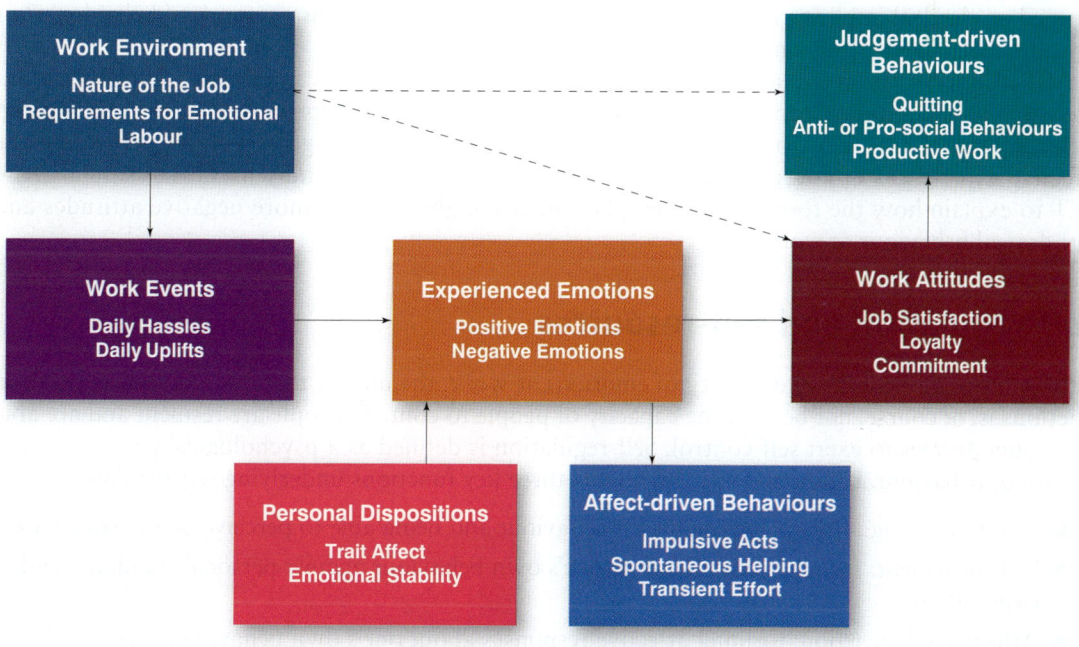

Figure 3.4 Affective Events Theory

- The crux of the model is the link between events and emotions. The theory suggests that daily work events elicit emotional reactions, either positive or negative. The intensity of those emotional reactions is regulated by personal characteristics. These include trait affect, and personality traits such as Emotional Stability and Extraversion.

- The first set of outcome behaviours lead straight from emotional reactions and are therefore described as affect-driven behaviours. These include impulsive or spontaneous acts, and the nature of the behaviour will depend on the experienced emotion. An example of a negative affect-driven behaviour might be losing your temper or saying something that you later regret.

- The second outcome of emotional reactions is related to attitudes. Emotion and mood can positively or negatively influence attitudes like job satisfaction, organizational commitment and loyalty, and we have already considered some of the outcomes that might follow as a consequence.

- In the AET model, attitudes lead to judgement-driven behaviours, which are behaviours that result from changes in work attitudes. These will include performance-related behaviours, and withdrawal behaviour such as absence and turnover.
- Dashed arrows in the model serve to recognize that not all of the effects of work environments on attitudes and behaviour act through emotional experiences, and rather job demands and characteristics have direct influences on attitudes and performance.

The AET model is a very neat framework for understanding how emotional reactions regulate the effects of events on attitudes and behaviour. How does it stand up to empirical tests? One recent meta-analytic study used the model to examine how breaches in the 'psychological contract' (i.e. the unwritten set of expectations that a person has about their relationship with their employer, and what they expect to give and receive at work) were related to outcomes such as trust, job satisfaction and effectiveness (Zhao, Wayne, Glibkowski, & Bravo, 2007). The findings of the study were consistent with AET. Affective or emotional reactions were an important mediator of the relationship between psychological contract breach and work outcomes. When people perceive that their employer has reneged on the deal implicit in their psychological contract, their response in terms of behavioural or attitudinal change depends on how they respond emotionally.

AET also serves as an explanatory purpose for framing how people's experience of work play out over time. For example, Cropanzano, Dasborough, and Weiss (2017) propose that the relationship between leaders and their followers (termed leader–member exchange) develops as through the affective experiences of interpersonal exchanges. Ashkanasy, Ayoko, and Jehn (2014) similarly use AET to explain how the features of open plan offices might result in more negative attitudes and withdrawal behaviour at work.

Self-regulation and self-resources

Although people experience a variety of emotions at work, the impact they have on behaviour and reactions is, of course, not beyond the capacity of people to control. People are resilient and are able to varying degrees to exert self-control. Self-regulation is defined as a psychological process of self-control of behaviour. Bandura (1991) highlights three key functions underlying self-regulation:

- Self-monitoring: monitoring one's own behaviour and being able to perceive one's own actions.
- Self-judgement: forming judgements of one's own behaviour against personal standards and expectations.
- Affective self-reaction: forming affective responses about one's own behaviour, such that it is evaluated positively or negatively.

Self-regulation is therefore about actively monitoring and managing our behaviour against certain internalized standards. It does not involve external influences on behaviour, and rather represents self-imposed interventions and controls. Interestingly, Muraven and Baumeister (2000) propose that such self-control is like a muscle, and argue that self-regulation is a limited resource, use of which depletes energy or resource available for subsequent use. They also argue that like a muscle, self-control can be rested or strengthened through exercising it. Bandura (1991) also highlights the role of self-efficacy, relating to self-belief about ability to control behaviour.

In the organizational field, self-regulation has featured in goal-setting theory. In these perspectives, self-regulation is applied to the processes of goal establishment, planning, striving to achieve goals and revision of engagement to goals (Vancouver & Day, 2005). Goals that are subject to self-regulation are necessarily internalized, and become desired states to be attained through behaviour. The self-regulatory processes here serve to monitor progress and influence behaviour and effort as a consequence.

Kanfer (2005) highlights potential applications around promoting commitment to difficult goals at work, and to providing people with competencies for perceiving and overcoming obstacles encountered in goal-directed behaviour, therefore promoting goal attainment. Recent studies have found that helping team leaders develop self-regulatory competencies improves team performance. Yeow and Martin (2013) reported this effect in a longitudinal field experiment in a business simulation context. Similarly, in learning and development, Sitzmann and Johnson (2012) found that interventions designed to promote people planning their learning and development were only effective when combined with interventions to promote self-regulatory processes.

In the context of emotion and well-being at work, self-regulation is combined with perspectives on self-resources, which are the internal psychological resources that each of us has for dealing with situations at work (whether they are problem focused such as skills, or emotion focused such as resilience). The conservation of resources model (Hobfoll, 1989) proposes that people's action is directed towards the acquisition and preservation of resources (which might include, for example, externally-derived resources like money or seniority of position, or internal resources such as skills, but also positive emotions such as self-efficacy and optimism; Hobfoll, Halbesleben, Neveu, & Westman, 2018). Self-regulation in part determines how people decide to use resources in specific situations (Halbesleben, Neveu, Paustian-Underdahl, & Westman, 2014).

The theoretical principles of the model argue that people must invest resources to deal with demands and that as a consequence those resources are depleted (Halbesleben et al., 2014). For example, if a person experiences a difficult exchange with a colleague, they may need to invest resources related to emotion control and self-efficacy for conflict resolution in order to preserve the resource of the working relationship with the colleague. If the outcome of this effort is positive, the latter resource is preserved and the former resources are also bolstered (e.g. people may feel better about resolving conflict in the future). Problems such as stress occur when the outcome of such an exchange is negative and effectively resources are lost. If subsequent events fail to replenish the resources, and further loss is incurred, then the theory holds that people become desperate to preserve the few remaining resources and become defensive, irrational and aggressive (Hobfoll et al., 2018).

The theory helps us to understand how demands and indeed affective events may lead to exhaustion at work. On the positive side, the model also helps to illustrate how support from organizations and managers can help; providing support to deal with demands and to reduce damaging outcomes of experiences would help people to both preserve and gain personal resources. In the example above, facilitating conflict resolution would be such an example.

PERCEPTION AND DECISION-MAKING

Perception represents the judgements that people make about their environments and people they encounter. They are important processes because they affect the way that people respond to others and to situations they encounter in organizations (Huczynski & Buchanan, 2007). By this reasoning, objective reality is relegated as an influence on outcomes, meaning it is the perception of that reality that counts. In work psychology, interpersonal perception has been the focus of attention, largely because person perception is a key process in activities that involve judging or assessing other people. Activities such as selection assessment and performance appraisal require that managers and others make judgements about people at work.

People form perceptions based on a variety of cues. These include information gauged about the target, and the situation that frames the target. Information is processed by the perceiver, and is therefore filtered through their values, personality traits and emotions. People also develop shortcuts in perceptions that enable them to quickly make sense of the world around them. This idea features in Personal Construct Theory (Kelly, 1955), which proposes that people have a unique, but limited set of features that they instantly attend to when they make judgements about people. Some of the commonest perceptual shortcuts are shown in Box 3.2.

> **BOX 3.2**
> **Interpersonal perceptual shortcuts**
>
> - Selective Attention. This happens when people pay attention primarily to information that they understand or are familiar with. People tend to have a bias for perceiving and remembering aspects of situations or characteristics of people that are in some way important personally. Imagine a manager listening to a presentation from their CEO, who judges the effectiveness of the speech afterwards. The process of selective attention suggests that they would base their judgement primarily on the points that were relevant for their area of the business, neglecting wider aspects of the presentation.
> - Stereotyping. Stereotypes are mental models that people hold about others, usually based on physical features or membership of demographic groups (based on factors like gender, ethnicity, sexual orientation or lifestyle preferences).
> - Halo Effect. The halo effect occurs when you perceive something positive about a person and then tend to evaluate everything about that person overly positively. This usually involves neglecting any negative information.
> - Contrast Effects. This occurs when a person is judged in comparison to a recently perceived other. This is a key issue in selection, where interviewers, for example, might see groups of people one after another, each being judged in relation to the performance of the previous interviewee.
> - Similar-to-me Effects. This happens when an individual perceives positively those characteristics that appear to be consistent with their own.

Attribution theories

One of the most informative aspects of research and theory in perception is attribution theories, a set of theories that aim to understand how people perceive the behaviour of others and, importantly, how they attribute cause to that behaviour.

The fundamental attribution error (Ross, 1977) describes how people overemphasize the role of internal forces (dispositions, characteristics, personality traits) when attributing cause to the behaviour of others, when, in fact, situational factors also have important influences. Moreover, Watson (1982) suggested that in comparison to causal attribution in perceptions of the behaviour of others, people tend to more strongly attribute their own behaviour to situational factors. So my perception is likely to be that I submitted a recent article manuscript late because my workload was high that month, making it impossible to complete it. On the other hand, when my colleague down the hall is late in delivering manuscripts and reports, it is because they are disorganized and generally tardy about getting things done. This error in perception represents a major weakness in the way that people perceive the behaviour of others at work.

Decision-making

A closely allied field of study to perception and judgement is decision-making or choice. People in organizations have to make decisions on a daily basis, ranging from small decisions like how to organize their working day, right through to huge decisions that might affect large groups of people inside or outside the organization. The major contributions of psychology to understanding decision-making have focused on how people choose or decide between competing options or problem solutions. You might assume that a rational approach to problem-solving or decision-making is most desirable or effective in organizations. The choice of solution depends on the analysis of evidence relevant to the problem. However, is it reasonable to say that any human decision is ever really completely rational?

> **DISCUSS WITH A COLLEAGUE**
>
> Do you think that you have ever made a biased decision about a colleague or person you have worked with? (Most of us have at one stage or another, the problem is failing to acknowledge it.) What could you do differently to avoid this in the future?

Many argue not, and an influential idea in decision-making research is the concept of bounded rationality, proposed by Simon (1972). In the theory of bounded rationality, human decision-makers are conceived as limited in their capacity to understand problems objectively. People appraise situations and problems based on their own limited perspectives, and Simon (1972) identifies three main limitations of people's capacity to understand problems:

- Introduction of Risk and Uncertainty: People are not good at evaluating probability and risk when making decisions and choices. Decision-making under uncertainty was the theme of Nobel Prize-winning research by Kahneman and Tversky (e.g. Kahneman & Tversky, 1973; Kahneman, 2003). Their experiments suggest that a major determinant of how people weigh up risk in decisions depends on the likelihood of experiencing losses as a result of the decision. People are essentially loss averse, and are much more likely to appraise risk positively if the alternative is a loss. One of the fascinating findings of Kahneman's and Tversky's research, however, is that this aversion is so powerful that the way in which decisions are framed can influence choices, even when the net results of those choices are exactly the same. Box 3.3 illustrates this.

- Incomplete Information about Alternatives: People may be required to make decisions based on incomplete information, or assume that they have all of the information when actually they do not. This would happen in cases where people's searches for information are limited in scope, meaning that they may feel they have evaluated alternatives accurately, when really they have failed to test alternatives thoroughly.

- Complexity: In many cases, a complete set of problem parameters would be so complex for people to appraise that they would simply be unable to rationally evaluate them. Rationality in this case is bounded by the limitations of people's capability to weigh up the parameters of decisions.

> **BOX 3.3**
> **Loss aversion in decision-making**
>
> Here is a decision problem. There has been an outbreak of a serious virus in a small town. There is no risk of the virus spreading further afield, but after conducting investigations within the town, doctors expect that 600 residents will die from the illness. You are in charge of making a decision about what to do next, and you have to decide between two vaccination programmes to combat the virus:
>
> Programme 1: If adopted, 400 people will definitely die.
>
> Programme 2: If adopted, there is a one-third chance that nobody will die, but a two-thirds chance that 600 people will die.
>
> Which would you choose?
>
> In this situation, most people choose the risky option (Programme 2). Now consider the following two choices:
>
> Programme 1: If adopted, 200 people will definitely be saved.
>
> Programme 2: If adopted, there is a one-third chance that everyone will be saved, but a two-thirds chance that nobody will be saved.
>
> When the problem is presented this way, most people opt for Programme 1, avoiding the risky choice. You will, of course, have noted that the two sets of options are identical, except that in the first example, the options are presented in terms of losses, and in the second, the options are presented in terms of gains.
>
> Kahneman and Tversky (1979) used a similar scenario in their research that showed that framing of problems alters people's decisions. The key factor is that people tend to be loss averse – they take a gamble to avoid certain loss, but avoid a gamble in order to ensure certain gain.

Intuition

Are people really always striving for rationality in their decision-making, or is there a role for intuition in decisions? In organizations, people often go with their gut feeling or use intuition to make decisions. Typically, such decision-making strategies have been derided as weak or flawed, but there is some emergent literature that examines the concept of intuition and which may, in time, help to establish when intuition results in good decisions.

Intuitions have been captured in a variety of theories and research studies on decision-making and are generally considered to represent decisions that are emotionally or affectively charged, arising through fast, non-conscious processes, in which problems are viewed holistically rather than as constituting components for analysis (Dane & Pratt, 2007; Burke & Miller, 1999). Hodgkinson, Langan-Fox, and Sadler-Smith (2008) address the problem of defining what intuition really is and how it feels:

> *Intuiting is a complex set of inter-related cognitive, affective and somatic processes, in which there is no apparent intrusion of deliberate, rational thought. Moreover, the outcome of this process (an intuition) can be difficult to articulate. The outcomes of intuition can be experienced as an holistic 'hunch' or 'gut feel', a sense of calling or overpowering certainty, and an awareness of a knowledge that is on the threshold of conscious perception.* (p. 2.)

Dane and Pratt (2007) propose a theory of intuitive decision-making, which includes some implications about when intuitive decision-making is likely to be most effective. They propose that intuition is likely to be most beneficial when:

1 Decision-makers have developed deep knowledge of the context of problems and the domain areas that frame problems. Such deep knowledge includes so-called 'mental schema' for dealing with situations. These are not merely comprised of facts, but rather of routines, ways of thinking and ways of behaving in response to particular problems.

2 Problems and the tasks associated with them are judgemental rather than intellectual. Judgemental problems are those in which outcomes are context dependent (i.e. right and wrong outcomes are subjective). For example, assume a situation in which a person is repeatedly absent from work. A manager's intuition might lead them to adopt a supportive stance, trying to help the employee and to understand the reasons for the absence. In one organization, this might be deemed effective and responsible; in another it may be viewed as weak and capitulating. The theory implies that because intuition takes account of things like organizational values, the intuitive decision is likely to reflect, and be right for, the context. Intellectual problems have objective markers of outcome success (i.e. right and wrong solutions are objective, and the same regardless of context), and in those cases, rational rather than intuitive decisions are more likely to be effective.

Dual-process theories such as the Cognitive-Experiential Self Theory (e.g. Epstein, 1994) help to explain how intuition and rational decision-making processes play out in daily life (Hodgkinson & Healey, 2014; Akinci & Sadler-Smith, 2013). According to these theories, there exist two systems of decision-making: system 1, which is intuitive, automatic and affectively driven (i.e. decisions are *felt*), and system 2, which is rational, cognitive and analytical. The dual-process model argues that both systems operate in parallel. Generally this operation acts seamlessly and in parallel (Hodgkinson & Sadler-Smith, 2018) as people take decisions day to day, but occasionally results in conflict, experienced as a clash of 'heart and head'. Effective decision-making in organizations is to some extent, therefore, necessarily dependent on being aware of the influence of both kinds on processing and the impact they have on behaviour.

SOCIAL INFLUENCES ON BEHAVIOUR

What are the effects of social context on behaviour in organizations? Research into social context and influence are rooted in social psychology, producing some of the most fascinating findings about people and their behaviour. The ideas tell us much about how factors such as group membership determine people's reactions, interactions and behaviour at work. In the final section of this chapter, we consider the social context of behaviour in organizations. The intention is not to pre-empt Part Three of this book on organizations, but rather to highlight some of the major social influences on the way that people behave in organizations.

People in groups

Hogg and Vaughan (2008) define a group as:

> *Two or more people who share a common definition and evaluation of themselves, and behave in accordance with that definition.* (p. 268.)

> **DISCUSS WITH A COLLEAGUE**
>
> List all the groups that you consider yourself to be a member of inside and outside of work or university.

You can see from this definition that 'group' can be used to refer to a very wide range of different collections of individuals, including teams, bigger departments or groups in organizations, clubs or interest groups, ethnic groups, religious groups, families, friendship groups and so on.

Behaviour in groups is affected by the mere fact that people are acting in groups rather than acting alone, and there are social processes that drive these changes in behaviour. One intriguing process is called social facilitation, which refers to changes in individual behaviour when others are present or observing. You will have experienced this yourself. In the presence of others, people typically raise their game slightly and perform better than they would ordinarily (Zajonc, 1965). There is an element of competitiveness or 'being seen to be performing well' in this effect. Allport (1920) speculated that this social facilitation of performance was down to the simple presence of others.

Social loafing

One of the special features assumed in social facilitation theories is that individuals are accountable, that is to say that others can observe their behaviour and hold them responsible for the outcome. In other words, the outcome of behaviour may be attributed to one person. You may be thinking to yourself that you have plenty of anecdotal evidence of how individuals perform less well or poorly in the presence of others. These examples (assuming you have some) are probably drawn from group-working activities, in which a group is working together on a task or activity. The effect is a real one, which has been considered by social psychologists and termed social loafing (Latane, Williams, & Harkins, 1979). Social loafing occurs when people make less effort on tasks because they perceive that others are also working on them. Importantly, social loafing applies when results or outcomes of group tasks are attributable to whole groups and not individuals. People sometimes feel that they are more anonymous in a group and therefore they are less concerned with being held responsible for performance. It is a robust social effect, demonstrated across multiple studies in a meta-analysis by Karau and Williams (1993). Their study showed that in research on social loafing, 80 per cent of comparisons between individual performance and group performance showed reductions in performance in groups. It has obvious implications for organizations, where tasks and performance are almost always mobilized in groups. It highlights why it is so important for managers to understand things like performance management and effective teamworking.

Classical concepts and studies in social psychology

Conformity

Conformity is a classical concept in social psychology, and the most famous experiments on conformity were conducted by Solomon Asch (1952, 1956). There is some excellent video footage of the experiments on the web (search Asch conformity on YouTube or similar) and this really gives a feel for the experiments. They were designed to test whether group pressure would lead individuals to conform in a very straightforward task, which involved judging the length of lines.

Participants were presented with four lines as shown in Figure 3.5. All they had to do was say which of the comparison lines was the same as the standard line. In a control experiment, Asch recorded that out of 37 participants, 35 made no errors at all on the task, one person made one error and one person made two. In sum this equates to 0.7 per cent errors.

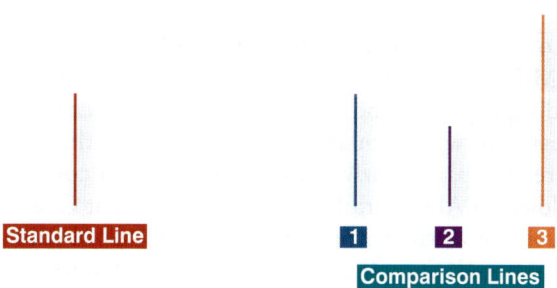

Figure 3.5   Example trial in Asch's experiment
Participants were asked which of the comparison lines was identical in length to the standard lines

In the experiment, the participant was placed in a line of confederates. The confederates had been instructed to give consistent, but incorrect answers on 12 out of 18 trials. The participant heard six people give the incorrect response, and then had to call out their answer. Asch found that compared with 95 per cent in the control, only 25 per cent of participants made no errors at all in the task, and that overall errors rose to 37 per cent.

The findings showed that the majority of participants gave incorrect answers in the task, even though those answers were obviously incorrect. The distortion of their judgement can be viewed on two levels, and both are relevant in organizations:

1. Distortion of perception. In this distortion, people genuinely believe that the group are correct. This might be seen in organizations where a person listens to the views of a group or team, and although incongruent with their views, they believe that the weight of consensus must mean that the group view is true.

2. Distortion of response. This represents the alteration of response due to normative pressure (e.g. Van Avermaet, 2001), but not belief. An example at work might be if a person listened to views of colleagues during a team meeting, all of whom agreed with one another. They might go along with the group to avoid the discomfort of disagreeing, even though deep down, their view had not changed. Such conformity could be damaging in organizations, as people may be inclined to agree in public, but privately continue to behave in ways that are inconsistent with the needs or objectives of the organization. Alternatively, they may simply avoid voicing dissent with group decisions.

Additional conditions were added in Asch's experiments to explore potential moderators. For example, conformity was reduced when one of the confederates gave the correct answer, acting as an ally for the participant. Likewise, conformity was reduced when participants were asked to privately write their answers rather than publicly announce them. The conformity experiments have been replicated on several occasions, with similar results evident in the 1980s (e.g. Vine, 1981) and 1990s (e.g. Abrams, Wetherell, Cochrane, Hogg, & Turner, 1990; Neto, 1995) challenging the assumption that levels of conformity reflect the particular historical context of the Asch experiments. Critical perspectives on the findings are apparent, however (e.g. Hodges & Geyer, 2006), with a significant criticism being that the experimental situation was very peculiar and the findings may not therefore generalize to everyday situations. Nevertheless, the paradigm is an enduring one, and is certainly informative in respect of why people conform to group pressure in organizations. The role of culture in conformity is explored in the Key Theme Box for this chapter.

Obedience to authority

A similarly fascinating set of studies of social influence on behaviour were those of Stanley Milgram in the 1960s and 1970s (Milgram, 1963, 1965, 1974). As with the experiments of Asch, you can watch these on video, and replications and the originals can be accessed online if you search for them. Milgram was interested in why regular people could bring themselves to commit atrocities during war. His questions related particularly to the Holocaust, but could similarly be applied to the behaviour of American soldiers at Abu Ghraib prison in Iraq, and at Guantanamo Bay. His question was whether people who commit terrible atrocities are evil, or just obedient. In other words, would regular people in the general population obey authority if instructed to cause harm to others?

The experiment involved two confederates and a participant. One confederate played the role of the experimenter, who was dressed in a white coat with clipboard, and who coordinated the experiment. The participant was informed that the experiment was about punishment on learning. In a faked random allocation, they were assigned the role of teacher, and a second confederate (playing the role of a second participant) was assigned the role of learner. The participant watched the learner being strapped into a chair with electrodes placed on their arms. They were then taken away to another room, where they sat down in front of a machine that administered electric shocks from 15V up to 450V in a series of stages. The highest levels were even labelled as 'Severe Shock' or 'XXX'. The participants themselves were given a shock of 45V to gauge the feeling of the shock. They were asked to read out a series of memory questions, and to administer electric shocks to the learner if they answered incorrectly, increasing the voltage each time an incorrect answer was given. Of course, no electric shocks were administered, but the participants were played recordings of the learner crying out in pain, asking for the experiment to stop, and even complaining of a heart condition. If the participant objected, the experimenter simply said that the experiment required that they continue, or that they must continue with the experiment.

The startling finding was that contrary to expectation, 62.5 per cent of the participants continued right up to the highest shock level, even after hearing the learner in obvious pain. Subsequent manipulations demonstrated that the influential factor was the authority figure insisting that the experiment continue. Without threatening sanctions or punishment to the participant, the simple insistence of the experimenter caused the majority of participants to administer lethal electric shocks to another person, who was obviously in discomfort. Ah, you may say, but that was then; surely now people are far too independent minded to obey such authority. Burger (2009) reported a replication of Milgram conducted in 2006, and the findings were near identical. The majority of people in the replication obeyed and continued to administer harmful electric shocks. The findings of these studies tell us much about why people carry out appalling behaviour when instructed to do so by an authority figure.

What are the implications of these findings for organizations though? Quite simply, they tell us about the role of leaders and managers in organizations, who hold positions of authority. At a basic level, they show how obedience to authority keeps organizational hierarchies intact and leads people to obey instructions from managers and leaders. When you think about it harder though, there are implications for understanding unethical behaviour in organizations. Are people who work for pharmaceutical companies all evil, cure-withholding mercenaries? Unlikely, but they might obediently make decisions that cause problems for people who need access to drugs in the poorest nations. Are oil and gas engineers all careless, callous polluters, exploiting the world's resources and the people who live among them? No, but the vast majority will obey authority when asked to make decisions about, or contribute to, activities that cause damage or harm.

The bottom line is that OB results from more than just individual factors. Social influences such as social facilitation, social identity, conformity and obedience have important effects on how people behave at work.

Social identity

How do social groups shape our sense of personal identity? This is the question that has motivated the development of social identity theory over the past 40 years (Hogg, 2006; Tajfel, 1969; Tajfel & Turner, 1979). Social identity theory is concerned with examining group membership and intergroup relations and behaviour, from the perspective of understanding how group members see themselves in relation to their own group and other groups.

Your personal identity represents the idiosyncratic traits and individual differences that give you a sense of who you are. Your social identity on the other hand represents the way in which you perceive yourself as a result of being a member of a particular social group. You might attribute part of your identity as being defined by your nationality, for example 'I am resilient as is typical of the English'. Alternatively, people can derive aspects of their identity from much smaller social groups, which can include membership of organizations or teams or groups within organizations.

The very essence of social identity is the idea of the prototype that represents the typical member of a group. The prototype is a mental representation held by people about the main or dominant characteristics or features of a group member. Importantly, these perceptions are held about the groups of people by members (in-groups) and those that are not (out-groups). The effect of thinking in prototypical ways is depersonalization (Hogg & Vaughan, 2008). This occurs when people are no longer seen as individuals in their own right, but rather simply as members of a group. Social identity becomes the only way in which others are perceived. It causes people to reinforce social identity by behaving more like their own group prototype, in order to differentiate themselves further from out-groups. Such behaviour serves to bolster or enhance our own view of ourselves.

Some of the consequences of social identity have clear relevance for organizations. One consequence is concerned with how positive people feel about their social group. If people perceive that others see their group positively, then social identity is likely to be enhanced. People like to be seen positively by others. This perception might, of course, depend on the values of the individual and the extent to which the social group reflects those values. These issues become particularly important when either individuals change, or social or societal contexts change. When others perceive a group negatively, the individual members, as a consequence of their social identity, are also perceived negatively. This can have a number of outcomes. The first is that individual members attempt to leave the group and find a more positive social identity elsewhere. However, this can be difficult in many cases. Take, for example, prejudiced negative evaluations of people based on their nationality or ethnicity. The alternative outcomes include bolstering in-group identities by comparison with lower-status groups (i.e. finding an enemy to galvanize social cohesion) or conflict with those that perceive the in-group as negative. This is one of the major processes behind intergroup conflict.

In organizations, people hold social identities based on memberships of teams or professional groups. Important aspects of individual identities are grounded in those group memberships, and when people feel that those social identities are threatened in some way, they react. For managers and others in organizations, an awareness of the salience of group memberships and social identities is important, as it helps them to understand intergroup behaviour, cooperation and conflict.

This can extend to informal groups as well as formal teams. You probably have your own examples of informal groups among your work or university colleagues. These can be as important, and in some cases more important, to people's sense of self than formal groups. Interventions or systems in organizations that threaten such groups can meet resistance and difficulties, and social identity theory helps us to understand why.

Workgroup diversity

One particular area of interest for organizations around social identity and its influence on people's interactions and performance at work is the issue of diversity and how to make it work in business. The word 'diversity' is most commonly taken to mean variation in ethnic or cultural background within a workgroup. However, diverse groups might equally be made up of people with wide differences in other characteristics such as age, disability, or individual differences such as personality traits.

Research literature offers two main perspectives on the issue of diversity and work performance (van Knippenberg, de Dreu, & Homan, 2004; Williams & O'Reilly, 1998). The social categorization perspective draws on the social identity literature and proposes that people adopt different orientations to group members based on perceived similarity or dissimilarity to the self. This social categorization may lead to problematic sub-group relations, leading to conflict and lower cohesion. The information/decision-making perspective, by contrast, adopts a positive view of diversity, and proposes that diverse workgroups benefit from having a wider array of skills and backgrounds that may be drawn upon for problem-solving. In challenging tasks, such groups are likely to be more innovative and creative in the way that they approach tasks. By one perspective, diversity seems positive, yet by another, more negative.

The challenge of reconciling these two perspectives was taken on by van Knippenberg and colleagues (van Knippenberg et al., 2004), who proposed the Categorization Elaboration Model (CEM). In the model, the two perspectives are combined with moderators of the effects of diversity based on workgroup and task characteristics. The model explains that social categorization may lead to intergroup biases under certain conditions of identity threat (when people feel threatened by diversity in their group). This opens the possibility of cohesion resulting from diversity, if members of the workgroup are positively oriented towards diversity (e.g. van Dick, van Knippenberg, Hagele, Guillaume, & Brodbeck, 2008). Likewise, the benefits of information elaboration and generation of diverse solutions to problems are also dependent on certain conditions, specifically that the task being undertaken is sufficiently complex to require sophisticated problem-solving. When tasks are simple, too many perspectives and opinions on how to carry out the task may be detrimental. Combining the two, van Knippenberg et al. (2004) also theorized that conflict that may arise from intergroup bias and interaction would interfere with task-related performance and information elaboration. Therefore, the extent to which the positives of diversity in task performance are realized depends upon the nature of the task being undertaken, and the social processes occurring within the group.

- Working from this foundation, there have been many research studies examining what specifically determines whether the presence of diversity enhances team effectiveness. For example, Hoever, van Knippenberg, van Ginkel, and Barkema (2012) found that perspective-taking was important in team design to promote creativity in diverse teams. This involved team members being instructed to take the perspective of other team members when trying to solve problems. In an integrative review of the literature on the moderating factors of the effects of workplace diversity, Guillaume, Dawson, Otaye-Ebede, Woods, and West (2017) identified two themes in the literature that help to explain how diversity can be managed:

- Shared perceptions of psychological safety, trust and justice that promote social integration and well-being: this involves the creation of team climates that encourage social contact, enable people to feel that they can speak up without receiving negative reactions, feeling they can depend on others and that decisions are taken fairly.
- Shared perceptions that information sharing is encouraged: this involves designing the work of diverse groups so that information is shared within the group, in turn promoting the use of that information in problem-solving.

The foundations of the CEM are certainly from work and organizational psychology theory. Recognizing the need to integrate this more closely with the HRM research literatures in order to facilitate application of theories of diversity, Guillaume et al. (2013a) reviewed both literatures and presented an integrative model of managing diversity in organizations. The model is shown in Figure 3.6. Like the CEM model, social categorization and innovation perspectives feature. However, the key additions are the management practices that influence, for example, whether diversity is perceived positively by workgroups, and therefore less likely to result in negative biases and conflict. Guillaume et al. (2013a) examine these influences on different levels. Societal factors such as legislation and culture set the context for diversity management, and there are obvious international differences about how diversity is perceived. Societal perspectives are also changeable, of course, and may evolve slowly, or change rapidly in response to significant local or world events.

The societal context influences how organizations respond, and top management are responsible for developing organizational policy and procedures around diversity management. Top management beliefs about diversity are influential at this stage. Moving to more operational levels, diversity management then requires the implementation of policy and procedure, and Guillaume et al. (2013a) highlight the importance of managers and leaders creating a climate in which individual differences are integrated, equitable employment practices are applied and decisions are taken inclusively. These practices in combination facilitate the individual psychological factors that enable diversity to lead to positive innovation, effectiveness and well-being.

The modelling of multiple influences on the outcomes of diversity at work challenges the simple assumption that diversity is always positive. Rather, these models show that obtaining the benefits of diversity requires careful awareness and management of the factors that contribute to those positive outcomes.

Inclusion

An evolution of diversity management is the development of inclusive approaches to management (see e.g. Roberson, 2006). Inclusion is a potential answer to the issue of how to promote the attainment of the positive benefits of diversity, and involves the adoption and application of management practices that serve to include rather than exclude people from key processes in teams and groups. Following this reasoning, diversity in groups and organizations is seen as a product or outcome of management decision-making, but somewhat neglects the specific practices that create the work environment. A critical observation is that managing diversity does little to address the inequality felt by women and minorities, for example, in accessing groups and teams in the first place. This is a problem of *exclusion*.

Inclusion, by contrast, is a concept that extends to capturing the policies and practices of management (Roberson, Ryan, & Ragins, 2017). Practices that promote inclusion aim to promote the participation of all employees in decision-making and work processes (Roberson, 2006). Examples would include composing stakeholder groups to be representative or taking steps to ensure all people within an organization are involved in strategy development and have access to key information and resources.

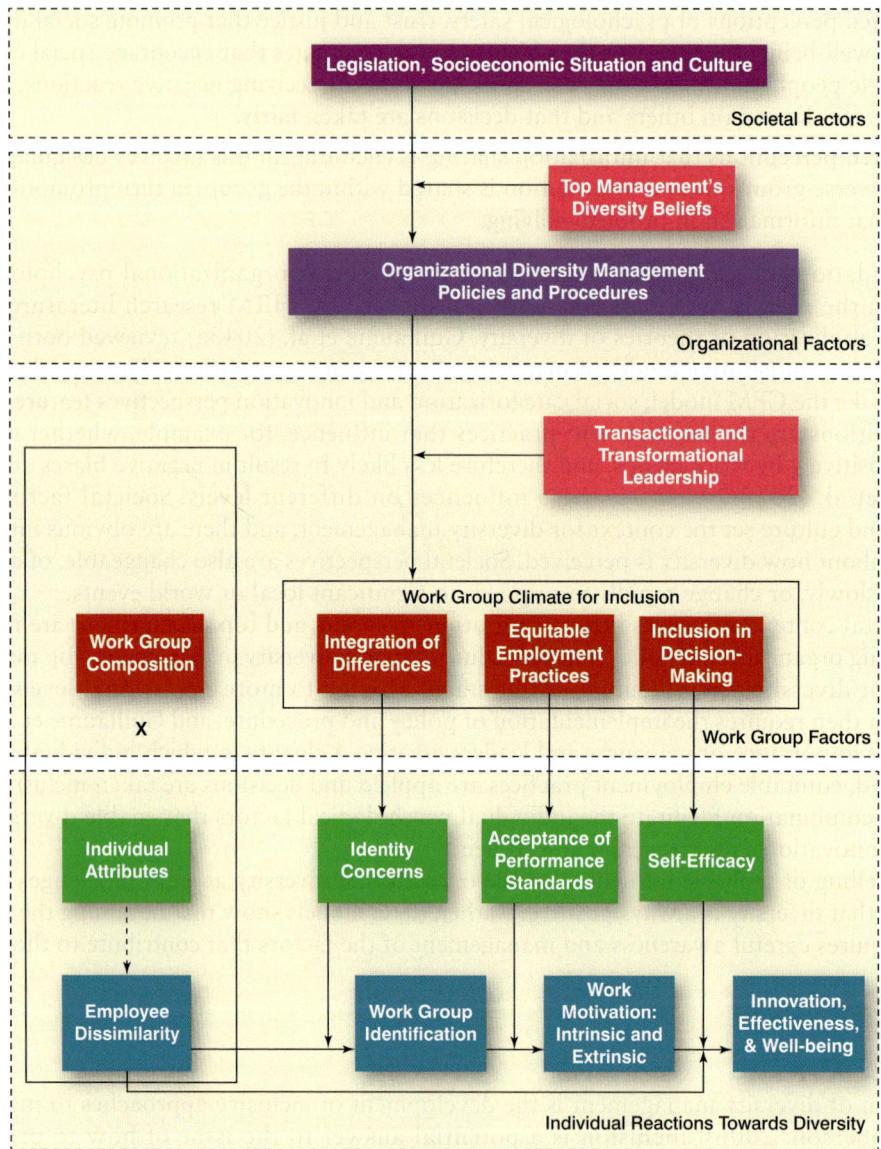

Figure 3.6 A model of managing diversity in organizations

Feelings of exclusion, of course, result in negative attitudes (Findler, Wind, & Mor Barak, 2007), but more than this they create the kinds of teams where people will inevitably feel unfairly treated, hurt, and of lower self-worth. By contrast, building inclusive organizations and teams would significantly improve job attitudes and performance (e.g. Cho & Mor Barak, 2008), but also will create the kinds of positive work experiences we describe through this book, characterized by higher engagement and trust (Downey, van der Werff, Thomas, & Plaut, 2015), and above all, fairness and justice.

PIONEERING WORK PSYCHOLOGISTS

Professor Quinetta Roberson

Professor Quinetta Roberson is Fred J. Springer Endowed Chair in Business Leadership and Professor of Management at Villanova University Business School. Professor Roberson's pioneering work on fairness, diversity and inclusion is striking for the clarity that it brings to understanding these critical issues in business and organizations.

Professor Roberson's work especially emphasizes the value of inclusivity in management, and of creating inclusive workplaces and teams. You can search online for some of Professor Roberson's presentations and talks. In a recent example, she shared that fostering inclusive workplaces goes beyond hiring practices: inclusion is 'more about participation, more about the contribution, more about the involvement of the workforce' and giving people 'the opportunity to be involved meaningfully in the work the organisation does'.

This kind of approach is important in contemporary work for many reasons, but at its core is about making workplaces more positive environments in which to cooperate and interact, to imbue them with greater justice and fairness. These are changes that can make a difference to whole societies, with work and organizations again acting as catalyst.

Key example papers:

Roberson, Q. M. (2019) Diversity in the workplace: A review, synthesis, and future research agenda. *Annual Review of Organizational Psychology and Organizational Behavior*, 6, 69–88.

Roberson, Q., Ryan, A. M., & Ragins, B. R. (2017). The evolution and future of diversity at work. *Journal of Applied Psychology*, 102(3), 483–499.

Roberson, Q. M., & Park, H. J. (2007). Examining the link between diversity and firm performance: The effects of diversity reputation and leader racial diversity. *Group & Organization Management*, 32(5), 548–568.

See also: www.lse.ac.uk/management/news/quinetta-roberson-091018

Professor Roberson's work especially emphasizes the value of inclusivity in management, and of creating inclusive workplaces and teams.

KEY THEME

Diversity and inclusion

When we encounter issues of diversity and inclusion in the popular media, and to some extent in social sciences research, the pressing focal issue remains *distributional* fairness. That is, the gap in opportunity for attainment of employment, and the benefits of employment like salary, promotion and so forth. These are rightly at the forefront of work to address unfairness and promote greater equality.

What we have seen, however, in research on diversity management is that there is another important side to the challenges of making organizations positive environments where people from diverse backgrounds can work and thrive. This is the challenge of creating workplaces that foster and promote the value of diversity, whether it is demographic (e.g. gender, race, age) or psychological (e.g. personality and skills).

The literature on diversity management (e.g. see Guillaume, Dawson, Woods, Sacramento, & West, 2013b) offers guidance, for example, on how to compose teams so that functional diversity does not lead to creation of 'fault-lines' that cut across demographic groups. There are also pointers about how to design work tasks so that they require a diverse set of inputs, and so that people work interdependently, thereby making a unique contribution.

These are simple example interventions, but they represent the building blocks of creating inclusive climates and cultures that *by design* value and encourage the contributions of everyone within a team or organization. Alone, these kinds of interventions are certainly not the solution to the pervasive issues of distributional unfairness (e.g. the gender and race pay gaps). But conversely, fixing distributional unfairness is not the complete answer to the challenge of creating inclusive workplaces, and of getting diversity at work *to work*.

Guillaume, Y. R., Dawson, J. F., Woods, S. A., Sacramento, C. A., & West, M. A. (2013). Getting diversity at work to work: What we know and what we still don't know. *Journal of Occupational and Organizational Psychology, 86*(2), 123–141.

POSITIVE WORK

A new strategic question for management

Strategic management in organizations is typically approached from the perspective of delivering the optimal organizational performance as a primary function. High-performance work systems are then implemented for the purpose of ensuring that strategic objectives are cascaded into goals for individual staff members and that achievement of those goals is enabled through, for example, training, development and performance management.

Some of the most powerful research findings reviewed in this chapter are those that show the role of job attitudes in explaining the relations of performance systems and other organization macro-factors, and actual performance outcomes. These tell us that positive staff attitudes are good for firm performance. However, it remains the case that staff positivity is generally seen as the by-product of good strategic management, not the main objective. That is, strategizing asks the question: 'how will organization performance be delivered?', rather than 'how can work be organized so that it is optimally positive for staff?'

Given the evidence of the impact of making work positive and rewarding, it would seem that addressing the latter question is very much a viable strategic approach. Managers could take a view that the prime objective for strategy should be to make work that is engaging, satisfying and that promotes commitment from staff (especially affective and normative commitment). With work tasks then oriented based on organizational performance objectives, research tells us that performance is likely to follow.

Such an approach fundamentally changes how work and organizations are designed, and provides the basis for putting person-focused employment practices at the heart of work: for example, also in this chapter, research on the benefits of adopting an inclusive approach to management practices and policies for employee trust and engagement. There would therefore be clear justification for incorporating this approach into organization strategy, not just because it would improve performance, but because it makes work more positive. The added impact of taking this approach, illustrated effectively by this latter example, is that by extension, organizations would simultaneously serve a function of improving society, for example by improving opportunity and equality. Think about this: you might not find the concept to be quite as radical or outlandish as it first sounds.

SUMMARY

The complexities of behaviour at work have been examined from numerous perspectives by work and organizational psychologists, and by researchers in management and organizational behaviour, their interest sustained and promoted because of the complex entwinement of individual attitudes, behaviour and performance.

Basic management influences on behaviour are explored in the behaviour modification literature, which draws heavily on behaviourism. Key processes in this perspective are social learning (through observation of behaviour of others) and reinforcement of behaviour. Reinforcement involves applying strategies such as reward and punishment to manipulate and control employee behaviour.

The link between attitudes and behaviour is a key area of research in social psychology, with obvious implications for organizations. The theory of planned behaviour explains how attitudes lead to behaviour, and the mechanisms that promote or inhibit the translation of attitude to intention, and intention to behaviour. Key attitudes at work include job satisfaction and organizational commitment. Research evidence reviewed in this chapter suggests that people who are satisfied and committed at work do tend to perform better, as do organizations whose members are positive and satisfied. There is evidence that higher satisfaction is also related to better outcomes at the level of groups, and to fewer withdrawal behaviours (e.g. lower frequency of absence from work).

Wider individual influences on behaviour include emotion and perception. Emotional reactions to the daily hassles and uplifts at work influence the way that people react and respond. The Affective Events Theory suggests that emotions can lead to behaviour in two ways. Spontaneous or impulsive behaviour results directly from emotions; judgement-driven behaviour results from formation or alteration of attitudes. Into this mixture of influences we can add self-management of behaviour (referred to as self-regulation), in which people monitor and manage their own behaviour.

Perceptions of the work environment, and particularly of people at work, are influential in behaviour and decision-making. Attribution theories tell us how people tend to incorrectly judge the causes of the behaviour of others, and research on decision-making shows how people appraise risk and use intuition to make decisions and solve problems at work.

Alongside individual influences on behaviour are social influences that come from the group and social context of work in organizations. Important social contextual processes such as social facilitation and social loafing influence individual behaviour. Decisions and behaviour are also affected by social pressure, as demonstrated by classic experiments in social psychology on conformity and obedience. Social context also gives rise to the formation of social identity, and theory in this area helps to explain how people perceive different groups at work, and how prejudice, conflict and cooperation arise between different groups. These issues have clear implications for managing diversity at work, expanding understanding beyond social factors to more complex interactions of task performance, problem-solving and HRM factors. Inclusion provides an integrated approach to managing these factors in the context of diversity and, alongside what we know about attitudes and behaviour at work, offers directions for the creation of positive and rewarding workplaces of the future.

DISCUSSION QUESTIONS

1. Looking back at your experiences of work and education, what are the ways in which your behaviour was modified or influenced by reinforcement interventions?

2. This question involves some reflective thought. Can you think of an attitude that you held at work or university that you either did or did not act on? Use the theory of planned behaviour to explain why your attitude did or did not lead to behaviour.

3. Which form of organizational commitment do you think is commonest among people at work in your country currently? Why?

4. How have your perceptual biases led you to make assumptions about people this week?

5. Think of a recent difficult decision you had to make. Use theories of decision-making to help explain the decision you made.

6. How could a manager use research on social influences on behaviour to more effectively manage a team?

7. What do you understand to be the difference between diversity and inclusion in organizations? What are examples that help explain the difference from your own experience?

FURTHER READING

Ajzen, I. (2005). *Attitudes, personality and behaviour.* Maidenhead, England: Open University Press.

Hogg, M. A., & Vaughan, G. M. (2008). *Social psychology.* Harlow, England: Pearson Education.

Judge, T. A., Thoresen, C. J., Bono, J. E., & Patton, G. K. (2001). The job satisfaction–job performance relationship: A qualitative and quantitative review. *Psychological Bulletin, 127,* 376–407.

Judge, T. A., Weiss, H. M., Kammeyer-Mueller, J. D., & Hulin, C. L. (2017). Job attitudes, job satisfaction, and job affect: A century of continuity and of change. *Journal of Applied Psychology, 102*(3), 356.

Robbins, S. P., & Judge, T. A. (2015). *Organizational behavior* (Pearson International Edition). London, England: Pearson/Prentice-Hall.

Roberson, Q., Ryan, A. M., & Ragins, B. R. (2017). The evolution and future of diversity at work. *Journal of Applied Psychology, 102*(3), 483–499.

REFERENCES

Abrams, D., Wetherell, M., Cochrane, S., Hogg, M. A., & Turner, J. C. (1990). Knowing what to think by knowing who you are: Self categorization and the nature of norm formation, conformity and group polarization. *British Journal of Social Psychology, 29,* 97–119.

Ajzen, I. (1988). *Attitudes, personality and behaviour.* Chicago, IL: Dorsey.

Ajzen, I. (1991). The theory of planned behaviour. *Organizational Behaviour and Human Decision Processes, 50,* 179–211.

Ajzen, I. (2002). Perceived behavioural control, self-efficacy, locus of control and the theory of planned behaviour. *Journal of Applied Social Psychology, 32,* 665–683.

Ajzen, I., & Fishbein, M. (1977). Attitude-behaviour relations: A theoretical analysis and review of empirical research. *Psychological Bulletin, 84,* 888–918.

Ajzen, I., & Fishbein, M. (1980). *Understanding attitudes and predicting social behaviour.* Englewood-Cliffs, NJ: Prentice-Hall.

Ajzen, I., & Fishbein, M. (2005). The influence of attitudes on behaviour. In D. Albarracín, B. T. Johnson, & M. P. Zanna (Eds.), *The handbook of attitudes* (pp. 173–221). Mahwah, NJ: Lawrence Erlbaum Associates.

Akinci, C., & Sadler-Smith, E. (2013). Assessing individual differences in experiential (intuitive) and rational (analytical) cognitive styles. *International Journal of Selection and Assessment, 21*(2), 211–221.

Allport, F. H. (1920). The influence of the group upon association and thought. *Journal of Experimental Psychology, 3*(3), 159.

Armitage, C. J., & Conner, M. (2001). Efficacy of the theory of planned behaviour: A meta-analytic review. *British Journal of Social Psychology, 40*, 471–499.

Asch, S. E. (1952). *Social psychology.* Englewood Cliffs, NJ: Prentice-Hall.

Asch, S. E. (1956). Studies of independence and conformity. A minority of one against a unanimous majority. *Psychological Monographs, 70*(9), 416.

Ashkanasy, N. M., Ayoko, O. B., & Jehn, K. A. (2014). Understanding the physical environment of work and employee behavior: An affective events perspective. *Journal of Organizational Behavior, 35*(8), 1169–1184.

Ashkanasy, N. M., & Daus, C. S. (2002). Emotion in the workplace: The new challenge for managers. *Academy of Management Executive, 16*, 76–86.

Bandura, A. (1977). *Social learning theory.* Englewood Cliffs, NJ: Prentice Hall.

Bandura, A. (1986). *Social foundations of thought and action.* Englewood Cliffs, NJ: Prentice Hall.

Bandura, A. (1991). Social cognitive theory of self-regulation. *Organizational Behavior and Human Decision Processes, 50*(2), 248–287.

Barsade, S. G., & Gibson, D. E. (2007). Why does affect matter in organizations? *Academy of Management Perspectives, 21*(1), 36–59.

Bem, D. J. (1967). Self-perception: An alternative interpretation of cognitive dissonance phenomena. *Psychological Review, 74*(3), 183–200.

Bentein, K., Vandenberghe, C., Vandenberg, R., & Stinglhamber, F. (2005). The role of change in the relationship between commitment and turnover: A latent growth modeling approach. *Journal of Applied Psychology, 90*(3), 468.

Breckler, S. J. (1984). Empirical validation of affect, behaviour and cognition as distinct components of attitude. *Journal of Personality and Social Psychology, 47*, 1191–1205.

Brief, A. P., & Weiss, H. M. (2002). Organizational behavior: Affect in the workplace. *Annual Review of Psychology, 53*(1), 279–307.

Burger, J. M. (2009). Replicating Milgram: Would people still obey today? *American Psychologist, 64*(1), 1–11.

Burke, L. A., & Miller, M. K. (1999). Taking the mystery out of intuitive decision-making. *Academy of Management Executive, 13*(4), 91–99.

Burns, S., & Roberts, L. (2013). Applying the theory of planned behaviour to predicting online safety behaviour. *Crime Prevention and Community Safety, 15*(1), 48–64.

Castanier, C., Deroche, T., & Woodman, T. (2013). Theory of planned behaviour and road violations: The moderating influence of perceived behavioural control. *Transportation Research Part F: Traffic Psychology and Behaviour, 18*, 148–158.

Cervone, D., & Shoda, Y. (Eds.) (1999). *The coherence of personality: Social-cognitive bases of consistency, variability and organization.* New York, NY: Guilford Press.

Cho, S., & Mor Barak, M. E. (2008). Understanding of diversity and inclusion in a perceived homogeneous culture: A study of organizational commitment and job performance among Korean employees. *Administration in Social Work, 32*(4), 100–126.

Cropanzano, R., Dasborough, M. T., & Weiss, H. M. (2017). Affective events and the development of leader–member exchange. *Academy of Management Review, 42*(2), 233–258.

Cropanzano, R., & Wright, T. A. (2001). When a "happy" worker is really a "productive" worker: A review and further refinement of the happy-productive worker thesis. *Consulting Psychology Journal: Practice and Research, 53*(3), 182.

Cropley, M., Plans, D., Morelli, D., Sütterlin, S., Inceoglu, I., Thomas, G., & Chu, C. (2017). The association between work-related rumination and heart rate variability: A field study. *Frontiers in Human Neuroscience, 11*, 27.

Crano, W. D., & Prislin, R. (2006). Attitudes and persuasion. *Annual Review of Psychology, 57*, 345–374.

Dalal, R. S., Lam, H., Weiss, H. M., Welch, E. R., & Hulin, C. L. (2009). A within-person approach to work behavior and performance: Concurrent and lagged citizenship–counterproductivity associations, and dynamic relationships with affect and overall job performance. *Academy of Management Journal, 52*(5), 1051–1066.

Dane, E., & Pratt, M. G. (2007). Exploring intuition and its role in managerial decision-making. *Academy of Management Review, 32*(1), 33–54.

Das, E. H. H., De Wit, J. B. F., & Stroebe, W. (2003). Fear appeals motivate acceptance of action recommendations: Evidence for a positive bias in the processing of persuasive messages. *Personality and Social Psychology Bulletin, 29*, 650–664.

Downey, S. N., van der Werff, L., Thomas, K. M., & Plaut, V. C. (2015). The role of diversity practices and inclusion in promoting trust and employee engagement. *Journal of Applied Social Psychology, 45*(1), 35–44.

Eagly, A. H., & Chaiken, S. (1993). *The psychology of attitudes*. Orlando, FL: Harcourt Brace Jovanovich College Publishers.

Elliot, A. J., & Devine, P. G. (1994). On the motivational nature of cognitive dissonance: Dissonance as psychological discomfort. *Journal of Personality and Social Psychology, 67*, 382–394.

Epstein, S. (1994). Integration of the cognitive and the psychodynamic unconscious. *American Psychologist, 49*, 709–724.

Erdheim, J., Wang, M., & Zickar, M. J. (2006). Linking the big five personality constructs to organizational commitment. *Personality and Individual Differences, 41*, 959–970.

Festinger, L. (1957). *A theory of cognitive dissonance*. Stanford, CA: Stanford University Press.

Findler, L., Wind, L. H., & Mor Barak, M. E. (2007). The challenge of workforce management in a global society: Modeling the relationship between diversity, inclusion, organizational culture, and employee well-being, job satisfaction and organizational commitment. *Administration in Social Work, 31*(3), 63–94.

Fugas, C. S., Silva, S. A., & Meliá, J. L. (2012). Another look at safety climate and safety behavior: Deepening the cognitive and social mediator mechanisms. *Accident Analysis & Prevention, 45*, 468–477.

Glasman, L. R., & Albarracin, D. (2005). Forming attitudes that predict future behavior: A meta-analysis of the attitude–behavior relation. *Psychological Bulletin, 132*(5), 778–822.

Guillaume, Y. R., Dawson, J. F., Otaye-Ebede, L., Woods, S. A., & West, M. A. (2017). Harnessing demographic differences in organizations: What moderates the effects of workplace diversity? *Journal of Organizational Behavior, 38*(2), 276–303.

Guillaume, Y. R., Dawson, J. F., Priola, V., Sacramento, C. A., Woods, S. A., Higson, H. E., … West, M. A. (2013a). Managing diversity in organizations: An integrative model and agenda for future research. *European Journal of Work and Organizational Psychology, 23*(5), 783–802.

Guillaume, Y. R., Dawson, J. F., Woods, S. A., Sacramento, C. A., & West, M. A. (2013b). Getting diversity at work to work: What we know and what we still don't know. *Journal of Occupational and Organizational Psychology, 86*(2), 123–141.

Halbesleben, J. R., Neveu, J. P., Paustian-Underdahl, S. C., & Westman, M. (2014). Getting to the "COR" understanding the role of resources in conservation of resources theory. *Journal of Management, 40*(5), 1334–1364.

Harmon-Jones, E., & Mills, J. (1999). An introduction to cognitive dissonance theory and an overview of current perspectives on the theory. In E. Harmon-Jones and J. Mills (Eds.), *Cognitive dissonance: Progress on a pivotal theory in social psychology* (pp. 3–21). Washington, DC: American Psychological Association.

Harrison, D. A., Newman, D. A., & Roth, P. L. (2006). How important are job attitudes? Meta-analytic comparisons of integrative behavioural outcomes and time sequences. *Academy of Management Journal, 49*(2), 305–325.

Harter, J. K., Schmidt, F. L., & Hayes, T. L. (2002). Business-unit-level relationship between employee satisfaction, employee engagement and business outcomes: A meta-analysis. *Journal of Applied Psychology, 87*(2), 268–279.

Hobfoll, S. E. (1989). Conservation of resources: A new attempt at conceptualizing stress. *The American Psychologist, 44*(3), 513–524.

Hobfoll, S. E., Halbesleben, J., Neveu, J. P., & Westman, M. (2018). Conservation of resources in the organizational context: The reality of resources and their consequences. *Annual Review of Organizational Psychology and Organizational Behavior, 5*, 103–128.

Hochschild, A. R. (1983) *The managed heart: Commercialization of human feeling*. Berkeley, CA: University of California.

Hodges, B. H., & Geyer, A. L. (2006). A nonconformist account of the Asch experiments: Values, pragmatics and moral dilemmas. *Personality and Social Psychology Review, 10*(1), 2–19.

Hodgkinson, G. P., & Healey, M. P. (2014). Coming in from the cold: The psychological foundations of radical innovation revisited. *Industrial Marketing Management, 43*(8), 1306–1313.

Hodgkinson, G. P., Langan-Fox, J., & Sadler-Smith, E. (2008). Intuition: A fundamental bridging construct in the behavioural sciences. *British Journal of Psychology, 99*(1), 1–27.

Hodgkinson, G. P., & Sadler-Smith, E. (2018). The dynamics of intuition and analysis in managerial and organizational decision making. *Academy of Management Perspectives, 32*(4), 473–492.

Hoever, I. J., van Knippenberg, D., van Ginkel, W. P., & Barkema, H. G. (2012). Fostering team creativity: Perspective taking as key to unlocking diversity's potential. *Journal of Applied Psychology, 97*(5), 982.

Hogg, M. A. (2006). Social identity theory. In P. J. Burke (Ed.), *Contemporary social psychological theories* (pp. 111–136). Palo Alto, CA: Stanford University Press.

Hogg, M. A., & Vaughan, G. M. (2008). *Social psychology.* Harlow, England: Pearson Education.

Hong, Y., Liao, H., Hu, J., & Jiang, K. (2013). Missing link in the service profit chain: A meta-analytic review of the antecedents, consequences, and moderators of service climate. *Journal of Applied Psychology, 98*(2), 237.

Huczynski, A., & Buchanan, D. A. (2007). *Organisational behaviour: An introductory text.* Harlow, England: Pearson Education Limited.

Judge, T. A., Heller, D., & Mount, M. K. (2002). Five-factor model of personality and job satisfaction: A meta-analysis. *Journal of Applied Psychology, 87*, 530–541.

Judge, T. A., & Hulin, C. L. (1993). Job-satisfaction as a reflection of disposition: A multiple-source causal analysis. *Organizational Behaviour and Human Decision Processes, 56*, 388–421.

Judge, T. A., Thoresen, C. J., Bono, J. E., & Patton, G. K. (2001). The job satisfaction–job performance relationship: A qualitative and quantitative review. *Psychological Bulletin, 127*, 376–407.

Judge, T. A., Weiss, H. M., Kammeyer-Mueller, J. D., & Hulin, C. L. (2017). Job attitudes, job satisfaction, and job affect: A century of continuity and of change. *Journal of Applied Psychology, 102*(3), 356.

Kahneman, D. (2003). A perspective on judgement and choice. *American Psychologist, 58*, 697–720.

Kahneman, D., & Tversky, A. (1973). On the psychology of prediction. *Psychological Review, 80*, 237–251.

Kahneman, D., & Tversky, A. (1979). Prospect theory: An analysis of decisions under risk. *Econometrica, 47*, 263–291.

Kaiser, F. G., Schultze, P. W., & Guericke, O. (2009). The attitude–behaviour relationship: A test of three models of the moderating role of behavioural difficulty. *Journal of Applied Social Psychology, 39*(1), 186–207.

Kammeyer-Mueller, J. D., Wanberg, C. R., Glomb, T. M., & Ahlburg, D. (2005). The role of temporal shifts in turnover processes: It's about time. *Journal of Applied Psychology, 90*(4), 644.

Kanfer, R. (2005). Self-regulation research in work and I/O psychology. *Applied Psychology, 54*(2), 186–191.

Karau, S. J., & Williams, K. D. (1993). Social loafing: A meta-analytic review and theoretical integration. *Journal of Personality and Social Psychology, 65*(4), 681–706.

Kelly, G. A. (1955). *The psychology of personal constructs.* New York, NY: Norton.

Komaki, J., Coombs, T., & Schepman, S. (1996). Motivational implications of reinforcement theory. In R. M. Steers, L. W. Porter, & G. A. Bigley (Eds.), *Motivation and leadership at work* (pp. 34–52). New York, NY: McGraw-Hill.

Lapkin, S., Levett-Jones, T., & Gilligan, C. (2015). Using the theory of planned behaviour to examine health professional students' behavioural intentions in relation to medication safety and collaborative practice. *Nurse Education Today, 35*(8), 935–940.

Latane, B., Williams, K., & Harkins, S. (1979). Many hands make light work: The causes and consequences of social loafing. *Journal of Personality and Social Psychology, 37*, 822–832.

Luthans, F., & Stajkovic, A. D. (1999). Reinforce (not necessarily pay) for performance. *Academy of Management Executive, 13*, 49–57.

McFarlin, D. B., & Sweeney, P. D. (1992). Distributive and procedural justice as predictors of satisfaction with personal and organizational outcomes. *Academy of Management Journal, 35*(3), 626–637.

Meyer, J. P., & Allen, N. J. (1991). A three-component conceptualization of organizational commitment. *Human Resource Management Review, 1*, 61–89.

Meyer, J. P., Stanley, D. J., Herscovitch, L., & Topolnytsky, L. (2002). Affective, continuance and normative commitment to the organization: A meta-analysis of antecedents, correlates and consequences. *Journal of Vocational Behavior, 61*, 20–52.

Milgram, S. (1963). Behavioural study of obedience. *Journal of Abnormal and Social Psychology, 67*, 371–378.

Milgram, S. (1965). Some conditions of obedience and disobedience to authority. *Human Relations, 18*, 57–76.

Milgram, S. (1974). *Obedience to authority: An experimental view*. New York. NY: Harper & Row.

Mowday, R. T., Porter, L. W., & Steers, R. M. (1982). *Employee-organization linkages. The psychology of commitment, absenteeism and turnover*. New York, NY: Academic Press.

Mowday, R. T., & Sutton, R. I. (1993). Organizational behaviour: Linking individuals and groups to organizational contexts. *Annual Review of Psychology, 44*, 195–229.

Muraven, M., & Baumeister, R. F. (2000). Self-regulation and depletion of limited resources: Does self-control resemble a muscle? *Psychological Bulletin, 126(2)*, 247.

Neto, F. (1995). Conformity and independence revisited. *Social Behavior and Personality, 23*, 217–222.

Petty, R. E., & Cacioppo, J. T. (1986). The elaboration likelihood model of persuasion. In L. Berkowitz (Ed.), *Advances in experimental social psychology* (Vol. 19, pp. 123–205). New York, NY: Academic Press.

Petty, R. E., Tormala, Z. L., & Rucker, D. D. (2004). Resisting persuasion by counterarguing: An attitude strength perspective. In J. T. Jost, M. R. Banaji, & D. A. Prentice (Eds.), *Perspectivism in social psychology: The yin and yang of scientific progress* (pp. 37–51). APA science series. APA decade of behavior series. Washington, DC: American Psychological Association.

Rafaeli, A., & Sutton, R. I. (1989). The expression of emotion in organizational life. *Research in Organizational Behavior, 11(1)*, 1–42.

Riketta, M. (2002). Attitudinal organizational commitment and job performance: A meta-analysis. *Journal of Organizational Behavior, 23*, 257–266.

Robbins, S. P., & Judge, T. A. (2015). *Organizational behaviour* (Pearson International ed.). London, England: Pearson/Prentice-Hall.

Roberson, Q. M. (2006). Disentangling the meanings of diversity and inclusion in organizations. *Group & Organization Management, 31(2)*, 212–236.

Roberson, Q. M. (2019). Diversity in the workplace: A review, synthesis, and future research agenda. *Annual Review of Organizational Psychology and Organizational Behavior, 6*, 69–88.

Roberson, Q. M., & Park, H. J. (2007). Examining the link between diversity and firm performance: The effects of diversity reputation and leader racial diversity. *Group & Organization Management, 32(5)*, 548–568.

Roberson, Q., Ryan, A. M., & Ragins, B. R. (2017). The evolution and future of diversity at work. *Journal of Applied Psychology, 102(3)*, 483–499.

Ross, L. (1977). The intuitive psychologist and his short-comings. In L. Berkowitz (Ed.), *Advances in experimental social psychology* (Vol. 10, pp. 173–220). San Diego, CA: Academic Press.

Ruch, W. A., Hershauer, J. C., & Wright, R. G. (1976). Toward solving the productivity puzzle: Worker correlates to performance. *Human Resource Management, 15*, 2–6.

Rusting, C. L., & Larsen, R. J. (1998). Personality and cognitive processing of affective information. *Personality and Social Psychology Bulletin, 24(2)*, 200–213.

Schneider B. (1985). Organizational behaviour. *Annual Review of Psychology, 36*, 573–611.

Senior, C., Lee, N., & Butler, M. (2011). PERSPECTIVE–organizational cognitive neuroscience. *Organization Science, 22(3)*, 804–815.

Simon, H. A. (1972). Theories of bounded rationality. In C. B. McGuire & R. Radner (Eds.) *Decisions and organization: A volume in honor of Jacob Marschak* (pp. 161–176). London, England: North-Holland.

Sitzmann, T., & Johnson, S. K. (2012). The best laid plans: Examining the conditions under which a planning intervention improves learning and reduces attrition. *Journal of Applied Psychology, 97(5)*, 967.

Stajkovic, A. D., & Luthans, F. (2003). Behavioural management and task performance in organisations: Conceptual background, meta-analysis and test of alternative models. *Personnel Psychology, 56*, 155–194.

Sung, S. Y., & Choi, J. N. (2014). Do organizations spend wisely on employees? Effects of training and development investments on learning and innovation in organizations. *Journal of Organizational Behavior, 35(3)*, 393–412.

Tajfel, H. (1969). Social and cultural factors in perception. In G. Lindzey & E. Aronson (Eds.) *Handbook of social psychology* (Vol. 3, pp. 315–394). Reading, MA: Addison-Wesley.

Tajfel, H., & Turner, J. C. (1979). An integrative theory is intergroup conflict. In W. G. Austin

& S. Worchel (Eds.) *The social psychology of intergroup relations* (pp. 33–47). Monterey, CA: Brooks/Cole.

Tett, R. P., & Meyer, J. P. (1993). Job satisfaction, organizational commitment, turnover intention and turnover: A path analysis based on meta-analytic findings. *Personnel Psychology, 46*, 259–293.

Thoresen, C. J., Kaplan, S. A., Barsky, A. P., Warren, C. R., & de Chermont, K. (2003). The affective underpinnings of job perceptions and attitudes: A meta-analytic review and integration. *Psychological Bulletin, 129*(6), 914–945.

Tormala, Z. L., & Petty, R. (2004). Resistance to persuasion and attitude certainty: The moderating role of elaboration. *Personality and Social Psychology Bulletin, 30*, 1446–1457.

Van Avermaet, E. (2001). Social influence in small groups. In M. Hewstone & W. Stroebe (Eds.), *Introduction to social psychology* (3rd ed., pp. 403–443). Oxford, England: Basil Blackwell.

van Dick, R., van Knippenberg, D., Hagele, S., Guillaume, Y. R., & Brodbeck, F. C. (2008). Group diversity and group identification: The moderating role of diversity beliefs. *Human Relations, 61*(10), 1463–1492.

van Knippenberg, D., de Dreu, C. K., & Homan, A. C. (2004). Work group diversity and group performance: An integrative model and research agenda. *Journal of Applied Psychology, 89*(6), 1008.

Vancouver, J. B., & Day, D. V. (2005). Industrial and organisation research on self-regulation: From constructs to applications. *Applied Psychology, 54*(2), 155–185.

Vine, I. (1981). [Letter to the editor]. *Bulletin of the British Psychological Society, 34*, 145.

Warr, P. (2011). *Work, happiness, and unhappiness*. Hove, England: Psychology Press.

Watson, D. (1982). The actor and the observer: How are the perceptions of causality divergent? *Psychological Bulletin, 92*, 682–700.

Weiss, H. M. (2002). Deconstructing job satisfaction: Separating evaluations, beliefs and affective experiences. *Human Resource Management Review, 12*(2), 173–194.

Weiss, H. M., & Cropanzano, R. (1996). Affective events theory: A theoretical discussion of the structure, causes and consequences of affective experiences at work. In B. M. Shaw & L. L. Cummings (Eds.), *Research in organizational behaviour* (Vol. 18, pp. 1–74). Greenwich, CT: JAI Press.

Williams, K., & O'Reilly, C. A. (1998). Demography and diversity in organizations. In B. M. Staw & L. L. Cummings (Eds.), *Research in organizational behavior* (Vol. 20, pp. 77–140). Greenwich, CT: JAI Press.

Woods, S. A., Poole, R., & Zibarras, L. D. (2012). Employee absence and organizational commitment. *Journal of Personnel Psychology, 11*(4), 199–203.

Yeow, J., & Martin, R. (2013). The role of self-regulation in developing leaders: A longitudinal field experiment. *The Leadership Quarterly, 24*(5), 625–637.

Zablah, A. R., Carlson, B. D., Donavan, D. T., Maxham, III, J. G., & Brown, T. J. (2016). A cross-lagged test of the association between customer satisfaction and employee job satisfaction in a relational context. *Journal of Applied Psychology, 101*(5), 743.

Zajonc, R. B. (1965). Social facilitation. *Science, 149*, 269–274.

Zhao, H., Wayne, S. J., Glibkowski, B., & Bravo, J. (2007). The impact of psychological contract breach on work-related outcomes: A meta-analysis. *Personnel Psychology, 60*, 647–680.

CHAPTER 4
MOTIVATION AT WORK

LEARNING OBJECTIVES

- Define motivation at work.
- Understand, evaluate and know how to apply theories of motivation: need theories, trait perspective of motivation, self-determination theory, cognitive theories of motivation (expectancy theory and goal-setting theory).
- Understand how fairness, justice and equity in different aspects of work affect motivation.
- Describe perspectives in job design and motivation (the job characteristics model, sociotechnical systems theory, job demands, control and resources) and the concept of work engagement as bridging motivation and well-being research.
- Integrate different theories of motivation to understand strategies for their application.

One appealing feature of motivation theories in work and organizational psychology is their diversity. Work motivation has been considered from many different perspectives and, rather than competing with one another, they can be seen as complementary, each offering a different insight into the concept of motivation at work. In this chapter, we examine four perspectives, grouping similar theories together according to the themes within them. Collectively, these perspectives consider how people are motivated:

- by personal needs and traits
- in response to cognitive processes related to work (i.e. how people perceive and respond to features of the work environment)
- when they feel fairly treated at work
- by the ways in which their jobs are designed.

There are plenty of general definitions of motivation, but the two below capture the essence effectively:

1 'A set of energetic forces that originate both within as well as beyond an individual's being to initiate work-related behaviour and to determine its form, direction, intensity and duration'. (Pinder 1998, p. 11)
2 'The processes that account for an individual's intensity, direction and persistence of effort toward attaining a goal'. (Robbins & Judge, 2009, p. 209)

Taking these two definitions together, you can see that the study of work motivation is concerned with why people initiate behaviour and effort at work, and the processes that determine its intensity, direction towards goals and maintenance over time. In short, how can we account for the reasons why people are motivated to attain goals at work, and how can we understand the processes that promote and sustain that effort?

> **DISCUSS WITH A COLLEAGUE**
>
> What motivates you at work or in your studies at university? Based on your intuition and discussion with a colleague, write down five ways in which you are motivated. See how many of them correspond to, or are explained by, the theories in this chapter.

NEED THEORIES OF MOTIVATION

Early theories of motivation focused on the needs of employees as the main source of motivation. Ask most managers about theories of motivation, and the one they tend to remember is Maslow's hierarchy of needs. Maslow's theory is a need theory of motivation, which describes how people are motivated to satisfy inner needs such as the need for affiliation with others. According to the theories, people with unfulfilled needs will be motivated to initiate action to satisfy them (Wright, 1989). Need theories therefore aim to identify what motivates employees at work. The theories are simple to understand and have high face validity with managers and practitioners, which is undoubtedly part of their appeal. They are less popular with work and organizational psychologists traditionally, for reasons that we will see shortly.

Maslow's hierarchy of needs

Maslow (1943; 1954) identified a hierarchy of five needs, which he suggested exist within all human beings. The theory proposed that people are motivated to fulfil each of these needs in a series of sequential steps whereby higher needs become dominant as lower ones become satisfied. The needs are presented in a hierarchical fashion in Figure 4.1, which shows the order in which Maslow proposed they operate. The five sets of needs are:

- Physiological. These are the basic needs that people need to fulfil in order to survive. They include hunger, thirst, sex and other needs that relate to basic physiological processes.
- Safety. Safety needs include the need for security, stability, freedom from physical and psychological harm and fear.

- Social. Maslow originally referred to these as 'love' needs, and they relate to the need for affiliation and close relationships with others.
- Esteem. This group of needs may be broken into two subsets. The first refers to the need for mastery of tasks, striving for personal accomplishment and competence. The second refers to the need for reputation and prestige, in other words, the esteem of others.
- Self-actualization. The final set of needs in the hierarchy is characteristic of many theories like Maslow's, which come from the humanistic tradition. They represent the need to self-actualize, which essentially refers to the need for people to fulfil their potential and to become all that they can possibly be.

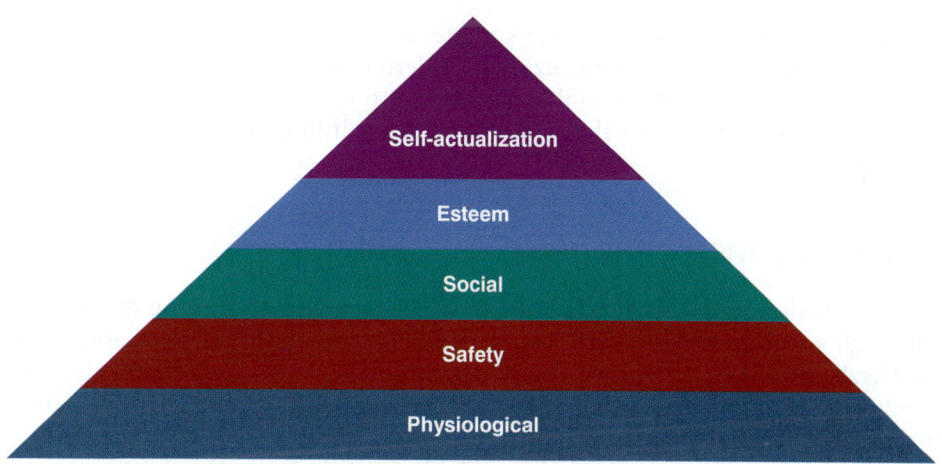

Figure 4.1 Maslow's hierarchy of needs

The hierarchical nature of the theory suggests that people are most strongly motivated to fulfil basic needs before the higher needs such as esteem and self-actualization come into play. However, there is a common misconception of the theory in which once basic needs are fulfilled, they cease to drive behaviour. Rather, Maslow believed that behaviour was multi-motivated (Pinder, 2008), suggesting that the satisfaction of lower-order needs diminishes rather than extinguishes their effects on behaviour.

At work, Maslow's theory gels with managerial intuition about motivation. In a work context, the theory implies that in order to motivate an individual, it is necessary to 1) promote motivation to fulfil higher-order needs by ensuring that the lower-order needs are fulfilled through work design (e.g. through providing pay, job security, a supportive social environment); 2) identify ways in which work tasks can fulfil the higher-order needs, thereby helping to motivate individuals to work on those tasks. An employee who is concerned about job security, or who is struggling to provide for their own basic needs and the needs of their family, is unlikely to be concerned to any great degree with mastering new skills or tasks or becoming the very best they can be at work. Their concerns would be more basic and based around fulfilling the lower-order needs.

Is there evidence that the theory works? One would have to say the evidence is marginal at best. Although the grouping of the needs has been supported empirically (Kluger & Tikochinsky, 2001; Ronen, 2001; Van-Dijk & Kluger, 2004), studies consistently failed to validate the theory, leading to the pessimistic conclusion that unsatisfied needs do not necessarily lead to motivation in the workplace (Lawler & Suttle, 1972; Rauschenberger, Schmitt, & Hunter, 1980; Wahba & Bridwell, 1976).

Alderfer ERG theory

Alderfer (1969; 1972) presented an alternative model, representing a reclassification and reorganization of human needs. The model contains three basic groups of needs, and is therefore simpler than Maslow's model:

- Existence needs include aspects similar to physiological and safety needs in the Maslow hierarchy.
- Relatedness needs are similar to the social needs in Maslow's theory and the needs for prestige and reputation (esteem of others).
- Growth needs refer to needs for self-esteem and self-actualization.

In addition to reorganizing needs, Alderfer's model is also different from Maslow's because it removes the hierarchical structural organization. Alderfer suggested that people are consistently motivated by all three sets of needs simultaneously, but to varying degrees at different times. The implication for management is that the aspects of work fulfilling the different needs need to be provided in a steady supply.

Herzberg's two-factor theory

The theories of Maslow and Alderfer describe how people are motivated by the inner fulfilment of needs through situation and life experiences. A different emphasis on motivation at work was adopted in Herzberg's (1959) two-factor theory. The two-factor theory, which has also been termed motivation-hygiene theory (Herzberg, Mausner, & Snyderman, 1959), was developed from research into factors at work that promote satisfaction and dissatisfaction. Herzberg examined the reasons that led people to feel either very good or very bad about their work, asking them to describe situations that illustrated these feelings. His analysis of people's responses revealed a distinction between factors that cause dissatisfaction and those that promote satisfaction. He termed these as hygiene factors and motivators respectively, although they have also been termed extrinsic and intrinsic motivators:

- Hygiene factors. Hygiene or extrinsic factors include things like pay, quality of supervision, work conditions, company policies and administrative procedures. When these do not meet expectations of employees, they tend to result in dissatisfaction and demotivation.
- Motivators. Motivators are factors that tap into internal or intrinsic needs. These include achievement, advancement and promotion, recognition, nature of work and responsibility at work.

The implications of motivation at work are based around the separation of extrinsic and intrinsic motivators. The removal of job characteristics that are dissatisfying only serves to reduce dissatisfaction in Herzberg's theory. Such measures do not promote satisfaction or enhance motivation. To do this, organizations and managers need to provide opportunities for intrinsically rewarding experience at work by providing things like promotion opportunities, interesting work tasks, and decision-making latitude, autonomy and responsibility.

As with all theories, the utility of the two-factor theory depends on how well it stands up to empirical tests. Early studies offered mixed support for the theory (Ewen, Smith, Hulin, & Locke, 1966; House & Wigdor, 1967; Soliman, 1970), with the majority of criticisms directed at the methodology used by Herzberg to derive his theory. These criticisms included questions about the reliability of the procedures used in the research. Another important problem for the theory is the assumed link between satisfaction, on the one hand, and effort and productivity on the other. The factors identified by Herzberg are those that lead to either satisfaction or dissatisfaction, and as we saw in Chapter 3, the relationships between satisfaction and performance are far from simple.

Perhaps more fundamentally, the argument behind Herzberg's model faces problems in the wider motivational literature. As highlighted by Tang (1992), the proposal that hygiene factors cannot motivate people in their jobs goes against a body of research demonstrating the motivational effectiveness of one specific hygiene factor: money (Lawler, 1981; Opsahl & Dunnette, 1966; Whyte, 1955). Sachau (2007) points out that Herzberg recognized that money could 'move' people, and that the assertion that pay is a hygiene factor, and thereby not a motivator, should not be taken too literally. Either way, this conceptual fuzziness and the lack of empirical support, alongside questions over the methodological groundings of Herzberg's motivation theory, raise serious doubts about its validity in organizations. Similar to Maslow's theory of motivation, Herzberg's model provides clear practical recommendations, but lacks a solid evidence base. Interestingly, though, some of the ideas about job factors that promote motivation at work have permeated through to more recent perspectives and ideas about motivation. These are picked up later in the chapter.

BOX 4.1
Money and motivation

To what extent are you motivated by money? Would you work without pay? The debate about the motivating properties of money is an old one, and within your peer group you will always find people willing to take the two sides of the argument. Those who tend to believe that money is a significant motivator tend to point to people's reliance on money for life satisfaction. They have scientific evidence on their side. Furnham and Argyle (1998) report overall correlations between money and life satisfaction of 0.25, which is weak, but meaningful. At work, there is a significant literature on the motivating properties of financial incentive, used as a form of reinforcement for performance behaviour (see Chapter 3).

Yet the relationship between pay and performance is not as high as you might think. In a meta-analysis, Mitra, Jenkins, Gupta, and Shaw (1997) report a relationship of 0.24. Moreover, the way that individuals perceive money as a motivator also varies, such that money motivates different people in different ways (Mitchell & Mickell, 1999). For example, materialistic people tend to value and seek high pay, individualists prefer pay schemes that are individually focused, and people who are risk averse value fixed pay schemes (Cable & Judge, 1994; Judge & Bretz, 1992). By focusing on the provision of money alone, it is possible to miss some of the more subtle motivating properties of reward, such as the methods by which it is distributed.

An often-quoted example that would seem to dispute the motivating properties of money is concerned with voluntary work. Why do people do charity work and voluntary work for no personal reward, if money is a fundamental motivator? What do you think? How realistic is it in contemporary society for people to work for intrinsic reward alone through volunteering?

MOTIVATION AS A TRAIT

McClelland's (1961) theory of motivation integrates concepts of individual differences with need theories of motivation, proposing motivation as stemming from trait-like inner needs for achievement, affiliation and power:

- Need for Achievement (nAch): This represents the need for achievement or the drive to excel and achieve success.
- Need for Affiliation (nAff): The need to develop close and meaningful interpersonal relationships.
- Need for Power (nPow): The need to control or influence the behaviour of others.

McClelland supposed that these inner needs were trait-like, so that people differed in the extent to which they were motivated by achievement or power needs, for example. He also suggested that these traits stemmed from experience and therefore that they could be developed. He believed that achievement motivation, for example, could be developed during childhood, through provision of experiences that lead to success and positive outcomes (Pinder, 2008). Ideas such as these are consistent with our understanding of factors such as self-efficacy (people's beliefs about their own capability and probability of success in activities).

The most widely studied of the three needs is nAch. Early research documented an association between nAch and success in entrepreneurial roles that require innovation and planning for the future (Hundal, 1971). This has since been supported by a meta-analysis conducted by Collins, Hanges, and Locke (2004) who showed that a high need for achievement predicted the choice of an entrepreneurial career as well as performance in an entrepreneurial role. High nAch tends to give budding entrepreneurs and business owners an advantage.

People with high need for achievement prefer tasks that are challenging, but which do not carry very low probabilities of success. This dependence on the link between success and effort differentiates the need for achievement from a more general form of ambition (Judge & Kammeyer-Mueller, 2012). One of the limitations of McClelland's theory is concerned with its application in organizations. In the theory, the needs are proposed to be unconscious processes, meaning that people are not directly aware of their influences on behaviour and performance at work. This has a knock-on implication for the measurement of the three needs, which must be done in a way that accesses unconscious processing. One measure that has been widely applied in research is the Thematic Apperception Test (TAT), which requires participants to tell a story based on a series of pictures. Once coded, the stories are intended to reveal the person's aspirations and fantasies and thereby provide a measure of their need for achievement, power and affiliation. The test is a projective measure, which means that responses need to be judged by expert raters, and this makes research and application dependent on the expertise of specific individuals. The technique also lacks psychometric accountability.

SELF-DETERMINATION THEORY

Theories reviewed so far in this chapter position motivation as a function of inner needs, extrinsic rewards, and intrinsic commitment and interest in work activity. The challenge of bringing these concepts together in a coherent theory is taken up in the formulation of *self-determination theory* (Deci & Ryan, 1985; Gagné & Deci, 2005; Ryan & Deci, 2000).

Basic concepts of intrinsic versus extrinsic motivation (e.g. Porter & Lawler, 1968) propose that total job satisfaction occurs when work is designed to make it intrinsically appealing, and sufficient extrinsic reward is provided. Yet paradoxically, providing an extrinsic reward linked to an activity may actually detract from the intrinsic motivation to carry it out (Deci, 1971). Based upon a line of theoretical advances (see Gagné & Deci, 2005 for a review), self-determination theory developed to propose a set of psychological processes that resolve this previously unexplained effect.

The theory first differentiates controlled motivation (i.e. reward linked and externally driven) from autonomous motivation (i.e. self-determined action, whether rewarded or not), and sets out a continuum of motivation from based on this distinction:

- amotivation: absence of any motivation
- external regulation: derived from reward and punishment
- introjected regulation: performance driven by external factors, but linked to feelings of self-worth
- identified regulation: reward attained from activity in which goals and underlying values represent important aspects of the self
- integrated regulation: full coherence between the goals, values and regulations of work and self
- intrinsic motivation: activity undertaken only for interest and enjoyment of the task.

According to self-determination theory, optimal motivation is attained when the work people do represents an important part of who they are. Work goals and values that are aligned to people's self-determined goals and values are internalized and serve to guide effort and behaviour in a way similar to intrinsic motivation. Even if such work is extrinsically regulated, and managed by an organization, motivation feels intrinsically derived. Under these conditions, people feel that they are working volitionally; they do not work to attain a reward, rather they work because the activity is important to them.

The theory also sets out the inner needs that must be satisfied to attain *integrated regulation* of work activity. Gagné and Deci (2005) describe three psychological needs: competence, autonomy and relatedness. Competence relates to the need to be able to carry out those tasks effectively and influence attainment of performance goals. Autonomy represents the need to decide on the goals that are pursued and the ways in which they are undertaken. Relatedness is the need for people to feel connected to the social world, to be playing a part in it and contributing. When our work satisfies all three of these needs, some of the core psychological conditions of internalization of work goals are fulfilled, leading to a greater sense of self-determination. Unlike McClelland's need theory, self-determination theory does not position needs as individually different, rather they are seen as core aspects of psychological health for all people.

Self-determination theory, once grasped, is a powerful unifying concept in work and organizational psychology. For management of motivation, there are implications for how work is designed, and the involvement of staff in goal-setting and activity-planning. However, there are also implications for personnel selection and occupational choice, given that fit between work and self are core concepts in both of these human resource processes. Work that helps people attain their personal strivings will inevitably be more positive and rewarding, and ultimately motivating.

COGNITION AND MOTIVATION

One of the mechanisms by which people are motivated, highlighted at the start of this chapter, is through the ways that they think about their work and work environment. These factors can be grouped under the heading of cognition or cognitive processes. In this section, we cover two theories about how cognition affects motivation. The first examines how people are motivated by their expectations about outcomes at work. The second is probably the most influential idea in contemporary motivation theory and research, and concerns how people think about and respond to goals at work.

Expectancy theory

Think about something that you want in your life that could feasibly be provided through working hard. How important is it to you? How likely is it that working hard will result in you achieving your goal? Are you working to achieve this goal right now?

If you are working to gain something important in your life right now, then chances are that you have made the following decisions:

1. I really want this outcome.
2. By performing well, I can get access to this outcome.
3. By working hard, I will be able to perform well, so working hard is what I will do to get access to the outcome.

These are the basic elements of Vroom's (1964) expectancy theory of motivation, which explains motivation in terms of the factors that influence an employee's decision to exert effort at work. Specifically, the theory identifies three factors that determine work effort:

- Valence: the desirability of an outcome to an individual, which can be positive or negative. This represents the extent to which a person values some outcome at work.
- Instrumentality: the perceived probability that effective performance will result in the desired outcome.
- Expectancy: the perceived probability that effort will result in the required level of performance.

Collectively, these are referred to as the VIE variables, and Vroom represented them in an equation:

$$F = V \times I \times E$$

$F = Effort\ or\ Force;\ V = Valence;\ I = Instrumentality;\ E = Expectancy$

The logic of the equation reveals the implications of the theory. People tend to expend most effort at work when they perceive that their efforts will result in good performance, leading to a valued, desirable outcome. People are likely to work less hard if:

1. They do not perceive a desirable or positive outcome resulting from their efforts.
2. They perceive that no amount of effort will result in the level of performance required to gain the outcome.
3. They do not believe that performance, however effective, will lead to the positive outcome.
4. Combinations of 1, 2 and 3 together.

If you are not working to achieve the outcome you identified at the start of this section, then it is likely for one of these reasons.

> **DISCUSS WITH A COLLEAGUE**
>
> Think about a time when you have felt intrinsically motivated in your work. Can you use *self-determination theory* to explain this experience?

The implication of expectancy for motivating people at work, and encouraging and promoting performance, is that managers need to ensure that people perceive that work will lead to desirable outcomes, and that these can be accessed through effort-related performance. Understanding the things that matter to people is a key component of this approach to motivation. This has led to the emergence of measures of individual preferences for particular outcomes at work (e.g. the Motives, Values and Preferences Inventory; Hogan & Hogan, 1996).

Evaluation of expectancy theory

The appealing logic of expectancy theory is backed up by scientific evidence. Early examinations generally accepted the theory as a valid explanation for motivation at work (Pritchard & Sanders, 1973). A meta-analysis by Van Eerde and Thierry (1996) also provided moderate support for the theory. Their analysis examined the relation of the VIE variables with a range of work-related criteria. One less encouraging finding for managers applying expectancy theory was that it tended to predict attitudinal components of motivation such as intentions and preference much more effectively than behavioural components of motivation such as actual performance and effort. This is perhaps unsurprising given the complex processes that determine whether attitudes and intentions lead to behaviour (see Chapter 3), but the failure to develop a clearer account of the pathway from the VIE equation to performance and action, alongside the absence of advances in the theory generally, must be seen as a weakness (Ambrose & Kulik, 1999).

Nonetheless, researchers have continued to examine the model. A study by Erez and Isen (2002) provided support for the motivational effects of the VIE model as part of their wider analysis of the influence of emotion and affect on motivation. The study found that more positive perceptions of valence, instrumentality and expectancy did increase levels of motivation, and that all three perceptions were associated with having a generally more positive outlook in life (positive affect).

Vansteenkiste, Lens, De Witte, and Feather (2005) used expectancy theory in research into unemployment, and their study illustrates how the theory could be misunderstood, with potentially damaging consequences. They considered the influence of valence and expectancy on unemployed individuals' motivation to seek work. Results predictably revealed a positive relationship between valence and job-search motivation in that those who strongly valued being employed were more motivated to engage in job-search activities. By contrast, a negative relationship was reported between expectancy and job-search motivation. How could this be explained? The researchers provided numerous hypothetical explanations for the unhypothesized negative relation, which seemingly contradicts the proposals of expectancy theory, but the most likely one is a misconception of the 'expectancy' variable. In the study, this represented participants' expectation that they would get a job in the near future. Put differently, it consisted of a judgement of how likely it would be that they would get a job soon, and not the extent to which they thought that job-seeking behaviour would lead to employment. People who felt confident that they would get their desired outcome did not see the need to expend additional effort to achieve it. Viewed in this way, the finding seems to support expectancy theory rather than contradict it.

Expectancy theory may also serve an explanatory function for understanding the impact of work attitudes on performance. For example, Downes, Kristof-Brown, Judge, and Darnold (2017) hypothesized that perceptions of person–organization fit were related to goal accomplishment because when people felt that accomplishing goals was beneficial to both themselves and the organization, instrumentality and expectancy were higher, especially as organizational support was also perceived as greater. The danger in applying expectancy theory is that desirable outcomes may be seen as too easy to obtain. If that is the case, then people are likely to be less motivated to work hard to achieve them. The processes by which people judge the difficulty of achieving outcomes is just one aspect of another cognitive perspective on motivation: goal-setting theory.

Goal-setting

Goal-setting theory is the most influential of all motivation theories in management practice, and with good reason given the extent of research on the theory and its development over time. The seed of the theory was planted by Locke (1968), who was interested to answer a very simple question in a basic research study (Latham & Locke, 2007): Does goal-setting affect a person's performance on a task? The answer was 'yes', and what followed was the evolution and development of goal-setting theory by Latham and Locke, integrating their own research with a multitude of studies conducted and published by others. This theory development may be considered as 'live' in that new perspectives on the original ideas continually emerge in the literature. Broadly speaking, the theory examines what types of goal are most successful in generating high levels of motivation, when these effects occur and why they occur.

Goal-setting and job performance

The value of setting goals for employees at work was underlined in the meta-analysis of Locke and Latham (1990). This study showed that performance was markedly higher when employees were set goals, as compared with no goal-setting. Recent meta-analytic research has also underlined the importance of goal-setting in teams (Kleingeld, van Mierlo, & Arends, 2011). Moreover, Locke and Latham (1990) also identified a number of features of goals that made them either more or less effective:

1. Goals must be specific and challenging. Goals that urge people to 'do their best' result in lower performance than specific, challenging goals, a robust finding about the influence of goal-setting on performance supported in numerous studies (e.g. Zetik & Stuhlmacher, 2002). 'Do your best' goals are subjective and do not identify a standard of performance. Consequently people are unable to evaluate the value or acceptability of their work.
2. Motivating goals must be measurable. There should be an objectively measurable outcome that indicates accomplishment of the goal, providing further scope for evaluation of performance.
3. Goals must be attainable and time-bound. Together, these two properties of goals motivate a person to perform highly at work. Goals that are unattainable are demotivating, because people perceive that regardless of the effort they put in, the goal will not be accomplished. Goals should stretch people, but still be achievable. Time-boundedness is encouraged through applying deadlines and timescales for goals, and enables people to decide how much effort is required to achieve a goal within the specified time.

Goals and motivation

Given that there is strong evidence of the link between goal-setting and performance, it is important to understand the mechanisms by which goal-setting promotes performance. There are four, and they are at the heart of the role of goal-setting in motivation:

1 Goals direct attention and effort towards activities that are relevant for achieving the goal. Goals therefore affect cognition and behaviour. This mechanism has been reported in several early studies of goal-setting (Locke & Bryan, 1969; Rothkopf & Billington, 1979).
2 Goal-setting energizes behaviour. Goals lead people to expend effort to facilitate their achievement.
3 Goals induce persistence and prolonged effort. Evidence from LaPorte and Nath (1976) showed that when subjects were allowed to control the amount of time they spent on a task, difficult goals led to sustained effort.
4 Goals influence the acquisition and use of task-relevant knowledge and strategies that increase the chances of task success (Wood & Locke, 1990). Indeed, a study by Knight, Durham, and Locke (2001) found that difficult goals affected job performance by influencing how people used particular job-relevant strategies.

The motivational properties of goals are tied to these four mechanisms. Imagine a salesperson is set a target of doubling their monthly sales income in six months. We will assume that the goal is attainable, it is certainly measurable, and the deadline means that it is time-bound. The theory suggests the motivational effects of the goal will first serve to focus the salesperson's attention on the challenge of doubling monthly sales. Behaviour to achieve the goal will be energized so that the person exerts effort and takes steps to improve, and that effort will be prolonged until such time as the goal is achieved, with further effort applied as needed to maintain the improved performance. In order to do all of these things, the salesperson might examine their performance behaviours and develop new strategies to improve.

When do goals lead to motivation and performance?

More precisely, under what conditions do goals lead to motivation and performance? The mere presence of a goal is not enough to ensure that people will be both motivated and that they will perform as a result. There are a number of factors that help to explain why some people are motivated by goals and others are not:

- Locke and Latham (2002) argue that the relationship between goal-setting and job performance is at its strongest when individuals are committed to their goals. Furthermore, when goals are difficult, commitment becomes even more significant because challenging goals demand increased effort and have a lower success rate compared to easy goals (Erez & Zidon, 1984; Klein, Wesson, Hollenbeck, & Alge, 1999). Goal commitment in turn is affected by two key factors: the importance of the goal to the individual and their personal belief that they are capable of achieving their goal (self-efficacy; Locke & Latham, 2002). People are likely to be more committed to their goals when they perceive that goal achievement is associated with a valued outcome, and that the outcome is attainable. Echoes of expectancy theory are evident here.

- Feedback on progress and performance enhances goal-related behaviour. Feedback increases the effectiveness of goals because it enables individuals to better understand how they are progressing towards the attainment of their goals. Without this information, the person cannot alter important factors such as strategy and level of effort to match goal requirements (Locke & Latham, 2002). People also use feedback in alternative ways depending on their individual differences. For example, Brown, Ganesan, and Challagalla (2001) found that individuals with high self-efficacy use feedback to decrease anxiety and increase their motivation, effort and task focus.
- The goal-setting–performance relationship is moderated by task complexity. The link between goals and performance is clearest for low-complexity tasks. For highly complex tasks, goal attainment is likely to be much more strongly affected by the extent to which a person has the ability to discover and use appropriate strategies and skills (Locke & Latham, 2002).
- The final constraints on the link between goal-setting and performance are situational or contextual (Latham & Locke, 2007). Aspects of work and organizational design might interfere or prevent people achieving or working towards goals, as indeed would non-work factors that affect performance and that are beyond people's control.

A model of goal-setting and performance

A number of models of the processes and mechanisms of goal-setting and its effects on performance have been presented (e.g. Latham & Locke, 2007; Locke & Latham, 2002), with a particularly comprehensive representation termed the High Performance Cycle (HPC). An adapted version of this model is shown in Figure 4.2. It highlights all of the factors relevant in determining the effectiveness of goals in promoting motivation and performance, but also adds reward mechanisms, tying the model more closely to performance management (the role of goal-setting in performance management is discussed in Chapter 7). Contingent reward is tied to goal accomplishment, non-contingent reward refers to general rewards and features of employment related to satisfaction and commitment.

Processes and concepts in goal-striving

Kanfer, Frese, and Johnson (2017) describe research on goal-striving as bridging the 'chasm between goals and performance', addressing how people approach goal-related activity and manage it towards attainment. Two key concepts are introduced in this respect in this section.

The goal-orientation concept (Dweck, 1986; Dweck & Leggett, 1988) posits that people are generally inclined to adopt one of two orientations in work-related activities:

1 To adopt a learning goal orientation (LGO), in which they strive to master tasks and learn all that they can about a particular task or activity, a style in which errors are central to the learning process.
2 To adopt a performance goal orientation (PGO), in which they strive to meet certain performance benchmarks, avoiding activities or strategies in which they might be seen as unsuccessful.

Goal orientation has been shown to be associated in various ways with the outcomes of goal-setting. 'Do your best' goals, used in situations where people have high autonomy and low influence from work and organizational structures, tend to be associated with higher performance for people with high LGO. The same goals are associated with low performance for those with high PGO (Seijts, Latham, Tasa, & Latham, 2004). By contrast, when people are set specific and challenging

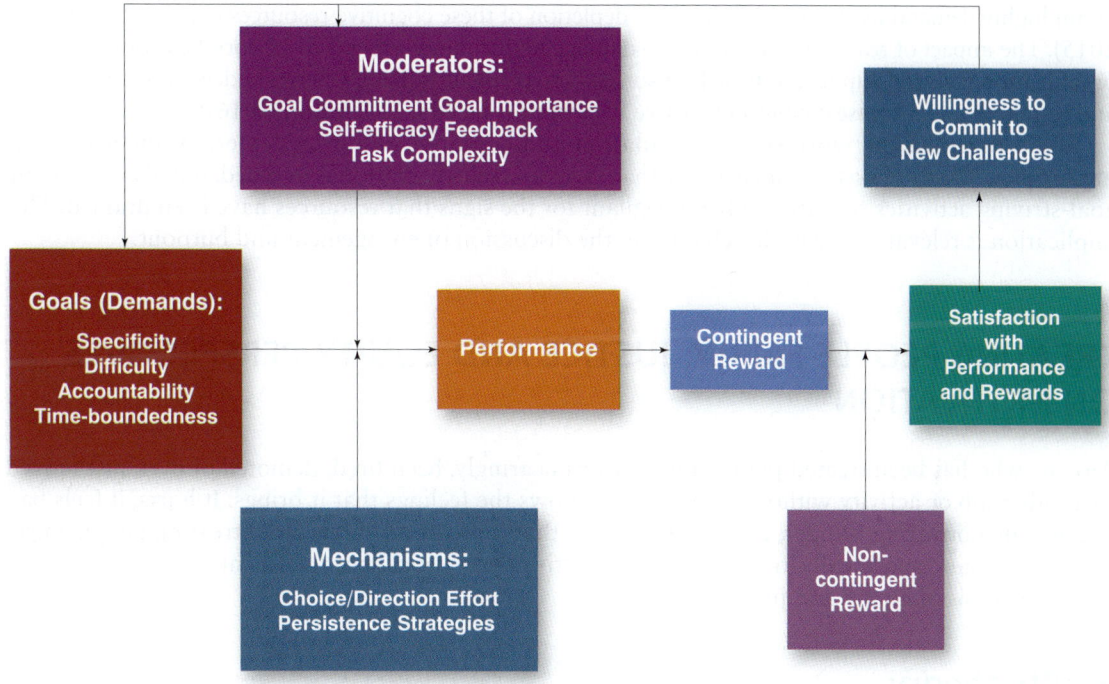

Figure 4.2   Model of goal setting: the high performance cycle

goals, which include objectives around learning and acquiring new performance strategies, differences in outcome performance between people with LGO and PGO are extinguished. This indicates that LGO and PGO may be better conceptualized as states that are specific to particular tasks or objectives at work. The implication is that people's typical or preferred goal orientation seems to influence task motivation and performance if people are left to organize their own work. Effective goal-setting can help to overcome the effects.

Self-regulation and cognitive resources

Self-regulation is a process by which people monitor and manage goal-related activity (e.g. Carver & Scheier, 1981; Kanfer, 1977). Self-regulation comprises three interrelated processes:

- Self-monitoring involves giving attention to behaviour and activity related to goal achievement.
- Self-evaluation is self-assessment of progress towards goal achievement.
- Self-reactions produce changes to behaviour and effort if self-evaluations indicate that goals will not be achieved.

Self-regulation is therefore instrumental in understanding how people manage their own performance and progress towards goal attainment. However, there are potential psychological costs to self-regulation. Ego-depletion theory (Muraven, Tice, & Baumeister, 1998) proposes that people have a limited set of cognitive resources available for self-regulation. Sustained self-regulation (such as in the case of striving to attain highly demanding work goals) leads to depletion of these cognitive resources (e.g. Lin & Johnson, 2015). The impact of resource depletion is to damage performance and positive work behaviours such as organizational citizenship (e.g. Lin & Johnson, 2015; Trougakos, Beal, Cheng, Hideg, & Zweig, 2015), and to potentially increase counterproductive behaviour (Lin, Ma, & Johnson, 2016).

Taken together, the work on self-regulation and cognitive resource depletion underlines the importance of setting goals in such a way that excessive self-regulation is avoided, but also managing goal-striving activities of staff and being vigilant for the signs that resources have been drained. This implication is relevant later in this chapter in the discussion of engagement and burnout.

TREATING PEOPLE FAIRLY: JUSTICE AND EQUITY PERSPECTIVES ON MOTIVATION

Anyone who has been treated poorly, unfairly or uncaringly, been fired, demoted or even just moved to another job or activity without consultation knows the feelings that it brings. It hurts, it feels bad and it is demotivating (Pinder, 2008). The notion that motivation stems from treating people fairly at work, or more specifically, from people's subjective perceptions that treatment at work is just and fair, is the basis of equity and justice theories.

Equity theory

Equity theory (Adams, 1963) posits that people decide on how fairly they are being treated by examining their inputs and outputs, and then comparing them with others at work. The basic equity equation that guides equity theory is shown in Box 4.2. People feel equitably treated if they perceive that their input and outcome ratio is equivalent to others. If people perceive inequity, then the theory suggests that people experience inequity tension: in the case of over-reward, guilt; in the case of under-reward, anger. The comparison 'others' in equity theory are typically thought of as co-workers and colleagues, as these individuals provide the closest and most accessible comparison points. However, people can use other reference points in determining equity:

- Previous job. A person could compare their current input/outcome ratio with that in a previous job role, either within or outside the organization. A person may look back fondly on treatment by a past employer, or conversely may have left past employment because of poor treatment, making them more tolerant of inequity in a new job.
- External company employee. People may look outside their current organization to judge how fairly they are being treated. Examining the working conditions of network colleagues in alternative companies allows people to judge the acceptability of their own experience. This kind of comparison might prompt people to leave the organization if they feel that their lot is unlikely to improve.

The predicted outcomes of equity theory are all based on the idea that people behave in ways that will restore equity. If they are under-rewarded, then they will reduce their inputs to restore equity; if they are over-rewarded, then they will work harder to restore equity. Mowday (1991) reviewed the evidence for the accuracy of these predictions, concluding that although there was generally positive support for equity theory in research, methodological problems abound in empirical studies of the theory, and so one could not be totally confident about the validity of the theory.

BOX 4.2
The equity equation

$$\frac{\text{Outcomes}_{\text{self}}}{\text{Inputs}_{\text{self}}} = \frac{\text{Outcomes}_{\text{Others}}}{\text{Inputs}_{\text{Others}}} \quad \text{Equity}$$

$$\frac{\text{Outcomes}_{\text{self}}}{\text{Inputs}_{\text{self}}} = \frac{\text{Outcomes}_{\text{Others}}}{\text{Inputs}_{\text{Others}}} \quad \text{Inequity due to under-reward}$$

$$\frac{\text{Outcomes}_{\text{self}}}{\text{Inputs}_{\text{self}}} = \frac{\text{Outcomes}_{\text{Others}}}{\text{Inputs}_{\text{Others}}} \quad \text{Inequity due to over-reward}$$

Organizational justice

More recently in work and organizational psychology, the basic ideas of equity theory have been developed and extended in the concept of organizational justice. The essence is still around fairness and people's perceptions of how fairly they are treated at work. Research has differentiated various forms of justice perceptions that collectively reflect not only the distribution of rewards, but also the mechanisms by which they are distributed, the respect people receive in interactions and the clarity, openness and honesty of information that is communicated (Kanfer et al., 2017). Four categories of justice are:

1. **Distributive justice** captures the essence of equity perceptions, based on the extent to which a person feels fairly rewarded for the work they provide, in relation to others.
2. **Procedural justice.** This form of justice perception is targeted towards the organizational systems used to determine how rewards are distributed. The definition could also be broadened to encompass perceptions of the fairness of systems generally in an organization.
3. **Interpersonal justice** concerns the extent to which people feel treated with respect and dignity. It moves beyond the transactional perspective on justice.
4. **Informational justice** refers to the ways in which decisions or procedures at work are communicated and explained. At the start of this section, we highlighted the example of being moved or reassigned without consultation. This would be an example where employees would likely perceive low informational justice.

As with equity theory, perceptions of justice at work are hypothesized to affect motivation and ultimately work behaviour. Hirschman (1970) presented a model of responses to inequity that is still relevant in understanding reactions to perceptions of injustice at work. He presented three typical responses:

- Exit: leaving the organization.
- Voice: protesting, or making dissatisfaction known.
- Loyalty: accepting unfairness, and remaining generally committed.

Pinder and Harlos (2001) add silence to the list of responses, which represents quietly taking, but not accepting, unfairness at work, and harbouring resentment as a result. This is the kind of response that might lead to presenteeism at work, a state of being at work, yet not being productive or engaged.

Research on organizational justice continues to build our understanding of the effects of justice perceptions. Perceptions of distributive justice exert effects on motivation and behaviour in ways similar to inequity tension. More interesting findings have examined the effects of the wider aspects of justice. Brocker and Siegel (1996) examined both procedural and distributive justice, studying their interaction. They reported that if people perceived procedures and systems as unjust, they tended to perceive decisions favourably, provided that distributive justice was high. This suggests a self-serving tendency. People might reason that 'the system is bad, but at least I am fairly treated overall'. When procedural justice was high, distributive justice became less important. People effectively had trust in the system and the people that used it to make decisions.

Zapata-Phelan, Colquitt, Scott, and Livingston (2009) examined the effects of procedural and interactional justice on intrinsic motivation and task performance. Results showed that procedural justice was positively related to intrinsic motivation and, further, that intrinsic motivation, in turn, affected task performance. This suggests that perceived fairness of procedures in organizations can have a positive effect on intrinsic motivation, leading to improved job performance.

Zapata-Phelan et al.'s (2009) study failed to report any significant relationships between interactional justice, intrinsic motivation and task performance. The researchers note the body of evidence revealing an inconsistent link between interactional justice and job performance, some studies reporting significant relationships (e.g. Aryee, Budhwar, & Chen, 2002) and others disconfirming the link (e.g. Colquitt, Scott, Judge, & Shaw, 2006). Part of the reason for inconsistent findings may be that the influences are not direct, and rather mediated. Colquitt, LePine, Piccolo, Zapata, and Rich (2012) reported that experienced trust was a mediator between justice perceptions and performance. People trusted their employer more as a consequence of high justice perceptions, which led to better performance. Aryee, Chen, Sun, and Debrah (2007) reported that perceptions of interactional justice mediate the pathway from perceived abusive supervision to performance outcomes and organizational commitment. When people felt badly treated by their supervisor, this affected their sense of interpersonal treatment at work generally, and led to reduced citizenship behaviour and lower organizational commitment. There are other supervisory effects as well. Ambrose, Schminke, and Mayer (2013) reported that supervisory perceptions of interactional justice were associated with subordinate perceptions, and that this was strongest in teams that had a flexible, decentralized structure.

Feeling fairly treated has potentially deeper and longer-standing effects too. For example, the negative consequences of the day-to-day hassles of work on performance are related to a feeling that they are *unfair*, whereas demanding work challenges are perceived as a fair expectation from work (Zhang, LePine, Buckman, & Wei, 2014). Leadership style moderates this pattern of fairness perceptions. Having a more inspirational leader conveys a greater sense of purpose and makes challenging tasks seem more achievable and simply part of the work culture of the team. From another perspective, justice perceptions may serve to maintain performance levels in difficult situations. In a study of the impact of job insecurity on job performance, people perceiving lower levels of justice performed more poorly when they felt insecure in their jobs. Job insecurity had no effect on performance for those with positive perceptions of justice in their teams and organizations (Wang, Lu, & Siu, 2015).

Organizational justice is a concept that has influenced research broadly in work and organizational psychology, and we will return to this in other chapters of the book. It appears that justice perceptions influence attitudes and behaviour in relation to a wide variety of HR functions and processes, including selection and recruitment (Bell, Wiechmann, & Ryan, 2006), training and learning (Liao & Tai, 2006) and appraisal and performance management (Roberson & Stewart, 2006).

KEY THEME

Environment and sustainability – motivation to act at work and beyond

One of the craziest (and increasingly saddest) aspects of the impending environmental catastrophe that human beings are presiding over on Earth is the reticence of people to do anything about it. World leaders attend numerous summits and conferences attempting to make progress on agreeing measures for reducing emissions of carbon dioxide and other greenhouse gases that are causing the climate emergency.

Yet what are we as citizens doing right now while we wait for one of these meetings to end well? If most of us are honest, quite little, and probably we could all do more. Why? Why are we not motivated to do more?

Equity theory could help to understand why people are not motivated to reduce their consumption. How many of you are thinking right now: 'I could cut back, but then why should I, when people in other parts of the world consume more?'. A sense of inequity demotivates us from changing. Is this belief rational, or indeed based on evidence?

Moreover, consider goal-setting theory for a moment, and then consider the kind of advice that most of us are given about recycling and other ways to be more energy efficient. Essentially it comes down to 'do your best to do your bit', and we now know that 'do your best' goals are the least effective of any goal that could be set. When people are given targets for improvement, they tend to meet them. In some parts of the UK, people are required to reduce their waste, with government refuse collection being limited to a set amount each week. People whinge about it, but they do it. The specific quantifiable target is met on a weekly basis.

These are prospective ideas, but since the writing of our second edition of this book an exciting paper has been published on specifically the issue of motivation and sustainable behaviour (see Unsworth & McNeill, 2017). In this paper, three studies are reported that collectively show how *self-concordance theory* (an extension of self-determination theory) can be used to promote sustainable behaviour. In the first study, it was reported that sustainable behaviours were more likely when they served a personal goal (i.e. concordant with self-goals). Then, in two experiments, that self-concordance of sustainable behaviour with goals was enhanced by encouraging reflection on how those behaviours would help achieve those personal goals. So, a motivational solution is to motivate sustainable behaviour not by appeal to higher environmental concern, but rather to show how those behaviours serve personal goals. From a psychological perspective, enhancing self-concordance may be the key to environmental behaviour change.

In what other ways could motivation theory be applied to understanding why people fail to change behaviour in respect of climate change?

JOB DESIGN AND MOTIVATION

For some people, the content and nature of the work that they do is all they need to motivate them. The nature of work as a source of motivation is the focus of the job characteristics model (JCM; Hackman & Oldham, 1980), which examines the features of work that lead to intrinsic work motivation. The theory proposes that a standard set of features should be built into jobs in order to make them rewarding and motivating. The purpose is to foster three work-related psychological states, which are associated with motivation:

- Sense of personal responsibility. Jobs should provide opportunities for individuals to feel personally responsible for the outcomes of work.
- Meaningfulness. This concerns people's sense of purpose about work. Meaningfulness is a perception that work *matters* in some way.
- Knowledge of results. Individuals should be able to determine how they are performing, so that they develop a sense of their own effectiveness at work.

Hackman and Oldham (1980) identify five job characteristics that promote the three psychological states. The first three create meaningfulness, the fourth fosters responsibility and the fifth facilitates knowledge of results:

1. Skill variety. The extent to which people are required to draw on a diverse set of job skills and abilities. Meaningful work requires that people use their capabilities.
2. Task identity. The extent to which a job allows people to complete a whole, identifiable piece of work, the outcome of which they can perceive.
3. Task significance. The extent to which the output of work has an impact on others, either people at work, or outside, such as service/product users.
4. Autonomy. Freedom to decide how to work and to accomplish goals. Autonomy at work is central to developing a sense of personal responsibility.
5. Feedback. Performance feedback (see Chapter 7) is critical for enabling people to gain knowledge of the results of their work.

There are elements of Herzberg's theory in the model, and the basic tenet of the JCM is that intrinsic motivation will be higher if these characteristics are present in people's jobs. In organizations, this means paying attention to job design, structuring jobs and work activities to ensure that the characteristics are present as far as is possible. How likely is it that such intervention would actually improve motivation?

Convincing support for the theory was provided by the meta-analysis by Fried and Ferris (1987), who found that the five job characteristics identified by the JCM were strongly positively related to internal job motivation and job satisfaction, although relationships with job performance and absenteeism were far weaker. Some studies have also tested specific aspects of the model.

Grant (2008) looked specifically at the effect of task significance on job performance. In the first experiment, fund-raising callers were given a task-significance intervention in which they read stories about how the work of former callers had benefited others. Those subjects who received the intervention significantly increased the number of pledges made and the amount of money raised one month later. In the second experiment, lifeguards were given a similar task-significance intervention in which they read stories about other lifeguards rescuing victims. Those subjects who received the intervention significantly increased the number of voluntary hours worked and the frequency of helping behaviours one month later. These two studies illustrate the positive impact emphasis on task significance can have on performance.

The empirical support for the JCM has maintained research interest in the model, and very recent studies have sought to develop and extend it. Through this development, the JCM might be seen as a precursor to wider perspectives on *job design*, rather than as a definitive model.

Sociotechnical systems approach to job design

The elements described in the JCM represent universal features of work that are theorized to make it more positive and rewarding. However, the model is less specific regarding the implementation of these features in specific job situations, and the differentiated needs and opportunities afforded by different roles. A different line of job design research provides insight in this respect: the sociotechnical systems approach.

The guiding principle of the sociotechnical approach is that work should be designed around human and technical aspects of work (Cherns, 1976; Clegg, 2000). These principles have been developed to extend to more detailed guiding principles for overall design approaches (e.g. *work design should reflect the needs of the business, its users and managers*), content (e.g. *systems should be simple in design and make problems visible*), and processes (e.g. *evaluation is an essential aspect of design*) (see Clegg, 2000, p. 465). More generally, the sociotechnical approach is discussed by Clegg, Robinson, Davis, Bolton, Pieniazek, and McKay (2017).

The essence of sociotechnical systems approaches is that each design situation is unique, contingent upon the combination of demands placed on the organization and its workers by its environmental, temporal, functional, social, technological and economic conditions. Design is not about ensuring standardized features, but rather ensuring harmony and alignment between the key elements of the job.

However, there is also a theme running through the approach about autonomy and ownership of design by the organization itself, and the people working in it. One widely researched implication of the approach was therefore the implementation of autonomous work teams: units established to complete whole tasks, and decide on how work should be set up and accomplished (Parker, Morgeson, & Johns, 2017). By design, many of the positive aspects of work captured in the JCM are inherent in this approach to team design. Evaluation of the impact of autonomous team design was generally positive in terms of benefits for productivity and well-being (e.g. Cohen & Bailey, 1997), although some studies indicate a bigger impact on well-being (e.g. Wall, Kemp, Jackson, & Clegg, 1986).

The trend towards greater freedom and autonomy in jobs generally means that the autonomy characteristic has taken on contemporary relevance. Morgeson, Johnson, Campion, Medsker, and Mumford (2006) examined the consequences of moving from a traditional workgroup setup to a semi-autonomous team structure over a 12-month period. Results showed an increase in effort expended, skill usage and problem-solving in employees who moved into semi-autonomous teams. Autonomy in this respect does appear to relate to increased effort and motivation.

Extending the scope of job design and motivation

Humphrey, Nahrgang, and Morgeson (2007) present a comprehensive model of job design features, differentiating motivational, social and work context characteristics, all of which they propose affect work outcomes such as performance, satisfaction, commitment and well-being. They maintain that the links between job characteristics and outcomes at work operate through the three psychological states in the JCM. Their model is shown in Figure 4.3, and was tested through meta-analysis.

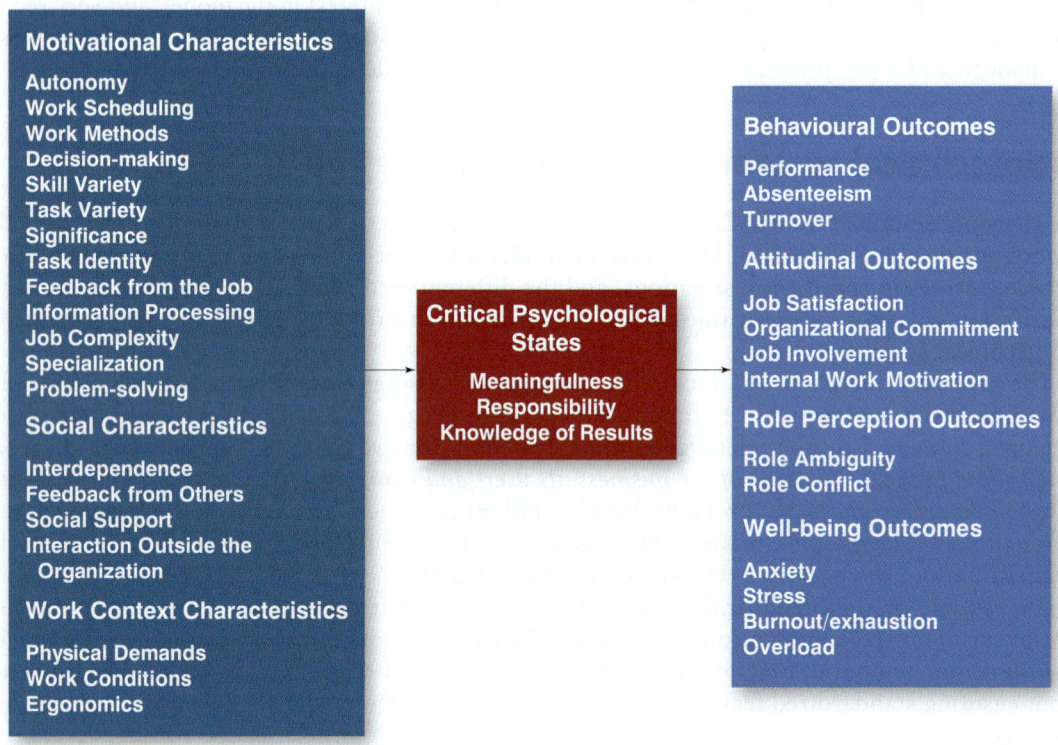

Figure 4.3   Job characteristics, psychological states and work outcomes

The results suggested substantial relationships between job characteristics and outcomes, providing further support for the idea that motivation can be improved through job design. Among the most interesting of findings were:

- Motivational and social characteristics accounted for 64 per cent of variance in organizational commitment, 87 per cent of variance in job involvement, 35 per cent of variance in subjective job performance, 7 per cent of variance in absence levels and 26 per cent of variance in turnover intentions.
- Motivational, social and work context characteristics accounted for 55 per cent of variance in job satisfaction, 38 per cent of variance in people's experience of work stress and 23 per cent of variance in burnout and exhaustion.

For managers and practitioners in organizations, the results of this meta-analysis clearly point to the value of considering carefully, and investing in, job design. The returns in terms of performance, well-being and, importantly, motivation appear well established in the research literature.

Humphrey et al.'s study also showed strong relationships between job characteristics and the three psychological states, and some support for the role of responsibility and meaningfulness as mediators. However, it appears that not all of the effects of job characteristics can be explained by the three psychological states, and this had led some to call for further refinements of the theory to really understand the mechanisms by which job characteristics lead to outcomes at work, including motivation, satisfaction and performance. Other attitudes such as engagement may need to be factored into theorizing (e.g. Woods & Sofat, 2013).

Pierce, Jussila, and Cummings (2009) propose a promising line of enquiry based on a single, integrative concept: psychological ownership. They suggest that the five core job characteristics give rise to a state of job-related psychological ownership. This comprises a sense of *mine-ness* about one's job – that it is more than simply a job role, rather it is *'my job, I own it, and control it, and it matters to me'* (Pierce, Kostova, & Dirks, 2003). Job characteristics are theorized to give rise to psychological ownership. For example, Pierce et al. (2009) suggest that autonomy is likely to provide employees with more opportunities for control over their work, while task identity requires the person to invest themselves personally into the job and establish an intimate relationship with their work. Both could develop a person's sense of job-related psychological ownership. This theory remains to be tested empirically, but does provide a good illustration of how the JCM continues to be relevant in research and practice, and how it might develop in the future.

Job demands, resources and control: Keys to work engagement

A separate stream of research in work and organizational psychology examines the issue of job design through the lens of work's impact on stress and health (Parker et al., 2017). Karasek's (1979) model of job demands and control proved to be highly influential in this track. The model positions job demands and controls as two key dimensions of job design. Motivation and well-being are enhanced by having greater control, whereas work has the greatest negative impact on health when demands are high and control low.

An enhancement to this approach was presented in seminal work on engagement by Demerouti, Bakker, Nachreiner, and Schaufeli (2001; see also Bakker & Demerouti, 2007). The job demands–resources model contrasts engagement and burnout as outcomes of the ways in which work is designed. They proposed that the outcome would be determined based on the balance of work demands versus the resources afforded by or to the worker, and importantly that resources could be represented by more than just autonomy, control and decision latitude.

The concept of work engagement has grown substantially from this work, and is important in as far as it bridges the conceptual gap between research lines on motivation and well-being (see e.g. Bakker, Schaufeli, Leiter, & Taris, 2008). Engagement is proposed as a motivational state representing high work-related well-being, and characterized by three psychological components:

- Vigour: having high levels of energy and mental resilience, investing effort and persistence.
- Dedication: being highly involved, experiencing a sense of significance and enthusiasm for work.
- Absorption: being fully concentrated and engrossed in work, whereby time passes quickly and detachment is difficult.

There has been much research into the predictors and effects of engagement. However, with respect to job design, the evidence for the pattern of effects of job demands and resources is compelling (see e.g. Crawford, LePine, & Rich, 2010). Resources are consistently related to higher engagement, and demands (provided they are seen as challenges rather than hindrances) also lead people to be more engaged.

Research in engagement from the perspective of job demands and resources also explores the role of the worker in seeking out more resources, a practice referred to as *job crafting* (literally crafting or developing one's job to enable acquisition of more resources to deal with demands). Demerouti, Bakker, and Gevers (2015) reported that such resource-seeking behaviour positively predicted greater engagement, which in turn predicted higher performance.

KEY THEME

The digital workplace – digital interactions at work: motivating or damaging

We are all familiar with the challenges that mobile technology brings for disengaging from work. Global working in combination with the portability of digital communication means that people are potentially connected to work constantly. On the other hand, in the concept of engagement, *finding it difficult to detach from a task* could simply be a sign of greater engagement. What are the impacts of digital interactions such as email, text and messaging on work motivation?

Research studies have looked at a number of aspects of this issue. For example, a study by Lanaj, Johnson, and Barnes (2014) examined the impact of late-night work-related smartphone use on engagement the next day. They found, unsurprisingly, that late-night use depleted people's energy through its effect on sleep, resulting in lower engagement as a consequence.

These findings are consistent with the effects observed for general information and communication technology, when it is characterized by greater volume, tighter response expectations and less functional effectiveness (Day, Paquet, Scott, & Hambley, 2012). However, this general negative consequence may not be the whole story. Provision of support, for example in the form of personal assistance and better functional support, were, in the same study, found to predict lower strain and stress. Also, there are likely to be individual differences in what works for people in terms of dealing with email and other forms of digital interactions (Russell, Woods, & Banks, 2017). For example, people who are highly conscientious are more likely to prefer to deal with emails right away, yet doing so may take them away from a core task. In Russell et al.'s study, resisting dealing with an email interruption when working on a task led to depleted well-being afterwards.

Overall, it seems critical that organizations address these potentially damaging and demotivating effects of digital communication, while realizing the obvious benefits of greater connectivity and flexibility about where and when to work.

PIONEERING WORK PSYCHOLOGISTS

Professor Evangelia Demerouti

Professor Evangelia Demerouti is a Full Professor at Eindhoven University of Technology (TU/e) and Chair of the Human Performance Management Group. Her research focuses on the processes enabling performance, including the effects of work characteristics, individual job strategies (including job crafting and decision-making), occupational well-being and work–life balance.

Professor Demerouti's pioneering work on the consequences of job demands and resources for well-being, burnout and engagement has founded new ways of understanding positive well-being at work and how it can be fostered through the design of work. Importantly, this work affords control to managers and people at work in making work positive and health-enhancing. For managers this is about designing jobs so that they include sufficient resources to deal with work demands. Workers can also exert some control by *crafting* their jobs to be more engaging through attaining more resources.

Overwhelmingly, Professor Demerouti's work offers great optimism for the prospect of improving the impact of work on people's psychological well-being and health.

Key example papers:

Bakker, A. B., & Demerouti, E. (2007). The job demands–resources model: state of the art. *Journal of Managerial Psychology, 22*(3), 309–328.

Demerouti, E., Bakker, A., & Gevers, J. M. (2015). Job crafting and extra-role behavior: The role of work engagement and flourishing. *Journal of Vocational Behavior, 91*, 87–96.

Demerouti, E., Bakker, A. B., Nachreiner, F., & Schaufeli, W. B. (2001). The job demands–resources model of burnout. *Journal of Applied Psychology, 86*(3), 499–512.

DISCUSS WITH A COLLEAGUE

Talk to a colleague about a current or past job (full- or part-time). Try to establish the extent to which the five job characteristics in the JCM are present in that job.

POSITIVE WORK

Putting theories of motivation to work

One of the barriers to applying theories of motivation in practice is a sense of which one to apply and when. With so many implications coming from the theories, how would managers be best advised to motivate their staff, and more broadly, how would an organization use the ideas to make a positive difference and motivate all of their employees? To answer these questions, the main theories of motivation need to be integrated and viewed alongside one another so that interventions draw jointly on multiple theories. In this section, we will discuss and explore the main emergent recommendations from theory and research on motivation. These are grouped into six strategies for promoting motivation at work.

Strategy 1. Remove sources of demotivation and treat people fairly

Herzberg's theory, along with equity theory and organizational justice research, all point to the potential for hygiene factors, including pay and rewards, to cause demotivation if people are dissatisfied with them. Research on justice suggests that one strategy to address potential sources of demotivation is to ensure that people feel they are receiving adequate return for the work that they give to an organization. More importantly, perceptions of the fairness of systems used to distribute benefits and rewards are critical, captured the concept of procedural justice. Systems and procedures in organizations, including those used to determine reward, have high potential for creating demotivation and dissatisfaction. Avoiding the negative consequences associated with these factors is likely to depend on improving systems and procedures, and ensuring people feel adequately and fairly rewarded for their work compared to others.

Strategy 2. Set people goals and objectives

The overwhelming evidence for the effectiveness of goal-setting as a performance improvement strategy underlines its importance in management. Goals should be specific and challenging, attainable, measurable and subject to deadlines that indicate the time frame for achieving them.

Setting goals is only part of ensuring their effectiveness, however. Commitment to goals is important to address, and it is likely that this can be encouraged in two ways: 1) by ensuring that outcome rewards are visible and valued (as in Strategy 5 below), so that employees feel that achieving the goal will be recognized and rewarded in ways that they appreciate; 2) through participative goal-setting, in which people contribute to the development of their own goals.

Not addressed in this chapter is the issue of capability, competence and skill. Goal accomplishment will obviously be dependent on people having the right knowledge, skills, abilities and competencies to achieve them, and so systems of employee development are important to integrate with goal-setting interventions.

Strategy 3. Provide autonomy and control

The benefits of having greater autonomy and control over work are evident in several theories and models in this chapter. From a work design perspective, the JCM includes autonomy as one of the key motivating characteristics of work. In Karasek's (1979) job demands–control model, the dimension of control and decision-making freedom is positioned as a key means of dealing with demands, a concept extended in job demands–resources models. Involvement and control are also important in attaining more advanced motivational states in self-determination theory. In practice, making a positive impact in this respect involves listening to staff at work, taking feedback and ideas, and releasing decision-making control so that people have choice about how to accomplish work objectives.

Strategy 4. Give people feedback

Feedback on performance has been included as a key motivational process in goal-setting theory and in the JCM. Feedback on performance allows people to determine whether they are on track to achieving goals, and to better understand the results of their work. Both are important for directing effort and behaviour, and thereby for influencing motivation. The mechanisms for providing feedback may need careful consideration, and some important issues in feedback are picked up in Chapter 7.

Strategy 5. Ensure an abundance of valued outcomes of work

Expectancy theory tells us that people are motivated to work on tasks and activities that lead to valued outcomes. Part of the challenge for managers is to understand those things that are important to people as individuals, essentially those outcomes from work that are valued by people. The next task in this strategy is to ensure that those things are abundant as far as is possible in the individual's work environment. This strategy is only likely to result in increased motivation if people are able to perceive the link between effort and performance on the one hand, and attaining the desired outcome on the other. Access to valued outcomes should be contingent on performance.

Strategy 6. Design jobs in ways that make them rewarding to people

The features or characteristics of work are important sources of motivation. Again, the ideas of motivation factors in Herzberg's theory provide a basic idea about the kinds of work features that are important to people, but the literature on job design specifies these much more precisely and clearly. Moreover, the there are many elements that can be designed into work that have been clearly demonstrated to be linked to positive work outcomes. Managing the features and characteristics of jobs is at the heart of job design. However, simply recommending that managers include rewarding features in job design is probably neglecting the practical realities of management in organizations. For example, most managers have limited control over the ways that they can change the design of work for their staff, which may rather be under the control of HR or other corporate groups. Second, the characteristics in Figure 4.3 seem like a long shopping list to attend to, which may dissuade managers from attempting to intervene in issues of work design.

However, such barriers can be overcome, and the application of models of motivation through job design may be more straightforward than it would appear. There is no research to suggest that motivation requires all of the job characteristics to be present. Certainly, it is likely to be highest when they are, but nevertheless the effects of rewarding job characteristics are likely to be additive. This means that implementing subsets of the characteristics is likely to be beneficial, provided that they are thought through clearly.

Moreover, the principles of sociotechnical systems design emphasize the value of having people involved in the design of their work. For example, a manager might introduce more autonomy into people's work, giving greater freedom for people to decide how to organize their work. However, without goal-setting, increased autonomy is unlikely

continued

to work. How would people organize their work if they did not know what they were working towards? Unhelpful systems and procedures that interfere with work would also need to be considered, and may need to be revised or redesigned. Otherwise, the combination of autonomy with administrative barriers of *hindrances* may provoke frustration.

The key point in this strategy is that work design can be addressed in various ways and to varying degrees to improve motivation, engagement and well-being, but that regardless of the scale of the intervention, careful attention needs to be given to the interaction of work requirements with organization systems and procedures. On a grand scale, work design is a key part of organization design, a subject that we return to later in this book.

Motivating people at work: From science to practice

These six strategies tie together some of the key practice implications of motivation theory and research. They provide a good illustration of how core theory in work and organizational psychology can translate through to practical application. The most important aspect of the strategies from the perspective of work and organizational psychology is that they are backed up by theory and sound science. This harks back to science, research and evidence-based practice and problem-solving. As we approach the end of this first part of the textbook, having covered a substantive volume of core theory and research in work and organizational psychology, it is useful to reflect on motivation theory as a clear illustration of the links between science and practice. The illustration makes it easy to see the value of sound scientific theory, which gives managers and practitioners confidence in making important decisions in organizations. These kinds of links feature even more strongly in Part Two of the book.

SUMMARY

The study of work motivation is concerned with why people initiate behaviour and effort at work, and the processes that determine its intensity, direction towards goals and maintenance over time. Theories of motivation abound in the work and organizational psychology literature, each addressing the topic in slightly different ways.

Simple early motivation theories examined the role of work in satisfying basic employee needs. Humanistic theories of Maslow, and later Alderfer, suggested that people were motivated to satisfy internal needs, and that work was one way of doing so. An alternative perspective was Herzberg's theory, which looked at work features specifically, differentiating hygiene factors from motivators, or extrinsic from intrinsic motivation.

McClelland considered motivation as trait-like, suggesting that people were more or less driven to satisfy inner needs for achievement, power and affiliation. Although trait-like, McClelland supposed that the needs could be developed. Research on this theory has focused on the performance-enhancing effects of need for achievement.

A powerful perspective on the role of psychological needs is self-determination theory, which examines how intrinsic motivation stems from the alignment of personal goals and values with work goals and values. Attaining this alignment helps to explain when and how work becomes internally motivated rather than externally regulated.

Two cognitive theories of motivation examine how motivation arises from thought processes. Expectancy theory describes how perceptions of desirable outcomes, and the belief that effort and performance will lead to those outcomes, combine to influence motivation and behaviour. Expectancy theory stands up reasonably well to empirical tests, and is practically very useful. Goal-setting theory has received more attention in research than any other motivation theory. Research clearly supports the idea that goal-setting increases effort and performance, and more recent elaborations of the theory provide thorough explanations of why they do so, and when they do so. The nature and content of goals are also critical to their effectiveness.

The role of fair treatment at work in motivation and demotivation is considered in equity theory and in research on organizational justice. As organizations become more concerned about corporate social responsibility, models of organizational justice will become increasingly important. The most recent models consider how people feel treated fairly in terms of the rewards they receive, by the systems for delivering those rewards and by other people at work.

A broader perspective on motivation examines how it is linked to job design. There are several approaches that consider the role of job design in motivation and well-being (for example, the JCM and the sociotechnical systems approach). Theories and models of work demands, control and resources bring a well-being and health dimension to the study of motivation, with work engagement offering a prospect for bridging the two. These models of the impact of job design on well-being and motivation stand up well in empirical research studies.

There are a variety of ways in which managers in organizations may apply theories and models of motivation at work in practice. Effective application involves integrating some of the concepts to develop overall strategies for improving motivation. Motivation serves as a good illustration of how sound research and scientific theory can be applied in practice.

The application of science and theory to practice is the central theme of Part Two of this book, which considers the professional applications of work and organizational psychology, building on the foundations established in this and the preceding three chapters. We hope that the topic of motivation at work has whetted your appetite.

DISCUSSION QUESTIONS

1. A manager of a customer services team has noticed that many staff in the team do not seem to be motivated to give the best possible service to customers. What could the manager do to improve motivation in this area?

2. Does Maslow's hierarchy of needs have any value as a theory of motivation in contemporary organizations?

3. Think about a time when you felt really motivated to accomplish something. Use motivation theories to explain this experience to colleagues.

4. Goal-setting is an individual-specific exercise, yet organizational justice tells us that people compare their own experiences with others in determining whether they are treated fairly. How can these two observations be reconciled?

5. How could you persuade a manager of the importance of fair treatment of employees at work?

6. How could a manager motivate employees in ways consistent with the ideas of the job demands–resources model?

7. Using the continuum of motivation in self-determination theory, try to identify the kind of motivation you have for different aspects of your current job or learning.

FURTHER READING

Kanfer, R., Frese, M., & Johnson, R. E. (2017). Motivation related to work: A century of progress. *Journal of Applied Psychology, 102*(3), 338–355.

Latham, G. P. (2012). *Work motivation: History, Theory, research and practice*. Thousand Oaks, CA: SAGE.

Latham, G. P., & Pinder, C. C. (2005). Work motivation theory and research at the dawn of the 21st century. *Annual Review of Psychology, 56*, 485–516.

Parker, S. K., Morgeson, F. P., & Johns, G. (2017). One hundred years of work design research: Looking back and looking forward. *Journal of Applied Psychology, 102*(3), 403–420.

Pinder, C. C. (2008). Work *Motivation in organizational behaviour*. New York, NY: Psychology Press.

REFERENCES

Adams, J. S. (1963). Toward an understanding of inequity. *Journal of Abnormal Psychology, 67*, 422–436.

Alderfer, C. P. (1969). An empirical test of a new theory of human needs. *Organizational Behaviour and Human Performance, 4*, 143–175.

Alderfer, C. P. (1972). *Existence, relatedness and growth*. New York, NY: Free Press.

Ambrose, M. L., & Kulik, C. T. (1999). Old friends, new faces: Motivation research in the 1990s. *Journal of Management, 25*(3), 231–292.

Ambrose, M. L., Schminke, M., & Mayer, D. M. (2013). Trickle-down effects of supervisor perceptions of interactional justice: A moderated mediation approach. *Journal of Applied Psychology, 98*, 678–89.

Aryee, S., Budhwar, P. S., & Chen, Z. X. (2002). Trust as a mediator of the relationship between organizational justice and work outcomes: Test of a social exchange model. *Journal of Organizational Behavior, 23*, 267–285.

Aryee, S., Chen, Z. X., Sun, L. Y, & Debrah, Y. A. (2007). Antecedents and outcomes of abusive supervision: Test of a trickle-down model. *Journal of Applied Psychology, 92*(1), 191.

Bakker, A. B., & Demerouti, E. (2007). The job demands–resources model: State of the art. *Journal of Managerial Psychology, 22*(3), 309–328.

Bakker, A. B., Schaufeli, W. B., Leiter, M. P., & Taris, T. W. (2008). Work engagement: An emerging concept in occupational health psychology. *Work & Stress, 22*(3), 187–200.

Bell, B. S., Wiechmann, D., & Ryan, A. M. (2006). Consequences of organizational justice expectations in a selection system. *Journal of Applied Psychology, 91*, 455–466.

Brocker, J., & Siegel, P. (1996). Understanding the interaction between procedural and distributive justice: The role of trust. In R. M. Kramer & T. R. Tyler (Eds.), *Trust in organizations: Frontiers of theory and research*. Thousand Oaks, CA: SAGE.

Brown, S. P., Ganesan, S., & Challagalla, G. (2001). Self-efficacy as a moderator of information-seeking effectiveness. *Journal of Applied Psychology, 86*, 1043–1051.

Cable, D. M., & Judge, T. A. (1994). Pay preferences and job search decisions: A person–organization fit perspective. *Personnel Psychology, 47*, 317–348.

Carver, C. S., & Scheier, M. F. (1981). The self-attention-induced feedback loop and social facilitation. *Journal of Experimental Social Psychology, 17*(6), 545–568.

Cherns, A. B. (1976). Principles of socio-technical design. *Human Relations, 29*, 783.

Clegg, C. W. (2000). Sociotechnical principles for system design. *Applied Ergonomics, 31*(5), 463–477.

Clegg, C. W., Robinson, M. A., Davis, M. C., Bolton, L. E., Pieniazek, R. L., & McKay, A. (2017). Applying organizational psychology as a design science: A method for predicting malfunctions in socio-technical systems (PreMiSTS). *Design Science, 3*.

Cohen, S. G., & Bailey, D. E. (1997). What makes teams work: Group effectiveness research from the shop floor to the executive suite. *Journal of Management, 23*(3), 239–290

Collins, C. J., Hanges, P. J., & Locke, E. A. (2004). The relationship of achievement motivation to entrepreneurial behaviour: A meta-analysis. *Human Performance, 17*(1), 95–117.

Colquitt, J. A., LePine, J. A., Piccolo, R. F., Zapata, C. P., & Rich, B. L. (2012). Explaining the justice–performance relationship: Trust as exchange deepener or trust as uncertainty reducer? *Journal of Applied Psychology, 97*(1), 1.

Colquitt, J. A., Scott, B. A., Judge, T. A., & Shaw, J. C. (2006). Justice and personality: Using integrative theories to derive moderators of justice effects. *Organizational Behaviour and Human Decision Processes, 100*, 110–127.

Crawford, E. R., LePine, J. A., & Rich, B. L. (2010). Linking job demands and resources to employee engagement and burnout: A theoretical extension and meta-analytic test. *Journal of Applied Psychology, 95*(5), 834.

Day, A., Paquet, S., Scott, N., & Hambley, L. (2012). Perceived information and communication technology (ICT) demands on employee outcomes: The moderating effect of organizational ICT support. *Journal of Occupational Health Psychology, 17*(4), 473.

Deci, E. L. (1971). Effects of externally mediated rewards on intrinsic motivation. *Journal of Personality and Social Psychology, 18*(1), 105.

Deci, E. L., & Ryan, R. M. (1985). *Intrinsic motivation and self-determination in human behavior*. Berlin, Germany: Springer Science & Business Media.

Demerouti, E., Bakker, A., & Gevers, J. M. (2015). Job crafting and extra-role behavior: The role of work engagement and flourishing. *Journal of Vocational Behavior, 91*, 87–96.

Demerouti, E., Bakker, A. B., Nachreiner, F., & Schaufeli, W. B. (2001). The job demands–resources model of burnout. *Journal of Applied Psychology, 86*(3), 499.

Downes, P. E., Kristof-Brown, A. L., Judge, T. A., & Darnold, T. C. (2017). Motivational mechanisms of self-concordance theory: Goal-specific efficacy and person–organization fit. *Journal of Business and Psychology, 32*(2), 197–215.

Dweck, C. S. (1986). Motivational processes affecting learning. *American Psychologist, 41*, 1040–48.

Dweck, C. S., & Leggett, E. L. (1988). A social-cognitive approach to motivation and personality. *Psychological Review, 95*, 256–273.

Erez, A., & Isen, A. M. (2002). The influence of positive affect on the components of expectancy motivation. *Journal of Applied Psychology, 87*(6), 1055–1067.

Erez, M., & Zidon, I. (1984). Effects of goal acceptance on the relationship of goal setting and task performance. *Journal of Applied Psychology, 69*, 69–78.

Ewen, R. B., Smith, P. C., Hulin, C. L., & Locke, E. A. (1966). An empirical test of the Herzberg two-factor theory. *Journal of Applied Psychology, 50*(6), 544–550.

Fried, Y., & Ferris, G. R. (1987). The validity of the job characteristics model: A review and meta-analysis. *Personnel Psychology, 40*(2), 287–322.

Furnham, A., & Argyle, M. (1998). *The psychology of money*. London, England: Routledge.

Gagné, M., & Deci, E. L. (2005). Self-determination theory and work motivation. *Journal of Organizational Behavior, 26*(4), 331–362.

Grant, A. M. (2008). The significance of task significance: Job performance effects, relational mechanisms and boundary conditions. *Journal of Applied Psychology, 93*(1), 108–124.

Hackman, J. R., & Oldham, G. R. (1980). *Work design*. Reading, MA: Addison-Wesley.

Herzberg, F., Mausner, B., & Snyderman, B. (1959). *The motivation to work*. New York, NY: John Wiley & Sons.

Hirschman, A. O. (1970). *Exit, voice, and loyalty: Responses to decline in firms, organizations, and states*. Cambridge, MA: Harvard University Press.

Hogan, J., & Hogan, R. (1996). *Motives, values, preferences manual*. Tulsa, OK: Hogan Assessment Systems.

House, R. J., & Wigdor, L. A. (1967). Herzberg's dual factor theory of job satisfaction and motivations: A review of the evidence and criticism. *Personnel Psychology, 20*(4), 369–389.

Humphrey, S. E., Nahrgang, J. D., & Morgeson, F. P. (2007). Integrating motivational, social and contextual work design features: A meta-analytic summary and theoretical extension of the work design literature. *Journal of Applied Psychology, 92*(5), 1332–1356.

Hundal, P. S. (1971). A study of entrepreneurial motivation: Comparison of fast and slow progressing small scale industrial entrepreneurs in Punjab, India. *Journal of Applied Psychology, 55*, 317–323.

Judge, T. A., & Bretz, R. D. (1992). Effects of work values on job choice decisions. *Journal of Applied Psychology, 77*, 261–271.

Judge, T. A., & Kammeyer-Mueller, J. D. (2012). On the value of aiming high: The causes and consequences of ambition. *Journal of Applied Psychology, 97*(4), 758.

Kanfer, F. H. (1977). The many faces of self-control, or behavior modification changes its focus. In R. B. Stuart (Ed.), *Behavioral self-management: Strategies, techniques, and outcomes* (pp. 1–48), New York, NY: Brunner/Mazel.

Kanfer, R., Frese, M., & Johnson, R. E. (2017). Motivation related to work: A century of progress. *Journal of Applied Psychology, 102*(3), 338.

Karasek, Jr., R. A. (1979). Job demands, job decision latitude, and mental strain: Implications for job redesign. *Administrative Science Quarterly, 24*(2), 285–308.

Klein, H. J., Wesson, M. J., Hollenbeck, J. R., & Alge, B. J. (1999). Goal commitment and the goal setting process: Conceptual clarification and empirical synthesis. *Journal of Applied Psychology, 84*, 885–896.

Kleingeld, A., van Mierlo, H., & Arends, L. (2011). The effect of goal setting on group performance: A meta-analysis. *Journal of Applied Psychology, 96*(6), 1289.

Kluger, A. N., & Tikochinsky, J. (2001). The error of accepting the 'theoretical' null hypothesis: The rise, fall and resurrection of commonsense hypotheses in psychology. *Psychological Bulletin, 127*, 408–423.

Knight, D., Durham, C. C., & Locke, E. A. (2001). The relationship of team goals, incentives and efficacy to strategic risk, tactical implementation and performance. *Academy of Management Journal, 44*, 623–639.

Lanaj, K., Johnson, R. E., & Barnes, C. M. (2014). Beginning the workday yet already depleted? Consequences of late-night smartphone use and sleep. *Organizational Behavior and Human Decision Processes, 124*(1), 11–23.

LaPorte, R., & Nath, R. (1976). Role of performance goals in prose learning. *Journal of Educational Psychology, 68*, 260–264.

Latham, G. P., & Locke, E. A. (2007). New developments in and directions for goal setting research. *European Psychologist, 12*(4), 290–300.

Latham, G. P., & Pinder, C. C. (2005). Work motivation theory and research at the dawn of the 21st century. *Annual Review of Psychology, 56*, 485–516.

Lawler, E. E. (1981). *Pay and organization development*. Reading, MA: Addison-Wesley.

Lawler, E. E., & Suttle, J. L. (1972). A causal correlation test of the need hierarchy concept. *Organizational Behaviour and Human Performance, 7*, 265–287.

Liao, W., & Tai, W. (2006). Organizational justice, motivation to learn and training outcomes. *Social Behavior and Personality: An International Journal, 34*(5), 545–556.

Lin, S. H. J., & Johnson, R. E. (2015). A suggestion to improve a day keeps your depletion away: Examining promotive and prohibitive voice behaviors within a regulatory focus and ego depletion framework. *Journal of Applied Psychology, 100*(5), 1381.

Lin, S. H. J., Ma, J., & Johnson, R. E. (2016). When ethical leader behavior breaks bad: How ethical leader behavior can turn abusive via ego depletion and moral licensing. *Journal of Applied Psychology, 101*(6), 815.

Locke, E. A. (1968). Toward a theory of task motivation and incentives. *Organizational Behavior and Human Performance, 3,* 157–189.

Locke, E. A., & Bryan, J. (1969). The directing function of goals in task performance. *Organizational Behaviour and Human Performance, 4,* 35–42.

Locke, E. A., & Latham, G. P. (1990). *A theory of goal setting and task performance.* Englewood Cliffs, NJ: Prentice Hall.

Locke, E. A., & Latham, G. P. (2002). Building a practically useful theory of goal setting and task motivation: A 35-year odyssey. *American Psychologist, 57,* 705–717.

Maslow, A. H. (1943). A theory of human motivation. *Psychological Review, 50,* 370–396.

Maslow, A. H. (1954). *Motivation and personality.* New York, NY: Harper & Row.

McClelland, D. C. (1961). *The achieving society.* New York, NY: Van Nostrand Reinhold.

Mitchell, T. R., & Mickell, A. E. (1999). The meaning of money: An individual difference perspective. *Academy of Management Review, 24,* 568–578.

Mitra, A., Jenkins, J. D., Gupta, N., & Shaw, J. D. (1997). *Financial incentive and performance: A meta-analytic review.* Paper presented at the annual meeting of the Society for Industrial and Organizational Psychology, St. Louis. Cited in: Mitchell, T. R., & Mickell, A. E. (1999). The meaning of money: An individual difference perspective. *Academy of Management Review, 24,* 568–578.

Morgeson, F. P., Johnson, M. D., Campion, M. A., Medsker, G. J., & Mumford, T. V. (2006). Understanding the reactions to job redesign: A quasi-experimental investigation of the moderating effects of organizational context on perceptions of performance behaviour. *Personnel Psychology, 59*(2), 333–363.

Mowday, R. T. (1991). Equity theory predictions of behavior in organizations. In R. M. Steers & L. W. Porter (Eds.), *Motivation and work behavior* (5th ed., pp. 111–130). New York, NY: McGraw-Hill.

Muraven, M., Tice, D. M., & Baumeister, R. F. (1998). Self-control as limited resource: Regulatory depletion patterns. *Journal of Personality and Social Psychology, 74*(3), 774–789.

Opsahl, R. L., & Dunnette, M. D. (1966). The role of financial compensation in industrial motivation. *Psychological Bulletin, 66*(2), 94–118.

Parker, S. K., Morgeson, F. P., & Johns, G. (2017). One hundred years of work design research: Looking back and looking forward. *Journal of Applied Psychology, 102*(3), 403.

Pierce, J. L., Jussila, I., & Cummings, A. (2009). Psychological ownership within the job design context: Revision of the job characteristics model. *Journal of Organizational Behaviour, 30,* 477–496.

Pierce, J. L., Kostova, T., & Dirks, K. T. (2003). The state of psychological ownership: Integrating and extending a century of research. *Review of General Psychology, 7*(1), 84.

Pinder, C. C. (1998). *Work motivation in organizational behaviour.* Upper Saddle River, NJ: Prentice Hall.

Pinder, C. C. (2008). *Work Motivation in organizational behaviour* (2nd ed.). New York: Psychology Press.

Pinder, C. C., & Harlos, K. P. (2001). Employee silence: Quiescence and acquiescence as responses to perceived injustice. *Research in Personnel and Human Resources Management, 20,* 331–369.

Porter, L. W., & Lawler, E. E. (1968). *Managerial attitudes and performance.* Homewood, IL: Richard D. Irwin.

Pritchard, R. D., & Sanders, M. S. (1973). The influence of valence, instrumentality and expectancy on effort and performance. *Journal of Applied Psychology, 57,* 55–60.

Rauschenberger, J., Schmitt, N., & Hunter, J. E. (1980). A test of the need hierarchy concept by a Markov model of change in need strength. *Administrative Science Quarterly, 25*(4), 654–670.

Robbins, S. P., & Judge, T. A. (2009). *Organizational behaviour* (Pearson International ed.). London, England: Pearson/Prentice-Hall.

Roberson, Q. M., & Stewart, M. M. (2006). Understanding the motivational effects of procedural and informational justice in feedback processes. *British Journal of Psychology, 97*(3), 281–298.

Ronen, S. (2001). Self-actualization versus collectualization: Implications for motivation theories. In M. Erez, U. Klenbeck, & H. K. Thierry (Eds.), *Work motivation in the context of a globalizing economy* (pp. 341–368). Hillsdale, NJ: Lawrence Erlbaum.

Rothkopf, E., & Billington, M. (1979). Goal-guided learning from text: Inferring a descriptive processing model from inspection times and eye movements. *Journal of Educational Psychology, 71,* 310–327.

Russell, E., Woods, S. A., & Banks, A. P. (2017). Examining conscientiousness as a key resource in resisting email interruptions: Implications for volatile resources and goal achievement. *Journal of Occupational and Organizational Psychology, 90*(3), 407–435.

Ryan, R. M., & Deci, E. L. (2000). Self-determination theory and the facilitation of intrinsic motivation, social development, and well-being. *American Psychologist, 55*(1), 68.

Sachau, D. A. (2007). Resurrecting the motivation–hygiene theory: Herzberg and the positive psychology movement. *Human Resource Development Review, 6*(4), 377–393.

Seijts, G. H., Latham, G. P., Tasa, K., & Latham, B. W. (2004). Goal setting and goal orientation: An integration of two different yet related literatures. *Academy of Management Journal, 47*(2), 227–239.

Soliman, H. M. (1970). Motivation–hygiene theory of job attitudes: An empirical investigation and an attempt to reconcile both the one- and the two-factor theories of job attitudes. *Journal of Applied Psychology, 54*(5), 452–461.

Tang, T. L. (1992). The meaning of money re-visited. *Journal of Organizational Behaviour, 13*(2), 197–202.

Trougakos, J. P., Beal, D. J., Cheng, B. H., Hideg, I., & Zweig, D. (2015). Too drained to help: A resource depletion perspective on daily interpersonal citizenship behaviors. *Journal of Applied Psychology, 100*(1), 227.

Unsworth, K. L., & McNeill, I. M. (2017). Increasing pro-environmental behaviors by increasing self-concordance: Testing an intervention. *Journal of Applied Psychology, 102*(1), 88.

Van-Dijk, D., & Kluger, A. N. (2004). Feedback sign effect on motivation: Is it moderated by regulatory focus? *Applied Psychology: An International Review, 53*, 113–135.

Van Eerde, W., & Thierry, H. (1996). Vroom's expectancy models and work-related criteria: A meta-analysis. *Journal of Applied Psychology, 81*(5), 575–586.

Vansteenkiste, M., Lens, W., De Witte, H., & Feather, N. T. (2005). Understanding unemployed people's job search behaviour, unemployment experience and well-being: A comparison of expectancy-value theory and self-determination theory. *British Journal of Social Psychology, 44*(2), 268–286.

Vroom, V. H. (1964). *Work motivation.* New York. NY: John Wiley & Sons.

Wahba, M. A., & Bridwell, L. G. (1976). Maslow reconsidered: A review of research on the need hierarchy theory. *Organizational Behaviour and Human Performance, 15*, 212–240.

Wall, T. D., Kemp, N. J., Jackson, P. R., & Clegg, C. W. (1986). Outcomes of autonomous workgroups: A long-term field experiment. *Academy of Management Journal, 29*(2), 280–304.

Wang, H. J., Lu, C. Q., & Siu, O. L. (2015). Job insecurity and job performance: The moderating role of organizational justice and the mediating role of work engagement. *Journal of Applied Psychology, 100*(4), 1249.

Whyte, W. F. (1955). *Money and motivation: An analysis of incentives in industry.* New York, NY: Harper & Row.

Wood, R., & Locke, E. (1990). Goal setting and strategy effects on complex tasks. In B. M. Staw & L. L. Cummings (Eds.), *Research in organizational behaviour* (Vol. 12, pp. 73–109). Greenwich, CT: JAI Press.

Woods, S. A., & Sofat, J. (2013) Personality and work engagement: The mediating role of psychological meaningfulness. *Journal of Applied Social Psychology, 43*(11), 2203–2210).

Wright, P. (1989). Motivation and job satisfaction. In C. Molander (Ed.), *Human resource management.* Lund, Sweden: Studentlitteratur.

Zapata-Phelan, C. P., Colquitt, J. A., Scott, B. A., & Livingston, B. (2009). Procedural justice, interactional justice and task performance: The mediating role of intrinsic motivation. *Organizational Behaviour and Human Decision Processes, 108*(1), 93–105.

Zetik, D. C., & Stuhlmacher, A. (2002). Goal setting and negotiation performance: A meta-analysis. *Group Processes and Intergroup Relations, 5*, 35–52.

Zhang, Y., LePine, J. A., Buckman, B. R., & Wei, F. (2014). It's not fair… or is it? The role of justice and leadership in explaining work stressor–job performance relationships. *Academy of Management Journal, 57*(3), 675–697.

CASE STUDIES FOR PART ONE: FOUNDATIONS OF WORK AND ORGANIZATIONAL PSYCHOLOGY

CASE STUDY 1.1

Switch Appliances: Aiming to Improve Staff Satisfaction and Happiness at Work

Switch Appliances is South Africa's leading manufacturer and distributor of major domestic appliances. It was founded in 1987 by Christopher Miller and his brother Mathew Miller, when they started manufacturing electric stoves.

Switch Appliances now offers customers a full range of kitchen and laundry appliances, including a bespoke design service, with a customer satisfaction warranty. The company's head office is in Silverton, Pretoria. It also owns three factories, operating at the following locations:

- East London – manufactures refrigerators and freezers
- Cape Town – manufactures stoves, washing machines and dishwashers
- Kimberly – manufactures electric and gas ovens, hobs and tumble dryers.

All factories have been accredited to standards of ISO 9001:2015. Switch Appliances also markets microwaves and air conditioners.

The organization has the strongest appliance brand positioning in South Africa with the slogan *'Turn your house into a home with just a switch'*.

It generates high revenue and was recently awarded 'best household appliance manufacturer in South Africa' at the Homemakers Expos in 2017 and 2018, recognizing its quality service. Consumers value the quality, user-centred design and after-sales service that Switch Appliances offers.

The organization has also started exporting its appliances to other African countries to expand its market base, and is seeking to export further afield.

Switch Appliances employs around 800 staff from diverse backgrounds. These staff are primarily based at the Pretoria head office. Brand manager Mike Thompson states: 'We stand for forward thinking and planning, continuity of values and goals, good relationships, and an employee-orientated corporate and leadership culture.'

The working hours for administrative and managerial staff are 8:00–17:00, Monday to Friday, while the assembly-line staff at the factories work three eight-hour shifts every week. Owing to the large number of employees in the organization, Switch Appliances has an HR manager and team to deal with all the employee-related matters that may arise. They do not currently have a work and organizational psychologist on their staff.

Two of the most important concerns of HR managers in South Africa today are employee productivity and job satisfaction, and how to manage these two critical factors together. South Africa's average productivity has been steadily growing in recent years compared to the global average. Switch Appliances strives for employee satisfaction and aims to bring this about in a manner that balances employee needs with the organization's goals. Switch Appliances attempts to increase employee morale and does so by rewarding success and good performance.

Sources and Further Reading

Wärnich, S., Carrell, M. R., Elbert, N. F., & Hatfield. R. D. (2018). *Human resource management in South Africa* (6th ed.). Andover, England: Cengage Learning EMEA.

continued

Case Questions

1. The HR manager at Switch Appliances is very concerned about increasing employee productivity and job satisfaction. How could job design interventions and other theories of motivation help to address these concerns?

2. What are the individual differences that might facilitate effectiveness for employees in Switch Appliances? How could these help to address issues of productivity?

3. What kinds of management issues should leaders consider to make a positive difference to work at Switch Appliances?

4. Muhammad is a social media marketing manager at Switch Appliances. He is responsible for marketing and advertising the organization's products on all social media platforms. Muhammad has two children. His wife, Fatima, who used to drop the children at school and fetch them afterwards, has started attending lectures in the evening to complete her honours degree. Muhammad approaches the HR manager, saying that he needs to take on additional family responsibilities such as picking up his children from school in the afternoons before the day-care centre closes. He needs to leave work at 16:00 to do so. The HR manager is aware that the employees at the organization are diverse individuals from various backgrounds. As a mother herself, she recognizes the need for workplace flexibility to accommodate employees' diverse needs.

How could the leadership and the HR manager strive to make the organization more inclusive and flexible for employees like Muhammad?

CASE STUDY 1.2

Unilever Plc

Unilever is one of the world's biggest consumer goods companies. It is estimated that every day, 2.5 billion people use Unilever products. The company has an annual turnover in excess of €50 billion and employs around 160,000 people.

Unilever has been pursuing a vision that is distinctive in businesses of its sector and size. Its vision is stated as:

> *"Unilever has a simple but clear purpose – to make sustainable living commonplace. We believe this is the best long-term way for our business to grow."*

The vision is applied in a strategic direction:

> *"[Unilever's] distinct Purpose and our operational expertise across our business model will help realise our vision to grow our business, whilst decoupling our environmental footprint from our growth and increasing our positive social impact."*

In practice this means pursuing growth in a sustainable way and providing consumers with the 'products they need to look good, feel good and get more out of life'. This is reflected in the company's priorities and principles:

- a better future for children
- a healthier future
- a more confident future

- a better future for the planet
- a better future for farming and farmers.

Former CEO Paul Polman is quoted as saying:

"we cannot close our eyes to the challenges that the world faces. Business must make an explicit and positive contribution to addressing them. I'm convinced we can create a more equitable and sustainable world for all of us by doing so, but this means that business has to change. The Unilever Sustainable Plan is a blueprint for sustainable growth."

Unilever's values and principles

Corporate behaviour standards and the way that Unilever does business and interacts with colleagues, partners, customers and consumers are founded on four core values:

- always working with integrity
- positive impact and continuous improvement
- setting out our aspirations
- working with others.

Unilever's business model

Unilever is guided by the principle that profitable growth should be responsible growth. This ethos is carried into the business model that the company follows. This is represented as a cycle (Exhibit 1.2.1).

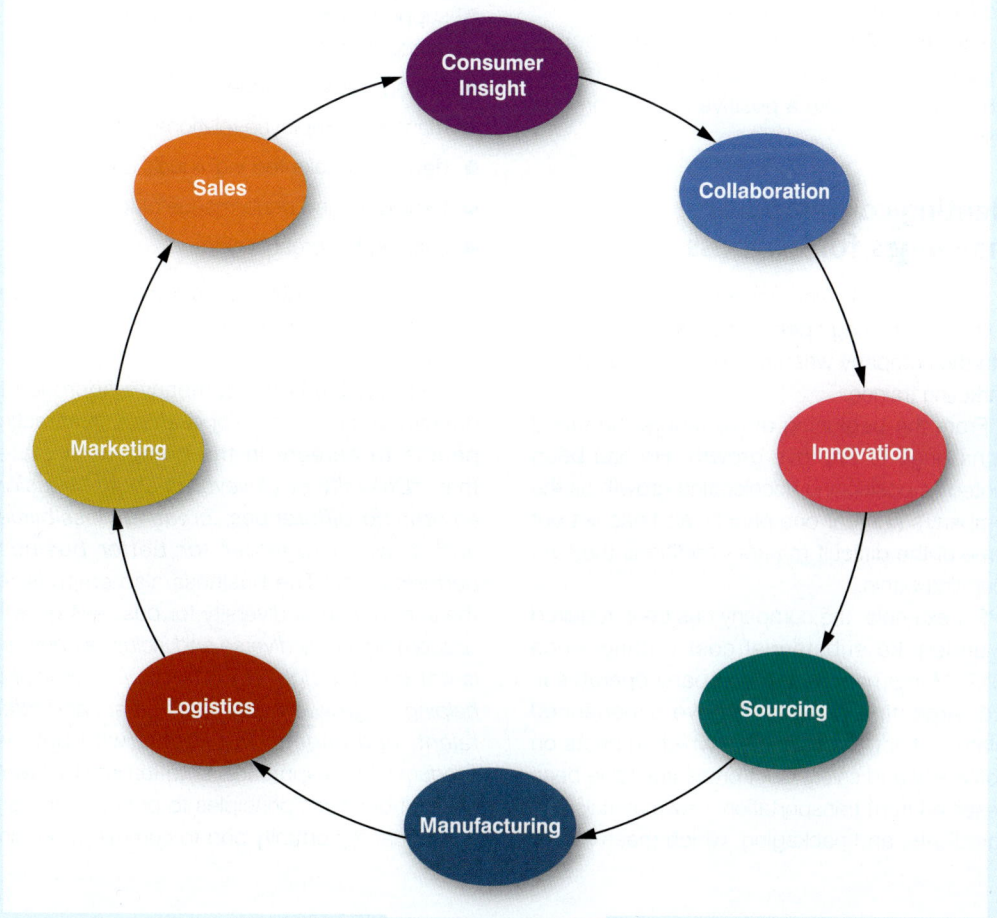

Exhibit 1.2.1 Unilever's business model

continued

The purpose of the business model is to combine insight from the various stakeholders of the Unilever business to deliver products that meet the company's vision, with the capacity for market success and growth.

Attracting people to work at Unilever

The philosophy and business approach of Unilever is strongly embedded in the way that it attracts people to work for the company. It emphasizes that *"Unilever is the place where you can bring your purpose to life through the work that you do, creating a better business and a better world. You will work with brands that are loved and improve the lives of our consumers and the communities around us."*

The appeal that it makes to prospective employees is to believe in purpose-led business and to seek to make a positive impact through their work.

Meeting contemporary challenges for business

In January 2019, Alan Jope took over as CEO of Unilever, having spent his career since 1985 with the company when he joined as a graduate marketing trainee.

From the beginning of his tenure, he faced a challenge to improve growth. He has been quoted as positioning accelerating growth as the company's number one priority, and has set out some of the difficult market conditions they are operating within.

For example, the company has been required to undertake substantial cost-cutting since 2017. Many markets the company operates in (e.g. Argentina and Brazil) have experienced volatility affecting currencies, which impacts on profitability and sales. Cost pressures have been presented from transportation, raw materials and ingredients, and packaging, which mean higher prices for consumers. In 2019, Unilever also faced the uncertainty of Brexit (by which the UK – where Unilever's HQ is located – prepared to leave the European Union).

These challenges reflect the state of the world and its economies more widely. Volatility, uncertainty, complexity and ambiguity are characteristic of the environments that businesses operate in. Running alongside is the rapid advancement of technology.

Managing the people of Unilever

The Human Resources group in Unilever have responsibility for core people management functions in the company, working on, for example:

- supporting well-being and championing success of staff
- driving culture change
- managing employee relations
- developing talented individuals and leaders
- turning around performance of teams
- shaping the organization.

Unilever seeks to develop its own purpose-driven leaders and encourage innovative thinking among its employees.

Also notable is the company's approach to diversity and inclusion. For example, in attracting people to careers in the company it states that: *"Diversity at Unilever is about inclusion, embracing differences, creating possibilities and growing together for better business performance."* The business also emphasizes the importance of diversity for business growth: *"Becoming a truly diverse and inclusive company is not only the right thing to do, it is crucial to helping us grow our business, attract and retain talent, and engage the people who buy our products."* This approach is written into Unilever's code of business principles to promote diversity and equal opportunity and to commit to building a work environment where there is mutual trust, respect for human rights and no discrimination. The company aspires to build a gender-balanced organization with an inclusive work culture. In 2017, 47 per cent of Unilever's managers were women, and in the UK, men on average earned 1.9 per cent more than women (although median pay was 2.2 per cent higher for women than for men). The distribution of men and women across roles in the company, however, is important in understanding the context of these differences in earnings (for example, men are proportionally more likely to work in the factories that Unilever operates, and in senior positions in the company).

What next for Unilever?

The direction of Unilever is set out in its corporate information online and elsewhere. However, pursuing a strategy of growth while maintaining commitment to its core vision and value will be a difficult task. This is the reality facing many organizations, which strive to make a positive impact in the work they do while protecting the financial sustainability of the business at the same time.

Unilever is undoubtedly distinctive in signalling its commitment to a new way of doing business and placing sustainable living (which includes both environmental and social sustainability) at the heart of its vision. The people who work for Unilever will be instrumental in ensuring that this is protected while the required business growth is delivered.

References and further reading

Information Correct as of March 2019, sourced from: www.unilever.co.uk/about/who-we-are/introduction-to-unilever/

www.unilever.co.uk/about/who-we-are/our-vision/

www.unilever.co.uk/about/who-we-are/purpose-and-principles/

www.unilever.co.uk/about/who-we-are/our-strategy/

www.standard.co.uk/business/unilever-s-new-boss-alan-jope-warns-of-tough-market-ahead-as-sales-disappoint-a4054081.html

www.ft.com/content/95eec1ec-252b-11e9-8ce6-5db4543da632

www.unilever.co.uk/careers/graduates/diversity-and-inclusion.html

www.unilever.co.uk/about/who-we-are/diversity-and-inclusion/

www.unilever.com/sustainable-living/enhancing-livelihoods/opportunities-for-women/advancing-diversity-and-inclusion/

www.unilever.com/Images/unilever-gender-pay-report-2017-final_tcm244-514178_en.pdf

Case questions

1. Based on Unilever's values and business model, what individual differences are likely to influence success for people working in the organization? How can Unilever seek to develop these in staff?

2. How can motivation theories help Unilever to embed the values and purpose-driven nature of the business in the way that people work?

3. Managers and leaders may be faced with difficult choices as they grow revenues and cut costs in the business. How would self-determination theory help to understand ways to ensure that the purpose – making sustainable living commonplace – is retained and protected in business development?

4. Some of the activities of HR involve organizational change and will likely involve attitude change. How does the material from the foundations of work and

continued

organizational psychology inform how this might be achieved?

5   As all staff will need to contribute to delivering growth, what are some of the attitudes and other people-factors that Unilever may need to monitor to ensure that staff well-being is maintained?

6   What are some of the ways that Unilever might seek to achieve its aims around diversity and inclusion?

7   To what extent would digital technology play a part in the some of your ideas and discussions in the questions above? What issues might the use of technology present?

PART TWO

PROFESSIONAL PRACTICE OF WORK AND ORGANIZATIONAL PSYCHOLOGY

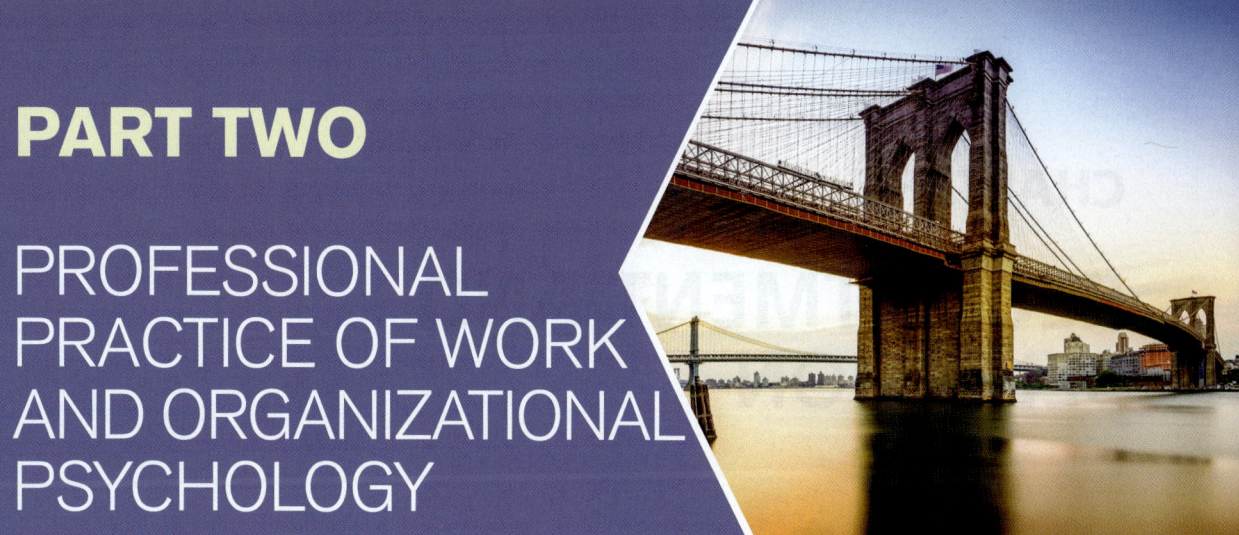

Areas of professional practice in work and organizational psychology have the potential to make important contributions to improving people management processes and systems in businesses, resulting in more positive psychological and physical health, higher engagement, and better performance and effectiveness. It is the critical intersection where psychology can be put into practice directly in organizations.

Part Two of this book will explore how our knowledge base can make a direct positive impact by informing how we manage key processes and discharge responsibilities to the people working in organizations. The chapters will show you how businesses and organizations can improve decisions about recruitment and selection, ensuring that those decisions are ethical and fair; make better investments in training, learning and development; and manage people's individual contributions more effectively through improved performance management.

From the perspective of individuals themselves, these and other experiences at work are accumulated over many years and even decades, representing careers. We will see how organizations have a role to play in facilitating career development and understanding the new expectations of people about work and its role in their lives. With work forming such a significant part of our lives, we should strive to do all we can to understand how people can thrive in their jobs and workplaces.

Furthermore, we'll also look at the effects of work on health. The demands of work and modern life are very different from those experienced by our ancestors, and humans have not evolved to cope with these new kinds of life pressures. Organizations have a responsibility to ensure that the demands of work in the 21st Century are not damaging to people's health and well-being, and this study of safety, stress and health at work has a pivotal role to play.

The next five chapters encourage you to think in new ways about people management practice and systems in organizations, identifying practical ways in which they can be changed and improved to make a positive difference to work and organizational life.

5   Recruitment and Selection
6   Learning, Training and Development
7   Performance Management
8   Careers and Career Management
9   Safety, Stress and Health at Work

CHAPTER 5

RECRUITMENT AND SELECTION

LEARNING OBJECTIVES

- Describe the importance and features of effective recruitment and selection in organizations.
- Describe and understand the systematic process of recruitment and selection, and key foundations of job analysis, reliability and validity.
- Understand and critically evaluate selection assessment techniques and their evidence base, including the impact of new and digital technology.
- Understand macro perspectives on recruitment and selection and the experience of recruitment and selection from the applicant's perspective.
- Critically evaluate concepts and methods for establishing fairness in recruitment and selection.

Take a walk through the nearest city to your home and marvel at the vast array of jobs being done by the people who work in it. You will see public services being provided, transportation, governmental, construction and maintenance, policing and emergency support, community development and enforcement. You will see retail and commerce, shopping centres, property sales and development, professional services. There will be medical practices and hospitals. Perhaps legal and financial services firms and education providers. Just try to build a picture in your mind of the diversity of the jobs that exist in these different organizations. Now try to think about what kinds of knowledge, skills, abilities and characteristics would be needed for those different roles. The skills required to work with children in a hospital are quite different from those required by your average solicitor or investment banker. Moreover, jobs that appear similar may have quite different requirements based on the specific work styles or organizational cultures of different businesses.

The extent to which people are suited for different kinds of jobs of course depends on their individual attributes. On meeting people for the first time, it is almost always difficult to perceive their traits, and even harder to perceive anything about their skills and abilities. Yet this is exactly the same situation as a job interview, which is usually the first time that an employer is able to meet a prospective employee.

The challenge facing recruiters and selectors in organizations is therefore three-fold. First, they need to be able to measure individual differences that are often hard to perceive. Second, they need to be able to make a judgement about whether those individual differences are suited to a particular job role in a particular organization. Finally, they need to understand how the needs of specific organizations, and the business environments that they exist within, should be incorporated into selection decisions. Recruitment and selection are therefore about identifying people who will thrive, be engaged and perform in specific jobs and organizations.

THE ORGANIZATIONAL IMPERATIVE

The challenge to recruit highly skilled or talented people into organizations is increasingly important. Globalization and continual developments in technology mean that product innovations are quickly adopted by competitors (Cooper, Robertson, & Tinline, 2003), and so do not offer persistent competitive advantage. Cooper et al. also point out that the brand advantage can easily be eroded by customer experiences. Competitive advantage in organizations therefore arguably lies in the people it can attract, recruit and retain. Their performance has a critical impact on the performance of the organization. Utility analysis (the analysis of the financial benefits of increased employee productivity; Schmidt & Hunter, 1983) indicates that the difference in productivity between a below average performer and an above average performer is worth about 80 per cent of their salary. This underlines why selecting those people who are likely to be high performers is so important. This chapter will explore some of the ways that organizations recruit and select their employees, focusing on the contributions of psychologists to recruitment and selection methodology.

EFFECTIVE RECRUITMENT AND SELECTION

It is possible to examine recruitment and selection from both micro and macro perspectives. The micro perspective (not to be confused with *simple*) is concerned with the processes and procedures of recruitment and selection. The macro perspective considers the wider factors and demands that influence how recruitment and selection are applied in organizations. These include strategic demands of the organization that may apply at a specific point of time. Cutting through both of these perspectives is the issue of fairness, which represents the need to ensure that recruitment and selection are free from bias and unfair discrimination. In this chapter, we begin from the micro perspective, and look at specific procedures and techniques of recruitment and selection, considering relevant evidence in each case. We then consider these in the context of the macro perspective, before outlining the critical relevance and implications of fairness. Taking what we know from these perspectives, we may define an effective approach to recruitment and selection as one that is:

- Evidence based – this means that research and empirical evidence is used to inform the processes and procedures of recruitment and selection.
- Systematic – this means that processes follow a logical pathway whereby decisions are made sequentially and on the basis of sound analyses.
- Fair – this means free from bias and unfair discrimination.
- Strategic – this means that recruitment and selection are performed with due attention to the strategic context of the HR function and the strategic needs of the organization.

Recruitment and selection is best conceptualized as a longitudinal process, comprising a series of stages. Figure 5.1 is a good representation of the process. It shows the practical tasks of recruitment and selection as well as the activities that underpin them. The aim of these activities is to ensure that the process is undertaken systematically and according to methodological best practice. The emphasis in most of this literature is towards the effectiveness of such systematic or structured techniques of selection (Zibarras & Woods, 2010). These might be defined as techniques that have a high degree of procedural methodology and clear processes of measurement and evaluation. The research literature, virtually without exception, points to the merits of such techniques (e.g. Schmidt & Hunter, 1998). If followed, the benefits are that relevant job competencies are assessed reliably and fairly, giving the most adequate indication of later job performance.

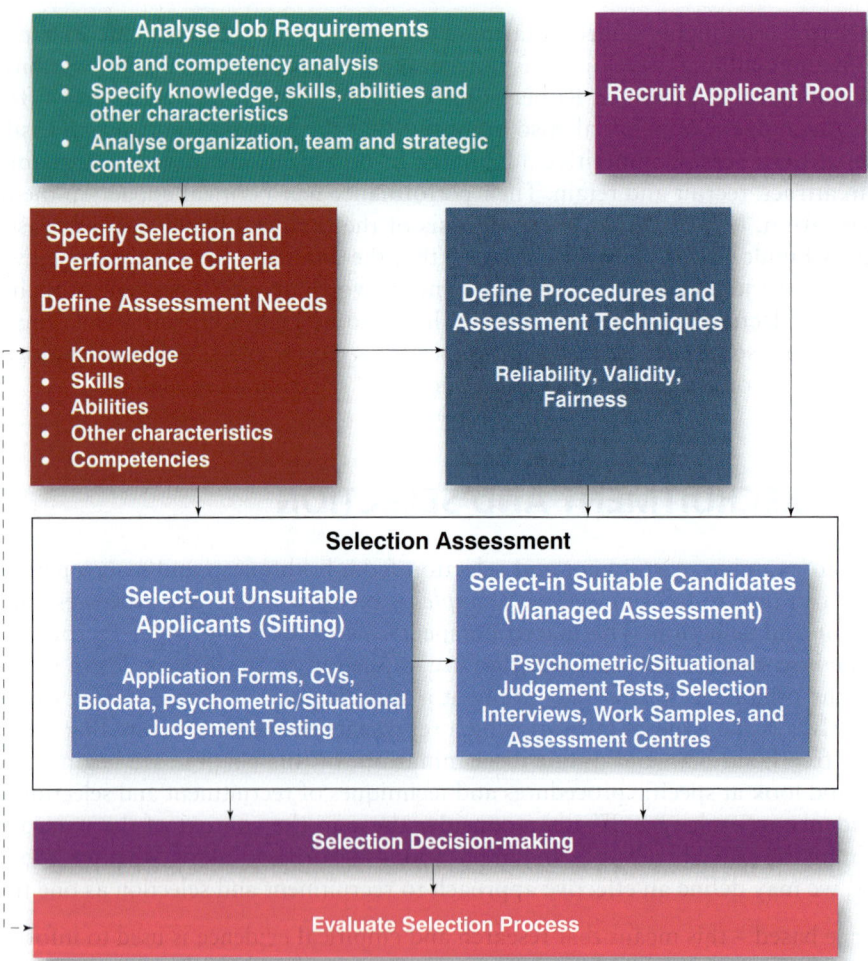

Figure 5.1 A model of the recruitment and selection process

Systematic approaches to selection follow a series of sequential steps and apply problem-solving logic to the recruitment and selection problem (see Figure 5.1). The selection process starts with an analysis of the job to be selected for. Information about the job role and its associated tasks is used to derive a specification of the knowledge, skills, abilities and other characteristics (KSAOs) that are essential or desirable for a person performing the job role. Based on the job analysis, recruitment activities are carried out to advertise and communicate job vacancies and attract job applicants by describing the tasks and person requirements alongside benefits and other information.

Job analysis information is also used to define selection criteria (i.e. the criteria that determine whether someone should be selected or rejected), reflecting the eventual performance requirements of the employee. Practitioners must then decide how best to assess job applicants and candidates against those criteria, and there are a range of different assessment methods that may be used to do this. Some of the major methods used in organizations are shown in the figure, and information about the reliability and validity of selection assessments also guides choices about which techniques to use. Technology has profoundly transformed the practices of recruitment and selection, with the use of social media, big data and the 'HR Tech' industry introducing new ways of managing and implementing processes. However, the fundamental steps of a systematic approach and the use of science to evaluate its effectiveness remain relevant.

Finally, best practice in selection includes an evaluation phase, in which selectors investigate whether the process was successful. The practical job of recruitment and selection is to attract a pool of job applicants, *select-out* unsuitable applicants, *select-in* potential candidates, and finally make a hiring decision.

Fit with wider organizational systems

Recruitment and selection can be viewed as core HRM activities (Davis & Scully, 2008), and it is useful to conceptualize them alongside other HR functions. Broadly speaking, recruitment and selection aim to identify, from a group of individuals, the person or persons with the highest potential for job success as indicated by a profile of KSAOs. The key word there is potential. Realizing the potential for success depends on a variety of other HR processes, including job design, management and leadership, training and socialization, and performance management systems. These interact to determine whether the individuals who are selected will go on to perform effectively in the organization (Figure 5.2). It is, of course, possible to extend this reasoning further to encompass the effects of team climate, organizational cultures and ultimately market environments on individual performance (see Part Three of this book).

Figure 5.2 Selection in the context of other human resource systems

Systematic selection: Perspectives in work and organizational psychology

Psychologists have a reputation for designing and implementing effective selection systems, and this is an important area where some psychological techniques have proven potential to contribute to practice. Psychologists have contributed significantly to recruitment and selection through the development, improvement and evaluation of an array of assessment approaches and methodologies, drawing on some of the core principles of psychological testing outlined in Chapter 2.

Much of the work that psychologists have undertaken has aimed to reduce the subjectivity of selection, minimizing the biases that selectors bring to the assessment processes, the most common of which are shown in Box 5.1. Although assessments of people to determine their suitability for particular jobs can be traced back centuries, the first applications of psychological assessment in selection were carried out by the military after the First World War. A basic personality inventory (Woodworth's Personal Data Sheet) was used to differentiate soldiers predisposed to experiencing 'shell shock' (a condition that may now be referred to as post-traumatic stress disorder; Winter & Barenbaum, 1999). This first venture into assessment for selection has developed over the past 90 years into a variety of different assessment methods. The most widely applied psychological assessment techniques include psychological or psychometric testing, biodata, and work-sample techniques such as assessment centres. Psychologists have also improved the understanding and application of more traditional techniques such as interviewing and the use of application forms. A more recent approach, which is gathering popularity and much evidence in the literature, combines techniques for measuring situational judgements. Psychologists have also contributed substantially to job analysis methods that form the foundations of recruitment and selection, and other HR functions.

BOX 5.1
Subjective biases in people perception

Beautyism: The tendency for assessors to rate candidates they perceive to be attractive more highly than those they do not.

Halo effect: Perceiving a person as positive and henceforth seeing only their positive features.

Horns effect: Same as the halo effect, but perceiving only negative information about a person.

Similar-to-me: Holding oneself as the 'gold standard' and comparing all others to one's own attributes.

Stereotyping: Making prejudiced assumptions about a person based on their appearance or demographic background (ethnicity, gender, age, regional dialect/accent).

Self-delusion: Believing oneself to be immune from subjective bias.

JOB ANALYSIS

What exactly are we trying to assess in selection processes? Overall, the purpose of selection assessment is to measure those attributes that enable an effective decision about the suitability of a particular job candidate. How would one identify and prioritize such attributes? Methods of job analysis represent the way that work psychologists answer this question, and are essential foundations of personnel selection processes. Job analysis is the catch-all label given to a range of techniques that are designed to help us understand what people do at work, and why some people do it better than others. Brannick, Levine, and Morgeson (2007) give a clear definition of job analysis.

> *Job analysis is the systematic process of discovery of the nature of a job by dividing it into smaller units, where the process results in one or more written products with the goal of describing what is done on the job or what capabilities are needed to effectively perform the job.* (Brannick et al., 2007, p. 8.)

The purpose of job analysis is to determine the characteristics of the job, to use these to state the KSAOs that should be demonstrated by the employee and ultimately to define the performance criteria for the job. Traditional job analysis is described as 'work-oriented' analysis, because the focus of the analyst is on the job and its associated tasks. There are a variety of different methods for conducting job analyses, and most are covered in depth in specialist sources or texts (e.g. Pearn & Kandola, 1988; Searle, 2003; Smith & Robertson, 1993; Woods & Hinton, 2017). Box 5.2 provides a summary of the main methods that are used in organizations. These methods supplement basic desk research techniques used by practitioners, for example reference to existing sources such as training manuals and past job specifications.

The product of job analysis is a job description, which describes concisely the main tasks and responsibilities of the job. The production of such task lists assumes that the tasks associated with the job remain stable over time (Robertson, Bartram, & Callinan, 2002). This may be a false assumption for some jobs, and the incorporation of anticipated changes to the job tasks is not something that is clearly addressed by conventional job analysis methods.

Once the job description has been produced, the next step is to translate the information into measurable performance outcomes and to produce a specification of the KSAOs (Knowledge, Skills, Abilities and Other attributes/characteristics; see Box 5.3; Woods & Hinton, 2017) and behaviours to be demonstrated by the employee. This step relies heavily on the expertise of the practitioner, who may draw on their experience and knowledge of the job, combined with consultation with managers and other relevant stakeholders to produce a specification of KSAOs. This process is therefore quite intuitive, and often based on the specific knowledge of the analyst. The product of 'worker-oriented' analysis is a specification of competencies to be demonstrated by the employee. There are a number of methods that may be used for worker-oriented analysis, also listed in Box 5.2.

BOX 5.2
Methods of job and competency analysis

Job analysis methods (work-oriented)

Questionnaires: There are several off-the-shelf questionnaires that can be used for job analysis. They contain lists of job tasks that are endorsed by job holders to indicate the extent to which they characterize their job role. An example is the Position Analysis Questionnaire (PAQ).

Observations: Workers are observed carrying out specific job tasks, and the behaviours demonstrated are recorded.

Shadowing: An individual worker is observed working for a specific period of time (generally longer in duration than for simple observations).

Self-records/Diary methods: Workers can be asked to talk through particular job tasks, or to keep a diary of activities for a short period of time.

Hierarchical task analysis: Broad work tasks are sequentially broken up into increasingly narrow tasks to result in a hierarchy of job responsibilities and activities.

continued

Worker-oriented methods

Critical incidents interviewing: Critical incidents interviewing involves conducting interviews with workers about particularly important or critical job occurrences. The aim of the interview is to understand the behaviours that made the outcome of the situation either particularly effective or ineffective.

Repertory grid: The repertory grid examines the personal attributes that make effective workers different from ineffective workers. Interviewees nominate effective and ineffective workers. Two effective and one ineffective worker are drawn at random from the list and the interviewee must identify what makes the ineffective person different from the two effective workers (e.g. the former is disorganized, whereas the latter are organized). The interviewer then probes the competency to identify exactly what the interviewee means when they describe the attribute.

Combination job analysis methodology

The combination job analysis method (CJAM) is one of the most useful and complete techniques for job analysis. It comprises a systematic approach to job analysis that can incorporate information from a variety of methodologies, combining them to produce a job description and person specification for use in selection and other HR activities. The CJAM uses a team of subject matter experts and job analysts (e.g. work psychologists) to guide the process, and proceeds in a series of steps (Brannick et al., 2007; Pearn & Kandola 1988):

- The team generate lists of tasks associated with the target job, using a variety of work-oriented methods to supplement their own ideas about tasks of the job.
- Sets of tasks are combined together to generate broad job activities or duties. These are rated by the group, and other key stakeholders, to determine their relative difficulty and importance in the job.
- Job activities and duties are considered by the team and used to generate lists of KSAOs or competencies that are required for effective performance.
- Generated KSAOs and competencies are combined, defined and elaborated to give a clear, parsimonious set. These are rated by the group, and other stakeholders, to determine their relative importance in newly appointed employees.

BOX 5.3
Defining KSAOs

Knowledge: The learning required to perform the tasks of a job effectively (product knowledge; knowledge of processes and procedures).

Skills: Acquired physical, mental and social capabilities related to specific job tasks, acquired through experience and strengthened through practice (machinery operation; leadership).

Abilities: Generalized physical and cognitive capabilities that can be applied flexibly to a number of different job tasks (verbal reasoning; manual dexterity).

Other attributes: Any other relevant characteristics of a person that cannot be classified into one of the categories above, and which in the context of job analysis are relevant to the work under scrutiny (motivation; attitudes; personality traits; values).

In contemporary HRM practice, a very widely used approach to job analysis is competency modelling or profiling. Competencies can be defined as *"observable workplace behaviours* [that] *form the basis of a differentiated measurement* [of performance]" (Bartram, 2005, pp. 1185–1186). So generally, competencies are seen as behaviour patterns that are performance related (Cooper et al., 2003; Woodruffe, 1997), and in that sense they may integrate attributes from K, S, A and O (Roberts, 2005).

Competency modelling involves the construction and design of frameworks of competencies that may be applied to a range of different job roles in an organization. The frameworks are usually quite generic, specifying behaviours that would contribute to job success in a variety of contexts. Practitioners may select relevant competencies from the framework that apply to a particular job role based on their own judgement or by seeking contributions from managers and others. These can then be assessed as part of a selection process. One exception to this practice is where competency frameworks are designed to apply in their entirety to a specific employee group. This applies frequently to leadership and management roles, with many organizations having company-wide corporate competency frameworks that reflect strategic goals and values.

By their nature, competencies are flexible, allowing them to be applied across jobs at different levels of seniority, and to remain relevant as job requirements change over time. For these reasons, many organizations favour the competency approach over other forms of job analysis (Campion et al., 2011). Research on the structure of competencies (e.g. Tett, Guterman, Bleier, & Murphy, 2000) have aimed to standardize the main classifications of job competencies (e.g. planning and organizing, communicating and presenting), for example by relating them to core aspects of individual differences in personality, motivation and ability (Bartram, 2005).

In recruitment and selection, the goal of job analysis is to provide an evidence-based specification of attributes that act as criteria for decision-making during the selection to guide the choice of assessment techniques, and therefore to establish their content validity (Schmidt, 2012). Assessments are selected based on correspondence between the attributes they assess and those identified in the job analysis.

> **DISCUSS WITH A COLLEAGUE**
>
> Try to list the KSAOs required for a job that you are familiar with. Write down around ten different person requirements. If you have time, search for your chosen job on the O*NET (www.onetonline.org) database to compare your person requirements with the listings on the site.

RECRUITMENT: ATTRACTING PEOPLE TO WORK

Recruitment refers to the 'broad set of activities that connect applicants to organizations and their jobs' (Ployhart, Schmitt, & Tippins, 2017, p. 293). The success of any recruitment and selection process hinges on attracting a pool of good applicants, yet critics point out that many findings from recruitment research are somewhat obvious (e.g. see critical evaluation by Ployhart, 2006). However, there is sufficient evidence to help practitioners in applying systematic approaches. For example, Breaugh (2008) identifies the following key steps in recruitment activities:

- Recruitment objectives: identifying the specific recruitment need, the kinds of individuals to be recruited (drawing on findings of the job analysis), the time frame, and the required levels of performance and retention needed from the process.
- Strategy development: working out a strategy for the recruitment activity, in which key questions about who and where to recruit, how to reach targeted people and what to communicate during the recruitment process are all considered.
- Recruitment activities: application of specific methods of recruitment to attract the applicant pool, typically involving decisions about who will do the recruitment, whether it will be outsourced, the nature of the information to be conveyed and the use of various media.

Breaugh (2008) also highlights the moderating effects of applicant characteristics. Applicant perceptions of the company and the attractiveness of the job, alongside their own expectations and relevant job interests, all impact on decisions to apply. This kind of thinking features clearly in Schneider's Attraction–Selection–Attrition model (ASA; Schneider, 1987). The ASA framework describes how people are attracted to organizations principally on the basis of their judgement about whether they fit with the job and organization. Initial decisions may be based on perceptions of job fit, but during the recruitment and selection phase, according to the ASA model, applicants and organizations undertake a mutual fact-finding exercise, designed to ascertain the degree of fit between them. When person–organization fit is high, people are more likely to be selected. Within the organization, employees who are a poorer fit to the organization are more likely to leave (attrition), resulting in an iterative homogenization of the organizational culture. This model highlights the importance of subjective fit perceptions in decision-making, with implications for how jobs are marketed during recruitment. A further implication is that recruiters should be mindful about whether their objective is to recruit 'for fit' or 'for diversity' to avoid creating overly homogeneous teams and groups.

Other research has examined specific practices, which can be interpreted against contingencies of recruitment and selection. For example, in situations in which there is likely to be a large applicant pool for a particular job, recruiters often use realistic job previews (RJPs) to ensure a good fit between person and job characteristics. Such previews might highlight any negative aspects of the job in order to ensure the seriousness of job applications. The administration of this and other practices is equally important. Chapman, Uggerslev, Carroll, Piasentin, and Jones (2005) found that receiving timely responses to enquiries and applications led to higher perceptions of the attractiveness of the recruiting company.

The internet now provides the main medium through which information about jobs and organizations is shared with potential applicants, and the pace with which practice accelerates has left research catching up (Ployhart et al., 2017). The use of social media means that organizations can connect very widely to the labour market. A question remains about how much more effective recruitment is through these means. For example, although the reach of recruitment is undoubtedly wider through the use of the internet, the main objective of recruitment is to attain a high-quality applicant pool. Creating a high volume of poor applications is problematic from a selection efficiency perspective. The use of big data and insights into potential applicants alongside adaptive marketing might present a future direction that will resolve these issues. Dineen and Noe (2009) examined the role of customizing the presentation of online adverts based on applicant user profiles and found that the quality of applicants was highest (i.e. the best fit between applicant and job/organization) when such customization was applied.

Of course, not all recruitment happens through external marketing. Van Hoye and Lievens (2009), for example, examined word-of-mouth influences on applicant behaviour (i.e. receiving word-of-mouth recommendation from specific others). They found that word-of-mouth effects were dependent upon characteristics of the applicant and the source. Alongside certain personality characteristics, source credibility and independence were important. Interestingly, the influences of word-of-mouth went beyond those of exposure to mass media, and were particularly positive when received early on in the recruitment process.

SELECTION: ASSESSING AND HIRING PEOPLE

Foundations of selection assessment: Reliability and validity

Reliability and validity are fundamental concepts in psychological assessments and are reviewed in that context elsewhere is this book. Assessments of individuals for selection in organizations are also very strongly underpinned by these concepts. In a critical approach to selection assessment, questions over reliability and validity must always be addressed.

Reliability

Reliability in selection assessment relates to two particular aspects of the assessment:

- Internal consistency reliability of the selection assessment, which provides an index that tells us whether tests and other assessments are consistently or accurately measuring the attribute of interest. Internal consistency is generally used to evaluate assessments made using self- or other-report scales or tests (such as biodata, personality tests or cognitive ability tests).
- Interrater reliability, which provides an indication of the extent to which two different assessors agree in their assessments of a particular job candidate. If a selection process is to be objective, then different individuals should be able to use the assessment process and system and agree on their findings. This would provide evidence that the assessment reflected the competencies or attributes of the candidate, rather than the idiosyncratic judgements of the assessor.

Validity

Validity takes several forms, all discussed in Chapter 2, and summarized in Box 5.4. Robertson et al. (2002) point out that among these different types of validity, construct and criterion validity are particularly important. Construct validity is concerned primarily with whether the assessment measures the competencies or attributes that it claims. While these analyses are straightforward for psychometric tests, construct validity is harder to establish for other selection assessments, and the approach that most practitioners take is to build a case for the validity of a particular assessment. Triangulation of measurement can be a useful way to do this. Selection processes that measure multiple attributes or competencies using several different methods are often referred to as a multi-trait, multi-method approach (MTMM). The essence of these approaches is that each competency or attribute is measured using a number of different methods. One way of checking the construct validity of the process as a whole is to establish that the scores on each construct converge across assessment methods, and diverge from other attribute scores where expected.

> **BOX 5.4**
> **Main types of validity in selection, and the questions answered by each**
>
> *Face validity:* Does the assessment look appropriate to job candidates?
>
> *Content validity:* Does the assessment look relevant to job experts (managers, job holders) in terms of its relevance to job requirements?
>
> *Convergent validity:* Does the assessment correlate with other relevant measurements? Do assessment components correlate strongly with a common 'factor' or construct, extracted through factor analyses?
>
> *Divergent validity:* Is the assessment uncorrelated with other non-relevant measurements?
>
> *Construct validity:* Can an overall case be made to support the validity of the assessment?
>
> *Criterion validity:* Does the assessment correlate with job performance or some other relevant work criterion measured at the same time (concurrent validity) or at a later date (predictive validity)?

These techniques tell us about the quantitatively aspects of validity, but they do not tell the whole story in terms of the comprehensiveness or relevance of the assessment. To address these issues, practitioners can pay attention to the face and content validity of the assessments:

- Face validity in selection relates to how relevant the assessment looks to the job candidates. It is often overlooked by the statistically minded, but in practice it is among the best predictors of perceptions of procedural fairness (Hausknecht, Day, & Thomas, 2004). This means that job candidates are more likely to feel that they have been treated fairly by the selecting organization if they believe the assessment to be relevant to the job they have applied for.
- Content validity is a similar qualitative judgement, made by subject experts rather than job candidates. In the case of tests, these are usually test designers and researchers, but for other forms of assessment, job holders could review assessments to determine their relevance to tasks and attributes that feature in their design.

The fixation of most selection research conducted over the past 50 or so years has undoubtedly been criterion validity, and with good reason. Criterion validity reflects the ultimate aim of selection assessments in organizations – to predict individual job performance. Asking a job candidate to participate in an assessment is a waste of time unless we know that it predicts how people tend to perform in the job we are selecting for. How can this be established? There are two approaches to criterion validation, and both involve correlating assessment scores with outcome criteria, usually job performance measures:

- The concurrent approach: Assessment scores are correlated with job performance measured at the same time (i.e. concurrently). This approach is generally used in the development of assessments with current job holders.
- The predictive approach: Assessment scores are correlated with job performance measured at some point in the future. This can be used to evaluate selection processes, enabling practitioners to check that the assessments of candidates made during the selection predicted their future job performance. A challenge with this approach is that only high-scoring candidates are selected, and we are unable to measure the performance of low-scoring candidates who were rejected from the selection process. This effect is called range restriction, which must be addressed in validity evaluations.

A challenge for practitioners seeking to evaluate criterion validity is the so-called 'criterion problem'. The criterion problem refers to the typical unavailability of robust job performance measures in organizations. In many organizations, job performance indices are either absent or unreliable. This is critical for criterion validity evaluations. Selection processes might be incorrectly judged as having high or low validity as a result of poor measurement of criteria.

The picture is not all bad, however. Some organizations do collect relevant job performance data, and moreover, it is probably short-sighted to view criterion validation solely from the perspective of job performance. In some jobs, organizations may not require high-flying performers, instead valuing reliable workers who are likely to stay with the organization for some time. One could think of the example of call centres, where turnover of staff has traditionally been problematic. In such cases, a well-defined, objectively measurable criterion such as tenure, absenteeism or turnover could be constructed and used.

Evidence of validity, reliability and fairness (see later in this chapter) are essential in verifying the effectiveness of selection processes. These therefore act as important evaluation criteria for selection processes. Many organizations and practitioners do not conduct robust evaluations of selection processes, despite sizable investment in assessments upfront. The reluctance to invest in evaluations makes life easier for selectors and comfortable for assessment suppliers, who may rarely need to prove that selection tools or processes work for specific jobs in specific organizations. When done well, examining the reliability and validity of selection processes and assessments is extremely valuable. First, it helps us to determine whether the selection process worked or not. Second, demonstrable validity ensures that selection systems are defensible. Third, it allows the calculation of utility or the financial benefit of selection.

Reliability and validity in digital selection methods

The general stability of selection methodology for several decades prior to the internet has arguably led to simplified mental models of reliability and validity in which 'rules of thumb' or consensus benchmarks for quality are applied without critical consideration (Woods, 2018). A good example is the concept of construct validity of new methods of capturing job-relevant psychological data through, for example, gamification, or AI-based analyses of video interviews and written content (e.g. postings, emails).

The conceptual challenge for such techniques is to determine what exactly has been measured (i.e. establishing construct validity). It will be important in the future to adopt a broad perspective on how indicators of psychological attributes combine to build an overall representation of the person. The continued relevance of methods of reliability and validity assessment depends on psychologists engaging with rather than rejecting outright the validity of new assessment methodologies. This is especially important in establishing that new technological forms of assessment are not simply fads or fashion, but are rather evidence based and fair.

Utility analyses

Related to the issue of communication of validity research is the technique of utility analysis, first applied to selection processes by Schmidt, Hunter, McKenzie, and Muldrow (1979) and Schmidt and Hunter (1983). They proposed a method that estimated the financial benefits of improvements in selection processes based on the validity of the process, ratios of selected to rejected candidates, and estimates of the monetary value of different levels of job performance. Recent developments to the technique have retained many of these original features (e.g. Sturman, 2001). Schmidt and Hunter (1983) provided the well-cited estimate of the value of improved job performance. A one standard deviation improvement in job performance is estimated to equate to 40 per cent of the employee's salary in productivity gains. We can use this assumption to evaluate the productivity returns of improving validity and consequently selecting people with higher levels of job performance.

Psychologists originally developed utility analysis to help them communicate the benefits of their assessments to managers in clearer business language. They believed that managers would be more convinced by the bottom-line financials than by explanations of validity. However, it appears that their belief may have been incorrect. Latham and Whyte (1994) reported that managers were more likely to endorse a new selection method if the validity of the assessment was explained clearly. However, the presentation of utility analyses has no influence on their decision-making. Perhaps psychologists should just try to make a better job of explaining what validity means rather than trying to express the effects financially.

Selection assessment methods

Assessment methodologies are the specific techniques applied to measure the KSAOs of prospective workers for the purpose of making hiring decisions. Early-stage assessment is designed to select-out unsuitable applicants. Those individuals remaining (job candidates) are assessed using more detailed assessment methods, designed to thoroughly assess their competencies. The purpose of these later-stage assessments is to select-in the most suitable candidates. There are constantly evolving changes to the techniques used in practice in organizations and developed through research. In this chapter, we set out the most commonly applied and research methods, but it is important to see these as the foundations rather than the totality of selection methodology. Recent innovations through technology are described in the Key Themes box. What is crucial to absorb from the review of conventional selection assessment methodologies is the critical approach taken in research to the establishment of their evidence base. It is essential that this is retained in the way that we investigate and improve all new forms of selection assessment methodology.

CVs, application forms, and biodata

The first contact that a job applicant has with an organization is usually through a curriculum vitae (CV) or application form, and this means that they have a high potential for affecting the outcomes of the selection process (Robertson & Smith, 2001). CVs provide a summary of relevant biographical information such as education and previous job experience. The unstandardized nature of CVs has led to questions about the effect it has on selection outcomes (Robertson & Smith, 2001; Searle, 2003). Many applicants include personal statements or other descriptive content highlighting relevant KSAOs, and these, along with the inclusion of applicant photographs, can affect the evaluation of the CV and the assessment of the applicant at later stages of the selection process (see Bright & Hutton, 2000 for a review). When poorly managed, another downside to using CVs for sifting is that it is relatively resource-intensive to sort through them in high volume, even when using some form of CV management system (Maheshwari, Sainani, & Reddy, 2010).

Application forms often contain similar information to CVs, but are organization-led, allowing some control over the format and contents of the initial submission by the applicant. The evaluation of application forms is open to bias, and in some cases to mistakes or failures of procedure (such as failure to verify information). While one might assume that people screening job applications act consistently with established selection criteria, there does appear to be some evidence of the potential for subjective biases in the decision to select or reject an applicant (McKinney, Carlson, Mecham, D'Angelo, & Connerley, 2003). Moreover, meta-analyses show that typical factors that are examined on application forms (e.g. years of job experience and education) are poor predictors of job performance.

Biodata are information about previous experiences provided by job applicants, which are scored or rated to determine their suitability. They represent a method for obtaining additional information for early-stage selection decisions. The data may be captured quantitatively through answers to questionnaires (see e.g. Oswald, Schmitt, Kim, Ramsay, & Gillespie, 2004), or qualitatively through provision of narrative text. Qualitative biodata questions are open-response and ask applicants to provide a descriptive account of a job-relevant example from their past experience. The key to the effectiveness of biodata is in the ways that they are scored or rated. A competency framework could be used with *behaviourally anchored rating scales (BARS)*, which define the behaviours that constitute particular scores. The assessor might alternatively seek to confirm specific points from the applicant's answers, which could then be scored on a Yes/No or True/False binary basis.

Psychometric testing

Psychometric testing (sometimes referred to as psychological testing) can be used in two ways in selection. It can be used to sift and reduce applicant pools to manageable sizes. It can also be used as part of a more detailed assessment of job candidates. It therefore covers both select-out and select-in activities, and the way that it is applied depends very much on the context of the selection process. Common forms of psychological test are:

- Tests of maximum performance. These consist of tests of ability and aptitude, linked to general intelligence, or specific facets of intelligence, such as verbal, numerical, abstract, spatial or mechanical abilities.
- Tests of typical performance. In selection these are almost exclusively trait assessments of personality.

Tests are popular for selection because they are easy to use and cost effective, and there is a huge volume of compelling evidence for their validity (see e.g. Schmitt, 2014). Logistically, many people can complete a test at the same time, requiring minimal supervision and input from selectors, and developments in online testing mean that people do not even need to visit the organization in order to complete a psychometric test.

Tests of ability and aptitude

Tests of ability and aptitude can be designed to measure overall reasoning ability or conversely to assess a very narrow aspect of an individual's ability, depending on job requirements. They may be used to establish a candidate's learning potential, or because requirements of the test are aligned to job tasks (Schmidt, 2012):

- Jobs that involve working with numerical data are likely to require a reasonable level of numerical ability, for example. Similar cases could be made for verbal abilities, with most jobs drawing to some extent on skills in comprehending, understanding, and communicating verbally either orally or in writing.
- Jobs involving the mental manipulation of three-dimensional shapes or spaces (such as for architects, air traffic controllers or firefighters) draw on spatial ability, and jobs that involve an appreciation of how things move require job holders to apply mechanical abilities.
- Abstract ability (the ability to recognize and use patterns presented in abstract forms) taps into an individual's fluid or novel problem-solving ability, and in that sense is often applied to jobs that require flexible problem-solving or systems thinking. For these reasons, they are popular for changeable or complex roles.

Tests also vary in their difficulty, and pitching this correctly determines the utility of the information that is gained from the testing process. Tests that are too easy will produce data that are skewed to the top end of the ability range and those that are too difficult will likely produce very low scores across all candidates. Test suppliers have addressed this issue by providing guidelines on the appropriateness tests for different job types. Developments in test design have also moved towards 'item banking', which allows tests to be constructed flexibly to suit different levels of ability. Increasingly, ability tests are delivered online, adding to their procedural practicality (see Bartram, 2005).

The use of psychometric testing can be viewed as one of the successes of work psychology in the sense that the methodology draws on important psychological theory and research, and is widespread with organizations. One of the reasons for its success is the high criterion validity values reported for ability testing, particularly in the research literature. In Hunter and Schmidt's (1998) meta-analysis, general ability tests are right up there with work samples and structured interviews with a validity of 0.51. In combination with an integrity test (which would extend to a personality assessment drawing on integrity-relevant traits), the validity rises to 0.63. In a European context, Salgado and Anderson (2003) reported extraordinarily high validities for the use of general mental ability (GMA) (0.60–0.70).

Theoretically speaking, the mediating pathway from ability to performance is learning (Schmidt & Hunter, 2004). People with higher ability tend to acquire job knowledge more quickly and in greater quantity, and to proceduralize that knowledge more effectively (Kuncel, Ones, & Sackett, 2010). As a consequence they adopt a steeper learning curve or performance trajectory. This theory helps to understand when ability assessment is most relevant: when jobs are complex and require fast learning. Job complexity is an important moderator of the validity of ability tests (Salgado, Anderson, Moscoso, Bertua, De Fruyt, & Rolland, 2003), with tests working best in more complex jobs.

However, the major downside of ability testing is based on their potential to cause adverse impact in recruitment and selection, thereby having strong potential to unfairly discriminate against some ethnic groups. This is especially critical in light of meta-analytic evidence suggesting that the predictive validity of ability tests is lower for some ethnic subgroups than it is for the white majority (Berry, Cullen, & Meyer, 2014). This is a significant issue, which we discuss later in the section on fairness.

KEY THEME

Work psychology in the digital economy

The increasing use of digital methods of selection assessment raises questions about how measurement using digital techniques might affect validity. The issues are made more complex as digital forms of assessment depart further from conventional techniques. However digital methods are incorporated into selection, robust measurement science is critical in order to ensure that selection is effective and fair. This presents a challenge for work psychologists to apply and adapt methods of validation in order to meet the demands of new technology. Two examples of the most prevalent early uses of digital technology in selection serve to illustrate.

The first is the use of social media for the purposes of selection assessment. This practice is often the subject of ethical concerns. Yet, many acknowledge that the practice of viewing social media to assist in hiring decisions is widespread, and it has been suggested that most people expect (and are comfortable with) potential employers checking their social media footprint (Chamorro-Premuzic, Winsborough, Sherman, & Hogan, 2016). Van Iddekinge, Lanivich, Roth, and Junco (2016) examined the psychometric properties of this form of social media screening and reported zero correlation between recruiter ratings of social media profiles and supervisor ratings of job performance. The evidence suggests that simply looking at people online gives little relevant insight into their job potential and may conversely have a high potential for bias or unfairness.

Digital developments in interviewing have led to new AI-based techniques for evaluating candidate performance. These are provided by HR technology providers like HireVue (see hirevue.com) and Montage (see montagetalent.com). Despite the rapid uptake of the technology, we know very little indeed about what is measured in such interviews (i.e. construct validity) and their criterion validity. There is cause for some optimism, however, about their potential because part of the technology used in the analysis of digital interviews uses transcribed text of answers to determine personality characteristics, drawing on research on language use and traits (see e.g. Schwartz et al., 2013; Tausczik & Pennebaker, 2010).

These new techniques serve to illustrate the speed of development in the digital economy around the use of technology for HR processes like selection. This next stage of digitization of selection presents new challenges in evaluating their effectiveness and requires psychologists and researchers to quicken their pace in keeping up.

Personality assessment

Personality traits are assessed in a number of different ways during the selection process. Selectors make informal judgements about personality traits during interviews and observational assessments. However, the assessment of traits is formally operationalized in personality trait inventories or questionnaires.

These are self-report inventories that require candidates to respond to questions or statements, rating their agreement with them, or their perceptions of their accuracy as a description of their personality.

There are a multitude of different personality tests available on the market for practitioners to use, and these are of variable quality. Well-designed tests can be highly useful in selection. Poorly designed tests are at best useless, and at worst potentially damaging to businesses and the well-being of job candidates. Training in the use of personality testing is therefore essential to help distinguish good from poor assessments and for the ethical use of assessments in organizations. Key differences in personality measures are how they measure the personality domain. Underlying each personality inventory is a personality structure, representing the dimensions or traits that are measured by the inventory. Inventories might measure broad traits similar to the Big Five personality factors, or at the facet level. The relative merits of each approach really depend on the performance criteria that selectors are trying to predict. If criteria are broad, then broad trait assessment is typically more useful; if the criteria are narrow, then more accurate assessment may be achieved through measuring at facet level (this is known as the bandwidth–fidelity trade-off).

The most prevalent approach to using personality assessment for selection is to seek to match candidate trait profiles to job demands. This usually draws on the practitioner's detailed knowledge of a specific personality instrument and the different traits that it assesses. Relevant traits are matched to aspects of the personnel specification, and an overall 'ideal' or 'desirable' personality profile constructed. For example, for jobs requiring social confidence, high Extraversion is ideal, whereas for jobs requiring lone working, low Extraversion may be a better fit. Candidates are then evaluated in terms of how well their profile fits with the ideal profile. This approach may be thought of as theoretically driven, because there are good conceptual reasons established as to why certain traits are more or less desirable. For example, Shaffer and Postlethwaite (2013) reported that Conscientiousness has strongest validity for predicting performance in jobs that were highly routinized, reflecting the alignment of job requirements with the organized, structured and planned approach taken by those high on Conscientiousness. The way in which personality assessment is used has a clear impact on its validity.

There has been criticism of personality assessment validities (Morgeson et al., 2007), but the overwhelming evidence is that when they are used in the right way, reliable assessments of personality do predict job performance. Traits are associated with performance in two ways. First, Conscientiousness particularly appears to predict performance fairly consistently (e.g. Barrick, Mount, & Judge, 2001). This probably reflects the association of Conscientiousness with organizational citizenship behaviour, which is important to some extent in almost all jobs. More relevant for selection, however, are the improvements in validity that result from adopting the theory-driven approach as described above. Hogan and Holland (2003) showed that when traits were matched to job demands, the validities of all of the Big Five were substantially improved. They reported validities of 0.43 for Emotional Stability, 0.35 for Extraversion, 0.34 for Agreeableness, 0.36 for Conscientiousness and 0.34 for Openness. Judge and Zapata (2015) similarly examined the validity of traits in relevant performance contexts, drawing on Trait Activation Theory (Tett & Burnett, 2003). As in other studies, they found that traits predict performance when criteria are trait-relevant.

Finally, there is emergent evidence that personality assessment validities may change and increase for predicting performance after several years. Lievens, Ones, and Dilchert (2009) examined this effect in medical school students, but their theory is relevant for assessment for selection. In their analyses, they observed increases in the validity of Extraversion and Openness for predicting performance at year 7 compared to year 1. The theoretical rationale is that later-stage training drew more on these dimensions as trainees interacted with real patients to solve medical problems. Thoresen, Bradley, Bliese, and Thoresen (2004) observed that personality validities changed for predicting performance at different job stages, and Minbashian, Earl, and Bright (2013) also reported that Openness was associated with better performance maintenance over time. Using personality assessment in selection may therefore have dual benefits of predicting performance in the short term where traits are matched to job requirements, but also in the long term by influencing motivation and emergent skills as people become more experienced in their work.

Criticisms about personality assessment by practitioners tend to focus on the potential for faking one's responses to personality inventories. There is substantive literature on this issue (see Box 5.5) and a variety of different perspectives. Some researchers believe it to be problematic for selection practice (e.g. Murphy & Dzieweczynski, 2005; Morgeson et al., 2007), and others do not (e.g. Hogan, 2005). One thing that is clear is that the effects of faking in selection are not fully understood, or well communicated, and while this remains the case, the concerns of practitioners are probably justified. Efforts to explore the nature of faking versus honest responding (e.g. König, Merz, & Trauffer, 2012) represent the most effective starting point to improve this situation.

BOX 5.5
Social desirability in personality testing

One of the most well-cited concerns of managers and practitioners in respect of personality assessment in organizations is the potential for faking or socially desirable responding. The principle is straightforward: personality measures do not have right and wrong answers and so, in theory, test-takers could a) try to make themselves seem more desirable than they really are, or b) try to spot what the selectors are looking for and respond in a dishonest way to make themselves appear more suitable than they really are. On the face of it, it is a valid concern, but there are those who argue against the importance of the issue.

Among the most direct of critics are Robert Hogan and Joyce Hogan. Robert Hogan (2005) makes the point that the issue of faking or socially desirable responding is blurred in assessment in the same way that it is blurred in life. All people make efforts to conform to social norms and expectations, suppressing their true urges, inclinations and desires. All people take steps to create a good impression in particular life situations. Think about the last time you went on a first date, or indeed the last job interview that you attended. You probably managed your behaviour and impression somewhat. The point is that perhaps impression management should not be viewed as faking *per se*.

Hogan, Barrett, and Hogan (2007) note three observations on socially desirable responding. First, individuals are able to fake their personality profile when instructed to do so. Second, the base-rate of faking in selection is quite low, a finding supported by Hogan et al.'s (2007) study and by Ellingson, Sackett, and Connelly (2007). Third, and perhaps most curiously, there is mixed evidence about the effects of response distortion on validities of personality measures. Hough, Eaton, Dunnette, Kamp, and McCloy (1990) argued that they remain stable, even if distortion is present. This may be because socially desirable responding represents an important individual difference in its own right. Others argue that validity is affected (e.g. Birkeland, Manson, Kisamore, Brannick, & Smith, 2006).

Numerous methods are available for detecting and reducing socially desirable responding in selection assessment. These include validity or social desirability scales designed to detect faking and impression management, instructional warnings about faking, and forced-choice items. The effectiveness of these interventions is unclear in the research literature, although instructional warnings do appear to mitigate the risk of faking (Dwight & Donovan, 2003), but all continue to be used to address the practical concerns of managers and practitioners.

Situational judgement tests

Situational judgement tests (SJTs) are designed to assess a candidate's judgement about typical job situations. Applicants are presented with hypothetical work-based scenarios describing a problem and asked to choose a response from a list of alternatives (Lievens, Peeters, & Schollaert, 2008b). SJTs can take two forms, being either behaviour based – in which a candidate indicates the way that he or she would be most likely to behave – or knowledge based – in which candidates indicate what they judge to be the most appropriate response (McDaniel, Hartman, Whetzel, & Grubb, 2007). This distinction can have an impact on the SJT in terms of its criterion-related validity (McDaniel & Nguyen, 2001) and how resistant it is to faking (Nguyen, Biderman, & McDaniel, 2005).

SJTs are developed on the basis of a thorough job analysis, to ensure that the content reflects situations that employees may face in the working environment (Christian, Edwards, & Bradley, 2010). In this sense, SJTs can be considered bespoke to each job setting, with the content and format of the SJT altered to fit the specific job role (Lievens et al., 2008).

Evidence suggests that SJTs are reliable (McDaniel et al., 2007) and have good criterion-related validity (i.e. they predict subsequent performance) across a range of occupations (Patterson et al., 2009), including prospectively in the long term (Lievens & Sackett, 2012). Additionally, SJTs have been demonstrated to predict other important behaviours such as organizational citizenship behaviours (OCB; Rockstuhl, Ang, Ng, Lievens, & Van Dyne, 2015).

Selection interviewing

Interviews are the most commonly experienced and applied selection assessment method and involve an interaction between the job candidate and one or more interviewers for the purpose of determining their suitability for the job. Judgements about the candidate's suitability are made based on his or her orally presented responses to orally presented questions. The delivery of the interview by the organization varies considerably (Cook, 2016). For example, interviews can vary in their duration, the number of interviewers present, and in terms of how candidate input is prompted and evaluated. All of these points affect the reliability, validity and candidate reactions to the interview process and so are important to consider in the design of interviews.

The broad finding from a wide range of research sources is that structured interviews comprehensively outperform unstructured interviews in terms of their validity and reliability (Moscoso, 2000; Robertson & Smith, 2001). Structure is defined as 'any enhancement of the interview that is intended to increase psychometric properties by increasing standardization or otherwise assisting the interviewer in determining what questions to ask or how to evaluate responses' (Campion, Palmer, & Campion, 1997, p. 656).

In Salgado's (1999) review of selection interviewing, the validities of highly structured and highly unstructured interviews were 0.56 and 0.20, respectively. Moreover, structured interviews achieve higher levels of interrater reliability than unstructured interviews (0.92 and 0.69, respectively, between the most and least structured panel interviews; Conway, Jako, & Goodman, 1995), a finding replicated in meta-analyses by Huffcutt, Culbertson, and Weyhrauch (2013). Schmidt, Oh, and Shaffer (2016) presented a more optimistic perspective on the validity of unstructured interviews, placing them at about equivalent validity to structured interviews. However, this finding corrects for the greater unreliability and higher range restriction observed in unstructured interviews. It would be expected that, in practice, organizations would observe lower validities for unstructured interviews as a consequence of their weaker reliabilities. One of the key aims of adding structure to interviews is to reduce the subjective biases that affect interviewers' questioning and evaluation during the interview process. Generally, these structural enhancements apply to either the content and interaction in the interview or the methodology for evaluating the interviewee answers (Levashina, Hartwell, Morgeson, & Campion, 2014). Some examples are:

- Standard questioning could be adopted to ensure that each candidate is asked exactly the same questions. This ensures that comparisons between candidates are made based on consistent information.
- Scoring and evaluation procedures are also key foci for adding structure. The use of competency dimensions or scales for the scoring of candidate performance improves the structure of assessment during the interview. This involves providing interviewers with definitions and notes about how to evaluate particular answers or candidate behaviours, which helps to improve consistency.
- Further structure can be added to the scoring of candidate performance by the use of rating scales.
- Information provided to interviewers about the job under scrutiny can be standardized.
- Multiple rather than single interviewers can be used.
- Procedural guidelines around aspects such as follow-up questions and overall interview duration can be applied.

Specific approaches to interviewing also help to add structure. More common structured formats are behavioural, competency and situational interviews. Examples of question formats from all three kinds of interviews are shown in Box 5.6.

BOX 5.6
Example interview questions

Behavioural

Describe a recent project that involved you working as part of a team. How did you keep the group on track? How did you ensure that everyone's opinions were taken on board?

Competency

Competency questioning is similar to behavioural, but focused on a specific competency.

An example question for teamwork could ask you to describe a project that involved you working as part of a team. What was your role and how did you contribute? Give an example of how you contributed to cooperation within the team.

Situational judgement

Imagine a situation where you were part of a team working on a product design project. How would you help to ensure cooperation in the team and facilitate the achievement of the team's objective?

The example interview questions in Box 5.6 can be explained as follows:

- Behavioural interviews are based on key job requirements and ask interviewees to describe past experiences of performing such tasks. Behavioural interviews reflect the theory that past behaviour predicts future behaviour. The aim is to uncover positive job behaviours through past examples of fulfilling similar job requirements. Interviewers look for actual behavioural evidence (e.g. specific examples of the behaviour in question).
- Competency-based interviewing (e.g. Roberts, 1997) has proved popular with practitioners, most likely because it allows interviews to be integrated with other forms of assessment such as assessment centres. Like behavioural interviews, the method uses questioning that requires the candidate to provide specific examples from their past experience to highlight relevant performance of job-relevant behaviours. However, in competency interviewing, questions are designed to tap into particular competency areas, and candidate responses are evaluated against competency definitions. Behavioural and competency interviews focus on past behaviour.
- Situational interviews are based on the theory that intentions predict behaviour (Sue-Chan & Latham, 2004). Candidates are presented with a particular situation and forced to describe how they would respond. Their answers are evaluated by comparing them with a pre-defined set of responses that vary in desirability.

Despite the relative straightforwardness with which structure can be introduced to interviews, and the consistent evidence of improved reliability and validity, the use of less effective, unstructured interviews is generally more common in organizations (Van der Zee, Bakker, & Bakker, 2002). Some argue that the technical or prescriptive design of structured interviews can put off managers and practitioners from using them (e.g. the multi-modal interview; Schuler & Moser, 1995). Managers may even favour unstructured methods in some cases, perhaps because of convenience or habit, or a perception that structured methods are beyond their control or capability (Van der Zee et al., 2002). It is clear that more needs to be done to clarify the ways in which research implications in this area are communicated (Huffcutt, 2010; Roulin & Bangerter, 2012).

Research on the validity of interviews is procedurally focused, but some studies also take a broader view of the social exchange that occurs during the interaction between interviewer and interviewee (Melchers, Ingold, Wilhelmy, & Kleinmann, 2015). For example, interviewees approach the interaction with a motivation to impression-manage, and the extent to which interviewers are attuned to this will impact the effect on the process (Buehl, Melchers, Macan, & Kühnel, 2018; Melchers et al., 2009). Impression management does seem to enhance interview ratings (Levashina et al., 2014). Faking tendencies in interviews are likely in part to reflect the attitudes and characteristics of interviewees (Buehl & Melchers, 2017), but also the questions that are asked. Levashina et al. (2014) reported that in past behaviour questions, candidates are more likely to self-promote, whereas in situational questions, candidates are likely to try to tailor the answer to what they feel the interviewer wants to hear. Conversely, interviewers also engage in impression management during interviews, generally to enhance the attractiveness of the organization as a place to work and thereby sell the job to candidates (Wilhelmy, Kleinmann, König, Melchers, & Truxillo, 2016).

Assessment centres

Assessment centres are processes that enable the in-depth assessment of job candidates. They are used in a variety of formats, and defined by the International Taskforce on Assessment Center Operations (2014) as:

> *a standardized evaluation of behavior based on multiple inputs. Any single assessment center consists of multiple components, which include behavioral simulation exercises, within which multiple trained assessors observe and record behaviors, classify them according to the behavioral constructs of interest, and (either individually or collectively) rate (either individual or pooled) behaviors. Using either a consensus meeting among assessors or statistical aggregation, assessment scores are derived that represent an assessee's standing on the behavioral constructs and/or an aggregated overall assessment rating.* (Rupp et al., 2015, p. 6.)

The definition captures the key components of assessment centres: multiple exercises, multiple assessment dimensions, multiple assessors. The strength of assessment centres is undoubtedly the richness of the assessment system and the data they produce.

Assessment centre design

Assessment centres are often described as multi-trait, multi-method approaches to selection. This reflects their design, which is based around the idea of assessing multiple competency dimensions in multiple exercises or activities. Competency dimensions form the basis of the assessment of candidates at the assessment centre. Exercises are designed to elicit specific competency dimensions, and the essence of the assessment centre design is to include a variety of activities that give an adequate representation of the different elements of the job. The exercises themselves are referred to as work samples. This is because they simulate job tasks, enabling candidates to provide a 'sample' of their job behaviour. Work samples may be used in combination in an assessment centre, or on their own as standalone assessments. Some common forms of work samples are listed in Box 5.7. Once the competencies are selected and exercises designed, a matrix of competencies against exercises is constructed (Figure 5.3). This shows which competencies are assessed in each exercise and is used by assessors to guide their evaluations of candidates.

Competency	Exercises		
	Group Activity	In-tray	Presentation
Communication	X		X
Planning	X	X	
People Management		X	X
Decision-making	X	X	
Problem-solving		X	X
Assertiveness	X		X

Figure 5.3 An example competency X exercise matrix

BOX 5.7
Common forms of work-sample tests

Inbox exercises. In these activities, candidates provide responses to a typical set of email inbox items. They are usually assessed based on the content of responses and overall prioritization.

Group tasks. These can include business games and team activities. Candidates are assessed on interpersonal and leadership competencies, among others.

Group discussions. These activities involve group discussion of a work-related issue or task, generally with the purpose of reaching a decision or conclusion. The discussions can be leader-assigned or leaderless, and can have assigned or unassigned roles (i.e. participants can be given a brief or purpose in the discussion, or be given no guidance on how they should contribute). Assessors consider the interactions of group members to assess communicative, interpersonal and leadership competencies.

Role-play or fact-finding interviews. These often involve examples of one-to-one management of people, or face-to-face interviews for conducting investigations. For example, the activities might require the candidate to deal with a staff performance issue.

Presentations. Presentations tend to be used for jobs that require people to present in public, such as sales or managerial roles. Candidates are asked to present on a particular topic, or given a free choice. They are usually assessed on communicative competencies, as well as on the content of the presentation.

Assessors and assessment procedures

Assessors at the assessment centres are usually a variety of different stakeholders in the selection process. Lievens (1999) found that while psychologists tended to be most effective at differentiating competencies behaviours, managers tended to give ratings that more accurately reflected the values of the organization. Training of assessors has been found to affect the validity and reliability of their ratings (Lievens, 2001), and yet many organizations continue to provide very limited training to assessment centre assessors.

The assessment of candidates at assessment centres is structured and methodical. The most common format is the ORCE method of assessment (Observe, Record, Classify, Evaluate). In this method, the assessor is trained to observe candidate behaviour, recording (in writing) everything that the candidate says or does during the exercise. Once recorded, the behaviours are classified against competency dimensions before being evaluated or rated. This last stage is usually guided by anchored rating scales. An alternative is the frame-of-reference method (Lievens & Klimoski, 2001), which encourages assessors to compare episodes of candidate behaviour against specific models of job performance that incorporate behaviour set within an organizational context. Rather than focusing solely on behaviour as in the ORCE method, the assessor would be encouraged to draw on knowledge of effective performance as expressed in a particular work context, using this information to judge the overall performance of the candidate.

Assessment centres are set up so that each candidate is assessed by several different assessors. At the end of the assessment centre, their judgements are integrated in a 'wash-up' meeting. The purpose of the integration session is to standardize ratings to some extent (providing a check that each assessor is using the assessment procedures in a similar way), but mainly to pool the ratings of the candidates from the various exercises.

The validity of assessment centres varies depending on the effectiveness of their design. Meta-analyses have reported validities of 0.28 (Hermelin, Lievens, & Robertson, 2007) and 0.39 (Arthur, Day, McNelly, & Edens, 2006)

> **DISCUSS WITH A COLLEAGUE**
>
> Go back to the list of KSAOs that you generated for a familiar job earlier in this chapter. Identify how each one could be assessed at a selection process.

A recurrent concern for assessment centres is their construct validity. Within the assessment centre, the competency dimensions are set up as the constructs to assess. Their construct validity rests on the assumption that they are indeed individual attributes that can be measured in different contexts. For example, if a candidate is given a score of 3 for problem-solving in one exercise, then they should achieve a similar or identical score for problem-solving in other exercises. Remember that we are assuming that the rating reflects their level of competency. The problem for assessment centres is that this assumption is not confirmed in empirical investigations, and scores appear to be much more consistent within exercises than they are within competencies. Scores on different competencies within the same exercise are rated similarly. The result is low convergent and discriminant validity. This is referred to as the exercise effect and several sources have tried to explain why it occurs and how to reduce it (e.g. Lievens, Chasteen, Day, & Christiansen, 2006; Lievens, De Koster, & Schollaert, 2008a). Clearly more work is needed in this area to determine exactly what is being measured at assessment centres. For example, it may be unreasonable to expect competency scores to be equal across exercises. Each represents a unique situation, and people generally are more or less effective in different work contexts. More important is to understand the potential effects on criterion validity.

Selection assessments: What does research tell us works best?

In 1998, Schmidt and Hunter published a highly influential meta-analysis of selection techniques. As discussed in previous chapters, meta-analyses take account of the methodological artefacts that suppress validity coefficients, allowing a more accurate aggregation of results from different studies. Table 5.1 presents the findings from several of the most widely cited, and shows the validity coefficients for a variety of different assessments and for some combinations of assessments. A good updated review of criterion validities is presented by Schmitt and Fandre (2008), and Schmidt et al. (2016) presented a working paper updating the 1998 Schmidt and Hunter findings. Among other updates are psychometric test data specifically from Europe (Bertua, Anderson, & Salgado, 2005; Salgado et al., 2003).

Table 5.1 generally points to the validity of more structured methods over those with less structure. This underlines the proposition at the start of the chapter that effective recruitment and selection is systematic in its approach. The meta-analyses and all of the preceding literature reviewed in this section also indicate the evidence base to guide effective selection.

Table 5.1 Selection Assessments and Their Associated Validities

Assessment or combination of assessments	Criterion validity values
Test of general cognitive ability plus structured interview	0.63 (Schmidt & Hunter, 1998) 0.76 (Schmidt et al., 2016)
Test of general cognitive ability plus integrity test	0.63 (Schmidt & Hunter, 1998) 0.78 (Schmidt et al., 2016)
Test of general cognitive ability plus work-sample test	0.63 (Schmidt & Hunter, 1998) 0.65 (Schmidt et al., 2016)
General cognitive ability test	0.51 (Schmidt & Hunter, 1998) 0.50–0.60 (Bertua et al., 2005) 0.65 (Schmidt et al., 2016)
Structured interview	0.56 (Salgado, 1999) 0.44 (McDaniel et al., 1994) 0.58 (Schmidt et al., 2016)
Work-sample test	0.54 (Schmidt & Hunter, 1998) 0.33 (Roth et al., 2005) 0.33 (Schmidt et al., 2016)
Job tryout procedure	0.44 (Schmidt et al., 2016)
Personality assessment	0.34–0.43 (Hogan & Holland, 2003) 0.31 (Schmidt & Hunter, 1998) 0.08-0.32 (Schmidt et al., 2016)
Assessment centres	0.39 (Arthur et al., 2006) 0.28 (Hermelin et al., 2007) 0.36 (Schmidt et al., 2016)
Biodata	0.35 (Schmidt & Hunter, 1998) (Schmidt et al., 2016)
Unstructured interview	0.20 (Salgado, 1999) 0.33 (McDaniel et al., 1994) 0.58 (Schmidt et al., 2016)
Reference check	0.26 (Schmidt & Hunter, 1998) (Schmidt et al., 2016)
Job experience	0.18 (Schmidt & Hunter, 1998) 0.16 (Schmidt et al., 2016)
Years of education	0.10 (Schmidt & Hunter, 1998) (Schmidt et al., 2016)
Graphology (handwriting analysis)	0.02 (Schmidt et al., 2016)

However, it is important that the results of meta-analyses are kept in their proper perspective. For example, input studies for meta-analyses may be very dated (e.g. many of the input studies from the Hunter and Schmidt, 1998, and Schmidt et al., 2016 meta-analyses date to the 1950s–1970s). The working world was of course very different at that time, as were the kinds of capabilities needed to deal with the demands that people faced then compared to now. Moreover, there is comparatively limited literature on the validity of newer technology-enabled selection assessments (Woods, 2018). It is critical that research continues to address the question of criterion validity in the coming years and seeks to expand the methodologies that are studied and reported upon in the literature.

PIONEERING WORK PSYCHOLOGISTS

Professor In-Sue Oh

Dr In-Sue Oh is the Charles E. Beury Professor in the Department of Human Resource Management at the Fox School of Business, Temple University. His research interests include personnel selection constructs (e.g. personality, cognitive ability) and methods (meta-analysis, employment interviews), strategic human resource management and human capital resources, and person–organization relationships (e.g. person–organization fit, support). He has received prestigious awards in his field of research: the 2014 Early Career Achievement Award from the Academy of Management (AOM) HR Division, the 2016 Distinguished Early Career Contributions Award from the Society for Industrial and Organizational Psychology (SIOP), the 2016 AOM HR Division Scholarly Achievement Award and the 2017 and 2018 William A. Owens Scholarly Achievement Award from SIOP.

Professor Oh's work is pioneering because it is enabling on two levels. In the context of personnel selection, on one level, his contributions to much-needed updating of meta-analyses of the validity of different methods is the foundation that many practitioner psychologists will work from in the coming years. On another level though, his work to develop methods of meta-analysis and the statistical procedures that underpin them unlocks the prospect of others furthering work and organizational psychology through their scientific work.

Key example papers:

- Oh, I.-S., Kim, S., & Van Iddekinge, C. H. (2015). Take it to another level: Do personality-based human capital resources matter to firm performance? *Journal of Applied Psychology, 100*(2), 935–947.
- Oh, I. S., Wang, G., & Mount, M. K. (2011). Validity of observer ratings of the five-factor model of personality traits: A meta-analysis. *Journal of Applied Psychology, 96*(4), 762–773.
- Schmidt, F. L., Oh, I. S., & Shaffer, J. A. (2016). The validity and utility of selection methods in personnel psychology: Practical and theoretical implications of 100 years of research findings. [working paper]

MACRO PERSPECTIVES ON RECRUITMENT AND SELECTION

While the processes and procedures from the micro perspective are certainly robust, many see this methodology as quite traditional (Cascio & Aguinis, 2008). At the heart of such processes are validity and reliability of selection, and the seminal works on validity almost feel somewhat 'last century'; Hunter and Schmidt published their major meta-analyses more than 15 years ago (Hunter & Schmidt, 1998), drawing partly on work published more than 30 years ago (Hunter & Hunter, 1984).

Bringing the literature into the 21st century requires examining the evidence base for structured and systematic recruitment and selection against a more strategic perspective on HRM frameworks (e.g. Cascio & Aguinis, 2008; Ployhart, 2006). One key theme in the strategic HRM literature is the role of contingencies in the effectiveness of HR and management practices (e.g. Lengnick-Hall, Lengnick-Hall, Andrade, & Drake, 2009). Contingency theories emphasize that in certain scenarios, specific practices are likely to be more or less effective than in others. This is a point less frequently acknowledged in the work and organizational psychology selection literature, which, by contrast, treats systematic selection as universally effective (Lengnick-Hall et al., 2009).

This is reasonable given the evidence from meta-analyses is consistently that structured selection is more effective than unstructured, informal techniques. Nevertheless, the utility of such techniques is predicated on being able to be very selective in decision-making. The fact is that in some economies, there is a dramatic under-supply of people with key skills and knowledge, meaning that selectors often do not have the luxury of selecting one person from a candidate pool of 20. Rather they may be required to select one from three, one from two, or even two from every three candidates. So selection ratio, based on economic context, is a key contingency that influences the effectiveness of structured selection practice.

Contingencies such as these and other strategic demands and objectives of organizations influence how best to deploy effective strategic recruitment and selection. Tsui, Pearce, Porter, and Tripoli (1997) identify how organizations typically have multiple HR systems used for different purposes. The challenge is to adapt the approach taken to fit the objectives of selection. For example, Lepak and Snell (1999) proposed that positions in a company should be classified on two dimensions: uniqueness of skills (how specific skills were to the company need) and value of skills (strategic importance). Where jobs are high uniqueness and high value, employee development is key and, correspondingly, selection might focus on capacity to learn. Where jobs are low uniqueness but high value, a market-based external approach to recruitment and selection is needed, where assessment might follow closely the models we have reviewed and invest heavily in the late-stage select-in techniques.

Occupational setting also presents a contingency to the application of selection methods. Within the literature on selection assessment methodologies, for example, there is an implicit 'professional settings' bias, in that the methods described and evaluated often tend to be most relevant to conventional organizational environments. Many mainstream research studies do not easily generalize to different settings (for example in construction, or for teachers in schools). This leads to a divergence in research rather than an integrated understanding of selection effectiveness.

RECRUITMENT AND SELECTION IN SPECIFIC CONTEXTS

Developing effective selection systems calls for adapting approaches to meet specific or strategic needs in organizations. Two high-impact recruitment and selection tasks are the recruitment and identification of talented and high-potential employees, and leadership and managerial selection.

Talent and high potential selection

Talent management is an often-quoted activity in HRM that might range in meaning from managing people generally, through to managing top-level managers and directors. However, it broadly refers to (e.g. Collings & Mellahi, 2009):

1 Identification of key positions in a business that contribute to the achievement of strategic business objectives.
2 Identification of high-potential individuals, either externally or internally, that can be developed and managed into those positions.

There is obviously a clear need and role for sound and robust assessment and selection in the process of talent management. Identifying high potential, selecting such individuals and keeping them is a critical strategic organizational task.

The challenge for assessment and selection is first to understand the nature of high potential. Also relevant is to understand the career context for high-potential employees. When an employee or recruit is added to a high-potential pool of people, that person is entered onto a steep career trajectory that will involve experience of multiple areas of a business, and fast progression quickly to leadership roles. The person is not so much selected for a job, rather for a career that involves frequent learning and adaptation.

Defining the nature of high potential has attracted surprisingly little research attention until recently. Silzer and Church (2009) review the literature on high potential and formulate a model capturing three key elements that define high-potential individuals:

- Foundation aspects: high cognitive ability to facilitate learning, and key personality traits such as achievement orientation.
- Growth aspects: motivation to learn and master things, and resilience to grow and develop.
- Career aspects: typically leadership, but also career-specific specialty or competence that might include technical excellence in a field.

For deploying assessments for selection, one implication for assessment and selection is that a combination of assessments is needed. For foundation aspects, *prospective assessment* is needed to inform decisions, looking forward at predictors of learning and performance maintenance such as personality traits and cognitive ability. For career aspects, *retrospective assessment* is needed to examine capability and competencies developed through the career to date. Interviews or work samples might be used, or potentially peer-assessments for current employees. For growth aspects, a combination of these techniques may be needed to look at prospective and actual past learning and adaptation.

Managerial and leadership selection

Managerial and leader selection is a preoccupation of many organizations, understandably so, given the impact leaders have on businesses. Most people can connect with the obvious issue that technical expertise and excellence is not enough for effective leadership and management. Promoting people or selecting leaders for technical excellence often means losing an excellent technician and gaining an average leader.

Fiedler (1996) considered the issue of leadership and management selection and pointed to the contradictory findings of the validity of intelligence assessments in this context. Intelligence was, it appeared, an inconsistent predictor of effectiveness as a leader.

In unpicking the literature, Fiedler identified some key issues in these findings. First, intelligence is only important to the extent that the leader has subsequent capacity and autonomy to learn and solve problems. Leaders and managers operating under hierarchical systems of control are likely to have less such autonomy, and in such contexts cognitive ability is less important. Second, leadership effectiveness itself is highly contingent. Leader behaviour, for example varies in terms of two dimensions: person-orientation (the focus of the leader on people and their welfare), and initiation of structure (task focus of the leader). Neither approach to leadership is universally effective, and so the context of the leadership role is critical.

The case of leadership selection is one that illustrates the issue of context. The context within which the leadership role is performed requires a contextualized assessment approach, in which the demands of the organization and the job environment are built into assessment design. Assessment centres are a good example, which may simulate aspects of the organization. Lessons from literatures on frame-of-reference techniques (Lievens, 2001) are likely to improve selection. Likewise, Cascio and Aguinis (2008) describe 'in-situ' performance, which represents understanding of both performance and the context within which performance occurs. The incorporation of contextual information to assessment is therefore highly relevant for effective managerial and leadership selection.

The literature on personality and leadership may also inform the selection of leaders and managers. For example, Judge, Bono, Ilies, and Gerhardt (2002) report a meta-analysis of the associations of personality traits with leader emergence and leader effectiveness. They reported that:

- Traits related to Extraversion and Conscientiousness in the Big Five model were associated with leader emergence.
- Traits related to Conscientiousness, Extraversion, Emotional Stability and Openness were associated with leader effectiveness.

The use of personality assessment as a component of leadership and managerial selection therefore seems sensible from an evidence-based perspective.

At its heart, the selection of leaders is a good example of a situation in which the components of effective selection may seem to be in conflict. If it is acknowledged that the demands of each senior leadership role is unique, and that candidates with sufficient experience also have very peculiar individualized profiles (i.e. requiring high strategic customization), how can a systematic approach be maintained? The construction of bespoke assessment strategies for individuals in such positions have been referred to simply as 'individual assessments' (Morris, Daisley, Wheeler, & Boyer, 2015). They are defined as *"any employee selection procedure that involved: 1) multiple assessment methods, 2) administered to an individual examinee, and 3) relying on assessor judgment to integrate the information into an overall evaluation of the candidate's suitability for a job"* (Morris et al., 2015). In their meta-analyses, Morris et al. report that these forms of assessment were generally more valid in managerial settings, with the inclusion of cognitive ability assessment and the use of the same assessor across all candidates. These findings suggest that it is possible to manage the strategic and systematic demands of managerial and leader selection with careful assessment procedure design.

APPLICANT PERSPECTIVES: THE EXPERIENCE OF RECRUITMENT AND SELECTION

The methods that have been explored so far in this chapter conform to a single paradigm in selection practice – the positivist or psychometric paradigm. Bilsberry (2007) comments that this paradigm considers selection primarily from the perspective of the organization, focusing on how good selection decisions should be made in order to maximize performance. Neglected by the paradigm is the perspective of the applicant or candidate. As highlighted earlier, the social process or constructionist perspective focuses on the social nature of the selection process. Bilsberry identifies that the social process approach is rarely integrated into the selection literature adequately, and rather serves as a theoretical counterpoint, presented as a critical perspective to the psychometric paradigm. However, some of the issues raised by the social process approach have been developed in empirical research.

Perhaps the most widely investigated area among those that he covers concerns applicant reactions and perceptions of the selection process and the organization. In a review of 40 studies conducted between 1985 and 1999, Ryan and Ployhart (2000) identify two trends in this research. The first is the influence of applicant perceptions on attitudes and behaviours towards the organization. The second is the influence of applicant perceptions on their subsequent performance at the selection process. These two sets of relationships were elaborated by Hausknecht et al. (2004) and included in a theoretical model of the antecedents, contents and outcomes of applicant perceptions of selection processes (see Figure 5.4).

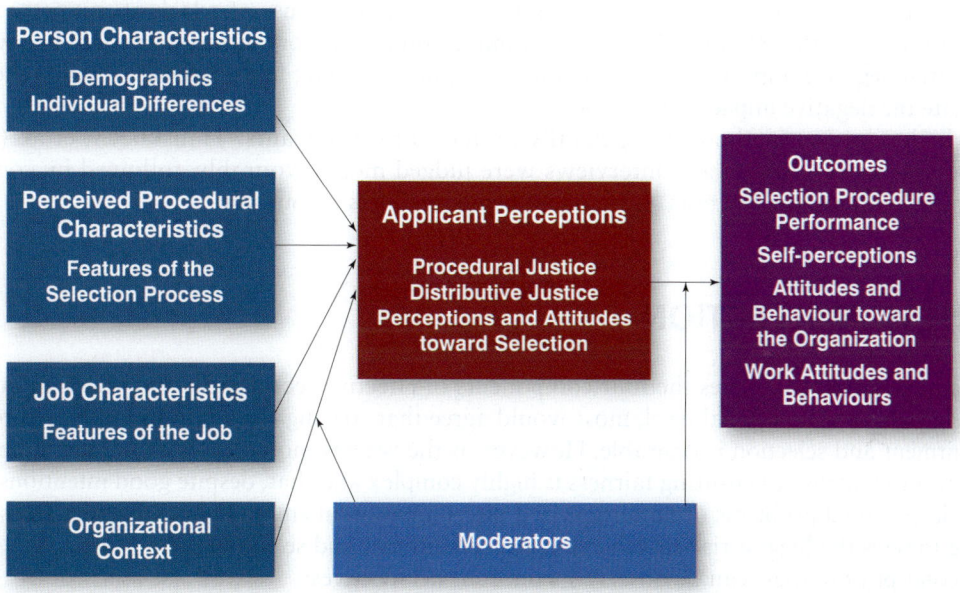

Figure 5.4 A model of applicant perceptions of selection processes, plus antecedents and consequences

A key element of the model concerns organizational justice, with the most commonly studied aspect being perceptions of procedural justice (perceptions of the overall fairness of the procedures used in the selection). In their meta-analyses of the components of their model, Hausknecht et al. (2004) reported clear associations between applicant perceptions of face and predictive validity, and positive perceptions of the fairness of the selection process. Moreover, those who perceived the selection positively were more likely to perceive the organization favourably, accept job offers and recommend the organization as an employer to others. Note also that perceptions of fairness are not necessarily aligned with actual fairness (Anderson, 2011), and so organizations need to consider both the process and presentation of selection.

New technology is once again critical in understanding the currency of research into applicant reactions to selection procedures. For example, McCarthy et al. (2017) cite a future challenge for this area of research in understanding how applicants respond to internet- and digital-mediated assessment. They describe that research generally indicates positive reactions to internet-based techniques, but that this is likely to be moderated by the extent to which people feel that the technology helps rather than hinders them to show their potential. For example, in a selection interview, both verbal and non-verbal interactions are typically seen as important to the content and conduct of the exchange. To the extent that technology degrades that opportunity, it might be seen as negative. As with criterion validity research, a next challenge for applicant perspectives research is to incorporate new technologies such as gamified and AI-based assessment.

As you may expect, however, the effects of perceived selection fairness may not be so straightforward. In a study of real job applicants, Schinkel, van Vianen, and van Dierendonck (2013) reported that affective well-being was related differently to perceptions of fairness depending on the selection outcome. Those who were selected reported higher well-being if they perceived the selection to be fair. However, for those who were rejected, well-being was higher if they thought the selection was unfair. This makes sense when you think about it: people could compensate for the negative effects of rejection by at least feeling that it was not because of a lack of competence, but rather a problem in the selection. The practical implication is that organizations should be aware of the potential negative impacts of rejection and, alongside designing fair processes, should take steps to mitigate the negative impacts of rejection.

So which selection methods are generally preferred by applicants? Hausknecht et al. (2004) reported that work samples and interviews were judged most favourably, followed by cognitive ability tests, with personality tests and biodata being rated less favourably.

FAIRNESS IN SELECTION

Fairness in selection completes the four components of effective recruitment and selection outlined in this chapter. At a superficial level, most would agree that striving for a fair and unbiased process of recruitment and selection is desirable. However, as the issue is more deeply examined, it becomes clear that the challenge of ensuring fairness is highly complex and that, despite good intentions, there remain deep-rooted problems of unfairness and discrimination in employment selection. Denying or ignoring these is the biggest risk to achieving fair recruitment and selection.

The concept of fairness can be observed from four perspectives:

1 bias and prejudice from people
2 procedural adverse impact and differential validity
3 legal concerns
4 professional standards.

Bias and prejudice

Interpersonal perceptual biases were highlighted at the outset of this chapter as sources of poor decision-making in selection. The answer to the problem of such bias is to adopt a systematic and evidence-based approach to recruitment and selection as discussed throughout the chapter.

There are, of course, many other overt prejudices that people carry about others based on their demographic characteristics (i.e. gender, race/ethnicity, sexual orientation). While espoused prejudiced opinions may be less prevalent in the discourse of people in organizations, it does not mean that such views have disappeared and no longer impact personnel decision-making (Kandola, 2018).

An example of this prejudice is the persistent observation of the impact of applicant name on the evaluation of CVs. The paradigm for studies in this area involves experimental studies that present recruiters with identical CVs with names that are typically from majority versus minority groups or male versus female. The results provide clear evidence that bias pervades in such evaluations. In the case of ethnicity, Derous, Ryan, & Serlie (2015) showed in a study in the Netherlands that identical CVs with Arabic-sounding names received systematically lower suitability evaluations than Dutch names. Meta-analyses of the same bias effects in gender show that men consistently receive higher evaluations in male-stereotyped occupational settings than women (again where CVs are identical, but gender is experimentally manipulated; see e.g. Koch, D'Mello, & Sackett, 2015).

In these studies, the observed effects are not necessarily purported to reflect overt racism; that is, people are not necessarily consciously evaluating minorities and women lower. Rather the effect is at the level of the decision-making and perception, and may reflect implicit or unconscious prejudices against others based on their background (Greenwald, Poehlman, Uhlmann, & Banaji, 2009). These implicit biases may represent some of the foundations of discrimination in decision-making observed in selection (see also Kandola & Kandola, 2013).

Procedural adverse impact and differential validity

Adverse impact (sometimes referred to as indirect discrimination) is related to individual assessments, as well as selection processes overall, and is a measure of the extent to which biases in assessment impact the outcomes of selection. Adverse impact occurs when one particular demographic group scores lower than others on a particular assessment (i.e. their mean score is lower than that of other groups). The net result is that a smaller proportion of candidates from that group will make it through the selection process compared to others. The group is systematically disadvantaged as a result of the use of the assessment technique. This form of discrimination can be contrasted with direct discrimination, which reflects particular prejudices of the selector. Indirect discrimination does not imply that the assessor or selector is prejudiced; rather it is an unseen form of discrimination – a property of the assessment rather than the assessor.

The four-fifths rule of thumb is a statistical convention for judging the severity of adverse impact. The rule states that the proportion of one group 'passing' a component of the selection should not be less than four-fifths or 80 per cent of another. If the proportion is less than 80 per cent, then adverse impact is effectively confirmed. A variety of procedures for determining adverse impact according to this rule of thumb have been developed (Collins & Morris, 2008). Hough, Oswald, and Ployhart (2001) reviewed adverse impact evidence for a variety of assessment methods, collating data on the differences in assessment scores between different demographic groups (e.g. men, women, black candidates, white candidates, older and younger workers). Their findings are summarized in Table 5.2.

According to some perspectives, on its own, adverse impact does not necessarily constitute unfairness, and it is actually validity that is the key to deciding whether a method is unfair. Criterion validity tells us the extent to which an assessment predicts job performance. If the assessment is valid, then selecting high-scoring candidates will give the highest probability of selecting a high-performing employee. Organizations cannot be challenged on these grounds, and even if the assessment causes adverse impact, using it to select job candidates is justifiable. This holds true unless the assessment is found to predict performance differently for different demographic groups. This is referred to as differential validity. The implication of differential validity is that estimates of job performance are different depending on the demographic group of the candidate (e.g. different performance estimates could be derived from two candidates with the same assessment scores). Procedures for determining differential validity were proposed by Cleary (1986), but are very difficult to implement, particularly in small samples of candidates (e.g. Woods, 2006). If differential validity is demonstrated, then the assessment can be considered to be unfair.

Table 5.2 Assessment Methods and Adverse Impact (potential for adverse impact highlighted where appropriate) (summarized from Hough et al., 2001)

Assessment Method	Potential Adverse Impact
Cognitive ability tests	**High potential for adverse impact:** **Moderate potential for adverse impact: Ethnicity, Gender, Age** - In US data, white groups score higher than black groups on many forms of ability test, higher than Hispanic groups and lower than East Asian groups on measures of g. - Men and women score equally on general ability tests, women score higher on verbal tests, men on spatial and numerical. - Older workers tend to score lower on measures of g.
Personality measures	**Moderate potential for adverse impact: Gender** - Small or negligible differences on the Big Five across ethnicities. - Women score higher on Agreeableness, and traits relating to affiliation and dependability.
Biodata	- Small differences in scores across ethnicities, gender and younger/older workers. If scores captured educational background, potential for adverse impact against some ethnic groups increases.
Assessments centres	**Moderate potential for adverse impact: Ethnicity, Age** - In US data, black candidates score lower than whites. - Older candidates surprisingly score lower than younger ones, considering that managerial skills supposedly develop with experience. - No information on gender differences, but higher performance on work-sample test may lead to higher AC score
Interviewers	- Whites scored slightly higher than blacks and Hispanic groups in US data. - Evidence less clear for gender, but difference likely to be negligible overall (Moscoso, 2000), but moderated by perceptual factors such as interviewer biases.
Work-sample tests	**Moderate potential for adverse impact: Ethnicity** - In US data, black groups score lower than white groups, men score lower than women. Ethnic differences are much smaller than those on cognitive ability test difference for the same participants, however, and so are preferable in terms of reducing advance impact.

The failure of work and organizational psychology to adequately grasp and tackle matters of fairness in procedures is laid bare in reviews of the literature (see e.g. Colella, Hebl, & King, 2017). There remain too few solutions to issues of procedural adverse impact such as that observed in cognitive testing (Berry et al., 2014). This is despite evidence of potential differential validity for different race groups and too little contemporary understanding of the problems. Using interviews as an example, Levashina et al. (2014) showed that adverse impact in interviews was observable in pre-1996 studies, but almost non-existent in post-1996 studies. Continuing to work from an outdated evidence base compounds research effort to address instances of adverse impact and unfairness.

Legal concerns

Globalization of organizations means that they may operate selection processes in a variety of different legal contexts, each treating fairness in selection differently. In Europe and the USA, there are some common threads, however. Employment law generally covers discrimination based on gender, ethnicity, disability and age. Recruitment material such as advertisements are prohibited from stating preferences for individuals from specific groups, unless it is essential for fulfilling a job requirement (e.g. in the case of disability, if the organization could not make a reasonable adjustment to the job).

Indirect discrimination is covered in most employment laws (e.g. the Equality Act 2010 in the UK), but only in the USA is it operationalized in the four-fifths rule of thumb. The essence of most legislation in respect of selection is that adverse impact or indirect discrimination is only unlawful if it cannot be shown to be a reasonable method of assessment. This usually means that assessments are judged fair if they can be shown to be job relevant through *a priori* job and competency analyses, and if there is some evidence of their validity. US law is peculiar in its specification of differential validity as grounds for unlawful practice, although employers can present a case to show that it was not practically possible to conduct a validity study. A major future challenge is to understand how research findings and implications relate to the legal environments in different countries (e.g. Myors et al., 2008).

A related question in this area concerns the difference between legal practice and ethical, responsible practice.

KEY THEME

Diversity and Inclusion

Any organizational strategy for diversity and inclusion must address procedures of recruitment and selection. In this chapter, we have considered some of the key issues and parameters of fairness in selection and what contributes to ensuring that a process is fair and justifiable. Some of the foundations of fairness include ensuring that processes are systematic, free from bias and based on sound evidence of their effectiveness. The issue of adverse impact and indirect discrimination is also critical for taking decisions that serve to improve diversity.

However, beyond these issues, there are further questions about how to make selection inclusive as a social process of introducing employer and employee and bringing people into teams in as positive a way as possible.

continued

This involves finding ways to ensure that all employees are able to participate and contribute to processes in ways that protect the systematic and fair nature of selection, but nevertheless promote involvement.

Salgado, Moscoso, García-Izquierdo, and Anderson (2017) consider ways to achieve this through developing what they refer to as *inclusive and discrimination-free personnel selection systems*. Some of the goals that they outline for inclusive personnel selection introduce new ways of thinking about how to implement selection. For example, they consider the role of employee voice in the process of selection. They propose that workers should be given chance to express their views about how selection procedures might be implemented to make them fairer and discrimination free. They also highlight that employees should be involved in the process of organizational entry. These suggestions are just some ways in which recruitment and selection processes could be made more inclusive, and less the exclusive preserve of senior managers. The presence of more voices in decision-making could contribute in important ways to making processes fairer and more representative of the needs of people working in organizations.

For example, an assessment method could cause adverse impact, yet still be lawful on the grounds that it is a legitimate way to identify individuals with the highest potential for performance.

On the issue of adverse impact, organizational culture and values are relevant. This might seem to contradict the majority of this chapter, which has primarily drawn on the technical and evidence-based application of selection methods, removing subjectivity in decision-making. Yet culture and values are important on this point. In work psychology research, we know about the potential adverse impact associated with some selection methods, most obviously with cognitive ability testing. Research has established that differences exist across ethnicities, and that even when combined with non-cognitive predictors, adverse impact or indirect discrimination may still occur. Plus, international working raises the issue of the effects of non-native speakers completing tests in the same language as native speakers. Evidence shows that our estimates of ability are suppressed when the test-taker completes verbal tests in non-native languages, with the test tapping into language proficiency rather than ability (e.g. te Nijenhuis & van der Flier, 2003).

The fairness of the test depends on whether it predicts performance differently across demographic groups. There is little reported evidence of differential validity in the research literature (e.g. Hunter, Schmidt, & Hunter, 1979), and many organizations are not in a position to carry out their own validity investigations. Organizations are therefore faced with a dilemma about trying to balance the demands of valid selection and a diverse workforce. According to De Corte and Lievens (2003), this dilemma is 'one of the most perplexing problems facing the practice of personnel selection today' (p. 87). Using a cognitive ability test will certainly help to identify high performers, but will most likely reduce diversity in the organization – in different ways for different tests. Even the most recent attempts to develop an empirical account of the problem are limited (e.g. De Corte, Lievens, & Sackett, 2007), because conceptualizing and modelling the selection quality–adverse impact trade-off is highly complex, and beyond the technical capabilities of most practitioners.

At present then, organizations must therefore make the decision about whether to use cognitive ability tests for selection based on their own values, and these are likely to include consideration of values around CSR. If the organization values productivity over diversity, then the use of a fair test with some adverse impact is justifiable. If the organization values diversity first, then the test is best avoided, particularly if it is unaccompanied by other supporting evidence in the selection process.

The question for work psychologists is whether they should present a position on the issue, and if so, what it should be? From our own perspective in this book, and in practice as psychologists, the answer is quite clear. Methodologies that create adverse impact and damage diversity are not the means to make a positive impact in work and organizations. This is especially the case when there are alternative valid selection tools that do not demonstrate the systematic adverse impact of cognitive testing.

> **DISCUSS WITH A COLLEAGUE**
>
> Review again the selection proposal you developed in the previous discussions. How could you ensure that this process was fair?

Professional standards

A further determinant of fairness concerns the extent to which best-practice guidelines have been followed in the selection process. There are some important sources of guidance on best practice in selection that can be drawn upon. Psychometric testing has well-defined guidelines for use. The International Testing Commission (2013) has developed a comprehensive set of guidelines, which are similar to those set down by the British Psychological Society in the Occupational Test User qualifications. There are similar guidelines for assessment centres (International Taskforce on Assessment Center Operations, 2014). In the UK, the Chartered Institute for Personnel and Development (CIPD) publish best-practice guidance, and in the USA, the Uniform Guidelines on Employee Selection Procedures (US Employment Opportunities Commission, 1978), although dated, are also comprehensive.

Many of these professional standards reflect conventional and established recruitment and selection approaches. There is an urgent need for similar professional standards for internet and digital forms of selection and recruitment. A good illustration of the need is the use of social media in recruitment screening. There is no evidence that the use of social media (i.e. screening and searching job applicants' online footprints) demonstrates any criterion-related validity (McCarthy et al., 2017). There is, however, evidence of potential adverse impact based on ethnicity (Van Iddekinge et al., 2016). Some countries such as Germany have banned this practice outright, yet we know that it does occur increasingly often (McCarthy et al., 2017; Roth, Bobko, Iddekinge, & Thatcher, 2013). There are calls for more research into such digital methodologies, but just as important in the future will be robust professional standards about how, if social media and other digital screening are ever used in selection, it could and should be done fairly.

POSITIVE WORK

The fairness imperative in recruitment and selection

Research in recruitment and selection in applied psychology has accumulated a huge literature on the validity of different selection methodologies. By comparison, research has advanced much less in the study of fairness and discrimination (Colella et al., 2017). There is a question about whether this trend in research reflects an organizational and business prioritization of performance over diversity and fairness that may have persisted in the past. Whatever the reason, one contrarian proposition for making recruitment and selection more positive is to change the primary emphasis in selection from validity to fairness.

Arguably in the past, validity of assessment methodology has superseded fairness (how else do we have in research the concept of the validity–diversity 'trade-off'?). In an evidence-based approach, methodology is to be ruled out in the absence of validity evidence. Valid methods are sometimes evaluated to determine their adverse impact, but the findings tend to have little influence on their application in selection practice.

Prioritizing fairness in recruitment and selection means positioning fairness as the primary concern. If there is evidence that a methodology is unfair or discriminatory (either by creating adverse impact, or differential validity), then it could be ruled out on that basis. Validity is, of course, still critical to establish. A method that does not create adverse impact, but which is also not valid as a predictor of performance, remains *unfair*. In this approach though, the importance of fairness conceptualized from all perspectives is raised to equivalent status to validity in decision-making about how to recruit and select staff.

Designing selection procedures in this way would not necessarily result in poorer performance prediction. There are multiple methodologies that show simultaneously high validity and lower adverse impact than cognitive testing, for example, or no adverse impact at all (such as structured interviewing as reported in post-1996 studies by Levashina et al., 2014).

Moreover, unaccounted for in the micro perspectives of assessment validity research are the organizational benefits of adopting an approach to recruitment and selection that would promote a greater sense of procedural justice, trust, and consequently improved engagement and well-being. These are brought into sharper focus against the negative impact of unfair recruitment and selection, namely damaged self-esteem, resentment and social injustice when scaled up to a societal level. Fair processes of assessment, recruitment and selection are in this context a prerequisite for positively improving work and organizations. So why not, in this case, make fairness our priority?

SUMMARY

Recruitment and selection are key activities for work psychologists in organizations. Effective recruitment and selection processes are those that are evidence based, systematic, strategic and fair. Such processes draw on sound science, proceed logically and methodically, and serve the specific strategic needs of particular organizations, or jobs and roles within them, and are free from bias and unfair discrimination.

From a practical perspective, recruitment and selection are best conceptualized as a longitudinal process following a series of sequential steps. The process starts with job analysis (an examination of the work to be carried out) and the knowledge, skills, abilities, other characteristics and competencies to be demonstrated by the worker. The resultant information is recorded in a job description and personnel specification, which are used to define selection criteria and assessment needs. The information also feeds into recruitment (attraction of job applicants).

Once assessment needs are defined, assessments are chosen on the basis of their match with needs, and their associated reliability, validity and fairness. Among the most common assessment methodologies are CVs, application forms and biodata, psychometric and situational judgement testing, selection interviewing and assessment centres. Advances in research, most notably meta-analyses, have enabled a huge volume of literature on the criterion validities of different assessment methods to be accumulated. Despite this, new and digital technology have transformed recruitment and selection methodology and practices and research has not kept pace, resulting in significant gaps in understanding about digital methods of assessment in particular. Macro perspectives on recruitment and selection explore how organizational contingencies guide how recruitment and selection are deployed in various ways in different organizations and for different purposes within organizations. Recent examples include a focus on assessment and identification of high-potential staff. Other wider perspectives focus on the experience of job candidates at selection processes and the impact that their experiences have on behavioural, attitudinal and affective outcomes.

Fairness in recruitment and selection requires appraisal of multiple perspectives, including research on prejudice and bias, procedural adverse impact and discrimination, legal versus ethical concerns, and professional standards. There remain many challenges for work and organizational psychology in the future to examine and better prioritize fairness of recruitment and selection in practice.

At the start of this chapter, you were invited to walk through the nearest city to your home and consider the wide diversity of jobs that people do in the organizations and businesses that you might encounter. What might the impact be of applying effective and fair selection practice in all of these organizations? Businesses could benefit because productivity and performance could be improved, and people would potentially be happier in their jobs, if their unique skills and attributes found expression and utility in their work. They might also feel more fairly treated by organizations. Then imagine this potential impact at the level of the whole city – interacting and co-dependent organizations all performing their functions more effectively, led and staffed by happier, more satisfied employees.

DISCUSSION QUESTIONS

1. What advice would you give to a manager who wanted to select a new administrator for their group?
2. Are tests of cognitive ability the best way to assess people in selection? Why?
3. If you were a selection candidate, what would be important in terms of helping you feel fairly treated?
4. Think about your own judgemental biases. How might they influence your decisions if you were interviewing a job candidate?
5. People can manage their behaviour and the impression they create at a selection process (i.e. they could fake a personality test, or act in a particular way in an interview). How would you advise an organization to protect against this possibility?
6. What are the key issues to consider in ensuring that selection processes are fair?

FURTHER READING

Cook, M. (2014). *Personnel selection: Adding value through people* (4th ed.). Chichester, England: John Wiley & Sons.

Kandola, B. (2018). *Racism at work: The danger of indifference.* Oxford, UK: Pearn Kandola Publishing.

McCarthy, J. M., Bauer, T. N., Truxillo, D. M., Anderson, N. R., Costa, A. C., & Ahmed, S. M. (2017). Applicant perspectives during selection: A review addressing "So what?," "What's new?," and "Where to next?". *Journal of Management, 43*(6), 1693–1725.

Ployhart, R. E., Schmitt, N., & Tippins, N. T. (2017). Solving the supreme problem: 100 years of selection and recruitment at the *Journal of Applied Psychology*. *Journal of Applied Psychology, 102*(3), 291–304.

REFERENCES

Anderson, N. (2011). Perceived job discrimination: Toward a model of applicant propensity to case initiation in selection. *International Journal of Selection and Assessment, 19*(3), 229–244.

Arthur, W., Day, E. A., McNelly, T. L., & Edens, P. S. (2006) A meta-analysis of the criterion-related validity of assessment centre dimensions. *Personnel Psychology, 56*(1), 125–153.

Barrick, M. R., Mount, M. K., & Judge, T. A. (2001). Personality and performance at the beginning of the new millennium: What do we know and where do we go next? *International Journal of Selection and Assessment, 9*, 9–30.

Bartram, D. (2005). The great eight competencies: A criterion-centric approach to validation. *Journal of Applied Psychology, 90*(6), 1185–1203.

Berry, C. M., Cullen, M. J., & Meyer, J. M. (2014). Racial/ethnic subgroup differences in cognitive ability test range restriction: Implications for differential validity. *Journal of Applied Psychology, 99*(1), 21–33.

Bertua, C., Anderson, N., & Salgado, J. F. (2005). The predictive validity of cognitive ability tests: A UK meta-analysis. *Journal of Occupational and Organizational Psychology, 78*(3), 387–409.

Bilsberry, J. (2007). *Experiencing recruitment and selection.* Chichester, England: John Wiley & Sons.

Birkeland, S. A., Manson, T. M., Kisamore, J. L., Brannick, M. T., & Smith, M. A. (2006). A meta-analytic investigation of job applicant faking on personality measures. *International Journal of Selection and Assessment, 14*(4), 317–335.

Brannick, M. T., Levine, E. L., & Morgeson, F. P. (2007). *Job and work analysis: Methods, research, and applications for human resource management* (2nd ed.). Thousand Oaks, CA: SAGE.

Breaugh, J. A. (2008). Employee recruitment: Current knowledge and important areas for future research. *Human Resource Management Review, 18*(3), 103–118.

Bright, J. E. H., & Hutton, S. (2000). The impact of competency statements on resumes for short-listing decisions. *International Journal of Selection and Assessment, 8*(2), 41–53.

Buehl, A. K., & Melchers, K. G. (2017). Individual difference variables and the occurrence and effectiveness of faking behavior in interviews. *Frontiers in Psychology, 8*, 686.

Buehl, A. K., Melchers, K. G., Macan, T., & Kühnel, J. (2018). Tell me sweet little lies: How Does faking in interviews affect interview scores and interview validity? *Journal of Business and Psychology*, 1–18.

Campion, M. A., Fink, A. A., Ruggeberg, B. J., Carr, L., Phillips, G. M., & Odman, R. B. (2011). Doing competencies well: Best practices in competency modeling. *Personnel Psychology, 64*(1), 225–262.

Campion, M. A., Palmer, D. K., & Campion, J. E. (1997). A review of structure in the selection interview. *Personnel Psychology, 50*, 655–702.

Cascio, W. F., & Aguinis, H. (2008). Staffing twenty-first-century organizations. *The Academy of Management Annals, 2*(1), 133–165.

Chamorro-Premuzic, T., Winsborough, D., Sherman, R. A., & Hogan, R. (2016). New talent signals: Shiny new objects or a brave new world? *Industrial and Organizational Psychology, 9*(3), 621–640.

Chapman, D. S., Uggerslev, K. L., Carroll, S. A., Piasentin, K. A., & Jones, D. A. (2005). Applicant attraction to organizations and job choice: A meta-analytic review of the correlates of recruiting outcomes. *Journal of Applied Psychology, 90*(5), 928.

Christian, M. S., Edwards, B. D., & Bradley, J. C. (2010). Situational judgment tests: Constructs assessed and a meta-analysis of their criterion-related validities. *Personnel Psychology, 63*(1), 83–117.

Cleary, T. A. (1986). Test bias: Prediction of grades of Negro and white students in integrated colleges. *Journal of Educational Measurement, 5*, 115–124.

Colella, A., Hebl, M., & King, E. (2017). One hundred years of discrimination research in the *Journal of Applied Psychology*: A sobering synopsis. *Journal of Applied Psychology, 102*(3), 500–513.

Collings, D. G., & Mellahi, K. (2009). Strategic talent management: A review and research agenda. *Human Resource Management Review, 19*(4), 304–313.

Collins, M. W., & Morris, S. B. (2008). Testing for adverse impact when sample size is small. *Journal of Applied Psychology, 93*(2), 463–471.

Conway, J. M., Jako, R. A., & Goodman, D. F. (1995). A meta-analysis of interrater and internal consistency reliability of selection interviews. *Journal of Applied Psychology, 80*(5), 565.

Cook, M. (2016). *Personnel selection: Adding value through people* (5th ed.). Chichester, England: John Wiley & Sons.

Cooper, D., Robertson, I. T., & Tinline, G. (2003). *Recruitment and selection: A framework for success*. London, England: Thomson.

Davis, A. J., & Scully, J. (2008). Strategic resourcing. In Aston Centre for Human Resources (Eds.), *Strategic human resource management* (pp. 95–128). London, England: CIPD.

De Corte, W., & Lievens, F. (2003). A practical procedure to estimate the quality and the adverse impact of single stage selection decisions. *International Journal of Selection and Assessment, 11*, 87–95.

De Corte, W., Lievens, F., & Sackett, P. R. (2007). Combining predictors to achieve optimal trade-offs between selection quality and adverse impact. *Journal of Applied Psychology, 92*(5), 1380–1393.

Derous, E., Ryan, A. M., & Serlie, A. W. (2015). Double jeopardy upon resumé screening. *Personnel Psychology, 68*(3), 659–696.

Dineen, B. R., & Noe, R. A. (2009). Effects of customization on application decisions and applicant pool characteristics in a web-based recruitment context. *Journal of Applied Psychology, 94*(1), 224–234.

Dwight, S. A., & Donovan, J. J. (2003). Do warnings not to fake reduce faking? *Human Performance, 16*, 1–23.

Ellingson, J. E., Sackett, P. R., & Connelly, B. S. (2007). Personality assessment across selection and development contexts: Insights into response distortion. *Journal of Applied Psychology, 92*(2), 386–395.

Fiedler, F. E. (1996). Research on leadership selection and training: One view of the future. *Administrative Science Quarterly, 41*(2), 241–250.

Greenwald, A. G., Poehlman, A. T., Uhlmann, E. L., & Banaji, M. R. (2009). Understanding and using the implicit association test: III. Meta-analysis of predictive validity. *Journal of Personality and Social Psychology, 97*(1), 17–41.

Hausknecht, J. P., Day, D. V., & Thomas, S. C. (2004). Applicant reactions to selection procedures: An updated model and meta-analysis. *Personnel Psychology, 57*, 639–683.

Hermelin, E., Lievens, F., & Robertson, I. T. (2007). The validity of assessment centres for the prediction of supervisory performance ratings: A meta-analysis. *International Journal of Selection and Assessment, 15*, 428–433.

Hogan, J., Barrett, P., & Hogan, R. (2007). Personality measurement, faking, and employment selection. *Journal of Applied Psychology, 92*, 1270–1285.

Hogan, J., & Holland, B. (2003). Using theory to evaluate personality and job-performance relations: A socioanalytic perspective. *Journal of Applied Psychology, 88*(1), 100.

Hogan, R. (2005). In defense of personality measurement: New wine for old whiners. *Human Performance, 18*(4), 331–341.

Hough, L. M., Eaton, N., Dunnette, M., Kamp, J., & McCloy, R. (1990). Criterion-related validities of personality constructs and the effect of response distortion on those validities. *Journal of Applied Psychology, 75*, 581–595.

Hough, L. M., Oswald, F. L., & Ployhart, R. E. (2001). Determinants, detection and amelioration of adverse impact in personnel selection procedures: Issues, evidence and lessons learned. *International Journal of Selection and Assessment, 9*, 152–194.

Huffcutt, A. I. (2010). From Science to practice: Seven principles for conducting employment interviews. *Applied HRM Research, 12*(1), 121–136.

Huffcutt, A. I., Culbertson, S. S., & Weyhrauch, W. S. (2013). Employment interview reliability: New meta-analytic estimates by structure and format. *International Journal of Selection and Assessment, 21*(3), 264–276.

Hunter, J. E., & Hunter, R. F. (1984). Validity and utility of alternative predictors of job performance. *Psychological Bulletin, 96*(1), 72–98.

Hunter, J. E., Schmidt, F. L., & Hunter, R. (1979). Differential validity of employment tests by race: A comprehensive review and analysis. *Psychological Bulletin, 86*(4), 721–735.

International Task Force on Assessment Center Guidelines. (2014). *Guidelines and ethical considerations for assessment center operations.* Pittsburgh, PA: DDI Inc.

International Testing Commission. (2013). *International guidelines on computer-based and internet delivered testing.* Retrieved from www.intestcom.org/files/guideline_computer_based_testing.pdf

Judge, T. A., Bono, J. E., Ilies, R., & Gerhardt, M. W. (2002). Personality and leadership: A qualitative and quantitative review. *Journal of Applied Psychology, 87*, 765–780.

Judge, T. A., & Zapata, G. P. (2015). The person–situation debate revisited: Effect of situation strength and trait activation on the validity of the big five personality traits in predicting job performance. *Academy of Management Journal, 58*(4), 1149–1179.

Kandola, B. (2018) *Racism at work: The danger of indifference.* Oxford, England: Pearn Kandola Publishing.

Kandola, J., & Kandola, B. (2013) *The invention of difference: The story of gender bias at work.* Oxford, England: Pearn Kandola Publishing.

Koch, A. J., D'Mello, S. D., & Sackett, P. R. (2015). A meta-analysis of gender stereotypes and bias in experimental simulations of employment decision making. *Journal of Applied Psychology, 100*(1), 128–161.

König, C. J., Merz, A. S., & Trauffer, N. (2012). What is in applicants' minds when they fill out a personality test? Insights from a qualitative study. *International Journal of Selection and Assessment, 20*(4), 442–452.

Kuncel, N. R., Ones, D. S., & Sackett, P. R. (2010). Individual differences as predictors of work, educational, and broad life outcomes. *Personality and Individual Differences, 49*(4), 331–336.

Latham, G. P., & Whyte, G. (1994). The futility of utility analysis. *Personnel Psychology, 47*, 31–46.

Lengnick-Hall, M. L., Lengnick-Hall, C. A., Andrade, L. S., & Drake, B. (2009). Strategic human resource management: The evolution of the field. *Human Resource Management Review, 19*(2), 64–85.

Lepak, D. P., & Snell, S. A. (1999). The human resource architecture: Toward a theory of human capital allocation and development. *Academy of Management Review, 24*(1), 31–48.

Levashina, J., Hartwell, C. J., Morgeson, F. P., & Campion, M. A. (2014). The structured employment interview: Narrative and quantitative review of the research literature. *Personnel Psychology, 67*(1), 241–293.

Lievens, F. (1999). Development of a simulated assessment center. *European Journal of Psychological Assessment, 15*, 117–126.

Lievens, F. (2001). Assessor training strategies and their effects on accuracy, interrater reliability, and discriminant validity. *Journal of Applied Psychology, 86*(2), 255–264.

Lievens, F., Chasteen, C. S., Day, E. A., & Christiansen, N. D. (2006). Large-scale investigation of the role of trait activation theory for understanding assessment center convergent and discriminant validity. *Journal of Applied Psychology, 91*(2), 247–258.

Lievens, F., De Koster, L., & Schollaert, E. (2008a). Current theory and practice of assessment centers: The importance of trait activation. In S. Cartwright & L. Cooper (Eds.), *The Oxford handbook of personnel psychology*. Oxford, England: Oxford University Press.

Lievens, F., & Klimoski, R. J. (2001). Understanding the assessment center process: Where are we now? In C. L. Cooper & I. T. Robertson (Eds.), *International review of industrial and organizational psychology* (Vol. 16, pp. 245–286). Chichester, England: John Wiley & Sons.

Lievens, F., Ones, D. S., & Dilchert, S. (2009). Personality scale validities increase throughout medical school. *Journal of Applied Psychology, 94*, 1514–1535. doi:10.1037/a0016137

Lievens, F., Peeters, H., & Schollaert, E. (2008b). Situational judgment tests: A review of recent research. *Personnel Review, 37*(4), 426–441.

Lievens, F., & Sackett, P. R. (2012). The validity of interpersonal skills assessment via situational judgment tests for predicting academic success and job performance. *Journal of Applied Psychology, 97*(2), 460–468.

Maheshwari, S., Sainani, A., & Reddy, P. K. (2010). An approach to extract special skills to improve the performance of resume selection. In *International Workshop on Databases in Networked Information Systems* (pp. 256–273). Berlin, Germany: Springer.

McCarthy, J. M., Bauer, T. N., Truxillo, D. M., Anderson, N. R., Costa, A. C., & Ahmed, S. M. (2017). Applicant perspectives during selection: A review addressing "So what?," "What's new?," and "Where to next?". *Journal of Management, 43*(6), 1693–1725.

McDaniel, M. A., Hartman, N. S., Whetzel, D. L., & Gubb, III, W. L. (2007). Situational judgment tests, response instructions, and validity: A meta-analysis. *Personnel Psychology, 60*(1), 63–91.

McDaniel, M. A., & Nguyen, N. T. (2001). Situational judgment tests: A review of practice and constructs assessed. *International Journal of Selection and Assessment, 9*(1–2), 103–113.

McDaniel, M. A., Whetzel, D. L., Schmidt, F. L., & Maurer, S. D. (1994). The validity of employment interviews: A comprehensive review and meta-analysis. *Journal of Applied Psychology, 79*(4), 599.

McKinney, A. P., Carlson, K. D., Mecham, III, R. L., D'Angelo, N. C., & Connerley, M. L. (2003). Recruiters' use of GPA in initial screening decisions: Higher GPAs don't always make the cut. *Personnel Psychology, 56*, 823–845.

Melchers, K. G., Ingold, P. V., Wilhelmy, A., & Kleinmann, M. (2015). Beyond validity: Shedding light on the social situation in employment interviews. In *Employee recruitment, selection, and assessment* (pp. 166–183). London, England: Psychology Press.

Melchers, K. G., Klehe, U. C., Richter, G. M., Kleinmann, M., König, C. J., & Lievens, F. (2009). "I know what you want to know": The impact of interviewees' ability to identify criteria on interview performance and construct-related validity. *Human Performance, 22*(4), 355–374.

Minbashian, A., Earl, J., & Bright, J. E. H. (2013). Openness to experience as a predictor of job performance trajectories. *Applied Psychology: An International Review, 62*, 1–12. doi:10.1111/j.1464-0597.2012.00490.x

Morgeson, F. P., Campion, M. A., Dipboye, R. L., Hollenbeck, J. R., Murphy, K., & Schmitt, N. (2007). Are we getting fooled again? Coming to terms with limitations in the use of personality tests for personnel selection. *Personnel Psychology, 60*, 1029–1049.

Morris, S. B., Daisley, R. L., Wheeler, M., & Boyer, P. (2015). A meta-analysis of the relationship between individual assessments and job performance. *Journal of Applied Psychology, 100*(1), 5–20.

Moscoso, S. (2000). Selection interview: A Review of validity evidence, adverse impact and applicant reactions. *International Journal of Selection and Assessment, 8*(4), 237–247.

Murphy, K. R., & Dzieweczynski, J. L. (2005). Why don't measures of broad dimensions of personality perform better as predictors of job performance? *Human Performance, 18*(4), 343–357.

Myors, B., Lievens, F., Schollaert, E., Van Hoye, G., Cronshaw, S. F., Mladinic, A., ... Rolland, F. (2008). International perspectives on the legal environment for selection. *Industrial and Organizational Psychology, 1*, 206–246.

Nguyen, N. T., Biderman, M. D., & McDaniel, M. A. (2005). Effects of response instructions on faking a situational judgment test. *International Journal of Selection and Assessment, 13*(4), 250–260.

Oswald, F. L., Schmitt, N., Kim, H. B., Ramsay, L. J., & Gillespie, M. A. (2004). Developing a bio-data measure and situational judgement inventory as predictors of college student performance. *Journal of Applied Psychology, 89*, 187–207.

Patterson, F., Carr, V., Zibarras, L., Burr, B., Berkin, L., Plint, S., ... Gregory, S. (2009). New machine-marked tests for selection into core medical training: Evidence from two validation studies. *Clinical Medicine, 9*(5), 417–420.

Pearn, M., & Kandola, R. (1988). *Job analysis: A manager's guide*. Oxford, England: IPD.

Ployhart, R. E. (2006). Staffing in the 21st century: New challenges and strategic opportunities. *Journal of Management, 32*(6), 868–897.

Ployhart, R. E., Schmitt, N., & Tippins, N. T. (2017). Solving the supreme problem: 100 years of selection and recruitment at the *Journal of Applied Psychology*. *Journal of Applied Psychology, 102*(3), 291–304.

Roberts, G. (1997). *Recruitment and selection: A competency approach*. London, England: CIPD.

Roberts, G. (2005). *Recruitment and selection*. London, England: CIPD.

Robertson, I. T., Bartram, D., & Callinan, M. (2002). Personnel selection and assessment. In P. Warr (Ed.), *Psychology at work* (pp. 100–152). London, England: Penguin.

Robertson, I. T., & Smith, M. (2001). Personnel selection. *Journal of Occupational and Organizational Psychology, 74*, 441–472.

Rockstuhl, T., Ang, S., Ng, K. Y., Lievens, F., & Van Dyne, L. (2015). Putting judging situations into situational judgment tests: Evidence from intercultural multimedia SJTs. *Journal of Applied Psychology, 100*(2), 464–480.

Roth, P. L., Bobko, P., & McFarland, L. Y. N. N. (2005). A meta-analysis of work sample test validity: Updating and integrating some classic literature. *Personnel Psychology, 58*(4), 1009–1037.

Roth, P. L., Bobko, P., Van Iddekinge, C. H., & Thatcher, J. B. (2016). Social media in employee-selection-related decisions: A research agenda for uncharted territory. *Journal of Management, 42*(1), 269–298.

Roulin, N., & Bangerter, A. (2012). Understanding the academic–practitioner gap for structured interviews: 'Behavioral' interviews diffuse, 'structured' interviews do not. *International Journal of Selection and Assessment, 20*(2), 149–158.

Rupp, D. E., Hoffman, B. J., Bischof, D., Byham, W., Collins, L., Gibbins, A. ... Thornton, G. (2015) Guidelines and ethical considerations for assessment center operations. *Journal of Management, 41*(4), 1244–1273.

Ryan, A. M., & Ployhart, R. E. (2000). Applicants' perceptions of selection procedures and decisions: A critical review and agenda for the future. *Journal of Management, 26*, 565–606.

Salgado, J. F. (1999). Personnel selection methods. In C. L. Cooper & I. T. Robertson (Eds.), *International review of industrial and organizational psychology* (pp. 1–54). New York, NY: Wiley.

Salgado, J. F., & Anderson, N. (2003). Validity generalization of GMA tests across countries in the European Community. *European Journal of Work and Organizational Psychology, 12*, 1–17.

Salgado, J. F., Anderson, N., Moscoso, S., Bertua, C., De Fruyt, F., & Rolland, J. P. (2003). A meta-analytic study of general mental ability validity for different occupations in the European community. *Journal of Applied Psychology, 88*(6), 1068–1080.

Salgado, J. F., Moscoso, S., García-Izquierdo, A. L., & Anderson, N. R. (2017). Inclusive and discrimination-free personnel selection. In A. Arenas, D. Di Marco, L. Munduate, & M. C. Euwema (Eds.), *Shaping inclusive workplaces through social dialogue* (pp. 103–119). Cham, Switzerland: Springer.

Schinkel, S., van Vianen, A., & van Dierendonck, D. (2013). Selection fairness and outcomes: A field study of interactive effects on applicant reactions. *International Journal of Selection and Assessment, 21*(1), 22–31.

Schmidt, F. L. (2012). Cognitive tests used in selection can have content validity as well as criterion validity: A broader research review and implications for practice. *International Journal of Selection and Assessment, 20*(1), 1–13.

Schmidt, F. L., & Hunter, J. E. (1983). Individual differences in productivity: An empirical test of estimates derived from studies on selection procedure utility. *Journal of Applied Psychology, 68,* 407–414.

Schmidt, F., & Hunter, J. E. (1998). The validity and utility of selection methods in personnel psychology: Practical and theoretical implications of 85 years of research findings. *Psychological Bulletin, 124,* 262–274.

Schmidt, F. L., & Hunter, J. (2004). General mental ability in the world of work: Occupational attainment and job performance. *Journal of Personality and Social Psychology, 86*(1), 162–173.

Schmidt, F. L., Hunter, J. E., McKenzie, R. C., & Muldrow, T. W. (1979). Impact of valid selection procedures on work-force productivity. *Journal of Applied Psychology, 73,* 46–57.

Schmidt, F. L., Oh, I. S., & Shaffer, J. A. (2016). The validity and utility of selection methods in personnel psychology: Practical and theoretical implications of 100 years of research findings.

Schmitt, N. (2014). Personality and cognitive ability as predictors of effective performance at work. *Annual Review of Organizational Psychology and Organizational Behavior, 1*(1), 45–65.

Schmitt, N., & Fandre, J. (2008). Validity of selection procedures. In S. Cartwright & C. L. Cooper (Eds.) *The Oxford handbook of personnel psychology* (pp. 163–193). Oxford, England: Oxford University Press.

Schneider, B. (1987). The people make the place. *Personnel Psychology, 40*(3), 437–453.

Schuler, H., & Moser, K. (1995). Validity of the multimodal interview. *Zeitschrift fur Arveitund Organisationspsychologie, 39,* 2–12.

Schwartz, H. A., Eichstaedt, J. C., Kern, M. L., Dziurzynski, L., Ramones, S. M., Agrawal, M., ... Ungar, L. H. (2013). Personality, gender, and age in the language of social media: The open-vocabulary approach. *PLoS ONE, 8*(9), e73791.

Searle, R. H. (2003). *Selection and recruitment: A critical text*. Milton Keynes, England: Open University Press.

Shaffer, J. A., & Postlethwaite, B. E. (2013). The validity of conscientiousness for predicting job performance: A meta-analytic test of two hypotheses. *International Journal of Selection and Assessment, 21*(2), 183–199.

Silzer, R., & Church, A. H. (2009). The pearls and perils of identifying potential. *Industrial and Organizational Psychology, 2*(4), 377–412.

Smith, M., & Robertson, I. T. (1993). *Systematic personnel selection*. London, England: Macmillan.

Sturman, M. C. (2001). Utility analysis for multiple selection devices and multiple outcomes. *Journal of Human Resource Costing and Accounting, 6*(2), 9–28.

Sue-Chan, C., & Latham, G. P. (2004). The situational interview as a predictor of academic and team performance: A study of the mediating effects of cognitive ability and emotional intelligence. *International Journal of Selection and Assessment, 12*(4), 312–320.

Tausczik, Y. R., & Pennebaker, J. W. (2010). The psychological meaning of words: LIWC and computerized text analysis methods. *Journal of Language and Social Psychology, 29*(1), 24–54.

te Nijenhuis, J., & Van der Flier, H. (2003). Immigrant–majority group differences in cognitive performance: Jensen effects, cultural effects, or both? *Intelligence, 31*(5), 443–459.

Tett, R. P., & Burnett, D. D. (2003). A personality trait-based interactionist model of job performance. *Journal of Applied Psychology, 88*(3), 500–517.

Tett, R. P., Guterman, H. A., Bleier, A., & Murphy, P. J. (2000). Development and content validation of a "hyperdimensional" taxonomy of managerial competence. *Human Performance, 13*(3), 205–252.

Thoresen, C. J., Bradley, J. C., Bliese, P. D., & Thoresen, J. D. (2004). The big five personality traits and individual job performance growth trajectories in maintenance and transitional job stages. *Journal of Applied Psychology, 89,* 835–853. doi:10.1037/0021-9010.89.5.835

Tsui, A. S., Pearce, J. L., Porter, L. W., & Tripoli, A. M. (1997) Alternative approaches to the employee–organization relationship: Does investment in employees pay off? *Academy of Management Journal, 40*(5), 1089–1121.

US Employment Opportunities Commission. (1978). *Uniform guidelines on employee selection procedures (1978)*. Retrieved from www.uniformguidelines.com/uniformguidelines.html

Van der Zee, K. I., Bakker, A. B., & Bakker, P. (2002). Why are structured interviews so rarely used in personnel selection? *Journal of Applied Psychology, 87,* 176–184.

Van Hoye, G., & Lievens, F. (2009). Tapping the grapevine: A closer look at word-of-mouth as a recruitment source. *Journal of Applied Psychology, 94*(2), 341.

Van Iddekinge, C. H., Lanivich, S. E., Roth, P. L., & Junco, E. (2016). Social media for selection? Validity and adverse impact potential of a Facebook-based assessment. *Journal of Management, 42*(7), 1811–1835.

Wilhelmy, A., Kleinmann, M., König, C. J., Melchers, K. G., & Truxillo, D. M. (2016). How and why do interviewers try to make impressions on applicants? A qualitative study. *Journal of Applied Psychology, 101*(3), 313.

Winter, D. G., & Barenbaum, N. B. (1999). History of modern personality theory and research. In L. A. Pervin & O. P. John (Eds.), *Handbook of personality: Theory and research* (2nd ed., pp. 3–27). New York, NY: Guilford.

Woodruffe, C. (1997). *Assessment centres: Identifying and developing competence.* London, England: Institute of Personnel Management.

Woods, S. A. (2006). Cognitive ability tests and unfairness against minority ethnic groups: Two practical ways to check for unfairness in selection. *Selection and Development Review, 22*(3), 2–7.

Woods, S. A. (2018). Assessment in the digital age: Some challenges for test developers and users. *Assessment and Development Matters, 10*(2).

Woods, S. A., & Hinton, D. P. (2017). What do people really do at work? Job analysis and design. In N. Chmiel, F. Fraccaroli, & M. Sverke (Eds.), *An introduction to work and organizational psychology: An international perspective* (pp. 1–24). Chichester, England: John Wiley & Sons.

Zibarras, L. D., & Woods, S. A. (2010). A survey of UK selection practices across different organization sizes and industry sectors. *Journal of Occupational and Organizational Psychology, 83*(2), 499–511.

CHAPTER 6

LEARNING, TRAINING AND DEVELOPMENT

LEARNING OBJECTIVES

- Understand learning and development against the context of organization and HR strategy.

- Describe and evaluate the learning and development cycle, its components and associated methods; learning needs assessment, design and delivery of training and other development interventions, training evaluation.

- Understand and evaluate learning theories, models of learning outcomes.

- Understand factors that contribute to the success and failure of learning, development and training, and how training affects organizational outcomes.

- Understand practices and research on workplace coaching and its impact on learning and performance outcomes.

Work and organizational psychology has conventionally prioritized selection as the area of professional practice in which research and practice dominates. However, with increasing fluidity of work demands, and greater recognition of the capacity of people to learn and develop at work, not just in terms of skills but also in their core psychological characteristics, the role of development is critical. Harnessing the diverse capabilities and skills of all people within an organization remains a critical path to creating effective and healthy work. Sound recruitment and selection helps with this, but training, learning and development, alongside performance management, makes the difference once employees are selected. This chapter is about learning, training and development in organizations and the contribution of work psychology to understanding and improving it.

LEARNING, TRAINING AND DEVELOPMENT IN ORGANIZATIONS

The development of job-relevant knowledge, skills, abilities and competencies in organizations is called many things (Harrison, 2009). Training is the term traditionally used in work psychology sources (e.g. Goldstein & Ford, 2002; Salas & Cannon-Bowers, 2001), but this is restrictive, because training is only one way of developing people in organizations. Harrison (2009) points out that the terms employee development and human resource development (HRD) are disliked by some practitioners, because they seem to imply that people are either subservient or 'a resource'. In the UK, the CIPD use the terms learning and development, simply because these two terms represent what is important in practice: the learning (however it is facilitated) needed to support individual, team and organizational development.

Figure 6.1   A model of the influence of learning and development strategy

However conceptualized, learning, training and development serve a strategic function in organizations. In strategic performance management, individual performance indicators and targets are linked to strategy, which is filtered down from organizational goals, through unit and team goals to individuals. Strategic learning and development is concerned with facilitating the development of people in ways that enable them to perform effectively. Blanchard and Thacker (2007) identify a number of ways that issues of learning and development can be built into wider organizational strategy:

1 Learning and development specialists can provide overviews of current KSAOs in the organization that can help strategists to determine the gap between actual and required capability in the organization.

2 Information could be provided about the interventions needed to achieve the strategic goals. These might include information about the best ways to develop capabilities, the specific areas of the organization that would benefit most from intervention, and the associated costs.

3 Learning and development are central to the successful implementation of organizational change, helping managers to identify potential barriers to behaviour and performance change.

Figure 6.1 shows the progression from organizational strategy to individual performance goals, and the role of learning and development in helping to determine whether those goals are achieved in organizational, unit/team and individual performance. The figure also shows how valuation of performance change can inform the development of more learning and development strategy. The strategic importance of learning, training and development means that it is a key area of practice for work psychologists.

This chapter explores the field within three main sections. The first considers the processes and implementation of learning, training and development in organizations. The second looks at factors that influence whether learning, training and development are successful. The third section examines the growth and effectiveness of workplace coaching as a specific form of learning and development intervention.

THE PROCESS AND IMPLEMENTATION OF LEARNING, TRAINING AND DEVELOPMENT

The learning and development process in organizations is almost always presented as cyclical. Depending upon which books or publications you read, the cycle might appear slightly different, but the basic components do not really change that much. The form represented in Figure 6.2 (the training cycle) represents the basic elements of Goldstein's Instructional System Design (ISD) model (Goldstein, 1991; Goldstein & Ford, 2002).

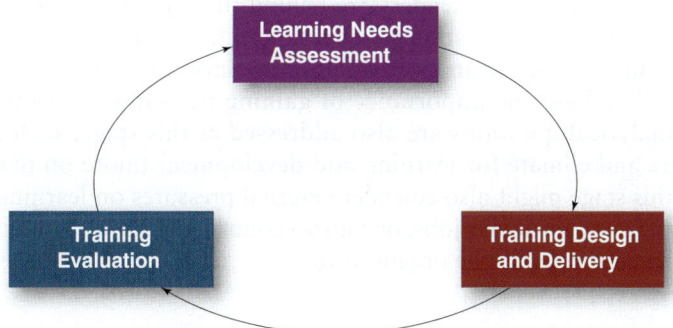

Figure 6.2 The learning and development cycle

The cycle begins with a needs assessment phase. This phase involves the analysis of learning and development needs at different levels of examination (organizational, team/unit, individual). From this analysis follows the specification of learning and development objectives designed to meet those needs. Once set, objectives guide the design and delivery of learning and development interventions. These may involve formal training, or other kinds of development activity. Careful consideration of individual differences and contextual factors is required in this step. The final step of the cycle is evaluation, which involves systematic examination of whether the objectives have been met and whether the learning and development interventions have had the desired effect. The cyclical nature of the model becomes apparent at this stage as the outcomes of the evaluation will inform the next round of needs assessment. In much of the work psychology literature, this model is simply called the training cycle.

Learning and development needs assessment

The needs assessment phase is designed to identify where learning and development interventions are required in the organization. Goldstein and Ford (2002) describe a systematic approach to conducting the needs assessment. Their model is summarized in Figure 6.3. Note that the needs assessment is carried out at different levels within the organization, starting with organizational factors and moving through to individuals. The general approach advocated in the model is to start with broad needs assessments, and to focus these down to the level of individuals.

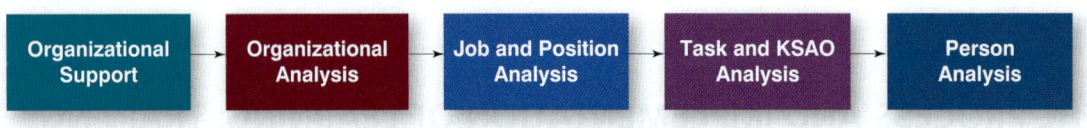

Figure 6.3 The needs assessment process

Organizational needs and analysis

Examination of the organization comprises a few key steps. The first is to determine the level of support for learning and development in the organization. The thinking behind this step is that interventions and activities in organizations tend to stand a better chance of being implemented and being effective if senior managers and leaders are behind them. Part of establishing such support would require an understanding of the strategic direction of the organization and how learning and development might fit in with that strategy. In addition to liaison with top management, Goldstein and Ford (2002) also highlight the importance of gaining the support of other stakeholders in the process. Wider analytical questions are also addressed at this stage, such as determining the organizational culture and climate for learning and development (more on that later). Moreover, needs assessment at this stage might also consider external pressures on learning and development, such as legal requirements of particular jobs, or future economic pressures. All of these factors act as a context to jobs being performed in the organization.

Job and position analysis

Although the terms job and position are often used interchangeably, there is a difference between them. A 'job' is defined by the nature of the work that is carried out by people with the same or similar job titles. A 'position' refers to a role in a specific organization, including duties and activities that are specific to the position. The purpose of this step of the needs assessment is to understand both.

First, the relevant positions in the organization need to be identified and examined. The nature and objectives of the position are considered, and in some cases compared with information available about similar jobs elsewhere. Part of this stage would also involve talking to line managers and job incumbents about their experiences of the positions of interest, as well as the team context. The team context can also be useful to consider, especially the division of roles in the team. It would be important to gauge, for example, whether a person is required to carry out all aspects of a particular job, or whether they work collaboratively with others contributing only part of the 'job requirements'. Future requirements of the business are also critical, particularly in contemporary rapidly changing environments (Dachner, Saxton, Noe, & Keeton, 2013).

Task, KSAO and competency analysis

This stage of the needs assessment is focused on defining the tasks required in the target positions, and, based on task requirements, defining the KSAOs (knowledge, skills, abilities and other characteristics) and competencies required. This is another process in work psychology where methods of job analysis are critical. Methods of job analysis are covered elsewhere in this book (see Chapter 5), and the same kinds of methods are applied in learning and development needs assessment. The basic steps involve using a variety of methods to help specify the tasks and duties associated with the target job or position, analyzing them where possible to identify clusters that are related to one another (e.g. Carlisle, Bhanugopan, & Fish, 2013), and then to use further methods to translate these into person requirements, expressed as KSAOs or job competencies. The differences between these aspects of person requirements are as follows:

- Knowledge. Required foundation learning about the context, content, processes or procedures of the job.
- Skills. Capability to carry out tasks relating to the use of tools or equipment, or the application of abilities to specific job tasks or contexts.
- Abilities. Core physical, mental or social capabilities that can be applied in a variety of contexts.
- Other characteristics. Personality traits, attitudes and motivation.
- Competencies. Performance-related behaviours.

Person analysis

The final step in the needs assessment returns to the focus of learning and development of individual people working in the organization. The purpose is to determine where there are gaps between the KSAO requirements of a position and the KSAO profile of the job incumbent. Performance measurement and management techniques are used in this step, which aim to establish whether or not someone is performing various aspects of their job satisfactorily. Some work may be required to supplement existing performance assessment systems, however, so that the measurement is clearly focused on understanding where learning or development is required. For example, an overall or objective performance measure (such as sales figures) is unlikely to be helpful in this respect as there is no information about which aspects of behaviour or performance are problematic. Assessment needs to be multidimensional so that people's strengths and weaknesses can be distinguished.

Some organizations use competency-based or psychometric assessments to help define gaps in KSAOs of current employees. The value of these methods is dependent on the extent to which they focus on KSAOs or competencies that are required in the target position. Participative discussion and input from the incumbent is also valuable, and may help them to self-assess their own training needs.

Learning and development interventions

Once gaps in KSAOs are identified through training needs analysis, interventions can be devised to address them. For work psychology, interventions are, in part, based on an understanding of how people learn. Two perspectives on learning in work psychology are behavioural and cognitive perspectives, and each has implications for training delivery and development interventions (Blanchard & Thacker, 2007).

From a strategic HRM perspective, in addition to individual learning interventions, practitioners are equally or more interested in learning at team or organizational level (Shipton & Zhou, 2008). The difference in implementing team and organizational learning interventions is that the purpose of learning and development is conceptualized as overall capability within the organization, rather than specific KSAO needs of individuals. In practice, methods are varied, and typically adopt a blended format of activities suited to meeting the learning needs. Some of the more common techniques are listed in Box 6.1.

BOX 6.1
Techniques and methods of training and development

Lectures The advantage of lectures is that a lot of information can be conveyed in a short amount of time. The disadvantage is that if badly implemented, the lecture can be perceived as dull or dry, and this is likely to inhibit learning and retention. Lecture and discussion also facilitate exploration and discussion with trainees on specific issues. This kind of approach works best in reasonably small participant groups.

Demonstrations Where a procedure or skill is to be learned by trainees, demonstration is highly effective, particularly if there is a standard or ideal way of performing. Demonstrations may be less effective for highly complex tasks, and the provision of follow-up information and explanation is likely to be important.

Simulations Simulations are useful for developing skills or cognitive strategies for problem-solving. Equipment simulators can be used to allow trainees to get a feel for how to use them prior to starting the job.

Role-play Role-play activities are used to simulate activities at work or in interpersonal situations. They can be set up so that participants work alone or in groups and can vary in terms of their structure.

Development centres Development centres are a variation of assessment centres that are used in selection. The basic format is much the same – performance is observed in multiple exercises or simulations by a team of assessors. However, the purpose is the production of in-depth development reports, which are usually fed back to the participant in a face-to-face interview. Some development centres allow for instant feedback that can be applied right away in a follow-up development exercise.

Case studies or critical scenario exercises These techniques comprise in-depth exercises relating to specific scenarios or situations. They can be used to train and observe how, for example, teams of professionals respond to complex events in real time.

On-job training Proactive on-job training involves structured guidance on developmental activities, supported by a work programme, shadowing activities and mentoring. A special kind of on-job training is an apprenticeship, which represents a partnership between several parties to sponsor the development of a junior worker (usually the employer, government and trade unions are involved to some degree).

E-learning The group of learning and development methods that are delivered by computer is referred to as e-learning, and a whole literature on the integration of technology into workplace learning is emerging (e.g. Bell & Kozlowski, 2009). One driver of e-learning is the combination of the demands of providing ever more development to staff, while cutting the costs of that development. Different forms of e-learning include:

- Programmed instruction. Online courses comprising text, graphics and multimedia enhancements.
- Intelligent development systems. Intelligent systems are adaptive in the sense that the nature of the course changes depending on the responses or input of the participant.
- Simulations. Computer-based simulations of situations or scenarios encountered at work. An important variable in simulation is its level of fidelity (the extent to which it replicates the reality of performance and the environment in which it occurs; e.g. Beaubien & Baker, 2004).

Secondment Secondments are short-term postings to new areas of the organization or partner companies. Individuals might complete specific projects or work within teams during the secondment, with the aim of bringing learning back to improve their own team. A particular kind of secondment is the expatriate or international assignment, increasingly valued as organizations become more globalized (e.g. Schuler, Budhwar, & Florkowski, 2002).

Job rotation Within teams, individuals can be asked to work in a variety of different positions with the express purpose of learning about different areas of business, clients, systems and processes.

Competitor and client placements The purpose of these kinds of learning and development techniques is to raise awareness and develop knowledge of services provided by similar businesses or the perspective of service users.

Team training Team training involves having complete teams attend training or development programmes and is a useful strategy where team members work interdependently on work tasks (Kozlowski, Gully, Nason, & Smith, 1999).

Communities of practice Groups of like-minded employees with shared concerns in an organization, working together to learn from each other and develop new approaches and ways of working have recently been referred to as Communities of Practice (Shipton & Zhou, 2008). Such groups tend to be self-managing, without much direction or management intervention on how they should conduct their work.

Behavioural theories of learning

Behaviourism is a basic form of learning theory. The work of Skinner emphasized the role of positive and negative reinforcement in the 'operant conditioning' of behaviour. In this theory, people learn to behave in particular ways either to access more rewards or to avoid punishment. In organizations, the approach could be adopted in structured environments to modify and control organizational behaviour. More useful is the work of Bandura (e.g. Bandura, 1977), who extended behaviourism to encompass two additional concepts:

- Observational learning. The idea that people learn by observing role models. Part of the process of observational learning involves perceiving a role model receiving some kind of outcome that is valued as a result of behaving in a particular way. That behaviour is likely to be mimicked or copied by the observer.
- Affect and cognition. In the more up-to-date social cognitive theories (e.g. Mischel & Shoda, 1995), behaviour is generated from interacting cognitions and affective responses that result from situational perceptions. The outcome of behaviour is observed and used to update cognition and affect. In an iterative process, ways of thinking, feeling and behaving are learned and increasingly automated (i.e. eventually behaviour, thought and emotion become habitual so that people no longer have to think about their reactions).

A social learning and behavioural approach to learning would facilitate learning in the following ways:

- Learning of new behaviours would be prioritized, and these could be modelled by the trainer to promote observational learning.
- Behavioural procedures might be practised in simulations as part of the training or development activities.
- Affect and cognition would also be targeted, perhaps by explaining the value of new learning. The purpose would be to change the way that trainees perceive and think about aspects of their work.

Cognitive learning

Anderson has proposed a cognitive theory of learning, catchily titled the Adaptive Character of Thought (ACT) model (Anderson, 1996). The model has developed slowly since the 1980s (e.g. Anderson, 1983), and has a strong logical emphasis on how people learn (see Figure 6.4).

Figure 6.4 Acquisition of cognitive skills

The most basic form of knowledge in Anderson's model is declarative knowledge. Declarative knowledge may be thought of as sets of disconnected facts called 'knowledge chunks'. These chunks are simple components of more complex knowledge but, for Anderson, they underpin everything that human beings do. A major task of learning is to accumulate basic knowledge chunks and to compile them. In this step, the knowledge chunks are compiled and organized into procedures for problem-solving. The result is procedural knowledge about how to solve problems or complete tasks.

In its initial form, procedural knowledge is described as 'weak', as it is untested (i.e. when a person decides how to address a problem at work, they have no indication initially about whether it will be successful). Procedural knowledge is strengthened when it is used and found to be successful, eventually becoming automatic. Anderson comments on an interesting implication of his work, which is that human learning develops in parallel with the experience of problems in the environment. People learn because there is some pressing need to do so, and the complexity of human beings is a reaction to the complexity of the environments in which they live. If the world were simpler, there would be no need for people to continually learn and adapt.

A cognitive approach to learning and training would adopt different emphases from a behavioural approach, and would facilitate learning in the following ways:

- Knowledge development would be emphasized, starting with the declarative knowledge and communication of facts of knowledge chunks.
- Activities would be designed to facilitate problem-solving using the knowledge, but trainees would probably be allowed to approach problems without seeing examples or modelling. The purpose would be development of procedural knowledge.
- More difficult problem scenarios could be used to strengthen and extend cognitive strategies for problem-solving.

In practice, training and development interventions in organizations tend to blend both kinds of approach. The extent to which a particular method is likely to be effective depends on a number of factors. These include the participants or trainees and their individual differences, the learning and development objectives, and the organizational context.

> **DISCUSS WITH A COLLEAGUE**
>
> List all the kinds of learning activity you have experienced. Rate them based on how effective they were at helping you learn. Compare and discuss your ratings with a course colleague.

Training evaluation

The third stage in the learning and development cycle is evaluation. Understanding the outcomes of training and other learning interventions allows organizations to determine the impact and benefits, and ultimately the value of learning (Kearns, 2005). Work psychologists have focused on two main issues in training evaluation:

- defining evaluation criteria to judge the effectiveness of training
- designing systematic methods and procedures for training evaluation.

Evaluation criteria

One of the first questions to address in training evaluation is what should be measured to help decide whether learning, training and development interventions have worked. Kirkpatrick's (1976) widely used framework of evaluation criteria proposes that training should be evaluated against four levels of criteria:

1 *Reactions:* Trainee attitudes about the training they have received. These are generally measured through the distribution of satisfaction surveys that ask people about the delivery and outcomes of the training.
2 *Learning:* Knowledge, skills and abilities that trainees have learned. These can be assessed through tests or assessments of post-training learning. There is no rule of thumb about when the assessment should be made.
3 *Behaviour:* Changes in trainee behaviour at work (training transfer). Assessments in this area would be made at work, and could vary in terms of specificity.
4 *Results:* Organization or team-level performance outcomes. These assessments are likely to be tangential to the aims of the training, and focused rather on improvements in quality, productivity or profitability.

The four levels of criteria are progressively more difficult to measure. Reactions to training are routinely collected by trainers and are highly accessible. Some courses also employ tests of learning to determine whether the learning objectives of the course have been achieved. Behaviour change is less commonly examined, but can often be adequately tapped by standard appraisal or performance management assessments (see Chapter 7), provided they reflect the content or aims of the training. Typically, if well designed, these kinds of criterion measures can achieve reasonable reliability.

The fourth level of Kirkpatrick's model, training results, presents a major practical challenge for organizations. This is because it is difficult to conceptualize and measure performance outcomes at the level of the organization. A basic model of organization-level outcomes is a combination of profitability, survival and growth of the organization or business (Hamblin, 1974). However, these criteria do not map clearly to the objectives of many training programmes, which are often designed to improve processes rather than outcomes (e.g. through the development of new technical or interpersonal skills). The 'balanced scorecard' (Kaplan & Norton, 1992) approach suggests that the performance of organizations should be judged against a range of relevant criteria. In this vein, organizational outcomes of training can be gauged by evaluating their impact in a variety of organizational performance indicators (e.g. HR outcomes, organizational performance improvements, profitability and financial outcomes; Tharenou, Saks, & Moore, 2007). This kind of approach is adaptable, and criteria may be modified so as to be relevant in different kinds of organization. For example, in healthcare organizations, patient/client satisfaction, community engagement, research and learning could all be examples of relevant criteria (Schalm, 2008).

Despite its practical utility, Kirkpatrick's model is criticized in the research literature as being overly simplistic or restrictive (e.g. Kraiger, Ford, & Salas, 1993), and there are alternative models that elaborate definitions of the outcomes of learning in organizations. The most notable of these focus specifically on individual learning outcomes.

Modelling individual learning outcomes

Gagné and colleagues (e.g. Gagné, Briggs, & Wager, 1992) designed a framework for learning outcomes, in which they distinguished between five kinds of learning outcome:

1 *Verbal information:* Declarative information that can be stated or recalled by the individual.
2 *Intellectual skills:* Procedural knowledge about concepts, rules and procedures that can be applied to solve problems.
3 *Cognitive strategies:* Rules for deciding when to bring verbal information and intellectual skills into play in order to solve a specific problem. Such strategies are important for people when they encounter novel problems for which there is no obvious learned solution.
4 *Attitudes:* Changes in the way people think and feel about specific aspects of their work environment.
5 *Motor skills:* Physical or movement-based skills such as using tools or physical labour.

A second model of learning outcomes is that of Kraiger et al. (1993). In response to criticisms about psychologists' weak understanding of training outcomes (e.g. Tannenbaum & Yukl, 1992),

Kraiger et al. examined a number of learning and educational taxonomies and proposed a classification system based on three important learning outcomes (see Table 6.1):

- Cognitive outcomes: Declarative and procedural knowledge, and cognitive strategies for problem-solving. The concept of metacognition is also highlighted, referring to the process by which a person examines and evaluates their own ways of thinking, identifying areas for development. In learning and development, this could be important in respect of changing the way that people think about the way they work.
- Skill-based outcomes: These are behavioural outcomes, such as learned performance behaviours and the extent to which they can be performed easily, quickly and without error.
- Affective outcomes: Two constructs are defined in the affective outcome category: attitudes and motivation. Attitudes are related to the way that a person feels about a particular object or target. Motivation comprises a number of different aspects, but notably goal setting, and the nature and difficulty of targets that people set for themselves after training. Self-efficacy is the final aspect of this category. Recall that self-efficacy concerns the belief that one can perform. This is obviously important for transfer of training to the work environment, since the application of learning at work will depend to some degree on whether a person believes it will be successful.

Table 6.1 The Learning Outcome Framework of Kraiger et al. (1993)

Learning outcomes	Sub-categories	Learning constructs
Cognitive outcomes	Verbal knowledge	Declarative knowledge
	Knowledge organization	Mental models
	Cognitive strategies	Self-insight metacognitive skills
Skill-based outcomes	Compilation	Composition proceduralization
	Automaticity	Automatic processing tuning
Affective outcomes	Attitudinal	Targeted object attitude strength
	Motivation	

Despite the enhanced classification of learning outcomes, research development has still focused on those areas that tap into simple cognitive dimensions (e.g. declarative and procedural knowledge; Bell & Kozlowski, 2002; Kozlowski & Bell, 2006), and motivational dispositions (Ford, Kraiger, & Merritt, 2009). Some of the more complex nuances of the model remain to be justified, and part of that involves explaining the practical utility of these complex quantitative models to people working in organizations.

Evaluation methods and procedures

The essence of evaluation is an assessment of change following some form of intervention. Whatever the evaluation criterion (knowledge, skill, ability, competency, behaviour, results and so on), the aim of the evaluation should be to establish whether there is any difference in that criterion before and after the learning and development intervention. Experimental methods are a logical choice, and in an ideal world all training evaluations would be conducted according to the principles of experimental research design.

Experimental designs allow practitioners to determine the benefits of training by comparing the performance of trained and untrained (control) groups of employees. By taking relevant measurements pre- and post-training, practitioners are able to assess changes in the performance of the two groups; the control group is important because it helps rule out the possibility that any observed change could have occurred regardless of the intervention. For example, imagine that we have observed change in a group of trainees after a training course. We might conclude that the training is effective, when in fact changes to work design or job characteristics could be the real reason that performance has changed, with improvements observed regardless of whether people have attended the training.

In experimental design, control groups are not subject to any treatment at all, other than criterion measurement. Experimental design is therefore desirable for training evaluation because it allows performance change to be attributed to the training intervention rather than to confounding or unmeasured variables.

In practice, training evaluations tend to adopt a quasi-experimental design (Goldstein & Ford, 2002). Trainees are selected for training because they have a particular training need, and their development is compared with colleagues who have not received training (i.e. the control group). The most common deviation from experimental design for many training evaluation procedures is to assess performance post-training only. This prevents the measurement of performance change, which is necessary for assessing the return on investment in training. A common alternative to the quasi-experimental design is the time-series design, in which performance change is tracked at several points before and after the training programme. This approach can determine whether there is a marked change in performance after the learning and development intervention. Figure 6.5 shows different evaluation methods side-by-side.

A final important issue in evaluation methodology is obviously measurement of outcomes. Practitioners need to think practically about the ways that different learning outcomes can be measured and assessed. At the individual level, aspects of performance measurement need to be considered that would help practitioners decide on how performance at work, and other learning outcomes, could be measured in organizations (see Chapter 7 for detailed discussion of performance measurement). Work psychologists also place a lot of emphasis on ensuring that measurements are reliable and valid. These are key issues to consider in the measurement of learning outcomes because they allow evaluation data to be viewed with more confidence. Even if research designs in training evaluation are very elaborate, poor measurement still equals poor decision-making.

CHAPTER 6 LEARNING, TRAINING AND DEVELOPMENT

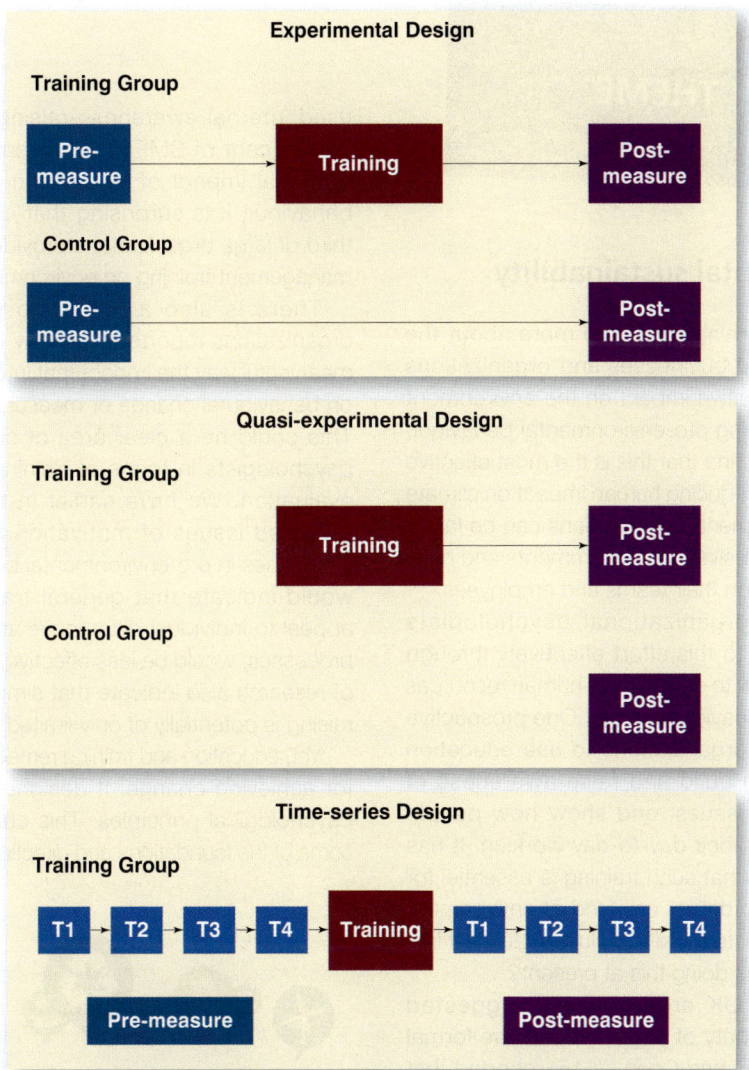

Figure 6.5 Training evaluation designs

DISCUSS WITH A COLLEAGUE

A sales manager has decided to put her sales team through a sales training programme. How would you advise her to evaluate the training?

KEY THEME

Environmental sustainability

We are learning more and more about the ways that businesses and organizations can make a positive impact on the environment through promoting pro-environmental behaviour. In time, we may find that this is the most effective mechanism for reducing human impact on climate and the environment. Organizations can be faster and more responsive than governments and have a direct impact on their teams and employees.

Work and organizational psychologists can contribute to this effort effectively through expertise on how to develop key human resources practices for behaviour change. One prospective strategy is for organizations to use education and training to build and raise awareness of environmental issues, and show how people can do more in their day-to-day working. It has been proposed that such training is essential for organizations to deliver any kind of environment management system (Daily & Huang, 2001). How are organizations doing this at present?

Surveys of UK organizations suggested that only a minority of organizations use formal training. Zibarras and Coan (2015) reported that around a third used training at least sometimes. Much more prevalent was provision of material for developing internal awareness (around 55 per cent). There were also differences across organizations according to their size. Training was used less in SMEs than large organizations, and while nearly 80 per cent of large organizations used internal awareness-raising, only around 30 per cent of SMEs did the same. Given the potential impact of leaders on environmental behaviour, it is surprising that only just over a third of large organizations provide leadership or management training on environmental issues.

There is also a follow-up problem: few organizations reported that they evaluate in any meaningful way the impact that interventions have on behavioural change or measurable outcomes. This could be a clear area of contribution for psychologists in terms of training and learning evaluation. We have earlier in this book also reviewed issues of motivation and individual differences in pro-environmental behaviour, which would indicate that general training, without appeal to individual differences and motivational processes, would be less effective. These insights of research also indicate that simple awareness-raising is potentially of only limited benefit.

Yet, education and training remain key prospects for achieving change, if designed around core psychological principles. This chapter provides some of the foundations and directions for doing so.

SUCCESS AND FAILURE OF LEARNING, TRAINING AND DEVELOPMENT

Why do learning, training and development succeed in some situations and fail in others? There are a number of factors that influence the likely success of training and development in organizations, and work psychologists have examined some of these. This section considers two perspectives:

- individual difference factors
- training transfer and organizational factors.

Individual differences

People learn in different ways, and individual differences in attributes, such as ability, personality and motivation, will all, to an extent, affect the way that people respond to learning and development at work. Gully and Chen (2009) developed a model of learning outcomes and individual differences (Figure 6.6). The key aspects of the model are:

- Trainee characteristics that affect learning outcomes include abilities, personality traits, demographics such as age (Bertolino, Truxillo, & Fraccaroli, 2011), interests and values.
- Individual differences act through intervening mechanisms to affect learning outcomes. Gully and Chen comment that 'training outcomes are determined by a combination of mechanisms that influence how people process information, focus their attention, direct their effort and manage their affect during learning'.
- The pathway from individual differences to learning outcomes is also moderated by attribute–treatment interactions. This means that learning outcomes for an individual depend on how they respond to a specific training and development intervention, and outcomes are a product of the interaction of learning methods and individual differences.

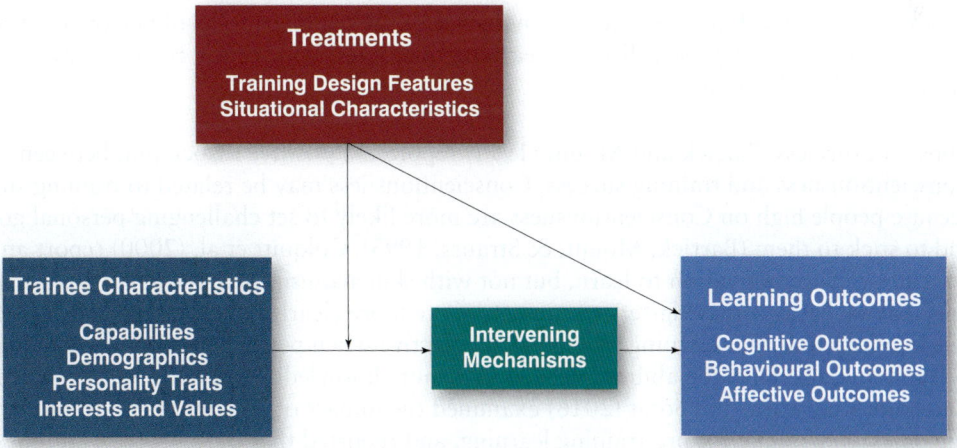

Figure 6.6   The pathway from individual differences to learning outcomes

Three areas of individual differences are particularly worth exploring to understand how individuals react to training and development:

1. ability and cognition
2. personality traits
3. goal orientation

Ability and cognition

General cognitive ability is an important predictor of learning outcomes. Remember that general cognitive ability is consistently predictive of job performance, particularly in complex jobs. One of the major pathways by which general ability predicts performance is through the acquisition of job knowledge. People with higher ability acquire job knowledge faster and in greater volume. Colquitt, LePine, and Noe (2000) reported moderate–strong associations between cognitive ability and learning outcomes of declarative knowledge, skill acquisition, training transfer and self-efficacy. If this result is viewed alongside the other models and theories of learning reviewed so far, then it is fairly straightforward to suppose why cognitive ability is so important for learning outcomes. People with higher ability are likely to absorb more information and to be able to organize, recall and adapt that information more effectively than those with lower abilities. One of the implications for learning and development is that people higher in cognitive ability learn and develop more effectively through exploration and problem-solving, whereas people with lower cognitive ability tend to respond better to more structured learning (Gully & Chen, 2009).

Another cognitive construct touched upon earlier is metacognition or self-regulation. People with greater metacognitive ability should learn more effectively because they are able to monitor their progress and improve where needed (Gully & Chen, 2009). The practical implication of this finding is that the process of reflection in training is important. People may not automatically reflect on their own progress and learning, or question their established styles of problem-solving and working. Guided reflection could encourage those lower in metacognitive abilities to think about their learning, and thereby promote better learning outcomes and transfer to the work environment. Furthermore, learning and development interventions in organizations should include some activities or components that facilitate reflection and metacognition.

Personality traits

As with other areas of work psychology, the emergence of the Big Five model of personality traits has clarified the associations of personality and learning outcomes. Four of the Big Five have exhibited associations with learning outcomes.

- Conscientiousness. Barrick and Mount (1991) reported a positive association between Conscientiousness and training success. Conscientiousness may be related to training success because people high on Conscientiousness are more likely to set challenging personal goals and to stick to them (Barrick, Mount, & Strauss, 1993). Colquitt et al. (2000) report an association with motivation to learn, but not with skill acquisition and declarative learning. This may be because these latter two outcomes are more clearly linked with cognitive ability. The implication is that learning may be most effective when people have a high motivation to learn, and also have the abilities needed to acquire knowledge and skills quickly. Woods, Patterson, Koczwara, and Sofat (2016) examined the impact of personality on training outcomes, controlling for pre-training learning, and reported that only Conscientiousness predicted post-training learning. They argued that some aspects of Conscientiousness such as dutifulness may reflect responsibility and commitment of people to engage with training and internalize individual development and change.
- Openness to Experience. Openness to experience was related to training success, but not job performance in the meta-analysis of Barrick and Mount (1991). Openness probably affects learning because people high on Openness are simply more likely to be open to new ideas.

- Extraversion. Extraversion was found to be positively associated with training success by Barrick and Mount (1991), although it is unclear exactly why. One possibility is that higher levels of Extraversion mean that people appraise learning opportunities more positively, and are more open to training in social or group-based scenarios. The majority of learning and development interventions involve some form of social or interpersonal interaction (with the exception of self-directed or e-learning). Esfandagheh, Harris, and Oreyzi (2012) reported that Extraversion was associated with higher training self-efficacy, which had a subsequent positive effect on learning outcomes.

- Emotional Stability. Emotional Stability was found to have a weak association with training success by Barrick and Mount (1991). However, facets of Emotional Stability related to anxiety seem to be most important. Colquitt et al. (2000) reported that anxiety was strongly negatively related to motivation to learn, self-efficacy post-training and acquisition of declarative knowledge and skills. Potential explanations for these findings include the negative effects of anxiety on learning experience – anxiety or nervousness may distract people's attention from learning activities, limiting their impact. Additionally, anxiety is related to negative affect, and high negative affect may mean that people feel less confident in the face of setbacks experienced during training or at work afterwards. For some people, the anticipation of setbacks or failure may be enough to lower motivation to learn or to engage with training.

Goal orientation

The concept of goal orientation emerged from the education literature, but has received a great deal of research interest in organizations in recent years. Dweck (1986) proposed that goal orientation was a motivational construct that explained some of the differences in achievement of children during their education. She suggested that goal orientation was linked to a child's belief about ability and intelligence. If they believed it to be fixed, then they were likely to adopt a performance goal orientation (PGO) based around avoiding negative feedback and gaining positive feedback. If they believed ability to be improvable, then they were likely to adopt a learning goal orientation (LGO), being driven to master a task for its own sake. Dweck (1986) suggested that LGO was associated with more positive outcomes than performance goal orientation.

The concept was quickly adopted by work psychologists (Farr, Hofmann, & Ringenbach, 1993) and it is easy to see why. On the face of it, these two different goal orientations seem immediately relevant to understanding why and how people learn and develop in an organization, and why the outcomes for some are more favourable than others. Some research in the area has examined the goal orientation construct in more detail. From the definitions, we might assume that the LGO and PGO are polar opposites, so that the presence of a strong learning goal orientation automatically prohibits the presence of a strong performance goal orientation. However, contrary to this belief, it appears that the two kinds of performance goal are independent, so that a person may simultaneously hold strong performance and learning goal orientations (Van de Walle, 1997).

Another important distinction in the literature is the difference between conceptualizing goal orientation as a trait or as a state. In the trait conceptualization, goal orientation is taken to be a stable disposition that does not really change over time. In the state conceptualization, goal orientation is a temporary orientation towards a particular task or activity that may change over time. Payne, Youngcourt, and Beaubien (2007) comment that it is likely that goal orientation could be conceptualized as both trait and state, with the experience of the state likely to be influenced in part by the trait. This means it is possible that goal orientation can change.

The attention given to goal orientation is justified because it appears to be a predictor of learning outcomes. In their meta-analysis, Payne et al. (2007) reported that LGO was linked to motivation and positive attitudes as well as learning and job performance. The implication is that if goal orientation is at least partly state-like, it would be sensible to promote the adoption of learning goals during training. However, the picture may not be that simple. There is some evidence that post-training self-efficacy is highest when training goal structure is consistent with goal orientation (Martocchio & Hertenstein, 2003). People feel more able to apply their learning if the learning environment has suited their goal orientation.

Furthermore, organizational climate and leadership are likely to affect goal orientation. Potosky and Ramakrishna (2002) report that people performed better and felt better able to learn and perform when they simultaneously had high LGO and perceived a supportive organizational climate for updating skills. Dragoni and Kuenzi (2012) reported that goal orientation of team members was associated with leader goal orientation. The benefits of LGO might therefore depend on the organizational context.

Training transfer

A marker of the success or failure of learning, training and development is whether learning is transferred to the work environment. Just because a person has acquired knowledge and skills, there is no guarantee that when they return to work, they will apply what they have learned. Most of us have our own experiences of this dilemma, particularly in respect of training courses. They are generally very useful, and during the course there is time to learn and reflect, but when we return to work it is too easy to slip back into the established ways of doing things. This is a big problem for organizations (Ford & Weissbein, 1997) because the benefits of learning and development can only be realized if learning is utilized and applied at work. To be justified, the investment in learning and development must result in some return such as improvements in quality or productivity.

Salas and Cannon-Bowers (2001) conceptualize training transfer as the extent to which KSAOs acquired in a training programme are applied, generalized and maintained over some time in the job environment.

There are a few immediate questions that emerge in respect of the issue of transfer. For example, is transfer a product of individual or organizational factors? What are the processes that facilitate application? What could an organization do to promote transfer?

Some researchers have developed models to disentangle the process of training transfer and answer some of these questions (e.g. Cheng & Hampson, 2008). Figure 6.7 summarizes these models, showing how different factors could combine to promote training transfer in organizations.

In the model, learning outcomes are affected by individual differences, training design and organizational factors, but these outcomes are not sufficient for transfer. The transfer of learning to the work environment requires 'intention to transfer' (Cheng & Hampson, 2008), with individual differences, training design and work environment factors influencing this intention (Beier & Kanfer, 2009). Perceived usefulness of training is also important (Alliger, Tannenbaum, Bennett, Traver, & Shotland, 1997; Van Eerde, Tang, & Talbot, 2008). When trainees perceive course content as having high relevance and utility, they are more likely to transfer their learning.

Organizational factors influence transfer intentions and transfer directly in the model, and there is some evidence for this from research. Quinones, Ford, Sego, and Smith (1995) highlight the importance of work design and 'opportunity to perform' at work. Their theory is simple and describes how transfer is promoted when people are given an opportunity to perform skills learned during learning and development activities. Building 'opportunity to perform' into learning and development plans is likely to enhance transfer. Arthur, Bennett, Stanush, and McNelly (1998) highlight the value of timely application, and reported that long delays between training and application at work result in significant learning decay. Opportunities for quick application of learning could help to facilitate transfer.

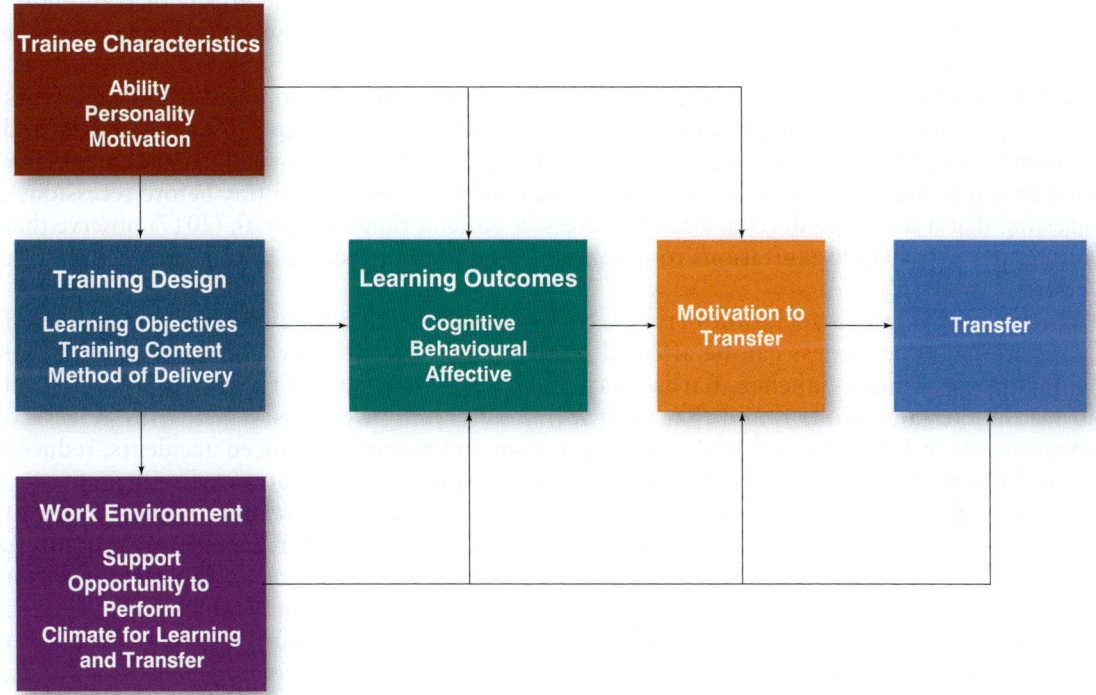

Figure 6.7 A model of training transfer

Wider organizational factors are also important. Social support from supervisors, peers and subordinates before and after training all helps to promote transfer (Salas & Cannon-Bowers, 2001). Saks and Belcourt (2004) reported that supervisor and trainee involvement in development planning, as well as supervisor and organizational support post-training, were all significantly related to training transfer.

Training, learning and development: organizational-level outcomes

There appears to be plenty of evidence that learning, training and development contribute to the overall performance of organizations. A recent meta-analysis (Tharenou et al., 2007) examined the effects of training on three categories of organization outcomes (HR outcomes, organization performance outcomes and financial outcomes). Training provision was associated with a range of beneficial HR outcomes. These included more positive employee attitudes such as higher satisfaction, involvement and commitment; lower incidence of grievances and absenteeism; higher employee retention and lower turnover. Training provision also predicted higher levels of overall human capital or employee skill levels, suggesting that training did transfer to some degree in the organizations studied.

With respect to organizational performance, training was found to predict key outcomes, specifically productivity, quality (including higher levels of customer satisfaction), objective organizational performance and managerial perceptions of performance. Training was also found to be associated with perceptions of the financial performance of organizations, but only negligibly related to actual financial outcomes. There was some evidence that the effects of training on organizational and financial performance were stronger when the training was clearly aligned to the organization's strategy.

Bell, Tannenbaum, Ford, Noe, and Kraiger (2017) also describe development of research work on the impact of training on organizational outcomes. They cite, for example, the study of Kim and Ployhart (2013), who examined the role of internal staff training on financial performance. They found that training was beneficial when economic conditions were good (i.e. before recessions), suggesting that it helped to develop slack resources in difficult times. Bell et al. (2017) observe that training may also help organizations to prepare to weather and recover from difficult economic conditions.

The strength of the association between training provision and managerial perceptions of organizational effectiveness can be affected by the design and delivery of training. A study of 457 managers (Aragon-Sanchez, Barba-Aragon, & Sanz-Valle, 2003) from a variety of small and medium organizations found that most forms of training were associated with perceived improvements in HR outcomes (reduced absenteeism and turnover, reduced accidents, reduced external recruiting of services), whereas only on-job training was associated with improved perceptions of service quality and profitability. Training provision is related to perceptions of the quality of innovation in organizations (Shipton, West, Dawson, Birdi, & Patterson, 2006). Organizations that train managers tend to perform more effectively than those that do not (Aragon & Sanz Valle, 2013). Moreover, training and development opportunities are included as one aspect of 'high performance HR practices', which are collectively associated with improved work-related attitudes such as commitment and satisfaction (Kooij, Jansen, Dikkers, & De Lange, 2010).

A meta-analysis of a wider range of training evaluation criteria (Arthur, Bennett, Edens, & Bell, 2003) examined all four of Kirkpatrick's criterion levels (reactions, learning, behaviour, results). Training was found to positively influence criteria in all four levels, importantly providing further evidence that training does lead to positive organizational outcomes.

A really powerful finding about the value of learning and development comes from the British National Health Service. As part of ongoing staff satisfaction and HR research in the Health Service, there have been a number of studies that have examined the organization-level outcomes of training, including benefits for patient care. Within these studies, it has been shown that the sophistication of, and satisfaction with, training policies within primary care trusts (PCTs) is directly related to patient mortality, even after controlling for hospital size, number of doctors per 100 beds and prior and region-specific mortality rates (West et al., 2002). Fewer patient deaths occur in hospitals where learning and development is organized effectively.

Success and failure of learning, training and development: summary

The message from research is that individual differences and organizational factors do have clear influences on learning and development outcomes in organizations, including transfer of learning. Learning and development outcomes depend on a combination of a person's abilities, personality traits, cognitive styles and motivational style. One method of development may be more effective for one person compared with another, and to complicate the picture, individual differences and organizational factors interact to determine whether a person applies their learning at work. There are a few key implications for learning and development strategies and interventions:

1. Organizations must aim to use a variety of learning and development techniques because a 'one size fits all' approach will certainly fail to appeal to a significant proportion of people regardless of the approach that is adopted.
2. Participative learning and development goal setting is important, but only so long as it genuinely allows for people's individual differences to be expressed and is taken into account during training and development planning. The purpose of developmental discussion should be to help find the most suitable and appealing learning and development activities to address learning needs.
3. Active intervention to promote successful outcomes from training can be used. For example, Sitzmann and Johnson (2012) reported that learning was more effective when people were instructed to create learning plans and to actively reflect on these plans as they undertook learning activity. Shantz and Latham (2012) reported similar benefits of writing 'self-guidance' for transfer of training, and goal setting also has the potential to increase application of training at work (Brown, McCracken, & Hillier, 2013).
4. Learning and development activities should take account of organizational performance management activities and climate so that learning outcomes are consistent with the way that people are expected to work in the organization. Moreover, managers should be aware of the effects that learning and development activities, and subsequent performance expectations, have on climate for learning in their organizations.
5. Work design and team processes should be considered and steps taken to give people timely opportunities to apply their learning, supported by peers and supervisors in the team.

KEY THEME

Diversity and inclusion

Training and development are part of the strategies that organizations use to help promote better outcomes in the management of diversity and creation of inclusive organizations. Psychologists have been at the forefront of this effort, with, for example, the American Psychological Association identifying, in 2013, diversity education as one of the five major learning goals for undergraduate education.

Diversity training has been defined as a *"distinct set of instructional programmes aimed at facilitating positive intergroup interactions, reducing prejudice and discrimination, and enhancing the skills, knowledge and motivation of participants to interact with diverse others"* (Bezrukova, Spell, Perry, & Jehn, 2016, p. 6). Different programmes employ a variety of methods and approaches, and given the centrality of training as an intervention on which we rely to attain the aims outlined in the definition above, it is important to understand how and in what ways the training works most effectively. To address this issue, Bezrukova et al. (2016) report a meta-analysis of diversity training outcomes.

continued

They point out that understanding the impact of diversity training is helpful only when accompanied by a theoretical account of why it works and why it may not work; only then can science be used to inform the design of better training. Their analyses indicated some key insights into how organizations can design diversity training to be most effective.

They report that there is an overall positive effect of diversity training, and that this includes change in attitudes and affective reactions to diversity. Training is more effective when it is part of an integrated strategy or set of management interventions for diversity. This means that training should be embedded as part of a wider organizational effort to address diversity management and inclusion. Training that includes elements of behavioural change works more effectively than training designed to raise awareness alone. Their findings suggest that programmes with single or multiple methods of instruction work equally effectively and that there is little difference in the impact whether the training is voluntary or mandatory. Longer training sessions were more effective than shorter (i.e. the number of hours was positively related to outcomes). The diversity of the trainee group was not found to moderate the impact of the training on learning outcomes; trainee group composition did not affect what people took away from the session.

The implications for diversity training design are notably that programmes really need to be part of an integrated inclusion and diversity strategy in an organization, and that behaviour change through skills development and awareness building should feature. Training should also be more than a short workshop – sufficient hours must be dedicated to allow exploration and learning. Overall, this reflects the kind of integrated approach to the psychology of management, work and organizations that we aim to develop in this book.

Bezrukova, K., Spell, C. S., Perry, J. L., & Jehn, K. A. (2016). A meta-analytical integration of over 40 years of research on diversity training evaluation. *Psychological Bulletin, 142*(11), 1227.

WORKPLACE COACHING

Coaching is generally defined as a collaborative relationship between a coach and coachee, which is formed for the purpose of supporting the coachee to attain their professional or personal goals (Grant, Passmore, Cavanagh, & Parker, 2010). It is a one-to-one learning and development intervention that uses a collaborative, reflective, goal-focused relationship to achieve professional outcomes that are valued by the coachee (Smither, 2011). Coaching has typically been perceived as an 'executive' development activity, yet is not necessarily only relevant for senior staff, and although the term continues to be used to describe a variety of activity, Jones, Woods, and Guillaume (2016) point out that there is general consensus about what constitute the core features or elements of coaching (e.g. see also Bono, Purvanova, Towler, & Peterson, 2009, and Smither, 2011). These are 1) formation and maintenance of a helping relationship between the coach and coachee; 2) a formally defined coaching agreement or contract, setting personal development objectives; 3) the fulfilment of this agreement (i.e., achievement of the objectives) through a development process focusing on interpersonal and intrapersonal issues; 4) striving for growth of the coachee by providing the tools, skills and opportunities they need to develop themselves and become more effective (Jones et al., 2016; Bono et al., 2009).

The coaching relationship is differentiated from other developmental working relationships (e.g. Mentoring, see Box 6.3) because of an absence of status assumptions guiding the interaction of coach and coachee (Jones et al., 2016). For example, in a formal performance management relationship between manager and staff, there is a clear status difference. In a peer-coaching relationship (Parker, Kram, & Hall, 2013), there is an assumption of equivalence.

Grant et al. (2010) highlight three forms of coaching at work:

- Skills coaching: designed to help people learn and apply a particular skill set at work.
- Performance coaching: designed to focus on the processes of goal setting and performance delivery over a period of time.
- Developmental coaching: a more widely strategic approach that aims to help people develop competencies and capabilities to deal with current and future demands.

The varied application and practice of coaching has often made the impact on organizational outcomes difficult to determine. This issue, however, was addressed by Jones et al. (2016), who conducted the first meta-analysis of coaching outcomes to focus exclusively on workplace coaching. The study examined 17 studies, representing data on the outcomes of coaching with 2,267 people. The study found that coaching overall had a positive effect on performance outcomes. This was a persistent observation across the studies. Jones et al. also examined the differential effects across criteria, reflecting approaches to training evaluation to define outcome criteria (reviewed earlier in this chapter). Coaching tended to have a stronger effect on individual results at work and affective outcomes (e.g. on well-being and attitudes), than on skill development. The study also examined some of the practical factors in the implementation of coaching that might affect the outcomes, such as whether a coach was internal or external (see Box 6.2).

BOX 6.2
Practice moderators of coaching

The meta-analysis of Jones et al. (2016), where available data permitted, examined several practice factors that they proposed might moderate the effectiveness of coaching.

Use of multi-source feedback: Multi-source feedback is commonly used to facilitate coachee self-awareness about performance, and to provide support from the coach to interpret the feedback (Luthans & Peterson, 2003). Despite the conceptual reasons to suppose that this kind of feedback enhances outcomes, in the meta-analysis coaching was less effective when multi-source feedback was included.

Format of coaching: Coaching is a relationship-based approach to development that is generally conducted face-to-face, but may also incorporate other forms of interaction (such as telephone, videoconference or email). The meta-analysis showed that there was no difference in the effectiveness of coaching conducted solely face-to-face, compared

continued

to adopting a blended range of interactions. This gives confidence in the application of coaching through digital means.

Internal or external coach: Coaches might be external to an organization and engaged on a consultative basis, or could be internal to an organization (although not in a position of line management responsibility). It might be tempting to assume that an experienced external coach would be the most effective for achieving positive work outcomes. The meta-analysis revealed, however, that although both internal and external coaches were effective, coachees working with an internal coach experienced the greatest impact. It could be that the inside knowledge of the work context of the coachee helps to put in perspective developmental activity.

Coaching may be used by organizations in a variety of ways to address poor performance issues, such as when an individual's performance declines; as a means of reducing exit costs for the organization by 'helping an individual to realize that they don't fit'; for leadership development, providing a 'safe' person to discuss organizational challenges with; to boost an individual's confidence following long-term absence from work; to help with a personal issue which is affecting work. The culture of the organization must be supportive of coaching since it is unlikely to be effective in a highly competitive environment (for example in a sales department where there is a high level of competition between staff).

The relationship between the coach and the coachee is clearly important, and, in well-developed coaching systems in organizations, there is a commitment to:

- Create a culture and a set of coaching procedures which are aligned with the philosophy of coaching.
- Build coaching responsibilities into people's jobs and providing appropriate time and recognition for this contribution.
- Assess the skills of coaches and ensuring they have appropriate training and supervision as well as opportunities for upgrading their skills.
- Select staff for coaching roles who have positive attitudes, emotional sensitivity and commitment to the role.
- Monitor the effectiveness of coaching and its impact within the organization and adapting the system as appropriate (Megginson & Clutterbuck, 2006).

A final consideration on the application of coaching is to consider when and for whom coaching is most effective. Jones, Woods, and Zhou (2018) found that job factors interacted with coaching practice factors to influence the outcomes that people report from coaching. For example, external coaches were found to be most beneficial for coachees in more complex jobs. It could be possible that a more bespoke pairing of coach and coachee could be needed when people's jobs are complex.

The growth of coaching has been explosive and it is now a substantial industry attracting many with psychology training and many more without. The ethical and competency issues raised are often not adequately addressed in many organizations, however. The continued professionalization of the coaching field in the coming years, combined with the growing robustness of the underlying research, will likely address these issues.

PIONEERING WORK PSYCHOLOGISTS

Dr Rebecca Jones

Dr Rebecca Jones is Associate Professor of Coaching at Henley Business School, and a leading researcher in the study of workplace coaching and its effectiveness. Her research is pioneering because it seeks to bring a scientific evidence base to the practice of coaching in the workplace. Coaching has been used extensively for people development in organizations, yet has in the past lacked a substantive evidence base for its effectiveness. Dr Jones' work has addressed this gap, most significantly in the publication of a meta-analysis showing that coaching has a positive impact on both learning and performance outcomes.

Her work has now moved on to look at some of the key questions that will shape how coaching should be carried out, including for whom coaching works best, the elements that enhance coaching and the kinds of jobs that it is most relevant for. You can hear about Dr Jones' work on her podcast, *The Coaching Academic*.

Key example papers

Jones, R. J., Napiersky, U., & Lyubovnikova, J. (2019). Conceptualizing the distinctiveness of team coaching. *Journal of Managerial Psychology*. doi.org/10.1108/JMP-07-2018-0326

Jones, R. J., Woods, S. A., & Zhou, Y. (2018). Boundary conditions of workplace coaching outcomes. *Journal of Managerial Psychology, 33*(7/8), 475–496. doi.org/10.1108/JMP-11-2017-0390

Bozer, G., & Jones, R. J. (2018). Understanding the factors that determine workplace coaching effectiveness: A systematic literature review. *European Journal of Work and Organizational Psychology, 27*(3), 342–361. doi:10.1080/1359432X.2018.1446946

Jones, R. J., Woods, S. A., & Guillaume, Y. R. F. (2016). The effectiveness of workplace coaching: A meta-analysis of learning and performance outcomes from coaching. *Journal of Occupational and Organizational Psychology, 89*(2), 249–277. doi:10.1111/joop.12119

BOX 6.3
Mentoring

Mentoring is similar to coaching in that it is a relational form of development, but is also distinguished from it in important ways (see Brockbank & MacGill, 2012). A mentoring relationship is conventionally long-term, between a highly experienced mentor and an inexperienced mentee. The mentor is assumed to be knowledgeable and advanced in the discipline or field in which the mentee is working (Eby et al., 2012). Whereas coaching is concerned with improving specific aspects of performance, mentoring involves providing generalized support and guidance to an individual (for example, the mentor typically provides guidance on career development and networking). Conventionally a mentor is a senior colleague within the mentee's organization, but sometimes may be a senior and experienced person outside the organization.

DISCUSS WITH A COLLEAGUE

Identify two issues that you face in your work for which you think coaching or mentoring would be helpful. How will you seek out this support?

POSITIVE WORK

Creating growth-oriented and resilient organizations

As Bell et al. (2017) observe in their review of 100 years of training literature, investment in learning and development seems to be an effective strategy for preparing organizations for difficult times. From the individual perspective, we have also reviewed in this chapter a wide variety of evidence that training is beneficial for people at work in terms of their effectiveness, motivation and well-being.

However, a positive agenda for learning and development in organizations goes beyond what we have found from historic research and considers the challenges of organizations in the future. Fundamentally, this is likely to involve a significant shift away from prescribed procedural training to accomplish fixed tasks, towards developing a responsive and resilient learning capability and culture across whole organizations. The value of this is underlined as the environments in which organizations operate become more volatile, uncertain and unclear. To this end, research and practice in work and organizational psychology points to three relevant directions.

First, it is important to ensure that people have the opportunity to be proactively in control of their own learning and development. This is in line with the philosophy of active learning, by which people influence what, when and how they learn. Doing so enables greater autonomy for people to improve their own effectiveness. The added benefit of this approach is that people are able to be responsive to changing needs. That is, when new challenges are encountered, people are able to quickly identify any development they need to do. Encouraging people to learn continually rather than episodically (put simply, to learn throughout one's career rather than at the outset, or on job transition) is also fundamental to promoting a growth-focused approach. Development and growth is a key benefit of work, and enriching to life experience.

Learning the skills for continuous development highlights the second direction afforded by applied psychology: coaching. Workplace coaching has the potential to provide a strong relationship for people to guide and facilitate their learning and development through working life. Blended approaches to coaching, combined with the evidence of the effectiveness of the intervention for performance and well-being outcomes, means that it is a resource that people could draw on as needed at key times in their careers. Furthermore, coaching is highly bespoke in the way that it encourages development to play out. This means that people could explore the best ways in which they could continually develop and grow; in short, to know how best they will learn through their working lives.

Thirdly, research on transfer tells us about the importance of creating the conditions for learning and development. This involves working on cultures and environments at team and organizational level. Simple practical steps include making space for learning, encouraging experimentation and providing management and peer support for implementing what has been learned in tasks and activities.

Absorbing these ideas into the design of management practices would encourage the learning capability and culture of an organization. They would promote a positive perspective on learning and growth at work too: as a privilege that comes from a fulfilling and meaningful working life.

BOX 6.4
Active learning

Active learning is an approach to learning and development in organizations whereby the employee has control over how and when they learn and develop (see Bell et al., 2017). They are given the freedom to decide how they will develop in particular areas, and to structure that development around their job responsibilities. In some cases, employees may also take the initiative to identify development areas. The use of e-learning is obviously useful to support active learning, as resources and courses are available constantly and employees are in control of the schedule and pace of their learning. A key advantage of active learning is also that it allows flexible adaptation to new job demands. In short, employees can monitor their own performance and elect to undertake some development if their job gets harder for some reason. There are some key issues in active learning, particularly around individual differences and learning outcomes. For example, does active learning assume that people have reasonable metacognitive ability, allowing them to question and identify their weaknesses? Bell and Kozlowski (2009) highlight the need for more understanding about the pathways from individual differences through active learning interventions to learning outcomes.

SUMMARY

This chapter has examined learning and development in organizations and the contribution of work psychology to understanding and improving learning and development systems and processes. Learning and development are important HR functions that help to ensure that people learn and apply knowledge, skills, abilities and competencies that are needed to deliver the strategy and goals of the organization.

The practice of learning and development is structured around the 'training cycle', which comprises a needs assessment phase, the design and delivery of training, plus systematic evaluation. Needs assessments are conducted at different levels, focusing on organizations, jobs and positions in team contexts, job tasks, required KSAOs and individual development needs. All are used to specify objectives for training and learning.

Behavioural and cognitive theories of learning are relevant to the design of training and development interventions and there are a variety of techniques that practitioners can use to help people develop in ways that they find rewarding. The concept of active learning describes how people take an active role in their own development by deciding on their own development needs, and when and how they will address them. New technology in the form of e-learning is likely to facilitate the development of this approach in future years.

Evaluations of training should ideally follow experimental research designs, which permit the analysis of change, and ultimately the examination of the value and benefits of learning and development. Such rigorous evaluation is quite rare in practice. Key challenges include defining and measuring outcome criteria, and psychologists have proposed several models of learning outcome criteria.

Success and failure of learning, training and development in organizations depend on many different factors, including individual differences, training design and organizational factors. Models of training transfer help to understand these issues more clearly. Getting learning, training and development right might be tricky, but it is worthwhile. Research examining the outcomes of training at an organizational level overwhelmingly points to the organizational and business benefits of investment in learning and development.

An increasingly popular and influential form of learning and development is workplace coaching. The evidence base for coaching at work has pointed to the effectiveness of the approach for learning and performance outcomes. It is likely to be an important component in an agenda for positive and growth-oriented learning and development helping organizations meet the demands of the future.

DISCUSSION QUESTIONS

1. Do you think you have a performance goal orientation or a learning goal orientation? What are the advantages and disadvantages of your approach?

2. Is investment in learning, training and development always a good idea? Why?

3. What kinds of job tasks would be best learned through behavioural approaches to learning and training? What kinds would be best suited to cognitive learning?

4. What are the key factors to consider in deciding whether to develop people through coaching versus training?

5. Should people always decide on their own development needs, as in active learning?

6. An organization has a very limited budget for learning, training and development, and the HR Director wants to ensure they get the most out of it. How would you advise them?

FURTHER READING

Bell, B. S., Tannenbaum, S. I., Ford, J. K., Noe, R. A., & Kraiger, K. (2017). 100 years of training and development research: What we know and where we should go. *Journal of Applied Psychology, 102*(3), 305–323.

Blanchard, P. N., & Thacker, J. W. (2007). *Effective training: Systems, strategies and policies.* Upper Saddle River, NJ: Pearson Education.

Goldstein, I. L., & Ford, J. K. (2002). *Training in organizations: Needs assessment, development and evaluation.* Monterey, CA: Brooks Cole. In S. W. J. Kozlowski & E. Salas (Eds.), *Learning, training and development in organizations* (pp. 65–98). New York, NY: Routledge.

Jones, R. J., Woods, S. A., & Guillaume, Y. R. F. (2016). The effectiveness of workplace coaching: A meta-analysis of learning and performance outcomes from coaching. *Journal of Occupational and Organizational Psychology, 89*(2), 249–277. doi:10.1111/joop.12119

REFERENCES

Alliger, G. M., Tannenbaum, S. I., Bennett, W., Traver, H., & Shotland, A. (1997). A meta-analysis of the relations among training criteria, *Personnel Psychology, 50*(2), 341–358.

Anderson, J. (1983). *The architecture of cognition.* Cambridge, MA: Harvard University Press.

Anderson, J. R. (1996). ACT: A simple theory of complex cognition. *American Psychologist, 51,* 355–365.

Aragon, I. B., & Sanz Valle, R. (2013). Does training managers pay off? *The International Journal of Human Resource Management, 24*(8), 1671–1684.

Aragon-Sanchez, A., Barba-Aragon, I., & Sanz-Valle, R. (2003). Effects of training on business results. *International Journal of Human Resource Management, 14*(6), 956–980.

Arthur, Jr., W., Bennett, Jr., W., Edens, P. S., & Bell, S. T. (2003). Effectiveness of training in organizations: A meta-analysis of design and evaluation features. *Journal of Applied Psychology, 88,* 234–245.

Arthur, W., Bennett, W., Stanush, P. L., & McNelly, T. L. (1998). Factors that influence skill decay and retention: A quantitative review and analysis. *Human Performance, 11,* 79–86.

Bandura, A. (1977). *Social learning theory.* Upper Saddle River, NJ: Prentice Hall.

Barrick, M. R., & Mount, M. K. (1991). The Big Five personality dimensions and job performance: A meta-analysis. *Personnel Psychology, 44,* 1–26.

Barrick, M. R., Mount, M. K., & Strauss, J. P. (1993). Conscientiousness and performance of sales representatives: Test of the mediating effects of goal setting. *Journal of Applied Psychology, 78,* 715–722.

Beaubien, J. M., & Baker, D. P. (2004). The use of simulation for training teamwork skills in health care: How low can you go? *Quality and Safety in Health Care, 13*(suppl 1), i51–i56.

Beier, M. E., & Kanfer, R. (2009). Motivation in training and development: A phase perspective. In S. W. J. Kozlowski & E. Salas (Eds.), *Learning, training and development in organizations* (pp. 65–98). New York, NY: Routledge.

Bell, B. S., & Kozlowski, S. W. J. (2002). Goal orientation and ability: Interactive effects on self-efficacy, performance and knowledge. *Journal of Applied Psychology, 87*(3), 497–505.

Bell, B. S., & Kozlowski, S. W. J. (2009). Toward a theory of learner centred training design: An integrative framework of active learning. In S. W. J. Kozlowski & E. Salas (eds.), *Learning, training and development in organizations* (pp. 263–300). New York, NY: Routledge Academic.

Bell, B. S., Tannenbaum, S. I., Ford, J. K., Noe, R. A., & Kraiger, K. (2017). 100 years of training and development research: What we know and where we should go. *Journal of Applied Psychology, 102*(3), 305–323.

Bertolino, M., Truxillo, D. M., & Fraccaroli, F. (2011). Age as moderator of the relationship of proactive personality with training motivation, perceived career development from training, and training behavioral intentions. *Journal of Organizational Behavior, 32*(2), 248–263.

Bezrukova, K., Spell, C. S., Perry, J. L., & Jehn, K. A. (2016). A meta-analytical integration of over 40 years of research on diversity training evaluation. *Psychological Bulletin, 142*(11), 1227.

Blanchard, P. N., & Thacker, J. W. (2007). *Effective training: Systems, strategies and policies*. Upper Saddle River, NJ: Pearson Education.

Bono, J. E., Purvanova, R. K., Towler, A. J., & Peterson, D. B. (2009). A survey of executive coaching practices. *Personnel Psychology, 62*, 361–404.

Brockbank, A., & McGill, I. (2012). *Facilitating reflective learning: Coaching, mentoring and supervision*. London, England: Kogan Page.

Brown, T. C., McCracken, M., & Hillier, T. L. (2013). Using evidence-based practices to enhance transfer of training: assessing the effectiveness of goal setting and behavioural observation scales. *Human Resource Development International, 16*(4), 374–389.

Carlisle, J., Bhanugopan, R., & Fish, A. (2013). Latent factor structures affecting the occupational profile construct of the training needs analysis scale. *The International Journal of Human Resource Management, 23*(20), 4319–4341.

Cheng, E., & Hampson, I. (2008). Transfer of training: A review and new insights. *International Journal of Management Reviews, 10*(4), 327–341.

Colquitt, J. A., LePine, J. A., & Noe, R. (2000). Toward an integrative theory of training motivation: A meta-analytic path analysis of 20 years of research. *Journal of Applied Psychology, 85*, 678–707.

Dachner, A. M., Saxton, B. M., Noe, R. A., & Keeton, K. E. (2013). To infinity and beyond: Using a narrative approach to identify training needs for unknown and dynamic situations. *Human Resource Development Quarterly, 24*(2), 239–267.

Daily, B. F., & Huang, S. C. (2001). Achieving sustainability through attention to human resource factors in environmental management. *International Journal of Operations & Production Management, 21*(12), 1539–1552.

Dragoni, L., & Kuenzi, M. (2012). Better understanding work unit goal orientation: Its emergence and impact under different types of work unit structure. *Journal of Applied Psychology, 97*(5), 1032.

Dweck, C. S. (1986). Motivational processes affecting learning. *American Psychologist, 41*, 1040–1048.

Eby, L. T., Allen, T.D., Hoffman, B.J., Baranik, L. E., Sauer, J. B., Baldwin, S., … Evans, S. C. (2013). An interdisciplinary meta-analysis of the potential antecedents, correlates, and consequences of protégé perceptions of mentoring. *Psychological Bulletin, 139*(2), 441–476.

Esfandagheh, F. B., Harris, R., & Oreyzi, H. R. (2012). The impact of extraversion and pre-training self-efficacy on levels of training outcomes. *Human Resource Development International, 15*(2), 175–191.

Farr, J. L., Hofmann, D. A., & Ringenbach, K. L. (1993). Goal orientation and action control theory: Implications for industrial and organizational psychology. In C. L. Cooper & I. T. Robertson (Eds.), *International review of industrial and organizational psychology* (pp. 193–232). New York, NY: Robertson Wiley.

Ford, J. K., Kraiger, K., & Merritt, S. M. (2009). An updated review of the multidimensionality of training outcomes: New directions for training evaluation research. In S. W. J. Kozlowski & E. Salas (Eds.), *Learning, training and development in organizations* (pp. 135–168). New York, NY: Routledge.

Ford, J. K., & Weissbein, D. A. (1997). Transfer of training: An updated review and analysis. *Performance Improvement Quarterly, 10*(2), 22–41.

Gagné, R., Briggs, L., & Wager, W. (1992). *Principles of instructional design* (4th ed.). Fort Worth, TX: HBJ College Publishers.

Goldstein, I. L. (1991). Training in work organizations. In M. D. Dunnette & L. M. Hough (Eds.), *Handbook of industrial and organizational psychology* (Vol. 2, 2nd ed., pp. 507–620). Palo Alto, CA: Consulting Psychologists Press.

Goldstein, I. L., & Ford, J. K. (2002). *Training in organizations: Needs assessment, development and evaluation.* Monterey, CA: Brooks Cole.

Grant, A. M., Passmore, J., Cavanagh, M. J., & Parker, H. (2010). The state of play in coaching today: A comprehensive review of the field. *International Review of Industrial and Organizational Psychology, 25*, 125–167.

Gully, S., & Chen, G. (2009). Individual differences, attribute-treatment interactions, and training outcomes. In S. W. J. Kozlowski, & E. Salas (eds.) *Learning, training and development in organizations* (pp. 3–64). New York, NY: Routledge.

Hamblin, A. (1974). *Evaluation and control of training.* London: McGraw Hill.

Harrison, R. (2009). *Learning and Development* (5th ed.). London: CIPD.

Jones, R. J., Woods, S. A., & Guillaume, Y. R. (2016). The effectiveness of workplace coaching: A meta-analysis of learning and performance outcomes from coaching. *Journal of Occupational and Organizational Psychology, 89*(2), 249–277.

Jones, R. J., Woods, S. A., & Zhou, Y. (2018). Boundary conditions of workplace coaching outcomes. *Journal of Managerial Psychology, 33*(7/8), 475–496.

Kaplan R. S., & Norton D. P. (1992) The balanced scorecard – measures that drive performance. *Harvard Business Review, 70*, 71–79.

Kearns, P. (2005). *Evaluating the ROI from learning.* London, England: Chartered Institute of Personnel and Development.

Kim, Y., & Ployhart, R. E. (2013) The effects of staffing and training on firm productivity and profit growth before, during, and after the Great Recession. *Journal of Applied Psychology, 99*(3). doi:10.1037/a0035408

Kirkpatrick, D. L. (1976). Evaluation of training. In R. L. Craig (Ed.), *Training and development handbook.* New York, NY: McGraw-Hill.

Kooij, D. T., Jansen, P. G., Dikkers, J. S., & De Lange, A. H. (2010). The influence of age on the associations between HR practices and both affective commitment and job satisfaction: A meta-analysis. *Journal of Organizational Behavior, 31*(8), 1111–1136.

Kozlowski, S. W. J., & Bell, B. S. (2006). Disentangling achievement orientation and goal setting: Effects on self-regulatory processes. *Journal of Applied Psychology, 91*(4), 900–916.

Kozlowski, S. W. J., Gully, S. M., Nason, E. R., & Smith, E. M. (1999). Developing adaptive teams: A theory of compilation and performance across levels and time. In D. R. Ilgen & E. D. Pulakos (Eds.), *The changing nature of work performance: Implications for staffing, personnel actions and development* (pp. 240–292). San Francisco, CA: Jossey-Bass.

Kraiger, K., Ford, J. K., & Salas, E. (1993). Application of cognitive, skill-based and affective theories of learning outcomes to new methods of training evaluation. *Journal of Applied Psychology, 78*(2), 311–328.

Luthans, F., & Peterson, S. J. (2003). 360-degree feedback with systematic coaching: Empirical analysis suggests a winning combination, *Human Resource Management, 42*, 243–256.

Martocchio, J. J., & Hertenstein, E. J. (2003). Learning orientation and goal orientation context: Relationships with cognitive and affective learning outcomes. *Human Resources Development Quarterly, 14*, 413–434.

Megginson, D., & Clutterbuck, D. (2006). Creating a coaching culture. *Industrial and Commercial Training, 38*(5), 232–237.

Mischel, W., & Shoda, Y. (1995). A cognitive affective system theory of personality: Reconceptualizing situations, dispositions, dynamics and invariance in personality structure. *Psychological Review, 102*(2), 246–268.

Parker, P., Kram, K. E., & Hall, D. T. (2013). Exploring risk factors in peer coaching: A Multilevel approach. *The Journal of Applied Behavioral Science, 49*(3), 361–387.

Payne, S. C., Youngcourt, S. S., & Beaubien, J. M. (2007). A meta-analytic examination of the goal orientation nomological net. *Journal of Applied Psychology, 92*(1), 128–150.

Potosky, D., & Ramakrishna, H. V. (2002). The moderating role of updating climate perceptions in the relationship between goal orientation, self-efficacy and job performance. *Human Performance, 15*(3), 275–297.

Quinones, M. A., Ford, J. K., Sego, D. J., & Smith, E. M. (1995). The effects of individual and transfer environment characteristics on the opportunity to perform trained tasks. *Training Research Journal, 1*, 29–48.

Saks, A. M., & Belcourt, M. (2004). An investigation of training activities and transfer of training in organizations. *Human Resources Management, 45*(4), 629–648.

Salas, E., & Cannon-Bowers, J. (2001). The science of training: A decade of progress. *Annual Review of Psychology, 52*, 471–499.

Schalm, C. (2008). Implementing a balanced scorecard as a strategic management tool in a long-term care organization. *Journal of Health Services Research Policy, 13*(1), 8–14.

Schuler, R. S., Budhwar, P., & Florkowski, G. (2002). International human resource management: Review and critique. *International Journal of Management Reviews, 4*(1), 41–70.

Shantz, A., & Latham, G. P. (2012). Transfer of training: Written self-guidance to increase self-efficacy and interviewing performance of job seekers. *Human Resource Management, 51*(5), 733–746.

Shipton, H., West, M. A., Dawson, J. F., Birdi, K., & Patterson, M. (2006). HRM as a predictor of innovation. *Human Resource Management Journal, 16*(1), 3–27.

Shipton, H., & Zhou, Q. (2008). Learning and development in organizations: Intervention or informality? In Aston Centre for Human Resources (Eds.), *Strategic human resource management* (pp. 159–188). London: CIPD.

Sitzmann, T., & Johnson, S. K. (2012). The best laid plans: Examining the conditions under which a planning intervention improves learning and reduces attrition. *Journal of Applied Psychology, 97*(5), 967.

Smither, J. W. (2011). Can psychotherapy research serve as a guide for research about executive coaching? An agenda for the next decade. *Journal of Business Psychology, 26*, 135–145.

Tannenbaum, S. I., & Yukl, G. (1992). Training and development in work organizations. *Annual Review of Psychology, 43*, 399–441.

Tharenou, P., Saks, A. M., & Moore, C. (2007). A review and critique of research on training and organizational-level outcomes. *Human Resource Management Review, 17*, 251–273.

Van de Walle, D. (1997). Development and validation of a work domain goal orientation instrument. *Educational and Psychological Measurement, 57*, 995–1015.

Van Eerde, W., Tang, K. C. S., & Talbot, G. (2008). The mediating role of training utility on the relationship between training needs assessment and organizational effectiveness. *International Journal of Human Resource Management, 19*, 63–73.

West, M. A., Borrill, C. S., Dawson, J. F., Scully, J., Carter, M., Anelay, S., … Waring. J. (2002). The link between the management of employees and patient mortality in acute hospitals. *International Journal of Human Resource Management, 13*, 1299–1310.

Woods, S. A., Patterson, F. C., Koczwara, A., & Sofat, J. A. (2016). The value of being a conscientious learner: Examining the effects of the Big Five personality traits on self-reported learning from training. *Journal of Workplace Learning, 28*(7), 424–434.

Zibarras, L. D., & Coan, P. (2015). HRM practices used to promote pro-environmental behavior: A UK survey. *The International Journal of Human Resource Management, 26*(16), 2121–2142.

CHAPTER 7
PERFORMANCE MANAGEMENT

LEARNING OBJECTIVES

- Understand the role of performance management in organization strategy.
- Understand and critically evaluate the process of performance measurement and management.
- Critically evaluate goal-setting theory and understand the conditions for positive performance.
- Understand the importance of feedback in performance management.
- Understand integrative and organizational perspectives on performance management practice.

So much of what we achieve as humans, whether in our own micro surroundings of life or at the various macro levels of society, is linked to the effectiveness with which people perform tasks or jobs. Human performance is instrumental in getting things *done*, getting problems *solved*, and ultimately directing how and in what ways our world changes and develops. The very reason that organizations exist is the need for collective performance; the recognition that some tasks and challenges require more than the individual to accomplish. And so, a logical consequence of organizing this collective performance is the management of the individual contributions, with the purpose of understanding how they combine to enable attainment of collective goals and objectives. This chapter is about the measurement and management of people's performance at work, and covers what we know about these processes from work psychology theory and research.

INTRODUCING PERFORMANCE MANAGEMENT

Performance management comprises several activities undertaken by managers and others in organizations in order to guide, measure and improve individual performance. It has been defined in the following ways:

> *A continuous process of identifying, measuring and developing the performance of individuals and teams and aligning performance with the strategic goals of the organization.* (Aguinis, 2009 p. 2.)

> *The wide variety of activities, policies, procedures and interventions designed to help employees improve their performance. These programs begin with performance appraisals, but also include feedback, goal setting and training, as well as reward systems.* (DeNisi & Murphy, 2017.)

Although work and organizational psychologists have concerned themselves principally with performance measurement and appraisal in respect of performance management, they have nevertheless made a contribution to understanding performance management. Performance measurement or appraisal is one part of performance management, with the key additions being processes designed to direct, improve or develop employee performance. Performance management therefore emphasizes development alongside assessment, and covers a variety of intervention and management strategies.

Murphy and DeNisi (2008) present a model of the performance management process (Figure 7.1). The model represents a flow diagram that shows the process of performance management. Beginning at the foundation of the model (the base), the first important point to note is the role of organizational strategy and goals in directing the whole performance management process. Individual goals and objectives need to be derived from the overall goal and objectives of the organization. This alignment is critical for ensuring that individual effort contributes to the performance of the whole organization (Aguinis, 2009). If you trace the arrows backwards in the figure, you see that the required performance standard is derived from corporate and individual goals. Performance goals should reflect the strategy of the organization, and the process of setting individual goals involves translating broad organizational strategies to smaller, measurable objectives for units, teams and ultimately individuals. For example, schools might set strategies that include objectives for students to achieve certain percentages of exam passes. These could be translated to individual targets for teachers for their specific classes.

The performance measurement box in the figure represents the assessment of performance. It denotes the observed level of employee performance, however it is measured, at the time of assessment. In practice, this is where performance appraisal occurs, as a process of determining how performance is modelled and quantified. In Murphy and DeNisi's model, performance measurement is considered alongside the required performance standard. This standard is based upon goals and objectives set in ways aligned with organizational need, and any ongoing performance improvement need.

Following the steps of the model leads to developmental processes. Performance assessment information is fed back to people in the organization. Where there is a discrepancy between observed and desired levels of performance (i.e. where performance is below the required standard), performance management interventions would be deployed to prompt improvement in performance. Expectations of performance improvement are then built into more goals and objectives, forming the basis of the next performance assessment. The cyclical nature of the model emphasizes the continuous nature of performance management. Performance management is ongoing and should not be viewed as episodic, or as a discrete intervention in organizations.

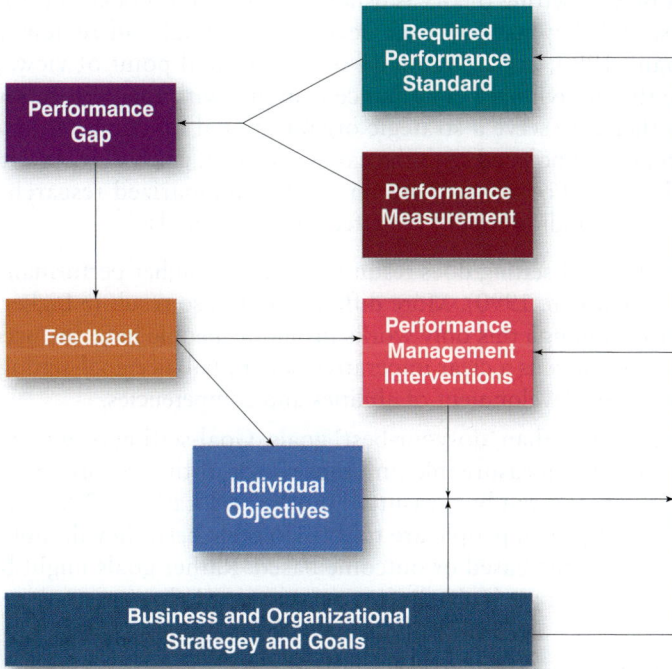

Figure 7.1 A model of performance management

This overall model identifies several important processes in performance management and these form the remainder of this chapter:

- *performance* goal-setting
- *performance* measurement
- *performance* feedback.

Not covered in this chapter, yet still relevant for performance management, are developmental processes (e.g. training, learning, coaching). These are covered elsewhere in this book. However, we do not cover issues of reward structure, which is more clearly aligned with HRM perspectives on performance management.

GOAL-SETTING

Goal-setting is a core part of performance management and is also one area of theory that is particularly well supported in the research literature. Although goal-setting theory was covered in our earlier chapter on motivation, the application of goals in performance management will be discussed here.

The development of goal-setting theory is usually attributed to Locke and Latham, two American work psychologists, and they have written several positional and review articles on the topic (e.g. Locke & Latham, 1990, 2002). From an organizational point of view, goals are important because they ensure that individual performance is in line with the performance standards for the organization. Goals therefore serve a strategic organizational function. However, research in work psychology has been more concerned with the extent to which goals are translated through to actual performance or behaviour. Locke and Latham (2002) summarized research in goal-setting, and presented some of the key findings about the effectiveness of goals:

- First and foremost, goal-setting does result in markedly higher performance than no goal-setting (Locke & Latham, 1990). More difficult goals also result in higher levels of effort and performance, although this only works insofar as people have the necessary abilities to meet their goals. There is a clear imperative here to balance goal-setting in performance management with the development of abilities and competencies.
- Specific goals are better than 'do-your-best' goals. Goal-setting results in higher performance if goals are specific and measureable (in other words, if the performance standards expected are clearly spelt out, and can be measured). Locke and Latham (2002) neatly surmise that in their research, when people are told to do their best, they do not do so. Goals are not necessarily results based or outcome based. Rather goals might blend aspects of results or outcomes with goals that refer to changes in behaviours or specific areas of job performance.
- Goals affect performance through four mechanisms. These are:
  1 Direction of behaviour. Goals direct behaviour towards goal-relevant activities and away from irrelevant activities.
  2 Energizing of behaviour. Goals lead people to expend greater effort on goal-relevant activities, with harder goals being associated with increased effort.
  3 Goals affect persistence. Harder goals tend to promote people prolonging their efforts to achieve those goals. Prolonged high-intensity effort cannot be maintained indefinitely, however. Tight deadlines tend to result in faster work pace for a short period of time.
  4 Goals lead people to develop their approach to work. Goals encourage people to develop achievement and performance strategies, learning job-relevant skills as a consequence.

The relationship between goals and performance is also moderated by a number of factors. This means that the extent to which goals result in performance depends on a number of additional factors:

- Goal commitment: The relationship between goals and performance is strongest when people are committed to their goals. There are two major predictors of goal commitment. The first is perceived importance of goals. People are more likely to be committed to their goals if they perceive them as important. One way of promoting this is to allow people to participate in goal-setting, although the evidence is mixed as to how effective this strategy is. In any case, participative goal-setting is likely to be perceived as fairer, even if it does not increase performance. Other ways of promoting perceptions of goal importance are to associate a valued incentive with the goal (such as monetary reward), or to communicate the goals in an inspirational way (bringing in clear interaction with leadership approaches). The second predictor of goal commitment is self-efficacy. Self-efficacy concerns the extent to which a person feels able to achieve their goals. It relates to self-perceptions of the extent to which a person has the relevant skills to achieve the goal and also of the achievability of the goal. Social psychologists have written much about the precursors and effects of self-efficacy (e.g. Bandura, 1997).

- Feedback: People perform better when they receive feedback about how they are performing in relation to their goals. Feedback allows people to see how they are doing in respect of their goals and to change their behaviour accordingly to ensure they meet their goals.
- Task complexity: Goals relate to performance most strongly for tasks which are low complexity. This is because for highly complex tasks, achieving a set goal might draw on a range of strategies and skills, and this in turn is related to people's abilities. Ability therefore becomes a limiter to the achievement of goals related to complex tasks for a great many people.

One area of research related to the task complexity moderator examines the differences between performance and learning goals (Dweck, 1986). Performance goals refer simply to achieving some level of performance and are typically simpler than learning goals, which might refer to the acquisition of new competencies or approaches to work. The picture is enriched further by the theory that people have a preferred style of working, which reflects how they interpret and understand their own goals. According to goal orientation theory, two learning approaches are differentiated, learning goal orientation (LGO) and performance goal orientation (PGO). People with LGO are motivated to learn and understand, whereas people with PGO are motivated to achieve their desired standard, but no more. Left to their own devices, people tend to work in their preferred styles, but a study by Seijts and Latham (2001) suggested that goal orientation effects could be overcome by setting goals in the right way. Regardless of preferred style, setting challenging learning goals resulted in similar performances from those with LGO and PGO styles. The implication for performance management is that for complex tasks, goal-setting should include learning goals in addition to performance goals.

Locke and Latham (2002) pull together many of these issues in a model of goal-setting and performance improvement (Figure 7.2). The model summarizes the processes by which performance is improved or managed through goal-setting. Note that a key part of the model is the association of goal achievement with satisfying and important rewards. The take-home of the model for performance management in organizations is that goal-setting is a crucial component of any performance management strategy, provided that it is implemented in the right way. Goal-setting is likely to be most effective when managers understand and are attentive to:

- the format and content of goals
- the mechanisms by which goals are achieved
- the moderators of the goals–performance relationship
- the satisfaction of individuals with the rewards they receive for achieving goals.

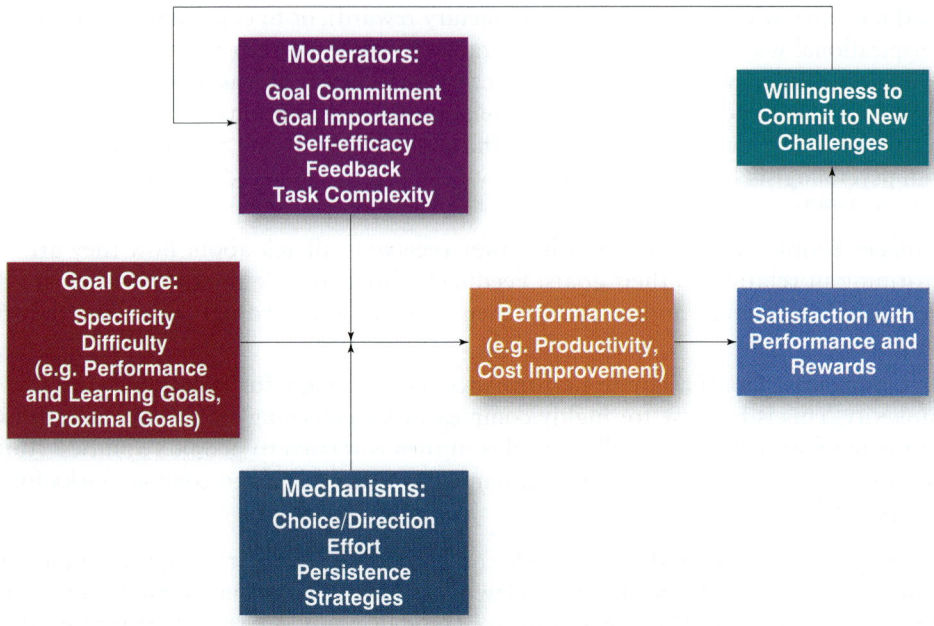

Figure 7.2 A model of goal setting

THE CONDITIONS FOR POSITIVE PERFORMANCE CHANGE

Performance management at its core is about understanding how and why people perform effectively in their work. Theories from a multitude of work and organizational psychology perspectives include aspects of performance, usually as outcomes of psychological characteristics and variables. Two that are notably helpful in understanding the conditions of positive performance and change are Trait Activation Theory (Tett & Burnett, 2003; see also Judge & Zapata, 2015) and the Theory of Work Adjustment (Dawis & Lofquist, 1984). These theories help to place the *person* in the performance management process, advancing our perspective beyond procedure and methodological issues.

Trait Activation Theory is a theory explaining the ways in which individual differences in personality are related to performance. However, the model is more than simply a trait-based performance model. Some key implications of the theory for performance behaviour are:

- Work demands serve to stimulate or activate individual characteristics. These demands could come from the task or from the organizational or social context.
- Individual performance behaviours stem from individual differences that are activated by the situation.
- Intrinsic and extrinsic rewards associated with the demonstration of performance behaviours also guide and shape what people do in response to situation demands.
- Where trait-related behaviour is consistent with the requirements of the job, then it is evaluated positively with respect to performance.

Judge and Zapata (2015) also examine the importance of situation strength in understanding performance differences. Strong situations are those in which individual characteristics are suppressed (that is, behaviour is managed by some aspect of the situation). Weaker situations allow for autonomy in how to respond to situational demands and offer greater scope for performance differences.

There are implications for understanding the conditions for people to perform at work. Demands must serve to activate individual differences and lead them to be expressed in behaviour. Reward should guide behaviour in the direction of positive performance. However, these models also imply that in order for performance to be most positive, traits need to be consistent with the job requirement or situation. While this effect is observable in data (e.g. Judge & Zapata, 2015), it offers little potential for development and performance improvement.

However, recent work on personality development and change at work (see e.g. Woods, Wille, Wu, Lievens, & De Fruyt, 2019), indicates that adopting concepts of work adjustment offers directions about the role of learning. The Theory of Work Adjustment describes how people respond to their work environment when their knowledge, skills, abilities, traits and competencies (KSAOs) are a misfit or poor fit to demands. In such situations, people have two options in order to ensure that performance standards are met and rewards attained. First, they might change some aspect of the job (e.g. through job crafting to improve performance; Rudolph, Katz, Lavigne, & Zacher, 2017). Second, they can act to develop themselves so that KSAOs are a better fit to job demands. This involves undertaking learning, which might be through training, coaching or other forms of development. Learning, training and development are covered in depth elsewhere in this book; however, they are key processes nevertheless for performance improvement.

The main implication of these observations for performance improvement is that development and learning interventions need to be used in conjunction with good information about the evaluation of individual performance. Exploring with people the ways in which their behaviour is suited to performance demands, and facilitating their growth to continually improve either through designing their jobs differently or helping them learn, is arguably where we most effectively understand positive performance growth and change.

MEASURING JOB PERFORMANCE

It is a common problem in management and human resource practice that a high proportion of managers tend to know intuitively whether staff are performing well or poorly, but are at a loss about exactly how to quantify performance (Woods, 2008). The problem of quantifying job performance is also prevalent in research in work psychology and management. Job performance is so important in work psychology that it is often known simply as 'the criterion' (Dalal, 2005), with the 'criterion problem' referring to the unavailability of robust job performance criteria in applied research (Austin & Villanova, 1992; Thayer, 1992). In the context of performance management, psychologists have also concentrated substantial effort on questions of how to measure job performance (DeNisi & Murphy, 2017). This is of real concern for researchers and practitioners because alongside performance management, many other activities also rely on job performance measurement: validation of selection systems and individual difference measures, training and development evaluation, and promotion planning, to name but a few. So performance measurement is an important process, but what exactly does it involve? Tannenbaum (2006) describes job performance measurement as:

> *The collection and use of judgements, ratings, perceptions or more objective sources of information to better understand the performance of a person, team, unit, business, process, program or initiative in order to guide subsequent actions or decisions.*

Highlighted in this definition are a number of potential ways that performance can be measured, but the basic issues that arise from all of them are around what actually constitutes job performance (i.e. what is job performance, and how could it be defined?) and how it should be measured (i.e. what methods should be used to measure performance?). The two issues are closely linked, such that the definition of job performance that is adopted will usually dictate how it is measured.

Objective measures of performance

A basic approach to performance measurement is to use objective outcome data collected by organizations, and this is relevant in specific kinds of jobs where data are easy to capture. Some objective measures reflect the core task or the job:

- Sales figures: Sales volume is easily measured in sales jobs and can be represented in various ways, including absolute monetary value, performance above target, or values adjusted for factors such as 'sales patch'.
- Service duration: Service jobs, such as those carried out in call centres, can be measured objectively, usually through examining call or service times.
- Utilization: Some organizations monitor the 'on-job hours' of employees. This is commonly used with consultants who are charged at daily rates. The time spent working on-contract versus off-contract could be measured.
- Results: Objectively measureable results are those that are not based on the perceptions of a rater or manager.
- Production: Any job that involves producing things can be measured by monitoring output.
- Quality: The products associated with some jobs have objective markers of quality (number of defects, for example), which can be measured.

Proxy measures are objective data that are not directly associated with the task or function of the job. These are actually a poor substitute for relevant job data:

- Absence: Absence from work is sometimes used as a performance indicator, as it is assumed to detract from productivity. Absence data are difficult to collect accurately.
- Safety record: These data might be collected in industrial jobs, recorded as number of accidents in a given period.
- Tardiness/Timekeeping: Where 'clocking-in' is used in an organization, records of tardiness at the start of the day, or during breaks, could be collected.

Objective measures are sometimes considered to be more robust and therefore more accurate indicators of performance compared with subjective measures. However, there are questions about exactly how objective such data are. Campbell (1990) argues that determining the boundaries for acceptable versus unacceptable objective performance is a subjective task (e.g. a supervisor has to decide what constitutes acceptable sales figures), and so many 'objective measures' could easily be conceptualized as subjective.

Perhaps more importantly, objective performance data are limited because they fail to tap into why some people perform better than others. To understand that, the focus of performance measurement needs to be on behaviour. Behaviour represents what people actually do at work, and Motowidlo, Borman, and Schmitt (1997) argue that behaviour should be the focus in performance measurement because results and outcomes can be affected by many factors outside the control of individuals. The results achieved by poorly performing employees and managers can be compensated by a buoyant business environment or co-worker support. Conversely, a person who performs all of the desirable behaviours required in their job might achieve poor results because the product or service that he or she is delivering is inadequate, or not in demand, factors that may be outside the employee's control. Does that make them poor performers, or is the shortcoming in the market research department of the organization? For work psychologists, the best way to establish fairly whether someone is performing at work is to examine behaviour at work.

Models of job performance behaviour

Think for a moment about your colleagues, or if you supervise people, your subordinates. You probably feel able to form an overall impression about their performance at work. There is likely to be some validity to your judgement (Viswesvaran, Schmidt, & Ones, 2005), but there are a number of problems with measuring performance in this way. First, your judgement is affected by bias, and particularly the halo effect (Viswesvaran et al., 2005). The halo effect is perceptual bias that affects how people perceive others. Before someone assesses another person's job performance, they form an impression about that individual's overall merit, and this influences the way that they evaluate the person's performance on a range of different performance dimensions. The halo effect occurs when people form a favourable impression and consequently overly positive judgements about a person's performance. The opposite is the horns effect. The second limitation is similar to that of objective measures; there is no information in the evaluation to determine which aspects of performance are weak or strong.

Jobs are diverse and therefore make diverse demands on people, eliciting a multitude of different behaviours, and this inevitably leads to multifaceted or multidimensional models of job performance. Multidimensional models allow us to make sense of complex behavioural phenomena, and to measure performance in ways that are more useful to people at work, and to organizations. Constructing them involves clustering performance behaviours into broad homogeneous dimensions. Each dimension is defined according to the common theme among its constituent behaviours. For example, key management performance behaviours include formulating short- and long-term team objectives, and organizing and prioritizing work. These two activities are conceptually related, and might be grouped under a broader heading of 'planning and organizing' (e.g. Borman & Brush, 1993). This multidimensional approach has led to two similar, yet divergent approaches to understanding job performance, explored in the next sections of this chapter:

- The first has examined the job performance in organizations generally, with the aim of understanding how performance can be conceptualized across all jobs.
- The second is the competency approach, which has drawn on the practice of competency modelling in organizations to construct broad models of job performance that can be applied in different ways across different jobs and organizations.

General models of job performance

While most psychologists emphasize the need to conduct thorough job analyses to define job performance in specific jobs, this does not mean that the basic elements of job performance change across different jobs (Viswesvaran & Ones, 2000). Research on models of job performance aims to define these basic elements. There is a huge and complex research literature examining the best way to model job performance, and the methods used in such studies are complicated, making it difficult for managers and HR practitioners to engage with the implications. However, once you cut through the complexity, these studies offer a wealth of information about job performance and how to measure it. The starting point is to break down overall performance into constituent parts. There are different ways of doing this, but by far the most widely supported approach to take is to differentiate task performance from organizational citizenship behaviours (OCB; Woods, 2008).

Task performance versus OCB

Probably the most influential advance in job performance modelling in the past 20 years is the differentiation of task performance and OCB (e.g. Motowidlo et al., 1997; Motowidlo & Van

Scotter, 1994). These two categories of job performance sit underneath general job performance in the hierarchical model. The traditional view of job performance restricted the domain of interest to the way that people performed the core tasks of their job. Task performance has a direct impact on organizational performance and is defined by Borman and Motowidlo (1997) as 'the effectiveness with which job incumbents perform activities that relate to the organization's technical core' (p. 99). Motowidlo et al. (1997) expand this definition to encompass two basic kinds of task performance activities:

- conversion of raw materials into goods and services that constitute the products of the organization (such as selling merchandise, operating machinery, teaching a class, performing surgical procedures)
- activities that maintain and service the technical core of the organization (such as the supervision of staff, planning core activities, distributing supplies and products).

Components of task performance. There are a variety of different perspectives in the research literature on how to break down task performance into more specific components, but an influential idea came from the Project A studies conducted by Campbell and colleagues (e.g. Campbell, 1990). Their simple model of performance distinguishes two aspects of task performance:

- Job-specific task performance: This can be thought of as core task proficiency, or performance of tasks that are central to a person's job role. Put simply, this is how well a person fulfils the tasks listed on their job description.
- Non-job-specific task performance: This is a general proficiency dimension, representing performance of tasks that may not be core to a person's role in the organization. This might be thought of as being performance on tasks or assignments outside areas of core responsibility (short-term projects, for example).

These two components are still rather abstract in their definition, and their purpose is to provide a framework around which more specific task performance behaviours can be organized. The use of job analysis, for example, could define the important task performance behaviours for different jobs.

Organizational citizenship behaviour

More recently, theories and models of job performance have acknowledged the importance of work behaviours that fall outside the domain of task performance, often referred to as discretionary or extra-role behaviours. In contemporary business environments characterized by flatter structures, international competition and increased employee autonomy, such behaviours are now considered critical to effective organizational performance (Podsakoff, MacKenzie, Paine, & Bachrach, 2000). The most widely used term for these aspects of job performance is OCB.

The concept of OCB was proposed by Organ in the late 1980s (e.g. Organ, 1988), who observed that to a varying extent, people tend to contribute to the continued existence of their organization beyond their core task activities. Such contributions include helping and cooperating with others, and general support for the organization and its mission. OCB was initially defined as extra-role behaviour, not directly recognized through formal reward systems. Such behaviour was therefore considered desirable, but not enforceable (Smith, Organ, & Near, 1983). This definition was modified by Borman and Motowidlo (1993), who proposed an alternative construct labelled contextual performance. They defined contextual behaviours as those that 'supported the organizational, social and psychological environment in which the technical core must function' (p. 74), elaborating this with examples such as helping co-workers, volunteering for extra work and describing the organization in a positive way. They noted that while task behaviour is job specific, contextual behaviours were desirable across all jobs. An important development of the theory was recognition that such behaviours need not fall outside formal job responsibilities, later recognized in Organ's model (Organ, 1997).

Components of OCB. There are several models of OCB in the research literature. The first was proposed by Organ (1988), who identified five dimensions labelled altruism, courtesy, conscientiousness, sportsmanship and civic virtue. A simpler two-dimensional structure was described by Williams and Anderson (1991), who distinguished between citizenship behaviours directed towards individuals (OCB-I) and organizations (OCB-O). These two dimensions are also represented in a model proposed by Coleman and Borman (2000), in the dimensions Personal Support and Organizational Support respectively. Their model incorporated a third dimension labelled Conscientious Initiative. Box 7.1, taken from Hanson and Borman (2006), describes the model. Hanson and Borman provide a fuller discussion of the overlaps and relationships between the various models of OCB.

When you start to think about OCB and its implications for job performance, it is also tempting to think about the opposite of citizenship behaviour. Counterproductive work behaviours are reviewed in Box 7.2, and there is a surprising conclusion from research about how they relate to OCB.

BOX 7.1
Dimensions of OCB

- **Personal Support** Helping others by offering suggestions, teaching them useful knowledge or skills, directly performing some of their tasks and providing emotional support for their personal problems. Cooperating with others by accepting suggestions, informing them of events they should know about and putting team objectives ahead of personal interests. Showing consideration, courtesy and tact in relations with others, as well as motivating and showing confidence in them.

- **Organizational Support** Representing the organization favourably by defending and promoting it, as well as expressing satisfaction and showing loyalty by staying with the organization despite temporary hardships. Supporting the organization's mission and objectives, complying with organizational rules and procedures and suggesting initiatives.

- **Conscientious Initiative** Persisting with extra effort despite difficult conditions. Taking the initiative to do all that is necessary to accomplish objectives even if not normally a part of own duties and finding additional productive work to perform when own duties are completed. Developing own knowledge and skills by taking advantage of opportunities within the organization and outside their own organization using own time and resources.

BOX 7.2
The flip-side of performance: counterproductive work behaviours

Theories of OCB tell us numerous ways that employees can engage in behaviours that enhance working practices, environments and relationships. Conversely, employees can engage in behaviours that are damaging to other individuals, to productivity and to the organization as a whole. Such behaviours fall under the overarching concept of counterproductive work behaviours (CWB). Viswesvaran and Ones (2000) include CWB as a third broad performance dimension next to task performance and OCB. They identify several kinds of common CWB:

- property damage (including theft and misuse of resources)
- substance abuse at work
- violence (which may also include workplace bullying)
- lateness, absenteeism, social loafing and turnover.

Viswesvaran and Ones (2000) point out that all of these behaviours are considered by supervisors when they rate the performance of their employees.

If one thinks for a moment about the kinds of things that a bad organizational citizen would be guilty of, some, if not all of the behaviours listed above intuitively spring to mind. The implicit perspective on OCB and CWB is therefore that they are at opposite ends of a single continuum. However, this assumption is misguided. In a meta-analysis addressing the question, Dalal (2005) reported an association of −0.32 between the two performance domains. This moderate negative relationship is too small to conclude that they are polar opposites. A better perspective is to view OCB and CWB as separate but related constructs (Kelloway, Loughlin, Barling, & Nault, 2002).

The competency approach to performance measurement

Models of job performance in the literature are not immediately accessible for managers and practitioners in organizations. More familiar are competencies and the competency approach to performance measurement. Competency modelling is a popular contemporary approach to analyzing job performance and the skills, abilities and attributes underlying performance. The approach has grown substantially in the past 20 years (Campion et al., 2011) and most large organizations now use some form of competency modelling or competency-based assessment as part of their HR strategy. There has been no general consensus in the academic literature about exactly how to define 'competencies'. However, recent commentaries in the literature (e.g. Campion et al., 2011; Soderquist, Papalexandris, Ioannou, & Prastacos, 2010), combined with past contributions (e.g. Bartram, 2005), point to a general definition as referring to the combined knowledge, skills, abilities and other characteristics that underlie effective performance, and are observable, measurable, and distinguish superior from average performance.

Critics of the concept of competencies correctly point out that competency definitions are currently a conceptual muddle. There is no standard format for how competencies might be represented (Voskuijl & Evers, 2008), yet significant advances have been made to describe and review best practice in competency modelling (Campion et al., 2011). Moreover, the major appeal of competency modelling as a tool for HRM lies in its applied benefits. Soderquist et al. (2010)

highlight that competency modelling allows horizontal integration of HRM processes, such that selection, development and performance management can all be aligned, and vertical integration, such that strategy and organization-level objectives can be built in directly to performance (i.e. competency) requirements of individual staff. The vertical integration aspect reflects the discussion earlier in this chapter regarding the importance of strategy in performance management.

A key property of job competencies is that they are behaviourally defined (Aguinis, 2009). Competencies used for assessment in organizations tend to comprise a label, a broad definition and several behavioural indicators or descriptors (see Figure 7.3). Box 7.3 presents an example job competency. Behavioural descriptors or indicators are used to facilitate assessment of competencies, to elaborate their meaning and to differentiate standards of proficiency. The behaviours described in the indicators, if observed in a person's performance, are taken as evidence of effective job performance, or presence of the competency. Some competency definitions also contain negative behavioural indicators (i.e. behaviours that constitute ineffective performance) to aid performance measurement. Assessment of competencies generally involves judgement based on observation about how effectively the individual has demonstrated the behaviours associated with the competency.

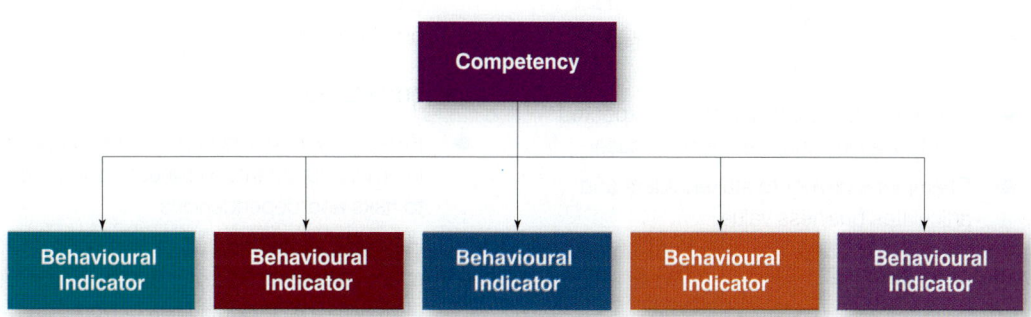

Figure 7.3   Competency and behaviour indicators

Competencies are a development of the behavioural perspective on measuring performance (Aguinis, 2009) and are used by organizations to help structure employee performance assessments. Competencies can be constructed to reflect different kinds of jobs in organizations, and conceptualized as narrow aspects of performance or very broad overarching constructs. Their flexibility is in some ways responsible for the criticisms around lack of structure and coherence associated with the competency approach.

From an applied perspective, it is possible to differentiate two approaches to the task of competency modelling. The first aims to identify universal competencies that apply across all jobs or within a specific kind of job. At a broad level of abstraction, Bartram (2005) identified the 'Great Eight' competencies. These were derived from considering the influence of major individual difference dimensions on work activity (the Big Five, general mental ability and need for power/achievement). The resultant eight competency dimensions (Box 7.4) were designed to be applied across jobs, with different jobs drawing more or less heavily on each of the eight.

BOX 7.3
Example competency

Project Management

Project Management is the art of creating accurate and effective schedules with a well-defined scope while being personally accountable for the execution and invested in the success of the project. People who exhibit this competency effectively and continuously manage risks and dependencies by making timely decisions while ensuring the quality of the project.

Proficiency Level 1

- Identifies risks and dependencies and communicates routinely to stakeholders.
- Appropriately escalates blocking issues when necessary.
- Understands project objectives, expected quality, metrics and the business case.
- Champions project to stakeholders and articulates business value.

Proficiency Level 2

- Develops systems to monitor risks and dependencies and report change.
- Works effectively across disciplines and organizational boundaries to gain timely closure on decisions that impact own project/portfolio/solution.
- Develops methods to track and report metrics, gains agreement on quality and relates it to business value.
- Asks the right questions to resolve issues and applies creative solutions to meet project objectives.

Proficiency Level 3

- Anticipates changing conditions and impact to risks and dependencies and takes preventative action.
- Effects timely, mutually beneficial outcomes on decisions that impact the whole product, multiple projects or portfolios.
- Evaluates quality and metrics based on return on investment and ensures alignment to business need.
- Proactively inspires others to take action on issues and implications that could prohibit projects success.

Proficiency Level 4

- Proactively identifies implications of related internal and external business conditions to risks and dependencies.
- Instils a system and culture that facilitates effective decision-making across organizations, product lines or portfolios.
- Evaluates project results against related examples and incorporates best practices and key learning for future improvements.
- Champions business value across multiple organizations and gains alignment and commitment to prioritization to ensure long-term project deliverables.

BOX 7.4
The 'Great Eight' competencies (from Bartram, 2005)

Leading and deciding
Supporting and cooperating
Interacting and presenting
Analyzing and interpreting

Creating and conceptualizing
Organizing and executing
Adapting and coping
Enterprising and performing

At a slightly less general level of abstraction are approaches that identify universal competencies for specific kinds of jobs (e.g. sales or management). Tett, Guterman, Bleier, and Murphy (2000) presented a hyperdimensional taxonomy of management competencies. Their model incorporated 53 management competencies, grouped into nine broader areas. The 53 management competencies are shown in Box 7.5. These competencies are designed to specifically tap into important managerial job performance behaviours.

The alternative to the universal approach might be termed a strategic or contextual approach. Rather than removing context and seeking general competencies that might be used across jobs and organizations, this approach begins with the context of performance and the strategy of the organization in mind. This enables competencies to be defined that fit with the strategic needs of the business, and that reflect the current and anticipated future performance needs (Campion et al., 2011). This approach recognizes the unique performance demands and requirements of different sectors and businesses.

Each of the two approaches has something to contribute to the process of using competencies to measure job performance. The more general and universal approach recognizes that at job level, there are common factors that influence successful performance across businesses. However, neglecting the context within which those competencies are performed may seriously limit their utility, which is the clear implication of a more organization-specific, contextual and strategic approach.

BOX 7.5
The 53 managerial competencies proposed by Tett et al. (2000)

Traditional functions

1. Problem awareness
2. Decision-making
3. Directing
4. Decision delegation
5. Short-term planning
6. Strategic planning
7. Coordinating
8. Goal-setting
9. Monitoring
10. Motivating by authority
11. Motivating by persuasion
12. Team-building
13. Productivity

continued

Task orientation

14 Initiative
15 Task focus
16 Urgency
17 Decisiveness
18 Compassion
19 Cooperation
20 Sociability
21 Politeness
22 Political astuteness
23 Assertiveness
24 Seeking input
25 Customer focus

Dependability

26 Orderliness
27 Rule orientation
28 Personal responsibility
29 Trustworthiness
30 Timeliness
31 Professionalism
32 Loyalty

Open Mindedness

33 Tolerance
34 Adaptability

35 Creative thinking
36 Cultural appreciation
37 Resilience
38 Stress management

Communication

39 Listening skills
40 Oral communication
41 Public presentation
42 Written communication

Developing self and others

43 Developmental goal-setting
44 Performance assessment
45 Developmental feedback
46 Job enrichment
47 Self-development

Occupational acumen and concerns

48 Technical proficiency
49 Organizational awareness
50 Quantity concern
51 Quality concern
52 Financial concern
53 Safety concern

DISCUSS WITH A COLLEAGUE

What are the key dimensions of performance in your current or past job? If you are a student, think about your performance as a student, or about a familiar job. Discuss and compare with a colleague.

The process of performance measurement: Appraisal

Models of job performance tell practitioners what to measure or assess in respect of a person's performance at work. The various models reviewed so far can be used in conjunction with information about people's jobs and the organizational contexts of those jobs (i.e. job or competency analysis information) to decide on the dimensions or competencies to measure. How is the performance assessment actually implemented in organizations? The process of measuring performance at work is usually referred to as performance appraisal. As we will see later in the chapter, the definition of appraisal might be broadened out to encompass performance improvement activities, but pragmatically for most practitioners, the measurement of employee performance is synonymous with performance appraisal. There are a number of different methods for collecting performance data, reviewed below.

Survey items and rating scales

Simple rating scales are perhaps the most common means of collecting performance judgements. Performance dimensions are broken down into their constituent parts, and raters are asked to indicate judgements about performance using specific rating scales. Some examples of different rating scales are shown in Box 7.6. You'll see that the scales are being used to rate 'Teamworking'. However, there is no information provided in the measure to allow the rater to see exactly what is meant by Teamworking. Performance appraisal survey items might take more detailed forms, breaking down performance dimensions into specific behaviours. An example is provided in Box 7.7. This measure is taken from Williams and Anderson (1991) and shows three scales measuring in-role behaviour, OCB directed towards individuals, and OCB directed towards the organization. These items have been designed to be behavioural, helping the rater to judge performance more clearly.

BOX 7.6
Different types of rating scales

Verbally anchored Likert scales

The level of this employee's Teamworking is:
1 = Unsatisfactory.
2 = Less than adequate.
3 = Fair.
4 = Good.
5 = Very Good.
6 = Outstanding.

Unanchored Likert scales

Unsatisfactory 1 2 3 4 5 6 Outstanding
Graphic Scale
Unsatisfactory [---------------] Outstanding

Comparative scales

In the area of Teamworking, this employee:
1 = Is one of the very poorest performers.
2 = Performs less well than most.
3 = Performs the same as most.
4 = Performs better than most.
5 = Is one of the top few performers.

BOX 7.7
Measuring three dimensions of job performance

Use the following items to rate the performance of a colleague, subordinate or supervisor. Use the rating scale below:

This person:

1. Adequately completes assigned duties.
   Almost Never 1 2 3 4 5 Almost Always
2. Fulfils responsibilities specified in the job description.
   Almost Never 1 2 3 4 5 Almost Always
3. Performs tasks that are expected of him/her.
   Almost Never 1 2 3 4 5 Almost Always
4. Meets formal performance requirements of the job.
   Almost Never 1 2 3 4 5 Almost Always
5. Engages in activities that will directly affect his/her performance evaluation.
   Almost Never 1 2 3 4 5 Almost Always
6. Neglects aspects of the job he/she is obligated to perform.
   Almost Never 1 2 3 4 5 Almost Always
7. Fails to perform essential duties.
   Almost Never 1 2 3 4 5 Almost Always
8. Helps others who have been absent.
   Almost Never 1 2 3 4 5 Almost Always
9. Helps others who have heavy workloads.
   Almost Never 1 2 3 4 5 Almost Always
10. Assists supervisor with his/her work (when not asked).
    Almost Never 1 2 3 4 5 Almost Always
11. Takes time to listen to co-workers' problems and worries.
    Almost Never 1 2 3 4 5 Almost Always
12. Goes out of way to help new employees.
    Almost Never 1 2 3 4 5 Almost Always
13. Takes a personal interest in other employees.
    Almost Never 1 2 3 4 5 Almost Always
14. Passes along information to co-workers.
    Almost Never 1 2 3 4 5 Almost Always
15. Attendance at work is above the norm.
    Almost Never 1 2 3 4 5 Almost Always
16. Gives advance notice when unable to come to work.
    Almost Never 1 2 3 4 5 Almost Always
17. Takes undeserved work breaks.
    Almost Never 1 2 3 4 5 Almost Always
18. Great deal of time spent with personal phone conversations.
    Almost Never 1 2 3 4 5 Almost Always
19. Complains about insignificant things at work.
    Almost Never 1 2 3 4 5 Almost Always
20. Conserves and protects organizational property.
    Almost Never 1 2 3 4 5 Almost Always
21. Adheres to informal rules devised to maintain order.
    Almost Never 1 2 3 4 5 Almost Always

To score your responses:
- In-role behaviour (task performance): (1+2+3+ 4+5+6R+7R) / 7
- Organizational citizenship behaviour – individual: (8+9+10+11+12+13+14) / 7
- Organizational citizenship behaviour – organization: (15+16+17R+18R+19R+20+21) / 7
- The scale calculations produce scores on the original 1–5 scale.

Improving rating scales and appraisal measures

Ratings collected using the basic kinds of appraisal measure shown in Box 7.7 are inevitably subjective. As such, the common biases that human judges bring to assessment are likely to affect ratings. As outlined earlier in this book, such biases include stereotyping, halo versus horns effect, similar-to-me effect and so forth. Such are the problems with performance appraisal ratings that some psychologists question their fundamental value in organizations (e.g. Adler et al., 2016). A challenge for work psychologists is therefore how to reduce the influences of subjective biases on ratings. Fletcher (2008) outlines a number of ways that rating scales might be improved to reduce bias:

- Training: Although rating scales are simple, they can still be used poorly by raters. Training of raters can help them to be aware of their own biases and to challenge them.
- Forced distributions: Using a five-point scale (Poor, Fair, Average, Good, Outstanding) to rate the performance of a group of employees should, by definition, result in most people being rated as average. However, the value that we attach to the word 'average' (people do not like to be labelled as average), combined with a reluctance among most people to rate the performance of others negatively, means that the majority of people are likely to be rated as 'good' or 'outstanding'. One way to overcome this problem is to use a forced distribution, whereby appraisers are forced to give 10 per cent the highest rating, 10 per cent the lowest rating and so on. Such approaches may be perceived negatively by people in organizations, and certainly seem to be at odds with the principle that performance should be evaluated on the basis of what people actually do (i.e. their behaviour). Rigid forced distribution systems are uncommon, although GE are famed for their system. Under the GE appraisal system, 10 per cent of managers each year are given the lowest performance rating. If they receive the same low rating the next year, they are asked to leave the company (Aguinis, 2009).
- Multiple raters: Combining the judgements of multiple raters overcomes the problem of the idiosyncratic judgement of one rater having a disproportionate effect on the appraisal rating. Several supervisors might rate the performance of the individual, or more commonly, supervisor ratings might be combined with ratings provided by peers, subordinates or even customers or clients. Multi-source appraisal (known as multi-source feedback) is a popular contemporary approach to performance assessment, and is discussed later in the chapter.
- Behavioural scales: In the behavioural approach to measuring performance, the role of the rater changes from 'judge' to 'observer'. In this approach, job performance ratings are based on the rater's perception of whether the target has demonstrated particular job-relevant behaviours, and to what frequency. These are Behaviourally Anchored Rating Scales (BARS; see Box 7.8) and Behavioural Observation Scales (BOS; see Box 7.8). BARS have very specific behavioural anchors that indicate the behaviour that a person should demonstrate to be awarded a specific rating. You can observe the increased effectiveness of these behaviours in respect of the performance dimension under scrutiny as the rating increases. By contrast, BOS are closer to the survey-item and rating scale approach outlined earlier. However, the items here are in the form of specific behaviours, and the rating scale requires that the rater makes an overall judgement about the frequency with which the employee demonstrates the behaviour.

> **BOX 7.8**
> **Behavioural scales used in appraisal and performance measurement**
>
> *Behaviourally-Anchored Rating Scale: Planning and organization*
>
> Identifies priorities, sets deadlines and plans schedules. Effectively manages own time to achieve goals. Gives considerations to wider implications of plans made.
>
> 1. The participant has not exhibited this competency in the exercise and/or has not followed instructions. Attempts to plan are ineffective through inappropriate prioritization or organization.
> 2. Plans are short-term, reactive and not related to objectives.
> 3. Plans linked to objectives, but these tend to be short term.
> 4. Plans are linked to objectives, are longer term and are based on priorities and deadlines.
> 5. Identifies priorities, sets deadlines and plans schedules. Effectively manages own time to achieve goals. Gives considerations to wider implications of plans made.
>
> *Behavioural Observation Scales: Teamworking*
>
> a. Tolerant with others and shows patience with them.
>   **Almost always 1 2 3 4 5 Almost never**
> b. Consistently seeks to offer help and support.
>   **Almost always 1 2 3 4 5 Almost never**
> c. Plays a balanced role in team discussions.
>   **Almost always 1 2 3 4 5 Almost never**
> d. Keeps colleagues informed where necessary.
>   **Almost always 1 2 3 4 5 Almost never**
> e. Volunteers for fair share of less popular duties.
>   **Almost always 1 2 3 4 5 Almost never**
> f. Willing to change own plans to cooperate with others.
>   **Almost always 1 2 3 4 5 Almost never**

Results-based appraisal

In the results-based appraisal method, employee performance is judged based on what they achieve rather than what they do. The foundations of results-based appraisal lie in the tradition of management by objectives (MBO). This approach to performance management holds that the key to motivating employees to perform at work is to set objectives and goals. Objective setting, when executed effectively, certainly has a central role to play in performance management. However, as an approach to measuring and judging performance, attending solely to outcomes is seriously limited for two reasons:

1. It is extremely difficult to compare different employees using the approach (Fletcher, 2008). This is because numerical ratings are not used to assess performance.
2. The assessment is over-simplistic, for the reasons outlined at the start of this chapter. In order to be perceived fairly by employees, the assessment would need to somehow account for wider contextual issues that might affect performance.

BOX 7.9
How reliable are performance assessments in organizations?

Like any other form of measurement in work psychology, a key question concerning ratings of job performance is their reliability. Reliability has been discussed at length in previous chapters, and the three forms of reliability are all relevant in performance assessment:

- Internal consistency: To what extent are performance rating scales internally consistent?
- Test–retest reliability: To what extent are performance ratings stable over time?
- Interrater reliability: To what extent do different people's ideas about and judgements of effective performance converge?

These three methods of assessing reliability present interesting applied interpretations when applied to job performance measures. Scale consistency can sometimes be interpreted as poor discrimination of performance dimensions by supervisors. Striving for stability in performance ratings goes against our intuitions that performance can change over time. Interrater reliability raises questions about the frame of reference that people apply when they rate job performance. To what extent does one rater's idea of effective performance generalize to other raters? These issues are important because job performance measurement is central to a substantive volume of work psychology research and HRM practice. For example, reliability estimates are critical in meta-analysis, where they are used to correct validity coefficients. Moreover, reliability is important for the practical use of job performance ratings, for example to determine pay, promotion and training requirements. None of these activities can be adequately carried out if performance measures are unreliable. Studies of the reliability of performance assessments have yielded the following findings:

- Viswesvaran, Ones, and Schmidt (1996) conducted a meta-analysis of the reliability of job performance ratings and reported modest interrater reliabilities for overall job performance assessments for supervisors (0.52) and for peers (0.42). Interestingly, reliabilities across dimensions varied, with the dimensions Quality, Productivity and Administrative Competence demonstrating the highest reliability and Communication and Interpersonal Competence the lowest. Borman (1979) suggests that such variations reflect the availability of evidence to raters. Some competencies or performance dimensions are more observable than others, and moreover, some are likely to be more visible to supervisors than peers and vice versa. The implication is that supervisor and peer ratings of job performance are most reliable when there is available evidence upon which to make a judgement. From their results, Viswesvaran et al. (1996) argued that interrater reliability was the most adequate reliability index for job performance as this reflects the basic question about whether two equally knowledgeable judges would rate the same individual's job performance similarly. As such, interrater reliability determines the effectiveness of, for example, applying single performance standards across organizations (where different supervisors rate the performance of different employees), or in placing team members in new positions or project teams, where their performance may be judged by someone other than their line supervisor. If you are investigating the reliability of appraisal ratings in your own organization, then interrater reliability is a key area to address.

continued

- Coefficient alpha reliabilities tend to be higher than interrater reliabilities. In Viswesvaran et al.'s (1996) analyses, internal consistency reliabilities were 0.86 for supervisors (range = 0.73–0.86) and 0.85 for peers (range = 0.61–0.85). The implication of this finding is that job performance scales can be reliable. One confound, however, refers back to the issue of the halo effect and the error it introduces into ratings. Recall that part of the reason that ratings of performance tend to be consistent across different dimensions is that all ratings are influenced by the bias associated with the halo effect. Viswesvaran et al. (2005) estimate the inflation effect on coefficient alpha reliabilities to be around 30 per cent for supervisory ratings and 60 per cent for peer ratings. In the analyses, supervisors were less influenced by halo than were peers. It seems, then, that supervisors are generally better at differentiating multiple aspects of job performance.
- An in-depth examination of the stability of performance measures over time was presented by Sturman, Cheramie, and Cashen (2005), and is highly informative in respect of test–retest reliability. Sturman et al. point out that we have to be very careful when we think about test–retest reliability in performance measures. We could test whether a performance measure gives the same result on two different occasions and conclude that the measure was stable, and thus reliable. However, this judgement is only sound if the performance of the people we are assessing is also unchanged. If performance has actually improved or worsened, then a stable measurement is inaccurate. Test–retest reliability should therefore be thought of as the stability of the measurement over time, assuming that performance has actually remained the same. By using statistical techniques, Sturman et al. (2005) were able to determine that in the short term, performance measurements can demonstrate acceptable reliability. However, when looking at stability in the long term (i.e. one year or more), the reliabilities of the measures decreased substantially. The practical implication of their work is that in order to be considered reliable, assessments of employee performance should be conducted regularly.

Competency-based appraisal

The competency approach to appraisal uses competencies and their definitions to structure the assessment of employee performance. The approach is similar to the behavioural approach to appraisal, except that behaviours are not rated in isolation, but are rather clustered together into the competency dimensions. The breadth and detail encapsulated in these dimensions make the competency approach useful for development purposes, as well as performance assessment. As described earlier, the definitions of competencies can give key information about the positive and negative behaviours associated with a particular dimension. These behaviours obviously help to structure the assessment and judgements of the rater, but also provide clear guidelines on the desirable levels and forms of performance. These can be discussed with ratees so that they can see how to improve. Moreover, a further advantage of this approach is that if competencies incorporate strategically important aspects, individual performance can be shaped around delivering business strategy.

PERFORMANCE FEEDBACK

Referring back to the original model of performance management presented at the start of this chapter shows that following performance evaluation, information needs to be shared and fed back to people. Already highlighted in the discussion of goal-setting is the importance of giving people feedback about their performance. Most managers are aware of the need to provide feedback to employees, but when you talk to people in organizations, the quality of the feedback they receive about their performance is a common source of dissatisfaction. Feedback should clearly communicate progress against objectives, but more importantly serve a developmental purpose. Good feedback allows employees to see what they are doing right, helping to build confidence, identifies areas for improvement, helping to build competence, and can also promote engagement and involvement with the organization. Aguinis (2009) lists some of the ways that feedback to employees can be generally improved (Box 7.10).

BOX 7.10
Characteristics of effective feedback

- Timeliness. Feedback delivered close to the event or performance episode.
- Frequency. Feedback provided regularly and continuously.
- Specificity. Specific behaviours or aspects of performance are reported.
- Verifiability. Focus on accurate, verifiable evidence, not rumour or inference.
- Consistency. The tone of feedback should be consistent, and not subject to huge variation.
- Privacy. Presented at an appropriate time and place to avoid embarrassment.
- Consequences. Consequences and potential outcomes of behaviour are communicated to contextualize feedback.
- Description first, evaluation second. Clear descriptions of performance behaviours precede evaluations of those behaviours.
- Performance as continuous. Focus on how to demonstrate more good behaviour and less ineffective behaviour, communicating that performance is not simply bad/good.
- Pattern identification. Patterns of poor performance behaviours identified rather than isolated mistakes.
- Confidence in the employee. Manager communicates confidence in the employee, emphasizing that negative feedback is targeted at behaviour and not the person.
- Advice and idea generation. Ways of improving performance offered by the manager (advice) and invited from the employee (idea generation).

Feedback provided to employees is likely to be a balance of positive and negative information, although it is the provision of negative feedback that typically concerns many managers. However, negative feedback is clearly crucial to performance management, as without it, employees have no information upon which to make a decision how to improve. A fundamental question in this area is the extent to which constructive or developmental feedback actually results in changes in behaviour. Evidence seems to suggest that giving feedback poorly can be less effective than giving no feedback at all. Indeed, reviews of the effects of feedback on performance indicate that there are robust findings showing that feedback can both enhance and have negative effects on performance (Kluger & DeNisi, 1996).

Research in this area in work psychology has examined the cognitive processes underlying people's responses and reactions to feedback on their job performance. The aim of such research is to examine the mechanisms that determine why one person might react positively to feedback, while someone else responds negatively. Kluger and DeNisi (1996) present a major review of the topic, and propose a model. Their model lacks something in applied value due to its complexity, but some of the major implications are informative. First, their analyses seem to suggest that perceptions of the nature of feedback are related to behaviour change. Feedback leads to performance improvement when it informs a person of a necessary change in behaviour, or when it challenges assumptions about the best way to do something at work. This is because such feedback leads a person to pay attention to the task at hand and to the way they are completing it. Feedback that is personal (which can include comparing the employee with other team members) promotes a focus on improving or defending oneself, thereby focusing attention away from the task at hand. A second important lesson from Kluger and DeNisi (1996) is that the way these processes work for individual employees is likely to depend on their personality, and on the situation.

Kinicki, Prussia, Wu, and McKee-Ryan (2004) tested a simpler model of feedback and performance improvement based on a model proposed by Ilgen, Fisher, and Taylor (1979). The model is shown in Figure 7.4. The main implications of their model are:

- Feedback is translated to performance through a series of sequential cognitive mechanisms, which represent individual reactions and judgements in respect of feedback.
- A fundamental judgement that employees make about feedback is its accuracy. The perceived accuracy of feedback depends on the credibility of the communicator, and the presence of a so-called 'feedback-rich environment'. A feedback-rich environment is one in which feedback is specific, provided frequently and is positive.
- Perceived accuracy is related to a desire to respond to the feedback, although the credibility of the person providing the feedback also has a direct effect on desire to respond.
- The desire to respond to the feedback leads to the formation of an intended response. There is a modest relationship between the intention to respond and actual performance change.

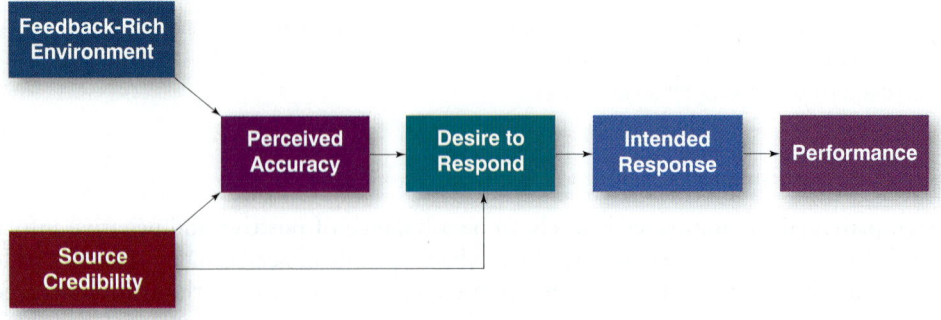

Figure 7.4   A model of performance improvement resulting from feedback

Parallels between this model and the theory of planned behaviour (Ajzen, see Chapter 3) are clear. In particular, the step from intention to behaviour is likely to be affected by a range of attitudinal and cognitive processes. Notably, Kinicki et al.'s model does have implications for the provision of negative feedback. It is well documented that people tend to perceive positive feedback as more accurate than negative feedback (e.g. Brett & Atwater, 2001), but perhaps creating a feedback-rich environment in which negative feedback is embedded could enhance the extent to which people see it as accurate.

> **DISCUSS WITH A COLLEAGUE**
>
> Think of an example when you received very effective feedback. Why do you think this feedback was so positive and impactful?

Multi-source feedback

Feedback is traditionally based on supervisor ratings of performance, but a popular contemporary approach to performance assessment and feedback is for ratings to be provided by a variety of people, including peers, subordinates and customers or clients. This form of performance assessment is usually referred to as 360-degree feedback, and has proved very popular with organizations. The profusion of such feedback systems appears to have been more popular initially in the USA, migrating to practice in the UK and Europe in the 1990s.

Multi-source performance ratings are valued by organizations because they appear to be more comprehensive than single sources, providing a more thorough assessment of performance across a range of different contexts. Supervisor ratings of performance may be based on limited evidence of employee competence because they may not observe the ratee in interactions with peers or subordinates. Despite practitioner enthusiasm for multi-source systems such as 360-degree appraisal, researchers have remained sceptical. Fletcher has written extensively on this topic in the UK, and points out that this scepticism often arises because 360-degree systems are sometimes poorly operationalized, and because the information collected is not always used effectively (Fletcher, 2001). He identifies some of the key practical components of 360-degree systems in organizations (Fletcher, 2008):

- Rating instruments. Feedback surveys are typically used to collect ratings of performance. As with other performance measures, raters use rating scales to indicate the effectiveness of particular performance behaviours.
- Raters. Self-ratings of performance are usually used, and the individual being rated is often asked to nominate the people who will assess him or her. The issue of anonymity is important in this respect, as subordinates particularly may feel uncomfortable about rating their boss, knowing that their boss will see their ratings.
- Feedback process. Data are collected and compiled by a central administrator or by the person giving feedback to the employee. Ratings are typically collated so that an average score is provided for each rating alongside a breakdown of the scores from each rating source. The average is important to report back, but the dispersion of scores across rating sources is often more informative.

A conceptual challenge in multi-source feedback systems is to understand whether different raters conceptualize performance dimensions similarly or differently. Understanding the validity and conceptual basis of multi-source ratings is important because it helps us to understand how best to use them. Studies generally support the measurement equivalence of performance ratings across sources (Facteau & Craig, 2001; Maurer, Raju, & Collins, 1998). Overall, it appears that measures of the same construct provided by different sources are conceptually similar. So, for example, a supervisory rating of leadership skill is likely to represent the same kinds of behaviours as a corresponding peer rating. These conclusions may not apply across all performance dimensions however.

Viswesvaran, Schmidt, and Ones (2002) examined convergence of supervisor and peer ratings on ten performance dimensions. They found that supervisor and peer ratings converged for some dimensions but not others. Supervisors and peers may therefore conceptualize some elements of performance differently. In 360-degree assessment systems, individuals may also rate their own job performance. Self–other convergence of performance ratings tend to be lower than other–other convergence (Conway & Huffcutt, 1997). This may be due to personality influences that inflate or suppress self-ratings of performance (e.g. Goffin & Anderson, 2007). People may be overly lenient, or conversely overly harsh on themselves, and this should be noted when implementing 360-degree assessment systems.

Practical concerns in multi-source feedback

If management in an organization decide to introduce 360-degree feedback, practitioners are faced with the choice of using it for either development or formal performance appraisal. There is no clear answer as to the best strategy to adopt, as the issues surrounding 360-degree feedback and its introduction are potentially complex. On the face of it, the approach appears to offer considerable advantages. People often feel that feedback or appraisal assessment based on the views of single individuals is limited, and may not reflect their true performance. Moreover, traditional appraisal assessments are hardly held up as a benchmark of accurate, objective measurement. A further benefit of the multi-source approach is that it empowers people to potentially influence the way they are managed. For subordinates, it offers a way for them to communicate their views about the way they are supervised.

The downside is that if 360-degree assessment was embedded in a company as part of formal performance appraisal, there could be various unintended effects (Fletcher, 2008). The ratings that people provide are likely to be compromised if they know that their assessments will affect the person's pay or status. There is some evidence that subordinate ratings are less useful if used for appraisal compared with development (Greguras, Robie, Schleicher, & Goff, 2003). Ratees might be less likely to take on board criticism from the process if it has consequences for them in the organization. There is also a risk that people may use the power that comes with rating performance to exercise influence over those they are rating. Many of these issues would be considered less critical if there were good evidence that 360-degree feedback is effective in terms of improving people's performance.

An important meta-analysis of this issue was conducted by Smither, London, and Reilly (2005). They examined only longitudinal studies, and were interested to see whether people improved their performance over time after a 360-degree assessment. Their findings suggest that only small performance improvements result from receiving 360-degree feedback. Interestingly it was subordinate ratings that seemed to increase the most. Smither et al. (2005) were unsurprised by their findings and suggest that there are, of course, a number of factors that will promote performance improvement following 360-degree feedback. These are summarized in their model (see Figure 7.5). Once again, some of the most important factors are around personal dispositions, beliefs about and reactions to the feedback. Beliefs about change in the model echo the issue of self-efficacy in goal-setting theory. As with other performance management mechanisms, the science tells us that simply using 360-degree or multi-source feedback is not enough for performance improvement; rather, it is the way the technique is applied in a specific context.

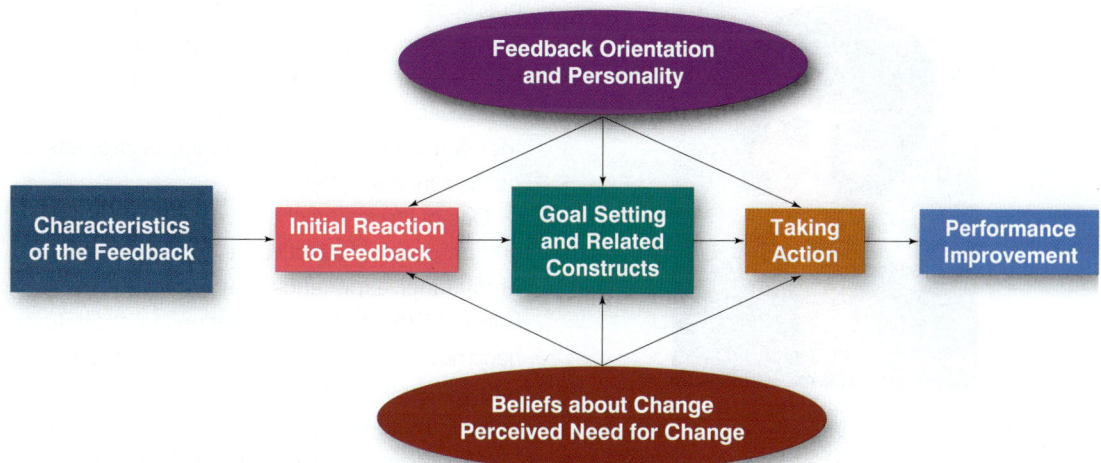

Figure 7.5   Theoretical model of performance improvement following multi-source feedback

CRITICAL PERSPECTIVES ON PERFORMANCE MEASUREMENT AND MANAGEMENT PROCESSES

Anecdotally, people in organizations do very often report that performance management reviews are handled ineffectively. However, some psychologists now extend this critique even further to suggest that the traditional processes of performance review are fundamentally flawed. Pulakos, Mueller-Hanson, and Arad (2019) provide a detailed review and critical position on traditional practices. They draw a number of conclusions about why performance management practices need to change and develop. For example, they highlight that the search for 'true' or accurate performance ratings may be futile because the very concept of a 'true' rating is potentially flawed. They point out that the relationship between leader (rater) and follower (ratee) affords a unique element, meaning that inevitably different raters see different levels of performance. They also highlight that raters are ineffective in making detailed or nuanced assessments.

Pulakos et al. (2019) press for a new approach to performance management in which the annualized review process is replaced with an alternative. This alternative, they propose, would be based on more continuous goal-setting, review and feedback. The process should be developmental, rather than confounded with pay and reward reviews that could otherwise derail processes of learning. Importantly, the role of the leader or manager becomes one of coach and facilitator rather than evaluator. This view is consistent with a general trend away from metric-driven performance evaluation in organizations towards more positive forms of management.

PIONEERING WORK PSYCHOLOGISTS

Professor Elaine D. Pulakos

Professor Elaine Pulakos has spent her career working with organizations to design and implement talent management systems and processes in the areas of performance management, leader and employee development, staffing, complex behaviour change, and adaptability. She also has extensive experience in organizational development and culture change. Her work has been recognized with several awards, including the Society for Industrial and Organizational Psychology's (SIOP) Distinguished Professional Contributions Award, the M. Scott Myers Award for Applied Research in the Workplace and the William A. Owens Scholarly Achievement Award for Best Professional Publication. Elaine is a Fellow of the American Psychological Association and SIOP, where she also served as President.

Professor Pulakos' research is pioneering in providing voice to the widespread dissatisfaction people hold about the process of annualized performance management. Her recent reviews of performance management research and practices spell out an alternative approach that would change how we think about performance evaluation in organizations. It would move processes from measurement focused to support focused and enable a continuous process of performance development.

One of the factors that give these observations and proposals distinctive weight is the work and practitioner experience that Professor Pulakos brings to them. These experiences show first-hand how the research that psychologists conduct may be applied, its limitations and boundaries. It is critical that the discipline maintains this input into scientific innovation and development.

Key example papers:

Pulakos, E. D., Arad, S., Donovan, M. A., & Plamondon, K. E. (2000). Adaptability in the workplace: Development of a taxonomy of adaptive performance. *Journal of Applied Psychology, 85*(4), 612–624.

Pulakos, E. D., Hanson, R. M., Arad, S., & Moye, N. (2015). Performance management can be fixed: An on-the-job experiential learning approach for complex behavior change. *Industrial and Organizational Psychology, 8*(1), 51–76.

Pulakos, E. D., Mueller-Hanson, R., & Arad, S. (2019). The evolution of performance management: Searching for value. *Annual Review of Organizational Psychology and Organizational Behavior, 6*, 249–271.

INTEGRATIVE AND ORGANIZATIONAL MODELS OF PERFORMANCE MANAGEMENT

In addition to perspectives on individual performance measurement and management, work and organizational psychologists are also increasingly interested in more macro and integrative perspectives on performance at work. This is in part due to challenges to the assumption that improving individual contributions at work will necessarily improve company-level performance (DeNisi & Smith, 2014), a link that remains somewhat elusive in the literature. We examine this research in this section and also consider how some of the core principles of performance management reviewed so far can be integrated in an overall approach.

ProMES: An integrative approach

The Productivity Measurement and Enhancement System (ProMES) is an integrative approach to improving the productivity of units in organizations through performance measurement and feedback (Pritchard, Harrell, DiazGranados, & Guzman, 2008). The system is built around an assumption that productivity represents how effectively an organization uses its resources to achieve its goals, and that performance management should involve effective measurement and intervention based on key indicators of productivity.

The model is distinctive in that it incorporates motivation theory such as expectancy and goal-setting theory to ensure that performance is guided and not just measured. The key steps in the ProMES approach are:

- Formation of a team to design the intervention based on the target unit and wider organization.
- Development and agreement of unit objectives and quantifiable measures of progress towards objectives (indicators). Indicators are objectively verifiable.
- Establishment of performance standards that determine the extent to which different levels of the indicator are effective.
- Measurement of the indicators and translation of measurement to effectiveness data by the work unit.
- Feedback of the measurement information to all members of the unit in writing.
- Communication and exploration of the feedback in meetings designed to promote continuous improvement.

The system builds in by design goal-setting (i.e. specifying standards to be attained and implicit guidance on what should and should not be done) and feedback that is specific, accurate and relevant to the work unit members. ProMES is also a good illustration of how performance management can take sound principles of theory, research and methodology and simultaneously make the approach to intervention bespoke or customized to specific settings and organizations (see also Schmerling & Scaduto, 2016). The empirical results supporting the potential performance benefits are also compelling. In a meta-analysis of multiple studies, Pritchard et al. (2008) reported overall improvements across 83 studies of around 1.44 standard deviations comparing baseline and post-feedback periods. This represents a very substantial unit-level improvement in productivity for the businesses implementing the system.

KEY THEME

Environmental sustainability – the role of performance management

One of the key ideas introduced in this chapter is that performance management is a critical process for enabling organizations to achieve goals and implement strategies. The key step is for organizational goals and objectives to be translated into unit, team and individual goals. Without this, it can be very hard for individuals to comprehend how they might contribute to the strategy.

Issues of environment and sustainable business are increasingly being addressed in organizational statements about mission, company culture and values, or strategies. This is not least because customers are more aware of the impact that business has on the environment and of the need for corporate social responsibility in this area more broadly. Companies that show a disregard for these issues may find people dissuaded from buying from them.

The weak link in these statements about sustainable business and management of environmental impact is how they are expressed in performance metrics and behaviours. If there is no clear inclusion of the issues in people's performance appraisal or objective setting, then it is all so much talk or lip service to the zeitgeist of socio-political progress.

The ProMES approach to performance measurement has at its heart the identification of real performance indicators that can be measured continuously and monitored. This could be applied to pro-environmental performance in teams, for example setting out indicators of environmental efficiency and resource usage. The major advantage of such an approach is that individual teams are tasked with developing the system of performance indicators and are therefore aware of their own impact. It is a significant step beyond the setting of vague organizational targets for resource consumption. The extent to which there is the will to make use of performance management and wider organizational systems to address issues of environment and sustainability probably gives an indication of the company's *real* appetite for change.

High-performance work systems

Research examining the impact of performance management of organization-level performance has captured performance management as a component of high-performance work systems (HPWS). These represent a 'system of HR practices designed to enhance employees' skills, commitment, and productivity in such a way that employees become a source of sustainable competitive advantage' (Datta, Guthrie, & Wright, 2005, p. 136).

This brings performance management together with the wider HR-related effort of people management for improved effectiveness. Research on the impact of HPWS is highly encouraging, with evidence of the impact of their implantation on the performance of companies (e.g. Combs, Liu, Hall, & Ketchen, 2006). This has led researchers to go on to examine the mechanisms by which they exert this effect. For example, Aryee, Walumbwa, Seidu, and Otaye (2012) found that HPWS had an impact on performance across 37 bank branches as a consequence of creating a greater climate of empowerment. People in the banks felt more empowered to perform and take decisions at work as a result of introducing HPWS, and this led to improved overall service performance and ultimately market performance. The effects are also observable at the individual level. So for example, Aryee, Walumbwa, Seidu, and Otaye (2016) reported that the extent to which HPWS were implemented impacted service orientation within business units, which in turn was observable in the individual behaviour of people in those units.

In summary, these studies show that performance management, when combined with other practices focused on HR performance, operates at different levels to produce enhanced effectiveness. On one hand, focusing on performance management of individuals does seem to have an impact on firm performance overall in these studies. Moreover, having effective systems also leads to observable effects in individual behaviour.

KEY THEME

Diversity and inclusion

High-performance work systems have been shown to be an effective integrated strategic approach to translating individual effort through to organizational performance. They illustrate how effective practices in the management of people in organizations have a real impact on how businesses perform. We have looked elsewhere in this book at the impact of practices designed to improve the effective management of diversity and promote inclusion, and concluded that, for example, diversity training works most effectively when it is embedded in a wider strategy and initiatives for diversity and inclusion. What impact do such strategies have on overall organization performance?

This was the question addressed by Armstrong, Flood, Guthrie, Liu, MacCurtain, and Mkamwa (2010), who looked at the impact of diversity and equality management systems (DEMS) on organization performance indicators. They theorized that DEMS would enhance performance beyond high-performance work systems because they would ensure that all employees had the opportunity to develop their skills, participate, feel valued and consequently be more motivated. They tested their theory by examining the performance of top companies in Ireland, and surveying their managers to find out about the management practices they employed.

DEMS were indicated by, for example, the proportion of employees receiving diversity training, the integration of diversity in strategy, and by monitoring recruitment, promotion and pay by gender, race, disability and ethnic background. The results were compelling. Even after controlling for the effects of high-performance work systems, the use of DEMS was associated with higher objective productivity,

continued

higher workplace innovation and lower employee turnover.

These results underline the business case for diversity and inclusion as part of an organization's strategy. Beyond general performance-oriented HR practices, specific actions to improve diversity management and inclusion do make an impact on organization-level performance.

POSITIVE WORK

An annual appraisal can be a worrying time for staff, who may be unsure about the kind of feedback they will receive. Performance measurement is necessarily evaluative and therefore will comprise both positive and developmental (or negative) information. Yet, there are so many opportunities for these processes to be very positive experiences that help people to realize their potential, grow and thrive in their work.

What are the collective lessons from the research and theory that we have reviewed in this chapter for making performance management positive?

1. Performance management is not simply performance appraisal. Measurement of performance is one aspect of performance management. It describes the past and, on its own, does not help people develop for the future. The impact of performance management is probably most compelling when it is combined with other positive HR systems like learning, training and development, such as in studies of HPWS.

2. Development is essential for performance improvement. When the conditions for positive performance change are conceptualized clearly, then the ideas of skills development and adjustment are the obvious mechanisms through which performance improves. This means that performance feedback must include some mechanism for exploring and discussing development and learning whether that is to close performance gaps or attain even higher standards.

3. Performance management could be most effective when staff are involved in the process rather than simply the targets. The ProMES approach (Pritchard et al., 2008) has the involvement of staff in the development of performance indicators at its heart. Moreover, they are involved in the measurement and feedback of performance information and in the problem-solving required to improve.

4. Honest and open communication is needed. The impact of feedback is dependent on many factors, but the presence of a feedback-rich environment and the credibility of the information resonate particularly. Where information is communicated clearly and non-judgementally, people are likely to feel a greater sense of fairness (see e.g. theories of organizational justice), and

when that communication on performance is simply part of a team's regular routines, there is less chance of people reacting badly and a greater chance that it is seen as constructive. It is a pity that many managers feel uncomfortable with rating performance negatively (evidenced in the tendency for performance ratings to be skewed towards higher ratings), as it would seem to indicate an environment in which constructive discussions about performance improvement are difficult. This is something that organizations need to address in terms of climate and culture to ensure that performance management makes a positive difference.

SUMMARY

Performance management in organizations is an important process by which organizational goals and strategies are achieved by using them to shape the objectives and management of individual behaviour. The process relies on effective goal-setting, measurement of job performance to determine whether people are performing in the required way, and feedback of that information to individuals. Performance management is inextricably linked to learning, training and development as a mechanism for supporting performance improvement where it is needed.

Examining performance management as a system or process helps to frame the core tasks involved. The system starts with objective- or goal-setting, and there is a huge body of literature on the value of goal-setting and how it can be implemented most effectively.

Performance measurement can take a variety of forms. Basic conceptualizations of job performance are based on objective data captured by organizations, but much more information can be examined and incorporated into measurement by focusing on performance behaviour. To help structure assessment of performance, work psychologists have developed broad models of job performance dimensions (notably task performance and OCB). They have also worked alongside other practitioners to develop models of job competencies.

The process of measuring job performance is synonymous with the term 'performance appraisal', and there are a number of methods that can be used to measure people's performance at work.

The impact of feedback in the process depends on the manner in which it is delivered, the organizational environment, and on the person giving the feedback. Work psychologists have considered all of these influences on feedback processes.

We began the chapter by considering how the big challenges that humans face require achievement of collective goals, which in turn are achieved by the contributions of individuals. Performance measurement and management are bridging processes in work psychology that sit very clearly at the intersection of work and organizational psychology. On the 'work' side, they contribute to understanding about how to select and develop people, and about how to manage organizational behaviour. On the 'organizational' side, they add significantly to a systems view of organizations and the way that people operate with them. Integrative studies of performance management as part of systems like ProMES and wider HPWS underline the potential impact of effective performance management. For practitioners, these are areas of great need in many organizations, and the theories, models and techniques identified in this chapter give plenty of guidance on how more organizations could improve and enhance the measurement and management of people's performance at work.

DISCUSSION QUESTIONS

1 An employee's appraisal has identified that they would benefit from development in interpersonal sensitivity. What should be done next?

2 Is 'no performance management' better than 'bad performance management'?

3 If a CEO wanted their company to be more innovative, how could they use performance management to achieve it? What else could they consider?

4 Is organizational citizenship behaviour important in all jobs? Why?

5 What are the issues that a manager should keep in mind before introducing multi-source feedback?

6 Is performance management worthless without effective performance measurement? Why?

7 How could performance management be implemented most effectively in innovation-driven businesses operating in fast-changing environments?

FURTHER READING

Budhwar, P. S., & DeNisi, A. S. (2008). *Performance management systems: A global perspective*. London, England: Routledge.

Denisi, A. S., & Murphy, K. R. (2017). Performance appraisal and performance management: 100 years of progress? *Journal of Applied Psychology, 102*(3), 421–433.

Pulakos, E. D., Mueller-Hanson, R., & Arad, S. (2019). The evolution of performance management: Searching for value. *Annual Review of Organizational Psychology and Organizational Behavior, 6*, 249–271.

REFERENCES

Adler, S., Campion, M., Colquitt, A., Grubb, A., Murphy, K., Ollander-Krane, R., & Pulakos, E. D. (2016). Getting rid of performance ratings: Genius or folly? A debate. *Industrial and Organizational Psychology, 9*(2), 219–252.

Aguinis, H. (2009). *Performance management*. Upper Saddle River, NJ: Pearson/Prentice-Hall.

Aryee, S., Walumbwa, F. O., Seidu, E. Y., & Otaye, L. E. (2012). Impact of high-performance work systems on individual-and branch-level performance: Test of a multilevel model of intermediate linkages. *Journal of Applied Psychology, 97*(2), 287.

Aryee, S., Walumbwa, F. O., Seidu, E. Y., & Otaye, L. E. (2016). Developing and leveraging human capital resource to promote service quality: Testing a theory of performance. *Journal of Management, 42*(2), 480–499.

Austin, J. T., & Villanova, P. (1992). The criterion problem 1917–1992. *Journal of Applied Psychology, 77*, 836–874.

Bandura, A. (1997). *Self-efficacy: The exercise of control*. New York, NY: Freeman.

Bartram, D. (2005). The Great Eight competencies: A criterion-centric approach to validation. *Journal of Applied Psychology, 90*(6), 1185.

Borman, W. C. (1979). Format and training effects on rating accuracy and rater errors. *Journal of Applied Psychology, 64*, 410–421.

Borman, W. C., & Brush, D. H. (1993). More progress toward a taxonomy of managerial performance requirements. *Human Performance, 6*, 1–21.

Borman, W. C., & Motowidlo, S. J. (1993). Expanding the criterion domain to include elements of contextual performance. In N. Schmitt & W. C. Borman (Eds.), *Personnel selection in organizations* (pp. 71–98). San Francisco, CA: Jossey-Bass.

Borman, W. C., & Motowidlo, S. J. (1997). Task performance and contextual performance: The meaning for personnel selection research. *Human Performance, 10*(2), 99–109.

Brett, J. F., & Atwater, L. E. (2001). 360° feedback: Accuracy, reactions and perceptions of usefulness. *Journal of Applied Psychology, 85*(5), 930–942.

Campbell, J. P. (1990). Modelling the performance prediction problem in industrial and organizational psychology. In M. D. Dunnette & L. M. Hough (Eds.), *Handbook of industrial and organizational psychology* (pp. 687–731). Palo Alto, CA: Consulting Psychologists Press.

Campion, M. A., Fink, A. A., Ruggeberg, B. J., Carr, L., Phillips, G. M., & Odman, R. B. (2011). Doing competencies well: Best practices in competency modeling. *Personnel Psychology, 64*(1), 225–262.

Coleman, V. I., & Borman, W. C. (2000). Investigating the underlying structure of the citizenship performance domain. *Human Resource Management Review, 10*, 25–44.

Combs, J., Liu, Y., Hall, A., & Ketchen, D. (2006). How much do high-performance work practices matter? A meta-analysis of their effects on organizational performance. *Personnel Psychology, 59*(3), 501–528.

Conway, J. M., & Huffcutt, A. I. (1997). Psychometric properties of multi-source performance ratings: A meta-analysis of subordinate, supervisor, peer, and self-ratings. *Human Performance, 10*, 331–360.

Dalal, R. S. (2005). A meta-analysis of the relationship between organizational citizenship behaviour and counterproductive work behaviour. *Journal of Applied Psychology, 90*, 1241–1255.

Datta, D. K., Guthrie, J. P., & Wright, P. M. (2005). Human resource management and labor productivity: Does industry matter? *Academy of Management Journal, 48*(1), 135–145.

Dawis, R. V., & Lofquist, L. H. (1984). *A psychological theory of work adjustment.* Minneapolis: University of Minnesota Press.

DeNisi, A., & Smith, C. E. (2014). Performance appraisal, performance management, and firm-level performance: A review, a proposed model, and new directions for future research. *The Academy of Management Annals, 8*(1), 127–179.

DeNisi, A. S., & Murphy, K. R. (2017). Performance appraisal and performance management: 100 years of progress? *Journal of Applied Psychology, 102*(3), 421.

Dweck, C. S. (1986). Motivational processes affecting learning. *American Psychologist, 41*, 1040–1048.

Facteau, J. D., & Craig, B. S. (2001). Are performance appraisal ratings from different rating sources comparable? *Journal of Applied Psychology, 86*(2), 215–227.

Fletcher, C. (2001). Performance appraisal and management: The developing research agenda. *Journal of Occupational and Organizational Psychology, 74*(4), 473–487.

Fletcher, C. (2008). *Appraisal, feedback, and development.* London, England: Routledge.

Goffin, R. D., & Anderson, D. W. (2007). The self-rater's personality and self-other disagreement in multi-source performance ratings. *Journal of Managerial Psychology, 22*, 271–289.

Greguras, G. J., Robie, C., Schleicher, D. J., & Goff III, M. (2003). A field study of the effects of rating purpose on the quality of multi-source ratings. *Personnel Psychology, 56*(1), 1–21.

Hanson, M. A., & Borman, W. C. (2006). Citizenship performance: An integrative review and motivational analysis. In W. Bennett, Jr., C. E. Lance, & D. J. Woehr (Eds.), *Performance measurement: Current perspectives and future challenges* (pp. 141–174). Mahwah, NJ: LEA.

Ilgen, D. R., Fisher, C. D., & Taylor, S. M. (1979). Consequences of individual feedback on behaviour in organizations. *Journal of Applied Psychology, 64*, 349–371.

Judge, T. A., & Zapata, C. P. (2015). The person–situation debate revisited: Effect of situation strength and trait activation on the validity of the Big Five personality traits in predicting job performance. *Academy of Management Journal, 58*(4), 1149–1179.

Kelloway, K., Loughlin, C., Barling, J., & Nault, A. (2002). Counterproductive and organizational citizenship behaviours: Separate but related constructs. *International Journal of Selection and Assessment, 10*(1–2), 143–151.

Kinicki, A., Prussia, G., Wu, B., & McKee-Ryan, F. (2004). A covariance structure analysis of employees' response to performance feedback. *Journal of Applied Psychology, 89*, 1057–1069.

Kluger, A. N., & DeNisi, A. (1996). The effects of feedback interventions on performance: A historical review, meta-analysis and a preliminary feedback intervention theory. *Psychological Bulletin, 119*, 254–284.

Locke, E. A., & Latham, G. P. (1990). *A theory of goal setting and task performance.* Englewood Cliffs, NJ: Prentice Hall.

Locke, E. A., & Latham, G. P. (2002). Building a practically useful theory of goal setting and task motivation: A 35-year odyssey. *American Psychologist, 57*(9), 705–717.

Maurer, T. J., Raju, N. S., & Collins, W. C. (1998). Peer and subordinate performance appraisal measurement equivalence. *Journal of Applied Psychology, 83*(5), 693–702.

Motowidlo, S. J., Borman, W. C., & Schmitt, M. J. (1997). A theory of individual differences in task and contextual performance. *Human Performance, 10*(2), 71–83.

Motowidlo, S. J., & Van Scotter, J. R. (1994). Evidence that task performance should be distinguished from the contextual performance. *Journal of Applied Psychology, 79*, 475–80.

Murphy, K. R., & DeNisi, A. S. (2008). A model of the appraisal process. In P. S. Budhwar & A. S. DeNisi (Eds.), *Performance management systems: A global perspective* (pp. 81–96). London, England: Routledge.

Organ, D. W. (1988). *Organizational citizenship behaviour: The good soldier syndrome.* Lexington, MA: Heath.

Organ, D. W. (1997). Organizational citizenship behaviour: It's construct clean-up time. *Human Performance, 10*(2), 85–97.

Podsakoff, P. M., MacKenzie, S. B., Paine, J. B., & Bachrach, D. G. (2000). Organizational citizenship behaviors: A critical review of the theoretical and empirical literature and suggestions for future research. *Journal of Management, 26*, 513–563.

Pritchard, R. D., Harrell, M. M., DiazGranados, D., & Guzman, M. J. (2008). The productivity measurement and enhancement system: A meta-analysis. *Journal of Applied Psychology, 93*(3), 540.

Pulakos, E. D., Mueller-Hanson, R., & Arad, S. (2019). The evolution of performance management: Searching for value. *Annual Review of Organizational Psychology and Organizational Behavior, 6*, 249–271.

Rudolph, C. W., Katz, I. M., Lavigne, K. N., & Zacher, H. (2017). Job crafting: A meta-analysis of relationships with individual differences, job characteristics, and work outcomes. *Journal of Vocational Behavior, 102*, 112–138.

Schmerling, D., & Scaduto, A. (2016). Use the best; leave the rest: The Productivity Measurement and Enhancement System (ProMES) for performance ratings. *Industrial and Organizational Psychology, 9*(2), 305–309.

Seijts, G. H., & Latham, G. P. (2001). The effect of distal learning, outcome and proximal goals on a moderately complex task. *Journal of Organizational Behaviour, 22*, 291–302.

Smith, C. A., Organ, D. W., & Near, J. P. (1983). Organizational citizenship behaviour: Its nature and antecedents. *Journal of Applied Psychology, 68*, 653–663.

Smither, J. W., London, M., & Reilly, R. (2005). Does performance improve following multi-source feedback? A theoretical model, meta-analysis and review of empirical findings. *Personnel Psychology, 58*, 33–66.

Soderquist, K. E., Papalexandris, A., Ioannou, G., & Prastacos, G. (2010). From task-based to competency-based: A typology and process supporting a critical HRM transition. *Personnel Review, 39*(3), 325–346.

Sturman, M. C., Cheramie, R. A., & Cashen, L. H. (2005). The consistency, stability and test-retest reliability of employee job performance: A meta-analytic review of longitudinal findings. *Journal of Applied Psychology, 90*, 269–283.

Tannenbaum, S. I. (2006). Applied measurement: Practical issues and challenges. In W. Bennett, Jr., C. E. Lance, & D. J. Woehr (Eds.), *Performance measurement: Current perspectives and future challenges* (pp. 297–320). Mahwah, NJ: LEA.

Tett, R. P., & Burnett, D. D. (2003). A personality trait-based interactionist model of job performance. *Journal of Applied Psychology, 88*(3), 500.

Tett, R. P., Guterman, H. A., Bleier, A., & Murphy, P. J. (2000). Development and content validation of a hyperdimensional taxonomy of managerial competence. *Human Performance, 13*, 205–251.

Thayer, P. W. (1992). Construct validation: Do we understand our criteria? *Human Performance, 5*, 97–108.

Viswesvaran, C., & Ones, D. S. (2000). Perspectives on models of job performance. *International Journal of Selection and Assessment, 8*, 216–26.

Viswesvaran, C., Ones, D. S., & Schmidt, F. L. (1996). Comparative analyses of the reliability of job performance ratings. *Journal of Applied Psychology, 81*, 557–574.

Viswesvaran, C., Schmidt, F. L., & Ones, D. S. (2002). The moderating influence of job performance dimensions on convergence of supervisory and peer ratings of job performance: Unconfounding construct-level convergence and rating difficulty. *Journal of Applied Psychology, 87*, 345–354.

Viswesvaran, C., Schmidt, F. L., & Ones, D. S. (2005). Is there a general factor in ratings of job performance? A meta-analytic framework for disentangling substantive and error influences. *Journal of Applied Psychology, 90*, 108–131.

Voskuijl, O. F., & Evers, A. (2008). Job analysis and competency modelling. In S. Cartwright & C. L. Cooper (Eds.), *The Oxford handbook of personnel psychology* (pp. 139–163). New York, NY: Oxford University Press.

Williams, L. J., & Anderson, S. E. (1991). Job satisfaction and organizational commitment as predictors of organizational citizenship and in-role behaviours. *Journal of Management, 17*, 418–428.

Woods, S. A. (2008). Job performance measurement: The elusive relationship between job performance and job satisfaction. In S. Cartwright & L. Cooper (Eds.), *The Oxford handbook of personnel psychology.* Oxford, England: Oxford University Press.

Woods, S., Wille, B., Wu, C. H., Lievens, F., & De Fruyt, F. (2019). The influence of work on personality trait development: The Demands–Affordances TrAnsactional (DATA) model, an integrative review, and research agenda. *Journal of Vocational Behavior*.

CHAPTER 8
CAREERS AND CAREER MANAGEMENT

> ### LEARNING OBJECTIVES
> - Describe the changing nature of careers in the 21st century.
> - Describe and critique developmental theories of careers and the role of work in identity development. Understand person–environment fit perspectives on careers, and especially research on vocational interests and environments.
> - Understand how gender, cultural, employability and other social factors influence career development.
> - Understand how theories and models of career interests and development can be applied in career management interventions to build positive environments for growth and thriving.

Careers might be thought of as the stories of our working lives. They represent a major part of our lives and, to differing degrees for people, are indicators of our successes – not just in terms of monetary or status outcomes, but also in respect of our own perceptions of whether we are achieving what we wanted in life. The story analogy for careers is a good one, and we can retrospectively look back over our decisions, the chances we took and missed, the rewards we gained as well as mistakes we made. Careers are good stories, which have moments of excitement, periods of prolonged happiness and usually some tough times marked by challenge, anxiety and, at times, disappointment. Almost like a novel, only with you as the heroic lead character.

What is your career story? How did you decide what kind of discipline you would like to work in? What kind of issues influenced your decision to work for a particular organization or in a particular career? Why did you decide to study, or learn about, work and organizational psychology by reading this book? These are all important questions, and work psychologists are concerned with understanding the answers to them. This chapter is about careers and their management. The chapter covers topics of career development, considering how theories of career development apply in the new world of work. The chapter also looks at career decision-making, and in particular at the development and influence of vocational interests and the interplay of individual differences and careers.

WORK, LIFE AND CAREERS IN THE 21ST CENTURY

Work represents a very substantial aspect of the social fabric of our lives. For example, social investment theory (Roberts, Wood, & Smith, 2005) proposes that investment in social institutions such as work shapes our development, and Warr (2008) argues that work provides key ingredients for a happy life, such as social interaction, opportunity for competence and status.

A stark representation of these propositions is what happens when people lose the influence of work in their lives and become unemployed. It has long been known, and demonstrated in research, that there is a substantial negative impact of unemployment on psychological well-being (see e.g. Clark & Georgellis, 2013; Young, 2012). Job loss is a dramatic life event that can have devastating effects on long-term happiness.

What is remarkable, however, is the evidence about what *restores* well-being after unemployment. In a study in the UK, Zhou, Zou, Woods, and Wu (2019) analyzed the well-being trajectories of people pre-, during and post-unemployment. They were able to differentiate what happens to people who, after becoming unemployed, either become re-employed or move into economic inactivity (i.e. leave work permanently). They found that only re-employment restored well-being in full. That means that work clearly provides something unique in our lives that cannot be easily substituted by other activity or life resources.

Much has been written about the changing context of work in the later part of the 20th century and the early 21st century. These important years have indeed witnessed striking changes to the landscape of organizations and to the jobs that people perform within them. Writers have tended to agree on some of the drivers of these changes (Kidd, 2002). Broadly, they comprise:

- Globalization and the internationalization of organizations and markets. Organizations have been required to change in order to meet the challenges of operating in many countries around the world. The pace of globalization has meant that the pace of organizational change has also increased. Employees have found themselves working within new organizational structures, designed to meet these challenges.

- Technological changes and innovations. In order to support rapid change, and to ensure competitiveness, organizations have developed and adopted new technologies. Technology has facilitated global working, so that people working in different countries can communicate and share ideas. Technology has also allowed people to work flexibly more easily. The most extreme example of this to date is the gig economy, which has enabled people to effectively work freelance in a variety of occupations, being connected to customers and clients instantaneously through the internet and digital connectivity. Looking back a little further, technology has completely changed the face of manufacturing, to the point that human input into manufacturing has become less and less important. The continued growth in robotics and artificial intelligence will make this kind of change increasingly prevalent in the future.

- Changes to employment law and regulations. Important changes to the relationship between employer and employee have occurred in the past 20–30 years. In the UK, the power of the trade unions has diminished, and consequently the enforcement of worker rights is a less pressing issue for many organizations (an issue exacerbated by the extension of the qualifying period for basic worker rights). This means that jobs are seen as more temporary, less secure and subject to fewer benefits. As highlighted above, this is a critical issue in the gig economy. In the past, lower security was juxtaposed against a steadily increasing minimum wage, whereby employees are essentially asked to accept higher remuneration in lieu of other benefits. However, this trend is no longer the case, especially since the 2008 financial crash and subsequent global recession.

- Changes to organizational structures. The biggest trend in organizations in recent history is restructuring, most notably de-layering and downsizing. Organizations have changed to become flatter and leaner. Such changes have important effects on people's careers. Leaving aside the associated increases in workload that accompany reductions in staffing levels, de-layering and downsizing inevitably result in fewer opportunities for promotion (because there are fewer levels within the organization), and require people to perform job tasks that are more diverse (because increasingly complex job tasks must be performed by fewer people). Employees should therefore expect fewer promotions and more horizontal moves within an organization, or across organizations, and should expect to be required to utilize a broader range of skills than previously.

Collectively, these issues mean that the traditional 'job for life' is less common in the majority of industries, and this has heralded changes in the mutual expectations of employers and employees. A career therefore is much more than being *employed* by an organization through life. Vocational psychology is the study of careers and the role work plays in development, and this discipline has approached the examination of careers through two main lenses: development and person–environment fit (see e.g. Wang & Wanberg, 2017). We review each of these in the next sections.

THE DEVELOPMENT OF CAREERS OVER TIME

Careers are metaphorically like stories, autobiographies created by individuals through their career aspirations and decisions. The nature and contents of career stories are inevitably about development, from childhood, to adulthood and eventually to old age. Psychologists are interested in this development, and developmental career theories aim to identify specific stages of careers.

Super's theory is arguably the most influential among the developmental theories, being focused entirely on career development rather than adult development generally (although if you wish to read further, also refer to the theories of Erikson and Levinson). In its original form, Super's theory proposed a set of five stages set around specific age ranges. They are shown in Table 8.1.

Table 8.1 The Five Stages of Super's Career Development Theory	
Growth (0–14)	The key phase for the development of career interests, capabilities and personality traits. At this stage, young people are starting to think about the kind of work that appeals to them.
Exploration (15–24)	This stage involves exploring the world of work and further development of the self-concept and identity, identifying jobs or roles that are consistent with it.
Establishment (25–44)	At this stage, the person finds a job or career that matches their identity and interests, and seeks to make a mark in their chosen field.
Maintenance (45–64)	Having established a position in a chosen field, the person now seeks to retain that position in the face of new challenges, such as changes in technology.
Decline/disengagement (65+)	Here the person begins to disengage from the work environment, focusing more on non-work interests. Retirement follows.

The theory is criticized on several grounds. First, it appears to be too inflexible about assigning ages to the five stages. In truth, however, the ages were deemed to be guidelines, and although Super persisted with organizing his stages across the lifespan (e.g. Super & Hall, 1978), he also acknowledged that the stages might apply to people at a variety of ages. Consider the person who opts for a career change during their 30s or 40s. Such a person might establish themselves within their new career later in life. Likewise, the decline stage is certainly unlikely to remain applicable to people aged 65 or over. We know that people are already deciding, and in some cases being forced, to work until age 70 or even later. In summary, it is the stages themselves, rather than the associated ages, that are the important components.

A second criticism is that, as with other developmental theories, Super focused primarily on male careers as the basis for his theory. There appears to be little consideration of career challenges faced by women (e.g. career breaks for having children), and in this sense, the theory is limited.

An interesting interpretation of Super's theory is presented by Savickas (2002, 2005). Adopting a social constructionist perspective, Savickas proposes that career development is triggered by social environmental changes (for example, societal expectations about how people develop during the course of their lives) rather than an internal impetus to develop. The criticism here is that Super's theory seems to neglect social context. In a similar vein, Fouad (2007) highlights that progressing through the various stages of a career depends on the opportunities and resources (skills, abilities, knowledge and external resources such as financial and social support) available to a person, and this varies in terms of associated ages for different people. This explains why some individuals seem to establish themselves more quickly in careers than others. It is a question of adaptability rather than maturity.

These two themes (the influences of social contextual factors, and also individual differences, on career development) are explored further by Woods, Lievens, De Fruyt, and Wille (2013). They presented a dynamic developmental model (DDM) of personality and work, in which personality traits dynamically influence, and are reciprocally influenced by, work activity and experience. In exploring the influences of individual differences on working life, they adopted Super's framework to consider the changing contexts of work over the course of a career.

Super's framework is appropriate in this regard because it reflects normative developmental challenges. That is to say that embedded within it are challenges that people face in the course of growing up, and despite changes to demography and lifestyle, people and society are both stubbornly traditional and therefore engage in social institutions at roughly the same times. So, for example, people are educated through to around age 18–25, and become increasingly specialized in that education. This necessitates their exploration of the working world, followed by entering a career and establishing themselves within it. That establishment is often fuelled by settling down and having children, which places greater financial burden on people, driving them to advance and maximize earnings. These demands eventually plateau, leading to the maintenance phase.

Super's stages may therefore be seen to represent the contexts against which career development plays out. In Woods et al.'s (2013) model, the course of career development is dynamically influenced by individual differences. At different stages, particular traits and characteristics are activated in response to contextual demands, influencing career and work outcomes, which may in turn give advantage or, in some cases, hindrance to progression (see also Chapter 2 for more discussion of these mechanisms).

> **DISCUSS WITH A COLLEAGUE**
>
> Spend ten minutes individually writing down in note form your career story to date on a blank sheet of paper. Think about the decisions you made at various stages of your education or career that have brought you to this point. What are your aspirations? Where do you see your career progressing from here? Have your aspirations changed at any point?

Work identity

Another perspective on the developmental impact of work and careers is the study of work identity. Identity is concerned with the fundamental question of who we feel we really are (Ashforth & Schinoff, 2016). Selenko et al. (2018) observe that work and identity are inextricably connected, in part because people spend a significant part of their life at work, and because work enables them to 'be and become someone'. Work is a place where we figure out what we are able to do, developing self-efficacy as a consequence (Bandura, 1982). Moreover, work fosters a sense of social inclusion, of belonging to society (Sen, 2000).

Our careers also help define our sense of self. We often tell people on first meeting what we do at work, our profession. It serves to indicate the social groups to which we belong, defining our place in society (Ashforth, Harrison, & Corley, 2008). Once developed, identity also influences the goals people set for themselves and the expectations and values they form (e.g. Miscenko & Day, 2016; van Knippenberg, 2000). Identity also matters for what people do and how they feel at work, determining motivation and performance (e.g. van Knippenberg, 2000), attitudes (van Dick, van Knippenberg, Kerschreiter, Hertel, & Wieseke, 2008) and well-being (Haslam, Jetten, Postmes, & Haslam, 2009).

In their review, Selenko et al. (2018) presented three ways in which work identity might develop through working life:

1 Passively, incrementally: the experience of work leads to gradual development of identity over time.
2 Actively, incrementally: people take decisions about careers, choosing pathways that fit with their identity and its associated values.
3 Actively, transformatively: people making choices that they want to be someone different, change their identity and pursue a different career pathway.

Work identity offers distinct conceptual advantages as a foundation for studying careers. First, it is individually focused; it enables consideration of the specific pathways of individual people rather than populations as a whole (such as in Super's theory). Second, it is able to adapt to sociohistorical context. For example, Kahn (2007) observed a trend for people to strive for meaningful work that fits their passion, something which is ever more the case in people entering the world of work. Selenko et al. (2018) consider the role of identity in new forms of atypical employment like the gig economy. Third, it enables the study of careers to be bridged to other areas of study, such as personality development, attitude formation and change, and social identity.

KEY THEME

Work psychology in the digital economy

The digital economy has given rise to a whole new range of jobs that are enabled through digital platforms and online connectivity. This has been referred to as the gig economy. Gig economy jobs are usually precarious in the sense that they are not tied to an employer, and the worker does not have employed status. Instead, they are classed as freelance, contracted to provide services to a digital platform host that connects them with prospective clients. Key examples are Uber, Grab, Hermes and Deliveroo. A critical issue for workers in these kinds of jobs concerns their access to basic employment rights. For example, in 2019, Hermes committed to classing its couriers as employees, offering minimum wages and holiday pay (UK *Guardian*, 2019).

However, there are also deeper psychological implications of such work in the digital economy that serves to illustrate the transformative effect that it is having on work and careers. Selenko et al. (2018) consider the issue of work identity for those in atypical employment. Atypical employment is characterized as, for example, ultra-short-term, zero-hours, on-call and digital platform managed. Selenko and colleagues point out that these forms of employment are absent from traditional studies of work identity. However, there are very particular issues that apply to people in these kinds of employment. For example, holding multiple forms of employment may lead to a fragmented sense of identity and working self. For example, a person might have followed a business degree, work part-time in retail and as a freelance courier for financial survival. How would such an individual perceive their work identity? The answer to this question is important because of the impact it has on well-being, self-esteem and future career decisions. While these atypical forms of employment provide autonomy, they also provide less of the positive elements of work that contribute to psychological health (e.g. time structure, security, opportunity for social relationships, and competence). Given the relative novelty of these forms of atypical employment, it could be possible that seeds are being sown for long-term impact on psychological health. It is a further illustration of how the digital world is transforming and evolving work in ways that we do not always anticipate.

Career moves: Job transition

So far we have discussed perspectives on career development as a whole. These theories tend not to focus on the individual jobs that make up a person's career, however. On this issue, theory and literature on job transition and socialization are relevant. Work-role transitions are broadly conceptualized as being a move in or out of a job or role, moves between jobs or alterations to work duties and responsibilities (Nicholson & West, 1988). Transitions might refer to entering into or retiring from employment, changing organizations, taking a new job, whether that be a promotion, demotion or sideways move, and changes to job tasks that are not necessarily associated with changes of employer or job titles.

Contemplating all of these potential work transitions, Nicholson (1990) put forward a flexible theory that helps to frame and understand the challenges and stages that people progress through during transitions. The transition cycle is shown in Figure 8.1 and comprises four steps.

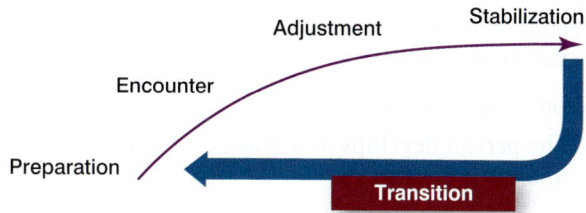

Figure 8.1   The transition cycle

1. **Preparation.** This stage refers to the period prior to entering a new job role. You may have your own experiences of starting a new job or role, and anecdotally one hears about organizations that provide very thorough guidance for new starters and those that provide very little. This stage involves the formation of perceptions by the individual about what the new role will be like.

2. **Encounter.** The second stage in the cycle refers to the first days and weeks in the new role. This involves a sort of reality check, by which the individual quickly learns about the basic characteristics of the job and the group of others that he or she will work with, inevitably comparing reality with previously held perceptions.

3. **Adjustment.** At this stage, the individual draws on the knowledge of the work and social environment that they have accumulated and develops their own style of fulfilling the work role. The individual might decide to conform to the requirements of the role as described by the organization, or to innovate and find their own way.

4. **Stabilization.** In this fourth stage, the work associated with the job role becomes routine, with the person becoming a veteran or 'old hand' at the job. This stage can prompt further job role change if the stabilization is associated with boredom.

The transition cycle is a very useful framework for understanding a variety of organizational behaviours, bringing our understanding of careers and career management closer to more mainstream management literature. One of the first important influences on the reaction of individuals to their job and organization is socialization. Fisher describes five learning outcomes of socialization:

- preliminary learning
- learning to adapt to the organization
- learning to function in the workgroup
- learning to do the job
- personal learning.

During the preparation and encounter stages of the transition cycle particularly, individuals acquire a high volume of information about their new work environment. Formal induction processes help to facilitate socialization, but more powerful is the informal learning that people acquire from their new colleagues and managers (Nicholson, 1990). The initial weeks in a new job role run the risk of being a period of disillusionment (Nicholson & Arnold, 1991), if the initial perceptions of the new employee turn out to be false or unrealistic. Socialization research has more recently examined the influence of individual differences such as proactive personality traits on the process and outcomes of socialization (e.g. Ashforth, Sluss, & Saks, 2007). The strategies that people adopt in respect of their first experiences in a new role do have an effect on socialization outcomes. Such outcomes include effective job performance and organizational commitment on the positive side, but also stress and negative well-being, turnover, disengagement or other escape strategies on the negative side – reason enough for organizations to do as much as they can to help new or existing employees to adjust to new work roles.

The transition cycle also tells us something about innovation at work. Schein (1971) identifies three approaches to adjusting to new work:

- Custodian: The person delivers work according to the formal job description.
- Content innovator: The person develops new ways of delivering the duties and outcomes associated with the role.
- Role innovator: The person rethinks or reshapes the work role and its position in the organization, including the deliverable responsibilities.

These three potential approaches represent adjustment strategies, and individuals might be influenced by their early encounters with the organization and aspects of its culture. Gabarro (1987) describes how initial innovation in a work role is aimed at 'taking hold' of the role. This is followed by a period of immersion where a person learns and reflects the detail of the job, before further 'reshaping' innovation takes place.

The models we have covered in this chapter lead us to think about how the process of lifelong development leads people to follow particular career paths. Theories about transition and socialization help us to understand how people navigate the various junctions and changes of direction on their journey. One of the biggest transitions that all people have to make at some point in their career is *out* of the work. Retirement brings its own benefits and challenges, and is currently a hot topic for economists and politicians as the population gets older and the proportion of retirees increases. The view of work psychologists is discussed in Box 8.1.

BOX 8.1
Retirement

Retirement represents a transition for people out of the working world. Unlike unemployment, retirement is a socially sanctioned move out of work (Warr, 2008), supported by an infrastructure of social and financial benefits, the latter of which are usually tied to success during people's careers, supplemented by government input that differs across countries. Retirement is also a choice, however, and has recently been framed as a part of career decision-making (Beehr & Bennett, 2015). Indeed, there are very regular normative motivations for retirement, such as health and family care needs, attitudes towards careers and work, and a desire to have more leisure time (Wang & Wanberg, 2017).

Retirement is part of the traditional development of careers across the lifespan, and is usually linked to age. In the UK, for example, traditional retirement ages were 65 for men and 60 for women, but these have risen because of the financial strain on pension schemes resulting from people living longer lives. Work Psychologists have been interested in the effects of retiring on health and well-being. There has been a prevalent myth over the years that retirement is bad for health and well-being (Ekerdt, 1987), but as with all such phenomena, the picture is not that simple. Work does provide important sources of life satisfaction (Warr, 2008), but that does not automatically mean that retirement is damaging in the long term.

There are positive changes in lifestyle that can result from retirement, including decreased stress and increased physical activity (Midanik, Soghikian, Ransom, & Tekawa, 1995). Some sources report increased well-being resulting from retirement (e.g. Kim & Feldman, 2000), but others report no differences between the well-being and physical health of retired and non-retired people of the same age (Ekerdt, Baden, Bossé, & Dibbs, 1983; Warr, Butcher, Robertson, & Callinan, 2004). One of the reasons for this is that people are likely to experience retirement in different ways. For example, Herzog, House, and Morgan (1991) found that physical and psychological health deteriorated if the decision to retire was constrained by non-controllable external factors. People who were forced to retire for some reason tended to experience retirement negatively. Warr et al. (2004) reported that people who were more committed to work before retirement tended to have lower happiness and well-being in retirement.

Retirement need not be the end of a person's career though, and it is common for retired people to return to work in some form, leading to continued growth and renewal (Wang, Olson, & Shultz, 2013). Such bridge employment is typically part-time, in a different organization to previous employment, and paid less than previous jobs (Warr, 2008). There is evidence that people who take bridge employment in retirement are more satisfied with life and with their retirement (Kim & Feldman, 2000), but this is also likely to be moderated by contextual factors.

PERSON–ENVIRONMENT FIT PERSPECTIVES

Super's career development framework describes an exploration phase in which individual differences in self-concept and job interests are formed, followed by choice of a particular career area and establishment within it. The development of individual differences in work preferences and vocational interests is a crucial step in determining how later career stages progress.

The person–environment fit (PE fit) perspective is concerned with the extent to which individual differences and preferences fit with the work environment. This line of research and practice has a long history in work, organizational and vocational psychology, founded in the work of Parsons (1909). Since then, the general concept has been developed to identify four main levels of fit, namely job, vocational, team/group and organizational (Su, Murdock, & Rounds, 2015):

- Person–job fit (PJ fit). The extent to which a person feels that their skills and characteristics are a fit to their job.
- Person–vocation fit (PV fit). The extent to which people's job interests match the characteristics of their occupation.

- Person–group fit (PG fit). The extent to which people feel that they are compatible with their team in terms of their contribution of skills and competencies, or in terms of the climate of the group (Anderson & West, 1996).
- Person–organization fit (PO fit). The extent to which a person feels that their values are matched well with their organization's culture.

The effects of PE fit on personal outcomes have been established in research and meta-analyses (e.g. Kristof-Brown, Zimmerman, & Johnson, 2005). Such studies show that attaining PE fit at work is associated with key positive outcomes, and what is striking is the consistency of the effects. Examining PJ, PO and PG fit, Kristof-Brown et al. (2005) reported that all were associated with job satisfaction, commitment, intention to leave (negatively), performance and organizational identification, among other criteria.

A distinction in the definition of fit is between complementary and supplementary fit. Complementary fit represents the degree to which individuals have the skills and abilities to meet the demands of the environment (Muchinsky & Monahan, 1987) and also the degree to which the environment meets the needs of the individual (Kristof, 1996). Supplementary fit represents simple congruence or similarity between person and environment.

Beyond these empirical effects of PE fit, its explanatory function has been utilized in multiple theories relevant to the study of personal and trait development. For example, at a career level, Super (1990) emphasizes the long-term career developmental trajectories as people optimize their fit to self-concept. At an organizational level, Schneider's ASA model elaborates how people are attracted to specific kinds of organizational cultures, selecting into those congruent environments.

This brings us to the major area of interest for work psychologists in respect of PE fit, careers and career management: the study of vocational interests. Work Psychologists have conducted influential work in this field, seeking to understand why people are attracted to particular kinds of job, and how those interests develop.

Take a moment to think about your ideal job. What kind of work would it involve? What would be some of the key features of that job? It is likely that the ideal job you have identified reflects your particular occupational interests, as does your choice of degree course, and learning activities. Occupational interests begin to develop early on, for most people during childhood and their education (Gottfredson, 1981), and remain relatively constant through their working life.

Recall from Chapter 2 that one of the key contributions of psychology to understanding individual differences is the construction of models and frameworks that help to explain the complexities of differences between people. Similarly, in the study of occupational interests, a key contribution has been a coherent model of occupational interests. This model was proposed by John Holland and formalized in the first edition of his book *Making Vocational Choices: Theory of vocational personalities and work environments* in 1973. His model has become highly influential in career counselling practice, particularly in the USA.

Holland's RIASEC model

In his work as a career counsellor, John Holland noticed that among his clients, preferences and interests for particular kinds of work or job environment tended to co-occur. This led him to believe that he could identify a set of distinct vocational interest types, which in his theory he describes as personality types. He extended this reasoning further to suggest that interests and work environments could be organized on the same typological framework. He explains the basic premises of the theory:

> *The theory consists of several simple ideas and their more complex collaborations. First, we can characterize people by their resemblance to each of six personality types: Realistic, Investigative, Artistic, Social, Enterprising and Conventional. The more closely a person resembles a particular type, the more likely he or she is to exhibit the personal traits and behaviours associated with that type. Second, the environment in which people live and work can be characterized by their resemblance to six model environments: Realistic, Investigative, Artistic, Social, Enterprising and Conventional. Finally, the pairing of persons and environment leads to outcomes that we can predict and understand, knowledge of the personality types and the environmental models. These outcomes include vocational choice, vocational stability and achievement, educational choice and achievement, personal competence, social behaviour and susceptibility to influence.*

Holland proposed six vocational personality types and six corresponding work environments, suggesting that people can be described in terms of their similarity to the six personality types, and that their most dominant type will give an indication of their preferred working style. Holland described work environments using these same six dimensions, and suggested that people are attracted to and find satisfaction in work environments that match their interests (i.e. that match their vocational personality type). The six personality types and corresponding work environments are summarized in Table 8.2.

Table 8.2 Holland's Six Vocational Personality/Environment Types

Personality/ Environment type	Personality traits and preferences	Typical work environments	Occupations
Realistic	A Realistic person prefers activities that involve the manipulation of objects, tools, machines and animals. They are typically conforming, practical, persistent, dogmatic and inflexible, among other traits.	Realistic occupations frequently involve work activities that include practical, hands-on problems and solutions. They often deal with plants, animals and real-world materials like tools and machinery. Many of the occupations require working outside, and do not involve paperwork or working closely with others.	Mechanic Labourer Surveyor Electrician Farmer
Investigative	An Investigative person prefers activities that involve observational, systematic or creative investigation of physical, biological or other scientific phenomena. They prefer abstract problem-solving, and often have an aversion to persuasive, social and repetitive activities. They are likely to be analytical, rational, independent and intellectual, among other traits.	Investigative occupations frequently involve working with ideas, and require an extensive amount of thinking. These occupations can involve searching out facts and figuring out problems mentally.	Scientist Anthropologist Engineer Laboratory technician

Artistic	An Artistic person prefers activities that involve the manipulation of physical, verbal or human materials to create art forms or products. They are likely to have an aversion to systematic or ordered activities, and enjoy an environment with few rules. They are likely to be imaginative, intuitive, nonconforming and expressive, among other traits.	Artistic occupations frequently involve working with forms, designs and patterns. They often require self-expression and the work can be done without following a clear set of rules.	Painter
Sculptor
Interior designer
Writer
Journalist
Social	A Social person prefers activities that involve working with others, usually teaching, developing or helping others. They are likely to be empathic, friendly, generous and altruistic, among other traits.	Social occupations frequently involve working or communicating with others or teaching people. These occupations tend to involve helping or providing services to others.	Teacher
Counsellor
Waiter/waitress
Nurse
Tour guide
Enterprising	An Enterprising person prefers activities involving managing others to attain organizational goals or economic gain. They are typically ambitious, assertive, extraverted and self-confident.	Enterprising occupations frequently involve starting up and carrying out projects, often dealing with businesses. These occupations can involve leading people, making decisions or risk-taking.	Sales person
Manager
Lawyer
Chief executive
Recruitment consultant
Conventional	A Conventional person prefers activities that are rule-regulated, such as working with data, record-keeping and other administrative work. They tend to be averse to ambiguous or unsystematic activities. They are typically careful, conforming, methodical and conscientious.	Conventional occupations frequently involve following set procedures and routines. These occupations can include working with data and details rather than with ideas. Usually there is a clear line of authority to follow.	Accountant
Auditor
Statistician
Cashier
Office clerk
Secretary
Administrator

The structure of vocational interests

Holland's theory proposed that the six types are arranged in a hexagon (see Figure 8.2). This hypothesis has stood up reasonably well in empirical tests (e.g. Armstrong, Hubert, & Rounds, 2003; Tracey & Rounds, 1993). The structure represents interests effectively from late adolescence onwards and seems to be largely invariant across gender and ethnicity (Armstrong et al., 2003; Darcy & Tracey, 2007). Each type is conceptually most similar to its adjacent types, and least similar to its opposing type (e.g. the Investigative type is similar to the Artistic type, and least similar to the Enterprising type).

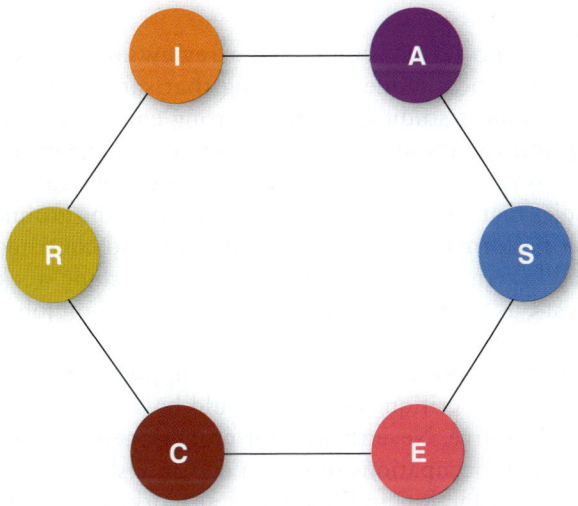

Figure 8.2   Holland's RIASEC hexagon

Application   Although Holland's model has been somewhat neglected in Europe and Asia, its impact is clearly visible in career counselling practice in the US. In the Dictionary of Occupational Titles (US Department of Labor, 1991) and more recently in the O*NET database (O*NET Resource Center, 2003), jobs are categorized according to Holland's six vocational types, and rated on continuous scales representing the degree to which they are characterized by each of the six types. Career counsellors use these resources to help people decide on the kinds of jobs that might best suit their individual interests. Interests are assessed using a number of different self-report questionnaires. Holland's own is the Self-directed Search (Holland, 1994), which continues to be used and can be completed online. Equally as popular is the Strong Interest Inventory (Harmon, Hansen, Borgen, & Hammer, 1994), and there are now at least two public-domain measures of the RIASEC model available for researchers and practitioners to use (e.g. Armstrong, Allison, & Rounds, 2008). All of these questionnaires tend to ask about preferences for jobs and for different work activities. The Self-directed Search also contains questions about people's self-rated competence in particular work activities.

Implications of Holland's theory   Like all good psychology theories, Holland's theory makes predictions about behaviour. The key predictive variable is congruence between interests and job environment, and the central tenet of the theory is that people seek out occupations that are consistent with their interests. When occupation and interests are matched, people are supposedly more satisfied and more likely to perform well. When interests and occupation are not matched, people tend to be less satisfied and to seek out ways to express their interests, which may include turnover from their current occupation in favour of something new. How well do these assumptions stand up?

The assumption that people gravitate to occupations that match their interests has been examined in a number of studies. A validation study for the Strong Interest Inventory found that RIASEC types predicted occupational group membership 12 years later (Hansen & Dik, 2005), and similar prospective results were reported by Donnay and Borgen (1996) and Betz, Borgen, and Harmon (2006), who also found that personality traits added to the prediction of occupational group membership beyond interest assessments. Recent studies such as these, in addition to an earlier review (Fouad, 1999), support the validity of measures of vocational interests as predictors of occupational membership.

Spokane, Meir, and Catalano (2000) conducted a review of studies testing the congruence hypotheses derived from Holland's model, indicating that satisfaction tends to correlate with congruence at about 0.25 in most studies, an effect strong enough to support the theory. Other investigators are less optimistic about the implications of congruence between interests and occupations. Arnold (2004) reviews a number of potential sources of weakness in the theory, drawing on two meta-analytic studies that strongly question the theory on the grounds that congruence does not predict satisfaction or performance at work convincingly and consistently (Assouline & Meir, 1987; Tranberg, Slane, & Ekeberg, 1993). Potential confounds include weak measurement of either the environment or interests, as well as neglect of wider influences on job satisfaction (such as job conditions and characteristics).

Overall, some of Holland's propositions appear to be supported in the literature, but combine these with some strong published critique and one would have to conclude that the implications of the theory are far from definitive. Nevertheless, for practitioners, understanding the congruence of people's interests and actual occupations offers an enormously heuristic approach for helping people explore preferences, satisfaction and happiness at work. It is a pity that the ideas are not used more often in job design in organizations. If a job does not naturally appeal to an individual's interests, then perhaps it could be redesigned or modified to allow some expression of interests and preferences, especially because different specialty pathways within an occupation can often present markedly different features (a point we return to shortly).

Schein's career anchors Taking a different perspective on individual differences in career development, Schein presented a set of career anchors (Schein, 1993), which he believed guided decisions about jobs and careers. Schein's contribution is an important one because it bridges the gap between theories of career development and vocational interests. He proposes that people develop a preference for a specific career theme, and that this influences their decision-making about how their career should progress. Like vocational interests, the anchors are supposed to lead people to gravitate to particular kinds of work (leading to the anchor analogy). The career anchors are:

- technical or functional competence
- general managerial competence
- autonomy/independence
- security/stability
- entrepreneurial creativity
- service/dedication
- pure challenge
- lifestyle.

Although the career anchors have had less impact than the theories of Holland and Super, the model and its associated assessment tools are increasingly popular in career counselling practice. The relationship between Prediger's two dimensions (1982) and Holland's six types is illustrated in Figure 8.3.

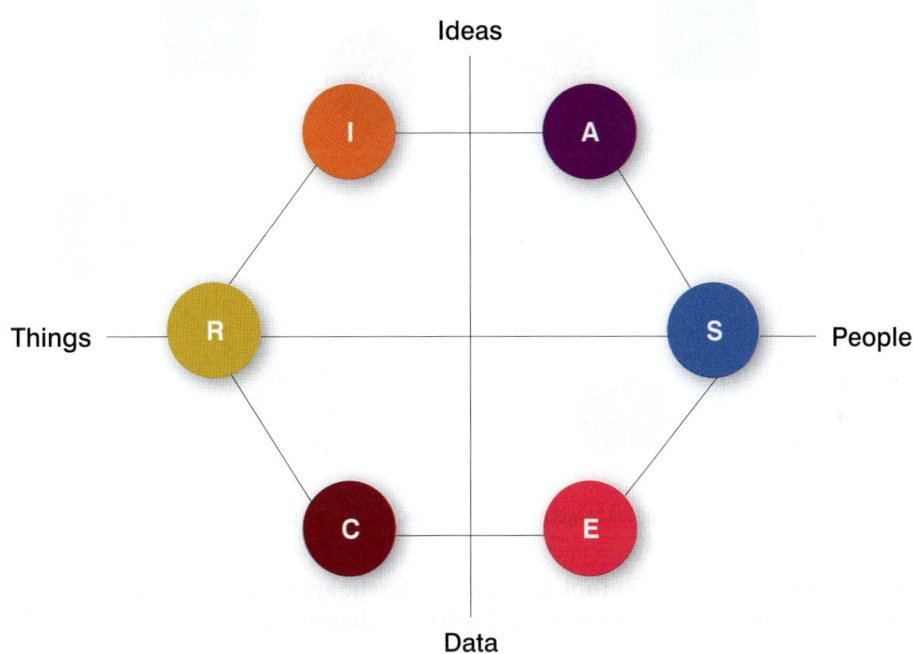

Figure 8.3 Holland's RIASEC hexagon, plus Prediger's dimensions

Personality traits and the RIASEC model

In Holland's theory, the RIASEC types are positioned as personality types. Parsimoniously, in the research literature, the constructs are more commonly described as based on interests rather than personality traits or variables *per se*. In this vein, six types of vocational interest stand alongside the two other important components of individual differences: cognitive ability/intelligence and personality traits. How are these different kinds of individual difference integrated to give an overall picture of the person?

There is plenty of research examining the associations of personality traits and the RIASEC types. These studies are summarized in two meta-analyses (Barrick, Mount, & Gupta, 2003; Larson, Rottinghaus, & Borgen, 2002). There were some differences in the findings of these two meta-analyses, but the most robust associations seem to be observed for Openness with Artistic/Investigative interests, Conscientiousness with Conventional interests, and Extraversion with Social and Enterprising interests. These associations are shown in Figure 8.4.

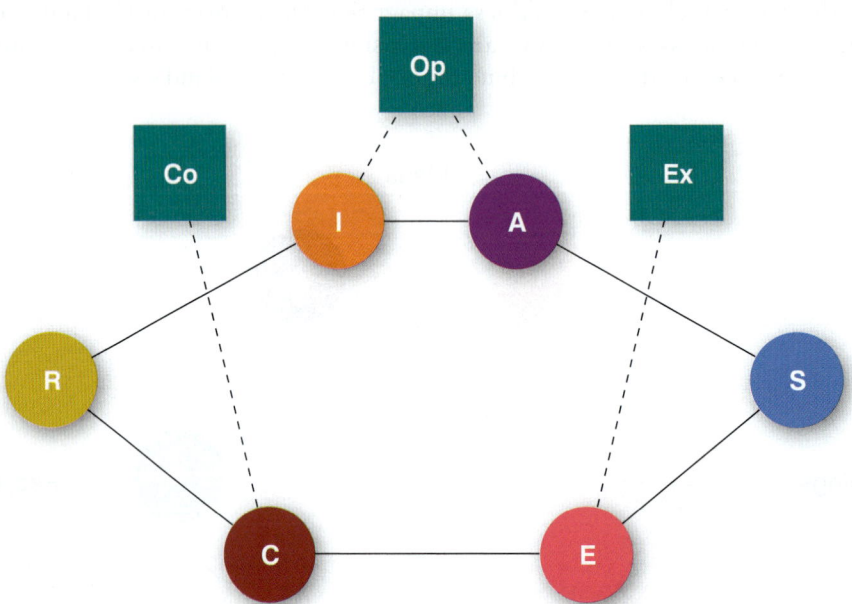

Figure 8.4 Associations between RIASEC types and the Big Five personality dimensions

Ackerman and Heggestad (1997) took a slightly different approach and examined how different forms of cognitive ability, personality traits and interests cluster together. They identified four types or clusters of characteristics:

1. Social: Enterprising and Social interests together with Extraversion from the Big Five model.
2. Clerical/Conventional: Conventional interests, Conscientiousness, and perceptual speed (with the latter representing an ability).
3. Science/Mathematics: Investigative and Realistic interests and numerical reasoning ability.
4. Intellectual/Cultural: Artistic and Investigative interests, Openness, and fluid and crystallized forms of general ability.

The associations between personality traits and the RIASEC types are also observed if occupational environments rather than interests are examined. Judge, Higgins, Thoresen, and Barrick (1999) reported that traits measured during adolescence predicted the RIASEC characteristics of participants' occupations many years later. Extending this to even earlier in childhood, Woods and Hampson (2010) reported associations between the Big Five personality dimensions measured at ages 6–12 and the RIASEC characteristics of job environments held by those same participants 40 years later, with Openness and Conscientiousness being particularly important (predicting later-life occupations characterized as Artistic/Investigative and Conventional/Social, respectively).

Woods and Hampson (2010) present a developmental theoretical model of childhood vocational development, and how this leads to adults working in particular occupational environments. They propose that early childhood personality traits such as Openness/Intellect, Conscientiousness and Extraversion direct children to particular activities and interests, which result in the acquisition of certain competencies. These eventually shape the development of vocational interests that in turn lead people to work in particular occupational environments.

Advancing the developmental perspective of personality and work further, Woods et al. (2013) consider the reciprocal influence of work on personality. Following the developmental process proposed by Woods and Hampson (2010), people select themselves into particular occupational environments in which their traits and associated competencies are activated, practised and strengthened. The strengthening and deepening of characteristics resulting from life experiences that draw on those traits is called the correspondive principle (Roberts, Caspi, & Moffitt, 2003). According to Woods et al. (2013), work influences our personality through these and other developmental processes. Their DDM has implications for how we understand the role of career development in people's lives more widely, and they propose that the development and maintenance of stable identities and personality characteristics may rely significantly on working life:

> *Longitudinal stability of personality may owe much to the processes of developing preferences for activities, practising them, applying them in a job, strengthening them, and then remaining in a career in which they are persistently activated from age 25 through to 65.* (Woods et al., 2013, p. S19.)

Career experiences have also been shown to be influential in the development of personality traits. Wille, Beyers, and De Fruyt (2012) showed that engagement in particular career roles (such as Director and Inspirator) over time led to the development of personality traits (e.g. Extraversion). This kind of finding is also reflected in the RIASEC characteristics of jobs, and their influence on how the Big Five develop (Wille & De Fruyt, 2014).

Another track of research extends the scope of focus of the Holland model beyond choice of occupations to choice of specialties within occupations. Different specialties within occupations may represent substantially different work environments. For example, a management pathway might represent a more Enterprising specialty, a teaching pathway more Social. Woods, Patterson, Wille, and Koczwara (2016) examined the associations of personality traits with the specialty choices of doctors in the UK NHS. These specialties were profiled on the RIASEC model. They found that Neuroticism and Agreeableness were the key associates of specialty choice. Doctors high on Neuroticism were less likely to work in Realistic specialties (e.g. Surgery) and more likely to work in Artistic specialties (e.g. Microbiology). Woods et al. (2016) proposed that Realistic specialties in medicine had a greater level of threat (e.g. high consequences of failure in surgical procedures) and were therefore avoided by people high on Neuroticism. Artistic specialties by contrast featured less threatening activities. Agreeableness was positively associated with Social specialties such as public health, most likely because of the opportunities in those specialties for prosocial helping, which might appeal to doctors with high Agreeableness.

This whole-career perspective on vocational interests is increasingly important as the developmental emphasis applied to the study of individual differences grows to include vocational interests. The person–environment fit model of Wille and De Fruyt (2019) proposes that vocational interests are not stable, and rather develop and change as a consequence of personal development decisions and trajectories. People may seek continuity, but also may seek change through change to their environment or themselves. Development processes serve to enhance person–environment fit over time, which may include change in preferences and interests.

PIONEERING WORK PSYCHOLOGISTS

Dr Bart Wille

Dr Bart Wille is Assistant Professor at Ghent University. He studies psychological individual differences and their role in work and career contexts. Dr Wille's research is pioneering because he has been central to enhancing the developmental perspective of individual differences in work and organizational psychology in a series of studies and papers. His work on personality development and the role of career-related factors in shaping that development has helped to bring exploration of the impact of work on who we are to the forefront of research on personality in work settings.

His latest research looks at vocational interest development. Again, in this area, the perspective on how interests develop over time challenges the assumptions that have existed for decades about how career advice and counselling is deployed. Whereas, in the past, interests were seen as stable and vocations advised accordingly, Dr Wille's work suggests otherwise, and provides the prospect that aspirational career goals can be facilitated to help people develop, rather than discouraged because of perceived 'misfit' to interests. This work will likely impact on how we use the concept of vocational interests in practice as psychologists.

Key example papers:

Wille, B., Beyers, W., & De Fruyt, F. (2012). A transactional approach to person–environment fit: Reciprocal relations between personality development and career role growth across young to middle adulthood. *Journal of Vocational Behavior, 81*(3), 307–321.

Wille, B., & De Fruyt, F. (2014). Vocations as a source of identity: Reciprocal relations between Big Five personality traits and RIASEC characteristics over 15 years. *Journal of Applied Psychology, 99*(2), 262–281.

Wille, B. & De Fruyt, F. (2019). The development of vocational interests. In C. D. Nye & J. Rounds (Eds.), *Vocational interests in the workplace: Rethinking behavior at work*. London, England: CRC Press.

In these studies, we can observe the interplay of personality and career development. Holland's RIASEC model provides a robust framework for examining the theoretical concepts and questions that such studies present. It is therefore an excellent example of a model that has both practical and theoretical value.

DISCUSS WITH A COLLEAGUE

Select the two RIASEC dimensions that you think best match your career interests. Use the O*NET database (www.onetonline.org/) to search for jobs that match those interests [Instructions for O*NET: Open O*NET > Find Occupations > Select Browse by Descriptor (Interests) > Click your preferred Interest].

What do you think of the results? Discuss the generated career options with a colleague.

SOCIAL, CULTURAL AND ORGANIZATIONAL INFLUENCES ON CAREERS

The theories and perspectives covered so far in this chapter are individual oriented. Career development and choices are conceptualized as a product of individual differences and developmental processes. However, these are not the only influences, and they neglect the realities of careers in which social, cultural and organization factors also play a part. In this section, we consider some of these influences and, at the same time, examine some more contemporary perspectives on careers.

Careers and gender

Gender is a major influence on the development of vocational interests and eventual career choices (Lent, Brown, & Hackett, 1994). From as young as two to three years, boys and girls aspire to careers that are gender stereotypic (Fouad, 2007). Much of the research on career development and vocational interests has neglected the issue of gender and yet most people are acutely aware of societal pressures and norms around gender and occupations. Kandola and Kandola (2013) point out that people still tend to automatically assume either a male or female job-holder for some occupations (e.g. nurse, carpenter), with the Think Manager–Think Male bias (Schein, 1973) being particularly persistent. What makes these stereotypes especially problematic is that they become tied up with stereotyped assumptions about the differences between men and women (Kandola & Kandola, 2013; see also Rudman, Greenwald, & McGhee, 2001). This gives rise to systematic and deeply engrained bias in perceptions of the relative fit of men and women for different kinds of occupations and jobs. You will observe the effects of this bias everywhere. For example, in media such as advertising and marketing, in television and film, in children's toys and games, and even in the digital world, systematic gender bias is prevalent (Google Image search 'nurse' and 'carpenter' and you will see the evidence of this).

Children absorb these cultural stereotypes in their early preferences for jobs and roles. Girls express preferences for female gender-stereotyped jobs (Miller & Budd, 1999) and girls who express preferences for non-traditional jobs are less likely to persist in their choice than those choosing traditional jobs (Farmer, Wardrop, Anderson, & Risinger, 1995; Fouad, 2007). Traditional career choices for men are those that typically confirm aspects of male identity, reflecting selection of masculine attitudes and traits over feminine ones and supporting self-perceptions of toughness and emotional restrictiveness (Jome & Tokar, 1998). Perhaps more interestingly, men and women often give different gender-stereotypic reasons for entering particular careers. For example, men explain entering engineering because of their interests in the field, whereas women tend to cite altruistic reasons such as helping others (Davey, 2001).

One of the most important and well-articulated theories of career and occupational aspirations and development is that of Gottfredson (1981). Her theory fills one of the key gaps in the career development theories outlined earlier because it focuses on children. Gottfredson identifies four stages of development for children in respect of their occupational aspirations:

- Orientation to size and power (ages 3–5): At this stage, children grasp the concept of becoming an adult and growing up.
- Orientation to sex roles (ages 6–8): Gottfredson suggests that gender (sex-role in her model) is the first influence on the development of a vocational self-concept. Children acquire stereotypes about male versus female roles early on in their development.

- Orientation to social valuation (ages 9–13): At this stage, demands of social class and ability become important determinants of behaviour and identity.
- Orientation to the internal, unique self: (age 14 and above): Children develop a greater awareness of their own individual, unique characteristics at this stage, and are able to deal with more complex aspects of their self-concept (this is related to Eriksson's 'identity crisis').

In examining the gender-stereotyped nature of occupations, Gottfredson explores gender preferences for occupation characteristics described on the RIASEC model. The most gender-stereotyped occupations are Realistic (male) and Conventional (female). Artistic and Social jobs are somewhat feminine whereas Investigative and Enterprising jobs are somewhat masculine.

In their study of personality and vocational environments, Woods and Hampson (2010) examined how gender and the Big Five dimensions measured in childhood interact to predict the kind of occupational environments that a person works in later in life. They found that women tended to work in jobs that were more Conventional, Social and Artistic, but also to a lesser extent more Enterprising. Men's jobs tended to be more Realistic, but equally Investigative compared to women. Gender and personality interacted in their study in some interesting ways. For example, men and women high on Openness were more likely to work in Artistic or Investigative jobs. However, low Openness predicted job environments differently for men and women. Women who were lower on Openness as children were more likely to work in Conventional jobs, whereas men lower on Openness as children were more likely to work in Realistic jobs. Later-life career environments for boys and girls low on Openness tended to diverge along gender-stereotypic lines. Woods and Hampson proposed that children high on Openness would be more likely to experiment with different activities and potentially buck the trend of gender stereotyping.

These findings have reflected the differences in the occupational preferences and choices of boys and girls as they develop. One other relevant consideration is opportunity. Career development is in part related to opportunities that a person has to attain the level of status or achievement that they aspire to, and although countries continue to take steps to address inequalities between men and women at work, there remain striking gaps and areas of inequity. These questions are reflected every year in the World Economic Forum's 'Global Gender Gap Report' (Schwab et al., 2018). The report examines a number of areas of inequality (work, health, education, and political empowerment), and rank orders countries according to the size of the gap between men and women. According to the 2017 report, no country in any part of the world has achieved equality, and although countries such as the UK, Germany, South Africa, Sweden, Norway and New Zealand are in the top 20 countries in the list, the rankings of some countries in terms of economic participation and opportunity are much lower than might be expected (e.g. out of 135 countries, UK 53rd, Germany 43rd, South Africa 89th). Scandinavian, African, Eastern European and Central Asian countries feature heavily in the top 30 countries, with the big economies of Brazil, China and India ranked 90th, 100th and 108th respectively. The USA ranks 49th overall, but 19th for economic participation and opportunity.

Depressingly, the report estimates that the gender gap will not be closed any time soon, and that current trends indicate it will be maintained globally for another 100 years. The biggest inequalities remain in the areas of economic participation and opportunity, and political empowerment, meaning there is significant work to do in the area of work and organizations.

Gender and leadership

A frequently cited metaphor for the barriers preventing women progressing into leadership positions is the glass ceiling; an invisible barrier hindering promotion of women to higher management. However, it appears that the social psychology of women in leadership is much more complex than this simple metaphor. Ryan and Haslam (2005) argue that although women are beginning to break through the glass ceiling, their performance once promoted is placed under close scrutiny. Moreover, there emerge some fascinating findings about the contexts in which women are typically perceived as desirable leaders, and indeed appointed to leadership roles. Examining the performance of the UK FTSE 100 companies, Ryan and Haslam (2005) found archival evidence that women were more likely to be appointed to boards at time of organizational crisis, and especially so when share prices had fallen over successive months. Those organizations that did appoint women in these circumstances tended to perform better in the months that followed. Ryan and Haslam (2005) termed this effect the glass cliff – the appointing of women to precarious positions of leadership at times of crisis.

Developing their work further, Ryan, Haslam, Hersby, and Bongiorno (2011) conducted a series of experiments in which they showed that women were perceived as more effective (i.e. ideal) leaders for companies in situations of crisis (confirming the Think Crisis–Think Female bias). However, their studies also showed that this applied specifically when the leader was expected to a) stay in the background and endure the crisis, b) take responsibility for the company failure, or c) manage people and personnel issues through the crisis. There was not female bias if the leader was expected to d) act as a spokesperson, or e) take control and improve performance. This research uncovers some troubling trends for perceptions around women in leadership, strengthening the case for the glass cliff hypothesis. Although more women may be breaking into top leadership, the social psychological forces associated with their appointment may mean that they are essentially set up to lead in situations in which they have a much higher probability of failure than is typically experienced by their male counterparts.

Gender, then, influences a child's aspirations for his or her career, including the career choices that he or she perceives as available. Persistent inequality acts to limit the career opportunities of women compared to men in a number of important ways, including most notably in terms of leadership, wages, and the proportions of women in professional and technical occupations.

Wider social inequality in careers

A final reflection on the issues of social inequality in careers is that these effects are not limited to gender inequality. Kandola (2018), for example, highlights similar observations regarding race at work, warning against making assumptions that racism in the workplace is something of the past. Minority employees are also grossly underrepresented in leadership of organizations (Eagly & Chin, 2010). For example, in 2017 there were only five black CEOs in the Fortune 500 list of top US companies (i.e. only 1 per cent). Similar findings have been reported in other forms of leadership such as in sport. In football, despite widespread intervention to stamp out racism and participation by increasingly diverse teams at player level, in leadership and management minorities are also underrepresented (Bradbury, 2013; Kandola, 2018).

Part of the glass ceiling for minorities may similarly have its roots in unconscious biased assumptions about leadership and race. Gündemir, Homan, de Dreu, and van Vugt (2014) reported that in implicit association tests, people showed significant pro-white leadership bias. Elsewhere in this book, we have considered the pervasive and persistent issues of discrimination in access to employment, recruitment and selection. Colella, Hebl, and King (2017) point out that the progress in applied psychology towards understanding discrimination from a theoretical perspective, and using theory to tackle it, has a long way to go. For example, beyond race and gender, there are many minority groups for whom bias and discrimination are under-researched and poorly understood (e.g. people with disabilities, LGBT+ employees). Colella et al. call psychologists to action in closing this gap in work and organizational psychology science and practice in future years.

Careers and culture

The theories of career development and choice that have been reviewed in this chapter are very clearly rooted in Western, and more specifically US, experiences of careers. Moreover, the major theories were conceived in the historical context of the USA between 1950 and 1980 (Wong & Slater, 2002). In this sense, the theories should be seen as limited in terms of their utility in other cultures. Culture has a strong influence on career appraisal, expectations and decisions. Derr and Laurent (1989) comment that:

> *National cultures have a significant impact on career dynamics in two major ways. First, national cultures shape the individuals self definition of a career ... Second, national cultures also shape the institutional context or design of work, and the individual's perception of it... through the norms, values and assumptions that the individual has already learned in the culture.* (Derr & Laurent, 1991, pp. 465–6, cited in Wong and Slater, 2002, p. 354.)

Schein (1984) explored how culture affected several aspects of careers. The very notion of a career is based on the aspiration for personal ambition, and this features more strongly in Western cultures. The concept of career in collectivist cultures would be very different. Societies also place values on careers that can determine their desirability. Compare the changing values attached to military careers in the USA currently to the negative stereotypes that were held in the late 1960s and early 1970s. The value of a career in life also varies across cultures. Hofstede (1980) found that employees in Singapore, Hong Kong, Columbia, Mexico and Peru did not value family time as an important feature of their careers. Employees in Japan, the Philippines and Taiwan valued it more, and those in New Zealand, Australia and Canada valued it most. Markers of success in careers are also different across cultures. For example, achieving results is valued strongly in the USA, creativity and health in Germany, education in the Netherlands and opinions of others in the UK (Laurent, 1991).

Comparative cross-cultural research is weak in vocational psychology, yet it has the potential to strengthen understanding about cultural differences more widely. Wong and Slater (2002) provide a good example of this. Their study used qualitative methods to explore the careers of managers in China. They comment on four relevant cultural traditions in China that differ from Western cultures:

- Importance of face: Giving respect to those of higher social status.
- Respect for hierarchy: Respect for seniority and age.
- Importance of collectivism: Thinking and behaving within accepted social norms.
- Importance of harmony: Keeping good relations by fulfilling reciprocal obligations and duties.

One of the emergent aspects of these values is guanxi, referring to relationships with others. In their interview data, Wong and Slater (2002) found that guanxi remained a significant influence on career progression and development of management careers in China, despite the significant economic and business reforms in the country. Many managers felt that maintaining good guanxi with subordinates and top management was important in career progression, and the implication is that part of maintaining good guanxi is respect for traditions and values.

Against this context of difference, there were also interesting similarities. Family upbringing, social status, individual values, motivation, environmental factors, life stages and organizations all had influences on career decisions and progression. Alongside the limitations of existing theories, there may also be some important strengths. What makes cultural comparison difficult in current times is cultural change. The exportation of Western working cultures and styles, driven in part by the biases that operate in management research, could bring changes to ways that careers are perceived in other cultures. Nevertheless, enduring cultural values are still vital to understanding when and how theories and models of careers are likely to be invalid across cultures.

The boundaryless career

The latest terminology to be applied to career theory in work psychology is the so-called 'boundaryless career'. Arthur and Rousseau (1996) originated the term, and Inkson (2008) identifies six specific meanings:

- moving across boundaries of separate employers
- validating work by seeking information outside the current employer
- sustaining work and role with information and networks that reach beyond the current employer
- breaking traditional career boundaries
- rejecting career opportunities for personal or family reasons
- perceiving one's career as without boundaries, regardless of current constraints.

The boundaryless career is one in which the individual is not constrained to career moves or indeed work activities that are restricted within one employer or organization. Although the roots of the idea can be traced back to Gouldner (1957), Inkson (2008) points out that the idea has found particular significance in the past 10–20 years as a result of some of the changes to work and organizations outlined earlier.

Thinking in respect of boundaryless careers has developed beyond the constraints of employer and organization. One focus has been the barriers or boundaries imposed by traditional aspirations and markers of career success. The closely related concept of the protean career (Hall, 2002) examines the subjectivity of goal setting, exploring how career goals might be understood as broad life goals, whereby an individual seeks to achieve more that the objective markers of success such as salary and status. These goals might be related to attaining happiness or contentment through achievement or validation of identity – essentially attaining meaning in life and career.

Other boundaries might also be broken down in the boundaryless career. These include geographical (location), occupational (actual job) and status (promotion, demotion, independence) boundaries. The notion of the boundaryless career incorporates a general rejection of the traditional structural constraints on decisions about careers, and is therefore timely. The ideas around rejecting structures and societal career traditions find expression because of the rapid development of social and cultural norms over the past 50 years. We now have more flexibility than ever before about how to live our lives and to decide on how we work. Increased access to education, travel and information has broken down some of the traditional boundaries of opportunity, mobility and access. Careers have therefore captured the attention of sociologists, acting as a lens for examining social change. It is naïve, however, to suppose that the boundaries of social class and opportunity have been broken or at least sufficiently eroded to move us closer to a true equality of opportunity. Issues of culture, class and privilege are pervasive in determining why young people of similar abilities aspire and gain access to careers with differing outcomes, including status and salary. Organizations could do more to promote social mobility, and this is explored in the key themes box.

The implication of seeking or simply having a 'boundaryless career' is a greater sense of agency and responsibility of the individual for managing and developing their career. The organization is seen as doing less to manage career progression, with people taking ownership of factors like development, networking and education for the purpose of initiating and furthering their careers. In this vein, Direnzo and Greenhaus (2011) present a model of job search and voluntary turnover. They argue that in the context of volatile economic conditions and removal of traditional career progression boundaries, people are more motivated to engage in proactive job-search activity. By maintaining a greater awareness of the job market, employees may be motivated to move jobs (voluntary turnover) or to engage in self-directed career development strategies such as up-skilling to maintain their marketability with prospective new employers. This marketability is referred to as employability, a concept reviewed in the next section.

Careers and employability

One impact of changing perspectives on careers and organizations is the concept of employability. The basic idea is that if careers are more fluid, less structured, less hierarchical and more boundaryless, then a person's career progression is enhanced or limited by their employability, or the extent to which they develop or possess a sought-after profile of abilities, skills and competencies. Employability has been defined as 'continuous fulfilling, acquiring or creating of work through the optimal use of one's competences' (Van der Heijde & Van der Heijden, 2006, p. 453) and studied from three perspectives (Nauta, Van Vianen, Van der Heijden, Van Dam, & Willemsen, 2009):

- Socio-economic perspective: Employability has been considered in relation to socio-economic factors such as culture, gender, ethnicity and disability. The focus in this perspective is often to understand why people from different backgrounds may find it more difficult to progress in their careers. Global boundaries are a current focus in this area, for example understanding the barriers for international workers with the right skills and abilities finding jobs in Europe and the USA (Brown, 2003).
- Individual perspective: Maintaining employability has been the focus of the individual perspectives. Key themes are adaptability to turbulent organizational changes and economies. Employability is a reaction or alternative to job security in this perspective (Forrier & Sels, 2003), and research has looked at some of the ways in which people stay employable, such as proactive learning across whole careers (Rothwell & Arnold, 2007). That learning seems especially important if it improves self-perceptions of employability. De Vos, De Hauw, and Van der Heijden (2011) reported that perceived employability mediated the relationship between competency development and career satisfaction.
- Organizational perspective: Employability has been flagged as beneficial for organizations too (Nauta et al., 2009). This is because employable people in organizations are, by definition, multi-skilled and flexible. They are able to move between organizations or between jobs within organizations. Consequently they help organizations to adapt quickly to new demands, and provide versatility because they are able to move between different tasks or jobs within their company.

People differ in the extent to which they are 'employability oriented', so that some are more inclined than others to seek out opportunities to increase employability. An interesting finding is that this orientation can be influenced by fostering a culture of employability in the organization, for example through HR initiatives that promote internal development or mobility, and the promotion of this kind of culture may have important organizational benefits (Nuata et al., 2009). In their study of health and welfare workers in the Netherlands, Nuata et al. reported that development of an employability culture increased employability orientation, but simultaneously reduced turnover intentions. The key factor was a reduction in 'push motives' for turnover (i.e. a desire to leave the company because of dissatisfaction). When people were given more opportunities to develop their employability within the organization, they were more likely to be satisfied with their careers and less likely to be 'pushed' out.

This finding is also relevant to understanding a practical concern that organizations may have that enhancing employability may increase the likelihood that people will find alternative employment.

For example, De Cuyper, Van Der Heijden, and De Witte (2011) reported a positive association between self-rated employability and turnover intention, so there appears to be some basis for this concern. This association may reflect complex supervisor–subordinate relationships. Supervisors may actually be less likely to promote some workers whom they perceive as highly employable, so as to keep them in their own teams (Van der Heijden, de Lange, Dermerouti, & Van der Heijde, 2009), which may lead those individuals to seek alternative employment.

By contrast, Yousaf and Sanders (2012) report a positive association between self-perceived employability and affective commitment, mediated most significantly by job satisfaction. So it appears that enhancing the employability of employees can be beneficial for organizations, provided it is against the context of creating an overall positive, satisfying job experience and a climate for competency development and career growth.

Employability is likely to be an increasingly important concept in understanding career development and decision-making, and in particular the differences in people's experiences of careers. Part of the motivation for greater understanding of the concept comes from the potential benefits of improving individual employability, which appear wide-ranging. Individuals could progress more easily and swiftly in careers, organizations could become more adaptable, and barriers to global and social mobility could be identified and weakened.

CAREER MANAGEMENT IN ORGANIZATIONS

How do organizations manage the careers of their employees in practice? How might the theories and research outlined in this chapter be applied to the management of careers? There are a number of ways that organizations can help to develop the careers of their employees and, likewise, there are things that individuals can do themselves. Not all interventions are equally useful for all people, all of the time. Rather, the theories and models of career development, career interests and work-role transitions lead to the conclusion that different kinds of career management strategies will be more or less relevant for people at different stages of their lives and careers. The theories and perspectives in this chapter point to the following broad aims for career management interventions:

- Counselling and advising people so that people better understand their individual differences and the kind of work that would appeal to their traits, skills, abilities and interests.
- Developing new knowledge, skills or abilities through formal learning, practical training or development or on-the-job development.
- Preparing for transition, either into new jobs or positions, or alternatively, out of the organization.
- Facilitating career progression with activities such as networking, or job-seeking skills.

Counselling and advising

Formal career counselling is the main contributor in this area of career management. Most career counselling is designed to explore a person's current situation, and to allow them to independently work out what might be the most suitable next steps in their career. Like other forms of counselling, career counselling is based on a relationship between the counsellor and the client, which may develop over a number of meetings held regularly over a lengthy period of time. The general stages of career counselling are to first understand the 'now', which is defined by understanding the client's career history to date and the resources they have available to them (including knowledge, skills, abilities and other characteristics). Preferred career options can be explored using models such as Holland's RIASEC typology, and the individual is then usually tasked with identifying a career goal and working out the action they need to take to achieve that goal.

Traditionally, career counselling has been employed most often at the start of people's careers (i.e. during education), but there is increasingly opportunity for counselling to be applied at various stages of people's careers (Arnold, 1997).

Developing people

If we take on board the implications of the literature on the changing psychological contract, then development would be considered the most useful career management provision from organizations to their employees. Development is empowering to employees in the sense that it allows them to address any self-identified weaknesses or skills gaps. The literature on development is covered in depth in Chapter 6, but a few general strategies are highlighted here:

- Developmental work assignments. Work and task assignments designed to allow employees to develop new skills and to experience new areas of responsibility or different parts of the organization.
- Development centres. A process of assessing employee competencies using the assessment centre method with the purpose of providing detailed feedback about performance and development needs.
- Mentoring. Partnering of an employee with an experienced colleague (usually more senior), who advises and develops them. The aim of mentoring is to provide the employee with an impartial source of support and learning in the organization, who is not his or her line manager.
- Self-directed development. Many organizations now use online and self-study development and e-learning materials that allow employees to work at their own pace and at convenient times. The internet has permitted wider use of self-directed development.

Preparing for transition

There are a number of interventions that organizations can make to help employees at stages of transition. The transition cycle is useful to remember when considering these interventions. In the preparation stage, the important task for employees is information seeking. A good example of assistance at this stage is the provision of realistic job previews, which provide an outline or demonstration of the uncensored requirements of the job, and often the organization's values and culture. After selection, the organization can provide an induction process for new employees. This intervention is relevant to the encounter stage in the transition cycle. During this stage, new employees are purported to seek as much information as possible about the job and organization. Induction processes can help them to do this, and provide a formal aspect of socialization that sits alongside the informal learning that new employees acquire from colleagues and other sources.

At some point, employees will leave the organization, either of their own volition, or involuntarily in the case of dismissal or redundancy. In the cases of redundancy and/or retirement, organizations can help employees at a potentially difficult stage of their careers by providing outplacement services. Outplacement is designed to support employees considering their options after leaving the organization and, with respect to redundancy, to help employees leaving the organization to find new jobs and careers. Outplacement services typically comprise career counselling and development planning, but might also involve wider counselling for employees suffering stress as a result of job loss, or financial planning and advice. Such services might actually offer little solace to those made redundant, but at least shows the organization to be fulfilling an ethical responsibility.

KEY THEME

Diversity and inclusion

In 2019, there are around 19,000 academic professors in the UK. Of these, only 25 are black and female. Nearly 70 per cent are white men. In 2019, a report by the University and Colleges Union highlighted that BAME professors also faced significant bullying, stereotyping and institutional neglect. It is a shocking and dismaying situation that is a blight on academic institutions that could be leading on issues of diversity and inclusion.

There is an obligation, however, for us to better understand the processes that give rise to the career blockages experienced by women and BAME academics as they develop and progress. By finding out more about why career progression stalls for some people and not others, we can do more to address and challenge issues.

One prospect for understanding the mechanisms of career opportunity inequality is the role of networking. This is especially acute in academic careers and serves to illustrate the impact of the issue across other careers too. Van den Brink and Benschop (2014) examine the experience of academic promotion through the lens of gender differences in networking. They identify the role of academics as gatekeepers to progression in the career. Senior academics are involved in recruitment and promotion and are therefore charged with the evaluation of promise and limitations of prospective new professors.

Networking with gatekeepers is a mechanism by which access to progression in a career can be attained. It involves getting insights into how to progress and developing relationships that can give an advantage in getting on in a chosen field. In respect of networking, Van den Brink and Benschop (2014) identify that women are at a disadvantage from two perspectives.

First, their access to networks is more limited than for men, reflecting a tendency in networking called *homophily*: the tendency for people to seek out and interact more easily with people similar to themselves. Van den Brink and Benschop (2014) state that 'when the gatekeepers are predominantly men, women have difficulty gaining access to desirable academic networks' (p. 464). Second, even if they have access to networks, the extent to which those networks are beneficial depends upon the ways in which working relationships are developed. Unless they interact in a way that conveys fit to the existing ways of doing things within these mainly male networks, women are placed at further disadvantage. As the authors conclude, *"through constructions of 'who you can trust' or 'who is a risk', gatekeepers exercise the power of inclusion and exclusion and contribute to the persistence of structural gender inequalities"* (p. 460).

Career management relies heavily on networking, and so access to influential networks and individuals must also play an important part in an organization's strategy for responsibly encouraging better inclusion through all layers of an organization. But this research shows that access alone is not enough; it is critical that the structural barriers that networks present are confronted and broken, otherwise we can expect that inequality persists.

Facilitating progression

A high proportion of new job roles never get formally advertised, and instead people are appointed through informal processes or managerial decision-making over task assignment. A key contributing factor in determining whether a person will be considered for new responsibilities is networking. Networking refers to the establishment of social relationships or connections with influential or important people and organizations, within and outside the organization. Effective networking can make the difference for speed of progression within an organization, and a good external network can also act as an information source for a variety of purposes (e.g. new developments in the industry, competitor information, new or forthcoming job roles). Organizations can support networking activities by funding travel and attendance of the employee at visits and meetings at different internal and external sites, as well as at professional events such as conferences.

Networking has been highlighted as a barrier for progression for minorities (Kandola, 2018) and women (Kandola & Kandola, 2013). It would therefore seem that improving access to networks is a good strategy for helping to address inequality. However, care is needed in organizations that networking itself does not become exclusive (for example, by happening solely in out-of-work, antisocial hours which might exclude people with care or family responsibilities or involving culturally insensitive activities).

A further set of skills that are very helpful in career development are job-seeking skills. It can be useful for mentors or managers to help those seeking promotion, or indeed jobs elsewhere, to develop skills in the preparation of CVs, or performing well at interview or other selection assessments. These skills will help facilitate career development, and are particularly welcomed by employees in contemporary careers where job moves are frequent. A concern of some is the extent to which such activities introduce bias into selection processes. My belief is that they do not. Many selection processes are built on the assumption that a person will perform at their best or give a fair and accurate picture of their skills and capabilities. A surprising number or people find it difficult to do this, and so effectively under-sell their skills and abilities. Development of job-seeking skills may actually help selectors to make sound decisions by helping candidates communicate their strengths more clearly.

POSITIVE WORK

Creating the platform for positive career development in organizations

Some of what is written and researched in the context of examining markers of career success seems to reflect striving for 'sufficiency': satisfaction, making effective decisions and so forth. A very clear exception to this is research on thriving at work (Spreitzer, Sutcliffe, Dutton, Sonenshein, & Grant, 2005). Thriving at work is a psychological state comprising the joint experience of learning and vitality. Porath, Spreitzer, Gibson, and Garnett (2012) describe people who are thriving as experiencing *"growth and momentum marked by both a sense of feeling energized and alive (vitality) and a sense that they are continually improving and getting better at what they do (learning)"* (Porath et al., p. 250).

Thriving at work matters because it enhances and develops health and personal growth of people at work. These are important as people are required to take control, move through protean careers and adapt to the new challenges that the working world presents. It might be thought of as a critical enabler of attaining positive career outcomes, but moreover, representative of having a meaningful and rewarding working life.

In this chapter, we have introduced different perspectives on careers and vocational psychology and have reviewed some of the strategies that organizations and practitioners can apply in the management of careers. By creating environments in which people thrive, however, it could be possible to create a platform for truly positive and life-enhancing career development. Such an environment would enable people to proactively do things that promote thriving, producing a model for career development and growth that reflects a balance of personal and organizational initiative. Spreitzer et al. (2012) refer to this strategy as moving towards achieving human sustainability in management and organizations, and provide a series of individual and organizational strategies.

Individual strategies

- Knowing when to take a break from high-demand learning activity: Activity such as job change or transition that involves a demanding degree of learning can have a negative impact on vitality. People are advised to monitor when vitality is waning so as to know when to take a break to recover.
- Craft work to be meaningful and impactful: Crafting involves building in activity that improves work. Examples are helping colleagues or working on tasks that evoke interest or passion.
- Find ways to innovate: Innovating at work helps to learn something new or develop new capability, both important to develop a sense of thriving.
- Find opportunities to learn and develop inside and outside work: In the case that learning may not be possible in work, opportunities outside work may still promote a sense of thriving.

Organizational strategies

- Provide autonomy and decision-making discretion: Individual strategies for thriving at work rely on the potential to take decisions about work and the way that it is carried out.
- Provide information about the organization: Open and honest communication about the organization and its direction helps to share understanding about the meaningfulness and impact of work.
- Minimize incivility: Incivility at work represents exchanges that violate conventions and norms of workplace conduct, leading to negative feelings on the part of receivers. Such exchanges, however small, are damaging to feelings of vitality.
- Provide performance feedback: Feedback provides information that might direct energy and learning.
- Promote diversity and inclusion: Promoting a climate of diversity fosters trust and respect, providing a sense that contributions are meaningful and valued, in turn promoting thriving at work.

These strategies in combination have the potential to make a positive impact on people's careers, setting a foundation for a working life in which they thrive.

SUMMARY

Modern and contemporary stories of people's working lives are different in important ways from those told in the past. Yet, we started this chapter by outlining the importance of work in life, and this fact remains as fundamental now as it ever was.

Careers have been studied in work psychology from a number of perspectives. One set of theories has examined how careers develop across the lifespan. Such theories collectively highlight traditional stages of development, and the challenges that people face at different stages of their lives. Navigating these challenges builds a sense of who we are, our work and personal identity.

A second dominant perspective examines the ways that people fit their environments, represented in characteristics of their jobs, occupations, groups and organizations. One of the most important decisions that people make in early adulthood is the kind of occupation in which they would like to work. Understanding why different people choose particular occupations is a central concern of Holland's theory of vocational personality types and environments. His theory suggests that work interests and environments can be described using the same six dimensions, and that people gravitate to environments that appeal to their interests. The process of choosing an occupation, specializing, establishing and maintaining one's career also has developmental implications, with emergent literature suggesting a reciprocal effect of work and careers on personality traits.

Work psychology has also considered some of the social, cultural and organizational influences on careers. Gender continues to be an important influence, and for women, it seems, a barrier to career development in all parts of the world. Inequality in career opportunity is not limited to gender, and future developments in work and organizational psychology should seek to better understand discrimination in career progression. Culture also affects careers on many levels, including career development and judgements about what constitutes career success. By attending to such issues, career stories can be seen as important reflections of social history and change.

Recent perspectives on careers have examined the changing nature of career progression, with some suggesting that careers are now more boundaryless than ever. However, the concept of employability mitigates this view and helps to explain why boundaries and barriers are experienced by some, but not others.

All of these perspectives have the potential to inform career management interventions in organizations, which take the form of counselling and advising, developing people, preparing people for change, and facilitating progression within and beyond the organization.

There is such a thing as a formula for a good story, and when you take the ideas introduced in this chapter together, it seems that there are similarly familiar formulae for the various sections of career stories. Theory helps us to make sense of, among other things, career choices and career development. Does that make the writing and telling of career stories predictable or less interesting? I do not think so – rather it enables work psychologists to help people with plot development, or to help organizations be better, more vibrant settings for career stories – in short, applying knowledge and understanding of the career stories of others, to help people thrive and flourish in the writing of their own.

DISCUSSION QUESTIONS

1 What could an organization do to manage issues of gender and race bias in career development strategies?

2 Why don't people always choose a career that matches their interests?

3 Are careers really boundaryless in the 21st century? Do people have clear work identities in the way they did in the past?

4 Suggest five ways that an organization could improve employability of staff.

5 Use the transition cycle to describe your experiences of job change, or of starting at your university. Discuss your experiences in a group.

6 Use theories and models to help make sense of your career story to date.

7 How can managers strive to enable people to thrive at work?

FURTHER READING

Arnold, J. (1997). *Managing careers into the 21st century*. London, England: SAGE.

Kandola, J., & Kandola, B. (2013) *The invention of difference: The story of gender bias at work*. Oxford, England: Pearn Kandola Publishing.

Wang, M., & Wanberg, C. R. (2017). 100 years of applied psychology research on individual careers: From career management to retirement. *Journal of Applied Psychology, 102*(3), 546–563.

Wille, B., & De Fruyt, F. (2019). The development of vocational interests. In C. D. Nye & J. Rounds (Eds.), *Vocational interests in the workplace: Rethinking behavior at work*. (Chapter 12) New York, NY: Routledge.

REFERENCES

Ackerman, P. L., & Heggestad, E. D. (1997). Intelligence, personality and interests: Evidence for overlapping traits. *Psychological Bulletin, 121,* 219–245.

Anderson, N., & West, M. A. (1996). The Team Climate Inventory: Development of the TCI and its applications in teambuilding for innovativeness. *European Journal of Work and Organizational Psychology, 5*(1), 53–66.

Armstrong, P. I., Allison, W., & Rounds, J. (2008). Development and initial validation of brief public domain RIASEC marker scales. *Journal of Vocational Behaviour, 73*(2), 287–299.

Armstrong, P. I., Hubert, L., & Rounds, J. (2003). Circular unidimensional scaling: A new look at group differences in interest structure. *Journal of Counselling Psychology, 50,* 297–308.

Arnold, J. (1997). *Managing careers into the 21st century*. London, England: SAGE.

Arnold, J. (2004). The congruence problem in John Holland's theory of vocational decisions. *Journal of Occupational and Organizational Psychology, 77*(1), 95–113.

Arthur, M. B., & Rousseau, D. M. (1996). *The boundaryless career: A new employment principle for a new organizational era*. New York, NY: Oxford University Press.

Ashforth, B. E., Harrison, S. H., & Corley, K. G. (2008). Identification in organizations: An examination of four fundamental questions. *Journal of Management, 34*(3), 325–374.

Ashforth, B. E., & Schinoff, B. S. (2016). Identity under construction: How individuals come to define themselves in organizations. *Annual Review of Organizational Psychology and Organizational Behavior, 3,* 111–137.

Ashforth, B. E., Sluss, D. M., & Saks, A. M. (2007). Socialization tactics, proactive behaviour and newcomer learning: Integrating socialization models. *Journal of Vocational Behaviour, 70*(3), 447–462.

Assouline, M., & Meir, E. I. (1987). Meta-analysis of the relationship between congruence and well-being measures. *Journal of Vocational Behaviour, 31*(3), 319–332.

Bandura, A. (1982). Self-efficacy mechanism in human agency. *American Psychologist, 37*(2), 122.

Barrick, M. R., Mount, M. K., & Gupta, R. (2003). Meta-analysis of the relationship between the five factor model of personality and Holland's occupational types. *Personnel Psychology, 56*, 45–74.

Beehr, T. A., & Bennett, M. M. (2015). Working after retirement: Features of bridge employment and research directions. *Work, Aging and Retirement, 1*(1), 112–128.

Betz, N. E., Borgen, F. H., & Harmon, L. W. (2006). Vocational confidence and personality in the prediction of occupational group membership. *Journal of Career Assessment, 14*, 36–55.

Bradbury, S. (2013). Institutional racism, whiteness and the under-representation of minorities in leadership positions in football in Europe. *Soccer and Society, 14*(3), 296–314.

Brown, P. (2003). The opportunity trap: Education and employment in a global economy. *European Educational Research Journal, 2*, 142–180.

Clark, A. E., & Georgellis, Y. (2013). Back to baseline in Britain: Adaptation in the British household panel survey. *Economica, 80*(319), 496–512.

Colella, A., Hebl, M., & King, E. (2017). One hundred years of discrimination research in the *Journal of Applied Psychology*: A sobering synopsis. *The Journal of Applied Psychology, 102*(3), 500–513.

Darcy, M. U. A., & Tracey, T. J. G. (2007). Circumplex structure of Holland's RIASEC interests across gender and time. *Journal of Counselling Psychology, 54*, 17–31.

Davey, F. H. (2001). The relationship between engineering and your women's occupational priorities. *Canadian Journal of Counselling, 35*, 221–228.

De Cuyper, N., Van der Heijden, B. I., & De Witte, H. (2011). Associations between perceived employability, employee well-being, and its contribution to organizational success: A matter of psychological contracts? *The International Journal of Human Resource Management, 22*(07), 1486–1503.

Derr, C. B., & Laurent, A. (1989) The internal and external career: A theoretical and cross-cultural perspective. In M. Arthur, B. S. Laurence, & D. T. Hall (Eds.), *The handbook of career theory* (pp. 454–471). New York, NY: Cambridge University Press.

De Vos, A., De Hauw, S., & Van der Heijden, B. I. (2011). Competency development and career success: The mediating role of employability. *Journal of Vocational Behavior, 79*(2), 438–447.

Direnzo, M. S., & Greenhaus, J. H. (2011). Job search and voluntary turnover in a boundaryless world: A control theory perspective. *Academy of Management Review, 36*(3), 567–589.

Donnay, D. A. C., & Borgen, F. H. (1996). Validity, structure and content of the 1994 Strong Interest Inventory. *Journal of Counselling Psychology, 43*, 275–291.

Eagly, A. H., & Chin, J. L. (2010). Diversity and leadership in a changing world. *American Psychologist, 65*(3), 216–224.

Ekerdt, D. J. (1987). Why the notion persists that retirement harms health. *The Gerentologist, 27*, 454–457.

Ekerdt, D. J., Baden, L., Bossé, R., & Dibbs, E. (1983). The effect of retirement on physical health. *American Journal of Public Health, 73*(7), 779–783.

Farmer, H. S., Wardrop, J. L, Anderson, M. Z., & Risinger, R. (1995). Women's career choices: Focus on science, math and technology careers. *Journal of Counseling Psychology, 42*, 155–170.

Forrier, A., & Sels, L. (2003). The concept employability: A complex mosaic. *International Journal of Human Resources Development and Management, 3*, 102–124.

Fouad, N. A. (1999). Validity evidence for interest inventories. In M. L. Savickas & R. L. Spokane (Eds.), *Vocational interests: Meaning, measurement and counselling use* (pp. 193–209). Palo Alto, CA: Davies-Black.

Fouad, N. A. (2007). Work and vocational psychology: Theory, research and applications. *Annual Review of Psychology, 58*, 543–564.

Gabarro, J. J. (1987). *The dynamics of taking charge*. Boston, MA: Harvard Business School Press.

Gottfredson, L. S. (1981). Circumscription and compromise: A developmental theory of occupational aspirations. *Journal of Counselling Psychology Monograph, 28*, 545–579.

Gouldner, A. (1957). Cosmopolitans and locals: Toward an analysis of latent social roles, part I. *Administrative Science Quarterly, 2*, 281–305.

Gündemir, S., Homan, A. C., de Dreu, C. K., & van Vugt, M. (2014). Think leader, think White? Capturing and weakening an implicit pro-white leadership bias. *PloS one, 9*(1), e83915.

Hall, D. T. (2002). *Careers in and out of organizations*. Thousand Oaks, CA: SAGE.

Hansen, J. C., & Dik, B. J. (2005). Evidence of 12-year predictive and concurrent validity for SII Occupational Scale scores. *Journal of Vocational Behaviour, 67*, 365–378.

Harmon, L. W., Hansen, J. C., Borgen, F. H., & Hammer, A. L. (1994). *Strong Interest Inventory applications and technical guide*. Palo Alto, CA: Consulting Psychologists Press.

Haslam, S. A., Jetten, J., Postmes, T., & Haslam, C. (2009). Social identity, health and well-being: An emerging agenda for applied psychology. *Applied Psychology, 58*(1), 1–23.

Herzog, A. R., House, J. S., & Morgan, J. N. (1991). Relation of work and retirement to health and well-being in older age. *Psychology and Ageing, 6*, 202–211.

Hofstede, G. (1980). *Cultures and organizations: Softwares of the mind*. Newbury Park, CA: SAGE.

Holland, J. L. (1973). *Making vocational choices: A theory of vocational personalities and work environments*. Odessa, FL: Psychological Assessment Resources.

Holland, J. L. (1994). *Self-directed search: Assessment booklet, a guide to educational and career planning*. Odessa, FL: Psychological Assessment Resources.

Inkson, K. (2008). The boundaryless career. In S. Cartwright & L. Cooper (Eds.), *The Oxford handbook of personnel psychology* (pp. 545–585). Oxford, England: Oxford University Press.

Jome, L. M., & Tokar, D. M. (1998). Dimensions of masculinity and major choice traditionality. *Journal of Vocational Behaviour, 52*, 120–134.

Judge, T. A., Higgins, C. A., Thoresen, C. J., & Barrick, M. R. (1999). The Big Five personality traits, general mental ability and career success across the life span. *Personnel Psychology, 52*, 621–652.

Kahn, W. A. (2007). Meaningful connections: Positive relationships and attachments at work. In J. E. Dutton & B. R. Ragins (Eds.), *Exploring positive relationships at work: Building a theoretical and research foundation* (pp. 189–206). LEA's organization and management series. Mahwah, NJ: Lawrence Erlbaum Associates.

Kandola, B. (2018). *Racism at work: The danger of indifference*. Oxford, England: Pearn Kandola Publishing.

Kandola, J., & Kandola, B. (2013). *The invention of difference: The story of gender bias at work*. Oxford, England: Pearn Kandola Publishing.

Kidd, J. M. (2002). Careers and career management. In P. Warr (Ed.), *Psychology at work* (pp. 178–202). London, England: Penguin.

Kim, S., & Feldman, D. C. (2000). Working in retirement: The antecedents of bridge employment and its consequences for quality of life in retirement. *Academy of Management Journal, 43*(6), 1195–1210.

Kristof, A. L. (1996). Person–organization fit: An integrative review of its conceptualizations, measurement, and implications. *Personnel Psychology, 49*(1), 1–49.

Kristof-Brown, A. L., Zimmerman, R. D., & Johnson, E. C. (2005). Consequences of individuals' fit at work: A meta-analysis of person–job, person–organization, person–group, and person–supervisor fit. *Personnel Psychology, 58*, 281–342.

Larson, L. M., Rottinghaus, P. J., & Borgen, F. H. (2002). Meta-analyses of Big Six interests and Big Five personality factors. *Journal of Vocational Behavior, 61*, 217–239.

Lent, R. W., Brown, S. D., & Hackett, G. (1994). Toward a unifying social cognitive theory of career and academic interest, choice and performance. *Journal of Vocational Behaviour, 45*, 79–122.

Midanik, L. T., Soghikian, K., Ransom, L. J., & Tekawa, I. S. (1995). The effect of retirement on mental health and health behaviours: The Kaiser Permanente Retirement Study. *The Journals of Gerontology Series B: Psychological Sciences and Social Sciences, 50B*(1), S59–S61.

Miller, L., & Budd, J. (1999). The development of occupational sex-role stereotypes, occupational preferences and academic subject preferences in children at ages 8, 12 and 16. *Educational Psychology, 19*, 17–35.

Miscenko, D., & Day, D. V. (2016). Identity and identification at work. *Organizational Psychology Review, 6*(3), 215–247.

Muchinsky, P. M., & Monahan, C. J. (1987). What is person–environment congruence? Supplementary versus complementary models of fit. *Journal of Vocational Behavior, 31*(3), 268–277.

Nauta, A., Van Vianen, A., Van der Heijden, B., Van Dam, K., & Willemsen, M. (2009). Understanding the factors that promote employability orientation: The impact of employability culture, career satisfaction and role breadth self-efficacy. *Journal of Occupational and Organizational Psychology, 82*, 233–251.

Nicholson, N. (1990). *On the move: The psychology of change and transition*. Chichester, England: John Wiley & Sons.

Nicholson, N., & Arnold, J. (1991). From expectation to experience: Graduates entering a large corporation. *Journal of Organizational Behaviour, 12*(5), 413–429.

Nicholson, N., & West, M. A. (1988). *Managerial job change: Men and women in transition*. Cambridge, England: Cambridge University Press.

O*NET Resource Center. (2003). *The O*NET analyst database*. O*NET Consortium. Retrieved from www.onetcenter.org/database.html#archive

Parsons, F. (1909) *Choosing a vocation*. Boston, MA: Houghton-Mifflin.

Porath, C., Spreitzer, G., Gibson, C., & Garnett, F. G. (2012). Thriving at work: Toward its measurement, construct validation, and theoretical refinement. *Journal of Organizational Behavior, 33*(2), 250–275.

Prediger, D. J. (1982). Dimensions underlying Holland's hexagon: Missing link between interests and occupations? *Journal of Vocational Behaviour, 21*, 259–287.

Roberts, B. W., Caspi, A., & Moffitt, T. E. (2003). Work experiences and personality development in young adulthood. *Journal of Personality and Social Psychology, 84*(3), 582.

Roberts, B. W., Wood, D., & Smith, J. L. (2005). Evaluating five factor theory and social investment perspectives on personality trait development. *Journal of Research in Personality, 39*, 166–184.

Rothwell, A., & Arnold, J. (2007). Self-perceived employability: Development and validation of a scale. *Personnel Review, 36*, 23–41.

Rudman, L. A., Greenwald, A. G., & McGhee, D. E. (2001). Implicit self-concept and evaluative implicit gender stereotypes: Self and ingroup share desirable traits. *Personality and Social Psychology Bulletin, 27*(9), 1164–1178.

Ryan, M. K., & Haslam, S. A. (2005). The glass cliff: Evidence that women are over-represented in precarious leadership positions. *British Journal of Management, 16*(2), 81–90.

Ryan, M. K., Haslam, S. A., Hersby, M. D., & Bongiorno, R. (2011). Think crisis–think female: The glass cliff and contextual variation in the think manager–think male stereotype. *Journal of Applied Psychology, 96*(3), 470.

Samnani, A. K., Boekhorst, J. A., & Harrison, J. A. (2013). The acculturation process: Antecedents, strategies, and outcomes. *Journal of Occupational and Organizational Psychology, 86*(2), 166–183.

Savickas, M. L. (2002). Career construction: A developmental theory of vocational behaviour. In D. Brown & Associates (Eds.), *Career choice and development* (4th ed., pp. 149–205). San Francisco, CA: Jossey-Bass.

Savickas, M. L. (2005). The theory and practice of career construction. In S. D. Brown & R. W. Lent. (Eds.), *Career development and counselling: Putting theory and research to work* (pp. 42–69). Hoboken, NJ: John Wiley & Sons.

Schein, E. H. (1971). The individual, the organization and the career: A conceptual scheme. *The Journal of Applied Behavioral Science, 7*(4), 401–426.

Schein, E. H. (1984). Culture as an environmental context for careers. *Journal of Occupational Behaviour, 5*(1), 71–81.

Schein, E. H. (1993). *Career anchors: Discovering your real values*. San Diego, CA: Pfeiffer.

Schein, V. E. (1973). The relationship between sex role stereotypes and requisite management characteristics. *Journal of Applied Psychology, 57*(2), 95.

Schwab, K. et al. (2018). The global gender gap report 2018. Cologny/Geneva, Switzerland: World Economic Forum.

Selenko, E., Berkers, H., Carter, A., Woods, S. A., Otto, K., Urbach, T., & De Witte, H. (2018). On the dynamics of work identity in atypical employment: Setting out a research agenda. *European Journal of Work and Organizational Psychology, 27*(3), 324–334.

Sen, A. (2000). *Social exclusion: Concept, application, and scrutiny*. Manila, Philippines: Asian Development Bank.

Spokane, A. R., Meir, E. I., & Catalano, M. (2000). Person–environment congruence and Holland's theory: A review and reconsideration. *Journal of Vocational Behaviour, 57*(2), 137–187.

Spreitzer, G., Sutcliffe, K., Dutton, J., Sonenshein, S., & Grant, A. M. (2005). A socially embedded model of thriving at work. *Organization Science, 16*(5), 537–549.

Su, R., Murdock, C. D., & Rounds, J. (2015). Person–environment fit. In P. J. Hartung, M. L. Savickas, & W. B. Walsh (Eds.) *APA handbook of career intervention* (Vol. 1, pp. 81–98). Washington, DC: APA.

Super, D. E. (1990). A life span, life-space approach to career development. In D. Brown & L. Brooks (Eds.), *Career choice and development* (2nd ed.). San Francisco, CA: Jossey–Bass.

Super, D. E., & Hall, D. T. (1978). Career development: Exploration and planning. *Annual Review of Psychology, 29*, 333–372.

Tracey, T. J., & Rounds, J. B. (1993). Evaluating Holland's and Gati's vocational-interest models: A structural meta-analysis. *Psychological Bulletin, 113*(2), 229–246.

Tranberg, M., Slane, S., & Ekeberg, E. (1993). The relation between interest congruence and satisfaction: A meta-analysis. *Journal of Vocational Behaviour, 42*, 253–264.

US Department of Labor. (1991). *Dictionary of Occupational Titles* (rev. 4th ed.). Washington, DC: US Government Printing Office.

Van den Brink, M., & Benschop, Y. (2014). Gender in academic networking: The role of gatekeepers in professorial recruitment. *Journal of Management Studies, 51*(3), 460–492.

Van der Heijde, C. M., & Van der Heijden, B. I. J. M. (2006). A competence-based and multidimensional operationalization and measurement of employability. *Human Resource Management, 45*, 449–476.

Van der Heijden, B. I., de Lange, A. H., Demerouti, E., & Van der Heijde, C. M. (2009). Age effects on the employability–career success relationship. *Journal of Vocational Behavior, 74*(2), 156–164.

van Dick, R., van Knippenberg, D., Kerschreiter, R., Hertel, G., & Wieseke, J. (2008). Interactive effects of work group and organizational identification on job satisfaction and extra-role behavior. *Journal of Vocational Behavior, 72*(3), 388–399.

van Knippenberg, D. (2000). Work motivation and performance: A social identity perspective. *Applied Psychology, 49*(3), 357–371.

Wang, M., Olson, D. A., & Shultz, K. S. (2013). Series in applied psychology. *Mid and late career issues: An integrative perspective*. New York, NY: Routledge.

Wang, M., & Wanberg, C. R. (2017). 100 years of applied psychology research on individual careers: From career management to retirement. *Journal of Applied Psychology, 102*(3), 546–563.

Warr, P. (2008). *Work, happiness and unhappiness*. Mahwah, NJ: LEA.

Warr, P., Butcher, V., Robertson, I., & Callinan, M. (2004). Older people's well-being as a function of employment, retirement, environmental characteristics and role preference. *British Journal of Psychology, 95*, 297–324.

Wille, B., Beyers, W., & De Fruyt, F. (2012). A transactional approach to person–environment fit: Reciprocal relations between personality development and career role growth across young to middle adulthood. *Journal of Vocational Behavior, 81*(3), 307–321.

Wille, B., & De Fruyt, F. (2014). Vocations as a source of identity: Reciprocal relations between Big Five personality traits and RIASEC characteristics over 15 years. *Journal of Applied Psychology, 99*(2), 262–281.

Wille, B., & De Fruyt, F. (2019). The development of vocational interests. In C. D. Nye & J. Rounds (Eds.), *Vocational interests in the workplace: Rethinking behavior at work*. New York, NY: Routledge.

Wong, A. L., & Slater, J. R. (2002). Executive development in China: Is there any in a Western sense? *International Journal of Human Resource Management, 13*(2), 338–360.

Woods, S. A., & Hampson, S. E. (2010). Predicting adult occupational environments from gender and childhood personality traits. *Journal of Applied Psychology, 95*(6), 1045.

Woods, S. A., Lievens, F., De Fruyt, F., & Wille, B. (2013). Personality across working life: The longitudinal and reciprocal influences of personality on work. *Journal of Organizational Behavior, 34*(1), S7–S25.

Woods, S. A., Patterson, F. C., Wille, B., & Koczwara, A. (2016). Personality and occupational specialty: An examination of medical specialties using Holland's RIASEC model. *Career Development International, 21*(3), 262–278.

Young, C. (2012). Losing a job: The nonpecuniary cost of unemployment in the United States. *Social Forces, 91*(2), 609–634.

Yousaf, A., & Sanders, K. (2012). The role of job satisfaction and self-efficacy as mediating mechanisms in the employability and affective organizational commitment relationship: A case from a Pakistani university. *Thunderbird International Business Review, 54*(6), 907–919.

Zhou, Y., Zou, M., Woods, S. A., & Wu, C. H. (2019). The restorative effect of work after unemployment: An intra-individual analysis of subjective well-being recovery through reemployment. *Journal of Applied Psychology*. doi.org/10.1037/apl0000393.

CHAPTER 9

SAFETY, STRESS AND HEALTH AT WORK

LEARNING OBJECTIVES

- Understand the concepts of occupational health and safety and how to reduce accidents at work.
- Understand the key theories of stress at work.
- Understand how task performance and mental and physical health are affected by stress.
- Identify the ways in which health and well-being can be protected and promoted at work.

POSITIVE EMOTION AT WORK

Positive emotions, such as hope, pleasure, happiness, humour, excitement, joy, love, pride and involvement, are important sources of human strength (Cameron & Spreitzer, 2011; Fredrickson, 2009; Lyubomirsky, King, & Diener, 2005). When we feel positive we think in a more flexible, open-minded way and consider a much wider range of possibilities than if we feel anxious, depressed or angry. This enables us to accomplish many tasks more effectively and to make the most of the situations we find ourselves in. We are also more likely to see challenges as opportunities rather than threats. When we feel positive, we exercise greater self-control, cope more effectively and are less likely to react defensively in workplace situations. The litany of benefits doesn't stop there. It spills over too into 'pro-social behaviour' – cooperation and altruism. When we feel positive emotion we are more likely to be helpful, generous and to exercise a sense of social responsibility.

We cannot create effective organizations by focusing simply on performance and ignoring the role of our emotions. Positive relationships and a sense of community are the product and cause of positive emotions. Working with human needs and capacities and potentials rather than against them helps in creating positive cultures and organizations that succeed and, at the same time, foster the health and well-being of those who work within them (Cameron & Spreitzer, 2011; Goleman, Boyatzis, & McKee, 2002; Layard, 2005). In organizations with positive climates, creativity, cooperation and citizenship are typical. And they are all factors that predict organizational performance.

Not surprisingly, the opposite of much of this is true too. Chronic anxiety and chronic hostility/anger lead to ill-health, failure to recover from illness and a generally depressed immune system. Pessimism, anger, anxiety, cynicism and apathy are corrosive in organizations, not just to organizational performance but also to the health and the well-being of the people who work within them. In this chapter we consider some of the dark sides of organizations and how they create tension, anger, ill-health and fear for employees. And we examine how the well-being of people at work can be understood, protected and promoted. We begin by examining the topic of health and safety at work.

OCCUPATIONAL HEALTH AND SAFETY

Addressing workplace safety is self-evidently important. In the USA in 2012, there were nearly five million workplace accidents requiring medical attention; the cost of the accidents was just under $200 billion (Hofmann, Burke, & Zohar, 2017). The World Health Organization estimates that there are 270 million occupational health injuries worldwide annually and 354,753 fatalities (Takala, 2002). Canada estimates the cost of such injuries at $6,000 per injury and $492,000 per fatality. In Bangladesh in 2013, the Rana Plaza building collapsed killing 1,127 workers and injuring 2,500 more. We have a long way to go to improve health and safety in the workplace.

The journey has been continuing in the UK since 1833 when the Factory Act was passed to protect children in the workplace, with successive Acts focusing on women at work (1844), inspections of workplaces (1867), requirements for accident reporting (1891) and means of escaping fires (1895). Today there are an estimated 596,000 people injured at work each year in the UK, with a corresponding annual cost in billions of pounds (Health and Safety Executive, 2013). Even though the number of injuries at work has dropped by 40 per cent over the past decade in the UK, the human costs in pain, misery or bereavement are still enormous.

How can work psychology help us prevent injury and illness? First we need to understand the phenomena we are faced with

> Occupational injury *represents a wound or damage to the body resulting from unintentional or intentional acute exposure to energy (kinetic, chemical, thermal, electrical and radiation) or from the acute absence of essential elements (e.g. heat, oxygen) caused by a specific event, incident or series of events within a single workday or shift.* (Bureau of Labour Statistics, 2013.)

> Occupational illness *represents any abnormal condition or disorder, other than one resulting from an occupational injury, caused by exposure to factors associated with employment. It includes acute and chronic illnesses or diseases that may be caused by inhalation, absorption, ingestion or direct contact. There are seven categories: occupational skin diseases, dust diseases of the lungs, respiratory conditions due to toxic agents, poisoning due to the systematic effects of toxic agents, disorders due to physical agents other than toxic materials (welding flash, sunstroke), disorders associated with repeated trauma (carpal tunnel syndrome, noise induced hearing loss) and all other occupational illnesses.* (Adapted from Bureau of Labour Statistics, 2013.)

What protects people from such occupational injuries and illness? 'Safety climate' is a key factor (Hofmann et al., 2017; Neal & Griffin, 2004). Zohar and colleagues' work (Zohar, 1980, 2003) has established that leaders and fellow team members play a key role in creating an effective safety climate (as one of us, MW, found during his work in the South Wales coal mines back in the 1970s). Safety climate refers to employees' perceptions of the policies, practices and procedures relating to safety (Zohar, 2003). It is highly influenced by what managers and leaders say and do in terms of making safety a priority (Hofmann, Morgeson, & Gerras, 2003). Their day-to-day behaviours in emphasizing, talking about and rewarding safe behaviours are a potent determinant of the safety behaviours of those they lead. And we know that safety training works, especially when it closely reflects the daily conditions and challenges that workers face on the job (Burke, Salvador, Smith-Crowe, Chan-Serafin, Smith, & Sonesh, 2011). Training supervisors in how to nurture a safety climate clearly improves safety at work (Zohar, 2002).

Turner and Parker (2004) have shown in a review of the literature (particularly research on cockpit crews in aircraft) that teams can have a very positive effect on safety in organizations since they provide a medium within which employees can influence decision-making. This is consistent with work in the UK National Health Service, suggesting that good teamworking is associated with fewer errors and injuries reported by staff (West & Lyubovnikova, 2013). Individual factors also affect occupational health and safety, such as anxiety and negative affect. Dunbar (1993) found that depression, anxiety and negative affect were associated with less use of protective equipment. And there is some indication that there are accident-prone individuals (Beus, Dhanani, & McCord, 2015), with Agreeableness and Conscientiousness negatively predicting accidents and sensation-seeking positively associated with accident proneness. However, safety climate perceptions – the individual's sense of the extent to which there is a strong emphasis on safety in their workplaces – is a more powerful predictor than any personality characteristics.

Probst and Brubaker (2001) found that job insecurity was associated with workplace accidents and injuries because it affected job satisfaction, which, in turn, influenced safety behaviours. These findings extend to casual work (important given the rise of the 'gig' economy). Quinlan and Bohle (2004) report consistent evidence that temporary work is associated with poor health outcomes. Quinlan, Mayhew, and Bohle (2001) reviewed 82 studies across 14 EU countries and Australia, and found that in 76 of them, compared with full-time work, contingent work led to higher injury rates and more strain. Benavides, Benach, Diez-Roux, and Roman (2000) found that, across Europe, fatigue, backache and muscular pain were more prevalent among those with precarious employment.

Age is another important factor in considering occupational health and safety. Loughlin and Frone (2004) report that non-fatal injuries at work are highest among young workers, especially males, in the 15–24 years age group. This is particularly important since young workers are not typically concentrated in dangerous industries such as mining, construction and petrochemicals. They are more likely to work in restaurants and groceries, yet typical injuries include lacerations, sprains, bruising, burns and fractures. Some researchers suggest this is because those in this age group are more likely to have perceptions of invulnerability, to be sensation-seeking, rebellious and to experience negative affect (disappointment at the quality of the work they are required to do). Moreover, young workers have less control in the workplace and are less likely to have union representation, so these protection factors are absent.

Occupational health psychology (OHP) aims to improve quality of work life by promoting the health, safety and well-being of workers by applying psychology. OHP researchers and practitioners focus on psychosocial work characteristics that lead to physical and mental health problems such as accidental injury, cardiovascular disease, psychological distress, burnout and depression. Two of the leading international OHP organizations are the Society for Occupational Health Psychology (sohp.psy.uconn.edu/) and the European Academy of Occupational Health Psychology (eaohp.org). Key journals related to this field are the *Journal of Occupational Health Psychology* and *Work and Stress*.

BOX 9.1
Making a positive difference: promoting health and safety

It is the responsibility of employers to protect the health and ensure the safety of employees at work, but it is taken seriously only to varying degrees across organizations and across nations. To what extent can HRM and other workplace practices promote health and safety in organizations? Zacharatos and Barling (2004) propose ten HRM practices that will influence workplace safety positively:

1. Employment security – since this encourages a long-term perspective, promoting trust and organizational commitment as well as building experience with safety procedures.

2. Selective hiring – to exclude accident-prone individuals based on drug addiction, alcoholism, emotional immaturity and untrustworthiness.

3. Extensive training – employees who have workplace safety training have fewer injuries (Colligan & Cohen, 2004).

4. Self-managed teams and decentralized decision-making – a number of studies have demonstrated higher levels of safety behaviour in teams. One example (Tjosvold, 1990) found that flight crews that worked as teams when facing dangerous situations were more effective than those that operated as a hierarchy.

5. Reduce status distinctions – where status distinctions are strong, expressed concerns about workplace safety are likely to be given weight only if the individual is of high status. Milanovich, Driskell, Stout, and Salas (1998) found that this was indeed the case among airline cockpit crews.

6. Share information – companies where there is more contact and information sharing between managers and front-line employees have fewer accidents.

7. Compensation contingent on safe performance – high pay communicates that the employee is valued. 'If you're getting paid a wage that you're happy with, then you're happy at your work, so you're switched on and alert. You don't mind doing your bit' (North Sea oil worker, Collinson, 1999, p. 591). And specifically rewarding all workers for group-level safety behaviour (lower rates of accidents across the whole organization) is likely to convey a message about the importance that managers and leaders place on safety (Fox, Hopkins, & Anger, 1987).

8. Compassionate and transformational leadership – will be effective in communicating to employees the importance of safety and inspiring them to work safely, a prediction supported among workers in the offshore oil and gas industry (O'Dea & Flin, 2000; West & Chowla, 2017).

9. High-quality work – high workload can lead to high levels of injury and errors at work (Hofmann & Stetzer, 1996). High job autonomy leads to safety at work (Parker, Axtell, & Turner, 2001), along with work-role clarity (Houston & Allt, 1997).

10. Measurement of variables critical to organizational success – these include employee attitudes to safety, organizational commitment, job satisfaction, engagement, trust in management, initiative taking in respect to safety and participation in safety processes and structures (such as health and safety committees); employment security; safety training experience; job quality; and the extent to which employees work in teams.

Overall, work psychologists and occupational health psychologists have made considerable advances in understanding the factors that influence occupational health and safety. But what about less visible forms of damage to people at work? If injuries are the visible part of the iceberg, many work psychologists argue that stress and strain at work are the invisible damage beneath the surface.

STRESS AND STRAIN AT WORK

The Health and Safety Executive estimates that the financial cost of work-related stress to UK employers is £531 million and to society nearly £4 billion per year. The total number of cases of stress in 2011/12 was 428,000 (40 per cent) out of a total of 1,073,000 for all work-related illnesses. The sectors with highest incidences are human health and social work, education and public administration, and defence. In particular, nurses, teachers, welfare and housing professionals are most likely to suffer from work-related stress. The main causes of stress they report are work pressure, lack of managerial support and work-related harassment and bullying.

The costs of stress stem not only from absenteeism and lost productivity, but also from compensation claims, health insurance and medical expenses. In the USA, annual stress insurance claims in the California workers' compensation system total approximately $383 million (Beehr, 1995).

What is work stress?

When our ancestors were trying to survive in a hostile natural world 80,000 years ago, the challenges were dangers from wild animals or other humans, and natural phenomena that were not fully understood (extreme weather or geological events), which occasionally must have made things a little tense. Today, sitting in an office, discussing the development of organizational strategy in the context of economic downturns, we imagine this does not have quite the same bite. Yet stress at work is a regular topic of conversation among those studying people at work. For some occupations it is easy to see why we might want to invoke this concept of 'stress'. The job of a soldier in combat is undoubtedly frightening, boring, dirty and lonely at times. Ambulance workers in inner cities face the threat of violence from people whose inhibitions have been lowered by alcohol. The call centre worker, with a large number of phone calls to deal with, some of which involve complaining customers crossing the line into personal abuse, might go home at the end of the day sad or tense and angry. The social worker, who is anxious about a family she thinks may be abusing or neglecting a young child, may lose sleep picturing herself in court over a failure to intervene. So, is stress modern-day, self-indulgent angst or a serious issue that needs tackling if we are to create positive work environments? Now we turn to explore this concept in detail and briefly describe the main theories to explain stress at work.

We can think of stress in a number of ways – as a cause of bad feelings or a stressor (the abusive customer, for example); as a process – the means by which work pressures results in loss of sleep; or as an outcome – elevated blood pressure and absenteeism. A brief review of the history of the concept will help us answer the questions we pose in this chapter.

Homeostasis and the 'fight or flight' response

Early theorizing is traced by most scholars to Cannon (1929), who coined the term 'fight or flight' and introduced the concept of homeostasis, referring to the deviation from 'normal' physiological processes when a person responds to perceived threat. When our ancient ancestor was confronted by a predator, her body instantly reacted to prepare her to do battle or fly with all speed. If you are crossing the street and a bus is suddenly upon you with the driver blasting his horn, you jump and run immediately to safety. Afterwards, you notice how fast your heart is beating and how quickly you are breathing. This is not simply a result of your leap to safety but a consequence of your bodily processes coordinating to prepare you for immediate and dynamic action – your heart rate speeds up immediately to pump blood to your muscles.

Consider another modern-day situation where you become involved in an argument with a colleague in a meeting about a report you failed to produce on time. Once again, you feel your face flushing and your heart rate speeding up, though you are not preparing to run away at all speed or beat him senseless with a club. However, your body is giving you the capacity to do both these things. The problem with this reaction is that it takes the body some time to return to a resting baseline (to achieve homeostasis), and the more frequently fight or flight reactions are produced, the less time the body is at rest. In a worst-case scenario, the failure to return to a state of relaxation leads to the basal level of arousal being permanently raised (homeostasis is reset at a higher level of arousal), with associated negative consequences such as high blood pressure and coronary heart disease (CHD).

General adaptation syndrome

Hans Selye (1956), a Canadian endocrinologist, built on Cannon's ideas and used the term 'stress' to describe a non-specific response of the body to any demand made on it. He distinguished between distress (harmful effects of demands) and 'eustress' (the enjoyment of challenging demands). Distress would be caused by conflicts with colleagues at work whereas eustress could occur in the process of running an exciting workshop developing ideas for new products for the future – demanding, yes, but also exhilarating. Selye proposed the 'general adaptation syndrome' (GAS) as a model for understanding how sustained stressors affect health. He described three stages: alarm, resistance and exhaustion.

In the first stage, the body produces an alarm reaction (for example in response to dealing with an abusive caller on the telephone) and secretes stress hormones – adrenalin, noradrenalin, epinephrine and cortisol, which all serve to raise arousal. The individual tries to adapt by coping with the stressors during the resistance stage and may well do so – there is sustained psycho-physiological arousal at a lower level of intensity than the alarm stage. However, resources are being used up and this impairs the ability to deal with other stressors. Managing angry customers is within her abilities, but having to deal with demanding colleagues may be beyond her resources. Finally is the stage of exhaustion in response to sustained exposure to stressors. Over time, resistance decreases, resulting in the person feeling 'burnt out', becoming ill or, in the extreme, dying (for example from a heart attack). The GAS model describes longer-lasting chronic stress, for example a sustained high level of workload, compared with the acute stress described in the fight or flight model.

A variety of theoretical approaches to understanding stress have been proposed since this early work and we briefly outline the main approaches below (for an excellent and more detailed review see Dewe, 2017).

THEORIES OF STRESS AT WORK
Role stress theory

Kahn and colleagues (e.g. Kahn, Wolfe, Quinn, Snoek, & Rosentbal, 1964) proposed that the characteristics of organizational roles, such as ambiguity (lack of clarity about job purpose), conflict (between quantity and quality of work, for example) and overload, impact on people's physiological and psychological well-being and their attempts to cope with these role stressors. Some principles emerging from this approach were that jobs should be reasonably challenging and have variety without overwhelming people; they should provide opportunities for learning; there should be opportunities for autonomous decision-making; people should have good social support and recognition in the workplace; and there should be opportunities for growth, learning or development.

Person–environment fit

In their 'Person–Environment Fit' model, French, Caplan, and Van Harrison (1982) developed the theoretical idea that the greater the extent to which our skills and abilities match the job requirements and work environment, the better will be our well-being. For example, a sociable, creative and well-travelled individual who seeks new projects continually is likely to make a good travel agent but not a software developer working on a long-term and detailed project. An anxious, attention-to-detail person who is highly risk avoidant and introverted may not make a good leader. We can separate out 'PE fit' into two sub-components: person–job fit and person–organization fit. The person–job fit concept relates to the extent to which the skills, abilities and interests of the individual are compatible with job requirements. Person–organization fit refers to whether the values of the organization are consistent with the values of the individual. One of the MBA students MW taught had a senior role and very high salary in a major defence industry organization but felt that his values and those of the organization were in conflict. He had been suffering increasing illness and strain when he left to join an international aid agency on a much lower salary. After two years in the new job, he was happier and healthier than at any time in his career. Verquer, Beehr, and Wagner (2003) performed a meta-analysis of PE fit and work attitudes confirming relationships between poor person–environment fit and intention to quit, and both low job satisfaction and organizational commitment.

Job demands, control and support

The Job Demands, Control and Support Model (Karasek 1979; Karasek & Theorell, 1990) highlighted the joint effects of work demands and job control or perceived decision latitude (autonomy/control), with high work demands and low control considered to be the most toxic cocktail. Indeed, Karasek and Theorell found that those in such positions were two or three times more likely to become ill than others at work. We can understand these concepts better by looking at some practical examples of different combinations of demands and control:

- High demands and low control – such as the work of a waiter, assembly line worker, Post Office worker, computer help desk.
- High demands and high control. Such a combination can be exciting and rewarding by offering what Csikszentmihalyi calls 'flow' (Csikszentmihalyi, 2008). Those who experience them are likely to include barristers, actors, surgeons and senior managers. These conditions are likely to be health promoting.
- Low demands and high control, e.g. gardener. The job is not particularly demanding and you can choose how to do it. The ideal job if you want a peaceful life.
- Low demands and low control, e.g. night watchman. The night watchman has little latitude about what there is to do on the job and what skills they can deploy. It is simply a case of 'keeping an eye on things' and getting through the night. Deeply boring but a great cure for insomnia!

Later formulations of the theory included a support dimension, such as support from colleagues and supervisors – think of firefighters, police or ambulance workers working in supportive pairs or teams. It was proposed that support moderates the relationships between demands, control and strain outcomes.

Research evidence supports the model. For example, Ganster, Fox, and Dwyer (2001) conducted a longitudinal study of 105 nurses and found that those who perceived high demands and low control were ill more often and incurred the highest overall healthcare costs. Many studies across cultures have confirmed that a combination of high demands and low control is damaging to human health.

Transactional model of stress

A major theoretical shift came with Lazarus and Folkman's (1984) proposal that the effect of stressors was dependent upon how the individual thought about (or 'cognitively appraised') them. In this approach, stressful experiences are construed as person–environment transactions. Primary appraisal is whether the individual perceives a potential stressor as harmful, threatening or challenging; and secondary appraisal describes how they feel they could manage or cope with the stressful situation. Coping processes produce a change in the person–environment situation which is then reappraised as favourable or not. The theory proposed that improving our planned coping responses to future or sustained stressors may be helpful.

The three major types of stress coping strategies described by the theory (in its modern form) are problem-focused, emotion-focused and appraisal-focused coping. The first strategy involves solving the problem by defining it, generating solutions and implementing solutions (Lazarus, 2000). For example, an office worker unable to respond to all the customer requests in a timely fashion, causing them to become irate, produces a Frequently Asked Questions website. Emotion-focused coping involves trying to manage anxiety via denial or wishful thinking, or distancing oneself from the problem. Appraisal-focused coping involves redefining the situation. For example, a junior manager might try to persuade herself that the presentation to the management team is not really important and it does not matter if she fails since the rest of her work is effective. Which approach is most successful? The research evidence suggests that problem-focused coping often helps to deal with a problem decisively and is most effective in preventing strain, while emotion-focused coping is the least effective. Avoidance – pretending the problem does not exist or it will go away – generally does not help (for example in relation to continued conflicts with someone in another department) (Cartwright & Cooper, 1997).

Effort–reward imbalance

The effort–reward imbalance model proposes that a lack of reciprocity between the expenditure of effort in work and consequent rewards leads to stress (Siegrist, 2017). Such an imbalance creates strong negative emotions and stress reactions that have long-term negative effects on health. Rewards include salary, promotion, job security and esteem or recognition at work. Considerable research reveals that chronic effort–reward imbalance is associated with elevated risks of depression, ischemic heart disease and other negative health outcomes. The model can also be applied to contexts other than paid work, such as volunteering, caring for a relative or other family work.

Conservation of resources

The conservation of resources theory proposes that people are motivated to retain, protect and foster resources because loss or threat of loss of resources leads to burnout (Hobfoll, 1989, 2001, 2011).

Resources are personal characteristics (skills, relationships), conditions (reputation at work, position in the organizational hierarchy) or energies (job satisfaction) valued for their own sake or for the role they play in helping us to acquire other resources. People strive to fulfil important roles, achieve important goals and offset despair and to minimize loss of resources. Feeling you have too many tasks to complete at work and that you are losing the space you need to think, take breaks or relax might make you feel you have to work even harder to achieve those valued outcomes. But that in turn makes you feel even more stressed and therefore anxious. The theory further proposes that because humans are more focused on loss than gain, attention turns more to workplace factors that threaten resources, such as negative feedback from one's boss or having to deal with a difficult conflict situation. Such resource-threatening factors are much more salient than rewards. Interpersonal conflict is particularly threatening (Leiter & Maslach, 1988). Moreover, there is evidence that the effects of loss of resources are chronic. Bakker et al. (Bakker, Schaufeli, Sixma, & Bosveld, 2001; Bakker, Schaufeli, Sixma, Bosveld, & Van Dierendonck 2000) studied 2007 general practitioners over five years and found a correlation of 0.5 in stress levels, showing that levels of stress appeared to be enduring over this period of time. Schaufeli and Buunk (2003) studied five different samples of workers over periods from three months to a year and found the correlation between stress levels at different points averaged 0.6.

Job demands and resources

This focus on resources characterizes a more recent approach to understanding stress – the Job Demands and Resources Model (JD-R model; Demerouti, Bakker, Nachreiner, & Schaufeli, 2001). This approach integrates theory and research on job design and job stress into one model (see also Schaufeli & Taris, 2014). Job demands and resources evoke two processes: health impairment results from chronic job demands (work overload and competing organizational demands), while motivational processes are stimulated by the presence of suitable job resources (e.g. social support from colleagues, good resources for doing the job). These motivational processes lead to job engagement (vigour, dedication and absorption in the work) and positive work outcomes. Job resources predict growth, learning and motivation and act as a buffer to strain. The theory has developed to include the notion of job crafting whereby people are encouraged to change their context by increasing resources and reducing demands through sculpting or crafting the characteristics of their jobs (Bakker & Demerouti, 2017).

Life events theory

A somewhat different view of stress was offered by theories that emphasized psychological reactions to stressors (Dohrenwend, 2006), particularly the influence of life events. However, research failed to find consistently strong relationships between life events and stress outcomes (strain), leading to new research emphasizing moderators of the relationship such as personality, perceived control over events, social support and the meaning of the event to the person affected (Bliese, Edwards, & Sonnentag, 2017). We describe some of the relevant research below.

INDIVIDUAL DIFFERENCES IN RESPONSE TO STRESS

While one person may find the prospect of working in a coal mine for six months rather scary, another person may see it as a great adventure. Taking responsibility for leading a team to introduce a culture of innovation in an organization might feel impossible to one person and exciting to another. Even with the same background of skills and experience, people differ considerably in how they respond to stress at work. The study of individual differences reveals that certain personality dimensions such as locus of control, hardiness and self-esteem relate to people's reactions to stressors.

Locus of control describes the extent to which people believe that they are in control of events in their lives versus being at the mercy of factors and events outside their control. Rotter (1966) proposed that having an internal locus of control (believing generally that you control what happens to you in life) moderates the relationship between stressors and strain such that a strong internal locus is associated with less strain.

Hardiness refers to the extent to which people have orientations of commitment, control and challenge in their approach to their work lives: commitment to being involved in events and change rather than being isolated; a determination to try to control and influence events rather than feeling paralyzed or powerless; and an orientation to see change as a challenge rather than as a threat. Maddi and Kobasa (1984) studied employees of the Illinois Bell Telephone Company during a mass redundancy programme over a one-year period, which involved cutting the 26,000 workforce by nearly half. Two-thirds of employees suffered health and psychological problems during the change process but one-third appeared to thrive, being healthier and more invigorated. Maddi and Kobasa (1984) found that the difference between the groups was accounted for by the commitment, control and challenge orientations described above. Maddi's Hardiness Institute now offers training programmes to help people change their perceptions of stressful situations to view them as a challenge to be overcome.

Emotional intelligence and optimism (which might be considered an aspect of hardiness) is consistently correlated with health outcomes at work, and this too is trainable (Matthews, Zeidner, & Roberts, 2012). Similarly, there are relationships between optimism, coping and well-being. For example, Tindale et al. (2009), as part of the Women's Health Initiative, gathered data from 95,000 women over 8 years. Optimists were less likely to develop CHD and they were 30 per cent less likely to die from it (and they had lower total mortality). Positive people appear to respond to workplace adversity in more adaptive ways and have better emotional well-being, more effective coping methods and better outcomes in terms of physical health. Furthermore, they are better liked and they manage to sort out their work problems more effectively. Partly as a consequence, they also keep relationships alive and vibrant – all of which is consistent with the proposals in the Conservation of Resources theory.

Type A personality describes those who have a '... chronic struggle to obtain an unlimited number of poorly defined things from their environment in the shortest period of time and, if necessary, against the opposing effects of other things or persons in this same environment' (Friedman, 1969, p. 84). Type A is also described as the coronary-prone personality. Friedman and Rosenman in their 1974 book, *Type A Behavior and Your Heart,* describe the coronary-prone personality as someone characterized by ambition, impatience, irritability and a sense of time urgency. They are engaged in a constant struggle to achieve more in even less time. Type B is described as relaxed, easy-going, patient and calm. It is noteworthy that Type A personalities achieve high work performance and career success. However, hostility is their main problem since they cannot help getting angry with others who fail to enable them to achieve their almost impossible aspirations (Krantz & McCeney, 2002).

Research has suggested that there are two sub-components of Type A: Achievement striving and Impatience and irritability. Achievement striving is associated with success and good health (Bluen, Barling, & Burns, 1990) and Impatience and irritability with illness and strain (Barling & Boswell, 1995).

A COMPREHENSIVE FRAMEWORK FOR UNDERSTANDING STRESS

What we have seen is that over the past 100 years, models of stress at work have developed to offer a more sophisticated representation of the phenomenon. One helpful model (Kahn & Byosiere, 1992) integrates work stressors, moderators, perceptions and cognitions and the consequences or strains (see Figure 9.1), and reveals the processes by which work stressors affect individuals. It helpfully distinguishes between the causes (stressors) and the outcomes (strain) while identifying the processes that mediate or moderate the relationship between stressors and strain.

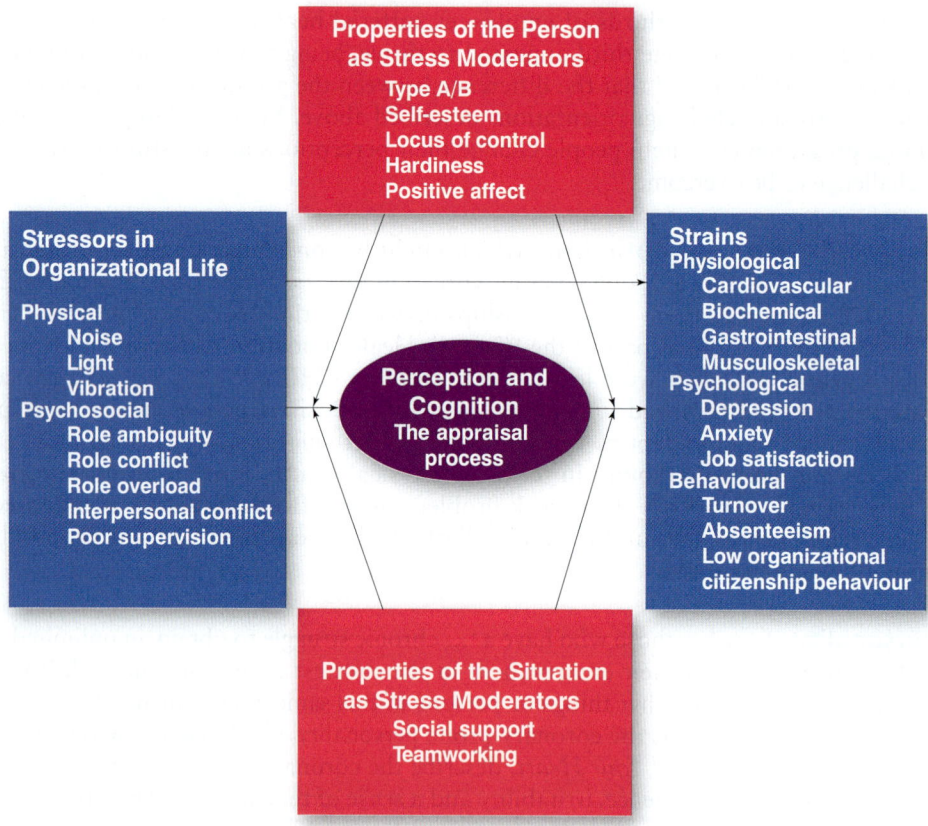

Figure 9.1 Theoretical framework for the study of stress in organizations

The figure describes:

- Work stressors such as interpersonal conflict at work or poor supervision (over-controlling, bullying or neglecting). Work stressors subsume both task and role stressors. They include:
    - Work overload (physically, psychologically or emotionally demanding work) or underload (too little stimulation) or fast pace.
    - Work schedule – shift work, night work, inflexible work schedules, rotas, unpredictable hours, long or unsociable hours.
    - Control/autonomy – little opportunity to influence decision-making, lack of control over workload, pacing etc.
    - Career development – stagnation, uncertainty, under- or over-promotion, poor pay, job insecurity, low social value to work.
    - Environment and equipment – dangerous, noxious or inadequate for the task.
    - Interpersonal relationships at work – social or physical isolation, poor relationships with supervisors, interpersonal conflict, lack of social support, presence of bullying or sexual (or other) harassment.
    - Underuse of skills.
    - Repetitive work/lack of variety.
    - Fragmented or meaningless work.
    - Lack of role clarity or role ambiguity, conflict, and onerous responsibility for people.
    - Effort–reward imbalance – making great efforts for very little reward.
    - Low support from supervisors or colleagues.
    - Job insecurity.
    - Poor supervision.
    - Organizational injustice.
    - Poor teamworking.
    - Threat-avoidant vigilance (experienced by police officers, soldiers and healthcare staff).
    - Bullying and discrimination.
    - Changes to work organization such as restructuring, downsizing, lowered staffing levels, the introduction of subcontracting temporary work.
- There are some damaging trends in the workplace that also act as stressors, such as the introduction of 'lean' or 'just in time' work. These initiatives can sometimes appear as modern versions of scientific management, leading to stressful multitasking (not multiskilling), tighter supervision and surveillance, and increased stress (Levi, 2017). There are trends too for people to experience more job insecurity, time pressure and work intensification. Indeed, time pressure at work increased for large proportions in Europe between 1977 and 1996. Similarly, the percentage of US workers who reported never having enough time at work increased from 40 to 60 per cent between 1977 and 1997 (Schnall, Dobson, & Landsbergis, 2017) and 25 per cent of salaried US workers now report working more than 50 hours a week.
- Moderators. These are factors that can reduce or increase the effects of stressors upon outcomes. Moderators of the stress process could include teamworking (good teamworking will reduce the impact of stressors), social support (having supportive family, friends or

colleagues buffers people from the effects of stressors), recovery activities – participating in engaging activities such as sports, cooking and gardening, as opposed to passive activities such as TV watching), helps people recover from stress and fatigue (Sonnentag, Kuttler, & Fritz, 2010), and individual differences – warm, positive, optimistic people are less likely to be affected by stressors than anxious people (Seligman, 2002).

- Perception and cognition. How we see, think about and interpret the world also affects the stressor–strain relationship. What to one person might seem a threat (giving a public talk) might be interpreted by another as an exciting challenge. How we appraise the world – our perceptions and cognitions – therefore affects whether stressors translate into strain or not. The appraisal process is vital in determining whether stress is damaging to our functioning (Lazarus, 1991).
- Strain or the consequences of stressors. These include: physiological consequences such as gastrointestinal and cardiovascular illness; psychological consequences such as depression and anxiety; and behavioural consequences such as absenteeism, spillover of tensions into home life and lower levels of organizational citizenship behaviour.

Figure 9.2 explores a model of work stress in the UK which examines the impact at national level.

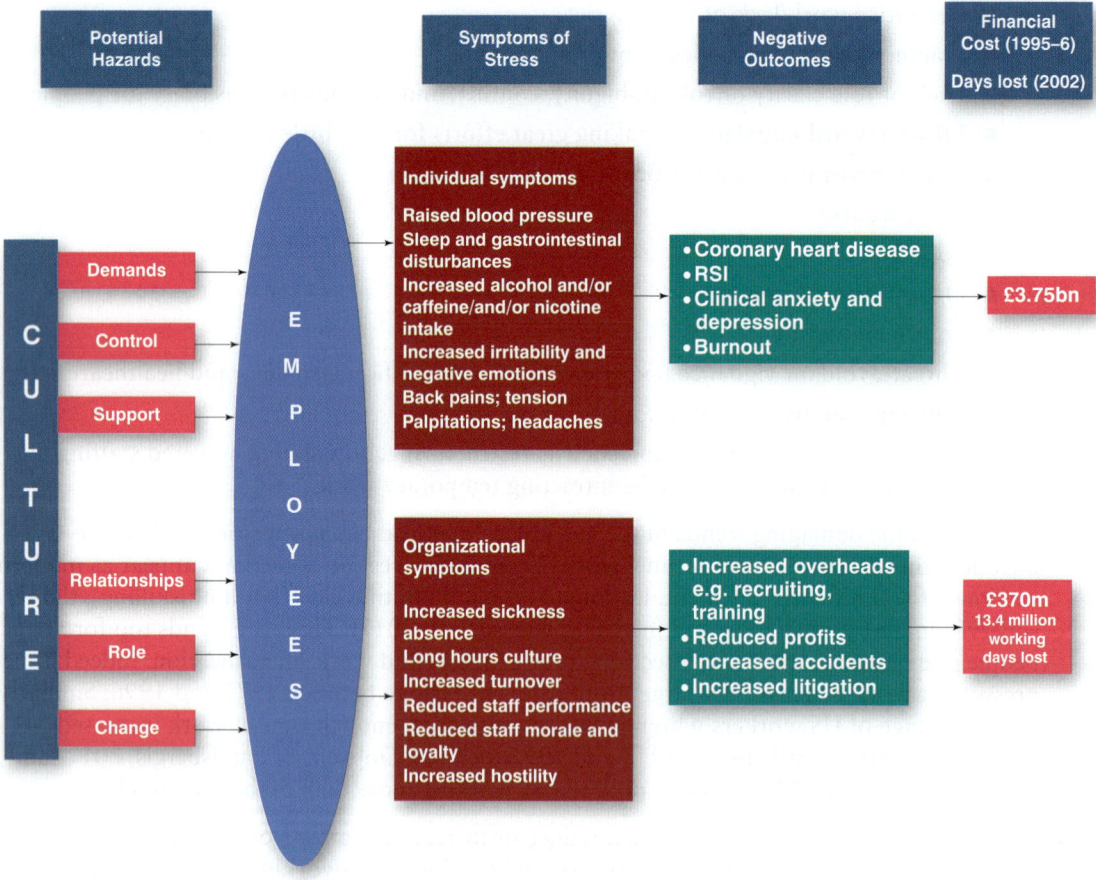

Figure 9.2 Model of work stress

Workplace stressors

We now explore some of these stressors in a little more depth. We begin with physical stressors.

- Physical stressors – with advances in technology and its pervasiveness in working life, the physical office environment is increasingly stressful (McCoy & Evans, 2004). Temperature may also affect work (Gifford, 1997); some studies have shown that productivity is reduced when temperatures are high (McCormick, 1976) and that fine movement is impeded under very cold conditions (Fox, 1967).

  Noise has been linked with increased risk of cardiovascular disease and increased mortality rates after long-term exposure (Ising, Babisch, & Günther, 1999; Melamed, Kristal-Boneh, & Froom, 1999; Zhao, Zhang, Selvin, & Spear, 1991). Evans and Johnson (2000) found that a noisy office environment was associated with elevated stress hormones and poor task performance. Perceived control over the source of the noise is also thought to be a factor (Cohen, Evans, Stokols, & Krantz, 1986; Wickens & Hollands, 2000). Glass, Singer, and Friedman (1969) presented participants with an aversive noise stimulus and gave one group the option of pressing a button to stop the noise (but with encouragement not to do so), while the control group did not have this option. In the experiment, no one used the button, meaning all participants were exposed to the same noise stimulus. However, those with the option of stopping the noise were less affected on subsequent tasks and showed less post-adaptive stress. Physical demands are also linked with stress. For example, continuous lifting and vibration has been shown to cause back and neck pain (e.g. Linton, 1990), as is poor ergonomic design such as poorly designed furniture (Goodrich, 1982; Wineman, 1986).

- Role stressors – role conflict, overload and role ambiguity (Rizzo, House, & Lirtzman, 1970). Role conflict describes a role where there are competing goals, such as between quality of care and costs in healthcare or for control versus support of clients among probation workers. Role ambiguity is the degree to which a worker is unclear about the expectations of her own, or others', roles. Research has consistently shown links between these role factors and strain (Day & Livingstone, 2001; Jackson & Schuler, 1985; Netemeyer, Johnston, & Burton, 1990).

- Workload. We described earlier how workload is a predictor of strain among healthcare workers. Some researchers have also distinguished between quantitative workload (the number of tasks, customers, products the role holder has to deal with) versus qualitative workload, which relates to the intensity of the work such as the complexity of the task. This distinction has not proved very helpful in practice, however.

- Work pace – for example, assembly line work where the worker has no control over the speed of the line; or time pressures, such as having to complete tasks within a specified period – for example, call centre workers may be told they have to complete all calls in an average of two minutes. Hurrell (1985) found, in a research study involving several thousand postal workers, that machine-paced workers suffered much more strain than those who controlled the pace of their work. Henning, Sauter, and Krieg (1992) proposed that stress may result from a lack of synchrony between a worker's physiological internal rhythms and the rhythm set by a computer, for example in data input tasks. Moreover, tasks with high repetition and short time cycles are likely to result in repetitive strain and also create risks of musculoskeletal disorders if office ergonomics are neglected (McCoy & Evans, 2004).

- Work schedule – for example, shift work is known to cause strain to varying degrees (Folkard & Monk, 1979). Typical shifts include the day shift (8 a.m. to 4 p.m.), afternoon shift (4 p.m. to midnight) and night shift (midnight to 8 a.m.). Rotating shift patterns typically require workers to rotate through the three shift patterns on a recurring basis (for example, a week on days, then a week on afternoons, then a week on nights). Research indicates a high level of sleep disturbance among those on rotating shifts (Barton, 1994; Smith et al., 1999). One problem is that such shift workers are unable to establish regular patterns of social activity since their leisure hours are constantly changing. Moreover, their leisure hours often do not coincide with those of their family and friends (Smith et al., 1999). Control over shift patterns seems to make a difference. Workers who choose to work night shifts when compared with those assigned to rotating shifts report fewer sleep problems, health or domestic difficulties (Barton, 1994).

- Time rigidity. Flexitime, where employees have some choice over the time they go to work while fulfilling their contractual obligations in relation to total hours, can be advantageous for childcare (dropping off and picking up from school) and thus reduce strain (Lee, 1981). For example, Baltes, Briggs, Huff, Wright, and Neuman (1999) found that flexitime had little effect on productivity, absenteeism and performance, but that employees on flexitime showed less strain than others. Lee (1983) found that increasing flexitime allowed fathers to spend more time with their children, thereby helping working mothers while reducing the stress caused by work/family relationships. Lee (1981) suggested that flexitime helped to alleviate stresses and strains directly related to childcare.

- Interpersonal conflict at work causes strain, especially where it is chronic (Reis & Gable, 2003). Passing conflicts do not appear to lead to problems. Conflict with co-workers, managers or clients all fall into the category of interpersonal conflict at work. De Dreu (2008) has reviewed research on conflict in teams and concludes that interpersonal conflict is damaging both to team effectiveness and to member well-being.

- Perceived control is now widely seen as a key factor in the stressor–strain relationship (Ganster & Murphy, 2000). A related concept in job design is autonomy (Hackman & Oldham, 1980; see Chapter 4) – the amount of freedom the individual has to do the job in their own way. Increasing control by increasing autonomy leads to reductions in stressors and therefore in strain.

- Emotional labour refers to the extent to which individuals at work have to manage their emotions in the course of their work. For example, cabin crew members in airlines have to smile and be helpful to passengers (not all of whom will be undemanding, pleasant or patient); police officers may have to deal with aggressive individuals on Saturday nights in city centres; ambulance workers have to manage the fear and pain of others while being confident and reassuring. Such emotional labour takes a toll and leads to strain. In short, the regulation of emotion to meet job or organizational demands produces strain over time. In particular, suppressing or showing false emotions is demanding and associated with job dissatisfaction, absenteeism, turnover and burnout (Brotheridge & Grandey, 2002). Grandey (2003) assessed 'surface acting' and 'deep acting' behaviour in employees in customer service roles. Surface acting can be described as modifying facial expression (smiling) in order to present a positive image (when the employee is not feeling positive themselves), whereas deep acting is when the employee modifies inner feelings in order to appear authentic to customers. In her research, Grandey found that those employees who exhibited more surface acting were more likely to experience emotional exhaustion. Conversely, there was no relationship between deep acting and emotional exhaustion. While this may seem counterintuitive due to the effort required to modify inner feelings, it is possible that by doing so, emotional dissonance is reduced. This, combined with the positive customer experience also associated with this behaviour, may restore the emotional resources of the employee while surface acting reduces the resources available (through emotional dissonance).

- Task content is itself a stressor and we describe some of the stressors in task content above in relation to the work of the police, ambulance workers and those in any organization dealing with customer complaints.
- Conflict between work life and non-work life (sometimes called work–family conflict). This refers to conflict between work roles and roles outside of work (mother, carer, etc.). Observation reveals that this is a particular problem for women, given their relatively heavy burdens in the home and with childcare. Such childcare also damage relationships between partners. There are clear effects of work–non-work conflict on employee well-being (Grant-Vallone & Donaldson, 2001). Frone (2000) reported that those experiencing such conflict are 30 times more likely to suffer a mental health problem (depression or anxiety) than others. Hoonakker, Carayon, and Schoepke (2004) found that employees with high work–family conflict experienced lower job satisfaction, high emotional exhaustion and increased turnover intention. Furthermore, they suggested that work–family conflict is negatively related to career opportunities and supervisory support, but that supervisors can help buffer their negative effects.

KEY THEME

Environment and sustainability

Organizations play a key role in climate change through their production of carbon dioxide and the widespread use of pollutants. Research has clearly established that natural settings enhance our mental health, with positive effects on cognitive, attentional, emotional and subjective well-being (Pryor, Townsend, Maller, & Field, 2006). Moreover, exposure to nature has positive effects on the health and well-being of office workers, prisoners and hospital patients. For example, when hospital patients have views of natural settings such as parkland and trees, they experience less pain and stress, have better post-surgical outcomes and leave hospital sooner (Devlin & Arneill, 2003; Ulrich, 2006). The noise of cities and workplaces is inherently stressful and interferes with good cognitive functioning. Spending time in the relative silence of nature, hearing largely non-jarring sounds, has restorative effects on our attention and well-being (Berman, Jonides, & Kaplan, 2008). Even children with attention deficit disorder function better after a walk in the park (Taylor & Kuo, 2009). Immersion in nature is good for us, and both creating and protecting natural environments makes good moral, business and people management sense for modern organizations. Surrounding workplaces with green spaces reduces stress and strain. There are many examples of where gardens and gardening are being used to improve health in areas such as social prescribing, community gardens, volunteering, recovery from illness, dementia care and end-of-life care (Buck, 2016). Lambeth's GP Food Co-op in London, England is a co-operative of patients, doctors, nurses and people living in Lambeth who have created a food-growing network for the benefit of all these groups. The Co-op has created gardens at 11 GP surgeries as well as at King's College Hospital, where patients learn how to grow food in a safe environment. The Co-op now sells some of the food it grows to the hospital.

Consequences of stressors – strain

Research reveals that the stressors described above, when chronic, are linked to cardiovascular disorders (CVD), recurrent cardiovascular disease, hypertension and depression (Schnall et al., 2017). Indeed, 10 to 20 per cent of all CVD deaths can be attributed to work (CVD is the leading cause of death in the world). There is also considerable evidence that there are industries and occupations at risk of stress-related addiction, including males in male-dominated industries, emergency response personnel (police, fire, paramedics), the military, and health and human service workers (such as nurses) (Roche, Kostadinov, & Fischer, 2017). Other physical outcomes include recurring common infections, diabetes, musculoskeletal pain, sleep problems, ageing and early mortality. Cognitive and emotional outcomes include negative effects on concentration, mood disturbance, depression, anxiety, health complaints and work performance. The consequences for work are considerable, such as low work ability, sickness absence, intention to quit, early retirement and disability pension. There are also effects on productivity, in-role performance, organizational citizenship behaviour, engagement and, inevitably, customer satisfaction.

A 2015 meta-analysis of 228 studies assessing ten workplace stressors and health outcomes found that high job demands raised the odds of diagnosed illness by 35 per cent and that long work hours increased mortality by almost 20 per cent. Excess job demands, low job control, job insecurity, low social support, long work hours and shift work, as well as unemployment, led to more than 120,000 deaths a year in the USA (Schnall et al., 2017).

Let us probe a little deeper beyond these figures. Strain can be divided into three main categories: behavioural, psychological and physiological.

Behavioural

Information processing – strain leads to deterioration in memory, reaction time, accuracy and task performance. People make more errors on cognitive tasks and this has particular implications for health and safety; for example, strain is associated with more medical errors among healthcare workers (Firth-Cozens, 1990). Hockey (1997) suggests that when perceived demands are unable to be met with normal work effort, either effort is increased, with consequent negative psychological (e.g. irritability, fatigue) and physiological (e.g. increased secretion of cortisol) effects; or the task performance is reduced, such as reduced levels of accuracy and speed. Lang, Thomas, Bliese, and Adler (2007) studied effects of job demand and strain on performance on leadership tasks in army cadets. They reported that job demands had a negative effect on performance, which was mediated through strain. That is, demands increased the strain experienced by an individual, which then resulted in a decrease in performance. Collet, Averty, and Dittmar (2009) showed that physiological data from the autonomic nervous system and subjective reports of strain matched task demands in air traffic controllers. They conclude that 'Emotional factors are integrated in each step of information processing and are shown, through pathological manifestations (particularly a cortical lesion of orbito-frontal areas), to influence cognitive activity' (p. 9).

Performance – strain has been suggested to have an 'inverted U' relationship with performance such that performance is best at moderate levels of strain or arousal and worst when strain or arousal is either very low or very high (Jex, 1998). However, any stress seems to impair performance in complex tasks (Motowidlo, Packard, & Manning, 1986). Motowidlo et al. (1986) found that stress was associated with less sensitivity, warmth and tolerance towards patients among a sample of nurses. The National Staff Survey for the NHS has repeatedly revealed associations between staff experience of stressful and unsupportive work environments and patient satisfaction, patient care and even patient mortality (West, Dawson, Admasachew, & Topakas, 2011).

Psychological

The most invoked concept to explain psychological consequences of sustained stress at work is that of 'burnout'. The metaphor is of an engine that has been run at a high speed for too long, creating such friction that eventually the level of heat in the engine causes sustained and catastrophic damage, resulting in engine failure. Psychological burnout, first described by Maslach and Leiter (1997), refers to three sub-dimensions of strain – emotional exhaustion, depersonalization (the healthcare worker becomes hardened and starts to treat patients like objects), sense of ineffectiveness and lack of accomplishment (Maslach, Schaufeli, & Leiter, 2001). This concept has been applied to and examined particularly among those in the caring professions. A measure to assess burnout (the Maslach Burnout Inventory; Maslach, Jackson, & Leiter, 1996) has proved valuable in identifying at-risk samples of workers. Examples of items include:

- I feel I'm working too hard on my job.
- In my work, I deal with emotional problems very calmly.
- I worry that this job is hardening me emotionally.

Schaufeli and Bakker (2004) measured burnout and its opposite, 'engagement', in employees from a number of organizations. They found that burnout was predicted mainly by job demands and, to a lesser extent, job resources; that it is related to turnover intention and health problems; and that it mediates the relationship between job demands and health problems.

Physiological

Sustained stress leads to chronic activation of the sympathetic nervous system, which in turn leads to ill-health because of excessive amounts of stress hormones circulating in the blood. Blood vessels also shrink and coronary arteries and the heart are damaged as a result of the thickening of plaque in the linings. Arteriolosclerosis (hardening and loss of elasticity in arterioles – often due to hypertension) is associated with increases in blood pressure and higher likelihood of heart attacks because the heart has to work so much harder. Because of the lack of oxygen associated with poorer cardiovascular function, the body requires more oxygen and this therefore results in increased blood pressure. The evidence is clear that people in sustained stressful situations are at a higher risk of heart attacks (Krantz & McCeney, 2002).

There are also gastrointestinal (digestive) problems associated with stress. Levy, Cain, Jarrett, and Heitkemper (1997) and Heitkemper et al. (2004) measured stress levels in women with and without irritable bowel syndrome (a dysfunction of the gastrointestinal system). They found that a positive relationship existed between daily symptoms and daily stress, and also that gastrointestinal patients reported higher stress levels than control groups.

Biochemical effects, such as the stress hormones, cortisol and catecholamine, increase when the individual experiences strain. Long-lasting stress hormone increases contribute to decreased functioning of the immune system and to CHD (Cohen & Herbert, 1996; Krantz & McCeney, 2002).

Overall, there is clear evidence that prolonged exposure to stressors can kill.

REDUCING AND MANAGING STRESS

Our journey so far has helped us to understand the stressor–strain relationship and the factors that account for, mediate and moderate that relationship. Work and organizational psychologists are (and should be) concerned with making a difference in the world of work, given the fact that so many workplaces worldwide are damaging to people's health and well-being. What can we do to make a difference in this domain?

Lennart Levi (2017) focuses on the general principles of prevention:

- Avoid risks.
- Evaluate the risks that cannot be avoided.
- Combat the risks at source.
- Adapt the work to the individual.

We can address the root causes of stress at work and change them (reducing workload, improving teamworking), and this is referred to as *primary prevention*. We can aim to reduce the effects of stressors on health by helping people to be more resilient or less stressed, using such interventions as mindfulness, exercise, and other health and well-being programmes, which fall into the category of *secondary prevention*. Or we can treat resulting ill-health – *tertiary prevention* (Quick, Wright, Adkins, Nelson, & Quick, 2013). Most organizations focus their efforts in the latter two areas despite lots of talk about primary prevention (Malzon & Lindsay 1992).

Let us look in more depth at these three types of intervention.

Primary interventions

Primary interventions are stressor-directed, so they are aimed at modifying or eliminating stressors in the work environment. This might include ensuring the right levels of heat, light or noise; giving people more control over their jobs and work environments; redesigning the tasks they are required to do; or giving them more flexible work schedules (Cartwright & Cooper, 2005). Such interventions might also take a problem-focused approach by reducing noise, improving quality of managerial support, reducing interruptions, time pressures, role ambiguity or number of hours worked.

Organizations can directly address job stressors by reducing demands and improving social relationships, for example, or by scheduling shift work effectively to ensure (for example) that rotating shifts are stable, longer term and rotate forward. They can help employees to recover from work by not expecting emails to be answered at night or weekends. Research with nurses (Greenberg 2006) examined underpayment inequity following a reduction in pay in two hospitals and comparing responses of nurses in two other hospitals where there was no change in pay. The affected nurses reported much higher levels of anger and upset and also more insomnia. Supervisors then received four hours of leadership training focused on promoting interactional justice, and this had the effect of reducing reports of insomnia and decreased feelings of being treated unfairly among nurses.

Workplace stress may also be prevented or counteracted by job redesign, such as empowering employees and avoiding both overload and underload; by improving social support; by promoting reasonable reward for effort invested; by adjusting physical settings to workers abilities', needs and reasonable expectations; and through promoting participative management, flexible work schedules and good career development. Overall, research suggests that efforts to increase employee participation and job control, social support and moderate job demands hold great promise. For example, Stockholm Municipal Transit agency reduced traffic congestion and improved passenger safety in response to driver and passenger concerns (Rydstedt, Johansson, & Evans, 1998). Bus routes were changed and the number and length of bus routes increased, with automatic green lights for buses and bus stops better located and built, as well as computerized passenger information systems. As a consequence, bus drivers were much less stressed and hassled and showed large improvements in blood pressure (Rydstedt et al., 1998). A study of Swedish office workers included stress management interventions plus worker committees to address sources of work stress. The intervention group reported increases in supervisor support and improvements in lipid profile (Orth-Gomér, Eriksson, Moser, Theorell, & Fredlund, 1994).

In Northern and Western Europe there have been concerted national efforts to reduce work stressors, resulting in lower prevalence of work strain in Denmark, Norway and the Netherlands (less job strain, bullying, work–family imbalance, long work hours, job insecurity and effort–reward imbalance). Even so, the prevalence of job strain across the European Union is still 26.9 per cent (Niedhammer, Sultan-Taïeb, Chastang, Vermeylen, & Parent-Thirion, 2014), affecting one in four of the working population (or over one hundred million people).

Designing interventions to reduce staff stress can focus on primary interventions that address five broad areas:

1 work tasks and responsibilities
2 work timing – shift work, pace etc.
3 work techniques – the methods used to get the job done
4 work team – cohesive or conflictual, for example
5 work environment (both the physical and social environment).

Primary interventions are not new in the workplace. Bennett, Weaver, Senft, and Meeper (2017) describe humanitarian approaches in modern organizations, but the Quaker movement in England played a leading role in designing good workplaces and homes for workers in the 19th century. And their legacy endures in Bournville in Birmingham, England and the history of the Cadbury company, and in modern workplaces such as John Lewis, Swann Morton in Sheffield, England (www.swann-morton.com/pages/history.php) and others. In the USA, Wannamker is an outstanding example of an enlightened employer.

The American Psychological Association promotes health workplaces through the APA Healthy Workplace Program. They propose that the key elements of a psychologically healthy workplace are:

- employee involvement
- growth and development
- work–life balance
- employee recognition
- health and safety (Grawitch & Ballard, 2016; Grawitch, Ballard, & Erb, 2015).

In 2009, workplaces that won the APA national psychologically healthy workplace awards had 28 per cent less turnover of employees, 14 per cent fewer reporting chronic work stress, 43 per cent more recommending as a place to work, and 24 per cent higher levels of satisfaction. And these figures remained stable over the years. Particularly good US examples are the American Cast Iron Pipe Company (manufacturing); the National Association of College Stores (retail); Steptoe and Johnson (law firm); and SAS Software. We can also promote primary interventions more broadly and in the longer term by adjusting curricula in business schools, technology, medical schools, etc. to train leaders, inspectors and so on in how to create healthy workplaces that enable people at work to flourish rather than languish.

Secondary interventions

Secondary interventions are more focused on people's response to stress. They target employees rather than changing aspects of the organization. So employees might be given relaxation exercises, stress management training and nutrition advice, or encouraged to undertake physical fitness training.

Sir Cary Cooper has called this the 'Band Aid approach' to stress management since it fails to deal with the underlying organizational causes, focusing instead on the symptoms (Cooper & Cartwright, 2001). Another example of secondary interventions is encouraging emotion-focused coping, such as telling staff to avoid, minimize or distance themselves emotionally from the stressors (e.g. the upset caused by unpleasant interactions). Other examples include training staff in negotiation and conflict resolution skills, and in stress management, including cognitive behavioural therapy-type training.

Stress inoculation programmes also fall under the heading of secondary interventions, such as teaching people about stress (educational component), having them learn about time management, relaxation and problem-solving methods (rehearsal), and then practising the skills in safe environments such as in workshops (application). Jones, Barge, Steffy, Fay, Kunz, and Wuebker (1988) found that using an organization-wide programme in hospitals led to fewer medical errors and malpractice claims. Many organizations recommend secondary interventions in the form of relaxation exercises, meditation or biofeedback. There is some evidence that the regular practice of exercises such as meditation and mindfulness can significantly reduce arousal and anxiety (West, 2017).

Mindfulness practice involves learning how to focus attention on our experience in the here and now without evaluation or intention, simply paying attention to our experience in the present moment. Research has demonstrated the beneficial effects of mindfulness practice in many domains, including lower levels of emotional disturbance, depressive symptoms, anxiety and stress; greater well-being, positive affect and life satisfaction; greater awareness, understanding and acceptance of emotions; greater ability to correct or repair unpleasant mood states (demonstrated via use of functional medical resonance imaging); less reactivity to emotionally threatening stimuli; more adaptive immune responses; better relationship quality, reduced reactivity to conflict, increased sustained attention to social exchanges and higher levels of emotional intelligence; and greater compassion among medical students (Brown, Ryan, & Cresswell, 2007). One study in the workplace found that mindfulness training was negatively associated with emotional exhaustion and positively associated with job satisfaction (Hülsheger, Alberts, Feinholdt, & Lang, 2013). It has led many organizations to introduce mindfulness to those in their workforces. What is the evidence for the effectiveness of mindfulness at work?

Murphy (1996) reviewed research on the health effects of interventions at work designed to alleviate stress. He looked at physiological and psychological outcomes, including blood pressure, headaches, anxiety and job satisfaction; muscle relaxation, biofeedback, meditation and cognitive behavioural training (CBT). His findings indicated that some interventions worked better for physiological outcomes (e.g. muscle relaxation) and others for psychological ones (e.g. cognitive behaviour skills). Meditation was the most effective intervention, providing the most consistent results. It was used in only six of the 64 studies included in his review, however. Using a combination of techniques (CBT and relaxation or meditation) was found to produce the most positive outcomes, rather than single techniques. He noted that none of the interventions was consistently effective in reducing job satisfaction or absenteeism.

A variety of mindfulness training programmes (MTs) have been developed for application in workplaces or to support leaders (Rupprecht, Koole, Chaskalson, Tamdjidi, & West, 2018). These programmes are usually adaptations of mindfulness-based stress reduction (MBSR) programmes. They vary greatly in length (1 day to 16 weeks) and delivery modes (phone apps, webinars, face-to-face training) to meet the demands and budgets of organizations. Adaptations of these include mindful communication, mindful emailing, mindfulness of transitions between tasks and moments of silence. To what extent do such programmes enable employees and leaders to thrive and be effective in the work environment? There is consistent evidence that mindfulness-based interventions are effective in reducing stress in working adults as well as symptoms of depression and addiction in clinical populations (Rupprecht et al., 2018). Most mindfulness intervention studies in workplaces have focused on stress and resilience as outcomes, and study quality (methodological sophistication) is generally not good. Consequently, there is only preliminary evidence of positive impacts on leadership, prosocial behaviour at work and performance. Studies have shown that mindful leadership is associated with humility and authenticity, follower well-being and citizenship, and good quality of leader–follower interactions, but these are generally correlational and cross-sectional studies. Mindfulness does seem to be associated with increases in prosocial behaviour at work, demonstrated by greater empathy and compassion and higher interaction quality. Some studies do show that mindfulness is associated with improved individual and team performance, but results are not consistent with others reporting negative or no effects (Rupprecht et al., 2018).

Other recommended secondary interventions include improving sleep (Carleton & Barling, 2017), drinking adequate quantities of water, ensuring a good diet, getting exercise, practising forgiveness in organizations, reflecting on three good things in life or work, using positive humour, thinking about something to be grateful for, sharing accounts of positive events, expressing gratitude to others and spending time in nature (Martin, Dixon, & Thomas, 2017). However, there is some evidence that those who take up such health and well-being programmes in organizations may be those who are well rather than those who are stressed (Jones, Molitor, & Reif, 2018).

Developing a strong social support network both in and outside work is also demonstrably valuable for helping people cope with stress at work. Another particularly important secondary intervention is encouraging those at work to ensure 'recovery'. After a heavy day at work we all want to unwind – letting go of the tension of the day and refreshing our resources in order to be effective at work the next day. What is the best way of doing this? Feet up in front of the TV for a few hours with a beer? A game of tennis or cooking a meal? There is evidence that the recuperative quality of the time to unwind is affected by the nature of leisure or non-work activities during those times (typically in the evenings after work). Sonnentag, Binnewies, and Mojza (2008) found that challenging non-work activities such as sport, hobbies, creative activities (cooking, painting, playing music) predicted positive affect among their participants the next day, whereas passive activities such as watching TV did not. After engaging in challenging activities during leisure time, people were more active, interested, excited, strong, inspired and alert than those who experienced more passive leisure time.

Having recovery time aids *psychological detachment* or disengaging mentally from work after the working day is over (Sonnentag & Fritz, 2007). It enables people to recover from job strain and is negatively related to health complaints, emotional exhaustion, depressive symptoms, negative mood, fatigue and sleep difficulties (Sonnentag, Mojza, Binnewies, & Scholl, 2008). Repeated incomplete recovery leads to sustained sympathetic and neuroendocrine activation, leading to fatigue, burnout, etc. and poor sleep (Sonnentag & Geurts, 2009).

What about holidays as a form of recovery? Toker and Melamed (2017) review the evidence showing that frequent breaks (e.g. monthly respites) are more effective than once-a-year vacations. And when people take work breaks more often they experience more positive mood, greater vigour and effectiveness, and reduced fatigue. Sonnentag and Fritz (2007) describe four types of recovery experience: psychological detachment, relaxation, task mastery (cooking, for example) and control.

Mastery is associated with positive moods and relaxation with serenity. Weekend relaxation is associated with joviality, self-assurance and serenity, and these effects appear to last through the following week; mastery and detachment predict positive moods for shorter periods of time (Fritz & Sonnentag, 2009; Fritz, Sonnentag, Spector, & McInroe, 2010). Vacations generally appear to increase energy and positive moods and reduce depression, though these effects tend not to be long lasting.

Organizations can create physical spaces for work and lunch breaks that allow exposure to nature. And it does appear important to give people autonomous choice of activities during their breaks. Organizations can also promote psychological detachment from work by restricting email and other forms of communication during evenings and weekends.

Tertiary interventions

Tertiary interventions are symptom directed. They are focused on helping individuals cope with consequences of stressors. Again this implies a focus on individuals rather than a focus on the organization – treating symptoms or outcomes of stress rather than the causes. One approach is to provide medical care in-house or outsourced for employees. Another is to use what are called employee assistance programmes (EAPs). EAPs have typically focused on employees' drug and alcohol problems, but have also been extended to dealing with employees' problems of stress at work. There is usually a significant counselling component to EAPs. Cooper and Sadri (1994) found improvements in mental health and esteem among those participating in EAPs. Nevertheless, they represent a reactive approach since they are used for dealing with employees' problems after they arise rather than focused on creating positive work environments that minimize stressors.

PIONEERING WORK PSYCHOLOGISTS

Professor Sir Cary Cooper

Professor Sir Cary Cooper is an American-born British psychologist and Professor of Organizational Psychology and Health at the Manchester Business School, University of Manchester, UK. He has been a pioneer in research but, equally important, in communicating the results of research in ways that have influenced leaders in public life and work organizations. He has had a powerful impact in improving people's lives at work during his career.

He was elected as Founding President of the British Academy of Management and in 2005 he was appointed head of the Sunningdale Institute, which brings international academics and industry figures together to advise UK public sector organizations. He was Chair of the Academy of Social Sciences, a body representing over 88,000 social scientists and 46 learned societies in the social sciences. He was recently President of Relate (an organization that helps couples manage their relationships), President of the Chartered Institute of Personnel and Development and past President of the British Association for Counselling and Psychotherapy. He was the founding editor-in-chief of the Journal of Organizational Behavior. He is always in demand by the media to comment on workplace issues.

He is the author/editor of over 160 books (on occupational stress, women at work, and industrial and organizational psychology), and over 100 chapters in books. He has written over 400 scholarly articles for academic journals.

In 2001, Cary was awarded a CBE in the Queen's Birthday Honours List for his contribution to occupational safety and health. In 2014 he was honoured with a knighthood for his services to social sciences. In November 2010, he was awarded the prestigious Lord Dearing Lifetime Achievement Award by Times Higher Education for his distinguished contribution to higher education.

Professor Cooper is the editor-in-chief of the international scholarly *Blackwell Encyclopedia of Management* (13-volume set), the editor of *Who's Who in the Management Sciences* and is on the editorial boards of many scholarly journals. He has been an adviser to two UN agencies, the World Health Organization and the International Labour Organization, and published a major report for the EU's European Foundation for the Improvement of Living and Work Conditions on 'Stress Prevention in the Workplace'. He was also the lead scientist for the UK Government Office for Science on their Foresight programme on Mental Capital and Wellbeing (2007–2008), and was appointed a member of the expert group on establishing guidance for the National Institute for Health and Clinical Excellence on 'promoting mental wellbeing through productive and healthy working conditions' (2009).

Some examples of his publications are included in the list of further reading at the end of this chapter, and below are links to two of his many presentations and interviews:

www.youtube.com/watch?v=y2zlNjE6D9M

www.hrreview.co.uk/analysis/sir-cary-cooper-cbe-interview-organisational-psychology/113366

Box 9.2
Positive work

Research has suggested some of the key elements in designing effective interventions for promoting well-being in workplaces (Bennett et al., 2017).

Define the outcomes desired, such as:

- Employees can transform the challenges of work into positive outcomes.
- Employees gain well-being and flourish through their employment.
- Employees develop a sense of personal efficacy.
- Employees feel interpersonally connected and supported in their work.
- The environment is such that there are both time and resources to enable people to reduce work demands and recover from them on a regular basis.
- Employees feel intrinsically motivated and thrive because they have autonomy, meaningfulness and control in their work (cf. Deci & Ryan 2008; Ryan & Deci, 2000).

And define the inputs:

- There are well-developed and applied protective HR practices, health promotion/wellness efforts, EAPs and training and professional development.

continued

- The work environment is physically supportive – well designed for their safety and health.
- Leaders genuinely seek employee input.
- Leadership engagement in the health and well-being of those they lead should be genuine, discerning and sustained.
- Leaders should see employee well-being as a fundamental dimension of effective teamwork.
- The design of programmes should see the involvement and support of all stakeholders (employees, trade unions, health and safety leads, family members, customers, leaders at every level).
- Interventions should be an integral part of the organization's culture, not simply an additional programme.
- Leaders and key change agents should assess organizational readiness for the programme.
- The most senior leaders must show commitment to the programme and appoint credible champions to lead it.
- The content of the programmes must be clear, coherent and credibly applicable from the outset.
- Establish measures of progress and success that all stakeholders endorse.
- Use tailored and personalized interventions for particular groups such as women in the workplace and staff from a BME background.
- Develop and implement a comprehensive communications strategy.
- Ensure the approach goes beyond a 'don't neglect' the environment for employees to how can we 'intentionally enhance' the environment so people thrive at work.
- Ensure the programme is integrated into as many relevant activities, processes and policies as possible – e.g. HRM, workforce, organization development, appraisal, performance management, socialization.

BURNOUT AND ENGAGEMENT

The Positive Organizational Scholarship movement focuses on how we can better understand human behaviour and well-being at work by paying at least equal attention to the strengths and potential in human behaviour rather than simply focusing on problems and weaknesses. A leading Dutch psychologist, Wilmar Schaufeli, has articulated this, particularly in relation to the literature on stress, suggesting that there is an opposite of stress or burnout: job engagement. He suggests that instead of simply preventing and treating stress, we should be promoting positive work environments that encourage job engagement. He and colleagues define engagement as 'a positive work-related state of fulfilment that is characterized by vigour, dedication and absorption' (Schaufeli, Salanova, González-Romá, & Bakker, 2002, p. 74). Engagement affects both individual outcomes such as well-being and organizational outcomes (Saks, 2006; Schaufeli & Bakker, 2004).

Job and organizational characteristics proposed to predict job engagement include those that create psychological growth by providing challenging, varied work (Saks, 2006) and a feeling of benefit to self and others as a result of role performance at work (Kahn, 1992); perceived fairness in how the organization manages employees will also encourage engagement. Harter, Schmidt, and Keyes (2003), in a meta-analysis of engagement and organizational outcomes, found that businesses that experienced high levels of employee engagement averaged $80,000 to $120,000 higher revenue or sales per month than other businesses. Erickson (2005) suggests that engagement is more than merely job satisfaction or loyalty to the organization; it is also about passion, commitment and activation.

Schaufeli et al. (2002) propose that job engagement among employees is described by five core elements:

1 urgency – the need to get this task done now
2 focus – on what is important now, not what might be most interesting
3 intensity – sense of significance and deep level of involvement in the work
4 adaptability – being proactive, not tied to job descriptions
5 personal initiative – thinking and working proactively and implementing new and improved ways of doing things.

Macey, Schneider, Barbera, and Young (2009) suggest that job engagement is a consequence of four interacting elements:

1 Employees have *capacity to engage* – as a result of the motivation and autonomy they experience in their jobs. The organization gives them the information they need to do their job well; gives learning opportunities; provides feedback, which builds confidence; and supports energy renewal through provision of flexitime and work–non-work balance.
2 Employees have the *motivation to engage* – as a result of good job design. Jobs are intrinsically interesting (Hackman & Oldham, 1980) and the organization ensures people feel valued, respected and supported at work.
3 Employees have the *freedom to engage* – there is support and safety for them to innovate, and this is explicitly and implicitly provided by their managers and the wider organization. They are treated fairly and trust their managers and the organization. People consequently feel safe to take action on their own initiative.
4 Employees focus their engagement on *the strategy and goals of the organization* – there is alignment between what employees do and the strategic goals of the organization. Staff know what the organizational priorities are and why, and when culture is aligned with these goals.

As a consequence, employees persist at tasks, even when the going is tough; they respond proactively to emerging threats and challenges; they expand their roles at work because they are continually innovating and learning; and they adapt more readily to change.

BOX 9.3
New technology, digital media and artificial intelligence (AI)

The future of work in the age of artificial intelligence

In 2017, a computer using machine learning (AlphaZero) spent just four hours studying chess and then played the 2016 world champion. The world champion was a computer (Stockfish 8) that could calculate 70 million chess moves per second while AlphaZero could only perform 80,000 calculations. AlphaZero simply developed its expertise by playing against itself using machine learning principles. Out of a hundred games between these two, 72 were tied and AlphaZero won all the remaining 28.

continued

Since the industrial revolution, the evolution of new technologies has led to incorrect predictions of mass unemployment. People have merely filled new and different jobs associated with the technology (motor car manufacturers and servicers rather than blacksmiths and farriers). This time it may be different. Work demands physical, cognitive and emotional capabilities, and as manual jobs were replaced by machines, humans tended to do jobs demanding more cognitive skills. Now AI is able to perform cognitive and emotional tasks and, most important, to learn far more effectively than humans. Where will that leave us?

With advances in neurosciences and psychology, we have come to understand that human decisions and judgements are not the result of free will but of pattern recognition by billions of neurons acting together. 'Good drivers, bankers and lawyers don't have magical intuitions about traffic, investment or negotiation – rather , by recognizing recurring patterns, they spot and try to avoid careless pedestrians, inept borrowers and dishonest crooks' (Harare, 2018, p. 20). But they also make mistakes by using heuristics that evolved to help us survive on the African savannah rather than in the complexity of modern cities. AI can outperform humans on tasks that we previously thought required this magical intuition. AI can better our neural networks in calculating probabilities and recognizing patterns. And it can already make better judgements about people's emotions by minutely analyzing facial expressions, gestures and postures.

AI also has superior connectivity and updateability. We would like doctors treating illness to be using the latest evidence-based practice in the diagnosis and treatment of cancers, for obvious reasons. They don't. It can take years for the latest knowledge to permeate into front-line practice. If diagnosis and treatments are being provided by AI doctors, they will all be instantly updated with the latest evidence. The same is true of self-driving cars, with instant updates on the latest traffic regulations, routes and hazards. AI doctors could provide safer and cheaper healthcare for people all over the world.

And self-driving cars and trucks could dramatically reduce the annual death rate for road traffic accidents (1.25 million people per year – twice the number killed by war, crime and terrorism). Nursing and social care are less likely to be easily replaced by AI because of the complexity of the physical and emotional skills involved (Chui, Manyika, & Miremadi, 2016).

Even art might be affected. If external algorithms are able to understand and manipulate emotions with the merging of skills in computing, neuroscience and biochemistry, the composition of music might be more successfully accomplished by machines (Fernández & Vico, 2013).

A major cause of stress for the future may be the threat of job loss for billions of people faced with the superior cognitive, physical and emotion recognition skills of computers (Harare, 2018). Or we may relax in the shared freedom and leisure that our technological advances could potentially offer us all.

POSITIVE WORK

Positive work – staying well

In 2008, the New Economics Foundation (NEF) was commissioned by the UK Government's Foresight Project to review the interdisciplinary work of over 400 scientists from across the world. The aim was to identify a set of evidence-based actions to improve well-being, which individuals would be encouraged to build into their daily lives (www.nhs.uk/Conditions/stress-anxiety-depression/Pages/).

The five evidence-based ways to well-being and the sorts of policy interventions that could help to enable them are described below.

Connect

Social relationships are critical to our well-being. Survey research has found that well-being is increased by life goals associated with family, friends, and social and community life. Governments can shape policies in ways that encourage citizens to spend more time with families and friends and less time in the workplace. For example, employment policies that actively promote flexible working and reduce the burdens of commuting, alongside policies aimed at strengthening local involvement, would enable people to spend more time at home and in their communities to build supportive and lasting relationships.

Be active

Exercise has been shown to improve mood and, of course, health, and has been used successfully to lower rates of depression and anxiety. Being active also develops the motor skills of children and protects against cognitive decline in the elderly. Yet for the first time in history, more of the world's population lives in urban rather than non-urban environments. Through urban design and transport policy, governments influence the way we navigate through our neighbourhoods and towns. To improve our well-being, policies could support more green space to encourage exercise and play and prioritize cycling and walking over car use.

Take notice

Research has shown that being in the present – practising awareness of sensations, thoughts and feelings – can improve both the knowledge we have about ourselves and our well-being (Brown et al., 2007). High levels of rumination about the past and worry about the future affect us negatively. But the 21st century's never-ending flow of messages from companies advertising products and services leaves little opportunity to savour or reflect on our experiences. Policy that incorporates emotional awareness training, mindfulness and meditation practice, and incorporates media education into education provision, may better equip individuals to navigate their way through the information super-highway with their well-being intact; regulation to create advertising-free spaces could further improve well-being outcomes.

Keep learning

Learning encourages social interaction and increases self-esteem and feelings of competency. Behaviour directed by personal goals to achieve something new has been shown to increase reported life satisfaction. While there is often a much greater policy emphasis on learning in the early years of life, psychological research suggests it is a critical aspect of day-to-day living for all age groups. Therefore, policies that encourage learning, including by the elderly, will enable individuals to develop new skills, strengthen social networks and feel more able to deal with life's challenges.

continued

Give

Studies in neuroscience have shown that cooperative and altruistic behaviour activates reward areas of the brain, suggesting we are hardwired to enjoy helping one another. Individuals actively engaged in their communities report higher well-being. But it is not simply about a one-way transaction of giving. Research by the NEF shows that building reciprocity and mutual exchange – through giving and receiving – is the simplest and most fundamental way of building trust between people and creating positive social relationships and resilient communities. Governments can choose to invest more in 'the care economy': the family, neighbourhood and community which, together, act as the operating system of society. Policies that provide accessible, enjoyable and rewarding ways of participation and exchange will enable more individuals to take part in social and political life.

… and sleep and shiftwork

We should add to this list of well-being factors the importance of sleep. Research demonstrates just how important sleep is to health and well-being and how work factors can lead to poor-quality sleep. For full-time employees the amount of time spent working has increased and sleep has decreased in recent years (Carleton & Barling, 2017; Walker, 2017). Yet people who consistently fail to get enough sleep are at an increased risk of chronic disease: cardiovascular disease (CVD), hypertension (myocardial infarction, hypertension etc.), type 2 diabetes, muscle pain, headaches, gastrointestinal disorders, obesity and negative psychological outcomes, including hostility, frustration, anxiety, paranoia and depression. Inadequate sleep is a risk factor for mental illness more generally. It is estimated that those who are getting by on only six hours sleep a night are 190 per cent more likely to develop hypertension, 110 per cent more likely to suffer from chronic depression and 63 per cent more likely to develop diabetes. They also take an average of 11.5 extra days' sick leave a year compared with others (Walker, 2017).

Shift work, not surprisingly, also causes health and well-being problems. Shift work is anything deviating from starting between 7 a.m. and 10 a.m., and this includes rotating shifts (such as afternoons, followed by evenings, followed by night shifts). Our drive to sleep is strongest at night and in the early afternoon (between 2 a.m. to 4 a.m. and 1 p.m. to 3 p.m.). Shift work disrupts this drive, so shift workers sleep an average of 30 to 60 minutes less a day and they have more difficulties in falling and staying asleep. In one study (Drake, Roehrs, Richardson, Walsh, & Roth, 2004), 18.5 per cent of shift workers reported sleep difficulties, twice the rate of day workers. Sleep difficulties are associated with CVD (40 per cent increased risk), gastrointestinal disorders, reproductive health problems and breast cancer (Carleton & Barling, 2017). One-third of nurses on shift work reported unintentionally falling asleep. Medical students and junior doctors are significantly more likely to make serious errors when working shifts (Barger et al., 2006). Nurses on rotating shifts are twice as likely to have work-related accidents or to make errors (Gold et al., 1992).

Work stress exacerbates sleep problems and particularly the effects of shift work and rotating shifts. Sleep difficulties are associated with worse task performance, less organizational citizenship behaviour, lower job satisfaction and engagement, and a greater likelihood of unethical behaviour. Lack of sleep leads to higher negative affect; impaired judgement of facial expressions, especially the anger and happy categories; lower emotional intelligence; and poorer interpersonal functioning. To this litany of negative outcomes we can add mood impairments, boredom and avoiding interactions; increased risk of safety incidents, errors and injuries (Dinges, 1995). Not surprisingly, sleep deprivation is associated with higher levels of absenteeism. In short, make sure you get eight hours of sleep a night!

SUMMARY

This chapter emphasized the roles of positive emotional climates, good working environments and supportive work relationships for human health and well-being and stressed that creating such workplaces is not only the ethical responsibility of employers and leaders. Strain at work has a huge impact on organizations' financial performance and effectiveness.

Levels of injuries and illness at work vary enormously depending on how well the workplace is managed to preserve the health and well-being of employees. Key indicators of problems in a work environment are high incidences of absenteeism and turnover.

Stress is the consequence when very high demands (or strains) are placed upon people at work, exceeding the physical, cognitive or emotional capacity they have to cope. Causes include physical role (such as nurses lifting patients in hospital), workload, work pace, relationships at work, perceived control, task content (the strain of some police work) and conflicts between work and home life.

The consequences of stress can be behavioural (inability to manage tasks such as memorizing material), poor performance on the job, burnout (emotional exhaustion, depersonalization and feeling ineffective) and ultimately physiological damage (e.g. heart disease). Stress coping strategies include problem-focused, emotion-focused and appraisal, with problem-focused appraisal appearing most effective.

Strategies for managing stress and strain at work include: primary – dealing with the stressors directly, such as reducing workload or improving the quality of supervision, teamwork and procedural justice (the most effective approach); secondary, which involves training people to deal with stress via relaxation exercises or providing social support; and tertiary, which involves dealing with the symptoms of stress such as through EAPs.

The chapter contrasts burnout with employee engagement, the latter characterized by workers' urgency, intensity, focus, adaptability and personal initiative. Prescriptions to promote the well-being and flourishing of people at work are offered, including the advice to connect, be active, take notice, keep learning and give in daily life. The chapter also revealed the importance of sleep and the damaging effects of shift work. Relatively new interventions such as mindfulness and structuring opportunities for detachment and recovery from work are enhancing our ability to intervene to create workplaces that enhance rather than damage employee well-being.

DISCUSSION QUESTIONS

1 How can the competing perspectives of maximizing shareholder value and employee health and well-being be reconciled?

2 To what extent should governments legislate to force companies to ensure employee health and well-being?

3 What would you include in a comprehensive health and well-being programme in an organization?

4 What evidence is there that interventions to reduce stress and strain actually make a difference?

5 To what extent is stress at work an individual or an organizational phenomenon?

FURTHER READING

Bakker, A. B. (2011). An evidence-based model of work engagement. *Current Directions in Psychological Science, 20*(4), 265–269.

Bakker, A. B., & Demerouti, E. (2017). Job demands–resources theory: Taking stock and looking forward. *Journal of Occupational Health Psychology, 22*(3), 273–285.

Bliese, P. D., Edwards, J. R., & Sonnentag, S. (2017). Stress and well-being at work: A century of empirical trends reflecting theoretical and societal influences. *Journal of Applied Psychology, 102*(3), 389–402.

Cameron, K. S., & Spreitzer, G. M. (Eds.). (2011). *The Oxford handbook of positive organizational scholarship*. Oxford, England: Oxford University Press.

Cooper, C. L., & Quick, J. C. (Eds.). (2017). *The handbook of stress and health: A guide to research and practice*. Chichester, England: Wiley Blackwell.

Grawitch, M. J., & Ballard, D. W. (2016). *The psychologically healthy workplace: Building a win–win environment for organizations and employees*. Washington, DC: American Psychological Association.

Hesketh, I., & Cooper, C. L. (2017). *Managing health and wellbeing in the public sector: A guide to best practice*. London, England: Routledge.

Hofmann, D. A., Burke, M. J., & Zohar, D. (2017). 100 years of occupational safety research: From basic protections and work analysis to a multilevel view of workplace safety and risk. *Journal of Applied Psychology, 102*(3), 375–388.

Macey, W. H., Schneider, B., Barbera, K. M., & Young, S. A. (2009). *Employee engagement: tools for analysis, practice and competitive advantage*. Chichester, England: Wiley-Blackwell.

Quick, J. C., & Tetrick, L. E. (2003). *Handbook of occupational health psychology*. Washington, DC: American Psychological Association.

REFERENCES

Bakker, A. B. (2011). An evidence-based model of work engagement. *Current Directions in Psychological Science, 20*(4), 265–269.

Bakker, A. B., & Demerouti, E. (2017). Job demands–resources theory: Taking stock and looking forward. *Journal of Occupational Health Psychology, 22*(3), 273.

Bakker, A. B., Schaufeli, W. B., Sixma, H. J., & Bosveld, W. (2001). Burnout contagion among general practitioners. *Journal of Social and Clinical Psychology, 20*(1), 82–98.

Bakker, A. B., Schaufeli, W. B., Sixma, H. J., Bosveld, W., & Van Dierendonck, D. (2000). Patient demands, lack of reciprocity, and burnout: A five-year longitudinal study among general practitioners. *Journal of Organizational Behavior, 21*(4), 425–441.

Baltes, B. B., Briggs, T. E., Huff, J. W., Wright, J. A., & Neuman, G. A. (1999). Flexible and compressed workweek schedules: A meta-analysis of their effects on work-related criteria. *Journal of Applied Psychology, 84*(4), 496–513.

Barger, L. K., Ayas, N. T., Cade, B. E., Cronin, J. W., Rosner, B., Speizer, F. E., & Czeisler, C. A. (2006). Impact of extended-duration shifts on medical errors, adverse events, and attentional failures. *PLoS Medicine, 3*(12), 2440–2448.

Barling, J., & Boswell, R. (1995). Work performance and the achievement-strivings and impatience-irritability dimensions of Type A behaviour. *Applied Psychology: An International Review, 44*(2), 143–153.

Barton, J. (1994). Choosing to work at night: A moderating influence on individual tolerance to shift work. *Journal of Applied Psychology, 79*, 449–454.

Beehr, T. A. (1995). *Psychological Stress in the workplace*. London, England: Routledge.

Benavides, F. G., Benach, J., Diez-Roux, A. V., & Roman, C. (2000). How do types of employment relate to health indicators? Findings from the Second European Survey on Working Conditions. *Journal of Epidemiology and Community Health, 54*(7), 494–501.

Bennett, J. B., Weaver, J., Senft, M., & Meeper, M. (2017). Creating workplace well-being. In C. L. Cooper & Quick, J. C. (Eds.), *The handbook of stress and health: A guide to research and practice* (pp. 570–604). Chichester, England: Wiley Blackwell.

Berman, M. G., Jonides, J., & Kaplan, S. (2008). The cognitive benefits of interacting with nature. *Psychological Science, 19*, 1207–1212.

Beus, J. M., Dhanani, L. Y., & McCord, M. A. (2015). A meta-analysis of personality and workplace safety: Addressing unanswered questions. *Journal of Applied Psychology, 100*(2), 481.

Bliese, P. D., Edwards, J. R., & Sonnentag, S. (2017). Stress and well-being at work: A century of empirical trends reflecting theoretical and societal influences. *Journal of Applied Psychology, 102*(3), 389.

Bluen, S. D., Barling, J., & Burns, W. (1990). Predicting sales performance, job satisfaction and depression using the achievement strivings and impatience-irritability dimensions of Type A behaviour. *Journal of Applied Psychology, 75*, 212–216.

Brotheridge, C., & Grandey, A. (2002). Emotional labour and burnout: Comparing two perspectives of 'people work'. *Journal of Vocational Behavior, 60*, 17–39.

Brown, K. W., Ryan, R. M., & Cresswell, J. D. (2007). Mindfulness: Theoretical foundations and evidence for its salutary effects. *Psychological Inquiry, 18*, 211–237.

Buck, D. (2016). *Gardens and health: Implications for policy and practice*. London, England: The King's Fund.

Bureau of Labor Statistics. (2013). Monthly labor review. Retrieved from www.bls.gov/opub/mlr/2013/

Burke, M. J., Salvador, R. O., Smith-Crowe, K., Chan-Serafin, S., Smith, A., & Sonesh, S. (2011). The dread factor: How hazards and safety training influence learning and performance. *Journal of Applied Psychology, 96*(1), 46.

Cameron, K. S., & Spreitzer, G. M. (Eds.). (2011). *The Oxford handbook of positive organizational scholarship*. Oxford, England: Oxford University Press.

Cannon, W. (1929). *Bodily changes in pain, hunger, fear and rage. An account of recent researches into the function of emotional excitement* (2nd ed.). New York, NY: Appleton.

Carleton, E., & Barling, J. (2017). Sleep, work and well-being. In C. L. Cooper & J. C. Quick (Eds.), *The handbook of stress and health: A guide to research and practice* (pp. 485–500). Chichester, England: Wiley Blackwell.

Cartwright, S., & Cooper, C. L. (1997). *Managing workplace stress*. London: SAGE.

Cartwright, S., & Cooper, C. L. (2005). Individually targeted interventions. In J. Barling, E. K. Kelloway, & M. R. Frone (Eds.), *Handbook of work stress*. Thousand Oaks, CA: SAGE.

Chui, M., Manyika, J., & Miremadi, M. (2016). Where machines could replace humans – and where they can't (yet). *McKinsey Quarterly*, July.

Cohen, S., Evans, G. W., Stokols, D., & Krantz, D. S. (1986). *Behaviour, health and environmental stress*. New York, NY: Plenum Press.

Cohen, S., & Herbert, T. B. (1996). Psychological factors and physical disease from the perspective of psychoneuroimmunology. *Annual Review of Psychology, 47*, 113–42.

Collet, C., Averty, P., & Dittmar, A. (2009). Autonomic nervous system and subjective ratings of strain in air traffic control. *Applied Ergonomics, 40*(1), 23–32.

Colligan, M. J., & Cohen, A. (2004). The role of training in promoting workplace health and safety. In J. Barling & M. R. Frone (Eds.), *The psychology of workplace safety* (pp. 223–248). Washington, DC: American Psychological Association.

Collinson, D. L. (1999). 'Surviving the rigs': Safety and surveillance on North Sea oil installations. *Organization Studies, 20*, 579–600.

Cooper, C. L., & Cartwright, S. (2001). Organizational management of stress and destructive emotions at work. In R. L. Payne & C. L. Cooper (Eds.), *Emotions at work: Theory, research and applications for management* (pp. 269–280). Chichester, England: John Wiley & Sons.

Cooper, C. L., & Sadri, G. (1994). The impact of stress counselling at work. In R. Crandall & P. L. Perrewe (Eds.), *Occupational stress: A handbook* (pp. 271–282). Bristol, PA: Taylor & Francis.

Csikszentmihalyi, M. (2008). *Flow: The psychology of optimal experience*. New York, NY: HarperCollins.

Day, A. L., & Livingstone, H. A. (2001). Chronic and acute stressors among military personnel: Do coping styles buffer their negative impact on health? *Journal of Occupational Health Psychology, 6*(4), 348–360.

de Dreu, C. K. W. (2008). The virtue and vice of workplace conflict: Food for (pessimistic) thought. *Journal of Organizational Behavior, 29*(1), 5–18.

Deci, E. L., & Ryan, R. M. (2008). Self-determination theory: A macrotheory of human motivation, development, and health. *Canadian Psychology/Psychologie canadienne, 49*(3), 182–185.

Demerouti, E., Bakker, A. B., Nachreiner, F., & Schaufeli, W. B. (2001). The job demands–resources model of burnout. *Journal of Applied Psychology, 86*(3), 499.

Devlin, A., & Arneill, A. (2003). Health care environments and patient outcomes: A review of the literature. *Environment and Behavior, 35*, 665–694.

Dewe, P. (2017). Demands, resources and their relationship with coping: Developments, issues, and future directions. In C. L. Cooper & J. C. Quick (Eds.), *The handbook of stress and health: A guide to research and practice* (pp. 427–442). Chichester, England: Wiley Blackwell.

Dinges, D. F. (1995). An overview of sleepiness and accidents. *Journal of Sleep Research, 4*, 4–14.

Dohrenwend, B. P. (2006). Inventorying stressful life events as risk factors for psychopathology: Toward resolution of the problem of intracategory variability. *Psychological Bulletin, 132*(3), 477.

Drake, C. L., Roehrs, T., Richardson, G., Walsh, J. K., & Roth, T. (2004). Shift work sleep disorder: Prevalence and consequences beyond that of symptomatic day workers. *Sleep, 27*(8), 1453–1462.

Dunbar, E. (1993). The role of psychological stress and prior experience in the use of personal protective equipment. *Journal of Safety Research, 24*, 181–187.

Erickson, T. J. (2005). Testimony submitted before the US Senate Committee on Health, Education, Labor and Pensions, May 26, p. 8. Retrieved from www.govinfo.gov/content/pkg/CHRG-109shrg21585/html/CHRG-109shrg21585.htm

Evans, G. W., & Johnson, D. (2000). Stress and open-office noise. *Journal of Applied Psychology, 85*(5), 779–783.

Fernández, J. D., & Vico, F. (2013). AI methods in algorithmic composition: A comprehensive survey. *Journal of Artificial Intelligence Research, 48*, 513–582.

Firth-Cozens, J. (1990). Source of stress in women junior house officers. *British Medical Journal, 301*(6743), 89–91.

Folkard, S., & Monk, T. H. (1979). Shiftwork and performance. *Human Factors, 21*, 483–492.

Fox, D. K., Hopkins, B. L., & Anger, W. K. (1987). The long-term effects of a token economy on safety performance in open-pit mining. *Journal of Applied Behavior Analysis, 20*, 215–224.

Fox, W. F. (1967). Human performance in the cold. Human Factors, 9(3), 203–220.

Fredrickson, B. L. (2009). *Positivity: Groundbreaking research reveals how to embrace the hidden strengths of positive emotions, overcome negativity and thrive*. New York, NY: Crown.

French, J. R. P., Caplan, R. D., & Van Harrison, R. V. (1982). *The mechanisms of job stress and strain*. Chichester, England: John Wiley & Sons.

Friedman, M. (1969). *Pathogenesis of coronary artery disease*. New York, NY: McGraw-Hill.

Friedman, M., & Rosenman, R. H. (1974). *Type A behaviour and your heart*. New York, NY: Knopf.

Fritz, C., & Sonnentag, S. (2009). Antecedents of day-level proactive behavior: A look at job stressors and positive affect during the workday. *Journal of Management, 35*(1), 94–111.

Fritz, C., Sonnentag, S., Spector, P. E., & McInroe, J. A. (2010). The weekend matters: Relationships between stress recovery and affective experiences. *Journal of Organizational Behavior, 31*(8), 1137–1162.

Frone, M. R. (2000). Work – family conflict and employee psychiatric disorders: The national comorbidity survey. *Journal of Applied Psychology, 85*(6), 888–895.

Ganster, D. C., Fox, M. L., & Dwyer, D. J. (2001). Explaining employees' health care costs: A prospective examination of stressful job demands, personal control, and physiological reactivity. *Journal of Applied Psychology, 86*(5), 954–964.

Ganster, D. C., & Murphy, L. R. (2000). Workplace interventions to prevent stress-related illness: Lessons from research and practice. In C. L. Cooper & E. A. Locke (Eds.), Industrial and organizational psychology (pp. 34–51). Oxford, England: Blackwell.

Gifford, R. (1997). *Environmental psychology: Principles and practice* (2nd ed.). Boston, MA: Allyn & Bacon.

Glass, D. C., Singer, J. E., & Friedman, L. N. (1969). Psychic cost of adaptation to an environmental stressor. *Journal of Personality and Social Psychology, 12*(3), 200–210.

Gold, D. R., Rogacz, S., Bock, N., Tosteson, T. D., Baum, T. M., Speizer, F. E., & Czeisler, C. A. (1992). Rotating shift work, sleep, and accidents related to sleepiness in hospital nurses. *American Journal of Public Health, 82*(7), 1011–1014.

Goleman, D., Boyatzis, R., & McKee, A. (2002). *The new leaders: Transforming the art of leadership into the science of results*. London, England: Little, Brown.

Goodrich, R. (1982). Seven office evaluations: A review. *Environment and Behavior, 14*, 353–378.

Grandey, A. A. (2003). When 'the show must go on': Surface acting and deep acting as determinants of emotional exhaustion and peer-rated service delivery. *Academy of Management Journal, 46(1)*, 86–96.

Grant-Vallone, E. J., & Donaldson, S. L. (2001). Consequences of work–family conflict on employee well-being over time. *Work and Stress, 15*(3), 214–226.

Grawitch, M. J., & Ballard, D. W. (2016). *The psychologically healthy workplace: Building a win–win environment for organizations and employees.* Washington, DC: American Psychological Association.

Grawitch, M. J., Ballard, D. W., & Erb, K. R. (2015). To be or not to be (stressed): The critical role of a psychologically healthy workplace in effective stress management. *Stress and Health, 31*(4), 264–273.

Greenberg, J. (2006). Losing sleep over organizational injustice: Attenuating insomniac reactions to underpayment inequity with supervisory training in interactional justice. *Journal of Applied Psychology, 91*(1), 58.

Hackman, J. R., & Oldham, G. R. (1980). *Work redesign.* Reading, MA: Addison-Wesley.

Harare, Y. (2018). *21 lessons for the 21st century.* London, England: Jonathon Cape.

Harter, J. K., Schmidt, F. L., & Keyes, C. L. (2003). Well-being in the workplace and its relationship to business outcomes: A review of the Gallup studies. In C. L. Keyes & J. Haidt (Eds.), *Flourishing: The Positive person and the good life* (pp. 205–224). Washington, DC: American Psychological Association.

Health and Safety Executive. (2013). *Annual Statistics Report for Great Britain.* Retrieved from www.hse.gov.uk/statistics/causinj/index.htm

Heitkemper, M. M., Jarrett, M. E., Levy, R. L., Cain, K. C., Burr, R. L., Feldii, A., Barney, P., & Weisman, P. (2004). Self-management for women with irritable bowel syndrome. *Clinical Gastroenterology and Hepatology, 2*(7), 585–596.

Henning, R. A., Sauter, S. L., & Krieg, E. F. (1992). Work rhythm and physiological rhythms in repetitive computer work: Effects of synchronization on well-being. *International Journal of Human–Computer Interaction, 4*(3), 233–243 [Special Issue: Part II: Occupational stress in human–computer interaction].

Hobfoll, S. E. (1989). Conservation of resources: A new attempt at conceptualizing stress. *American Psychologist, 44*(3), 513.

Hobfoll, S. E. (2001). The influence of culture, community, and the nested-self in the stress process: Advancing conservation of resources theory. *Applied Psychology, 50*(3), 337–421.

Hobfoll, S. E. (2011). Conservation of resources theory: Its implication for stress, health, and resilience. In S. Folkman (Ed.), *The Oxford handbook of stress, health, and coping* (pp. 127–147). Oxford Library of Psychology. New York, NY: Oxford University Press.

Hockey, G. J. (1997). Compensatory control in the regulation of human performance under stress and high workload: A cognitive-energetical framework. *Biological Psychology, 45*, 73–93.

Hofmann, D. A., Burke, M. J., & Zohar, D. (2017). 100 years of occupational safety research: From basic protections and work analysis to a multilevel view of workplace safety and risk. *Journal of Applied Psychology, 102*(3), 375.

Hofmann, D. A., Morgeson, F. P., & Gerras, S. J. (2003). Climate as a moderator of the relationship between leader–member exchange and content specific citizenship: Safety climate as an exemplar. *Journal of Applied Psychology, 88*(1), 170.

Hofmann, D. A., & Stetzer, A. (1996). A cross-level investigation of factors influencing unsafe behaviours and accidents. *Personnel Psychology, 49*, 307–339.

Hoonakker, P., Carayon, P., & Schoepke, J. (2004). Work–family conflict in the IT work force. *Journal of Organizational Behaviour, 13*, 389–411.

Houston, D. M., & Allt, S. K. (1997). Psychological distress and error making among junior house officers. *British Journal of Health Psychology, 2*, 141–151.

Hülsheger, U. R., Alberts, H. J., Feinholdt, A., & Lang, J. W. (2013). Benefits of mindfulness at work: The role of mindfulness in emotion regulation, emotional exhaustion, and job satisfaction. *Journal of Applied Psychology, 98*(2), 310–325.

Hurrell, J. (1985). Machine-paced work and the Type A behaviour pattern. *Journal of Occupational Psychology, 58*, 15–25.

Ising, H., Babisch, W., & Günther, T. (1999). Work noise as a risk factor in myocardial infarction. *Journal of Clinical and Basic Cardiology, 2*, 64–68.

Jackson, S. E., & Schuler, R. S. (1985). A meta-analysis and conceptual critique of research on role ambiguity and role conflict in work settings. *Organizational Behaviour and Human Decision Processes, 36*(1), 16–78.

Jex, S. M. (1998). *Stress and job performance: Theory, research, and implications for managerial practice.* Thousand Oaks, CA: SAGE.

Jones, D., Molitor, D., & Reif, J. (2018). What do workplace wellness programs do? Evidence from the Illinois Workplace Wellness Study. Washington, DC: National Bureau of Economic Research Working Paper 24229. Retrieved from www.nber.org/papers/w24229

Jones, J. W., Barge, B. N., Steffy, B. D., Fay, L. M., Kunz, L. K., & Wuebker, L. J. (1988). Stress and medical malpractice: Organizational risk assessment and intervention. *Journal of Applied Psychology, 73*, 727–735.

Kahn, R., Wolfe, D., Quinn, R., Snoek, J., & Rosentbal, R. (1964). *Organizational stress: Studies in role conflict and ambiguity*. New York, NY: Wiley.

Kahn, R. L., & Byosiere, P. (1992). Theoretical framework for the study of stress in organizations. In M. D. Dunnette & L. M. Hough (Eds.), *Handbook of industrial and organizational psychology* (2nd ed., pp. 571–650). Palo Alto, CA: Consulting Psychologists Press.

Kahn, W. A. (1992). To be fully there: Psychological presence at work. *Human Relations, 45*(4), 321–49.

Karasek, R., & Theorell, T. (1990). *Healthy work: Stress, productivity, and the reconstruction of working life*. New York, NY: Basic Books.

Karasek, R. A. (1979). Job demands, job decision latitude and mental strain: Implications for job redesign. *Administrative Science Quarterly, 24*(2), 285–308.

Krantz, D. S., & McCeney, M. K. (2002). Effects of psychological and social factors on organic disease: A critical assessment of research on coronary heart disease. *Annual Review of Psychology, 53*, 341–369.

Lang, J., Thomas, J. L., Bliese, P. D., & Adler, A. B. (2007). Job demands and job performance: The mediating effect of psychological and physical strain and the moderating effect of role clarity. *Journal of Occupational Health Psychology, 12*(2), 116–124.

Layard, R. (2005). *Happiness: Lessons from a new science*. London, England: Penguin Press.

Lazarus, R. (1991). *Emotion and adaptation*. New York, NY: Oxford University Press.

Lazarus, R. (2000). Evolution of a model of stress, coping, and discrete emotions. In V. H. Rice (Ed.), *Handbook of stress, coping and health: Implications for nursing research, theory, and practice* (pp. 195–222). Thousand Oaks, CA: SAGE.

Lazarus, R. S., & Folkman, S. (1984). *Stress, appraisal, and coping*. New York, NY: Springer.

Lee, R. A. (1981). The effects of flexitime on family life: Some implications for managers. *Personnel Review, 10*(3), 31–35.

Lee. R. A. (1983). Flexitime and conjugal roles. *Journal of Occupational Behaviour, 4*(4), 297–315.

Leiter, M. P., & Maslach, C. (1988). The impact of interpersonal environment on burnout and organizational commitment. *Journal of Organizational Behavior, 9*(4), 297–308.

Levi, L. (2017). Bridging the science–policy and policy–implementation gaps. In C. L. Cooper & J. C. Quick (Eds.), *The handbook of stress and health* (pp. 7–23). Chichester, England: Wiley Blackwell.

Levy, R. L., Cain, K. C., Jarrett, M., & Heitkemper, M. M. (1997). The relationship between daily life stress and gastrointestinal symptoms in women with irritable bowel syndrome. *Journal of Behavioral Medicine, 20*, 177–193.

Linton, S. J. (1990). Risk factors for neck and back pain in a working population in Sweden. *Work and Stress, 4*(1), 41–49.

Loughlin, C., & Frone, M. R. (2004). Young workers' occupational safety. In J. Barling & M. R. Frone (Eds.), *The psychology of workplace safety* (pp. 107–125). Washington, DC: American Psychological Association.

Lyubomirsky, S., King, L., & Diener, E. (2005). The benefits of frequent positive affect: Does happiness lead to success? *Psychological Bulletin, 131*, 803–855.

Macey, W. H., Schneider, B., Barbera, K. M., & Young, S. A. (2009). *Employee engagement: Tools for analysis, practice and competitive advantage*. Chichester, England: Wiley-Blackwell.

Maddi, S. R., & Kobasa, S. C. (1984). *The hardy executive: Health under stress*. Homewood, IL: Dow Jones-Irwin.

Malzon, R. A., & Lindsay, G. B. (1992). *Health promotion at the worksite: A brief survey of large organizations in Europe*. Copenhagen, Denmark: WHO Regional Office for Europe.

Martin, W., Dixon, B. J., & Thomas, H. (2017). Enhancing mental well-being. In C. L. Cooper & J. C. Quick (Eds.), *The handbook of stress and health: A guide to research and practice* (pp. 461–471). Chichester, England: Wiley Blackwell.

Maslach, C., Jackson, S. E., & Leiter, M. P. (1996). *Maslach burnout inventory manual* (3rd ed.). Palo Alto, CA: Consulting Psychologists Press.

Maslach, C., & Leiter, M. P. (1997). *The truth about burnout: How organizations cause personal stress and what to do about it*. San Francisco, CA: Jossey-Bass.

Maslach, C., Schaufeli, W. B., & Leiter, M. P. (2001) Job burnout. *Annual Review of Psychology 52*, 397–422. doi:10.1146/annurev.psych.52.1.397

Matthews, G., Zeidner, M., & Roberts, R. D. (2012). *Emotional intelligence 101*. New York, NY: Springer.

McCormick, E. (1976). *Human factors in engineering and design*. New York, NY: McGraw-Hill.

McCoy, J. M., & Evans, G. W. (2004). Physical work environment. In J. Barling, K. E. Kelloway, & M. R. Frone (Eds.), *Handbook of work stress* (pp. 219–266). London, England: SAGE.

Melamed, S., Kristal-Boneh, E., & Froom, P. (1999). Industrial noise exposure and risk factors for cardiovascular disease: Findings from the CORDIS study. *Noise and Health, 4*, 49–56.

Milanovich, D. M., Driskell, J. E., Stout, R. J., & Salas, E. (1998). Status and cockpit dynamics: A review and empirical study. *Group Dynamics: Theory, Research and Practice, 2*, 155–167.

Motowidlo, S. J., Packard, J. S., & Manning, M. R. (1986). Occupational stress: Its causes and consequences for job performance. *Journal of Applied Psychology, 71*(4), 618–629.

Murphy, L. R. (1996). Stress management in work settings: A critical review of the health effects. *American Journal of Health Promotion, 11*(2), 112–135.

Neal, A., & Griffin, M. A. (2004). Safety climate and safety at work. In J. Barling & M. R. Frone (Eds.), *The psychology of workplace safety* (pp. 15–34). Washington, DC: American Psychological Association.

Netemeyer, R. G., Johnston, M. W., & Burton, S. (1990). Analysis of role conflict and role ambiguity in a structural equations framework. *Journal of Applied Psychology, 75*(2), 148–157.

Niedhammer, I., Sultan-Taïeb, H., Chastang, J. F., Vermeylen, G., & Parent-Thirion, A. (2014). Fractions of cardiovascular diseases and mental disorders attributable to psychosocial work factors in 31 countries in Europe. *International Archives of Occupational and Environmental Health, 87*(4), 403–411.

O'Dea, A., & Flin, R. (2000, August). *Safety leadership in the offshore oil and gas industry*. Paper presented at the Academy of Management Annual Meeting, Toronto, Canada.

Orth-Gomér, K., Eriksson, I., Moser, V., Theorell, T., & Fredlund, P. (1994). Lipid lowering through work stress reduction. *International Journal of Behavioral Medicine, 1*(3), 204–214.

Parker, S. K., Axtell, C., & Turner, N. (2001). Designing a safer workplace: Importance of job autonomy, communication quality and supportive supervisors. *Journal of Occupational Health Psychology, 6*, 211–228.

Probst, T. M., & Brubaker, T. L. (2001). The effects of job insecurity on employee safety outcomes: Cross-sectional and longitudinal explorations. *Journal of Occupational Health Psychology, 6*, 139–159.

Pryor, A., Townsend, M., Maller, C., & Field, K. (2006). Health and well-being naturally: 'Contact with nature' in health promotion for targeted individuals, communities and populations. *Health Promotion Journal of Australia, 17*, 114–123.

Quick, J. C., & Tetrick, L. E. (2003). *Handbook of occupational health psychology*. Washington DC: American Psychological Association.

Quick, J. C., Wright, T. A., Adkins, J. A., Nelson, D. L., & Quick, J. D. (2013). *Preventive stress management in organizations*. Washington, DC: American Psychological Association.

Quinlan, M., & Bohle, P. (2004). Contingent work and occupational safety. In J. Barling & M. R. Frone (Eds.), *The psychology of workplace safety* (pp. 81–105). Washington, DC: American Psychological Association.

Quinlan, M., Mayhew, C., & Bohle, P. (2001). The global expansion of precarious employment, work disorganization and consequences for occupational health: A review of recent research. *International Journal of Health Services, 31*(2), 225–414.

Reis, H. T., & Gable, S. L. (2003). Toward a positive psychology of relationships. In C. L. M. Keyes & J. Haidt (Eds.), *Flourishing* (pp. 129–159). Baltimore, MD: United Books.

Rizzo, J. R., House, R. J., & Lirtzman, S. I. (1970). Role conflict and ambiguity in complex organizations. *Administrative Science Quarterly, 15*(2), 150–163.

Roche, A., Kostadinov, V., & Fischer, J. (2017). Stress and addiction. In C. L. Cooper & J. C. Quick (Eds.), *The handbook of stress and health* (pp. 252–279). Chichester, England: Wiley Blackwell.

Rotter, J. B. (1966). Generalized expectancies for internal versus external control of reinforcement. *Psychological Monographs: General and Applied, 80*(1), 1–28.

Rupprecht, S., Koole, W., Chaskalson, M., Tamdjidi, C., & West, M. (2018). Running too far ahead? Towards a broader understanding of mindfulness in organisations. *Current Opinion in Psychology*, 28, 32–36.

Ryan, R. M., & Deci, E. L. (2000). Self-determination theory and the facilitation of intrinsic motivation, social development, and well-being. *American Psychologist*, 55(1), 68–78.

Rydstedt, L. W., Johansson, G., & Evans, G. W. (1998). A longitudinal study of workload, health and well-being among male and female urban bus drivers. *Journal of Occupational and Organizational Psychology*, 71(1), 35–45.

Saks, A. M. (2006). Antecedents and consequences of employee engagement. *Journal of Managerial Psychology*, 21(7), 600–619.

Schaufeli, W. B., & Bakker, A. B. (2004). Job demands, job resources and their relationship with burnout and engagement: A multi-sample study. *Journal of Organizational Behaviour*, 25(3), 293–315.

Schaufeli, W. B., & Buunk, B. P. (2003). Burnout: An overview of 25 years of research and theorizing. In M. J. Schabracq, J. A. M. Winnubst, & C. L. Cooper (Eds.), *Work and health psychology* (2nd ed., pp. 383–249). Chichester, England: John Wiley & Sons.

Schaufeli, W. B., Salanova, M., González-Romá, V., & Bakker, A. B. (2002). The measurement of engagement and burnout: A two sample confirmatory factor analytic approach. *Journal of Happiness Studies*, 3, 71–92.

Schaufeli, W. B., & Taris, T. W. (2014). A critical review of the Job demands–resources model: Implications for improving work and health. In G. F. **Bauer** & O. **Hämmig** (Eds.), *Bridging occupational, organizational and public health* (pp. 43–68). Dordrecht, Netherlands: Springer.

Schnall, P. L., Dobson, M., & Landsbergis, P. (2017). Work, stress, and cardiovascular disease. In C. L. Cooper and J. C. Quick (Eds.), *The handbook of stress and health* (pp. 99–124). Chichester, England: Wiley Blackwell.

Seligman, M. E. P. (2002). *Authentic happiness: Using the new positive psychology to realize your potential for lasting fulfillment*. New York, NY: Free Press/Simon & Schuster.

Selye, H. (1956). *The stress of life*. New York, NY: McGraw-Hill.

Siegrist, J. (2017). The effort–reward imbalance model. In C. L. Cooper & J. C. Quick (Eds.), *The handbook of stress and health: A Guide to research and practice* (pp. 24–35). Chichester, England: Wiley Blackwell.

Smith, C. S., Robie, C., Barton, J., Smith, L., Spelten, E., Totterdell, P., & Costa, G. (1999). A process model of shiftwork and health. *Journal of Occupational Health Psychology*, 4, 207–218.

Sonnentag, S., & Fritz, C. (2007). The Recovery Experience Questionnaire: Development and validation of a measure for assessing recuperation and unwinding from work. *Journal of Occupational Health Psychology*, 12(3), 204–221.

Sonnentag, S., & Geurts, S. A. (2009). Methodological issues in recovery research. In S. Sonnentag, P. L. Perrewé, & D. C. Ganster (Eds.), *Current perspectives on job-stress recovery* (pp. 1–36). Emerald.

Sonnentag, S., Binnewies, C., & Mojza, E. J. (2008). 'Did you have a nice evening?' A day-level study on recovery experiences, sleep and affect. *Journal of Applied Psychology*, 93(3), 674–684.

Sonnentag, S., Kuttler, I., & Fritz, C. (2010). Job stressors, emotional exhaustion, and need for recovery: A multi-source study on the benefits of psychological detachment. *Journal of Vocational Behavior*, 76, 355–365.

Sonnentag, S., Mojza, E. J., Binnewies, C., & Scholl, A. (2008). Being engaged at work and detached at home: A week-level study on work engagement, psychological detachment, and affect. *Work and Stress*, 22, 257–276.

Takala J. (2002). Introductory report: *Decent Work – Safe Work*. Paper presented at the XVIth World Congress on Safety and Health at Work, Vienna: ILO.

Taylor, A. F., & Kuo, F. E. (2009). Children with attention deficits concentrate better after walk in the park. *Journal of Attention Disorders*, 12, 402–409.

Tindale, H. A., Chang, Y., Kuller, L. H., Manson, J. E., Robinson, J. G., Rosal, M. C., ... Matthews, K. A. (2009). Optimism, cynical hostility, and incident coronary heart disease and mortality in the Women's Health Initiative. *Circulation*, 120, 656–662.

Tjosvold, D. (1990). Flight crew collaboration to manage safety risks. *Group and Organization Studies*, 15, 177–191.

Toker, S., & Melamed, S. (2017). Stress, recovery, sleep and burnout. In C. L. Cooper and Quick, J. C. (Eds.), *The handbook of stress and health: A guide to research and practice* (pp. 168–185). Chichester, England: Wiley Blackwell.

Turner, N., & Parker, S. K. (2004). The effect of teamwork on safety processes and outcomes. In J. Barling & M. R. Frone (Eds.), *The psychology of workplace safety* (pp. 35–63). Washington, DC: American Psychological Association.

Ulrich, R. (2006). Evidence-based health care architecture. *The Lancet, 368*, S38–S39.

Verquer, M. L., Beehr, T. A., & Wagner, S. H. (2003). A meta-analysis of relations between person–organization fit and work attitudes. *Journal of Vocational Behavior, 63*, 473–489.

Walker, M. (2017). *Why we sleep: The new science of sleep and dreams*. London, England: Penguin.

West, M. A. (Ed.). (2017). *The Psychology of meditation: Research and practice*. Oxford, England: Oxford University Press.

West, M. A., & Chowla, R. (2017). Compassionate leadership for compassionate health care. In P. Gilbert (Ed.), *Compassion: Concepts, research and applications* (pp. 237–257). London, England: Routledge.

West, M. A., Dawson, J., Admasachew, L., & Topakas, A. (2011). *NHS staff management and health service quality: Results from the NHS staff survey and related data*. London, England: Department of Health.

West, M. A., & Lyubovnikova, J. (2013). Illusions of teamworking in healthcare. *Journal of Health Organization and Management, 27*, 134–142.

Wickens, C. D., & Hollands, J. G. (2000). *Engineering psychology and human performance* (3rd ed.). Upper Saddle River, NJ: Prentice Hall.

Wineman, J. D. (1986). *Behavioural issues in office design*. New York, NY: Van Nostrand Reinhold.

Zacharatos, A., & Barling, J. (2004). High-performance work systems and occupational safety. In J. Barling & M. R. Frone (Eds.), *The psychology of workplace safety* (pp. 203–222). Washington, DC: American Psychological Association.

Zhao, Y., Zhang, S., Selvin, S., & Spear, R. C. (1991). A dose response relation for noise induced hypertension. *British Journal of Industrial Medicine, 48*, 179–184.

Zohar, D. (1980). Safety climate in industrial organizations: Theoretical and applied implications. *Journal of Applied Psychology, 65*, 96–102.

Zohar, D. (2002). Modifying supervisory practices to improve subunit safety: A leadership-based intervention model. *Journal of Applied Psychology, 87*(1), 156.

Zohar, D. (2003). Safety climate: Conceptual and measurement issues. In J. C. Quick & L. E. Tetrick (Eds.), *Handbook of occupational health psychology* (pp. 123–142). Washington, DC: American Psychological Association.

CASE STUDIES FOR PART TWO: PROFESSIONAL PRACTICE OF WORK AND ORGANIZATIONAL PSYCHOLOGY

CASE STUDY 2.1

University of South West England: Improving Diversity and Inclusion

This case study is set within a fictional UK university.

The University of South West England is a medium-sized higher education institution with approximately 15,000 students, employing around 1,600 academic staff and 1,300 administrative and support staff.

The University is divided into four faculties: Human Science, Physical Sciences and Engineering, Social Sciences, and Business & Economics.

Diversity and inclusion

For many years, the University's management and executive team have struggled to improve diversity and inclusion across the organization. Although their wish is for proactive improvement in these areas, issues are more pressing than ever because of the University's failure to attain a UK *Athena Swan* recognition for commitment to advancing the careers of women in science, engineering, maths and medicine in higher education. A high-profile tribunal case brought by a member of academic staff, who claimed he was turned down for promotion on grounds of race, has also highlighted significant shortcomings in policy and procedure in Human Resources.

Josephine Clark, the new Human Resources Director, has therefore initiated a project to transform diversity and inclusion in the University. Her first activity was to engage a group of independent consultants to establish the scale of issues to be addressed, and to find out more about the experience of people working at the University.

The consultancy report

The consultant group undertook research to investigate matters of diversity and inclusion at the University using three methods: an audit of employment statistics; a survey of experiences; and interviews with staff. Some of their main findings confirmed the concerns that had circulated informally:

- Diversity in staff groups (academic and administrative) existed at junior levels in the University. At senior academic and management level, representation of women and BAME staff was woefully low.

- Analyses of recruitment statistics indicated poor representation of women and BAME candidates at senior levels. Staff reported that they had witnessed poor selection practices and the majority had witnessed, at least occasionally, incidents of bias (e.g. sexism or racism).

- Promotion procedures were unclear and many considered them to be biased and politically driven. Women and BAME employees felt that they were denied access to key networks that would help with promotion. Managers and staff were dissatisfied with promotion procedures. Analyses revealed higher than expected rates of promotion failure for BAME employees.

- Staff at junior levels from all backgrounds reported that their views were seldom heard or taken into account in decision-making. Only a small percentage understood how decisions were taken at senior levels.

- BAME staff and women reported multiple incidents of incivility or disrespect. This ranged from, for example, academic staff being assumed to be support or administrative staff, professors excluded from senior staff informal meetings, inappropriate comments, or conduct such as being talked down to or treated in a dismissive fashion.

- In a few extreme cases, the consultants heard accounts which, if proven, may constitute harassment or bullying. Almost half of staff surveyed responded that they would feel intimidated or fearful for their career if they were to raise a grievance concerning harassment or bullying.

- While the University had a range of flexible working policies, few employees understood these and around two-thirds would feel that requesting flexible working or taking an extended maternity or paternity period would damage their promotion chances. Accounts of maternity provision indicated that return to work for mothers after maternity was managed poorly.

- The student population was diverse across the University, but around half of women, LGBT+ and BAME students also reported they had received or witnessed incivility or disrespectful behaviour by staff.

Developing an action plan

With such a devastating account of findings laid out in the report, Josephine was now tasked with the challenge of transforming diversity and inclusion across the University. But where to start? The next stage of her project was the formation of an action plan. The plan was to be comprised of two main classes of activity: 1) priority interventions to improve fairness; 2) long-term strategic change to make the University more diverse and inclusive.

Questions

1. Based on your reading of the main findings of the report, what are the main areas of management practice that need to be urgently addressed at the University?

2. What does work and organizational psychology tell us about how these key areas of management could be improved to encourage diversity and inclusion?

3. How could recruitment and promotion processes, in particular, be made fairer and more inclusive?

4. What are the key issues to consider in the long-term changes that are needed in order to build a more inclusive organization?

CASE STUDY 2.2

TESCO Plc Introduction

Tesco was created in 1919 by Jack Cohen, and the first store opened in 1929. Since then the company has grown exponentially, expanding into other sectors such as clothing and more recently banking and telecoms, and opening stores outside the UK. The first customer loyalty card, which allows Tesco to track the shopping habits of customers, was launched in 1995 and, soon after, Tesco was the UK's most visited supermarket. Sir Terry Leahy became the supermarket's chief executive in 1997 and presided over unprecedented supermarket expansion across the UK. In March 2011, Sir Terry Leahy retired

continued

and new CEO Philip Clarke arrived. Expansion into the USA was abandoned in 2013, after operating at a loss for several months, and Tesco experienced its first fall in profits for over 20 years.

Six-point plan

After spending some time overseeing UK operations, as well as continuing with the Group CEO role, in April 2012 Clarke announced a new plan to 'Build a Better Tesco'. This comprised six points:

1. Give better customer service through hiring more staff and specialist training.
2. Make the stores more inviting; changing layouts, signage and lighting.
3. More straight pricing and promotions that customers want.
4. Update products and relaunch Tesco brands.
5. Update branding and marketing with a new advertising agency.
6. Improve online offerings and allowing customers to collect an increased variety of items from more locations.

Purpose and values

As well as the six-point plan, Clarke introduced a new 'core purpose' for Tesco: 'We make what matters better, together'. This phrase highlights Tesco's increasing focus on CSR, being seen to do the right thing and to encourage trust and loyalty from customers, suppliers and employees. To strengthen this, an extra value was added to Tesco's two core values, which have been in place for over a decade. These two core values are: *"No one tries harder for customers"*, which is about providing excellent customer service and *"We treat everyone how we like to be treated"*, which is about respect and teamwork. The newest addition, *"We use our scale for good"*, is about CSR, with aims specifically around opportunities for young people, tackling obesity and reducing food waste.

The core purpose and values of the brand translate into how people are managed within Tesco. Employees are treated with trust and respect by the organization, in the belief that this will translate into excellent customer service. This culture also means that employees stay with the company for a long time; many members of staff have been working at Tesco for 25 years or more (including the CEO). Another aspect of this is that Tesco believe in developing staff that perform well, and around 80 per cent of managers have been appointed from internal positions.

'Be a great employer'

To be a great employer is one of the four Essential Elements of Tesco's approach. Tesco aim to ensure that staff are happy and proud in their work, to develop employee potential and to enable equal opportunities. As such, Tesco take the business of motivating, developing and rewarding their employees seriously, although this is a difficult job. The size and scope of Tesco's operations mean that the roles occupied by employees are extremely varied, spanning various market sectors and countries. For example, apart from their main business in the UK, Tesco now operate across countries in Europe and Asia, and as well as the main food retailing business, the company has arms in clothing, technology and telecoms. This means that the ways employees are motivated, the rewards they are offered and the development opportunities that are available need to be suited to such varied positions as customer assistants in-store through to customer analysts in head office; from warehouse pickers to marketing managers.

Reward and recognition

To ensure reward is managed in a structured way, despite these varying demands, Tesco have an overarching framework in place to motivate and recognize employees. This is called Tesco Reward Principles. This is implemented in ways that focus staff on the goals of the company, while promoting a sense of pride and loyalty towards the brand. The principles are:

- Competitive:
  - Assessed on a total rewards basis, including financial and non-financial rewards.
  - Reflects an individual's role, experience and contribution.
  - Set with reference to external market practices and internal relativity.
- Simple:
  - Simple, clear and easy to understand.
  - Avoids unnecessary complexity.
  - Delivered accurately.
- Fair:
  - Transparent and applied consistently and equitably.
  - Trusted and properly governed.
  - Legal and compliant.
- Sustainable:
  - Aligned to the business strategy, reflects performance and is affordable.
  - Flexible to meet the changing needs of the business.
  - Responsible.

There is a large range of benefits on offer to employees, as part of the reward package. A few of the more innovative financial incentives include the 'Shares in Success', 'Save as you Earn' and 'Buy as you Earn' (BAYE) schemes. The shares scheme entitles employees who have been with Tesco for at least one year to free shares and a proportion of the company's profits; the saving scheme encourages staff to save out of their salaries for a set time period, with tax-free incentives; and the BAYE scheme is an opportunity to buy shares with tax-saving advantages. Other benefits include the Privilege card, which gives staff 10 per cent off shopping, as well as discounts on a range of products and services, including gym memberships, private medical insurance and holidays. There is also the opportunity to take a career break after two years' service.

Tesco make their employees feel recognized in other ways too, as demonstrated by the Students At Tesco website. This website is specifically designed for, and accessible only to, the many students who work in stores for Tesco during A levels and university, and includes articles on a range of subjects as well as Tesco cooking recipes.

Development

As already acknowledged, Tesco are keen to develop internal talent for future roles in senior positions, as well as more generally provide opportunities for individuals to increase their skillsets and move around the organization. At any one time Tesco have around 7,000 staff members on development courses to enable them to change roles successfully within the company, and there are specific training programmes for each major career stage within Tesco. Where possible, these programmes are tailored to the individual's specific requirements. One training and development offering is the Options programme, which trains individuals for the next job level or a different role through on-the-job training and specific training courses to up-skill them in the required areas.

A well-known way of developing potential future leaders quickly within Tesco is the Graduate Scheme, although there are also Apprenticeship and A level leavers' schemes. There are three main strands to the scheme: Store Management, Distribution, and Offices (which incorporates many different strands from commercial food to supply chain to the dot.com side of the business). Each of these strands looks for different individual qualities in applicants. Store managers have to be good communicators, have the drive to implement change, be self-aware and able to influence others. Individuals are expected to be running their own store within two years. After five years they are expected to be working towards becoming a Store Director, managing a number of Store Managers around a certain location.

continued

In distribution, individuals need to be able to make decisions quickly and be able to work with individuals from all backgrounds. In this area of the company, graduates run projects to increase efficiency within the distribution networks, specifically focusing on how items are received in warehouses, picked and loaded for delivery. After the scheme Graduates take on senior management roles, with a more strategic role over distribution operations. The Offices graduate scheme strands are specific to the department involved, but all Graduate Scheme employees are developed quickly, often being promoted within one year and given a wide variety of training and development opportunities to propel them into more senior roles rapidly.

Communication

An additional way that Tesco engage their staff is through communication. Regular blog posts are made by selected members of the group about a range of topics, from activities in-store to partnering with charities. Importantly, the CEO and UK Managing Director, as well as Heads of Group in Asia and Europe, regularly contribute to the blog. The visibility of the senior team and their posts, which show them to be 'living the values' of the company, keep them in contact with staff and engage employees with what is happening in the wider business. Senior staff also take part in a programme called TWIST (Tesco Week In Store Together) for one week each year, where they spend five days on the shop floor. This helps to connect colleagues and promote conversations between employees who ordinarily work in separate areas of the business.

Another important part of this communication strategy is the annual anonymous staff engagement survey, where employees are free to comment about changes they would like to see. The senior team act on these suggestions; for example, a recent survey highlighted that employees wanted more opportunities to voice their suggestions and concerns, and subsequent efforts are being made to make this happen and ensure staff recognition for their suggestions. Tesco also measure how well they are meeting their aims of happy and proud workers, developing potential and providing equal opportunities through metrics collected from the survey. The 2012/2013 figures available show that the target for numbers of individuals on the Options programme was missed by 0.1 per cent, although other development opportunities have been in place for more staff as Tesco increased store staff numbers and provided specialist training.

Diversity

A key aim of Tesco's drive to be a great employer is around diversity and equal opportunities: 'To build an environment where all our colleagues contribute, make a difference and can be themselves'. The Group-wide plan also has a key element of 'Everyone is welcome'. Diversity in the leadership team is an important focus for Tesco, as they aim to increase the number of women working at the top level. Between 2007 and 2013, 93 per cent more women were appointed as Directors or Business Leaders, and as of April 2013, 30 per cent of the Tesco Plc Board were women (three people). In 2010 Tesco launched their Women in Leadership development programme in order to progress and retain women in senior positions. This programme is also working in other countries where Tesco operate, such as South Korea, where it is more unusual for women to take leadership roles.

Tesco UK also have a policy in place to encourage staff to work beyond the traditional retirement age if they wish to, and currently 2,500 individuals do so. Additionally, the company has policies and networks in place to encourage further diversity within the workforce. For example, there is a growing LGBT+ employee network, a new in 2011/2012 ABC (African, Black British and Caribbean) network and the longer-running Women in Business and Asian networks. Tesco also work with external organizations to encourage applications from individuals with disabilities and long-term unemployed people, as well as ex-service personnel and ex-offenders. All of these policies move Tesco closer to ensuring that their staff members reflect the wider society.

Teamwork

Many of the staff members at Tesco also talk about the camaraderie of the teams within the stores. One way this is fostered is through social events, as all stores have their own social committees, who organize events such as five-a-side football tournaments and fancy-dress competitions. The teamwork culture of Tesco is also highlighted by the fact that many senior staff members go to work on the shop floor during the busy Christmas period as part of the 'Helping Hands' programme. In 2013, over 5,000 members of staff from the Tesco offices spent time working in-store to help keep the shelves stocked.

References and further reading

www.tescoplc.com – search for careers and graduates

www.marketingweek.co.uk – search for article 'Sir Terry Leahy to retire in Tesco board overhaul' by Russell Parsons, 2010

www.telegraph.co.uk – search finance/newsbysector/ retailandconsumer for 'Tesco the six point turnaround plan' with Philip Clarke

www.bbc.co.uk/news/magazine – Tesco: How one supermarket came to dominate' by Denise Winterman, 2013

www.managementtoday.co.uk – search for 'Tesco boss Philip Clarke: I feel Bloody Great' by Chris Blackhurst, 2013

Questions

1. **a.** What Big Five personality traits do you think are important for the Store Manager and Distribution Manager graduate schemes, based on the information in the case?

   b. Why do you think these qualities would be important?

2. How do you think emotions, core self-evaluations and psychological capital would impact the work of Graduate Store Managers?

3. How can we apply information from Chapter 3 about social influences on behaviour in groups to the Tesco case?

4. How could we use the models of motivation from Chapter 4 to explain the policies and procedures in place at Tesco?

5. What evidence is there in the case that Tesco is attempting to create a satisfied and committed workforce? What else could they do?

6. How would you propose to design and deliver fair and effective selection processes for Store Managers and Distribution Managers graduate schemes? What kinds of competencies and characteristics would be needed and how could you assess them?

7. How could managers at Tesco use work and organizational psychology to achieve the company's aims around development?

8. What are some of the issues that Tesco should consider in managing diversity? Would you advise building more inclusive work cultures as part of their strategy?

9. Using what you know about work and organizational psychology, in what ways would you recommend that the policies and procedures at Tesco as outlined in the case could be improved to make a positive impact?

10. Do you think that Tesco's approaches would help to manage the careers of the people working for the company effectively?

11. How could Tesco most effectively safeguard against issues of workplace stress or burnout among its staff?

PART THREE

ORGANIZATIONS

This final part of the book gives a perspective on organizations as a whole. At this level, research and theorizing can become more complex since we have to take simultaneous account of individual- and group-level processes that shape organizational processes. It involves taking a systems perspective. We also have to take account of the external environment within which organizations operate: their markets, countries, cultures, competitors and governments.

And we have to remember that organizations vary considerably in size, purpose and processes. They are entities that can range from a small enterprise of perhaps 20 people working in a tool-making company, manufacturing parts for machinery used in car production, through AB InBev, a brewing and soft drinks company in South Africa with just over 9,000 employees, up to BP, one of the largest corporations in Europe, with 37,000 employees. Even that is tiny in comparison with the 1.4 million employees in the network of organizations that makes up the National Health Service in England.

Organizations are created to align the activities of employees towards achieving organizational goals. This involves structuring activities by specifying goals and strategies; providing effective leadership which directs, motivates and enables employees to successfully achieve what is required; building effective teams and ensuring inter-team working; developing and reinforcing values and norms within the organization that sustain effective performance; and managing the change which is essential for organizations to adapt continually to their ever-changing environments. The next chapters explore research and theorizing in these areas, providing a thorough grounding in understanding organizations, which we believe is essential for understanding the psychology of work and organizations.

10 Organizations: Strategy and Structure
11 Leadership in Organizations
12 Teams and Teamwork
13 Organizational Culture, Climate and Change

CHAPTER 10
ORGANIZATIONS: STRATEGY AND STRUCTURE

LEARNING OBJECTIVES

- To be able to compare and contrast the different perspectives on strategy adopted by theorists over the past 50 years.
- To be able to present the arguments for a value-based perspective on strategy.
- To understand the structure of organizations and be able to explain how this can affect culture, behaviour and work attitudes in organizations.
- To be able to explain how the environment of an organization affects its structure.

INTRODUCTION

Psychologists are interested in human behaviour – individual, social and organizational (such as the study of culture and climate). In this chapter, we consider organizational strategies, structures and environments and the relationships between them.

> *Picture the following scenario: It is the credit crunch and economic recession of 2009 and you are working in a large company that makes a range of products for supplying the automotive industry. The industry is highly competitive and suppliers' prices are driven down by the large car manufacturers. Very few people are buying cars. Not surprisingly, your company is suffering. Your company has always been highly participative and consults its staff about major decisions. The company is going to have to cut costs by at least 40 per cent or find new markets that will bring in an additional 40 per cent of revenue.*
>
> *The company seems faced with a choice between two strategies. The first is to encourage innovation, to develop better products that differentiate it from competitors, and find innovative ways of reducing costs. This will involve everyone in the company coming up with new and improved ways of doing things. The alternative is to make a substantial proportion of the staff redundant to achieve the necessary cost savings to help the company stay in business. Your instincts are to keep people in work and to go for the innovation strategy – but is that a recipe for failure? It may very well be, in the circumstances.*

And that is why those who study the psychology of work and organizations should have an understanding of strategy, structure and environment – because it provides and indeed shapes the context for their work. In this chapter we explore organizations and their relationships with their environments via the topics of strategy and structure. To begin though, we must think carefully about what an organization is.

Huczynski and Buchanan (2007) define 'organization' as *a social arrangement for achieving controlled performance in pursuit of collective goals* (p. 6) and as we saw earlier in this book, it is clear from that definition that organizations have been around for most of human history. We have had social arrangements for achieving controlled performance in pursuit of our collective goals for many thousands of years. Historically, few organizations, with the exception of the religious and the military, were ever bigger than about 30 people. Indeed, most people worked in small groups of three, four, five or six people. Organizations of 20 or more people tended to be unusual. All that changed with the Industrial Revolution, however, and for just the past 200 years, for the briefest eye blink of human history (probably about 0.2 per cent of our time here), large organizations have begun to proliferate, and now we struggle to understand and manage these much larger social organizations that we have created to meet our economic needs and to ensure that those who work in them flourish rather than experience chronic misery or boredom. What practitioners, academics and management consultants are all concerned about is finding ways of ensuring that organizations survive, prosper and succeed in increasingly turbulent and competitive environments, so strategy is a word that dominates their conversations. Strategy, as we have argued throughout, must also include plans to ensure the growth, development and well-being of those who work within our organizations.

ORGANIZATIONAL STRATEGY

The word strategy was always used to describe the tactics of generals in battle rather than the plans of organizational leaders. It is a concept embedded in the study of war. One of the earliest proponents of strategy as a concept taken out of the context of military manoeuvres was Niccolo Machiavelli. His writings in *The Prince* elucidated ideas about how Italian leaders in the 16th century could preserve their power and control their states, engage effectively with other states, and prosper and succeed without the necessity of going to war. His name became a byword for manipulation and intrigue in common parlance, but he was a master of power, politics and strategy. His writings on the subjects provide quotes for management scholars to this day. What he says about the challenges of innovation illustrate this by providing valuable insight into the psychology of the process of innovation:

> *... There is no more delicate matter to take in hand, nor more dangerous to conduct, nor more doubtful in its successes, than to set up as a leader in the introduction of changes. For he who innovates will have for his enemies all those who are well off under the existing order of things and only lukewarm supporters in those who might be better off under the new. This lukewarm temper arises partly from the fear of adversaries who have the laws on their side and partly from the incredulity of mankind who will never admit the merit of anything new, until they have seen it proved by the event.* (Skinner & Price, 1988.)

Although Machiavelli was therefore an early champion of the idea of strategy in collectives, be they organizations or states, we have to wait until the latter half of the 20th century before the concept was being applied systematically to thinking about organization development in work contexts:

> *The end is still the same – to be victorious in the field of battle – it is merely the arena that has shifted. Competition is war by other means and, so the story goes, you need strategy to win it.* (Carter, Clegg, & Komberger, 2008, p. 19.)

We will review its history from that point on, but first we must clarify what we mean by this word.

What is strategy?

Strategy is variously defined as a concern with the future and the goals of the organization; as a metaphorical road map to guide the organization towards a desired destination; and as a means of achieving goals through the use of its resources. Because organizations are in competition with other organizations (other car parts suppliers in the example we used at the beginning), they need strategies to ensure they win (or at least do not lose – since losing can be fatal to the organization). The assumption in scholarly as well as popular writings is that strategy is the business of top managers. They are the people with the knowledge, skills and abilities to shape and implement strategy – it is what they are paid to do:

> *usually it is a top management privilege to spend time at expensive management retreats arguing with even more expensive consultants about 'what if... scenarios'.* (Carter et al., 2008, p. 10.)

According to most theorists (though not all, as we will see), strategy is very much an organizational response to the environment and to changes in the environment. Just like an organism, an organization needs to adjust to changes in its environment in order to survive and prosper. Animals forage for food more widely when there is too little because of other predators; organizations seek new markets. Therefore, the strategy of the organization is a means of survival or defeating the opposition and it provides a plan for how to achieve these or other desired outcomes. Strategic decisions in turn lead to changes in the processes and operations of the organization. Indeed, theory suggests that strategy shapes the structure of the organization (in terms of hierarchies and divisions of operations) and influences its culture (values and practices).

If strategy shapes structure, determines policies and practices in organizations and influences values and behaviours, then, self-evidently, it should be of central concern to those concerned to understand the psychology of work and organizations. It would be convenient, therefore, to offer a consensus view of strategy, but the ground has shifted a great deal over the past 60 years and is energetically contested. In order to help the reader understand this elusive concept of strategy, we will briefly review the history of theorizing over the past 50 years.

The early history of strategic management

The development of strategic management as a discipline began in the 1950s when Philip Selznick (1957) introduced the idea that managers would need to 'fit' the organization to its external environment, 'strategy' being the set of decisions shaped by and responding to external factors. This led to the development of 'SWOT' analysis, in which managers carefully consider the Strengths and Weaknesses of their organizations, while also considering the Opportunities and Threats they face. Such an analysis, it was claimed, provided a basis for strategic planning.

The developing discipline of strategic management was given an intellectual coherence by the publication of Alfred Chandler's book *Strategy and Structure* in 1962. Until then, management had largely been seen as a series of separate activities – production, sales, marketing, R&D and finance. Chandler drew attention to the need for an integrated approach to management that took a long-term perspective, and this approach was named 'strategy'. The structure of the organization, he argued, would then be a consequence of the strategic choices made by senior managers. The departments and hierarchies would be structured in order to respond to the demands of the environment. Many theorists now argue that organizational structures (divisions, departments and hierarchies) are created to reduce uncertainty in the environment. There is a marketing department because it reduces uncertainty about customer needs and preferences; there is an R&D department because it reduces the uncertainty about how to create new products to meet shifting demands.

These models of strategy were based on a rational, neat and quasi-military approach to planning for the future. Environments were understood, decisions made and structures adapted in a rational, unambiguous and transparent way. The 'Rational Planning Model' had an early champion in Igor Ansoff (1965), an applied mathematician and business manager, who developed strategic management as a discipline by offering both dynamic models and a vocabulary that remains influential to this day. He distinguished between three broad activities in organizations:

- administrative activities – maximization of efficiency of administrative processes
- operational activities – direct production processes
- strategic activities – directed to managing the organization's relationship with its environment and anticipating strategic turbulence or continual change.

Ansoff introduced the idea of 'gap analysis', a process of identifying the space between where the organization is currently, where we would like it to be, and the necessary actions to reduce the gap. His Product Mission Matrix, which continues to influence thinking and practice today, integrates market and product analyses to produce the 2 by 2 matrix shown in Figure 10.1. Decisions about whether to focus on new or existing markets and to focus on existing or new products provide four broad strategies:

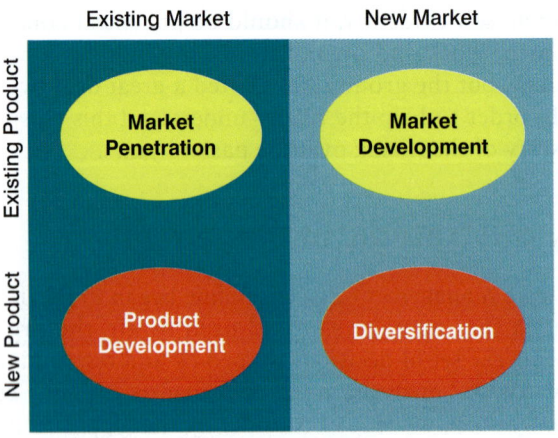

Figure 10.1 Ansoff's product market matrix

- *Market penetration* involves selling more existing products/services into existing markets. The aim is to maintain or increase market share through having the most competitive prices or effective advertising or using loyalty schemes so that customers always shop with you rather than your competitors because of the discounts they get. Dell computers has pursued this strategy very successfully, driving down prices and driving away competitors.
- *Market development* involves selling existing products into new markets. Examples might be generating markets in new geographical areas. Tobacco companies, restricted by legislation from advertising, have aggressively marketed their products in developing companies in recent years. Japan uses barcode recognition on most of its mobile telephone devices. The companies that make these systems have been adopting market development strategies by seeking to make them available in Europe and the USA, thereby creating huge new markets for these companies.
- *Product development* is a strategy based on selling new products or services into current markets. For example, a vehicle breakdown service may begin offering car insurance to its customers, followed by house and travel insurance.
- *Diversification* strategies involve selling new products or services into new markets. This means diversifying the products the organization seeks to sell and trying to sell them into markets the company has not operated in before. This might involve moving into the business of your suppliers: a car manufacturer deciding to make oil filters for its own cars and selling them to other car manufacturers; acquisition of other companies in order to diversify activities so the organization is not too dependent upon one market; or developing new product lines as a result of an accident (e.g. the weakly sticky Post-it note was the result of a failure to make a strong enough adhesive at 3M).

DISCUSS WITH A COLLEAGUE

Identify four different organizations that use one of these strategies. Try to discover what it is about their products or markets that leads them to adopt this strategy. Do you think it is the right strategy for them? What strategy would you recommend, given their products and markets? Talk to managers in different organizations (they may be family or friends, colleagues on your course) and ask them which strategy is pursued by their organization. Ask them if they are able to say why their organization pursues this strategy and whether one of the other three alternatives could work for them. Such conversations are likely to increase the sophistication of your understanding of strategy and enrich your appreciation of organizations more generally.

Having understood what we mean by strategy and explored briefly the beginnings of strategic management, we now explore major approaches to strategy in the past 60 years.

MAJOR PERSPECTIVES ON STRATEGY

Management by objectives

One of the most influential management theorists of the 20th century, Austrian-born Peter Drucker, asserted from a management perspective what work and organizational psychologists see as axiomatic – the importance of clear objectives. Drucker emphasized clear objectives for the organization as a means of ensuring survival and success. His work led to the influential approach dubbed 'management by objectives' – ensuring that the organization has clear objectives and that those of the departments, teams and individuals who make up the organization are derived from the organization's overall objectives. Managing by objectives is not just about setting objectives but also about monitoring progress towards them. He also gave credence to the notion of the *intellectual capital* of the organization – the fact that the knowledge that employees hold in their heads and that the organization retains in its 'memory' is a vital resource, as much as land, buildings and technology. Drucker's view was that understanding the behaviour of people within organizations was vital to both setting and managing strategy. For a good account of Drucker, his life and his extraordinary intellectual contribution to our understanding of organizations, see Elizabeth Edersheim's book, *The Definitive Drucker* (2007).

Bounded rationality perspectives on strategy

Academic thinking about strategy was profoundly influenced by the Nobel Prize-winning economist Herbert A. Simon (1945). He argued, in contrast to assumptions of rational planning models, that, in real life, decision-making was far from perfect, not entirely rational and could only be understood as approximations to rationality. He coined the term 'satisficing' to describe what managers do when developing strategies and making decisions, a word that combines 'sufficing' and 'satisfying'. Simon's work suggests that managers should be focused on doing enough to be acceptably effective rather than wasting time and energy seeking the very best decisions. Rationality is limited by lack of information, our cognitive limitations in processing a wide variety of complex and uncertain information, and simply the time available to manage complexity. What we see in organizational strategies and managerial decision-making, he proposed, is not rationality but 'bounded rationality': rationality bounded by these limitations. There are many other bounds to rationality, such as incorrect information, misinterpreted information, powerful interests dictating decisions and so on.

Cohen, March, and Olsen (1972) took this thinking further with their startlingly named *garbage can model of decision-making*. Their analysis of strategy offered surprising insights into the randomness and complexity of strategic decision-making. They proposed that there are streams of events in organizations, such as *problems* that can arise inside or outside the organization (loss of key personnel; economic downturn) and *solutions* (new product ideas; opportunities to sell into new markets; the serendipitous discovery of new products or processes). These solutions are not necessarily (or even usually) responses to problems and are often independent of them. Solutions are often discarded (in the metaphorical garbage can) without being used and managers then rummage around in the garbage can and find an appropriate solution when a problem occurs. The Post-it note adhesive was a failure, and it was only the persistence of one choral-singing employee, who saw the failed adhesive as a solution to marking the pages of his hymnal, that led to its identification as a potential new product. The failure became a solution, which produced a major new revenue stream for 3M.

There are also *choice opportunities* when organizations and their managers are expected to come up with a decision (even though there may be no rational need for a decision at that point). The advisory board is meeting and managers feel they should present a new strategy to them, so, even though there is no problem, a choice opportunity exists and a garbage can solution can be selected. And then there are *participants*. Their involvement in particular problems, solutions or choice opportunities is also far from rational. People may have preferences for particular strategic solutions, problems or choice opportunities depending upon, for example, who is watching. If the CEO prefers certain strategic solutions, problems or choice opportunities, participants are likely to be vigilant for those and pluck them smartly from the garbage can.

> **DISCUSS WITH A COLLEAGUE**
>
> Think of a decision you have been involved in – perhaps in a sports club, social organization or with a group of friends. Thinking back to the process, can you see how the garbage can model might offer a better description of what actually happened than a rational planning model of decision-making? Better still if you can think of an example from a work organization. Then discuss what the implications are for organizations and how we might train managers to make strategic decisions (e.g. by seeking solutions regardless of problems, by seeking participants and creating choice).

These ideas have been extended to suggest that organizations are action generators. They generate problems for which they already have solutions. Total Quality Management is a solution – this involves continually improving the quality of every part and process of the organization. Business Process Re-engineering is another solution that focuses on finding ways of dramatically speeding up and making more efficient the processes in the business, whether it is making products or responding to customer complaints. These are ready-made solutions waiting for problems, and each manager has their stock of them. Managers then generate problems (identifying situations as problems) to which these solutions are applied. The solutions are not driven by problems, but strategies emerge (e.g. introducing culture change or leadership development programmes) because these strategic solutions are available and favoured by particular managers. Lean Manufacturing is another example of a solution that generates problems. We may believe that lean manufacturing (optimizing production processes, for example) is successful. We therefore come to see our secretarial processes as a problem to which we can apply 'lean', though no one has said the secretaries are not functioning well. Applying lean manufacturing principles to streamlining secretarial processes becomes a new strategy for improving the performance of the organization.

Michael Porter's economic perspectives on strategy

This rapid transit through theoretical models of strategy takes us to the work of Michael Porter (1980, 1985), an industrial economist based at Harvard Business School. Porter argued that the potential of the organization and its strategy are dependent on the industry and the market within which it operates. The task of strategic decision-makers is to identify and exploit weaknesses and opportunities in these industries and markets. The airline industry might be in trouble right now and there are very few opportunities, so cutting costs is a priority. The pharmaceutical industry, on the other hand, is in good shape and companies are investing in long-term research and development for new products. Strategy is therefore very much dependent on the industry within which the organization is embedded. Indeed, according to Porter, understanding the industry context is central to understanding organizational strategy. Competitive strategy must focus on product quality, manufacturing costs and product price, sales promotion and services, and strength of sales channels – how effective the means of distributing products to retail outlets are. Note that we are using manufacturing terms here, but this equally applies to services such as insurance, selection and recruitment services, and charities.

Porter's analysis suggests three core strategies that organizations can pursue to secure competitive advantage in their markets:

- Product differentiation involves innovating to ensure your product is distinct from those of competitors in a way that will be attractive to potential customers. This might involve adapting the product to include some new device or quality – as in the case of watch manufacturers including a phone, fitness tracking, camera and messaging facility in the watch. It might also involve heavily advertising the product to give a sense that it has a unique and desirable quality. Coca-Cola is simply another highly sugared, fizzy vegetable drink, but massive global advertising presents it as 'the real thing'.
- Market segmentation involves analyzing the market and separating it out into discrete elements to enable you to target the different segments with appropriate products and advertising. This might be based on demography (people of different ages and genders will want different products and will be attracted by different advertising messages). It may also be done geographically (the climate in Greece is very different from that in Norway, so if you are advertising soft drinks, emphasizing qualities such as cool and refreshing may make sense in one place but not the other). Culture is another segment. Advertising in the USA often relies on images of women. This will not appeal in some Muslim countries. Organizations can also segment markets on the basis of psychological factors. Those people who have developed an identity characterized by a strong commitment to the environment will find 'green' messages and 'organic' products and services more appealing.
- Price policy and cost leadership usually involves reducing costs and prices. Supermarkets adopt such an approach because they can benefit from the very large volumes they buy and sell. This means they can demand lower prices from their suppliers, reduce their own processing costs and pass lower prices on to their customers. In some circumstances, pricing policy may mark the organization's products as high price but highly valued. A Luis Vuitton bag carries no more, no more safely and no more beautifully than the vast majority of other bags in the world. But the high price associated with it leads some people to value it highly and to buy one.

Porter's work also draws particular attention to the competitive environment, arguing that five forces determine bargaining power in negotiating prices with customers and suppliers. These five forces are listed below:

- *Rivalry among existing competitors* – this is the central competitive force. It is traditionally measured by industry concentration, which is the percentage of the market taken by the top four firms: the greater the percentage, the less the competition.
- *Entrants* – ease of entry into a market determines the level of competition or rivalry. Governments may restrict entry by granting monopolies or quasi-monopolies to organizations; some postal services in Europe are examples, along with utilities such as water

and energy. If a firm holds patents on a particular process or technology essential to the production of a product (e.g. pharmaceuticals with patents on a particular statin) this will restrict entry. Some products or services require highly specialized plants and technologies, which deter organizations from entering the industry, such as Norway's sophistication in oil and gas exploration. Finally, there are economies of scale that result from a firm having built up capacity over the years and producing large quantities of a product at a low price, making it very difficult for new entrants to enter the market and compete.

- *Buyers* – the fewer buyers there are, the more competitive the industry is. For example, governments buying military equipment for their armies from an arms production firm in the home country; or large car manufacturers buying air filters for their cars from a small number of companies. The more dependent a company is on large buyers, the greater the rivalry among competitors for that large contract, and the more competitively vulnerable the company is.
- *Substitutes* – the availability of substitutes also shapes the competitive environment. If it is easily possible to substitute one product for another then the environment is more competitive. Examples of substitutability are glass bottles and plastic bottles for aluminium drinks cans. Bus travel is a substitute for train travel, and both trains and ferries offer an alternative to air travel for travellers from France wishing to visit the UK.
- *Suppliers* – are powerful if there is a significant cost to a company to switch suppliers. Part of Microsoft's strength as a supplier of operating systems is that it would cost PC manufacturers a great deal to redesign their computers to use other operating systems. Suppliers are also powerful if they are few and concentrated, such as the pharmaceutical industry in its relationships with healthcare systems. The greater the power of suppliers, the more competitive the environment.

Strategic management then requires the organization's decision-makers to understand the complexity of these forces and their interactions in such a way that they can produce a plan that will enable them to increase their profitability and ensure long-term survival, exploiting opportunities to reduce the power of their competitors and gain a greater industry concentration.

Porter's influential work did not stop there. His 1985 book, *Competitive Advantage: Creating and Sustaining Superior Performance*, focused on the concept of the value chain in production processes. The processes of production or delivery of services can be conceived of as a 'value chain' which transforms inputs (such as people's efforts, raw materials, knowledge and creativity) into final products or services. Porter proposed that the industry value chain depicted how different steps in the process add value (or do not) to services and products. Added value is the difference between the costs of production and revenue from sales. Thus we may assess the value added by the addition of attractive packaging to a particular product – customers pay more because packaging is glitzy. We may also assess the extent to which bureaucracy in an organization (requiring three signatures on a requisition for more materials) adds value. In effect, such an analysis leads us to question what specific parts of the organization add value, for example the work of HR, R&D, sales team, etc. What does not add value? Does the ambience of a restaurant add to the final price that can be charged? Does the quality of raw materials make a difference? Does raising chickens organically and free range result in the ability to charge more? One of the consequences of such an analysis is that it reveals that some activities add less value than they would if the function was 'outsourced' (e.g. having a computing company provide email service and support rather than having this provided in-house).

Porter finally turned, at the request of US President Ronald Reagan, to consider the competitive advantage of nations in order to answer the question of what leads nations to success. It is important to be aware of this national level of analysis in understanding strategy since it identifies environmental factors that determine strategy, competitiveness and managerial decisions in organizations. As shown in Figure 10.2, Porter identified four key factors influencing competitive advantage and two secondary influencing factors.

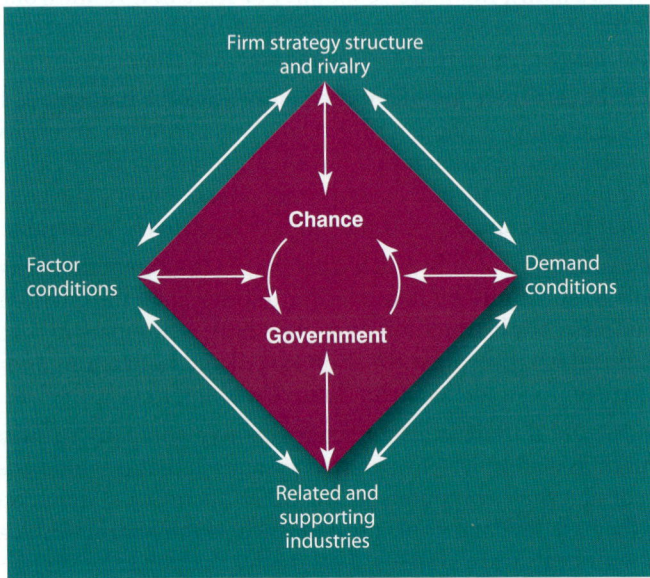

Figure 10.2   Porter's diamond model for the competitive advantage of nations

Factor conditions These include the availability of skilled labour and the infrastructure (education health services, roads, airports, telecoms, etc.). Obviously, the more the better. Traditionally, natural resources have been seen as offering huge advantages but this is by no means a given. Take, for example, countries that have large quantities of oil or diamonds. Many of these countries are held back by corruption, conflict and lack of industry development. Because of these natural resources, governments do not need to encourage industry, entrepreneurialism and innovation and do not invest sufficiently in education, infrastructure, regulation and training. Countries with few natural resources such as Japan and the Netherlands have become outstandingly entrepreneurial, whereas those with many natural resources such as Nigeria and Chad are among the poorest in the world (Collier, 2007).

Demand conditions The more sophisticated customers there are in the home market, the more competitive the country will be, since customers will drive product and service innovation. Russia has traditionally not had a sophisticated domestic market because of the legacy of communism. Customers had to put up with what they were given by the state system. The legacy continues today, with customers unlikely to be demanding in terms of services or product quality and therefore not forcing high levels of innovation and competitiveness on organizations. On the other hand, Japan's incredibly sophisticated customers for micro technology have meant that the country continues to lead the world in this sector.

Related and supporting industries Where there are related and supporting industries, nations and industries will be more competitive. The most famous example is the concentration of computing firms in the Silicon Valley area of California. There is an abundance of suppliers, skilled labour with strong knowledge bases and also a great deal of knowledge diffusion.

Firm strategy, structure and rivalry The level of domestic competition will affect an industry's and a nation's competitive advantage. Strong competition domestically ensures that companies become highly sophisticated and competitive, reducing thereby the likelihood of global competition. Domestic capital markets will also affect competitive advantage. For example, some countries emphasize a very short-term return on investments (e.g. the USA and UK), and this leads to the development of industries that give a quick return (such as the automotive industry); other countries emphasize longer-term returns, encouraging different types of industry (the chemical industry in Germany and the pharmaceutical industry in Switzerland are examples).

Secondary (and by implication less important) influencing factors are:

Government The state does or does not provide fiscal and economic stability; laws and systems that encourage enterprise – corruption discourages enterprise, for example; and subsidies to firms (directly through grants or indirectly through creating roads to the places where the firms wish to locate).

Chance Of course, chance also has a significant impact on competitive advantage. Carter et al. (2008) give the example of how American forces flooded Japan for strategic military reasons after the Second World War (because of the rise of the Soviet Union), but decided that bringing back empty ships made no sense. Those empty ships were instead filled with Japanese products, which were exported and sold in the USA, providing the basis for the extraordinary economic development of Japan in the 20th century.

This analysis is not restricted to nations' competitive advantage, but also helps us understand industries. A sector will have its own diamond within a given region, for example electronics in Eindhoven in the Netherlands. This will differ depending on sectors within a region. But the stronger a region's diamond within a sector, the more globally competitive the sector will be. In Sheffield, England, steel-making remains strong despite the huge drop in steel prices over the past 30 years because the factors in the diamond are strong and the region has innovative capacity.

Resource-based view of strategy

This perspective on strategy argues that it is the internal resources and unique capabilities of the firm that drive strategy. The resource-based view (RBV) of the firm suggests that resources determine the fit between the environment in which a firm operates and its capabilities or core competencies. This approach was articulated by Edith Penrose (1959), an American-born economist, who bravely defended colleagues against McCarthyism in the 1950s before moving to the UK. Her ideas were revised by Wernefelt (1984), who proposed that resources were the key to profitability.

Unique resources such as knowledge, technology, skilled staff, brand names, efficient processes, organizational culture and innovation capacity ensure organizational advantage and survival. Such resources could come from training employees, takeovers of other companies, hiring employees with new skills or developing new technologies. Theorists have distinguished between *tangible resources* such as physical plant, capital and intellectual property rights (IPR), and *intangible resources* such as reputation, brands, creativity and innovative capacity. Hamel and Prahalad (1996) extended these ideas by arguing, in contrast to Porter's industry emphasis, that the organization's resources are the key.

RBV theorists identify four types of resources:

- financial, e.g. equity, capital and loans
- physical, e.g. plant, equipment and land
- human, e.g. the knowledge, skills and attitudes of employees
- organizational, e.g. culture, climate and levels of trust within the organization.

Of course, it is not just any old resources that firms must have. The RBV specifies *valuable resources*. To be valuable they must have four characteristics (referred to as the VRIN model):

- Valuable in enabling firm to exploit opportunities and gain advantage (for example a new technology which captures solar power effectively and cheaply).
- Rare among competitor organizations.
- Imperfectly imitable – it is difficult to imitate this resource. Developing a highly trained and motivated workforce is one example. This is an imperfectly imitable resource since it is difficult to achieve without specialist knowledge and persistence.
- Not easily substitutable – having employees with a deep knowledge of the Alps working in the tourist industry in Switzerland is not easily substitutable, whereas the skills of call centre operatives in South Africa are.

According to RBV, strategists should look inside their organizations for resources that have these VRIN characteristics and not keep scanning the environment, if they are to develop brilliant strategies that will help them to win:

> *Sustainable competitive advantage can only be won by continuously developing existing resources incrementally while trying also to innovate products and services discontinuously in ways that play to the unique capabilities the organization has assembled, or can assemble, as it responds to changing market conditions.* (Carter et al., 2008, p. 58.)

Emergent process of strategy-making

Strategic management has been dominated by the thinking of economists and those who adopt rational planning approaches. We have briefly considered the work of those who question such models (for example the bounded rationality perspective) and now go on to consider more radical alternatives, packaged as 'emergent strategy'. Among the theorists questioning rational planning were Cohen et al. (1972), Lindblom (1959) and Weick (1995), all of whose thinking originally derived from the work of Herbert A. Simon that we considered earlier. Their collective views can be summed up by saying that highly complex and dynamic environments require emergent strategy.

Strategizing (they argue) is a process of making sense of complexity and ambiguity and this sense-making is an unfolding process. It is far more amorphous and fluid than is suggested by the models we have described thus far. Top-down approaches to sculpting strategy may be fine in stable and simple environments, but in the real world of complex, dynamic situations it is a messy and experimental process that must be driven from the bottom up, top down and sideways (Mintzberg, 1990). One view in the emergent school proposes that strategy is a process rather than a well-worked-out plan. For example, Pettigrew's comprehensive 1985 study of strategy in ICI suggested that power and politics often influenced strategic decisions more than rational planning. Indeed, what masquerades as rationality is often shaped by powerful influences within the organization. What the CEO and other leaders say is rational becomes rational. Alternative viewpoints from less powerful sources may be dismissed as uninformed or unintelligent.

Theorists in the emergent school question whether top management can ever know enough to come up with a sound strategic plan. They need information from all parts of the organization to have a sufficiently comprehensive understanding and they need information from the uncertain environment. To develop effective strategy requires employees to feed into the strategy or sense-making process because their experience at the sharp end of the business, interacting with customers and suppliers, gives them important intelligence. However, they are often not motivated to engage because it is not a part of their job and they are not paid anything like as much as top management. Their concerns are with their psychological contract and their immediate work environment, not with abstract notions of strategy.

BOX 10.1
W. L. Gore & Associates (UK) – engaged employees

W. L. Gore (a US company) is famous for its high-performance fabrics for outdoor activities, keeping clothes, boots and equipment protected from cold, wind and rain. Its 460 employees at the Livingstone plant in Scotland overwhelmingly believe they can make a valuable contribution to the success of the firm and are proud to work for the organization. The company has no job titles, no managers and no job descriptions. Employees are 'leaders' or 'associates' and they are paid according to their contribution, which is judged by their fellow associates. The most appropriate person (with the necessary skills) leads work groups at each stage of a project, and teamwork underpins the organization's activities. They manage their work time flexibly to deal with childcare or home deliveries, and have a range of benefits available, such as free dental care, health insurance, share options, childcare vouchers and sabbatical and career breaks. Moreover, employees say that they have fun at work and support their colleagues – team members care a lot about each other (adapted from www.sundaytimes.co.uk – best 100 companies).

Weick's (1995) work on the social psychology of organizing and on sense-making through strategy is particularly relevant to psychological orientations towards organizational strategy. He explains how strategy provides a way of making sense of complexity in a way that gives the reassurance of direction. He uses the story of a group of soldiers lost in the Alps. One of them finds an old map in his pocket that offers hope. Carefully following the map at each turn and twist, the soldiers find their way back down from the mountains. On arriving back in civilization, they show the map to someone who points out that it is, in fact, a map of the Pyrenees. But it had done the job. Strategies are similarly simply a means of orientation – they give people confidence, provide directions and routes, and help to provide orientation. Strategy defines the terrain as the Alps for everyone and helps them find a way. It is a social construction of reality – constructing a reality it appears to mirror. Weick says strategy therefore has a number of functions:

- It gets people to work together to think about where they are and where they want to get to.
- It provides a way of thinking about the future – and just happens to use a language of visions, missions, and of strengths, weaknesses, threats and opportunities (SWOT).
- It motivates people and organizations.

- It represents the dreams of the organization (the community of employees).
- It manages the anxiety of potentially frightening futures such as organizational failure and large-scale redundancies.

It should not be surprising that, when asked, emergent perspectives are less popular with managers than the clearly defined prescriptions of theorists such as Porter and those who offer the RBV. Popular management texts that offer simple, straightforward solutions sell well and managers are hungry for such guidance about how to develop strategy.

Cognitive perspectives

An important psychological perspective on strategy takes a cognitive orientation, arguing that strategy is often a consequence of the development of group mental models (Porac, Thomas, & Bade-Fuller, 1989). One study showed how managers from firms in the same sector in a geographic region developed a shared mental model of the nature of the competition in their sector in that region. Through their conversations and interactions they produced a model of the competitive domain which they came to believe, probably through a process of consensual validation. This led to the development of a rather narrow set of strategic alternatives – in effect, to a kind of 'groupthink' and to collective blind spots. Think of how Uber came along and radically disrupted the shared mental models of traditional taxi companies, changing the way they all had to do business.

Another cognitive perspective is provided by models of phases of strategic decision-making. Schwenk (1984) suggested three phases: problem identification, generation of alternatives (strategies) and selection. Based on documentary evidence, he showed that, in the first phase, people seek information that confirms their initial beliefs. This also influences, of course, their consideration of alternatives, along with a felt sense of personal responsibility as a strategic decision-maker. This sense of responsibility leads to group convergence, where decision-makers go along with group beliefs as a way of reducing personal responsibility. If the majority adopt this approach, the individual is somehow less culpable when the strategy proves ill founded. In the final selection stage, leaders may rely on past experiences as a guide to their choices, despite major changes in the environment. The use of heuristics to guide decision-making can result in illusions of control and in misplaced certainty (Hodgkinson & Sparrow, 2002). Such cognitive perspectives enrich our understanding of strategic decision-making and demonstrate the value of psychological perspectives.

Those studying strategic decision-making and those making strategic decisions would benefit enormously from developing knowledge and awareness of psychological processes, such as the 'too much invested to quit' phenomenon, and social psychological processes, such as conformity and group polarization that can affect the way we make important decisions (Hodgkinson & Starbuck, 2012).

Strategy as revolution

The approach adopted by some 'management gurus' proposes that strategy development should dramatically shake up the organization in order that its tendencies to inertia and unresponsiveness to a rapidly changing environment are counteracted. A leading proponent is Gary Hamel (1996), one of whose organizational exemplars was Enron, a company that failed spectacularly because of fundamental flaws in strategy and values. He puts forward ten propositions for great strategy-making:

1 Strategic planning should be about exploring the potential for revolution in the organization – for dramatic change.
2 It must be subversive – challenging accepted conventions within the organization and taken-for-granted assumptions.

3 The bottleneck is at the top of the bottle – the views of top managers are grounded in past experience. The need is for imagination and originality, not past experience.

4 Revolutionaries exist in every company, so the task is to identify and engage them.

5 Change is not the problem, engagement is – engage revolutionaries and others in a discourse about the future, deliberately seeking challenging views.

6 Strategy-making must be democratic.

7 Anyone can be a strategy activist within the organization.

8 Perspective is worth 50 IQ points – we can't make people smarter but we can give them new perspectives, which lead to shifts in thinking and practice.

9 Top down and bottom up are not the alternatives – both these and many more directions are needed (see Box 10.2 for an example of this).

10 You cannot see the end from the beginning – it is an open-ended process. It continually unfolds.

A more extreme version of these approaches to strategy development is offered by another 'management guru', Tom Peters (2003), whose messages include the recommendation to seek out the old and smash it. In a highly critical analysis of these ideas, Uchitelle (2006) points out in his book, *The Disposable American*, that these revolutionary ideas are associated with large-scale redundancy programmes and that the organizational revolutions these gurus advocate can lead to deep cost cutting, jobs lost and a cruel and dehumanizing culture:

> *At its core, the new cultural revolutionaries seek a totalizing creep into and envelopment of an increasing part of the organizational members' life world, in a manner that is difficult to see as other than corrosive or destructive.* (Carter et al., 2008, p. 96.)

BOX 10.2

Napp Pharmaceutical Holdings

This Cambridge, UK, firm employs 838 staff to produce new drugs and its staff say they have strong leadership, good pay (39 per cent earn over £35k) and benefits, and believe they are employed by a socially responsible company. A 'charter team' sets Napp's strategy by determining aims, direction and strategy. Half the team are senior managers and half are drawn from across the organization. The latter are people who will challenge conventional thinking and come up with radical innovations. Front-line staff who deal with customers and suppliers then decide on implementing the strategy, rather than this being a remote managerial decision. The company strives constantly to improve performance while maintaining a supportive culture. MD Antony Mattessich says: 'Our culture is very different from that of the usual pharmaceutical company. We're a bit less hard edged: we really look for balance between the heart, head and body. You need to have all the standard attributes required in any pharmaceutical company, such as drive and intellect. However, that isn't enough. You need to be human: a nice person'. Read further about this at www.napp.co.uk/.

KEY THEME

Environment and sustainability – it's not just about turning off the lights

How can leaders integrate actions to reduce their environmental impact into their strategies? According to IBM, every dollar they save in energy spending drives an additional $6 to $8 in operational savings. Rich Lechner, Vice President of Environment and Energy (Lechner, 2009), argues that it's not only cash benefits that arise from having an environmentally friendly strategy; there are brand and reputational benefits as well. He suggests organizations answer the following key questions as they seek to develop a strategy that incorporates environmental awareness:

- Are all aspects of the business, operations, IT and product lifecycle management, efficient and protective of our environment?
- Do we see environmental custodianship and energy consumption as key measures of our business success?
- Do we set challenging and public goals in our strategy related to environmental stewardship and energy consumption and make the data transparent?
- Are we acting as true leaders in these areas within our industry?
- Does our strategy involve reducing costs, complexity and inefficiency in all our activities so resources are saved?
- Are we simply reactive to regulation or do we take a proactive stance to energy and climate challenges, leading the way?
- Are energy conservation and environmental protection central to our business and brand strategies?

Lechner argues that the environmental strategy must include people, information, product, IT, property and business operations and be core and integrated into the overall business strategy:

- *People* The strategy should identify ways of reducing (for example) commuting and business travel time and costs by using new technologies wherever possible.
- *Information* Companies must find efficient ways of collecting and storing data in order to minimize their data footprint. The by-product is better information access and response.
- *Product* Companies must design products that have a lower environmental impact. Streamlining product development and manufacturing also results in less waste, fewer resources used and less energy usage.
- *Information technology* IT usage is costly in terms of power use and the need to keep machines cool. Businesses must focus their IT strategies to reduce energy costs and increase efficiency of IT systems in their contribution to the business goals.
- *Property* Companies need to ensure their buildings and transport systems are constantly reducing their environmental impact. When companies collaborate in transporting goods, for example, there are far fewer empty and half-empty trucks and containers travelling around the globe.

- *Business operations*: Reducing energy or water consumption leads to reduced costs. Using good measures to compare existing use and conservation benchmarks is one starting point.

Addressing these key components of a business in combination, in relation to environmental impact, makes companies more competitive as well as socially responsible.

Strategy as practice

Finally, the strategy as practice approach, perhaps similar to emergent strategy ideas, examines strategy as a process rather than an outcome. Researchers in this tradition are concerned to know where and how the work of strategizing and organizing is actually done. By researching the strategy process, it is suggested, we will better understand the nature of strategy. The approach seeks to answer questions such as who does it; what skills are needed; what are the common tools and methods; how is the work done; and how are the products of this work communicated and enacted? The focus is on strategy as a social practice; on the social interactions and negotiations of people throughout organizations as they engage in strategy formation (Jarzabkowski, 2005; Jarzabkowski & Spee, 2009). Studying strategy as practice, it is proposed, will help practitioners to develop reflexivity about their work by reflecting on what it is they are trying to achieve, how they are going about it and what they therefore need to change. It is an orientation that is consistent with a psychological perspective since it is grounded in research, focused on social interactions and social psychological processes, and advocates a learning-in-action orientation to strategy formulation.

Conclusion

Reflecting on these different approaches to developing strategy, from Machiavelli through to Jarzabkowski, the reader might react with bewilderment and ask: 'Which approach is right?' 'What should guide me in my work?' The answers are that all these approaches and ideas enrich our understanding of how to shape the decisions and directions of organizations. Each adds value (to borrow from Drucker's notions). However, some stand out as more consistent with psychological and sociological perspectives on organizations. These are the RBV of the firm, the strategy as practice view, and strategy as an emergent process. Psychologists can identify more easily with each of these rather more sophisticated approaches than perhaps they can with others such as the product market matrix, the rational planning model, strategy as revolution and economic models.

Finally, what is striking about this area is how strategy appears to be discussed in a moral vacuum. Even war has its Geneva Convention, prescribing what is acceptable morally and what not. Yet little of the writing about organizational strategy discusses the fundamental moral issues that should be at the heart of strategy development. In recent years we have seen organizations fail on a massive scale because of a failure of values, for example the collapse of Lehman Brothers. These include dishonesty with the public; failure to learn from past mistakes; lack of wisdom among leaders more concerned with individual success than integrity; failure of regulation (the excesses and imprudence of banks); the damage done to our environment by organizations denying the reality of the climate emergency; and the priority of organizational profit over contribution to the community. Integrating values with strategy development is essential. Two US psychologists, Peterson and Seligman (2004), have researched the fundamental human values in human communities cross-culturally, surveying more than a million people, and have identified six core areas of values – wisdom, courage, justice, love, temperance and wonder. These are described with annotations on how they might apply to strategy development in relation to the environment and sustainability in organizations (see Box 10.3).

This ends our exploration of strategy, but early in our exploration we noted how strategy determines structure, and it is to an exploration of organizational structure that we now therefore turn.

BOX 10.3
Sustainability and the environment

Integrating values into strategy

1 **Wisdom and knowledge** – the acquisition and use of knowledge within organizations.

   - **Creativity** [originality, ingenuity]: Thinking of novel and productive ways to conceptualize and do things within the organization that care for the environment and reduce global heating.
   - **Curiosity** [interest, novelty-seeking, openness to experience]: In relation to learning about the environment and sustainability, taking an interest in research in this area for its own sake not just for business profitability; finding subjects and topics relating to the climate emergency and protecting the environment fascinating; exploring and discovering relevant research.
   - **Judgement and open-mindedness** [critical thinking]: Thinking issues to do with the environment through and examining them from all sides; not jumping to conclusions; being able to change one's mind in light of evidence; weighing all evidence fairly.
   - **Love of learning:** Mastering new skills, topics, and bodies of knowledge about the environment, sustainability and the climate emergency, particularly as they relate to the organization.
   - **Perspective [wisdom]:** Valuing wise counsel; having ways of looking at the challenges of caring for the environment and managing the climate emergency in ways that make sense.

2 **Courage** – Emotional strengths that involve the exercise of will to accomplish environmental sustainability goals in the face of opposition, external or internal.

   - **Bravery** [valour]: Not shrinking from threat, challenge, difficulty or pain in the fight to protect the environment; speaking up for what is right even if there is opposition; acting on convictions in relation to sustainability even if they are unpopular in the organization.

- **Perseverance** [persistence, industriousness]: Finishing what the organization starts in relation to sustaining the environment; persisting in a course of action focused on minimizing the organization's negative impact on the environment in spite of obstacles.
- **Honesty** [authenticity, integrity]: Speaking the truth, but more broadly, leaders presenting themselves and the organization in a genuine way and acting in a sincere way in relation to protecting the environment.
- **Zest** [vitality, enthusiasm, vigour, energy]: An organization characterized by excitement and energy in its commitment to protecting the environment; not doing things halfway or half-heartedly; the climate emergency and sustainability work approached as an urgent adventure; an environmentally aware organization that is alive and active in bringing about positive change.

3 **Humanity** – An organizational strength that involves supporting and enabling all.
- **Caring:** Valuing close relations in the pursuit of the goal of protecting the environment, in particular those in which sharing and caring are reciprocated; being close to people in pursuit of the environmental sustainability mission.
- **Kindness** [generosity, nurturance, care, compassion, 'niceness']: Doing favours and good deeds for others; helping them; taking care of them and building a sense of kindness as a core value to others and to the environment.
- **Social intelligence** [emotional intelligence, personal intelligence]: Being aware of the motives and feelings of others as the organization pursues its vision in promoting a more sustainable environment.

4 **Justice** – civic strengths that underlie the commitment to protecting the environment as well as to a healthy community life.
- **Teamwork** [citizenship, social responsibility, loyalty]: Working well as groups and teams; loyalty to the group in pursuit of the common goal of environmental sustainability.
- **Fairness:** Treating all people the same according to notions of fairness and justice, not on whether they are sufficiently committed to the cause of environmental protection, for example; personal feelings about people's commitment to the cause not biasing decisions within the organization; everyone being given a fair chance.
- **Leadership:** Encouraging high performance on environmental issues and at the same time good relations within the organization.

5 **Temperance** – Strengths that protect against excess.
- **Forgiveness and mercy:** Forgiving those who have been judged as doing wrong; accepting the shortcomings of others; giving people a second chance; not being vengeful in the pursuit of the vision of an environmentally friendly organization.
- **Modesty and humility:** Letting accomplishments speak for themselves.
- **Prudence:** Being careful about organizational choices; not taking undue risks; not doing things that might later be regretted despite the passionate vision to protect the environment.
- **Organizational regulation** [control]: Regulating the organization; being disciplined; controlling organizational appetites and emotions in order to achieve the goal of caring for the planet as an organization.

continued

6   **Wonder and gratitude** – strengths that forge connections to the larger universe and provide meaning.

- **Appreciation of beauty and excellence** [awe, wonder, elevation]: Noticing and appreciating beauty, excellence in the environment and/or skilled performance in protecting the planet.

- **Gratitude:** Being aware of and thankful for the good things that happen within the organization in caring for the environment; taking time to express thanks.

- **Hope** [optimism, future-mindedness, future orientation]: Expecting the best in the future for our relationship with the planet and working to achieve it; communicating that a good future for our relationship with the planet is something that can be brought about within the organization.

- **Humour** [playfulness]: Laughter and fun within the organization; bringing smiles to the faces of people within the organization or served by it; the organization seeing the light side; organizational jokes, especially in relation to the organization's environmental activism.

- **Religiousness and spirituality** [faith, purpose]: Having coherent beliefs about the higher purpose and meaning of the universe and the contribution of the organization to this in its commitment to caring for the planet; knowing where the organization fits within the larger scheme of environmental and societal custodianship; having beliefs about the meaning of life and the value of our environment that shape the activities of the organization.

DISCUSS WITH A COLLEAGUE

Work with a group of fellow students (ideally in groups of six). Consider the strategies of six organizations in your home country (you can usually access these from websites or write to the company headquarters). Analyze the strategy statements in terms of the six values described in Box 10.3 and indicate on a scale of 1 to 7 the extent to which each of these values is present in the strategy document, with 7 indicating a dominant value in the document. Where possible, provide examples of how you judge the value to be present. What values are missing entirely? Given that organizations are human communities and these six values represent the most important emphases in human communities across the world, what does it tell us about the nature of work organizations? What values (aside from the six listed) emerge as dominant in the strategy documents? What does this tell us about the nature of work organizations as human communities? Discuss in your groups of six and try to reach some conclusions. As authors, we would be keen to hear your conclusions - please contact us.

PIONEERING WORK PSYCHOLOGISTS

Professor Yorelis Acosta

Yorelis Acosta is a professor at Universidad Central de Venezuela and is pioneering in her reaction to the tragic changes that have affected her country in recent years. Hyperinflation (as of early 2019, over 1 million per cent) and reductions in salary have meant she, like many Venezuelans, has virtually no income. She collects food, money and clothing for colleagues who are struggling to survive with even more difficulty than she is. Her research on the impact of the country's economic crisis on university staff has been harrowing. Many have joined the 1.9 million people leaving the country and those that remain are often experiencing mental health problems because of frustration, stress, fear and despair in response to the economic and political collapse of the country.

Professor Acosta has been mapping the emotional climate in the country, assessing the suffering across 11 different cities, exposing herself to potential harassment by some members of the security forces, because she is identifying widespread despair, fear and anger. To work at the university she must raise income to finance research and attendance at conferences, which is hugely difficult given the difficulties in the wider economy. Her commitment to using her psychological knowledge and research skills to make a positive difference to people's work lives is truly inspirational. Key example papers:

2018. Sufrimiento psicosocial del siglo XXI: Venezuela y la Revolución. *Revista de Psicologia Política, 1.* Bolivia.

2018. Psychosocial suffering of the 21st century: Venezuela and the Revolution. *Journal of Political Psychology*, *1*. Bolivia. www.scielo.org.bo/scielo.php?pid=S2223-30322018000100009&script=sci_arttext.

2017. Percepción del sistema normativo y desconfianza institucional: Sus implicaciones psicosociales. En: *Muchas Instituciones, un jefe. El desmontaje de la democracia venezolana.* Transparencia Venezuela.

2017. Perception of the normative system and institutional distrust: Its psychosocial implications. In: *Many institutions, one boss: The dismantling of Venezuelan democracy. Transparency Venezuela.*

2016. Emocion y politica: La fuerza de la esperanza. *Revista Comunicación, 174.* Caracas: UCAB.

2016. Emotion and politics: The force of hope. *Communication Magazine, 174.* Caracas: UCAB. gumilla.org/biblioteca/bases/biblo/texto/COM2016174_75-89.pdf

2016. *Mapa emocional de Venezuela: Sociológica de la Venezuela actual 2015.* Colección Visión Venezuela. Caracas: UCAB Ediciones, Cap. 3.

2016. *Emotional map of Venezuela: The sociological Reality of Venezuela in crisis.* Visión Venezuela Collection. Caracas: UCAB Ediciones, chap. 3.

A powerful testimony to Yorelis can be found here: factor.prodavinci.com/profesoraenvenezuela/

ORGANIZATIONAL STRUCTURE

Organization structure defined

Organizational structure is the formal system of task design and management reporting relationships that controls, coordinates and motivates staff so that they work together effectively to achieve the organization's goals.

Contingencies such as the environment, technology and strategy of the organization will influence and determine the structure of the organization. The technology might be call centre technology, drug development technology or nuclear power plant technology. The nature of the technology will clearly influence structural design. In a nuclear power plant, control and safety will be vital, so there will be tight control, clear hierarchy, role clarity, teamworking and a high level of recording and reporting. In a call centre, mass production and efficiency will be key so hierarchy, low levels of teamworking and clear job specification are the norm. In a pharmaceutical company, high-tech equipment and highly skilled technicians will be needed, so there is more teamworking, less bureaucracy and a flatter and more cross-functional structure.

The environment includes some of the economic forces we have already discussed (such as the stage in the economic cycle – 2013 was characterized by a prevailing economic slump in Western Europe); competitors' strategies; government actions and decisions; the behaviour of suppliers and distributors; environmental forces (particularly climate change); and international forces (such as a trade war between China and the USA). These environmental forces will influence the design of the organization and this, in turn, will affect the culture of the organization. Structure thus influences employees' experience (an innovative, entrepreneurial culture or a tight, control culture for examples).

A typical way of representing the structure is to depict it as a triangle – see Figure 10.3. The triangle is thin at the top where the CEO is located and broad at the bottom where the vast majority of employees are located in this typical hierarchical structure. In the figure there are seven levels in the organization, including the chief executive and the workers, and, for most small and medium-sized enterprises, this represents a rather hierarchical organization. An organization of less than 1,000 people could potentially manage within only three or four levels (John Lewis, a retail organization with 80,000 employees, has just three levels), thus improving communication and speeding up decision-making (the example of W. L. Gore earlier depicted only two or at most three levels). But to understand structure in a more sophisticated way, it is necessary to revisit the seminal work of Max Weber and then to appreciate the body of research and theorizing spanning three decades that came to be known as the 'Aston Studies' (Pugh, 1998a, 1988b, 1988c).

Max Weber was trained in law in Germany and wrote at the beginning of the 20th century about his theory of bureaucracy and its role in the development of society and of organizations. The key element of organizations, he suggested, was the hierarchy of authority that ensures members carry out the orders that underpin the organization. Organizational structure in his terms referred to the way authority was distributed. The rules of the organization are developed and implemented by a management group who also work to preserve their position of power. Weber viewed bureaucracy as a modern and superior organizational form that involved sets of jurisdictional areas ordered by rules. Duties, authority, qualifications, hierarchy, subordination, training, and knowledge of rules are all fundamental to an effective bureaucracy, according to Weber. He viewed modern organizations with their strong bureaucracies as an ideal form.

The largest body of research on modern organizations in the last half of the 20th century was conducted at Aston University in Birmingham and came to be known as the 'Aston Studies'.

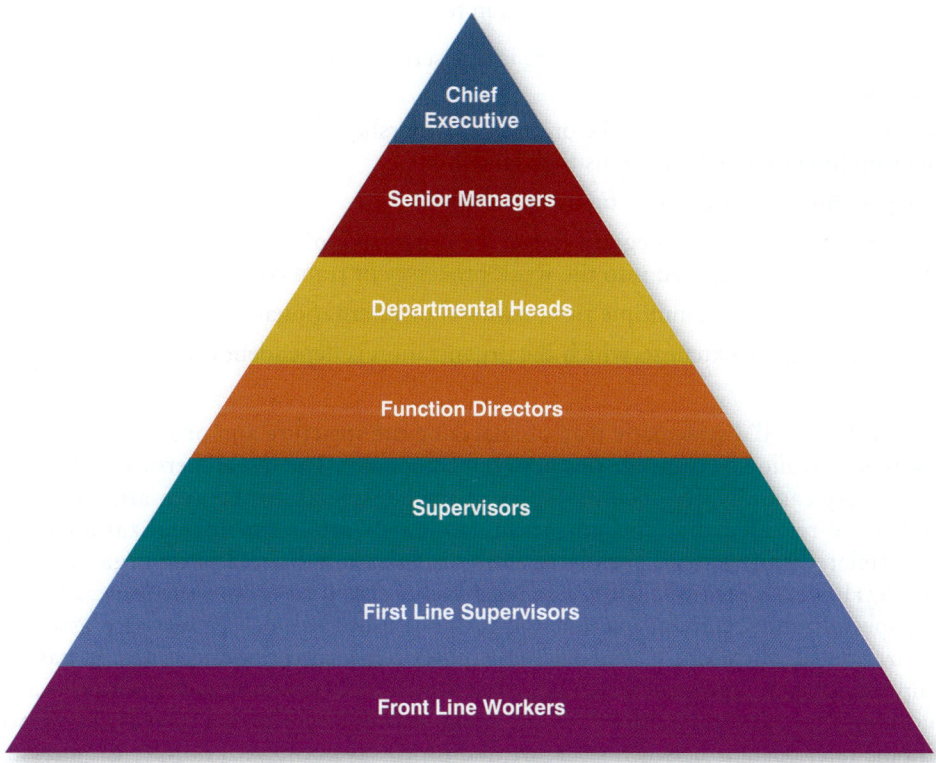

Figure 10.3   One view of organizational structure

The Aston Studies took a systematic approach to understanding organizational structure by developing constructs and standardized measures:

- Specialization – the extent of specialized roles within organizations (as opposed to people being multi-skilled and 'jacks of all trades') and the number of specialized roles (think of roles on the railways to understand what this means – drivers, train dispatchers, revenue protection officers (ticket checkers to you and me!), etc.
- Standardization of workflow activities – the degree to which there are standard rules and procedures in place to control work processes (think of call centres and you get the picture).
- Standardization of employment practices – processes for recruiting, promoting and disciplining employees.
- Formalization – the extent to which instructions and procedures are documented and saved (whether in electronic form or paper form). The civil service has been infamous for documenting everything and, prior to computerization, having everything in triplicate.
- Centralization – the degree to which decisions are made at the top of the hierarchy in the organization.
- Configuration – length of chain of command, span of control of managers and the percentage of specialized or support staff. Unlike the other measures, this has multiple dimensions and is less useful.

The context of the organization was assessed in terms of:

- Origin and history, e.g. when and where it was set up and as what type of business (e.g. family-owned originally).
- Ownership and control, e.g. public or private ownership and the degree of concentration of ownership (one shareholder versus thousands).
- Size, e.g. number of employees, financial turnover.
- Technology, e.g. degree of integration into the organization's work processes (the technology of trains is deeply integrated into the work processes of train companies, for example).
- Location, e.g. single site, multiple sites, national or international.
- Dependence, e.g. the extent to which the organization is dependent on customers, suppliers, banks.

This approach offered a systematic way of analyzing the structure and processes in organizations for the first time and allowed comparisons between companies. The researchers carried out their first studies, using very carefully designed measures of the constructs, in the area around Birmingham in England. They revealed that specialization, standardization and formalization were highly positively correlated and were all correlated with organizational size. Larger organizations meant more of each. However, centralization was negatively related to each – the more centralization, the less the specialization, standardization and formalization. Larger size was also associated with less centralization. Replications of the original studies reinforced these findings, in particular the relationship between size and structure. The Aston Studies provided a practical set of measures that researchers could use, and this influenced the design of research for many years as we sought to understand the relationships between structure and processes in organizations (e.g. Patterson, West, & Wall, 2004). You can use these measures to analyze any organization you encounter in your life to assess its structure and processes.

John Child (1984), one of the Aston Studies team members, offers a simpler way of describing or designing the structure of the organization. He identified five main questions:

1 Specialization. To what extent will jobs be specialized so that individuals complete rather narrow tasks but become very skilled in performing those tasks? The other extreme is to encourage workers to be 'jacks of all trades', able to do many jobs in the organization. The latter is typically necessary in much smaller organizations.

2 Hierarchy. How many levels will be needed to control and direct the organization? Will there be many layers of management to keep tight control? Alternatively, will the organization be 'flat' to encourage decision-making at the front line? If it is flat, the 'span of control' of each manager (the number of people who report to them) will be much greater. Decisions about hierarchy will influence employees' motivation and engagement (greater in flatter organizations), communication effectiveness within the organization, and costs.

3 Grouping. How are workers to be organized? Into functional groupings (production staff, R&D, HR, Sales and Marketing) or into cross-functional groups focused on particular products or services (all involved in commissioning and producing social science books working together and all those involved in commissioning and producing natural science books working together)?

4 Integration. How are the different parts of the organization going to integrate their work together appropriately, both vertically (workers influencing managers' ideas about strategy) and horizontally (HR working effectively with Finance)?

5 Control. What systems will be in place to ensure that quality is high across the organization, that costs are low and that managerial decisions are implemented? Will managers delegate authority to front-line teams or maintain strict control? And should there be extensive formalization with lots of standard operating procedures and written rules and regulations? Who will have responsibility (an obligation to perform a task or function) and accountability (an obligation to report back on the discharge of their responsibilities)?

Answers to these questions then determine the broad structure of the organization.

The structure is usually defined by an organization chart or organogram. Structures can be functional, product based or geography based. Figure 10.4a shows a functional structure (organized around the main functions of the organization). The disadvantages of such a structure are that it gets harder for the different functions to provide support for a wider and wider range of products as the business develops. Moreover, communication between the different functions may suffer, as they may operate like separate entities unless there are good integration mechanisms.

Figure 10.4b shows a product-based structure with its advantage of specialization and disadvantages of replication of resource (for example, HR) across the products and a lack of learning and development across boundaries. Good HR practice in science books in an international publishing company may not be replicated in arts books.

Figure 10.4c shows a geographically based structure. This has the advantage of focusing on the needs of particular segments of the market (e.g. Far East) but the disadvantages of increasing operating costs (duplication across divisions), poor communication and likely competition for resources between divisions.

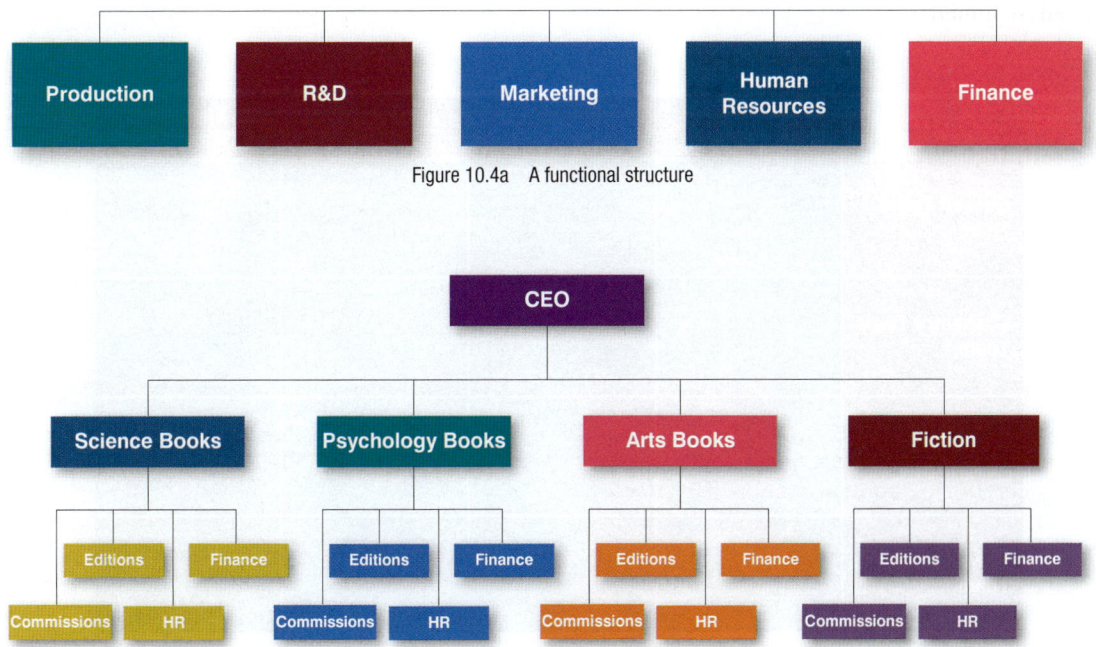

Figure 10.4a A functional structure

Figure 10.4b A product structure

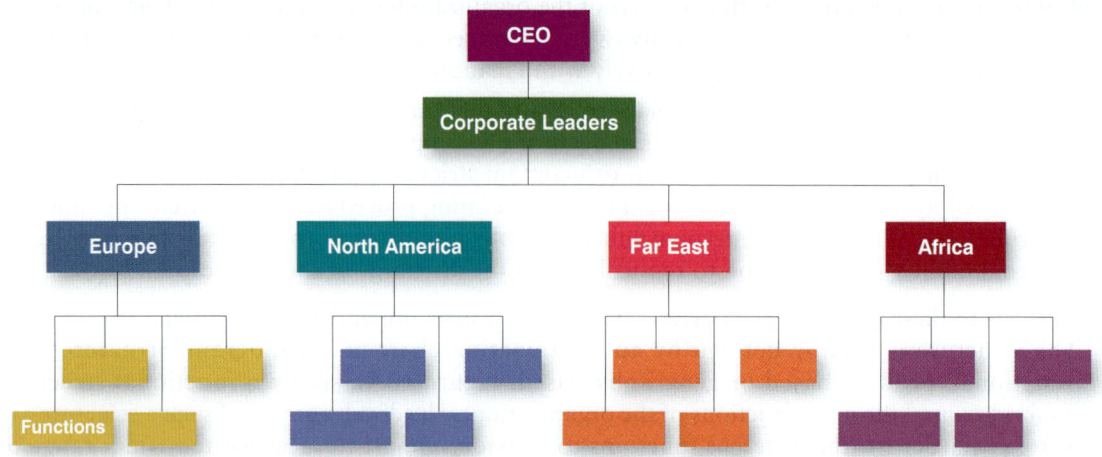

Figure 10.4c   A geographic structure

Figure 10.5 depicts a matrix structure in which the organization is structured around both products and functions. Thus there is a team working on developing, producing and selling garden tools; a team developing, producing and selling metal-working tools; and so on. Each team has members with R&D skills, with HR skills, manufacturing skills and sales and marketing skills, and each team member has two lines of reporting. Thus the R&D person on the garden tools team reports to the garden tools team leader and to the R&D team leader. Such a structure is likely to generate conflict between the competing needs of the different managers (R&D team leader and garden tools team leader). But, well managed and with excellent systems of communication, such structures can lead to high levels of innovation and responsiveness to the environment.

	R&D	HR	Manufacturing	Sales & Marketing
Garden Tools Team				
Carpentry Tools Team				
Metal Working Tools Team				
Car Repair Tools Team				

Figure 10.5   Matrix structure

Of course, there are many more advantages and disadvantages in all these forms of structure and they are presented far more simply than reality allows. There is no perfect structure because organization design is an approximate art, just like strategy development, and it is a constantly evolving process. The organization has to adjust continually to its environment and may do so successfully or unsuccessfully. The tendency to create hierarchical levels as a way of promoting people can be particularly dysfunctional. Organizational restructuring is dangerously attractive to senior managers since they can make such changes quickly and they appear to offer the chance of improving effectiveness. However, all the research evidence and practical experience suggests that it is culture that is the most important and most difficult area to address. Changing culture is much more difficult than changing structure, but is likely to have much more impact on organizational performance.

Another important distinction in thinking about organization structures is between *mechanistic* and *organic* organizations (Burns & Stalker, 1961). A mechanistic structure aims to ensure that the actions, decisions and processes in organizations are regulated, controlled and predictable. You can imagine that this would be necessary in a nuclear power plant, for example. Such organizations are characterized by a tall, centralized hierarchy of authority; top-down decision-making; detailed rules and standard operating procedures; and clearly specified tasks and roles. The major disadvantage of mechanistic organizations is that innovation and adaptability are inhibited. Given an unchanging environment and unchanging methods, such a structure may be appropriate, although employees are increasingly seeking enriched jobs that give them opportunities for growth and development. In a buoyant market they are likely to seek employment in less rigid organizations.

Organic organizations seek to decentralize decision-making to the front line and to encourage high levels of communication, integration and innovation. In this way, the organization is able to respond quickly and effectively in an unpredictable environment or when faced with new tasks. W. L. Gore, the US company that makes waterproofing for outdoor wear, is continually innovating and is a highly organic organization, restricting the growth of any one plant (by creating new plants when they reach a certain size – more than 450) in order to maximize cross-functional communication. Organic structures are characterized by a flat, decentralized hierarchy of authority; lateral communication and decision-making between people in different departments; great use of mutual adjustment in how the different parts of the operation work together; high levels of face-to-face communication in task forces and teams; deliberately ill-defined tasks and roles; and a loose division of labour. They can be experienced as chaotic and uncontrolled, of course, and some find them too unregulated for comfort.

Another way of conceiving of organizational structure is the team-based organization. Figure 10.6 depicts a team-based organization structure in a healthcare organization with the focus on the patient pathway (the various functions and teams the patient encounters on his or her journey through the healthcare system). This structure makes the team the unit of analysis rather than the individual, and focuses on inter-team working rather than on hierarchical control (West & Markiewicz, 2003). It also identifies teams outside the organization (GPs) as included within the team-based organization since the patient experience is much affected by the interaction between the patient's general practitioner and the hospital. Such a structure emphasizes communication and collaboration in teams, focused on the needs of the customer (or in this case, the patient). Moreover, the traditional stem and leaf diagram of the organization chart is not appropriate for depicting team-based organizations. A more appropriate metaphor might be a solar system, with the management team representing the sun and other teams as planets or moons, affected by each other's gravitational pull (interacting and cooperating together) and particularly by the gravitational pull of the management team. Alternative perspectives on structure, such as this, are needed as organizations experiment with new and ever more varied ways of structuring their activities.

Figure 10.6 A team-based health care organization

How does this description of organizational structures help our understanding of organizations? Just as in our consideration of strategy, it is important to recognize the powerful influence that structure has upon climate, culture and the experience of those working in organizations. Choices about structure should not be based on the preferences of senior managers but on the needs of the organization and on the fit between strategy, structure and environment. We turn now to consider the relationship between strategy and structure.

STRATEGY AND STRUCTURE

Thus far we have treated strategy and structure somewhat separately, occasionally pointing out the link between them. The most influential work on this relationship (Miles & Snow; 1986; Snow, Miles, & Coleman, 1992) suggested that organizations could be understood as having one of four strategies in relation to the competitive environment and that their structures should complement that environment.

Prospector The Prospector organization is the first to market with a product; they are innovators who make short-term products, moving on quickly to make new products as their competitors imitate them. Such organizations require a flexible structure with autonomous work groups responsible for local decision-making. At the same time, the organization is specialized and efficient. A good example would be Apple and its organization form – organic, with autonomous work teams.

Defender Defender organizations have a limited but stable product line. They compete on the basis of cost and reduce their costs by constantly increasing efficiency. Such cost competitiveness is a good way of seeing off potential new entrants. They have mechanistic structures with centralized decision-making and a high degree of specialization. Call centres are typically of this type, always seeking to reduce costs, which helps to explain why they often give bad service by keeping you waiting and assuming that tasteless piped music will mollify you!

Analyzer The Analyzer organization usually follows the Prospector, seeking to be second in the market. By copying the Prospector, but reducing costs and increasing quality, they can compete with them. Many Chinese companies have adopted the strategy of the Analyzer (it is a mix of both Prospector and Defender strategies). The Analyzer, according to Miles and Snow, should have a mix of functional and divisional structures to produce a matrix organization. Project and brand managers integrate project units and resource groups (such as Sales and Marketing). Some parts are flexible (such as R&D or parts of production to improve quality) while others are traditional and stable (such as other parts of production, reducing costs and increasing efficiency of production).

Reactor Finally we have the Reactor organization, which has no clear strategy. It simply responds ad hoc to whatever is going on in the environment at the time. The structure is therefore not stable and simply changes to fit the needs of the organization at that time.

This neat(ish) analysis provided by Miles and Snow is helpful in thinking about the relationship between strategy and structure. It should alert you to the fact that structure should follow strategy and reflect the environment within which the organization is operating. A dynamic, fast-changing, complex, unpredictable environment is no place for a hierarchical, tightly controlled organization. The point is to think carefully about the relationship between strategy, structure and environment in the organizations you encounter. Think about the extent to which their strategies and structures fit their environments and their cultures and what needs to change for the organization to be more effective.

DISCUSS WITH A COLLEAGUE

Discuss the organization you work in with a friend or relative, or a colleague. Analyze with them the strategy they adopt in relation to their products or services and try to categorize them in terms of the four types described by Miles and Snow. What are the implications for the structure and processes of the organization of their adoption of this approach? How does it affect the work experience, motivation and work roles of those who work within the organization? Is the organization a pure type or a mix of the different types, or does it not conform to any of the four types described?

Second, given the demands of each type, what structures and methods of organizing work would you recommend for each?

An example will serve to illustrate the point. The authors of this book both work in business and management schools, which compete with many other business schools worldwide, many of which are outstanding and most of which are competing to attract the same students (and professors). Economic recessions, flu pandemics and reputation can all have dramatic effects on the profitability of our schools. Our environment is dynamic, complex and challenging. We therefore need a strategy of innovation, quality and global appeal if we are to prosper, and protecting our reputation is vital. We encourage innovation via organic structures, but also retain control over quality by having standardized procedures for monitoring and controlling teaching and learning, research and administrative processes. Overall, we strive to be organic organizations but we also need some mechanistic elements to be successful.

New forms of organizing

While psychology may discover the enduring qualities of what it is to be human (such as the processes involved in short-term memory storage), organizations are swiftly evolving entities. What was true of organizations in the 1950s is not true today in many cases. Research suggests that new forms of organizing are developing and we need to monitor these new forms, learn from them and be vigilant about what organizational forms will enable people to give of their best, thrive, prosper and grow in organizations. Moreover, we need to recognize what forms of organizations are dehumanizing and do not take account of enduring human needs for connection, growth and development (call centres often sadly fit into this latter category).

Whittington et al. (1999) undertook research which charted the development of new forms of organizing. They studied, over four years, 450 European companies to discover what changes were associated with high performance and with reaping the benefits of organizational innovation. They found that companies had to make whole-system or holistic changes and that the most successful companies over those four years were those that changed structures, processes and boundaries:

- *Structures* Decentralization (but not of strategy development – this was retained within senior management); de-layering (reducing the number of hierarchical levels down from an average of 3.5 to 3.2); use of project teams; improving lateral communication; making better use of resources; and the introduction of sophisticated human resource management practices (including better systems of appraisal, induction, recruitment and selection).

- *Processes* The most successful companies made major investments in their IT and intranet systems to enable and encourage better communication and share knowledge horizontally to encourage high levels of innovation. They spread accountability vertically, making more people responsible for reporting on their fulfilment of responsibilities. Developing clear missions, investing in training and team-building were increasingly emphasized in the best-performing organizations.

- *Boundaries* These companies focused on their core competencies rather than diversifying and spreading their resources too thinly. They outsourced the functions they were not expert in (catering, cleaning) and set up joint ventures and strategic alliances so that they could gain the benefits of access to other companies rather than competing and drawing strict boundaries around their own activities. In effect, they changed their boundaries in strategic ways.

The research suggested that high performance was the consequence when the companies changed all or nearly all of the following nine elements: decentralizing, de-layering, project forms of organizing, 'downscoping' (reducing size), outsourcing, developing strategic alliances, communicating horizontally and vertically, investing in IT, and introducing new HRM practices. Andrew Pettigrew, one of the project team leaders, warns against trying to achieve effective organizational development with simple and single changes (just changing structure) to achieve success. Change efforts need to be wise, integrated, appropriate to the organization and to be introduced on multiple dimensions (compare this recommendation with systems approaches to change described in Chapter 13).

POSITIVE WORK

The UK National Health Service (NHS)

Most of Michael West's work is now conducted in the UK NHS, which has a workforce of 1.4 million people – the largest organizational workforce in Europe. It includes over 300 organizations responsible for providing primary healthcare, acute hospital care, mental healthcare and ambulance services.

However, those charged with running these organizations are constantly in the public eye. With a million patient contacts every 36 hours, some go wrong, and the press and politicians are quick to criticize. It is also not surprising that senior management struggle to articulate strategies and design structures that will succeed when faced with the increasing demands of patients, their relatives, staff, the media, national and local politicians, civil servants and pressure groups (such as Royal Colleges, unions and pharmaceutical companies). Staff are under intolerable pressure, reflected in staff survey data revealing high levels of stress, bullying, harassment, discrimination and highly variable levels of engagement.

The approaches to strategy of the constituent organizations vary enormously. Understandably, some are very cautious while others 'build the bridge as they walk on it' (Quinn, 2004). Some are brave in developing new structures that devolve responsibility to front-line teams delivering healthcare while others are defensively cautious, desperately trying to control procedures and set targets in almost every area of activity.

Our research has revealed the importance of how staff in these settings are managed, and has shown that this is strongly related to patient satisfaction and patient mortality (West et al., 2011). We also helped to run the NHS annual survey of staff experiences over a number of years, achieving a 55 to 60 per cent response rate each year (this is in the region of 250,000 responses a year – see www.nhsstaffsurveys.com).

Our research has led to many conversations with senior staff and government policy makers across the UK (and in other countries) about how to lead healthcare organizations to achieve the best possible patient care. These conversations often come back to strategy, culture and structure. Our ability to have these conversations and, at the same time, share perspectives from WO psychology, has influenced policy in the NHS in directions most WO psychologists would applaud. This has led directly to changes in HR policies and practices. Our ability to work and have influence with those charged with running the NHS at the most senior levels is a consequence of our knowledge of WO psychology and its methods, and our ability to engage intelligently in conversations about strategy and structure. Being able to use an evidence base is critical. It is a privilege and gratifying as a practitioner and as a researcher to feel that you have made a positive

continued

difference. That is also why these topics are so important in the training of WO psychologists. For an overview of our recent work on strategy and culture in the NHS, see Dixon-Woods et al. (2014) and these websites:

improvement.nhs.uk/resources/culture-and-leadership/

improvement.nhs.uk/resources/culture-and-leadership-programme-phase-2-design/

improvement.nhs.uk/resources/developing-people-improving-care/

Understanding organizational strategy, structure, culture and environment enables WO psychologists to understand other theoretical contexts for their work and to be able to influence senior managers more effectively in creating organizational environments that enable people to develop and thrive.

SUMMARY

In this chapter, we have proposed that strategy and structure are important topics since they are of fundamental concern to those charged with leading organizations. We have explained what we mean by organizational strategy. Strategy is defined as a metaphorical road map to guide the organization towards a desired destination and as a means of achieving goals through the use of its resources.

The chapter reviewed the major perspectives on strategy, thereby giving the reader a comprehensive and sophisticated understanding. These sought to achieve a fit between the organization and its environment. Market penetration, market development, product development and diversification are four approaches to strategy that have come to be known as the Product Market Matrix. Other major perspectives on strategy have included management by objectives (MBO) (Drucker); bounded rationality perspectives (Simon); and garbage can models (Cohen et al.). Economic perspectives on strategy have been dominated by the work of Michael Porter, which includes choices between market segmentation, product differentiation and price/cost leadership as strategies; industry perspectives such as the five forces model of industry competition and strategy, including the concept of the value chain; and national strategies for competitive advantage summarized in his diamond model.

The chapter also reviewed resource-based views of strategy, which argues that the unique resources of the firm should drive its strategy. Another perspective sees strategy as an emergent process of making sense of complexity and ambiguity, and this sense-making is an unfolding process. The strategy as revolution approach proposes that strategy development should dramatically shake up the organization in order that its tendencies to inertia and unresponsiveness to a rapidly changing environment are counteracted. Finally, the chapter described strategy as practice. Researchers in this tradition are concerned to know where and how the work of strategizing and organizing is actually done. The chapter particularly emphasized the importance of integrating values into the strategy development process and used a list of values recently developed by psychologists to show how values should be integrated into strategy development.

We have explored how and why organizations are structured the way they are. This reveals that structure plays an important part in influencing culture, behaviour and work attitudes. Organization structure is the formal system of task design and management reporting relationships. Contingencies such as the environment, technology and strategy of the organization will influence and determine the structure of the organization. The Aston Studies took a systematic approach to understanding organizational structure by developing constructs and standardized measures, including specialization, standardization, formalization and centralization. Functional, product, divisional and matrix structures are described, and mechanistic structures are contrasted with organic structures. We also described the emerging form of team-based organizations. The chapter described the relationship between strategy and structure and described a typology of Prospector, Defender, Analyzer and Reactor strategies in fitting structure to strategy and environment.

Finally, we described new forms of organizing in recognition that the organizational landscape is constantly changing and forms that worked well 30 years ago are giving way to new forms dictated by dramatically different environments.

This chapter illustrates why simplistic recommendations for managing strategy, changing structures and managing the environments of companies are not helpful. If we wish to ensure the development of organizations that are effective and to ensure that those who work within them flourish, we must understand and shape the strategy and structure of organizations.

DISCUSSION QUESTIONS

1. Why are both strategy and structure important topics for you to study?
2. What is organization strategy and how would you advise a management team about how to develop a coherent and powerful strategy?
3. Compare three different perspectives on strategy adopted by theorists over the past 50 years, identifying the strengths and weaknesses of each.
4. Why should we adopt a value-based perspective on strategy and how do we decide within each organization what those values should be?
5. How do strategy and culture relate to each other?
6. How should we go about analyzing the structure of organizations?
7. To what extent is structure likely to influence culture, behaviour and work attitudes in organizations?

FURTHER READING

Carter, C., Clegg, S. R., & Komberger, M. (2008). *A very short, fairly interesting and reasonably cheap book about strategy.* London, England: SAGE.

Edersheim, E. (2007). *The definitive Drucker: Challenges for tomorrow's executives – final advice from the father of modern management.* New York, NY: McGraw-Hill.

Houlder, D. (2004). *Strategy: How to shape the future of business.* Norwich, England: Format Publishing.

Hülsheger, U. R. (2016). From dawn till dusk: Shedding light on the recovery process by investigating daily change patterns in fatigue. *Journal of Applied Psychology, 101*(6), 905–14. doi:10.1037/apl0000104

Hülsheger, U. R., Alberts, H. J. E. M., Feinholdt, A., & Lang, J. W. B. (2013). Benefits of mindfulness at work: On the role of mindfulness in emotion regulation, emotional exhaustion, and job satisfaction. *Journal of Applied Psychology, 98*, 310–325.

Hülsheger, U. R., Lang, J. W. B., Depenbrock, F., Fehrmann, C., Zijlstra, F. & Alberts, H. J. E. M. (2014). The power of presence: The role of mindfulness at work for daily levels and change trajectories of psychological detachment and sleep quality. *Journal of Applied Psychology, 99*, 1113–1128.

Hülsheger, U. R., Lang, J. W. B., Schewe, A. F., & Zijlstra, F. (2015). When regulating emotions at work pays off: A diary and an intervention study on emotion regulation and customer tips in service jobs. *Journal of Applied Psychology, 100*, 263–277.

Weick, K. (1995). *Sensemaking in organizations.* Thousand Oaks, CA: SAGE.

Whittington, R., Pettigrew, A., Peck, S., Fenton, E., & Conyon, M. (1999). Change and complementarities in the new competitive landscape: A European panel study, 1992, 1996. *Organizational Science, 10*(5), 583–600.

REFERENCES

Ansoff, I. H. (1965). *Corporate strategy: An analytic approach to business policy for growth and expansion.* New York, NY: McGraw-Hill.

Burns, T., & Stalker, G. M. (1961). *The management of innovation.* London, England: Tavistock Press.

Carter, C., Clegg, S. R., & Kornberger, M. (2008). *A very short, fairly interesting and reasonably cheap book about strategy.* London, England: SAGE.

Child, J. (1984). *Organization: A guide to problems and practice* (2nd ed.). London, England: Harper & Row.

Cohen, M. D., March, J. G., & Olsen, J. P. (1972). The garbage can model of organizational choice. *Administrative Science Quarterly, 17*(1), 1–25.

Collier, P. (2007). *The bottom billion: Why the poorest countries are failing and what can be done about it.* Oxford, England: Oxford University Press.

Dixon-Woods, M., Baker, R., Charles, K., Dawson, J., Jerzembek, G., Martin, G., McCarthy, I., ... West, M. (2014). Culture and behaviour in the English National Health Service: Overview of lessons from a large multi-method study. *British Medical Journal: Quality and Safety, 23*(2), 106–115. doi:10.1136/bmjqs-2013-001947

Edersheim, E. (2007). *The definitive Drucker: Challenges for tomorrow's executives – final advice from the father of modern management*. New York, NY: McGraw-Hill.

Hamel, G. (1996) Strategy as revolution. *Harvard Business Review*, July–August, 69–82.

Hamel, G., & Prahalad, C. K. (1996). Competing in the new economy: Managing out of bounds. *Strategic Management Journal, 17*(3), 237–242.

Hodgkinson, G. P., & Sparrow, P. R. (2002). *The competent organization: A psychological analysis of the strategic management process*. Buckingham, England: Open University Press.

Hodgkinson, G. P., & Starbuck, W. H. (Eds.). (2012). *The Oxford handbook of organizational decision making*. Oxford, England: Oxford University Press.

Huczynski, A., & Buchanan, D. A. (2007). *Organizational behaviour: An introductory text*. London, England: Financial Times/Prentice Hall.

Jarzabkowski, P. (2005). *Strategy as practice: An activity-based approach*. London, England: SAGE.

Jarzabkowski, P., & Spee, A. P. (2009). Strategy as practice: A review and future directions for the field. *International Journal of Management Reviews, 11*(1), 69–95.

Lechner, R. (2009). The seven pillars of a 'green' corporate strategy. *Environmental Leader*, 10 March.

Lindblom, C. (1959). The science of muddling through. *Public Administration Review, 19*(2), 79–88.

Miles, R. E., & Snow, C. C. (1986). Organizations: New concepts for new forms. *California Management Review, 28*(3), 62–73.

Mintzberg, H. (1990). The design school: Reconsidering the basic premises of strategic management, *Strategic Management Journal, 11*(3), 171–195.

Patterson, M., West, M. A., & Wall, T. D. (2004). Integrated manufacturing, empowerment and company performance. *Journal of Organizational Behavior, 25*, 641–665.

Penrose, E. (1959). *The Theory of the growth of the firm*. Oxford, England: Blackwell.

Peters, T. (2003). *Re-imagine: Business experience in a disruptive age*. London, England: Dorling Kindersley.

Peterson, C., & Seligman, M. E. P. (2004). *Character strengths and virtues: A handbook and classification*. Oxford, England: Oxford University Press.

Pettigrew, A. M. (1985). *The awakening giant: Continuity and change in ICI*. Oxford, England: Blackwell.

Porac, J. F., Thomas, H., & Bade-Fuller, C. (1989). Competitive groups as cognitive communities: The case of Scottish knitwear manufacturers. *Journal of Management Studies, 26*, 397–416.

Porter, M. (1980). *Competitive strategy: Techniques for analyzing industries and competitors*. New York, NY: Free Press.

Porter, M. (1985). *Competitive advantage: Creating and sustaining superior performance*. New York, NY: Free Press.

Pugh, D. S. (1998a). *The Aston Studies* (Vol. 1). Aldershot, England: Ashgate.

Pugh, D. S. (1998b). *The Aston Studies* (Vol. 2). Aldershot, England: Ashgate.

Pugh, D. S. (1998c). *The Aston Studies* (Vol. 3). Aldershot, England: Ashgate.

Quinn, R. E. (2004). *Building the bridge as you walk on it: A guide for leading change*. San Francisco, CA: John Wiley & Sons.

Schwenk, C. R. (1984). Cognitive simplification processes in strategic decision making. *Strategic Management Journal, 5*, 111–128.

Selznick, P. (1957). *Leadership in administration*. New York, NY: Harper & Row.

Simon, H. A. (1945). *Administrative Behaviour* (2nd ed.). New York, NY: Free Press.

Skinner, Q., & Price, R. (1988). *Machiavelli: The prince*. Cambridge, England: Cambridge University Press.

Snow, C. C., Miles, R. E., & Coleman, H. J. (1992). Managing 21st century network organizations. *Organizational Dynamic, 20*(3), 5–21.

Uchitelle, L. (2006). *The disposable American: Layoffs and their consequences*. New York, NY: Knopf.

Weick, K (1995). *Sensemaking in organizations*. Thousand Oaks, CA: SAGE.

Wernefelt, B. (1984). A resource-based view of the firm. *Strategic Management Journal, 5*(2), 171–180.

West, M. A., Dawson, J. F., Admasachew, L., & Topakas, A. (2011). *NHS staff management and health service quality: Results from the NHS Staff Survey and related data* (Report to the Department of Health). Retrieved from www.gov.uk/government/publications/nhs-staff-management-and-health-service-quality

West, M. A., & Markiewicz, L. (2003). *Effective teamwork: Practical lessons from organizational research*. Oxford, England: Blackwell.

Whittington, R., Pettigrew, A., Peck, S., Fenton, E., & Conyon, M. (1999). Change and complementarities in the new competitive landscape: A European panel study, 1992, 1996. *Organizational Science, 10*(5), 583–600.

CHAPTER 11

LEADERSHIP IN ORGANIZATIONS

LEARNING OBJECTIVES

- Understand the concepts of leadership and leadership effectiveness.
- Know the key traits, motivations and competencies that predict leadership effectiveness.
- Describe the key elements, strengths and weaknesses of the trait, behavioural, contingency, leader–member exchange and transformational/transactional theories of leadership.
- Appreciate what is known about effective leadership behaviours in organizations.
- Know the main forms of leadership development and the extent to which research evidence supports their effectiveness.

INTRODUCTION

Leadership is the most researched area of work and organizational psychology; there are more research papers published in this area than any other. This is because leadership has an enormously important place in human society and in our thinking about our world. Whenever a group of people come together to perform a task or make a decision, implicit and explicit leadership processes occur.

We rely on leaders to help shape direction in teams and organizations, to encourage the alignment of efforts towards goals, and to encourage or nurture the commitment of those they lead (Drath et al., 2008). Tales of leadership populate our literatures, TV programmes, newspapers, mythologies and films. We constantly focus on those who lead us politically, examining every nuance of their behaviour and speech, in order to gauge their trustworthiness, their intentions and their fitness to lead us. In work, we pay far more attention to the content of what our leaders and managers say than we do to the speech of others. Leadership is fundamental in human society.

> **DISCUSS WITH A COLLEAGUE**
>
> Think of three leaders that you admire (past or present). They could be people you worked with or people whom you read about in the newspapers or see on television or they may be historical figures like Gandhi, Nelson Mandela or Martin Luther King. Think about these three leaders and what it is about them as individuals or their behaviour as leaders that makes you admire their leadership. Try to come up with four or five examples of their behaviours and their traits that exemplify what you admire about their leadership. You are then in a position to attempt a definition of leadership. Try to write this out before you read on.

What is leadership?

Offering a definition of leadership that would be accepted by most researchers and managers is a challenge, since approaches to understanding this complex subject vary so greatly. A simple definition might be that leadership is directing the activities of a group towards a shared goal. However, such a definition ignores the many nuances of leadership that the following definitions illustrate:

- Leadership is ... the influential increment over and above the mechanical compliance with the routine directives of the organization (Katz & Kahn, 1978, p. 528).
- Leadership is ... the process of influencing the activities of the group toward goal achievement (Rauch & Behling, 1984, p. 46).
- Leadership is ... the ability to step outside the culture. To start evolutionary change activities that are more adaptive (Schein, 1992, p. 2).
- Leadership is ... about articulating visions, embodying values and creating an environment within which things can be accomplished (Richards & Engle, 1986, p. 206).
- Leadership is ... to make decisions or take responsibility for the coordination or direction of other people (Nicholson, 2013, p. 12).

Leadership can be defined in terms of the traits or behaviours of the leader, as a set of influence processes, interaction patterns or role relationships. It may simply be defined also as the occupation of administrative positions (being the chief executive officer) regardless of traits, behaviours or processes. Yukl (2013a) says that most definitions of leadership see it as '... a process whereby intentional influence is exerted over other people to guide, structure and facilitate activities and relationships in a group or organization' (p. 21). Leadership can therefore be seen both as a specialized role that an individual occupies and as a process of influence. We can distinguish between leaders and leadership. When we adopt a perspective of understanding leaders, we are inevitably directed towards understanding who leaders and who followers are and why they occupy these roles. When we adopt the influence process perspective, we assume that anyone in a group or organization may exercise leadership at any point and that the complex interactions between people and situations will affect the emergence of leadership processes. Moreover, it is not either/or – leadership is both a specialized role and an influence process. Yukl (2010) concludes therefore that:

> *Leadership is the process of influencing others to understand and agree about what needs to be done and how to do it, and the process of facilitating individual and collective efforts to accomplish shared objectives.* (p. 26.)

Leadership effectiveness

Much writing about leadership over the years focuses on the factors that are associated with effective leadership – understandably given the importance of leadership in human affairs (for an excellent review of the history of leadership research in psychology, see Lord, Day, Zaccaro, Avolio, & Eagly, 2017). Implicitly, the question we want to answer is 'how can we identify those likely to be the most effective leaders?' This begs the question of 'what is effective leadership?' Is it the enthusiastic commitment of followers or their indifferent compliance or reluctant obedience? The answer seems obvious. But consider this example.

When Nelson Mandela was released from prison after more than a quarter of a century, the African National Congress could finally unite behind their leader and overthrow the apartheid regime. The world waited with horrified foreboding, anticipating a terrible civil war. Nelson Mandela went against the prevailing view of his followers and instead strained towards dialogue, reconciliation and negotiated transition rather than confrontation and violence. He achieved a reluctant obedience among his followers, which allowed a negotiated transfer of power without the bloodshed the world expected. So, at times, reluctant obedience of followers may indicate highly effective leadership. Early resistance to a leader's behests might lead to later commitment when the wisdom of the approach is revealed.

Effectiveness may also depend on who is defining the term. Followers might focus on the achievement of task objectives whereas the leader might focus on the personal benefits he or she gains, such as promotion to a more senior position. This may seem a surprising way of thinking about leadership, but many leaders are in it to a greater or lesser extent for what they can get – more power, more influence or more money. From 2008 to 2009 the world's economy teetered on the edge of collapse as a result of the actions of some of the most powerful leaders in the financial world, working for their personal benefits. Many leaders are successful for their organizations and for themselves at the same time, achieving great things for their organizations and very large salaries and bonuses for themselves. Leadership therefore has multiple motives, and it is hard to disentangle selfish from altruistic motives, comfortable though it might be to see leadership effectiveness simply as selfless.

Another approach to leadership effectiveness is to see it as the product of intelligent, rational minds applied to complex problem-solving. The effective leader analyzes the situation, develops effective strategies, allocates tasks, monitors performance and achieves goal outcomes. This was certainly a dominant perspective until the 1980s. In the past 25 years, we have seen much more emphasis on emotions and values, inspiration and motivation as hallmarks of effective leadership. Leaders are those who can inspire and motivate followers, and who can create positive, confident, optimistic work environments within which loyalty, commitment and engagement are dominant orientations.

Measures of effectiveness may therefore include the achievement of the group's or organization's goals via improved performance, including measures such as productivity, share prices, return on investment, etc.; follower attitudes to and perceptions of the leader; the leader's contribution to enhancing group and organizational processes, including cohesion, culture, climate, cooperation and readiness for change and crisis; and the career of the leader – has she or he had a rapid advance up the hierarchy within or across organizations? It is difficult, therefore, to find a single measure of effectiveness since there are so many potential trade-offs. Increases in productivity might be associated with decreases in quality and decreases in staff commitment, for example. A bigger share dividend might be achieved at the expense of caring for the environment. Moreover, when should we judge the leader's effectiveness? Is it fair to judge the new CEO of a manufacturing company on the basis of productivity targets achieved after only four months?

RESEARCH INTO LEADERSHIP

Below we consider five major streams of research into leadership: the trait, behaviour, contingency, dyadic and charismatic/transformational theories. The trait approach suggests that some people are natural leaders and many studies between 1930 and 1950 tried to identify what the traits of such people were. These were largely inconclusive, but improved research designs over the past 50 years have yielded more convincing results and we will review these.

In the 1950s and 1960s, the behavioural approach compared the behaviour of effective and ineffective leaders using survey research and examined correlations of questionnaire measures with measures of effectiveness. The approach has also been used to study how leaders and managers spend their time in order to probe the nature of managerial or leadership work, using direct observation, diary studies and job description questionnaires. The contingency approach examines leadership in the context of the characteristics of followers and of the task, context or organization. Dyadic approaches examine the varying nature of the relationships between the leader and his or her different followers and how favouritism can damage cohesion and leader effectiveness. Finally, charismatic/transformational leadership theories place particular emphasis on the leader's ability to inspire and motivate followers by articulating an attractive vision, by intellectually stimulating followers, by encouraging them and by giving time and energy to their skill and career development.

Research approaches vary also in relation to the level of analysis of leadership and leadership processes. At the *intra-individual* level, researchers might use psychological theories of decision-making, cognition and motivation; they may focus on self-management theory; or they may identify personal objectives and how leaders prioritize, manage time and monitor their own behaviour. The intra-individual approach has limited value because it neglects the social processes, which are at the core of leadership. The next level is *dyadic*, where the focus is on the relationship between two people. Leadership is a reciprocal influence process, usually with a focus on developing cooperative, trusting relationships in order to increase motivation and commitment. This approach too is limited, in this case by its failure to take account of the context within which dyadic relationships occur (for example in a team). Leadership can also be considered as a *group process*, where the team is taken into account, and research at this level would question how a leader contributes to group effectiveness and the role the leader plays in influencing the affective tone of the team. At the *organizational level*, leadership is conceived of as occurring in a larger open system in which groups or departments are subsystems characterized by intergroup relations and group-organizational relationships that the leader must manage. At this level, leadership research proposals might examine how effective leaders are at ensuring the organization adapts to its environment and acquires the resources needed to survive (see Chapter 13). And there is much interest also in system leadership in the public sector, which involves leaders working cooperatively to integrate the services for citizens, ensuring alignment between health and social care organizations, voluntary services and local governments (Hulks, Walsh, Powell, Ham, & Alderwick, 2017).

> **DISCUSS WITH A COLLEAGUE**
>
> If you now review your definition of leaders/leadership you developed earlier, what assumptions did you make about the concepts of leader, effectiveness, approach and level of analysis? And how would you change your definition having explored the concept of leadership a little further?

Our initial introduction to the concept of leadership makes clear some of the complexities of the subject. The concept of leader is itself problematic, as is the definition of effectiveness. We must also grapple with the decision about what approach we wish to take to understanding leadership and at what level of analysis. It should already be clear that this area of research yields few easy answers.

TRAIT APPROACHES TO LEADERSHIP

We now go on to consider each of the major approaches to leadership and leadership effectiveness. See Figure 11.1.

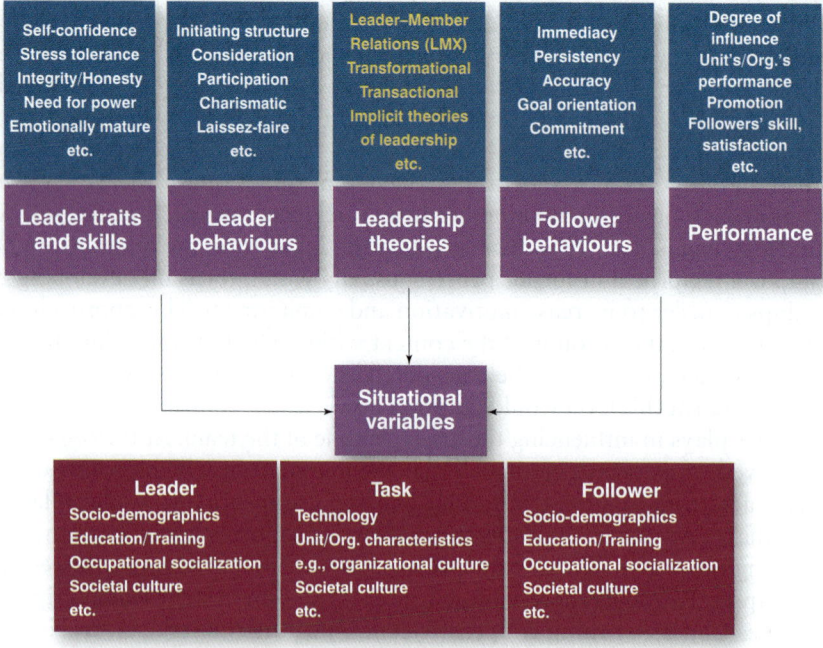

Figure 11.1   Approaches to understanding and effective leadership

First, we consider theories that focus on the extent to which leadership emergence and effectiveness can be predicted from the personality traits (e.g. Extraversion), motivations (e.g. need to achieve) and skills (e.g. specialist technical knowledge) of individuals (see Figure 11.2). This is the longest tradition in leadership research and represents a body of knowledge developed over the past 60 years. Those studies that use emergence as the outcome focus on who in a group becomes the eventual leader, whereas those that use effectiveness as the outcome are concerned with the extent to which leadership characteristics predict outcome measures as diverse as productivity, innovation, group member satisfaction, group cohesion and peer evaluations.

Figure 11.2 Leadership traits, skills and motivations

Traits are relatively enduring patterns of behaviour, and skills are abilities to perform a task effectively. Research has established that not only traits but also skills have a strong hereditary component (Arvey, Zhang, Avolio, & Krueger, 2007), so if research establishes a strong relationship between traits, skills and leadership effectiveness, it suggests that the notion of a born leader has some validity. Skills are usually divided into technical skills (knowledge about methods, processes and procedures), interpersonal skills and conceptual skills (knowledge of ideas and concepts), and we consider these later. For now, we will focus on personality traits and their relationship with leadership effectiveness.

One of the largest research initiatives combined the data from 124 studies conducted between 1904 and 1948 (Stogdill, 1948), and a follow-up of studies from 1949 to 1970 (Stogdill, 1974) confirmed and extended the original findings. Together they revealed that effective leaders were: adaptable to situations, alert to the social environment, ambitious, achievement oriented, creative, assertive, cooperative, decisive, dependable, dominant, energetic, persistent, self-confident, tolerant of stress and willing to assume responsibility. Key skills included cleverness, conceptual skills, diplomacy and tact, fluency, knowledge about the work, administrative ability, persuasiveness and social skills. However, such a list of necessary leadership requirements would rule virtually all humanity out of contention for leadership. Moreover, Stogdill pointed out that this was not a definitive list and none of the traits emerged as an absolute must for leadership. He also concluded that the situation that leaders operate in exerts a big influence on what is effective at any moment in time.

Considerable research effort has gone into identifying which of the Big Five dimensions of personality are associated with leadership effectiveness. Notwithstanding the fact that effectiveness has continued to be operationalized in research in different ways, three of the five dimensions appear to be associated with leadership effectiveness. Openness to Experience and Extraversion are positively correlated and Neuroticism is negatively correlated (e.g. Judge, Bono, Ilies, & Gerhardt, 2002). The desire to learn and explore new opportunities is clearly important for leaders in modern organizations, as is the commitment to seeing things through effectively, being dependable and having integrity. Moreover, being warm, positive, energetic and confident, as we have already seen, is important for effective leadership. However, being anxious, relatively pessimistic and emotionally unpredictable is problematic, not least because of the impact on followers. Agreeableness does not correlate with leadership effectiveness, consistent with the suggestion that need for affiliation is not a high priority for a leader. However, there are correlations between four of the five dimensions and leadership emergence (who emerges as a leader in a group situation). Again Extraversion, Emotional Stability (the opposite of Neuroticism) and Openness are positively correlated, but with Conscientiousness also proving to be quite strongly related (see Figure 11.3).

Leadership	Emergence	Effectiveness
	β / R	β / R
Neuroticism	−.09	−.10*
Extraversion	.30*	.18*
Openness	.21*	.19*
Agreeableness	−.14*	.10*
Conscientiousness	.36*	.12*
Multiple R	.53*	.39*

Based on 222 correlations from 73 samples with total N ~ 43.000 (Judge, et al., 2002)

Figure 11.3 Big Five and leadership emergence and effectiveness

Managerial motivation

McClelland and colleagues undertook a major programme of research to understand how achievement motivation of leaders was related to performance (McClelland, 1985). The research was conducted using the Thematic Apperception Test, which involves research participants telling a story based on ambiguous pictures of people. McClelland and colleagues discerned three motivational themes underlying the stories their leaders told: need for achievement; need for affiliation; and need for power. Need for power had two sub-dimensions: socialized power orientation and personalized power orientation. The latter refers to a motivation orientation to acquire power in order to advance the organization's aims, make a contribution or enable followers to develop their skills and careers. Nelson Mandela is a good example. Such leaders tended to have strong self-control. Another type of power orientation was 'personalized power orientation', characterized by a desire for power to advance the leader's own interests by dominating others in order to fulfil their own desires. Donald Trump is a good example. The research suggested that effective leaders or managers in large organizations have a moderately high need for achievement, a relatively low need for affiliation and a highly socialized rather than personalized power orientation (McClelland & Boyatzis, 1982).

Another approach to understanding the motivations of effective leaders (Berman & Miner, 1985; Miner, 1977) used a qualitative measure called the Sentence Completion Test. Again, content was investigated qualitatively to identify motivational themes in leaders'/managers' responses to the incomplete sentences. Miner used this approach to examine the motivations associated with advancement in large organizations. He identified six motivation themes and found that three were related to managers' advancement in their organizations' hierarchies. Those that correlated most consistently were: desire to exercise power; desire to compete with peers; and a positive attitude towards authority figures. Those that did not correlate consistently with advancement were: desire to stand out from the group; desire to perform routine administrative functions; and desire to be actively assertive. The results were not so clear for leaders in smaller organizations, indicating the importance of context in research into managerial and leader effectiveness; what may lead to career advancement in a large organization of 1,000 people may be irrelevant in small enterprises of, say, 10–15 employees.

Competencies

A body of research that has influenced both practitioners and researchers (Boyatzis, 1982) focused on the competencies related to managerial effectiveness. The competencies explored by Boyatzis include personality traits, motives, skills, knowledge, self-image and some specific behaviours. The main research method employed was the 'behavioural event interview'. This asked managers to identify critical incidents in their work and the ways in which they dealt with them. These were analyzed in depth to reveal underlying competencies. The sample included 253 managers who were rated as low or high in effectiveness.

Effective managers proved to have a strong efficiency orientation; high achievement motivation; high work standards; and a focus on task objectives. Confirming McClelland's earlier work, they had a strong socialized power orientation; a high desire for power; liked having power symbols such as grand titles and large offices; were assertive in their behaviour; had a strong tendency to attempt to influence others; were concerned about the reputation of the organization; had high self-confidence and were decisive rather than hesitant; made proposals in a firm manner, with appropriate poise, bearing and gestures; had high self-efficacy and a high internal locus of control; initiated action rather than waited for things to happen; took steps to circumvent obstacles; sought information from a variety of sources; and accepted responsibility for success or failure. The research also suggested that effective managers (unsurprisingly) had good interpersonal skills and good oral presentation skills, including the ability to use symbolic, verbal and non-verbal communication devices to make clear and convincing presentations. They were good at building team spirit and encouraging a sense of group identity and loyalty. Finally, effective managers had strong conceptual skills, including the ability to identify patterns or relationships in information and events (what the researchers called 'inductive reasoning') and the ability to communicate this effectively to the people they led.

This influential research has been taken up by many organizations, which have sought to build their leadership capacity by testing for, and developing, these competencies in managers. The major problem with this approach is the lack of parsimony. The list of competencies is so long that it suggests few people would have or could develop all these competencies effectively. What works for whom in what context is unclear.

Assessment centres

The advent of assessment centres in the past 40 years offered another means for determining which traits predicted advancement in an organization. The most outstanding research using this approach was conducted in the US AT&T company (a major telecommunications organization). The research focused on data gathered in assessment centres (Howard & Bray, 1990) and monitored each candidate's progress into middle management. Assessment centre scores were related to advancement 8 years and 20 years later. Such a long-term research study is unusual and the design offers fascinating insights into the personal attributes that predicted advancement. The traits that best predicted advancement were (not surprisingly) desire for advancement, along with dominance, interpersonal skills, cognitive skills (creativity and critical thinking) and administrative skills. Other important predictors included need for achievement, self-confidence, high energy levels and low need for security. Particularly interesting is that the individual's first job was an important moderator of the relationship between traits and ultimate advancement. The more opportunities for learning and development in the first role, the greater the job challenge (within limits) and the better the person's boss as a role model of success and achievement orientation, the quicker the individual advanced in their career from there on.

Derailing

Another way of gleaning understanding about what predicts effective leadership is to focus on what predicts failure. The Center for Creative Leadership (CCL) has studied what predicts the success and, unusually, the failure of top executives (Lombardo & McCauley, 1988). Failure is termed 'derailing'. Derailed managers are those who are dismissed, transfer, retire early or just fail to continue to advance. In the CCL study, there are many similarities between both those who succeeded and those who failed but certain traits seemed to be particularly important for predicting failure.

Emotional stability and composure Managers who derailed were less able to handle pressure. They were moody, had angry outbursts and displayed inconsistent behaviour.

Defensiveness Managers who derailed were more likely to be defensive about failure. They attempted to cover mistakes and blame other people.

Integrity Successful managers were more open, honest and focused on the immediate task and on the needs of their staff than on competing with rivals or impressing superiors.

Interpersonal skills Managers who derailed were likely to have less developed interpersonal skills and were often abrasive or intimidating towards others.

Technical and cognitive skills Those who derailed were often outstanding in terms of technical knowledge when they were at lower levels in the organization. As they moved up, this technical competence led to arrogance and over-confidence about their opinions and decisions. So the strength became a weakness.

Summary

Over the past 70 to 80 years a considerable amount of research has sought to determine the traits predicting leadership effectiveness and, though some commentators argue that this has been a blind alley, it is possible to identify some core personality traits associated with leadership effectiveness. Yukl (2010) identifies the following:

1. *High energy level and stress tolerance* Effective leaders are people who have high levels of stamina and can work effectively over long periods. They maintain relatively high levels of energy throughout the day. They are also less likely to be affected adversely by conflicts, crises and pressure, and being unable to maintain an equilibrium. In particular, they are able to think calmly in crisis situations and to communicate calmness and confidence to others.

2. *Self-confidence* They are self-confident, believing that they can be effective in difficult situations and giving those they lead a sense of confidence and efficacy. They tend to be optimistic in the face of difficulties, and this optimism is often a self-fulfilling prophecy. As a consequence they are more likely to deal with difficult situations rather than deny or avoid them. However, excessive self-confidence or self-esteem can make leaders prone to making highly risky or downright wrong decisions.

3. *Internal locus of control* Effective leaders believe that what happens around them is more under their control than the control of external forces and so are motivated to take action to influence and control events. This is associated with a tendency to be proactive rather than passive. They also believe that they can influence, persuade and motivate others as well as win their allegiance to courses of action.

4. *Emotional maturity* They have higher levels of emotional maturity, which includes emotional intelligence. They are less prone to moodiness, irritability and angry outbursts. Indeed, they are more likely to be positive and optimistic, communicating their positivity to others. Emotionally mature people have awareness of their own strengths, weaknesses and typical reactions to situations. They have a high level of moral integrity. Emotional maturity is associated with a socialized rather than a personalized power orientation.

5. *Personal integrity* Consistency between espoused values and behaviour is characteristic of those with high levels of personal integrity, along with honesty, transparency and trustworthiness. Such leaders also keep promises to staff and other stakeholder groups.

6. *Socialized power motivation* Effective leaders seek power, but primarily in order to achieve organizational objectives and to support the growth, development and advancement of those they lead.

7. *Moderately high achievement orientation* Not surprisingly, high achievement orientation is associated with leadership effectiveness. However, this is not a linear relationship. Those managers with very high achievement orientation can become insensitive to the effects of their desires on those around them who feel too driven by their leader's ambition.

8. *Low need for affiliation* Need for affiliation refers to the need to be liked and accepted by those around us. Effective leaders do not have high needs for affiliation. Those who did would be likely to put their need to be liked ahead of making good decisions in difficult situations or ahead of having to manage poor performance among their followers. Neither do they have extremely low affiliation needs, uncaring for the opinions or liking of others. That would suggest imperviousness to social relationships and the need for belonging, which is central to healthy human growth and development.

Turning to skills and competencies, the research to date suggests the following are important for leaders:

1. *Technical competence* is important because it wins the respect of followers. It includes knowledge about the organization, its strategy, structure and processes; knowledge about products and services and production methods and technologies; and knowledge about the organization's environment.

2   *Conceptual skills* are important because having an understanding of the complex environments of organizations (both internal and external) enables sense-making and reduces anxiety that the situation is too complex to be comprehended and therefore managed. The ability to analyze, organize, plan and make decisions is central to organizational functioning, so leaders who have conceptual skill will increase the confidence of followers within the organization.

3   Finally, *interpersonal skills* are vital to effective management and leadership. Understanding the needs and feelings of followers, monitoring the effects of one's own behaviours on followers and being aware of one's own emotional reactions are central to effective leadership.

Caveats that need to be born in mind in considering these conclusions are:

- Only a few studies have rigorously tested the assumption that personality traits have a causal impact on leader effectiveness or the emergence as a leader.
- For at least some personality traits, it is not clear which comes first, being in a leadership position or possessing the trait in question.
- Implicit theories of leadership held by followers can facilitate leadership emergence (e.g. leaders should be 'extraverted') rather than leader traits predicting emergence.
- The trait approach provides little guidance concerning what advice or training to give current or aspiring soon-to-be leaders.

BEHAVIOURAL THEORIES

Our discussion has concentrated on the personality and competencies of leaders. We now turn to considering the behaviour of leaders. Below, we consider two streams of research. The first looks at the nature of leadership and managerial work and the second at two important research programmes that adopted a behavioural approach, conducted respectively at the universities of Ohio and Michigan during the 1950s and 1960s.

The nature of leadership and managerial work

We have discussed leaders and leadership, but inevitably the words 'managers' and 'management' have also peppered the text. In this section we begin by asking who are the leaders and who are the managers? The reality is that leadership roles require a great deal of management, and managers are also required to be leaders. Different researchers have offered pithy differentiating statements: 'Managers are those who do things right, leaders are those who do the right things'; 'managers seek stability, leaders seek innovation'. However, the reality is that leading and managing are distinct processes, not different types of people (Bass, 1985). We have already defined leadership, and much of management can be understood as the day-to-day processes of ensuring that leadership goals are achieved via supporting, monitoring, directing and motivating performance.

What is it like to lead and manage in modern organizations? Yukl (2013a) shows the pace is unrelenting. Managers tend to work long hours and to deal constantly with requests for information, requirements for decisions to be made and requests for assistance or direction. The content of the work is varied and fragmented, each component necessarily of brief duration. Half of the tasks managers undertake take less than nine minutes and only one-tenth take an hour. A big challenge for leaders is finding the time to address the most pressing organizational problems (such as workforce shortages or promoting staff engagement and reducing staff stress). Consequently, interruptions are frequent, multitasking is essential and important activities are interspersed with relatively unimportant tasks. Indeed, Sumantra Ghoshal once observed that the challenge of leadership is to learn to focus on the difficult, tough, major tasks which really will make a difference to organizational performance, and not to manage the inevitable (see Birkinshaw & Piramal, 2006 for an appreciation of Ghoshal's work).

Because of the large number of tasks and requests, managers have to react to some and ignore or give minimal attention to others. There are always more challenges and problems than can be handled, so the need to make wise choices about which must be attended to and with how much attention and effort is a constant. Human beings are effort minimizers (as are all animal species), so there is a tendency to deal with easy problems, with problems for which solutions already exist, with problems for which solutions have been found in the past, or with problems where the people are amenable rather than difficult. Of course, problems that bosses raise tend to get dealt with first, though clearly customers' problems should also take precedence. These high levels of demands mean that managers may have little time for reflection and may avoid tasks that take time, such as team-building, confronting the most difficult challenges and reflecting critically on what the organization is trying to achieve, its processes and its successes. Instead, firefighting, responding to immediate demands and doing emails tend to attract the spotlight of attention. Good leadership and management means making wise choices about how scarce and valuable leadership time is used and how managers make decisions is not so much linear as a disorderly process with strong political elements. Decisions are made as a consequence of many conversations, new information and unfolding events, which often evolve haphazardly rather than as a result of a careful, rational process.

One response is to suggest that leaders will benefit from learning mindfulness practices that help them relate to the present moment of their leadership, by becoming more able to give attention to the totality of their present experience in an accepting and non-judgemental way. As a result, they are more likely to be able to offer effective leadership (see for example, Glomb, Duffy, Bono, & Yang, 2011) by developing response flexibility, affect regulation, empathy, persistence, better communication, improved memory, increased self-determination, coping more effectively with stress and developing less biased decision-making. Mindfulness may help them become more aware of their pre-judgements, prevarication, and the tendency to avoid the difficult and to manage the inevitable. Such mindfulness may also help them to build 'presence' – the leadership trait of being present and attentive when with team members or followers.

So far we have considered the skills, traits and motivations of leaders and how they relate to leadership effectiveness. During the 1950s and 1960s, research in this area focused more on which leadership behaviours were related to effectiveness (Figure 11.4). The research was concentrated in two centres: Ohio State University and the University of Michigan. The two centres produced similar conclusions about effective leadership behaviours.

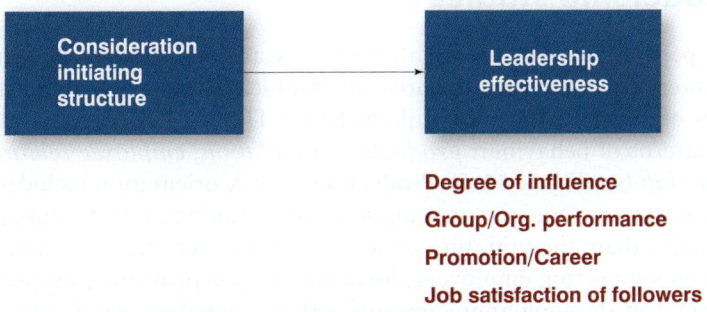

Figure 11.4 Behavioural theories of leadership

Ohio State leadership studies

Researchers from this group identified 150 good examples of leadership behaviours and developed a series of questionnaires to measure these behaviours. The questionnaires included the Leader Behaviour Description Questionnaire (LBDQ), the Supervisory Behaviour Description Questionnaire (SBDQ) and the Leader Opinion Questionnaire (LOQ). Factor analysis revealed two broad categories of leader behaviours: *consideration* and *initiating structure* (see Figure 11.5):

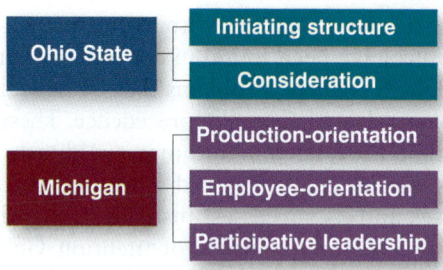

Figure 11.5   Ohio and Michigan behavioural studies

- *Consideration*: behaviour indicating that a leader trusts, respects and values good relationships with their followers.
- *Initiating structure*: behaviour that a leader engages in to make sure that work gets done and that team members perform their jobs acceptably.

Consideration describes leader behaviours focused on the employee, such as listening to and valuing employees, helping them solve problems, supporting them, giving positive feedback and being friendly, supportive and respectful in interactions with them. Initiating structure behaviours are focused on the task and include clarifying employees' roles and objectives, setting performance standards, monitoring task performance and correcting poor performance. The two factors proved to be relatively independent of one another, suggesting that leaders could have high levels of both, low levels of both or high levels of just one.

The key question is which of these behavioural styles predicted performance. It is not a surprise that consideration predicts employee satisfaction, but both styles had only weak relationships with effectiveness measured in terms of task performance (Judge, Piccolo, & Ilies, 2004).

Michigan leadership studies

During the same period, virtually identical research was being undertaken at the University of Michigan where interviews were used to gather data on leader behaviours and these were linked to objective measures of group productivity (Likert, 1967). The researchers found that effective leaders displayed three patterns of behaviour: *production orientation, employee relations orientation* and *participative leadership* (see Figure 11.5). Production or task orientation included setting objectives, finding necessary resources (equipment, supplies) and planning and scheduling. This was similar to, but rather broader than, the initiating structure pattern identified in Ohio. Relations-oriented behaviours included supporting employees, listening to their problems, supporting their skill and career development and showing appreciation for their contributions. Again, this was a broader category of behaviours than the consideration constellation identified at Ohio. The third category identified group-level behaviours such as working with a team rather than just individuals, setting up and facilitating meetings, ensuring participation in group decision-making and promoting cooperative group working.

Limitations of behavioural approach

The approach taken by these two centres (which were highly influential in their day) has been criticized on several grounds. First, it is difficult to determine causality in the studies – were the leaders displaying these behaviours because their teams had been successful, or were the teams successful because their leaders behaved this way? Many studies used only self-report questionnaires for both leader behaviour measures and outcome measures, so it is difficult to know whether relationships are the result of the measurement process rather than reflecting real relationships. For example, followers may see their leaders and their team's performance in a consistently positive (or rosy) light. Moreover, the questionnaires themselves have been criticized for the ambiguity of many items and the response bias they inadvertently create. Overall, the research suggests that increases in relations-oriented behaviours result in higher levels of staff satisfaction and that changes to task-oriented behaviours produce inconclusive results.

Blake and Mouton's managerial grid

It may have already occurred to you that it would be interesting to compare the effectiveness of leaders who display high levels of both consideration and task orientation or task structure with leaders low on both or just one dimension. Blake and Mouton (1964) (Figure 11.6) proposed such a model with four extreme categories:

- high consideration, high structure
- high consideration, low structure
- low consideration, high structure
- low consideration, low structure.

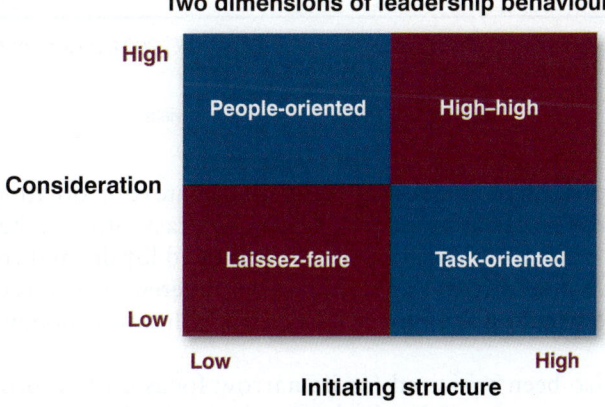

Figure 11.6 Blake and Mouton's managerial grid

Those low on both dimensions were termed laissez faire in their behavioural style, since they were likely to leave employees to largely manage themselves. The two high–low configurations were termed either people oriented or task oriented. The researchers were particularly interested in what came to be called the 'high–high' leader, predicting that this configuration of behaviours would be highly effective. Research has generally been inconclusive, which is not surprising given that the model assumes a simplicity that is at odds with reality. A leader's behaviour in any situation may have a complex mix of both consideration and task structuring, so it is not easy to categorize behaviour.

Amabile, Schatzel, Moneta, and Kramer (2004) used diary data from 26 project teams over several weeks. They found that effective leaders used more relations-oriented behaviours, such as giving psychological support, consulting with team members and recognizing their contributions. They also used task behaviours, such as clarifying roles and objectives, monitoring progress and dealing with problems. But the timing of these behaviours proved at least as important as the level of the behaviours. Negative behaviours by leaders, such as making mistakes, inappropriately chastising team members or failing to take appropriate action, created negative spirals.

Figure 11.7 shows the results of a meta-analysis of research on the relationships between the dimensions in the Ohio and Michigan studies and a variety of potential leadership effectiveness measures (Judge et al., 2004). What is clear is that the relationships between the consideration/employee relations measures and the outcomes are stronger than those between the structuring/task orientation measures and the outcomes.

Leadership behaviour	Consideration/People orientation	Initiating structure/Task orientation
	r/p	r/p
Leader effectiveness	.39*	.28*
Followers' motlivation	.40*	.26*
Satisfaction with leader	.68*	.27*
Job satisfaction	.40*	.19
Group/Org. performance	.23*	.23
Overall average	.49*	.29*

Based on 400 correlations from 200 studies with 300 samples (Judge et al., 2004, Journal of Applied Psychology)

Figure 11.7 Effects of leadership behaviours

Overall, the behavioural approach tends to ignore the context or situation within which leader behaviours occur. In some situations (crises, for example), task-oriented behaviour will be vital, whereas at other times, relations-oriented behaviour will build loyalty and commitment. It appears that initiating structure is more susceptible to situational differences than is consideration, because in some situations task orientation is positively associated with satisfaction, whereas in others it has negative effects.

The approach has also been criticized for its narrow focus on two broad behavioural areas (consideration and initiating structure). Leadership involves more than two dimensions of behaviour.

It includes scanning the external environment, developing visions and strategies, managing conflicts, establishing coalitions with other parts of the organization or other organizations, influencing external stakeholders and so on. The list is almost endless, but the management of change is a particularly important category.

In reviewing the extensive research in this area, Yukl (2010) argues for an integrative framework of leader behaviours subsuming three broad categories: task-oriented behaviours, relations-oriented behaviours and change-oriented behaviours. Change-oriented behaviours include:

- monitoring the external environment
- interpreting events to explain the urgent need for change
- studying competitors' ideas for innovation
- envisioning exciting new possibilities for the organization
- encouraging people to view problems and opportunities in new ways
- encouraging innovation
- encouraging and celebrating progress in implementing change.

The most serious criticism of this approach is that it fails to address the question of which leadership behaviours are appropriate in which situations. In a crisis, when a customer in a restaurant is complaining because the meal is late, using consideration as a style in the kitchen may not be at all helpful. After the dinner has been successfully served, it may be. We therefore need a much greater understanding of the situations in which different leader behaviours are most and least helpful. The major problem, therefore, with both trait and behavioural approaches is that they offer very simple answers to very complex questions.

CONTINGENCY APPROACH

The study of trait and behavioural approaches leads to the conclusion that the effectiveness of leadership is determined not just by leaders' traits or behaviours alone but is dependent on situational factors – leadership effectiveness is contingent upon factors such as the task, skills and motivation of followers and other aspects of the environment. This has led to the development of 'contingency' theories of leadership (Figure 11.8) and below we consider two examples: *situational leadership* and the *path–goal theory* of leadership.

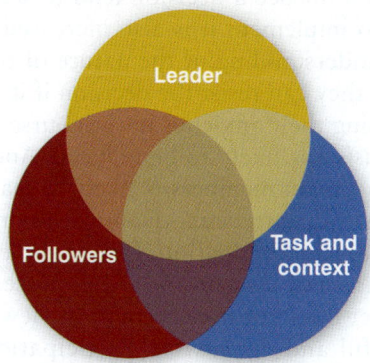

Figure 11.8 Contingency approaches to leadership. Leadership effectiveness is determined by both the personal characteristics of leaders and by various characteristics of the situation in which leadership takes place

Situational leadership theory

Hersey and Blanchard (1977) proposed that effective leadership was contingent on the maturity of followers. They distinguished between job maturity – how skilled the followers were at their jobs; and psychological maturity – how confident the followers were. The less mature the team members, the theory proposes, the more task orientation or structuring the leader needed to provide. At intermediate levels of maturity, leaders should use more consideration and less structuring. When followers were mature, leaders could withdraw and provide minimal structuring and support since followers were self-directed. There is little empirical support for the theory, but it does draw attention to the idea that leadership behaviours have to be adjusted to the characteristics of followers and that a participative approach may not be appropriate in every situation (Figure 11.9).

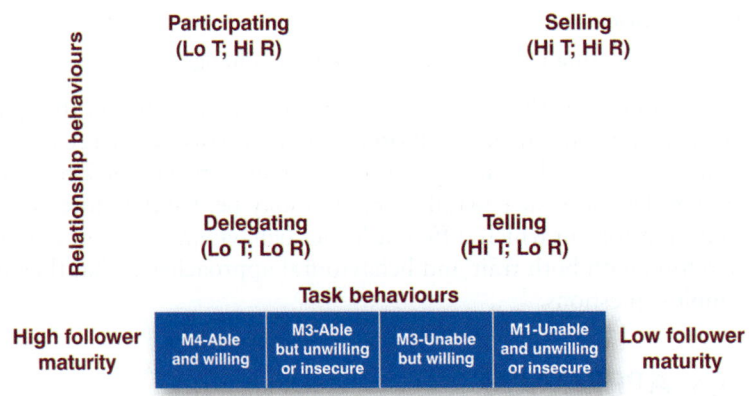

Figure 11.9   Situational leadership (T=task orientation; R=relations orientation)

Participative leadership

Participation in decision-making by followers seems like an obvious strategy for leaders to promote. Leaders who encourage those they lead to contribute to decisions gain a number of advantages from this style of leadership. Those who influence a decision tend to see it as more their own decision and support it. Their motivation to implement it is also increased. As a result of being involved in the process they have a better understanding of the nature of the decision and their anxieties are likely to be reduced. Moreover, they can resist the decision if it appears likely to threaten their interests. Finally, simply by expressing their anxieties in the course of participating in the decision process, their resistance to the decision is likely to be reduced. And, of course, incorporating the views, experience and knowledge of team members is likely to lead to a more sophisticated and comprehensive analysis of the issue, leading to better-quality decisions.

However, there are disadvantages to participation. For example, participation takes time, and time may not be available in a crisis. Staff may not be in full possession of the facts or may make self-interested decisions. If the leader does not take account of views expressed in the consultation process, they may become resentful and distrustful. Participation in some circumstances can be a recipe for avoiding making decisions, leading to organizational inertia. Participation is not necessarily a cost-free process.

Think through your own approach to leadership and times when you have been called upon to lead. When did you use one or more of the styles below? What was it about the situation or about you at that time that led you to use each of these styles? What conclusions do you draw about the relationship between leadership styles and situational factors affecting behaviour?

- *Autocratic decision* The leader makes the decision, not taking into account the opinions or suggestions of staff. They therefore have no direct influence on the decision. This style involves no participation.
- *Consultation* The leader invites staff to contribute their opinions and ideas. However, he or she still makes the decision alone after taking into account the views of staff.
- *Joint decision* The leader invites the views of staff in a meeting. Everyone's comments are contributed and the group collectively arrives at a decision. The leader does not make the final decision; this is made on the basis of consensus in the group.
- *Delegation* The leader asks staff to take responsibility for making the decision. The staff members given this responsibility may have to seek the leader's approval for the final decision. Delegation is greater to the extent that the individual staff member does not have to seek final approval.

Path–goal theory

Robert House (1971) offered a more sophisticated version of contingency theory in the form of *path–goal theory.* House suggests that the leader should make desired rewards available (goal) and clarify for the subordinate the kinds of behaviour that will lead to the reward (path). The theory proposes four types of leader behaviour and two situational variables (Figure 11.10). The four types of leadership behaviours are:

- Directive – sets goals and gives guidance.
- Supportive – shows concern for followers' needs.
- Participative – consults before decision-making.
- Achievement oriented – sets challenging goals and expects followers to perform at highest level.

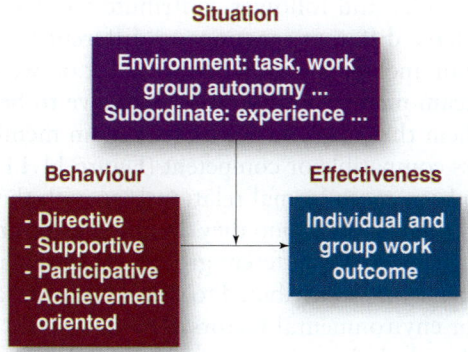

Figure 11.10 Path-goal theory

Each of these strategies is enacted by taking into account the nature of team members and their tasks.

Path–goal theory proposes two classes of situational or contingency variables that moderate the relationship between leadership behaviour and outcome:

- *environment*: task structure, formal authority system, workgroup autonomy
- *subordinate*: locus of control, experience, perceived ability.

When the leader compensates for things lacking in either the work setting or the employee, performance and employee satisfaction are likely to be high. If there is low task structure, the leader will need to be directive. Where there is high workgroup autonomy, the leader can be consultative. When team members have a low internal locus of control, leaders will need to be directive. If employees have high perceived ability and experience, then an achievement-oriented style makes sense. When the task is stressful, tedious or dangerous, supportive leadership is more appropriate as a style. Overall, this approach has produced more support than the other contingency approaches in terms of predicting effective leadership (Podsakoff, MacKenzie, Ahearne, & Bommer, 1995), but the results are not conclusive.

Contingency theories therefore take us a little further than trait or behavioural theories in representing more accurately the complexity of leadership in real organizations. They have been criticized for being too simplistic, despite their attempts to take account of situational factors. The criticism centres on the observation that real-life situations are too complex to be reduced to single variables (follower maturity, task structure). In practice, leadership situations are multifaceted, dynamic and subject to only limited control. Moreover, given the fast pace of their work, leaders and managers do not have the luxury of analyzing the situation using what may seem contrived or unrealistic models. Their value lies in reminding leaders of the need to monitor the changing situation.

A final criticism of contingency approaches is that followers are treated as a homogeneous group, assumed to share characteristics – all relatively mature, able and experienced; or all with a low internal locus of control. We now turn to examine a theory that presents a quite different approach by focusing on leader–follower relationships.

DYADIC THEORIES OF LEADERSHIP

The leader–member exchange model describes the relationships that may develop between a leader and a follower and what the leader and follower contribute and receive in the relationship. The model proposes that leaders have different reactions to different followers (Graen & Cashman, 1975). When the leader has team members with whom they get on well or who are similar to them (personal compatibility), or team members whom they perceive to be competent, they both trust and spend more time with them than they do with other team members. The reverse applies to those who are perceived as less compatible or competent (Figure 11.11). Not only do leaders spend less time with them, they also have more formal relationships with them. The theory also suggests that team members know very well which group they are in – the 'in-group' or the 'out-group'. The attributions of leaders to members of these different groups are systematically different.

The successes of in-group members are attributed to their ability or hard work, while their failures are attributed to situational or environmental factors. The reverse is true for out-group members. In-group members are trusted with the more interesting assignments and desirable tasks, are given more information and are taken into the leader's confidence more.

A widely used seven-item measure is available to test the nature of relationships – the LMX7. Subordinate ratings of their leaders are influenced by whether they see the leader as fair, whereas the ratings provided by leaders are influenced by whether they see their team members as competent. Research using this and other LMX measures generally supports the model (Martinko, Harvey, &

Douglas, 2007). Given its predictive validity and the obvious implications for practice, the model has been used to develop a set of prescriptions about how to correct performance deficiencies apparent among followers in ways other than adopting favourites (summarized by Yukl, 2010, pp. 243–246):

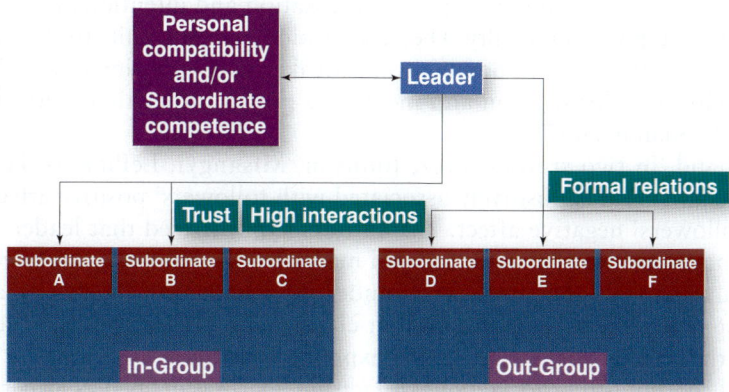

Figure 11.11 Leader-member exchange model

- Gather information about performance problems rather than jumping to conclusions about employees' motivation or competence.
- Try to avoid attributional biases that assume the problem lies with the person rather than the situation.
- Provide corrective feedback as soon as possible after the performance problem becomes apparent.
- Describe the problem briefly to the person.
- Explain the consequences (for the team, customer, organization) of the performance problem.
- Be calm and professional rather than angry, resentful or embarrassed.
- Work together with the employee to try to identify the reasons for the problems in performance.
- Invite suggestions for ways of correcting the performance problem.
- Express confidence in and support for the employee.
- Show a sincere commitment to helping the person.
- Agree on the steps forward to correct problems.
- Summarize and agree the content of the discussion.

CHARISMATIC AND TRANSFORMATIONAL LEADERSHIP

Another approach to leadership focuses on *charismatic* and *transformational leadership* behaviour. Charismatic leadership describes a self-confident, enthusiastic leader able to win followers' respect and support for their vision of how good things could be. Followers identify with such leaders because of their desire to please an individual who seems extraordinary because of their strategic insights, unconventional (even radical) views, strong convictions, high energy levels and self-confidence.

This attractive description should not blind us to the dangers of charismatic leadership. Both Winston Churchill (typically seen as a benevolent leader) and Adolf Hitler (a tyrant) have fitted the charismatic leader profile. Donald Trump also fits the mould. Theorists and researchers propose that negative charismatics have a personalized power orientation and intentionally seek devotion from followers rather than support and loyalty. They use ideology when it suits them, changing the rules for personal benefit, and they tend to dominate and weaken followers, increasing their dependence. Their concern is with self-glorification and increasing power rather than with the well-being of followers (Howell & Shamir, 2005).

On the other hand, in two studies, Erez, Johnson, Misangyi, LePine, & Halverson (2008) found that leader charisma was positively associated with followers' positive affect and negatively associated with followers' negative affect. The authors hypothesized that leaders' positive affect, positive expression and aroused behaviour would mediate the relationships between charisma and affect. Their research showed that firefighters under the command of a charismatic officer were happier than those under the command of a non-charismatic officer and that these relationships were mediated by the leader's positive affect and expressed positivity.

A closely related concept is *transformational leadership*, which is defined as leadership that inspires followers to trust the leader, to perform at a high level and to contribute to the achievement of organizational goals. Bass (1985) describes transformational leadership as having four key components:

- *Idealized influence* Leaders behave in admirable ways so that followers tend to identify with them (e.g. they display conviction; they portray role modelling behaviours consistent with a vision; they appeal to the commitment and loyalty of followers on an emotional level as well as rational level).
- *Inspirational motivation* Leaders articulate a vision which is appealing and inspiring to followers (e.g. this provides meaning for the work task; they set high standards and communicate optimism about the achievability of the vision).
- *Intellectual stimulation* Leaders stimulate and encourage creativity in their followers (e.g. challenge assumptions, take risks, ask followers for their ideas and for suggestions on how to develop them into practice).
- *Individualized consideration* Leaders attend to each follower individually (e.g. by acting as a mentor or coach, and by listening to their concerns and paying attention to their needs, including their skill and career development needs).

The theory contrasts two styles of behaviour called *transformational* and *transactional leadership*. Transactional leadership motivates followers by exchanging rewards for high performance and reprimanding team members for mistakes and substandard performance. Transactional leadership consists of three dimensions underlying leaders' behaviour:

- *Contingent reward* Leaders set up constructive transactions or exchanges with followers, e.g. clarifying expectations, and establishing rewards in order to motivate and shape their performance. Other examples include exchanging rewards for appropriate levels of effort, or responding to followers' self-interests as long as they are getting the job done.
- *Active management by exception* Leaders monitor followers' behaviour, anticipate problems and take corrective action before serious difficulties occur.
- *Passive management by exception* Leaders wait until the followers' behaviour has created problems before taking action.

These leader behaviours are therefore task-focused and behavioural rather than relational and emotional. Theorists such as Bass (1985) suggest that transformational and transactional behaviours are not mutually exclusive but that effective leaders use both styles. However, it is proposed that the most effective leaders use the transformational approach more since it increases follower motivation and performance. Figure 11.12 reveals what research suggests about the two styles. Transformational leadership does appear more effective than management by exception (passive management by exception appears to be negatively related to effectiveness). Both contingent reward and transformational leadership are positively and relatively strongly related to leadership effectiveness.

	Outcome*
	r/p
Transformational leadership	.44*
Transactional leadership	
Contingent reward	.39*
Active management by exception	.15
Passive management by exception	−.15
Laissez-faire leadership	−.37*

[a] A combined outcome measure of follower job satisfaction satisfaction wilth leader, motivation, leader performance, effectiveness and group/organization performance.

Based on 626 correlations from 87 studies with a total N > 38.000 (Judge, et al., 2004).

Figure 11.12   Relationships between transformational and transactional leadership outcomes

The final category, *laissez-faire leadership*, represents the absence of leadership. It differs from passive management by exception, where at least some influence is exerted. In effect, this involves leaving staff to manage themselves and make their own decisions regardless of their competence or of the need to structure the task. The meta-analysis in Figure 11.11 reveals that this approach is strongly negatively related to effectiveness. Why would anyone use either passive management by exception or laissez faire styles? Observation suggests the answer is 'out of necessity'. Where leaders must oversee very large groups of staff or where the task is simple, predictable and structured, leaders may be inclined to adopt these approaches. However, the research evidence suggests that such styles are nevertheless counterproductive.

Overall, the research evidence suggests that transformational leadership is effective, and that a combination of transformational leadership and contingent reward is powerful in producing desirable outcomes such as effectiveness (productivity, profitability), innovation, employee commitment and engagement, and employee well-being. Recent studies also suggest its value in encouraging employee creativity and corporate entrepreneurship. Gong, Huang, and Farh (2009) examined the relationship between transformational leadership, employee creativity and job performance. Transformational leadership predicted employee creativity, which in turn predicted employee sales and supervisor-rated employee job performance. Another showed the effects on top management teams (TMTs) of CEO transformational leadership. Ling, Simsek, Lubatkin, and Veiga (2008) proposed that transformational CEOs influence TMTs' consistency, risk propensity, decentralization of responsibilities and long-term compensation, and that these TMT characteristics impact corporate entrepreneurship. Data from 152 firms supported most of these hypothesized links, underscoring how the CEO–TMT interface helps explain transformational CEOs' role in promoting corporate entrepreneurship. Transformational leadership also predicts commitment to organizational change among followers (Herold, Fedor, Caldwell, & Yi, 2008).

KEY THEME

Diversity in leadership prototypes – Global Leadership and Organizational Behaviour Effectiveness (GLOBE)

Do leadership styles and follower preferences for leadership styles vary across countries? These questions led to the creation of the GLOBE programme in 1993, involving 170 researchers from 63 countries. The focus of the research was on the relationship between societal culture, organizational culture, leadership prototypes (what people implicitly expect of their leaders) and organizational effectiveness. Data were gathered from 17,000 middle managers in 900 organizations concentrated in three industry sectors (finance, telecommunications and food).

The GLOBE programme investigated leader behaviours and attributes reported to be effective or ineffective in each societal culture. The methodology relied primarily on the development of a questionnaire instrument, translated, back-translated and tested in each of the 63 countries, covering all major cultural regions in the world (Brodbeck et al., 2000; Den Hartog et al., 1999; House et al., 1999).

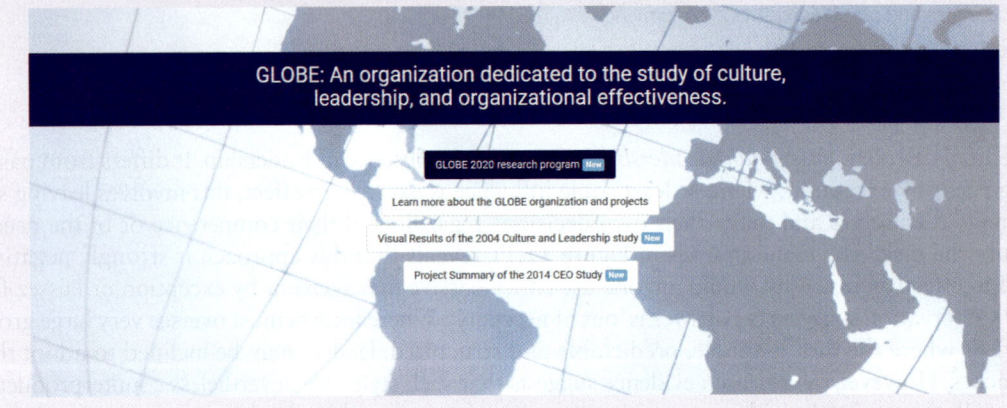

We now move on to examine three important questions in leadership research: Are there cross-cultural differences in leadership styles? Do men and women differ in their leadership styles? And can leadership be developed via training programmes and other interventions? We examine the key theme above in more depth, focusing on cross-cultural differences in leadership.

LEADERSHIP ACROSS CULTURES

Leadership is recognized by the fit between what the individual implicitly believes leadership constitutes and the behaviours observed in someone in a leadership role (Lord & Maher, 1991). The implicit model carried in the individual's mind is called their 'leadership prototype'. The better the match between the individual's leadership prototype and their leader's behaviour, the more they are influenced by the leader. For example, research on transformational leadership suggests that charismatic/transformational leadership styles are closer to followers' perceptions of 'ideal' leadership than other styles (e.g. transactional leadership). This research also suggests that when employees see a leader as close to ideal, the leader can influence them in ways that go well beyond the influence deriving from the formal authority position.

GLOBE tested the hypothesis that differences in leadership prototypes exhibit predictable within-country consistency and between-country differences and that the differing prototypes mirror cultural norms, values and assumptions deeply ingrained in societal culture. In other words, people develop leadership prototypes that mirror their societal cultures. Leadership prototypes will therefore be widely shared within particular cultures and there will be predictable cross-cultural differences in these prototypes. In our increasingly connected world, characterized by more interaction, global travel, global business and international working, understanding these variations becomes important. A style of leadership that works well in the USA may not go down so well in the Middle East or in Turkey. The leadership prototype in Germany may be discordant with the leadership prototype in Sweden. Understanding what works where and why is important for understanding which leadership styles work well in which countries and for training leaders to be more protean – changing their styles to suit the situation they find themselves in. It is also important because most research on leadership over the past 100 years has been conducted in the USA. Our knowledge is therefore biased towards US models and prototypes and highly ethnocentric. For the fast-growing economies of countries such as India, China and Brazil (for example), this research may have limited applicability or may be misleading.

The GLOBE research identified 21 leadership prototypical dimensions grouped into six broad categories (see Figure 11.13) which reliably differentiated leadership prototypes across cultures. The dimensions include some that vary across cultures ('culturally contingent leadership') and some that are valued across all cultures ('universal leadership concepts'). The latter include charismatic/value-based; team oriented; humane oriented; autonomous; self-protective and participative. The sub-elements making up these six dimensions from among the 21 are depicted in Figure 11.13.

1. Charismatic/Value-based

Charismatic 1: Visionary

Charismatic 2: Inspirational

Charismatic 3: Inspirational

Integrity

Decisive

Performance-oriented

2. Team-oriented

Team 1: Colloborative team orientation

Team 2: Team Integrator

Diplomatic

Malevolent (reverse scored)

Administratively competent

3. Self-protective

Self-centered

Status conscious

Conflict Inducer

Face saver

Procedural

4. Participative

Autocratic (reverse scored)

Non-participative (reverse scored)

5. Humane-oriented

Modesty

Humane-oriented

6. Autonomous

Autonomous

Figure 11.13 The GLOBE leadership dimensions

Culturally contingent leadership concepts

Those dimensions which varied across cultures included: ambitious, cautious, compassionate, domineering, formal, humble (self-effacing), independent, risk-taking and self-sacrificing.

Taking the European sub-sample, which involved more than 6,000 middle managers from 22 European countries, the results clustered into five broad groups of countries: Anglo, Nordic, Germanic, Latin and Near East countries. The results showed that leadership prototypes were similar within and different between the five culture clusters. Further analysis revealed three higher-order dimensions which differentiated countries by leader prototypes: 1) *Interpersonal Directness and Proximity* (i.e. low face-saving, low self-centred, low administrative; high inspirational and integrity); 2) *Autonomy* (i.e. individualistic, independent, autonomous, unique); and 3) *Modesty* (i.e. modest, self-effacing, patient). For example, the 'Interpersonal Directness and Proximity' dimension separates the South/East from the North/West European countries (the exceptions are former East Germany and Portugal). In the Germanic, Anglo and Nordic countries, people expect leaders to have high interpersonal directness and proximity, whereas this is not the case in South/East European countries. The Germanic cluster, Georgia and most prominently the Czech Republic expect and prefer leaders with high levels of autonomy (individualistic, independent, unique), and much more so than is the case in the Anglo, Nordic, Central, Latin and Near East European countries.

Universal leadership concepts

In at least 95 per cent of the 62 countries studied in GLOBE, three dimensions were always associated with effective leadership. These are Integrity, Inspirational and Team Integrator. Two were always found to be negatively related to effective leadership – Malevolent and Face Saver (Den Hartog et al., 1999). House et al. (1999) originally proposed that charismatic/transformational leadership (Integrity, Visionary, Inspirational, Self-sacrificing, Decisive and Performance oriented) is a universally endorsed leadership constellation. Though this hypothesis received some support, only two elements out of the five (Inspiration, Integrity) were universally endorsed. Across all countries the following items indicated leadership effectiveness: motive arouser, foresight, encouraging, communicative, trustworthy, dynamic, positive and confidence builder (Den Hartog et al., 1999). Figure 11.14 shows those clusters around the world in which particular prototypes are rated as high, medium or low.

Where a particular dimension is seen as prototypical across cultures, we should recognize that this does not mean that these characteristics are necessarily expressed in the same way. As we shall see in Chapter 13, there are major differences across cultures that influence values and behaviours. Inspirational or charismatic leadership may be valued across all societies, but may be seen in rather different ways. In some places, such leadership is seen as potentially dangerous because of the risk that the leader may exploit followers. The risk-taking associated with inspiration may be viewed ambivalently in cultures that are avoidant of uncertainty. Consequently, the expression of transformational leadership or charismatic leadership is likely to be moderated and expressed in different ways across cultures that nevertheless value that leadership prototype.

The GLOBE project serves to show how important cross-cultural issues are in our understanding of behaviour at work, and the extent to which reliance on findings largely from one or two cultures may blind us to understanding of leadership specifically and work behaviour in general across cultures (Chhokar, Brodbeck, & House, 2007; House, Hanges, Dorfman, & Gupta, 2004).

CHAPTER 11 LEADERSHIP IN ORGANIZATIONS

Societal cluster	Charismatic/ Value-based	Team-oriented	Participative	Humane-oriented	Autonomous	Self-protective
Eastern Europe	M	M	L	M	H	H
Latin America	H	H	M	M	L	M
Latin Europe	M	M	M	L	L	M
Confucian Asia	M	M	L	M	M	H
Nordic Europe	H	M	H	L	M	L
Anglo	H	M	H	H	M	L
Sub-Saharan Africa	M	M	M	H	L	M
Southern Asia	H	M	L	H	M	H
Germanic Europe	H	M	H	M	H	L
Middle East	L	L	L	M	M	H

Key: H a high score on this dimension; M a medium score on this dimension; L a low score on this dimension.

H, L indicate the highest or lowest score on this dimension in comparison with the other societal clusters

e.g., Eastern Europe had the highest score of all the culture clusters for 'Autonomous' and Latin America had the lowest.

Figure 11.14 Summary of societal rankings for GLOBE dimensions of leadership (adapted from Chhokar, Brodeck and House, 2007)

PIONEERING WORK PSYCHOLOGISTS

Dr Klodiana Lanaj

Dr Klodiana Lanaj is a researcher and associate professor in the Management Department at the University of Florida. She received a PhD in Business Administration from Michigan State University in 2013 after working first in a large European bank as a project manager of risk and as a credit analyst for small and medium enterprises. Her main areas of research are leadership, team processes and performance, and motivation and self-regulation. She has helped to advance our understanding of leader engagement and well-being, leader emergence and dominance in self-managing teams, the factors that contribute to team performance, and has also provided insights into daily behaviours and interactions that deplete and replenish people at work. Her research in these areas is published in the top academic outlets such as the *Academy of Management Journal*, *Journal of Applied Psychology*, *Organizational Behavior and Human*

continued

Decision Processes, *Personnel Psychology* and *Psychological Bulletin*. Equally impressive is how her research has attracted the attention of the press and popular media.

Her work on the costs and benefits of helping others at work attracted press coverage from NBC Today.com, CBS Local, Futurity, *Medical Daily*, *Business News Daily*, *Glamour*, Toronto Star and the *New York Magazine*. And her work on how men 'over emerge' as leaders in comparison to their leadership effectiveness was highlighted by *Forbes*, Business Insider, Futurity, Yahoo! Finance, the World Economic Forum and the US Government Executive. She has also studied how smartphone use at home after 9 p.m. can mean people not sleeping well and arriving for work the next day not fully recovered, reported in an influential paper in the journal *Organizational Behavior and Human Decision Processes*. This attracted press coverage from the *Financial Times*, Time.com, *The Wall Street Journal*, NPR, *Forbes*, Huffington Post, *The Globe and Mail*, Yahoo! News, *Toronto Sun*, *Men's Health*, Psychology Today, *Women's Health*, Michigan Radio, *Medical Daily*, WILX Channel 10, The State News, U.S. News & World Report, and *Psychology Today*.

Her striking ability to communicate the results of her research to general and business audiences is illustrated by her brilliant record in publishing in the prestigious *Harvard Business Review.* She has written articles for the *Review* on how self-reflection can help leaders stay motivated; how feeling powerful at work makes us feel worse when we get home; how helping colleagues brings many benefits, but it may carry a cost in exhaustion (the latter in LSE Business Review).

She has lectured widely on her work nationally and internationally, including in Switzerland, Singapore and throughout the USA.

GENDER AND LEADERSHIP

Despite decades of debate, discussion and awareness-raising, it remains the case that women are dramatically underrepresented as CEOs and on the boards of corporations, as well as in political life and in leadership positions generally. In effect, the leadership potential of many women is not fulfilled and their contribution to businesses, corporations and organizations is lost. There is a desperate need for leaders at senior levels of most organizations, yet the potential contributions of women are wasted. The effects on women aspiring to leadership positions are also deeply damaging. To quote the Business Editor of *The Observer*, Ruth Sunderland: 'Women are the single biggest – and least acknowledged – force for economic growth on the planet. This is not a claim made by rampant feminists, but by *The Economist*, which suggests that over the past few decades women have contributed more to the expansion of the world economy than either new technology or the emerging markets of China and India.'

What are some of the reasons for this discrimination, sometimes called the 'glass ceiling'? Lyness and Heilman (2006) suggest that women need more skills than men to advance to executive positions. Others offer the following explanations. Women are denied access to roles and positions that provide important experience or visibility that will enable promotion. Women are excluded from networks that provide connections and supports for promotion to senior positions. Women are less likely to focus on promotion and exert effort in that direction than men. Senior industry figures are less likely to provide mentoring for women than men because they do not see them as future leaders. Competing family demands, such as childcare duties, make career progress more difficult for women. Senior managers do not take decisive action to encourage equality of opportunity in their organizations. Senior managers are biased and tend to promote people with similar characteristics to themselves, including gender. Some men intentionally try to preserve the top echelons for men (see Yukl, 2010 for more discussion of these explanations). There is some evidence that all of these factors are at play within organizations and create the circumstances that prevent women from assuming leadership positions (for a good introduction, see also Lord et al., 2017).

Research has examined the extent to which there are differences between men and women in terms of leadership style and leadership effectiveness, since this might be one explanation for some of the differences. Eagly, Johannesen-Schmidt, and van Engen (2003) undertook a meta-analysis to investigate leadership styles and concluded that women used transformational leadership styles a little more than men. They were also more likely to use contingent reward as a transactional style, whereas men used passive management by exception more. Their transformational style involved more use of individualized consideration – supportive behaviour towards those they lead and a focus on developing team members' skills and confidence. Such findings, given our earlier analysis, suggest women should be more likely than men to be offered leadership positions, given this configuration of leadership style.

There is little difference in leadership effectiveness (Eagly, Karau, & Makhijani, 1995). Women are more likely to be effective when the role requires strong interpersonal skills and men are more likely to be effective in roles that require strong task skills. However, the differences in leadership style and role performance are small; so small in fact that it is safer to assume that there is no difference in leadership effectiveness between men and women.

The key is to ensure that organizations make best use of the talents that are available to them. Currently, the majority of organizations in Europe fail to do this because of their long-standing discrimination, favouring the promotion of men over women to senior positions.

BOX 11.1
Positive work and compassionate leadership

In the context of our discussion about developing positive organizational environments within which people at work flourish rather than languish, the concept of compassionate leadership offers great promise, we believe.

There has been considerable growth in theory and related research activity in the concept of compassion at work in the past decade, with the *Academy of Management Review* dedicating a special issue to the topic in 2012 (Rynes, Bartunek, Dutton, & Margolis, 2012). Compassion (in an organizational context) can be understood as having four components: *attending, understanding, empathizing and helping* (Atkins & Parker, 2012):

1 *Attending* paying attention to the other and noticing his or her difficulties, challenges or suffering.

2 *Understanding* understanding what is causing the other's difficulties, by making an appraisal of the cause, ideally through a dialogue.

3 *Empathizing* having an empathic response, a felt relation with the other's difficulties or distress.

4 *Helping* taking intelligent (thoughtful and appropriate) action to serve or help the other with the challenge or difficulty.

continued

Gilbert and Choden (2013) define compassion as 'a sensitivity to suffering in self and others with a commitment to try to alleviate and prevent it'. Because caring is a basic motivation we are motivated to notice and become aware of the distress of the other, and pay attention to this distress (Cole-King & Gilbert, 2011; Gilbert, 2017), while having an empathic insight into the needs of others. It also implies having the motivation to help. The 'commitment to alleviate/prevent suffering' requires courage and wisdom (Cole-King & Gilbert, 2011), that is, taking 'wise' action. De Zulueta views compassion as involving 'the motivation to relieve the suffering of another' (de Zulueta, 2016) and invokes the concept of cognitive empathy – 'stepping into someone else's shoes', which helps to guide an appropriate response (de Zulueta, 2016).

Compassion has facilitators and inhibitors. For example, it is easier to be compassionate towards people we like than those we don't; those we think will appreciate us rather than people we think will not; and people who share our values rather than those who do not. Inhibitors of compassion include poor working conditions, poor leadership, role confusion, role conflicts and work overload. It is therefore important to identify both the inhibitors and facilitators of compassion in the work context (Brown, Crawford, Gilbert, Gilbert, & Gale, 2014; Gilbert, 2017).

Based on our exploration of the concept of compassion above, compassionate leadership can be understood as having four components (West & Chowla, 2017):

1 *Attending* Since it is our motives that direct our attention, focused leaders will pay attention in a particular way to those they lead – what Nancy Kline (2002) calls 'listening with fascination'. In practice, this would involve leaders being motivated to take the time to listen to the accounts of the experiences of staff throughout their work – the challenges, obstacles, frustrations and hurts as well as the successes and delights. According to a model of compassionate leadership, the first task for leaders is to ensure they devote adequate time to listening deeply to those they lead in order that they have an appreciation of the situations they face and the abilities they have to face them.

2 *Understanding* The second component involves leaders appraising the situation others face and arriving at an understanding of the causes of their discomfort or distress. Simply responding to distress without exploring the underlying reasons may exacerbate the other's distress. For example, a team member may express strong frustration with a colleague because a particular task (e.g. completing a report) was taking longer than usual, resulting in the colleague feeling angry and hurt. Exploration of the incident might reveal that the nurse had experienced a verbal attack from a patient during the working day that led to her feeling threatened and overwhelmed. The second task of compassionate leadership is therefore appraising the causes of distress and arriving at an understanding of the causes. Ideally, this is best done in conjunction with the individual whose distress evokes compassion, because a shared understanding is likely to be both more accurate and helpful for the distressed person. These first two elements may seem obvious prescriptions for leadership, but in the context of highly pressured work situations, staff often feel they are not listened to and that their leaders do not understand the situations they face (West, Dawson, Admasachew, & Topakas, 2011).

3 *Empathizing* The third component of compassionate leadership is empathizing. In general, empathizing has two components, one that is linked to emotion and the second

to perspective-taking, which is cognitive. Compassionate leaders are motivated and able to emotionally 'tune in' to the distress of the other. In addition, perspective-taking enables an understanding of the sources and context of these difficulties. We are uniquely enabled as a species to feel the distress of others because of our neurophysiological capacity to mirror observed emotion. Compassion, as Gilbert and others have shown, has emotional, cognitive and behavioural responses that vary with context. Compassionate leaders therefore are emotionally in touch with, able to tolerate and not over-identify with the distress of others. This mirroring of emotion, in part, enables leaders to arrive at a deeper understanding of the other's situation and thereby be able to more effectively work out how to take steps to help the other.

4 *Helping* The fourth and final component is taking thoughtful and intelligent action to help the other. Leadership, according to all definitions, includes helping and supporting others. In the context of healthcare, for example, where staff face significant challenges on a daily or even hourly basis, supportive leadership is an important determinant of staff well-being and effectiveness. This fourth component is focused on taking action to help the person. Wisdom is needed to know what this actually involves – it could be by removing obstacles, supporting the implementation of solutions or otherwise taking thoughtful, appropriate action (it might simply be enough to listen). The helping element has four sub-components that are required for a competent compassionate response: *scope* – breadth of resources offered; *scale* – the volume of resources; *speed* – the timeliness of the response; and *specialization* – the extent to which the response meets the real needs of the other (Lilius, Kanov, Dutton, JWorline, & Maitlis, 2011).

LEADERSHIP DEVELOPMENT

A question asked of those who study leadership by many business people is: 'Are leaders born or is it possible to train people to be leaders?' That question reflects a lack of understanding about the nature of leadership. Certainly some traits with a strong genetic component are important for leadership, such as Extraversion (positively) and Neuroticism (negatively), but it is equally true that everybody is called upon at points in their lives to provide leadership. Moreover, leadership is highly dependent upon the situation in which people find themselves, as we have seen above.

Nevertheless, the question of whether leadership competence can be enhanced by training is an important issue. In Chapter 6, we saw that the effectiveness of training programmes depends on how well they are designed. They range in quality from the frankly hopeless to good. It is important to examine the design elements of such programmes (Baldwin & Ford, 1988; Lord & Hall, 2005; Salas & Cannon-Bowers, 2000; Tannenbaum & Yukl, 1992). Based on the existing research, Yukl (2010) identifies eight factors that determine the success of leader training:

1 *Clear learning objectives* – the training programme must specify a limited number of very clear objectives in order that it is appropriately focused.
2 *Clear meaningful content* – the content must be clear to the trainees in order that it can guide their thinking and behaviour and it must be meaningful in its relation to the objectives of

the training and the development of effective leadership. Periodic summaries of content help to ensure understanding. Models should be simple enough for people to understand and memorable enough for them to be able to access and apply in the workplace.

3 *Appropriate sequencing of content* – models should be presented before people are asked to acquire techniques derived from them. Material should progress from the simple to the more complex. And having intervals in training so that people can practise techniques and digest the learning between training sessions is valuable.

4 *Appropriate mix of training methods* – there should be a mix of training sessions rather than a diet of only one method. Formal lectures, practice sessions, role plays, coaching and experiential exercises can all be used, but should be appropriate both to the capacities of learners and to the particular skills being taught.

5 *Opportunity for active practice* – trainees should be asked to restate the principles they have been taught, try them out in a safe way (e.g. through role plays) and then put them into practice back in their workplaces, with an opportunity to review effectiveness.

6 *Relevant, timely feedback* – feedback is fundamental to all animal learning, and no less to humans. Therefore information about the success or otherwise of leadership behaviours during the training process is vital for effective training.

7 *Promoting the self-confidence of trainees* – by reassuring and praising them, their confidence is likely to be developed and their leadership skills to improve. Beginning with relatively simple tasks ensures trainees can experience success before moving on to more complex and challenging tasks.

8 *Follow-up activities* – in order to sustain learning it is helpful to have review sessions or to have trainees carry out specific leadership tasks back in their organizations and then to review their success and problems in order that learning can be sustained.

Leadership development is a huge industry in most countries, soaking up enormous amounts of money spent by organizations on training. Below we briefly review evidence on the effectiveness of different types of interventions to promote leadership effectiveness.

Multi-source feedback via questionnaire

This method of promoting leadership effectiveness involves the individual and several others with whom they work completing a questionnaire assessing the leader's behaviours and effectiveness. This is sometimes called 360-degree assessment because team members, peers and bosses are all asked to assess the individual. The leader is then encouraged to reflect on the differences between self-ratings and those of the others; to reflect on the ratings of those they work with or report to; and to reflect on how the ratings compare with those of other leaders in organizations, using the norm data available for that particular instrument. There are many variations of such instruments available with varying psychometric properties. Some are widely used personality questionnaires, which have poor validity data (such as Myers Briggs), while others are based on considerable research in psychology, such as some 'Big Five' measures. Feedback to the individual can be in the form of a written report (the least useful), a one-to-one discussion with someone expert in understanding the results, or a workshop with a group of leaders sharing and discussing their results together.

How effective is multi-source feedback? Studies have produced mixed results (Seifert, Yukl, & McDonald, 2003), some suggesting positive effects and others no effects. In a review that took in some 131 studies (not confined to leadership), Kluger and DeNisi (1996) found only a weak positive effect of multi-source feedback on performance. Indeed, in one-third of studies the relationship was negative. It may be that, used in conjunction with training or other interventions, this approach is useful, but there is no clear evidence for this. More research is needed to determine the effectiveness of this approach.

Developmental assessment centres

Assessment centres were described in detail in Chapters 5 and 6. Here we consider their effectiveness in promoting leader development. Assessment centres, usually spread over two to three days, involve multi-source feedback, in-basket exercises, aptitude tests, interviews, group exercises, writing assignments and intensive reflection processes. There is evidence that such combined processes do have positive effects on subsequent leader performance (Engelbracht & Fischer, 1995). The problem is that with such a mix of interventions, it is very difficult to know which elements are potent in enabling leadership development and which are redundant. The design of programmes is therefore a 'pick and mix in the dark' process for those charged with encouraging effective leadership development. More sophisticated questions, such as which elements are most effective for which leaders, cannot be addressed in the existing corpus of research.

Developmental assignments

The best way to learn to lead, many argue, is through experience rather than through formal training, so giving potential leaders challenging assignments can be helpful (McCall, Lombardo, & Morrison, 1988). These could include challenging projects on a 'task and finish' group, managing a new project, leading a 'blue sky' team proposing new products or services, working on a secondment in another part of the organization, having an assignment in another country or chairing a special task force.

The research at AT&T (Bray et al., 1974) suggested that experiencing diverse and challenging work enhanced subsequent career development. Research at the CCL (McCauley, Eastman, & Ohlott, 1995) reinforced that conclusion, suggesting that managers learned new and valuable skills, though this was dependent upon the project they were involved in. Research and anecdotal evidence indicates that having a challenging assignment is best, but this should not be to the point where the individual feels they are sinking or where they fail. The greater the variety of tasks, in general, the better the learning people derive. And the better and more timely the feedback, the more effective the learning from assignments is.

Job rotation

Job rotation is a system of encouraging leadership development by assigning people to multiple jobs consecutively within the organization in a short space of time. Managers are usually encouraged to work in up to five or six different jobs over periods usually up to two years. The purpose is for them to experience a range of aspects of the business, to interact with different customers, to get to know different technologies, to experience different country cultures in a multinational organization and to increase their network of contacts within the country. Participants report the value of such experiences, although the constant change and learning can be stressful and overwhelming. Campion, Cheraskin, and Stevens (1994) found that participants reported increased technical, managerial and business knowledge. However, there was also evidence of lower productivity because of the frequent requirements for new learning and there were negative effects on team members who reported lower satisfaction when exposed to constant changes of manager. Because job rotation is often employed to rapidly increase the skills and advance the careers of outstanding individuals (called 'fast tracking'), this can generate resentment among others at their exclusion from the programme. Overall, there is little research evidence to support the value of this method of encouraging leader development – simply because there have been too few studies to provide a clear picture.

Action learning

Action learning groups are formed of individuals who meet regularly together while working on a specific project in their work areas or organizations. They meet under the guidance of a facilitator to set objectives, review progress, problem-solve and share experiences. By working in such a group, motivation is increased and there is a strong sense of mutual support. This works best when a whole team works together. Participants report valuable outcomes; for example, knowing that they will have to report on progress at the next action learning group meeting spurs them to make progress on the project. Moreover, having the support and guidance of the group gives confidence. Very few published studies have evaluated outcomes, however. Prideaux and Ford (1988) report positive outcomes, but these are based only on retrospective self-reported benefits. This is another area of leadership development research where considerably more effort is needed to advance our understanding.

Mentoring

Mentoring refers to situations where an experienced manager works with a less experienced individual to support their leadership development. The role has two functions or advantages. The more senior person can advise, support and counsel the person based on their greater experience and knowledge. And they can help to advance the career of the mentee by promoting and protecting them and winning good assignments for them. Indeed, there is some evidence that mentees do have greater career success as a result of this patronage (Whitely & Coetsier, 1993). It is noteworthy, however, that women seem to have more difficulty finding a mentor within organizations (Ragins & Cotton, 1993). Mentees generally report better career advancement, higher levels of satisfaction, higher organizational commitment and lower turnover. The evidence suggests that mentoring is useful, but there is little to suggest that it leads to higher levels of leadership effectiveness.

Executive coaching

It is mainly high-level leaders and managers in organizations whose development needs are provided by executive coaches. The coach is usually a high-level (often retired) manager or specialist and coaches can be internal or external to the organization. The purpose of coaching is to help the individual leader learn new skills, handle difficult problems, manage conflicts or learn to work effectively across cultural boundaries. The relationship should be characterized (rather like a therapeutic relationship) by strict confidentiality, rules for ethical conduct and a sense of psychological safety and trust between the two parties. Executive coaching is usually contracted over a limited period and includes regular meetings between the coach and the leader.

The advantage of this approach to development is that there is a strong, clear focus on specific issues faced by the leader, in contrast to training programmes, which may be generic, abstract and not sufficiently relevant to participants' day-to-day work problems. The disadvantages are the cost and variable coach competency.

There has been limited research examining the effectiveness of coaching, but what there is has been favourable. Hall, Otazo, and Hollenbeck (1999) reported on a study of 75 people from six companies for whom executive coaching was helpful. However, this study was based on self-reports and was retrospective, limiting the confidence we can place in the findings. Olivero, Bane, and Kopelman (1997) assessed outcomes associated with a three-day training workshop, augmented by eight weeks of executive coaching focused on individual action projects. The results suggested the managers were more productive as a result of the training and these effects were augmented by the coaching; indeed, coaching had the stronger effects of the two interventions. A study by Bowles, Cunningham, De La Rosa, Picano, and Meekins (2007) produced similarly positive results. A careful review suggests that there are clear benefits from coaching but most studies are flawed, so solid evidence for effectiveness in predicting team and organizational performance outcomes is still lacking (de Haan, Duckworth, Birch, & Jones, 2013). Much depends on the quality of coach training, clarity of structure and processes of coaching, the underlying theoretical model, supervision of coaches and clarity about overall purpose.

Outdoor pursuits programmes

This approach to leadership development involves groups of participants engaging in challenging activities, usually in wild and wonderful places. Rock climbing, white-water rafting, building bridges, hiking and other challenging pursuits form the core of the experience. The aim is to make links between these activities and organizational leadership. There is usually an experienced facilitator whose role is to assist in this process. The experience is supposed to encourage personal growth, build self-confidence and self-control, encourage trust between participants and enable risk-taking in a controlled environment.

Very few studies have examined the efficacy of such interventions. In the area of team-building, the results are not encouraging (Tannenbaum, Salas, & Cannon-Bowers, 1996). Marsh, Richards, and Barnes report long-term improvements in leaders' self-confidence but Wagner, Baldwin, and Roland (1991) found only weak effects three months after the interventions. Perceptions of teamwork did improve where intact teams participated in programmes. There is little evidence that these programmes are effective (other than self-report evidence and it is clear from this that many participants do enjoy the experience). A few headline cases have resulted in serious injury to physical or mental health when the programmes are run by people without adequate training.

Reflections on leadership development

Overall, there is little consistent evidence for the effectiveness of specific leadership development programmes. Undoubtedly some programmes work for some people some of the time, but evaluating their effectiveness empirically is very challenging. The interventions are so diverse, the participants very often have quite different challenges, and those providing the programmes have hugely varying experience, knowledge and sensitivity. What is needed is research, which asks focused questions about what interventions work for what leadership development objectives with which individuals in which work contexts. We are very far from being able to answer such questions. Vast sums of money are spent on leadership development in organizations; if only 1 per cent were spent on research into effective interventions, there is no doubt we could save a great deal of wasted money and produce a great many more effective leaders. What is clear is that experience in the job of leadership is hugely valuable in enabling leaders to develop their skills, but without guidance and support, much of that experience can be wasted (Day, 2000; Day & Harrison, 2007).

> **DISCUSS WITH A COLLEAGUE**
>
> Given what you have learned about leadership in this chapter, design a training programme that you think would help leaders to become more effective in their work. Remember also to draw on the information contained in Chapter 6 to enable you to offer something more effective than that offered by most leadership development providers.

CONCLUSION

From the preceding discussion of our knowledge of leadership, it may feel difficult to identify the key elements of leadership. Gary Yukl, a leading theorist and researcher in the leadership area over many years, summarizes understanding of effective leadership behaviours in a helpful way. In reviewing the extensive research, Yukl (2013b) argues for an integrative hierarchical framework of leader behaviours subsuming four broad categories: task-oriented behaviours, relations-oriented behaviours, change-oriented behaviours and external behaviours.

Task-oriented	Clarifying
	Planning
	Monitoring operations
	Problem-solving
Relations-oriented	Supporting
	Developing
	Recognizing
	Empowering
Change-oriented	Advocating change
	Envisioning change
	Encouraging innovation
	Facilitating collective learning
External	Networking
	External monitoring
	Representing

POSITIVE WORK

Developing collective leadership in modern organizations

Collective leadership refers to a type of leadership culture which is the result of the collective actions of formal and informal leaders acting together to influence organizational success (McGuire & Rhodes, 2009; Kuenkel, 2016). This perspective proposes that it is not simply the number or quality of individual leaders that determines organizational performance, but the extent to which formal and informal leaders work collectively to nurture cultures that ensure high-quality performance and employee growth and well-being (West, Topakas, & Dawson, 2014). Leadership is therefore both the leaders themselves and the relationships among them, including how they cooperate and coordinate efforts to nurture leadership and thereby organizational culture. Fundamental to the concept of collective leadership is the extent to which leaders accept and act on their responsibility for the success of the organization overall, not just their own area of responsibility. A pithier definition is leadership of all, by all and for all. In effect, collective leadership means:

- Leadership is the responsibility of all – anyone with expertise taking responsibility when appropriate.
- Shared leadership in teams and across teams.
- Interdependent, collaborative leadership – working together across boundaries, prioritizing quality, well-being and performance across the system/organization.
- Consistent approach to leadership within the leadership community – authenticity, openness, humility, optimism, compassion, appreciation.

Take the example of healthcare organizations. Organizational culture in hospitals is shaped by the nature of its leadership. It is the behaviour of leaders, top to bottom and end to end, individually and collectively, in healthcare organizations that determine whether care quality is the priority; all staff have clear objectives; there is enlightened people management; there are high levels of staff engagement; learning and quality improvement are embedded; and good team and inter-team working is endemic. Research on climate and culture in healthcare internationally suggests that leadership cultures of command and control are less effective than more engaging leadership styles in healthcare systems across the world (Dickinson, Ham, Snelling, & Spurgeon, 2013; West et al., 2014), and implies that collective leadership approaches are likely to be most effective. One consistent lesson from investigations into failings in healthcare across the world is that safety is dependent on developing cultures in which staff at every level of organizations take responsibility for ensuring safe practice, including challenging unsafe behaviours no matter what the seniority of those involved.

Research and practice from the Center for Creative Leadership suggests that collective leadership is more effective in creating direction, alignment and commitment, particularly in organizations that face challenges of uncertainty and complexity (Drath et al., 2008). Direction is agreement on what the organization is seeking to achieve, such as – in a hospital, for example – care quality, good patient experience, compassionate care and staff and patient safety. It also means an understanding and acceptance of how decisions are made in the organization and by whom. Alignment is the coordination and integration of the work across the organization so that care is appropriately integrated. Task and role clarity are key preconditions for alignment. Commitment refers to all taking responsibility for the success of the organization as a whole, rather than focusing on just the success of their component.

SUMMARY

This chapter began by making clear the importance of leadership in human society and therefore the importance of understanding what constitutes effective leadership. Huge advances in understanding have been made in the past 100 years, but very large areas of ignorance remain. This is partly because defining leaders and leadership is complex and challenging. It was proposed that:

> *Leadership is the process of influencing others to understand and agree about what needs to be done and how to do it, and the process of facilitating individual and collective efforts to accomplish shared objectives.*

Leadership effectiveness is similarly complex and depends on which stakeholder group is defining it. Effectiveness can subsume productivity, innovation, personal benefits, employee attitudes, long-term outcomes or short-term outcomes, cohesion, culture, group identity and successful management of change. Effectiveness may also be defined in terms of the career of the leader – has she or he had a rapid advance up the hierarchy within or across organizations?

The chapter described trait theories that assess the extent to which personality predicts leader emergence and effectiveness. The Big Five personality dimensions correlate with leader effectiveness, with Extraversion and Openness correlating positively and Neuroticism correlating negatively. Four of the five dimensions correlate with leader emergence (Extraversion, Conscientiousness, Openness and – negatively – Neuroticism). Overall, leader effectiveness and emergence are predicted by traits such as high energy level and stress tolerance; self-confidence; internal locus of control; emotional maturity; personal integrity; socialized power motivation; moderately high achievement orientation; low need for affiliation; technical competence; conceptual skills; and interpersonal skills.

The behavioural approach has focused on the nature of leadership and management and illustrates the complexity of these roles – high demand and high variation. The Ohio State and Michigan University studies examined the extent to which leaders focus on managing relationships with followers or getting the job done. The former approach (relations orientation) appears more effective, with a task approach having a weak association with outcomes. The behavioural approach ignores the complexity and variety of situations that leaders face and assumes that certain leader behaviours will be effective across all situations. Moreover, they neglect the importance of leadership focused on changing organizations.

Contingency approaches seek to take account of the situation and explore both task and follower characteristics. Situational leadership examines the maturity (confidence and ability) of followers and proposes that, with greater maturity, less task structuring is required. House's path–goal theory proposes that the leader clarifies rewards for followers (goal) and the desired behaviours to achieve this (path). Two contingencies determine the appropriate leader style (directive, supportive, participative, achievement oriented): environment and followers. When the leader compensates for factors lacking in followers or in the environment, he or she will be most effective. There is some limited support for the contingency approach.

Dyadic theory focuses on the leader–member exchange process. Where followers are perceived by the leader to be similar to them or technically competent, they are treated as favourites and damaging 'in-groups' and 'out-groups' are created. The best leadership is apparent when there are few differences in relationships between leaders and followers in terms of preferences and when followers view their leaders as fair.

The chapter described the more recent focus on charismatic and transformational leadership, pointing out that charismatic leaders are attractive but can be dangerous. The transformational leader uses idealized influence, inspirational motivation, intellectual stimulation and individualized consideration to promote follower motivation and loyalty. This is contrasted with transactional leadership, which consists of three dimensions underlying leaders' behaviour: contingent reward, active management by exception and passive management by exception. The most effective styles appear to be transformational and contingent reward.

The chapter explored leadership across cultures, using the results from the GLOBE study. This describes six core dimensions of leadership behaviour: charismatic/value-based; team oriented; humane oriented; autonomous; self-protective and participative. Some descriptions of leadership are valued differently across cultures, such as ambitious, domineering and self-effacing. Some are valued in all cultures, including integrity, inspirational and team integrator. This research reminds us that leadership is culturally specific and that leaders must learn how to lead in different cultural settings. Moreover, reliance on research from only one culture will blind us to very real differences across cultures.

Women are massively underrepresented in leadership in companies around the world. There are many explanations for this, but differences in leadership style or effectiveness is not one of them. Although women tend to have a slightly more transformational and participative styles, these differences are so small as to be immaterial (and anyway should confer advantage). There is a desperate need for the widespread discrimination against women in the world of work to be ended.

Overall, there is little evidence for the effectiveness of leadership development programmes (for a good review, see Van Velsor, McCauley, & Ruderman, 2010). Undoubtedly some programmes work for some people some of the time, but evaluating their effectiveness empirically is very challenging. Much research remains to be done in this and other areas of leadership research.

DISCUSSION QUESTIONS

1. What is leadership and what is leadership effectiveness?
2. To what extent are leaders born rather than made?
3. What are the most effective leadership behaviours?
4. How can leaders have different relationships with team members and still be fair?
5. How can leaders learn to be charismatic and transformational?
6. How would you design a study to determine what aspects of leadership training are most effective?
7. How do you explain the fact that some leadership attributes are universally valued while others are culturally dependent? What is it about the former group of attributes or values that makes them so important?

FURTHER READING

Barnes, C. M., Lanaj, K., & Johnson, R. E. (2014). Research: Using a smartphone after 9 pm leaves workers disengaged. *Harvard Business Review*, January. Retrieved from hbr.org/2014/01/research-using-a-smartphone-after-9-pm-leaves-workers-disengaged

Bass, B. M., & Riggio, R. E. (2006). *Transformational leadership* (2nd ed.). Mahwah, NJ: Lawrence Erlbaum.

Chhokar, J. S., Brodbeck, F. C., & House, R. J. (2007). *Culture and leadership around the world: The GLOBE book of in-depth studies of 25 societies*. Mahwah, NJ: Lawrence Erlbaum.

Dinh, J. E., Lord, R. G., Gardner, W. L., Meuser, J. D., Liden, R. C., & Hu, J. (2014). Leadership theory and research in the new millennium: Current theoretical trends and changing perspectives. *The Leadership Quarterly, 25*(1), 36–62.

Eagly, A. H., Johannesen-Schmidt, M. C., & van Engen, M. L. (2003). Transformational, transactional and laissez-faire leadership styles: A meta-analysis comparing women and men. *Psychological Bulletin, 129*, 569–591.

Foulk, T. A., Lanaj, K., Tu, M-H., Erez, A., & Archambeau, L. (2018). Heavy is the head that wears the crown: An actor-centric approach to daily psychological power, abusive leader behavior, and perceived incivility. *Academy of Management Journal, 61*(2), 661–684.

Lanaj, K., & Hollenbeck, J. R. (2015). Leadership over-emergence in self-managing teams: The role of gender and countervailing biases. *Academy of Management Journal, 58*(5), 1476–1494.

Lanaj, K., Johnson, R. E., & Barnes, C. M. (2014). Beginning the workday yet already depleted? Consequences of late-night smartphone use and sleep. *Organizational Behavior and Human Decision Processes, 21*(1), 11–23.

Lord, R. G., Day, D. V., Zaccaro, S. J., Avolio, B. J., & Eagly, A. H. (2017). Leadership in applied psychology: Three waves of theory and research. *Journal of Applied Psychology, 102*(3), 434.

Meuser, J. D., Gardner, W. L., Dinh, J. E., Hu, J., Liden, R. C., & Lord, R. G. (2016). A network analysis of leadership theory: The infancy of integration. *Journal of Management, 42*(5), 1374–1403.

Nohria, N., & Khurana, R. (Eds.). (2010). *Handbook of leadership theory and practice: A Harvard Business School Centennial Colloquium*. Boston, MA: Harvard Business School.

Yukl, G. (2010). *Leadership in organizations* (8th ed.). Upper Saddle River, NJ: Pearson Prentice Hall.

REFERENCES

Amabile, T. M., Schatzel, E. A., Moneta, G. B., & Kramer, S. J. (2004). Leader behaviours and the work environment for creativity: Perceived leader support. *Leadership Quarterly, 15*(1), 5–32.

Arvey, R. D., Zhang, Z., Avolio, B. J., & Krueger, R. F. (2007). Developmental and genetic determinants of leadership role occupancy among women. *Journal of Applied Psychology, 92*, 693–706.

Atkins, P. W., & Parker, S. K. (2012). Understanding individual compassion in organizations: The role of appraisals and psychological flexibility. *Academy of Management Review, 37*(4), 524–546.

Baldwin, T. T., & Ford, J. K. (1988). Transfer of training: A review and directions for future research. *Personnel Psychology, 41*, 63–105.

Bass, B. M. (1985). *Leadership and performance beyond expectation.* New York, NY: Free Press.

Berman, F. E., & Miner, J. B. (1985). Motivation to change at the top executive level: A test of the hierarchic role-motivation theory. *Personnel Psychology, 38*, 377–379.

Birkinshaw, J., & Piramal, G. (2006). *Sumantra Ghoshal on management: A force for good.* London, England: Financial Times Press.

Blake, R., & Mouton, J. (1964). *The managerial grid: The key to leadership excellence.* Houston, TX: Gulf Publishing Co.

Bowles, S., Cunningham, C. J. L., De La Rosa, G., Picano, J., & Meekins, R. (2007). Coaching leaders in middle and executive management: Goals, performance, buy-in. *Leadership and Organization Development, 28*(5), 388–408.

Boyatzis, R. E. (1982). *The competent manager.* New York, NY: John Wiley.

Bray, D. W., Campbell, R. J., & Grant, D. L. (1974). *Formative years in business: A long-term AT&T study of managerial lives.* New York, NY: John Wiley.

Brodbeck, F. C., Frese, M., Akerblom, S., Audia, G., Bakacsi, G., Bendova, H, ... Wunderer, R. (2000). Cultural variation of leadership prototypes across 22 European countries. *Journal of Occupational and Organizational Psychology, 73*, 1–29.

Brown, B., Crawford, P., Gilbert, P., Gilbert, J., & Gale, G. (2014). Practical compassion: Repertoires of practice and compassion talk in acute mental healthcare. *Sociology of Health & Illness, 36*, 383–399.

Campion, M. A., Cheraskin, L., & Stevens, M. J. (1994). Career-related antecedents and outcomes of job rotation. *Academy of Management Journal, 37*, 1518–1542.

Chhokar, J. S., Brodbeck, F. C., & House, R. J. (2007). *Culture and leadership around the world: The GLOBE book of in-depth studies of 25 societies.* Mahwah, NJ: Lawrence Erlbaum.

Cole-King, A., & Gilbert, P. (2011). Compassionate care: The theory and the reality. *Journal of Holistic Healthcare, 8*(3), 29–37.

Day, D. V. (2000). Leadership development: A review in context. *The Leadership Quarterly, 11*(4), 581–613.

Day, D. V., & Harrison, M. M. (2007). A multilevel, identity-based approach to leadership development. *Human Resource Management Review, 17*(4), 360–373.

de Haan, E., Duckworth, A., Birch, D., & Jones, C. (2013). Executive coaching outcome research: The contribution of common factors such as relationship, personality match, and self-efficacy. *Consulting Psychology Journal: Practice and Research, 65*(1), 40.

Den Hartog, D. N., House, R. J., Hanges, P. J., Ruiz-Quintanilla, S. A., Dorfman, P. W., & Associates. (1999). Culture specific and cross-culturally generalizable implicit leadership theories: Are the attributes of charismatic/transformational leadership universally endorsed? *The Leadership Quarterly, 10*, 219–256.

de Zulueta, P. C. (2016). Developing compassionate leadership in health care: An integrative review. *Journal of Healthcare Leadership, 8*, 1–10.

Dickinson, H., Ham, C., Snelling, I., & Spurgeon, P. (2013). *Are we there yet? Models of medical leadership and their effectiveness: An exploratory study.* Birmingham, England: NIHR Service Delivery and Organisation Programme.

Drath, W. H., McCauley, C. D., Palus, C. J., Van Velsor, E., O'Connor, P. M., & McGuire, J. B. (2008). Direction, alignment, commitment: Toward a more integrative ontology of leadership. *The Leadership Quarterly, 19*(6), 635–653.

Eagly, A. H., Johannesen-Schmidt, M. C., & van Engen, M. L. (2003). Transformational, transactional and laissez-faire leadership styles: A meta-analysis comparing women and men. *Psychological Bulletin, 129*, 569–591.

Eagly, A. H., Karau, S. J., & Makhijani, M. G. (1995). Gender and the effectiveness of leaders: A meta-analysis. *Psychological Bulletin, 117*(1), 125–145.

Engelbracht, A. S., & Fischer, A. H. (1995). The managerial performance implications of a developmental assessment centre process. *Human Relations, 48*, 1–18.

Erez, A., Johnson, D. E., Misangyi, V. F., LePine, M. A., & Halverson, K. C. (2008). Stirring the hearts of followers: Charismatic leadership as the transferal of affect. *Journal of Applied Psychology, 93*, 602–616.

Gilbert, P. (Ed.). (2017). *Compassion: Concepts, research and applications.* Abingdon, England: Routledge.

Gilbert, P., & Choden. (2013). *Mindful compassion*. London, England: Constable & Robinson.

Glomb, T. M., Duffy, M. K., Bono, J. E., & Yang, T. (2011). Mindfulness at work. *Research in Personnel and Human Resources Management, 30*, 115–157.

Gong, Y., Huang, J.-C., & Farh, J.-L. (2009). Employee learning orientation, transformational leadership and employee creativity: The mediating role of employee creative self-efficacy. *Academy of Management Journal, 52*, 765–778.

Graen, S. G., & Cashman, J. F. (1975). A role-making model of leadership in formal organizations: A development approach. *Organization and Administrative Sciences, 6*, 143–165.

Hall, D. T., Otazo, K. L., & Hollenbeck, G. P. (1999). Behind closed doors: What really happens in executive coaching. *Organizational Dynamics, 29* (Winter), 39–53.

Herold, D. M., Fedor, D. B., Caldwell, S., & Yi, L. (2008). The effects of transformational and change leadership on employees' commitment to a change: A multilevel study. *Journal of Applied Psychology, 93*, 346–357.

Hersey, P., & Blanchard, K. H. (1977). *The management of organizational behaviour* (3rd ed.). Englewood Cliffs, NJ: Prentice Hall.

House, R. J. (1971). A path goal theory of leader effectiveness. *Administrative Science Quarterly, 16*(3), 321–339.

House, R. J., Hanges, P. J., Javidan, M., Dorfman, P. W., & Gupta, V. (Eds.). (2004). *Culture, leadership, and organizations: The GLOBE study of 62 societies*. Thousand Oaks, CA: SAGE.

House, R. J., Hanges, P. J., Ruiz-Quintanilla, S. A., Dorfman, P. W., Javidan, M., Dickson, M. W., Gupta, V., Koopman, P.L. (1999). Cultural influences on leadership and organizations: Project GLOBE. In W. H. Mobley, M. J. Gessner, & V. Arnold (Eds.), *Advances in global leadership* (pp. 171–233). Stanford, CN: JAI.

Howard, A., & Bray, D. W. (1990). Predictors of managerial success over long periods of time. In H. Clark & M. Clark (Eds.), *Measures of leadership* (pp. 113–130). West Orange, NJ: Leadership Library of America, .

Howell, J. M., & Shamir, B. (2005). The role of followers in the charismatic leadership process: Relationships and their consequences. *Academy of Management Review, 30*, 96–112.

Hulks, S., Walsh, N., Powell, M., Ham C., & Alderwick, H. (2017) *Leading across the health and care system: Lessons from experience*. London, England: The King's Fund.

Judge, T. A., Bono, J. E., Ilies, R., & Gerhardt, M. W. (2002). Personality and leadership: A qualitative and quantitative review. *Journal of Applied Psychology, 87*(4), 765–780.

Judge, T. A., Piccolo, R. F., & Ilies, R. (2004). The forgotten ones? The validity of consideration and initiating structure in leadership research. *Journal of Applied Psychology, 89*, 36–51.

Katz, D., & Kahn, R. L. (1978). *The social psychology of organizations* (2nd ed.). New York, NY: John Wiley & Sons.

Kline, N. (2002). *Time to think: Listening to ignite the human mind*. London, England: Cassell.

Kluger, A. N., & DeNisi, A. S. (1996). The effects of feedback interventions on performance: Historical review, meta-analysis, a preliminary feedback intervention theory. *Psychological Bulletin, 119*, 254–284.

Kuenkel, P. (2016). *The art of leading collectively: Co-creating a sustainable, socially just future*. White River Junction, VT: Chelsea Green Publishing.

Lanaj, K., & Hollenbeck, J. R. (2015). Leadership over-emergence in self-managing teams: The role of gender and countervailing biases. *Academy of Management Journal, 58*(5), 1476–1494.

Lanaj, K., Johnson, R. E., & Barnes, C. M. (2014). Beginning the workday yet already depleted? Consequences of late-night smartphone use and sleep. *Organizational Behavior and Human Decision Processes, 21*(1), 11–23.

Likert, R. (1967). *The human organization: Its management and value*. New York, NY: McGraw-Hill.

Lilius, J. M., Kanov, J., Dutton, J. E., Worline, M. C., & Maitlis, S. (2011). Compassion revealed: What we know about compassion at work (and where we need to know more). In K. Cameron & G. Spreitzer (Eds.), *The Oxford handbook of positive organizational scholarship* (pp. 273–287). New York, NY: Oxford University Press.

Ling, Y. A. N., Simsek, Z., Lubatkin, M. H., & Veiga, J. F. (2008). Transformational leadership's role in promoting corporate entrepreneurship: Examining the CEO–TMT interface. *Academy of Management Journal, 51*, 557–576.

Lombardo, M. M., & McCauley, C. D. (1988). *The dynamics of management derailment* (Technical Report No. 34). Greensboro, NC: Center for Creative Leadership.

Lord, R. G., Day, D. V., Zaccaro, S. J., Avolio, B. J., & Eagly, A. H. (2017). Leadership in applied psychology: Three waves of theory and research. *Journal of Applied Psychology, 102*(3), 434.

Lord, R. G., & Hall, R. J. (2005). Identity, deep structure and the development of leadership skill. *The Leadership Quarterly, 16,* 591–615.

Lord, R. G., & Maher, K. J. (1991). *Leadership and information processing: Linking perceptions and performance.* Boston, MA: Unwin-Hyman.

Lyness, K. S., & Heilman, M. E. (2006). When fit is fundamental: Performance evaluations and promotions of upper-level female and male managers. *Journal of Applied Psychology, 91,* 777–785.

Martinko, M. J., Harvey, P., & Douglas, S. C. (2007). The role, function, and contribution of attribution theory to leadership: A review. *The Leadership Quarterly, 18*(6), 561–585.

McCall, Jr., M. W., Lombardo, M. M., & Morrison, A. (1988). *The lessons of experience.* Lexington, MA: Lexington Books.

McCauley, C. D., Eastman, L. J., & Ohlott, P. J. (1995). Linking management selection and development through stretch assignments. *Human Resource Management, 34*(1), 93–115.

McClelland, D. C. (1985). *Human motivation,* Glenview, IL: Scott, Foresman.

McClelland, D. C., & Boyatzis, R. E. (1982). The leadership motive pattern and long-term success in management. *Journal of Applied Psychology, 67*(6), 737–743.

McGuire, J. B., & Rhodes, G. B. (2009). *Transforming your leadership culture.* San Francisco, CA: John Wiley & Sons.

Miner, J. B. (1977). *Motivation to manage: A ten-year update on the "studies in management education" research.* Atlanta, GA: Organizational Measurement Systems Press.

Nicholson, N. (2013). *The 'I' of leadership: Strategies for seeing, being and doing.* Chichester, England: John Wiley.

Olivero, G., Bane, D. K., & Kopelman, R. E. (1997). Executive coaching as a transfer of training tool: Effects on productivity in a public agency. *Public Personnel Management, 26,* 461–469.

Podsakoff, P. M., MacKenzie, S. B., Ahearne, M., & Bommer, W. H. (1995). Searching for a needle in a haystack: Trying to identify the illusive moderators of leadership behaviours. *Journal of Management, 21,* 423–470.

Prideaux, G., & Ford, J. E. (1988). Management development: Competencies, teams, learning contracts and work experience-based learning. *Journal of Management Development, 7,* 13–21.

Ragins, B. R., & Cotton, J. L. (1993). Gender and willingness to mentor in organizations. *Journal of Management, 19,* 97–111.

Rauch, C. F., & Behling, O. (1984). Functionalism: Basis for an alternate approach to the study of leadership. In J. G. Hunt, D. M. Hosking, C. A. Schriesheim, & R. Stewart (Eds.), *Leaders and managers: International perspectives on managerial behavior and leadership* (pp. 45–62). New York, NY: Pergamon Press.

Richards, D., & Engle, S. (1986). After the vision: Suggestions to corporate visionaries and vision champions. In J. D. Adams (Ed.), *Transforming leadership* (pp. 199–214). Alexandria, VA: Miles River Press.

Rynes, S. L., Bartunek, J. M., Dutton, J. E., & Margolis, J. D. (2012). Care and compassion through an organizational lens: Opening up new possibilities. *Academy of Management Review, 37,* 503–523.

Salas, E., & Cannon-Bowers, J. A. (2000). The anatomy of team training. In L. Tobias & D. Fletcher (Eds.), *Handbook on research in training.* New York, NY: Macmillan.

Schein, E. H. (1992). *Organizational culture and leadership* (2nd ed.). San Francisco, CA: Jossey-Bass.

Seifert, C., Yukl, G., & McDonald, R. (2003). Effects of multi-source feedback and a feedback facilitator on the influence behavior of managers toward subordinates. *Journal of Applied Psychology, 88*(3), 561–569.

Stogdill, R. M. (1948). Personal factors associated with leadership: A survey of the literature. *Journal of Psychology, 25,* 35–71.

Stogdill, R. M. (1974). *Handbook of leadership: A survey of the literature.* New York, NY: Free Press.

Tannenbaum, S. I., Salas, E., & Cannon-Bowers, J. A. (1996). Promoting team effectiveness. In M. A. West (Ed.), *Handbook of work group psychology* (pp. 503–529). Chichester, England: Wiley.

Tannenbaum, S. I., & Yukl, G. (1992). Training and development in work organizations. In P. R. Rozenzwig and L. W. Porter (Eds.), *Annual review of psychology* (pp. 399–441). Palo Alto, CA: Annual Reviews.

Van Velsor, E., McCauley, C. D., & Ruderman, M. N. (Eds.). (2010). *The center for creative leadership handbook of leadership development* (3rd ed.). San Francisco, CA: Jossey-Bass.

Wagner, R. J., Baldwin, T. T., & Roland, C. (1991). Outdoor training: Revolution or fad? *Training & Development Journal, 45*(3), 1991, 50–57.

West, M. A., & Chowla, R. (2017). Compassionate leadership for compassionate health care. In P. Gilbert (Ed.), *Compassion: Concepts, research and applications* (pp. 237–257). London, England: Routledge.

West, M. A., Dawson, J. F., Admasachew, L., & Topakas, A. (2011). *NHS staff management and health service quality: Results from the NHS Staff Survey and related data* (Report to the Department of Health). Retrieved from www.dh.gov.uk/health/2011/08/nhs-staff-management/

West, M. A., Topakas, A., & Dawson, J. F. (2014). Climate and culture for health care performance. In B. Schneider & K. M. Barbera (Eds.), *The Oxford handbook of organizational climate and culture* (pp. 335–359). Oxford, England: Oxford University Press.

Whitely, W. T., & Coetsier, P. (1993). The relationship of career mentoring to early career outcomes. *Organization Studies, 14*(3), 419–441.

Yukl, G. (2010). *Leadership in organizations* (7th ed.). Upper Saddle River, NJ: Pearson Prentice Hall.

Yukl, G. (2013a). *Leadership in organizations* (8th ed.). Upper Saddle River, NJ: Pearson Prentice Hall.

Yukl, G. (2013b). Effective leadership behavior: What we know and what questions need more attention. *Academy of Management Perspectives, 26*, 66–85.

CHAPTER 12
TEAMS AND TEAMWORK

> ### LEARNING OBJECTIVES
> - Explain what a work team is and be able to distinguish between real teams and other organizational groupings.
> - Identify what is and is not an appropriate task for a team to perform.
> - Understand the relationships between teamworking and key outcomes.
> - Understand the factors influencing the performance of teams.
> - Understand how to develop effective teamworking.

Think of a group of humans working together; some examples are:

- Early humans on the savannah 80,000 years ago, working together to catch an antelope so they could eat and survive.
- A lifeboat crew working to rescue a couple from a floundering yacht in a storm.
- A top management group, trying to ensure their company increases productivity and profitability so they can stay in business through a recession.
- Breast cancer care professionals working together to correctly diagnose and determine the best possible treatment for a mother who shows symptoms.
- A group of academics located in five different countries who are conducting a cross-national study of the effectiveness of virtual teamworking.
- A production cell, manufacturing the fascia of car dashboards for three different automotive companies and involving 20 different designs.
- An international women's football team, working to claw back a 2–0 deficit from the first round of the World Cup.

What they have in common is that they are trying to achieve shared objectives by working interdependently, communicating about their work together, playing specific roles in the process and sharing responsibility for the outcome of their work together. They are teams.

WHAT IS A TEAM?

What do we mean by a 'team'? It might be argued that the fans at the football game are a team; so are the rest of the people in the hospital or all of those working in the manufacturing company. As in many areas of social science, definitions are slippery (see Delarue, Van Hootegem, Procter, & Burridge, 2008; Hackman, 1987; Rasmussen & Jeppesen, 2006; West & Lyubovnikova, 2012; West, Tjosvold, & Smith, 2005, for debates on definitions of teams).

Our definition is:

> *A team is a relatively small group of people working on a clearly defined, challenging task that is most efficiently completed by a group working together rather than individuals working alone or in parallel; who have clear, shared, challenging, team-level objectives derived directly from the task; who have to work closely and interdependently to achieve these objectives; whose members work in distinct roles within the team (though some roles may be duplicated); and who have the necessary authority, autonomy and resources to enable them to meet the team's objectives.*

Unpacking this definition, we can see that members of the team have shared objectives in relation to their work – rescuing yachters, catching food, winning games, successfully diagnosing and treating breast cancer. Second, they have sufficient autonomy and control so that they can make the necessary team decisions about how to achieve their objectives. Third, they have both responsibility and accountability – they have to decide the tactics and put them into operation, so it is down to them if it doesn't work out. Fourth, they are dependent upon and must interact with each other in order to achieve their shared objectives. They have to discuss strategy, tactics and roles and adapt their individual work depending on what others in the team do. Fifth, they have an organizational identity as a work group with a defined organizational function (e.g. the HR team responsible for all aspects of personnel management). Finally, they are not so large that they would be defined more appropriately as an organization, which has an internal structure of vertical and horizontal relationships characterized by sub-groupings. In practice, this is likely to mean that a team is smaller than 10–15 members. Research evidence generally suggests that teams should be as small as possible to achieve their objectives efficiently, and ideally should be no bigger than six to eight members (Hackman, 2002).

Kozlowski and Ilgen (2006, p. 79) describe teams as:

> *(a) two or more individuals who; (b) socially interact (face-to-face or, increasingly, virtually); (c) possess one or more common goals; (d) are brought together to perform an organizationally relevant tasks; (e) exhibit interdependencies with respect to workflow, goals, and outcomes; (f) have different roles and responsibilities; and (g) are together embedded in an encompassing organizational system, with boundaries and linages to the broader system context and task environment.* (p. 79)

Both definitions refer to shared objectives and task interdependence. However, our definition focuses more on group-level features, such as autonomy, identity, teams' roles and cooperation, whereas Kozlowski and Bell's (2003) definition takes a more organizational-level perspective, looking at how the team interacts with, and is influenced by, the wider organization, a theme we will return to later. Both definitions offer useful and complementary perspectives in understanding teams.

Salas, Rosen, Burke, and Goodwin (2009) suggest that there are five core components of teamwork. The first is leadership, which incorporates the search for and structuring of information to help the team perform its task; the use of information to solve problems; the management of team members; and the management of resources (e.g. IT). Leadership may also be shared when the leadership function is transferred between members for particular tasks, depending on who has the knowledge, skills and abilities (KSAs) to enable the team to perform a particular task. Second is adaptability, which is the team's ability to adapt its performance processes in response to changes or cues in the environment. Third is mutual performance monitoring between team members to ensure teamwork is on track. Fourth is 'backup behaviour' – team members supporting each other when they have a workload problem. Fifth is team orientation, which refers to the team's robustness in maintaining effective teamwork even under pressure or stress. These components are facilitated by three coordination mechanisms: first, shared mental models, which are knowledge structures or representations of the team's work, processes or environment that are shared or distributed (to a greater or lesser extent) throughout the team and enable them to work in a compatible way. The second coordination mechanism is closed-loop communications, whereby a message is sent by team members, received by other team members and followed up by the sender to ensure the message was appropriately received and interpreted. The third is mutual trust, which exists when team members can rely on each other to do what they say they will do and when they support each other in their shared endeavour (see Dinh & Salas 2017).

Because many people report working in very large teams or in teams that do not have clear objectives, or whose members do not meet regularly, researchers have argued that what are often called 'teams' in organizations are in reality only 'pseudo teams' (Dawson, Yan, & West, 2008; West & Lyubovnikova, 2012), and such pseudo teams may lead to ineffectiveness rather than effectiveness in organizations.

'Real' versus 'pseudo' teams

A typical example of a pseudo team is where employees report that they are part of a team, but observation reveals that they merely work in close proximity to each other and have the same supervisor. Hackman (2002) argues that in such cases these are not real teams, as their task does not require them to work together collectively, nor are all members accountable for the task's completion. A team is a 'real' team when team members work closely and interdependently towards clear, shared objectives. Real teams also have regular and effective communication, usually in the form of team meetings, in which they reflect upon their performance and how it could be improved.

In contrast, pseudo teams do not have clear goals, or team members do not communicate, or team members do not work interdependently to achieve team goals. In these groups, members are less likely to be satisfied, committed and effective, and there are likely to be high error rates and low effectiveness. Indeed, in healthcare settings, research suggests that the more people who work in pseudo teams, the higher the levels of errors that could harm patients or staff, the higher the levels of violence by patients or their carers towards staff, and the poorer the quality of patient care, resulting in higher levels of patient mortality (Lyubovnikova, West, Dawson, & Carter, 2015). Having clarified the distinction between real teams and pseudo teams, it is helpful to consider the different types of (real) teams we find in organizations.

Types of teams in organizations

There are multiple types of teams in organizations, which can be grouped into categories such as these:

- Strategy and policy teams, e.g. management decision-making teams; university committees setting standards on teaching quality; politicians at cabinet level deciding on how to reduce carbon emissions in the nation's cars.
- Production teams, e.g. manufacturing assembly teams in a company producing mobile phones; production process teams in an aluminium smelting company; bottling teams in a brewery; teams in a garden nursery that grow plants and display them ready for sale.
- Service teams, e.g. teams that service photocopiers in client organizations; radiography teams in hospitals; advice centre teams for a computer sales organization; healthcare teams in primary care.
- Project and development teams, e.g. research teams; new product development teams; software development teams; problem-solving teams trying to determine the cause of defects in a carbon fibre coating system.
- Action and performing teams, e.g. surgical teams; negotiation teams; cockpit crews in commercial airliners; ambulance teams; firefighting teams; lifeboat crews; football teams; string quartets and rock bands.
- It is also important to recognize that in modern organizations teams may form and disband frequently and rapidly and that team members may be spread across multiple sites while working in several different teams simultaneously. Tasks may vary enormously and change significantly over time too.

Key dimensions on which they differ include:

- Degree of permanence – project teams have a defined lifetime that can vary from weeks to years; cockpit 'teams' are together for only hours.
- Emphasis on skill/competence development – breast cancer care teams must continually develop their skills over time to a high level, whereas decision-making committees usually have little emphasis on skill development.
- Genuine autonomy and influence – manufacturing assembly teams may have little autonomy and influence, whereas top management teams have considerable discretion and are powerful.
- Level of task from routine through to strategic – short-haul airline flights involve crews in routine tasks, whereas a government cabinet may be determining penal strategy for a ten-year period.

A very different approach to understanding the structure of teams is offered by an organizing framework (Hollenbeck, Beersma, & Shouten, 2012) that identifies three underlying dimensions that can be used to describe work teams: *skill differentiation, temporal stability* and *authority differentiation*. First, skill differentiation describes the extent to which members of a team have specialist knowledge, expertise or functional capabilities, which would make it difficult to interchange team member roles or substitute team members. Some may be described as unidisciplinary, such as a group of paediatric nurses working together in a hospital ward. Interdisciplinary (also referred to as multiprofessional/cross-disciplinary) teams are composed of members from a range of different occupational groups and disciplines with high levels of knowledge and skill differentiation. The second dimension is temporal stability, which refers to the extent to which a team has a history and is likely to remain intact in the future. Membership stability is argued to facilitate the development of shared mental models regarding both task and teamwork processes. The third team descriptor is authority differentiation, referring to the degree to which decision-making power lies with the team as a whole or individual members/subgroups who occupy leadership roles. Research has shown that a hierarchical authority structure, in combination with a culture deeply rooted in individual professional autonomy and poor communication, can create barriers to establishing a safe culture in healthcare teams.

Implicit in this exploration of types of teams is that there are certain tasks that are best performed by teams and others that are best performed by individuals or groups of individuals working serially or in parallel. The second learning objective of this chapter is to understand what tasks are best performed by teams.

WHAT DO TEAMS DO?

The point of having a team is to get a job done, a task completed, a set of objectives met, whether it is catching an antelope for meat, rescuing people at sea or developing a business strategy for financial survival. When teams are created to perform a task, the tasks they perform should be tasks that are best performed by a team. Building a house does not necessarily require the bricklayers to work interdependently and in close communication over decisions. Each of those laying bricks simply needs to know which is his or her section of the wall. On the other hand, a team of chefs preparing a dinner for 80 people will have to work very closely together with a high degree of communication and coordination to ensure the diners have a good dinner. Similarly, sports teams are called teams since they have to work interdependently, to communicate constantly, to understand each other's roles and to collectively implement a strategy in order to achieve their goal of winning.

What tasks are best performed by teams rather than individuals? The following dimensions can be used to analyze the appropriateness of tasks in organizations for teamwork:

- *Completeness, i.e. whole tasks* – not simply putting the studs on the car wheels but assembling the whole transmission system plus wheels. Just doing a small and routine element of a task is not motivating or enjoyable, nor does it require a team.
- *Varied demands* – the task requires a range of skills that are held or best developed by a number of different individuals, such as a hotel conference centre team, requiring audio-visual technical skills, planning skills, sales and marketing skills and people management skills.
- *Requirements for interdependence* – the task requires people to work together in interdependent ways, communicating, sharing information and debating decisions about the best way to do the job (as in the case of the breast cancer care team described earlier).
- *Task significance* – the importance of the task in contributing to the achievement of organizational goals or to the benefit of the wider society. Examples are a top management team in a £25 million turnover company or a crisis management team set up following a natural disaster that is working to provide shelter, food and safety for hundreds of people.
- *Opportunities for learning* – providing team members with chances to develop and stretch their skills and knowledge because the task demands and offers that.
- *Developmental possibilities for the task* – the task can be developed to offer more challenges to the team members, requiring them to take on more responsibility and learn new skills over time.
- *Autonomy* – the amount of freedom teams have over how to do their work, ranging from when and how often to have review days (during which they stop work to reflect, plan and take action) through to offering new products and services they have developed and to hiring new staff.

Working in teams is challenging, takes hard work, careful thought and may involve interpersonal conflict. Why would organizations therefore invest resources in teamworking if it is difficult? This brings us to the third learning objective: to understand how teamworking affects organizational performance.

WHY WORK IN TEAMS?

Why do modern organizations use teams as a means of structuring work and what evidence is there for their value? Teams have been used to accomplish large, complex tasks that individuals working alone cannot take on. Moreover, they offer the potential for innovation in responding to the requirements of customers and the demands of fast-changing environments. According to Cohen and Bailey (1997), there are several reasons for implementing team-based working:

- *Teams* are the best way to enact organizational strategy. Authority for decisions can be devolved to teams, rather than being taken by senior managers, and teams can respond quickly and effectively in the fast-changing environments most organizations encounter.
- *Teams* enable organizations to *speedily develop and deliver products and services* cost-effectively. Teams can work faster and more effectively with members working in parallel and interdependently whereas individuals working serially and separately are much slower.
- Teams *enable organizations to learn* (and retain learning) more effectively. When one team member leaves, the learning of the team is not lost. Team members also learn from each other during the course of teamworking.
- Cross-functional teams promote *improved quality management*. By combining team members' diverse perspectives, decision-making is better because team members can question ideas and decisions about how best to provide products and services to clients.
- Cross-functional design teams can undertake *radical change*. The breadth of perspective offered by cross-functional teams produces the questioning and integration of diverse perspectives that enables teams to challenge basic assumptions and make radical changes to improve their products, services and ways of working.
- *Creativity and innovation* are promoted within team-based organizations through the cross-fertilization of ideas (West, Tjosvold, & Smith, 2003).

Does teamworking really produce the goods? Delarue et al. (2008) reviewed the research evidence on the links between team-based working and various outcomes (operational, financial, structural and worker). They concluded that there were significant positive associations. Levine and D'Andrea-Tyson (1990) also found that employee participation leads to sustained increases in productivity and that teams effectively enable such participation. Cohen, Ledford, and Spreitzer (1996) reported associations between teamworking and both efficiency and quality when a work organization developed teams whose members were given a voice in decision-making. In a review of 12 large-scale surveys and 185 case studies of managerial practices, Applebaum and Batt (1994) concluded that team-based working led to improvements in organizational performance. A number of other surveys have also reported links between team-based working and improvements in both labour productivity and quality (e.g. Banker, Field, Schroeder, & Sinha, 1996; Batt, 1999; Benders & Van Hootegem, 1999; Elmuti, 1997; Mathieu, Gilson, & Ruddy, 2006; Paul & Anantharaman, 2003; Procter & Burridge, 2004; Stewart & Barrick, 2000; Tata & Prasad, 2004; West, Brodbeck, & Richter, 2004). Positive effects of teamwork on productivity have been recorded in settings as diverse as US steel mills (Boning, Ichniowski, & Shaw, 2001), the US apparel industry (Dunlop & Weil, 1996) and the Australian economy (Glassop, 2002). Overall, research suggests that well-managed teamwork is likely to have a positive impact on performance (Delarue et al., 2008).

There are similarly positive relationships between teamwork and financial outcomes. In a meta-analysis of 131 field studies on organizational change, Macy and Izumi (1993) found that interventions with the largest effects upon financial measures of organizational performance were team development interventions. Zwick's (2004) study of German organizations showed that economic value increased after the introduction of teamwork. Another meta-analysis of 61 independent samples found that teamworking had a significant though small positive relationship with both performance outcomes and staff attitudes (Richter, Dawson, & West, 2011). The analyses showed that teamworking had a stronger relationship with performance outcomes if accompanied by complementary HR measures.

A core purpose of team-based working is to decentralize decision-making to lower levels in the organization (Bacon & Blyton, 2000). Organizations that use self-managing work groups have been shown to be less hierarchical in structure and to have a broader span of control (Glassop, 2002). This enables them to be more adaptive and agile in response to changes in their environments, since there are fewer levels in decision-making to be negotiated when changes are proposed.

Do those working in teams feel more satisfied at work? In a survey of Canadian employees, Godard (2001) found that team-based working was associated with job satisfaction, empowerment, commitment, citizenship, task involvement and belongingness. Why should this be so? The activity of a group of people working cooperatively to achieve shared goals via differentiation of roles and using elaborate systems of communication is basic to our species. We have worked this way throughout most of our evolutionary history. Human beings work and live in groups because groups originally enabled survival and reproduction (Ainsworth, 1989; Buss, 1991). By living and working in groups, early humans could share food, easily find mates and care for infants. They could hunt more effectively and defend themselves against their enemies. Individuals who did not readily join groups would be disadvantaged in comparison with group members as a consequence (West, 2001). 'Over the course of evolution, the small group became the survival strategy developed by the human species' (Barchas, 1986, p. 212). The benefits of teamworking are therefore not only improved task performance (West, 1996), but also emotional benefits for team members (Carter & West, 1999; Patterson & West, 1999). It follows that organizations that make extensive use of teamworking have lower levels of employee turnover (Glassop, 2002), and reduced absenteeism (Delarue, Van Hootegem, Huys, & Gryp, 2004).

Overall, therefore, the evidence suggests that teamworking contributes to organizational performance in positive ways. But as the comments earlier in this chapter suggested, this is likely to be dependent on (or mediated by) how well the team works together. This brings us to our fourth learning objective – to understand the factors influencing the performance of teams. Critical to influencing the performance of teams are 'inputs' and 'team processes'. We will now turn to consider these.

WHAT MAKES AN EFFECTIVE TEAM?

What models might help us understand the functioning of teams, from lifeboat crews to top management teams to football teams? The model of choice over the past 30 years is the input–process–output (IPO) model (see Figure 12.1). More sophisticated representations can be used to guide research and practice (see Mathieu, Maynard, Rapp, & Gilson, 2008 for this and for a valuable review of research on team effectiveness), but the value of the IPO model is that it shows the relationships between team inputs and outputs. It also proposes that team processes mediate input–output relationships – team inputs (such as team member skills) affect team processes (such as communication) and thereby have an effect on outputs.

Figure 12.1   An input-output model of team performance

For example, having team members with diverse knowledge and experience leads to more informed and better decision-making and therefore to higher levels of team effectiveness. Moreover, inputs also directly affect outputs – having sufficient resources enables the team to respond quickly to customer orders, making the team more effective.

Figure 12.1 describes the broad categories of factors that influence team effectiveness and team-based working – the inputs, processes and outputs. In addition the figure shows the four core dimensions of inputs, the seven dimensions of processes and the five key dimensions of the outputs. Each of these 16 components is an important element of what influences team effectiveness and the effectiveness of team-based working across an organization.

Before describing the IPO model in detail, it is useful to have in mind the key criticisms of this approach. There are two. First, IPO models have been criticized for simplifying too far the complex processes of teamwork. Teams have multiple concurrent performance episodes that overlap, so there are often quite different processes occurring at the same time. Critics suggest that the IPO model should be used to understand each of these separately, not simply sum them all to present a rather simplistic picture of the team. Moreover, the model does not incorporate a feedback loop from outputs to inputs and processes, but clearly learning and change are consequences of performance and other outcomes. Second, the model is criticized because it takes too broad a time slice and offers a static picture that ignores the long-term development of the team. Teams learn, develop and mature over time and this is neglected in IPO models (Salas et al., 2009). An alternative model that answers these criticisms (and is aimed at researchers rather than practitioners) is the input–mediator–output–input framework (Ilgen, Hollenbeck, Johnson, & Jundt, 2005; Mathieu et al., 2008; Grossman, Friedman, & Kalra, 2017). The elements of the IPO model are now described in more detail.

TEAM INPUTS

Team task

Inputs include the most important aspect of any model of team – the task a team is required to perform. The task determines team members' roles, collective goals, task-related interactions and team coordination, and workflow processes (Kozlowski & Ilgen, 2006; see Table 12.1). We reviewed key dimensions of team tasks above. However, another very useful approach is offered by Mathieu, Hollenbeck, van Knippenberg, and Ilgen (2017), who distinguish between two dimensions of tasks: scope and complexity. Scope refers to the number of component acts that go into completion of the task. Complexity is sub-divided into component complexity, dynamic complexity and coordinative complexity. The first refers to the amount of information needed for decision-making and the variety of skills needed to implement decisions (a lifeboat crew, for example); dynamic complexity is the degree to which these components change over time (think of aid workers following a humanitarian disaster); and coordination complexity is indicated by the level of interdependence between components of the task and issues of sequencing and timing (imagine a highly complex surgical operation).

Table 12.1 Team inputs

Dimension	Components

Task design	Complete task
	    Autonomy
	    Task relevance
	    Feedback
	    Interdependence
	    Task complexity

Team effort and skills	Team member motivation and effort Appropriateness of team members' skill to the task in hand Team potency – team members' belief in likelihood of the team's ability to succeed
Organizational support	Information and communication Training for teamworking Climate in support of teamworking
Resources	Material and human resources, e.g. IT support, administrative support

Key dimensions of teamwork include degree of permanence; emphasis on skill/competence development; genuine autonomy and influence; level of task from routine through to strategic. Tasks best performed by teams have high levels of the following characteristics: completeness, varied demands, requirements for interdependence, task significance, opportunities for learning, developmental possibilities for the task, and autonomy.

Team composition

How do we go about selecting the right people for the team? We address this question by first asking whether diversity of team composition is an advantage or disadvantage. Then we consider the personalities of team members, their social skills and their teamwork KSAs. A key principle is focusing on the skills required to perform the task. If a hospital manager wishes to create a team that will provide breast cancer care services, he or she needs to ensure access to the skills to investigate biopsies and offer a diagnosis (a medical oncologist), operative skills for conducting biopsies and removing cancerous growths (a breast surgeon), the skills to undertake nursing care pre- and post-operatively (breast cancer care nurse) and the skills to provide ongoing support to someone recovering at home (such as a medical social worker). Research into team composition has focused increasingly on aspects other than task skills, including mix of personalities, gender, cognitive style, values, goals, affect and task cognitions (Mathieu et al., 2017 – for a comprehensive review see Wolfson & Mathieu, 2017). Research on diversity has also considered the effects of dissimilarity in personality, information and perspectives, demographic attributes, tenure and educational background (see Meyer, 2017). There is growing knowledge too about 'fault lines' – where multiple forms of diversity align to create robust sub-divisions that exacerbate problems in teams (Meyer, 2017). An example is demographic minorities all being new in the team and occupying the same functional role (women as HR specialists on the top management team, for example).

KEY THEME

Diversity – team diversity

A key issue to understand in composing teams is whether heterogeneity (or diversity) is advantageous or disadvantageous to teams and their members. Is it better to put together a team whose members are very different from each other? This may be in relation to observable characteristics such as age, gender, ethnicity or status in the organization; or to underlying dimensions such as skills, attitudes, experience; or even personality. Or is team functioning disadvantaged by such diversity?

Van Knippenberg and Schippers (2007) have reviewed the effects of team diversity on team performance. They define diversity as the degree to which there are objective or subjective differences between people within the team and conclude that we can view diversity from two theoretical perspectives.

The first is an Information/Decision-making Perspective. This suggests:

- Diversity is an informational resource since it creates a bigger pool of information for a team to draw from in its decision-making.
- Consequently this offers the prospect of better problem-solving, decision quality, creativity and innovation.
- Diversity is therefore good for performance.

The second, and competing, perspective is a Social Categorization Perspective that suggests:

- Diversity is a source of intergroup bias – we distinguish between those who are like us and not like us in our team and biases develop between 'us' and 'them'.
- This intergroup bias produces less liking for, trust in and cooperation with dissimilar

others in our team and leads to poor communication, interpersonal challenges, misunderstandings and incivility.

- This creates conflict, suspicion and lack of trust, and disrupts performance.

For the most part, the evidence suggests that diversity, when well managed through good team processes (such as clarifying objectives, clear roles, good communication and regular reviews of team effectiveness), leads to performance gains rather than losses in the long term (van Knippenberg et al., 2011). However, initial performance in heterogeneous teams is likely to be affected by process difficulties more than in homogeneous teams, and teams may never recover from this.

Research by van Knippenberg and his colleagues reveals that when team members believe in the value of diversity, diversity is more likely to have positive effects on team performance. The leader, in particular, plays a vital role in encouraging the development of positive beliefs about diversity in the team. Edmondson and Roloff (2009) argue that psychological safety and learning are key factors in effective collaboration in diverse teams.

Team size

The evidence suggests that teams should comprise the smallest number of members required to enable the team to accomplish its task. This is because having more team members than necessary leads to perceptions among team members that there is unequal distribution of workload and perceptions that some individuals are putting in more effort than others, creating feelings of resentment and reducing motivation (Hackman, 2002). And having more members than are needed is simply inefficient. Once the team gets above eight to ten members, coordination and communication become more difficult, and more formalized rules for working together have to be developed to ensure the team remains effective (West, 2012).

Personality and ability

How do people with different personalities work together in teams? This question has led to a variety of enormously popular models of team personality which suggest what mix of personalities is best for effective teams. The best known is Belbin's Team Roles Model, which proposes that a mix of team roles (dominant leader, facilitating leader, creative person, warm supporter, task completer, external networker) predicts team performance. This idea has intuitive appeal to managers, but researchers have found little or no supportive evidence. Moreover, the instruments developed to measure the team role types (Belbin, 1981, 1993) do not appear to have good psychometric properties (Anderson & Sleap, 2004; Furnham, Steele, & Pendleton, 1993).

Do more rigorous approaches suggest that a mix of personalities in teams predicts better team performance, or is it best for all team members to be agreeable people, primarily focused on getting on with other team members? The 'Big Five' model of personality (Goldberg, 1990; see Chapter 2) offers a robust personality model that we can use to analyze the mix of personalities in teams and the effects on team performance. The model describes five dimensions of personality:

- Extraversion – positive emotions, gregariousness and warmth.
- Agreeableness – trust, straightforwardness and tender-mindedness.
- Conscientiousness – competence, order and self-discipline.
- Emotional stability versus Neuroticism – calmness and stability versus anxiety, self-consciousness and vulnerability.
- Openness to experience – fantasy, actions and ideas.

Research evidence suggests that the particular personality dimensions that predict team effectiveness depend on the type of task. In interdependent teams where individual contributions to team success are easily recognized and rewarded, hardworking and dependable team members are most successful (Barrick, Stewart, Neubert, & Mount, 1998; Mount, Barrick, & Stewart, 1998). High levels of Conscientiousness accompanied by low variability of this trait between team members are associated with team effectiveness. Other team members see these conscientious individuals as valued team members because they can be relied upon to perform their part of the work. Conscientiousness is particularly important in team settings because hierarchical control is reduced, so there is a need for self-discipline.

Having high levels of Agreeableness *per se* in teams does not appear to be related to team performance, but having any very disagreeable individual in a team undermines effectiveness. One aggressive or manipulative member or someone who is low in Conscientiousness (and so does not pull their weight) can dramatically undermine team performance (de Dreu & Weingart, 2003). Task conflict is managed better in teams with high levels of Emotional Stability and Openness (Bradley, Klotz, Postlethwaite, & Brown, 2013). Teams with high levels of Extraversion are good at decision-making (for example management teams), probably because their warmth and optimism helps them in persuading others to accept their decisions. For teams requiring creative decisions or innovation, Openness rather than Conscientiousness or Extraversion is likely to be important. In general, however, the research evidence suggests that *teams composed of conscientious people with high levels of Extraversion are likely to be most effective.*

Teamwork skills

When we create teams, we need to consider the technical skills required to perform the task, such as a chemist, marketer and production specialist for an R&D team making cosmetics. However, we also need to consider other skills which we might label 'generic teamworking skills'. This includes people's preferences for working in teams; whether they have an individualist or collectivist approach to working with others; their basic social skills such as listening, speaking and cooperating; and their teamworking skills such as collaboration, concern for the team and interpersonal awareness. Do they express appreciation, build optimism, contribute to cohesion and enhance a sense of team potency?

Generic teamwork skills include social skills such as:

- Active listening skills – being able to listen to others and engage effectively in understanding their views and experiences.
- Communication skills – understanding how to communicate effectively, taking into account the receiver, the message and the appropriate medium; for example, email for routine communications, telephone conversation for more complex discussions and face-to-face for communications involving conflicts.
- Social perceptiveness – being aware of others' reactions and understanding why they react the way they do (this is often referred to as one dimension of 'emotional intelligence' – see Chapter 2).
- Self-monitoring – being sensitive to the effects of our behaviour on others (so called because it involves monitoring the effects of the self on others).
- Altruism – working to help colleagues without necessarily expecting reciprocity.
- Warmth and cooperation – smiles, appreciation, humour, support and small talk oil the wheels of teamwork.
- Patience and tolerance – accepting criticism and dealing patiently with frustrations (Peterson, Mumford, Borman, & Jeanneret, 2001).

The application of such skills builds a sense of trust, safety and mutual respect in teams. Selecting team members for these skills or coaching them to develop these skills creates better conditions for team effectiveness.

Another way of thinking about generic skills for working in teams is in relation to the KSAs for teamwork. In teamwork settings, employees need the abilities to perform the job as individuals as well as the abilities to work effectively in a team, because both are important for team performance. Stevens and Campion (1994, 1999) propose that effective team functioning depends on teamwork abilities, focusing on team members' knowledge of how to perform in teams that extends beyond the requirements for individual job performance. Based on the literature on team functioning, they identified two broad skill areas (interpersonal KSAs and self-management KSAs), consisting of a total of 14 specific KSA requirements for effective teamwork (see Table 12.2).

Stevens and Campion (1999) also developed a 35-item multiple-choice test in which respondents are presented with scenarios they may face in the workplace and asked to identify the strategy they would most likely follow. Examples are shown in Box 12.1.

The researchers found that team members' scores on this test were significantly related to team performance in several studies (McDaniel, Morgeson, Finnegan, Campion, & Braverman, 2001). Regardless of their task specialism or their preferred team role, there are certain attributes that all team members need to demonstrate if the team is to achieve its goal according to this model, and that is teamwork KSAs. (The correct answers by the way are B, A and C.)

So far, in our consideration of team inputs we have focused on the team's task, the mix of team members, including the team size, the task-related skills of members, their personalities, social skills and teamworking KSAs. Now we move on to consider the organizational context within which teams function. If teams are seeds, the organization is the seed bed within which teams grow. If the bed is rocky and infertile, teams will fail. If the bed is correctly prepared and maintained, teams will thrive and flourish.

Table 12.2 Steven's and Campion's KSAs for Teamworking

1 Interpersonal team member KSAs

A conflict resolution
1. Fostering useful debate, while eliminating dysfunction conflict
2. Matching the conflict management strategy to the cause and nature of the conflict
3. Using integrative (win–win) strategies rather than distribution (win–lose) strategies

B Collaborative problem-solving
4. Using an appropriate level of participation for any given problem
5. Avoiding obstacles to team problem-solving (e.g. domination by some team members) by structuring how team members interact

C Communication
6. Employing communication that maximizes an open flow
7. Using an open and supportive style of communication
8. Using active listening techniques
9. Paying attention to non-verbal messages
10. Warm greeting to other term members, engaging in appropriate small talk, etc.

2 Self-management team KSAs

D Goal-setting and performance management
11. Selling specific, challenging and acceptable team goals
12. Monitoring, evaluating and providing feedback on performance

E Planning and task coordination
13. Coordinating and synchronizing tasks, activities and information
14. Establishing fair and balanced roles and workloads among team members

---

BOX 12.1
Example items from a measure for selection into teams

Suppose you find yourself in an argument with several co-workers about who should do a very disagreeable, but routine task. Which of the following would likely be the most effective way to resolve this situation?

A. Have your supervisor decide, because this would avoid any personal bias.

B. Arrange for a rotating schedule so everyone shares the chore.

C. Let the workers who show up earliest choose on a first-come, first-served basis.

D. Randomly assign a person to do the task and don't change it.

continued

Your team wants to improve the quality and flow of conversations among its members. Your team should:

- **A** Use comments that build upon and connect to what others have already said.
- **B** Set up a specific order for everyone to speak and then follow it.
- **C** Let team members with more say determine the direction and topic of conversation.
- **D** Do all of the above.

Suppose you are presented with the following types of goals. You are asked to pick one for your team to work on. Which would you choose?

- **A** An easy goal to ensure the team reaches it, thus creating a feeling of success.
- **B** A goal of average difficulty so the team will be somewhat challenged, but successful without too much effort.
- **C** A difficult and challenging goal that will stretch the team to perform at a high level, but attainable so that effort will not be seen as futile.
- **D** A very difficult or even impossible goal so that even if the team falls short, it will at least have a very high target to aim for.

KEY THEME

Digital technologies and virtual teams

During the past century we have seen seismic shifts in our capacities for communication, including the widespread use of first fixed and now mobile telephony, air travel, the use of email and the internet, videoconferencing, teleconferencing, fax, podcasts, vodcasts, television and radio as well as a variety of application-sharing devices. All of these developments have influenced the way we work in teams, but the pace of change has been far quicker than the pace of our understanding of how these changes affect teamwork.

Consider the following case study from Verifone. Verifone, Inc. produces electronic payment solutions – the technology you see when you go to pay at the till in your supermarket or to buy a train ticket at a railway station. Its principal products are point-of-sale, merchant-operated, consumer-facing and self-service payment systems for multiple industries, including banks, shops, hotels, petrol stations and pharmacies. Verifone uses virtual teams in every aspect of its operation, whether it is groups of facility managers working to reduce toxins in their offices, manufacturing procurement groups working together to buy semiconductors, or marketing and development teams developing ideas for new products. Verifone has systematically planned how to make best use of virtual teams and advocate key steps in the process. They do so through these steps:

- *Define a purpose* for the virtual team. Verifone believes that members of such teams need to know what the purpose is at the outset. They must then identify the information they need to clarify that purpose. The teams also ensure they are clear about the time required for a solution or output – at what point does the organization or its customers expect the team to have delivered? They also agree, as a team,

continued

what they will and won't try to achieve as a team, specifying clear boundaries around the task. Team members also discuss what technologies they can use to enable them to work effectively as a team, such as group decision support systems, desktop videoconferencing and email and for what purposes. They also specify very precisely what defines success for the team in its work. Every virtual team has a start-up checklist to complete to ensure these issues have all been effectively discussed and decided.

- Through specifying the *duration* of the virtual team's life and the team task, the different types of team are identified:
  - Short-term teams – these are teams whose task is usually completed within minutes or hours. Typically they would be solving a problem for a customer very quickly.
  - Problem-solving task teams – these are teams of diverse membership focused on responding to specific problems such as technical problems with equipment that perhaps repeatedly malfunctions. Engineers from across the world will work together to solve such problems.
  - Process improvement teams – these teams may be involved in finding ways of dramatically improving the efficiency and effectiveness of processes within the company, such as streamlining the sales-to-order process and reducing turnaround from order to delivery by half. There are at least 60 such teams within the organization at any one time, each with a clear leader, and reporting progress to the company top management team. These virtual process improvement teams underpin a culture of continuous improvement.
  - Long-term operational teams – an example is the profitability team, focused on ensuring continued financial success for the organization. All business unit controllers from around the world are members and they meet for an hour each week by videoconference to review financial forecasts. Company-wide forecasts are distributed to them in advance by email to ensure they have the necessary information to conduct effective financial planning as a team.

- *Recruit members* to the virtual team. At Verifone this is typically no fewer than three and no more than seven per team. Members have a range of experience, knowledge, skills and abilities and in some cases will live in different time zones. This enables the team to work over the course of a much longer day than the typical 9 a.m. to 5 p.m. working day.

- *Select technology tools* for the team. Technologies are selected and team members are trained in how to use them. Typically, for keeping in contact they use beepers, mobile phones and voice mail; for disseminating information, the technologies of choice are fax, email and application sharing over the company intranet; for decision-making they rely on email, conference calls and videoconferencing. Marketing teams use remote application sharing to see and comment on slides being presented (using webinar technologies). Problem-solving teams have follow-up conference calls daily to ensure they are on track and on target.

continued

Kirkman and Mathieu (2005) propose that virtuality can be described by three core dimensions: teams that make more use of *virtual tools*, make less use of *synchronous communication* (members communicating with each other simultaneously) and require less *informational richness* in their communication are *more* virtual. They also propose three input factors that further determine the level of virtuality: the *number of boundaries* to be crossed, *proportion of co-located members* and *team size*. The more boundaries to be crossed (organizational, geographic, time zones), the lower the proportion of co-located members; and the greater the number of team members, the more likely are teams to work virtually. As can be seen from Table 12.3 below, working virtually necessitates less synchronous communication, less informational richness and greater the use of virtual tools.

Table 12.3 M. A. West (2012). Effective Teamworking: Practical Lessons from Organizational Research

	Benefits of virtuality	Disadvantages of virtuality
Individual	Flexibility	Isolation
	More control over when to perform particular tasks	Decreased interpersonal contact with team members
	Work–non-work-life balance	Work–non-work-life balance
	Motivation from autonomy	Misunderstandings
	Empowerment	Conflicts
Team	Flexibility	Conflicts
	Short-term teams can easily be formed	Poor decision-making
	Selection of team members on basis of KSAs not location	Communication problems
	Bigger skill pool	Less productive and effective than co-located teams for some tasks
Organization	Around-the-clock working	Difficulties of supervision
	Speed	Costs of technologies
	Flexibility	Data security
	Reduced travel costs	Loss of organizational citizenship
	Close connection to suppliers	Additional training required
	Close connection to customers	

continued

Society	Development of poorer regions by creating virtual teams in those areas (e.g. rural)	Increase of isolation and alienation
		Invasion of work into home and family time
	Integration of disabled people into the workforce	Use of technology to increase monitoring and control of staff
	Integration of carers into the workforce who would otherwise not be able to participate	
	Reduction in traffic congestion and air pollution	
	Decrease in commuting time	

Organizational supports

Developing teamwork in organizations requires that the organization provide the right context for teamworking. For example, encouraging the development of teamworking in an organization that has a high level of bureaucracy and many rules and regulations is unlikely to be successful. Teams, because of their diverse perspectives, are innovative. If that innovation is stifled by excessive bureaucracy, teamwork will be stifled too. Below are some of the key characteristics that are required to sustain teamworking in organizations.

Organization structure: Vertical and horizontal linkages

In considering the structure of the organization, including the layout of the organization chart, it is important to consider the number of hierarchical levels within the organization. The simplest way of doing this is to count the number of levels from the most senior manager to the person who is lowest in the organization hierarchy, including both in the count. Where there are more than three levels in a small to medium-sized organization (between 20 and 250 employees), there may well be a case for considering reducing the number of layers to increase the effectiveness of teamworking.

Another important element of the structure of the organization is the degree of integration between departments and functions. To what extent do different departments and functions interact together, share information and have influence over each other's decision-making? Organizations are sometimes described as constructed in separate silos where finance, production and marketing (for example) do not cooperate or interact. There are tensions and conflicts between departments. In other organizations there are cross-functional teams which ensure effective pooling of knowledge and expertise and good communication to provide a seamless service to customers.

One reason for the introduction of team-based working is to improve the degree of integration between departments, functions and especially between teams. A high degree of integration within the organization supports effective team-based working since innovations (which almost always require cooperation across team boundaries) can be facilitated rather than blocked. Mechanisms to ensure teams and departments communicate, cooperate, share best practice and innovate across boundaries will enable effective team-based working, since teamworking is as much about bridging across teams as it is about bonding within teams. A simple way is requiring every team to have as one of its five or six objectives: *improving the effectiveness and supportiveness with which we work with other teams in the organization.*

Organization culture

Organizations can be described in terms of their cultures – the shared meanings, values, attitudes and beliefs of members (Schein, 1992; see Chapter 13). Surface manifestations of culture include: the number of levels in the hierarchy; pay levels (how big the gaps are between the highest and lowest paid, for example); how rigid or inspirational the job descriptions are; informal practices and norms such as 'dress-down Friday' when everyone comes in to work dressed more informally; espoused values and rituals, stories, jokes and jargon; and the physical environment. The introduction of team-based working in the organization requires that a number of key elements of culture are in place or are developed in parallel. These key elements are likely to include:

- trust
- communication
- involvement and participation
- support for training
- support for teamworking.

DISCUSS WITH A COLLEAGUE

Work with a colleague and discuss and decide why it is suggested that these five elements of culture are important for effective teamworking in organizations. Explain why you think each cultural element is important for effective teamworking and try to develop practical examples to illustrate your arguments:

- communication
- involvement and participation
- trust
- support for training
- support for teamworking.

Climate for team-based working

This requires a commitment within the organization to this way of working and an organizational climate which promotes team-based working. Supportive and challenging environments are likely to sustain high levels of team performance, especially those which encourage risk-taking and idea generation. Also important are egalitarianism and valuing innovation. Where climates are characterized by distrust, poor communication, personal antipathies, limited individual autonomy and unclear goals, the implementation of these ideas is inhibited. HRM systems should be geared to support teamworking. This includes recruiting for teamworking, socializing people for effective team and inter-teamworking, and appraisal and reward systems focused on teams.

Appraisal and performance review systems

In a team-based organization attention should be focused on the development of performance criteria against which teams can be measured. These include:

- *Team outcomes* – the team's performance, be it producing parts, treating patients, or providing customer service is likely to be best defined and evaluated by the 'customers' of the teams.

- *Team member growth and well-being* – the learning, development and satisfaction of team members. In well-functioning teams, members learn from each other constantly.
- *Team innovation* – the introduction of new and improved ways of doing things by the team. Teams, almost by definition, should be fountains of creativity and innovation since they bring together individuals with diverse knowledge, orientations, skills, attitudes and experiences in a collective enterprise, thus creating the ideal conditions for creativity (West, 2002).
- *Inter-team relations* – cooperation with other teams and departments within the organization. Teams must not only be cohesive, they must also cooperate and work effectively with other teams and departments (West & Markiewicz, 2004).
- *Team goal setting* – perhaps the most powerful component of appraisal is goal setting, and this applies no less to teams. The overall direction of a team's work – its purpose – should be clearly articulated by the team leader or the senior management team. This purpose should link tightly to the overall purpose of the organization. Team goals should be operationalized as six or seven clear, challenging and measurable objectives that team members have been involved in setting. Where clear goals and objectives are not set for teams in organizations, conflict and ineffectiveness are likely consequences.

Reward systems

To encourage a focus on effective teamworking, rewards should be based on team performance to some extent. Where such rewards are related to the achievement of predetermined team goals, rewards may then be distributed equally to each member of the team or they may be apportioned by senior management, by the team leader or in a manner determined by the team itself. It is worth noting, however, that where team rewards are used, team members who do not pull their weight are seen even more so than usual as 'free riders' and their failures lead to resentment and demotivation among other team members.

Using systems of team rewards to complement individual and organization-based rewards focuses staff on the importance of teamwork. But the reward system has to be seen as transparent and fair and as not inappropriately rewarding those who do not pull their weight. Of course, team rewards may not always involve money. The organization may provide team-level rewards in other forms, such as an away day in a luxury spa, dinner for the team or new office furniture or equipment.

These, then, are the inputs into teamworking – the elements that make up the construction of the boat. Now we turn to explore team processes or the sailing of the boat out on the seas.

TEAM PROCESSES

The essence of teamwork is team members integrating their activities to ensure successful achievement of the team's goals. These team processes are important in and of themselves, but they also affect how team members feel and think, both individually and collectively, as a result of their work in the team. Marks and colleagues (Marks, Mathieu, & Zaccaro, 2001) distinguish between *team processes* – 'the cognitive, verbal and behavioural activities directed towards organizing taskwork to achieve collective goals' – and *emergent states*, which are the cognitive, emotional and behavioural outcomes of team processes. They describe three types of team process: transition, action and interpersonal. Transition processes include analyzing the mission of the team, setting goals and formulating action plans (Scott & Wildman, 2017). In the action phases, team members focus on getting the task done, monitoring progress and ways of working, and coordinating with and backing up or supporting their team mates. Interpersonal processes include communication, managing conflict, creating positive climates, encouraging each other and building motivation and confidence. Leadership is critical in this. All are important processes for team effectiveness. The key elements of team processes are shown in Table 12.4.

Table 12.4 Team processes

Transition processes	
Dimension	**Components**
Objectives	Clarity of objectives
	Team members' commitment to the objectives
	Agreement within the team about the appropriateness of the objectives
Reflexivity	Reflection on performance
Action processes	
Dimension	**Components**
Participation	Decision-making
	Communication
	Regular meetings
	Trust, safety and support
Task focus	Customer/client focus
	Concern with quality of work or commitment to excellence
	Constructive debates about task performance
	Error management
	Practical support for innovation
Interpersonal processes	
Dimension	**Components**
Team conflict	Task-related conflict
	Process conflict
	Interpersonal conflict
Creativity and innovation	Climate for creativity and innovation

Emergent states include morale, confidence, sense of efficacy, empowerment and motivation. Emergent states also include shared mental models and transactive memory systems (the division of labour within a team with respect to the storage and retrieval of knowledge from different domains) that enable the team to function most effectively. Finally, emergent states also include affective tone (positive or negative), psychological safety and the sense of justice within the team (Mathieu et al., 2017).

We explore below these key team processes and consider how they influence the effectiveness of teams. We begin by considering transition processes, including team objectives and reflexivity.

Team objectives

Fundamental to good teamworking is clarifying the objectives of the team and ensuring that team members are both committed to these objectives and agree with them. Their objectives will be dependent upon the nature of the task they are required to perform – making car parts, delivering computer support, providing Accident and Emergency services or providing cabin service in an airliner. Clarifying the objectives requires that the team state clearly no more than six or seven measurable aims. There should be a limited number since this helps the team to both focus and prioritize and, given the limitations of human short-term memory, six or seven is a suitable maximum. These objectives should be stated in a way that enables their achievement to be measurable, and they should be challenging (Locke & Latham, 2013). However, team members should also be committed to these goals since commitment is associated with higher levels of motivation (hardly surprising), and commitment is stronger when team members have together agreed their objectives. All teams embedded in organizations should have one goal focused on improving their inter-team cooperation and effectiveness – how they work with other teams in the organization.

A useful test of the clarity of team objectives is to ask all team members to write down their team objectives, without consultation with each other, and check how well they agree. In many teams there is a very low level of agreement (beyond vague aspirations such as 'to be really effective as a team' or 'to deliver great customer service'), and this leads to ineffectiveness, mistakes and team member dissatisfaction.

Reflexivity

Team reflexivity is the extent to which team members collectively reflect upon the team's objectives, strategies and processes, as well as their wider organizations and environments, and adapt accordingly. After open-heart surgery, the team comes together and reviews their performance – what went well, what was problematic, what can we learn from this and what do we need to change for next time? There is increasing interest in this concept because it is seen as a means for developing teamwork generally (Schippers, Den Hartog, Koopman, & van Knippenberg, 2008; Schippers, West, & Dawson, 2015; Schippers, West, & Edmondson, 2017; Widmer, Schippers, & West, 2009).

Team reflexivity is conceptualized as a process involving three stages or components: *reflection*, *planning* and *action or adaptation*. The first stage, *team reflection*, refers to a team's joint exploration of work-related issues and includes behaviours such as questioning, planning, exploratory learning, analysis and reviewing past events. This is what a good sports team does at half time and at the end of the game.

The second stage, *planning*, refers to the activities that enable reflections to change into action or adaptation. Effective teams translate their insights about their functioning into plans for change and action (West, 2000). The third stage is *action or adaptation* – putting plans into action.

Non-reflexive teams show little awareness of team objectives, strategies and the environment in which they operate, and they tend to rely on the use of habitual routines. In other words, they tend to repeatedly exhibit a similar pattern of behaviour when problems arise, without explicitly discussing other possible ways of action. This lack of exploration of alternative hypotheses ultimately leads to stagnation, lack of innovation and inability to adapt to a changing environment.

Research in both experimental and field settings has found positive effects of team reflexivity on team performance (Schippers et al., 2008, 2012, 2017; Widmer et al., 2009). These effects were observed in samples comprising management, production and teams, coming from a variety of sectors, including banking, government, healthcare, the chemical industry and R&D. In these studies, the impact of team reflexivity is particularly powerful in teams with complex tasks working in dynamic, uncertain environments.

Schippers et al. (2017) propose that the factors promoting reflexivity are a clear team goal, psychological safety, team leadership coaching and expertise diversity (a wide range of skills in the team). They also suggest that moderate time pressure, task complexity and task interdependence (team members have to rely on each other to get the job done) promote reflexivity. They suggest that team reflexivity is a powerful way of overcoming the problems inherent in team-based knowledge work, described earlier:

> The human capacity to reflect is a valuable but often underused resource. Using this capacity to overcome group information processing problems can enable team productivity, innovation and effectiveness ... (p. 473.)

Action processes

Participation

Being part of a team involves participation, the essence of teamwork, which includes *interacting*, *information sharing*, and *decision-making*.

In order for a group of individuals who share a common goal to be called a team, they must have some degree of *interaction* through meetings, teleconferences, email interchange, etc., on a regular basis, otherwise their efforts are essentially uncoordinated and unaggregated. Interaction provides opportunities for exchanging information, communicating, building trust, giving each other feedback and just generally 'touching base', which enables the team to coordinate individual member efforts to achieve their shared goals. By meeting, communicating and interacting, they learn to dance the dance of teamwork better. Imagine how successful a sports team would be if it only met to play together once or twice a year, never discussed or compared tactics or gave each other feedback on performance or planned playing strategies. Virtual teams in particular are faced with many challenges of not interacting regularly other than via electronic media (Hertel, Geister, & Konradt, 2005).

Information in a team context is data that alter the understanding of the team as a whole and/or of individual team members. Within teams, the ideal way of communicating information is in face-to-face meetings, except for giving routine messages, which can be done via email or in other written forms. Of course, there is a temptation to avoid such direct communication since this takes time. In general, teams err on the side of electronic mail messages and communicate too little face-to-face. Yet the whole basis of teamwork is communication, coordination, cooperation and transfer of information in the richest possible form (Dinh & Salas, 2017).

A principal assumption behind the structuring of organizational functioning into work teams is that teams will make better decisions about performing their task than individual team members working alone. However, there is much research to show that teams are subject to social processes that undermine their decision-making effectiveness:

1 One is the tendency for team members to focus on and discuss information all team members share before the discussion starts, and to ignore new information that only one or two team members know about (the 'hidden profile' phenomenon). Even when those one or two members introduce this information into the discussion, team members are likely

to ignore it since it is not information they all already share. Teams can avoid it by ensuring that members have clearly defined roles so that each is seen as a source of potentially unique and important information; by members listening carefully to colleagues' contributions; and leaders ensuring that each team member's voice is heard (Stasser, Vaughan, & Stewart, 2000). Poor medical decision-making often occurs when the unique information about the patient's symptoms offered by one member of the team (often of lower status) is ignored by the others.

2 Team members tend to go along with the majority opinion and are thus susceptible to social conformity effects, causing them to withhold opinions and information contrary to the majority view (Brown, 2000).

3 The team may be dominated by loud, confident or aggressive individuals who take up disproportionate 'air time' (how long you speak for in team meetings). 'Air time' and expertise are positively correlated in high-performing teams and uncorrelated in teams that perform poorly. In other words, time speaking on a topic in high-performing teams is apportioned most to those who have most expertise on the particular topic.

4 Status and hierarchy effects can cause problems because some members' contributions can be valued and attended to disproportionately. Leaders' views will always tend to have an undue influence on the outcome. Good team leaders hold their views in abeyance until all other team members' views have been heard.

5 'Group polarization' refers to the tendency of work teams to make more extreme decisions than the average of individual members' opinions or decision. Team decisions tend to be either more risky or more conservative than the average of individuals members' opinions or decisions (Semin & Glendon, 1973; Walker & Main, 1973).

6 In his study of failures in policy decisions, social psychologist Irving Janis identified the phenomenon of 'groupthink', whereby tightly knit groups may err in their decision-making because they are more concerned with achieving agreement than with the quality of the decisions made. This can be especially threatening to organizational functioning where different departments see themselves as competing with one another, promoting 'in-group' favouritism and groupthink. The crash of the space shuttle *Columbia* has been attributed directly to problems of 'groupthink'. It is also likely to occur when the leader of the team is especially dominating. Margaret Thatcher and Donald Trump both tend(ed) to reject disagreement, leading to flawed decision-making and foreign policy failures (see for example Nicholson, 2013).

7 The social loafing effect is the tendency of individuals in teams to work less hard than they do when individual contributions can be identified and evaluated. In organizations, individuals may put less effort into contributing to high-quality decisions in meetings if they perceive that their contribution is hidden in overall team performance (Karau & Williams, 1993).

8 The study of idea generation in groups (sometimes called 'brainstorming groups') shows that the quantity and often the creativity of ideas produced by individuals working separately are consistently superior to those produced by a group working together. Individuals working alone generate about 50 per cent more ideas than those working in a group for an equivalent period of time. They also produce ideas of at least equivalent and usually superior creativity. This is due to a 'production-blocking' effect. Individuals are inhibited from both thinking of new ideas and offering them aloud to the group by the competing verbalizations of others (Diehl & Stroebe, 1987). Yet almost everyone in organizations goes straight into the process of idea generation in groups, resulting in poor performance. By simply giving all team members five minutes to quietly develop their own ideas before all share their ideas in the group, idea generation in groups ('brainstorming') would be much more effective.

Task focus

Teams that are more concerned with agreeing than with doing a good job are ineffective and potentially dangerous. Task focus is the team's practice of examining their team performance critically. Dean Tjosvold coined the term 'constructive controversy' to describe the conditions necessary for effective questioning within a team (Tjosvold, 1998). His work shows that when teams explore opposing opinions carefully and discuss them in a cooperative context, quality of decision-making and team effectiveness are better (see also West et al., 2003):

> *Controversy when discussed in a cooperative context promotes elaboration of views, the search for new information and ideas and the integration of apparently opposing positions.* (Tjosvold, 1991.)

Tjosvold believes that a lack of constructive controversy can lead to poor team decisions and tragedies such as the *Challenger* space shuttle disaster. In the latter case, engineers suppressed controversy over the appropriateness of launching the shuttle in cold weather, with tragic consequences. Constructive controversy has three elements: elaborating positions; searching for understanding; and integrating perspectives:

1 Elaborating positions: team members carefully describe their positions on the issue under discussion, explaining how they have come to their conclusions. They also indicate to what extent they are confident or uncertain about the positions they have adopted.

2 Searching for understanding: people with opposing viewpoints seek out more information about each other's positions and attempt to restate them as clearly as possible. There are attempts to explore areas of common ground in opposing positions along with an emphasis on personal regard for individuals whose positions oppose their own.

3 Integrating perspectives: team members work together to reach a solution based on shared, rational understanding rather than attempted dominance.

4 Finally, members strive for consensus by combining team ideas wherever possible rather than using techniques to reduce controversy, such as majority voting. Box 12.2 shows the conditions within which team constructive controversy can exist.

BOX 12.2

Positive Work – encouraging constructive controversy in teams

- Teams can encourage constructive controversy by coaching team members to explore all team members' views in an open-minded way, so that creative ideas emerge.

- Independent thinking is encouraged by having the team consider all team members' views and suggestions.

- Team members should consider all team members' views based on whether their proposals would improve the team's service to its clients. They then base judgements on quality, not (for example) on the status of the person proposing the idea.

- Team members should have vigorous and supportive discussions of alternatives since

continued

- such comprehensive decision-making encourages all team members to develop their critical thinking and to learn from each other in the course of teamwork.
- Team leaders can encourage team members not to focus on winning in the process of making decisions. They should be primarily concerned with making excellent decisions that lead to the best products or services for their clients.
- Constructive controversy does not exist when there are competitive team climates.
- If team members publicly question their colleagues' competence, destructive arguments about team decisions erupt and quality of decision-making suffers.
- Team members should build cooperative team climates, characterized by trust, supportiveness, safety and a professional approach to work.
- Leaders should also encourage team members to communicate their respect for each other's competence and commitment.

Error management

How teams manage errors is a good barometer of their ability to achieve a high level of task focus in the interests of their customers or clients. Team members and leaders can respond to an error by seeking whom to blame or by asking: 'What can we learn from this?' A good example of this principle is a study on safety in teams. Edmondson (1996) studied newly formed intensive-care nursing teams and their management of medication errors (giving too much or too little of a drug, or administering the wrong drug). In some groups, members openly acknowledged and discussed their medication errors and ways to avoid their occurrence. In others, members kept information about errors to themselves. Learning about the causes of these errors, as a team, and devising innovations to prevent future errors was only possible in groups of the former type. Edmondson (1996, 1999) argues that learning and innovation only take place where group members trust other members' intentions – in a climate of 'psychological safety'. Where this is the case, team members believe that well-intentioned action will not lead to punishment or rejection by the team. Psychological safety '… is meant to suggest a realistic, learning-oriented attitude about effort, error and change – not to imply a careless sense of permissiveness, nor an unrelentingly positive affect. Safety is not the same as comfort; in contrast, it is predicted to facilitate risk' (Edmondson, 1999, p. 14).

Having considered action processes that affect team functioning, we now explore interpersonal processes that determine the outcomes of teamworking in organizations.

Interpersonal processes

Underpinning all team interpersonal processes should be a sense of mutual trust, safety and support. Otherwise, teamworking is like swimming against the current. Where team members feel they may be attacked by colleagues (verbally or physically), teamwork will fail. Each team member has a responsibility to promote safety. This involves encouraging others to offer their views and then supportively exploring those ideas. Trust in teams is vital to team members' preparedness to cooperate (Costa & Anderson, 2017; Korsgaard, Brodt, & Sapienza, 2003). Safety, trust and support are also essential for the team to manage disagreements and enable helpful debates about the best way to achieve the team's objectives (Edmondson, 1999).

Team conflicts

We can identify three clear types of conflict in teams: task, relationship and process conflict. Task conflicts are disagreements about the content of tasks, while relationship conflicts stem from interpersonal incompatibilities and tensions (Greer & Dannals, 2017). Task conflicts can also spill over into relationship conflicts (Yu & Zellmer-Bruhn, 2018). Process conflicts refer to disagreements about the practicalities around task completion, including roles, responsibilities and work arrangements.

Task conflicts have the potential to impact positively upon team outcomes, according to meta-analyses (De Wit, Greer, & Jehn, 2012). But such conflicts have to be non-personal, effectively managed and in a context of psychological safety in teams (Greer & Dannels, 2017). Relationship conflicts generally have negative effects on team outcomes (performance, satisfaction, innovation, etc.). It may be best to avoid relationship conflicts in teams or to try to reduce emotionality. Teams with a history of conflict (even intense task conflict), strong fault lines or a history of negative events (such as negative performance feedback) are likely to experience more relationship conflicts. Process conflicts have the most detrimental effects on outcomes, rooted as they are in perceptions of justice and fairness. They are also linked to issues of power and control over resources (Greer & Dannels, 2017), and task conflicts often spill over into process conflicts. Often process conflicts mask unexpressed but underlying concerns as members express their frustration via process conflict with issues of leadership, values, hierarchy, team norms and structures.

Constructive conflict is desirable in teams (Deutsch, 1973). Constructive team conflict can be a source of excellence, quality and creativity, but how can we achieve this?

Constructive controversy is different from task conflict in its effects. Conflict is emotionally uncomfortable, whereas constructive controversy is not personalized. Individuals feel supported rather than attacked. In productive and creative teams, constructive task conflict is not only endemic but desirable (Tjosvold, 1998). Team diversity and differences of opinion about how best to meet customers' needs should be a source of excellence, quality and creativity. *But too much conflict (whether it is about the task or not) or conflict experienced as threatening and unpleasant by team members can destroy relationships and the effectiveness of the team.* What may be a comfortable level of debate for you can be intensely uncomfortable for your colleagues, who may feel threatened, attacked or put down. When that happens, people withdraw and stop engaging open-heartedly and enthusiastically in the team.

How do we resolve conflict in teams? We can *avoid* the conflict by pretending it does not exist, probably just postponing the conflict if the issue is likely to recur. We can give in and *accommodate* the other person. They get what they want and I don't. I feel resentful and they expect me to accommodate them every time. We can *compete* to win against them and, if we do, their needs are not met and they may carry resentment into the next conflict we have and be determined to win whatever. *Compromise* sounds like a sensible way to manage conflict, but actually it means that neither of us gets our needs fully met. Or, we can *collaborate* to find an integrative, creative solution that meets (or even exceeds!) both our needs. This is a 'win–win' solution. It is the ideal since both parties are happy and their relationship is stronger because of the successful conflict negotiation. Here is an opportunity for team members to exercise their creativity and develop innovative solutions that promote the long-term effectiveness of the team.

Imagine two people in a top management team who are in a conflict. One wants innovative action taken quickly to achieve the aims of providing brilliant products and services to customers rather than being blocked and frustrated by bureaucracy. The other, who controls the budget, is anxious that there should be careful processes of review, probity and decision-making in place to control the situation. They keep finding themselves in conflict. Avoidance, compromise, competition and accommodation are not working. An integrative solution might be for them to meet weekly to discuss new ideas together, ahead of full team meetings, so that together they can deal quickly with new ideas. This is based on the principle of both of them committing to the principles of probity and innovation. They bring their integrative solutions in each case to the wider team for discussion and approval rather than using up time in team meetings in repeated conflicts.

Of course, team members will not necessarily be best friends. After all, we are thrown together by chance with people at work who are often very different from us. But if we are clear about, and committed to, a shared team vision and clear team objectives, we are less likely to allow our small differences to interfere with team success. We don't need to vote for the same political party in order to work together successfully to ensure we correctly diagnose breast cancer and offer the patient we are serving the best possible care and support.

Climate for creativity and innovation

Creativity is the development of ideas; innovation implementation is making them happen in practice. Innovation therefore includes both creativity and implementation (West, 2002). Team innovation is the introduction of new and improved processes, products or services by a team (see Box 12.3). Levels of team innovation are high when team members expect, approve and practically support attempts to introduce new and improved ways of doing things. Team members may reject or ignore ideas or they may offer both verbal and practical support. High levels of both verbal and practical support will lead to more attempts to introduce innovations in teams. Verbal support is most helpful when team members initially propose ideas. Practical support can take the form of cooperation in the development of ideas, as well as the provision of time and resources by team members to apply them (West, 2002).

BOX 12.3
Team creativity and innovation

How can teams promote their levels of creativity and innovation? Problem-solving has a number of distinct and important stages. Each requires different kinds of skills and activities. These are: problem exploration, developing alternative ideas, selecting an option and implementing the preferred option.

Exploration – Probably the most important stage of team problem-solving is clarifying and exploring the problem. Team members usually begin to try to develop solutions to problems before clarifying and exploring and, if necessary, redefining the problem itself. But the more time spent in exploring and clarifying a problem before attempting to seek solutions, the better the quality of the ultimate solution.

Ideation – Having suspended attempts at solution development during Stage 1, the next step is to develop a range of alternative solutions to the problem. When making decisions, teams generally seek for 'one way out'. One idea is proposed and the team goes with that idea, making appropriate modifications as are perceived necessary. Research on team problem-solving suggests that it is most effective to begin by generating a range of possible solutions. It should be a stage that is both playful and challenging, when all ideas are welcomed and encouraged.

Selection – In this stage, the aim is to encourage constructive controversy about appropriate ways forward; to be critical and judgemental, but in a way that is constructive and personally supportive.

Implementation – Teams that conduct the first three stages carefully will find that implementation is the least difficult and most rewarding stage of the problem-solving process.

These then are four distinct stages of problem-solving. If you would like to explore techniques which teams can use at each of these stages of creative problem-solving, see Van Gundy (1988) and West (2004).

Leadership

Probably the most significant influence on team processes is the leadership. Task- and person-focused leadership both predict team performance, but the research evidence suggests that person-centred leadership has twice the effect of task-centred leadership (van Knippenberg, 2017; Scott & Wildman, 2017). Leadership coaching behaviours seem particularly powerful in influencing performance. Coaching improves self-management, team member relationship quality, team climate and team member satisfaction. It helps team members to develop knowledge skills and abilities and to coordinate efforts effectively to enhance team effectiveness (see Scott & Wildman, 2017). Team leader displays of emotion – particularly positive affect – predict the mood of followers and team cooperation. Leaders displaying happiness are more effective in stimulating team performance.

Empowering team leadership is also positively related to team performance (van Knippenberg, 2017), and this is important to note because of increasing evidence relating to shared team leadership, where all team members take responsibility for leadership even when there is a designated hierarchical leader. The research suggests that shared team leadership is positively related to team effectiveness overall (Wang, Waldman, & Zhang, 2014).

TEAM OUTPUTS

If team inputs and team processes are well managed, team outputs should follow, according to the IPO model. Table 12.5 shows the main dimensions of team outputs.

Table 12.5 Outputs

Dimension	Components
Team effectiveness	Goal achievement
	Productivity
	Managerial praise
Innovation	Development of new processes, services, ways of working
Inter-team relationships	Cooperation with other teams
	Effectiveness in working with other teams
	Absence of destructive conflict with other teams
Team member satisfaction	With recognition for condition
	With responsibility
	With team member support
	With influence over decisions
	With team openness
	With how conflicts are resolved
Attachment	Attachment to the team and its members
	Sense of belonging in the team
Cognitive states	Shared mental models
	Transactive memory systems

The first is team effectiveness – is the team achieving what it is required to, whether rescuing people at sea, providing great customer services, building cars, etc.? (Brodbeck, 1996; see Scott & Wildman, 2017 for a discussion of measures of team performance). Second is innovation. In complex teamworking settings, innovation is likely to be one of the best barometers of team functioning. Bringing together a group of people with diverse skills and backgrounds to address a challenging task should lead to creativity and innovation, if team processes are effective. If not, something is wrong with those processes (West, 2002).

Key to team effectiveness is inter-team relationships. There is a danger that the development of a number of individually successful teams within an organization will lead to levels of inter-team competition which could in the long term be detrimental to organization performance (Richter, West, van Dick, & Dawson, 2006). Organizations must encourage the development of individual team identity while ensuring that communication and feedback flow between teams. This allows teams to avoid duplication of effort, to learn from each other's experiences and to coordinate efforts to achieve the broader goals of the organization. A key dimension of effective teamworking is therefore the extent to which teams work cooperatively and effectively with other teams within the organization (West & Markiewicz, 2004).

Then there are the 'softer' elements of team effectiveness, but none the less important for that. These are the satisfaction with, and attachment of team members to, their teams. Do they feel satisfied with how the team functions and do they have a sense of frequent interaction, continuity of the team, absence of conflict and presence of strong mutual support that are the hallmarks of belonging? (Baumeister & Leary, 1995). Given the importance of positivity in human relationships and human experience, we should recognize that optimism, cohesion and a collective sense of efficacy/potency are key outcomes of inputs and processes.

PIONEERING WORK PSYCHOLOGISTS

Professor Dora C. Lau

Professor Dora C. Lau is an Associate Professor in the Department of Management at The Chinese University of Hong Kong (CUHK) Business School.

She has done pioneering work in many areas related to teams, human well-being and interconnection. She has helped to advance our understanding of demographic diversity and fault lines in teams, how the dynamics of team composition affect team performance and well-being outcomes, and how we can promote interpersonal trust in teams. She has also helped us appreciate more the relationship between the composition of top leadership teams and their organizational impact, the challenges of top teams in family businesses (particularly relevant in China), and Chinese approaches to management and leadership. She is a leading international scholar publishing extensively in top-tiered journals such as the *Academy of Management Review*, *Academy of Management Journal* and the *Journal of Applied Psychology*. She is the Consulting Editor of the *Journal of Applied Psychology* and the Associate Editor of the *Journal of Trust Research*.

Finally, there are cognitive states, including shared mental models and transactive memory systems and strategic consensus. Shared mental models refer to shared knowledge and understanding about the task and the task environment. With better shared mental models, teams can better coordinate and adapt to the work they are required to do, as well as work more efficiently as a team (DeChurch & Mesmer-Magnus, 2010).

Transactive memory systems involve sharing information and knowledge between team members, updating each other, sharing learning and thereby promoting team knowledge of who knows what information within the team. Essentially this is about teams and learning and working together to understand who is best suited for what role and whom to go to for skills or information needed to reach team goals. Such systems are vital for team effectiveness.

Team development

This also then leads to the question of how we take a team that is not functioning well and develop it into a high-performing team. There is substantial research evidence to help us answer this question (for example, DiazGranados, Shuffler, Wingate, & Salas, 2017; Lacerenza, Marlow, Tannenbaum, & Salas, 2018). Salas and colleagues (2008) conducted a meta-analysis that revealed that team training interventions had significant positive effects on a range of team outcomes. The study revealed that the content of training mattered (as we will show below); the stability of the team (the longer the team had been together, the more effective the training was; and the size of the team mattered (the larger the team – 10 or more members, the more effective the interventions are, probably because the challenges are greater).

The most effective interventions appear to be cross-training, 'Crew Resource Management' (CRM) training, team-coaching, team-building, team debriefs and the use of team charters. *Cross-training* involves developing team members' knowledge of the skills and role responsibilities of their fellow team members. This is particularly important in action teams such as surgical teams, firefighting crews and paramedic teams. The most effective way of building such knowledge is getting team members to perform each other's roles (where this is possible) – this is called 'positional rotation' (Marks, Sabella, Burke, & Zaccaro, 2002).

CRM training involves interventions to improve communication, decision-making and adaptability in teams faced with critical situations such as an emergency on an airline. The crew is trained to employ strategies to reduce human error and accident by training team members to use their resources most effectively. This is accomplished by using simulations in environments that are designed to closely approximate what they may face in real life, for example by using computerized cockpit simulation systems with realistic visual displays. Although they were derived from the aviation industry, such CRM programmes are now widely used in healthcare environments (for example in anaesthetics) (Lacerenza et al., 2018).

Team-coaching is used to help teams establish their goals, ensure clear direction, make sense of their work and environment or to provide feedback to motivate team improvement. Think of sports teams and how they are coached top improve the way they play together to ensure success. Coaching can come from either internal or external leaders or the coaching process can be shared by several team members. Team-coaching is a powerful way of ensuring team effectiveness (Hackman, 2011).

Another approach to team development is team-building. Team training usually focuses on developing the KSAs of team members in relation to the task aspects of their work. Team-building is more focused on interpersonal interactions among team members and tends to emphasize one or more of goal setting, role clarification, interpersonal relations and problem-solving (DiazGranados et al., 2017). The most effective is goal setting followed by role clarification. There is little hard evidence that interventions focused on improving interpersonal relations in isolation have a reliable impact on outcomes. Problem-solving interventions help teams to work together on specific challenges have the benefit of bringing about positive change in specific areas (solving a quality problem, for example) while improving critical thinking skills, communication and potentially productivity and efficiency.

Another effective intervention is the use of team charters, which are documents stating shared team agreements about roles, responsibilities, values, behaviours, processes and norms. The aim is to ensure there is clarity and shared norms in relation to team functions, goals, roles and behaviours. The research evidence suggests that high-quality charters coupled with well-thought-through performance strategies significantly improve performance (Mathieu & Rapp, 2009; McDowell, Herdman, & Aaron, 2011).

Team debriefs refer primarily to review processes focused on addressing negative outcomes after a team experiences adverse events (DiazGranados et al., 2017), although they can also focus on successes. They are also referred to as after-action reviews. The research evidence suggests that they are powerful in improving team performance. Tannenbaum and Cerasoli (2013) conducted a meta-analysis (based on 49 published studies) of debriefing exercises and found that they enhanced team effectiveness by 38 per cent! Well-conducted debriefs offer great promise for the development of teams and organizations in terms of learning, performance gains and specific desired outcomes (such as reducing stress or improving safety) (Allen, Reiter-Palmon, Crowe, & Scott, 2018).

Given the importance of teamworking in organizations, it is not surprising that research into teamworking has grown exponentially over the past 100 years, building on the Hawthorne studies in the 1920s and 1930s (Mathieu, Wolfson, & Park, 2018). Now we see new research frontiers as psychologists extend team research into many areas of human enterprise such as polar expeditions, off shore oil rigs, undersea operations (Vessey & Landon, 2017), healthcare, emergencies, terrorism, long-distance space missions, and schools (see the themed issue of *American Psychologist* on teamwork: McDaniel & Salas (2018)). These are exciting teams for the development of effective teamwork and rightly so. To meet the challenges we face as a species (climate change, war, natural disasters), we will have to increasingly understand how to develop belonging and trust and create team climates and organizational cultures of cooperation, connection and compassion. Humans make up teams and organizations, and we must come to see our species as more collaborative, compassionate and caring in order to shape our future and the future of our world.

POSITIVE WORK

Based on the contents of this chapter, key elements of effective team leadership are:

- Ensure an inspiring vision and clear direction.
- Ensure regular and positive team meetings.
- Encourage positive, supportive relationships.
- Resolve and prevent intense conflicts.
- Promote positive group attitudes towards diversity.
- Be attentive and listen carefully to all team members' contributions.
- Lead inter-team cooperation.
- Nurture team learning, improvement and innovation.

By summarizing some of the key points from this chapter and our experience of working with teams in organizations, we can create a picture of what a high-performing team will look like. This includes:

- Having an inspiring vision.
- Holding regular and engaging, rather than turgid, team meetings.
- Generally positive, warm, supportive relationships in the team.
- An ability to quickly work through conflict; collectively avoiding intense or chronic conflicts.
- Showing compassion to each other.
- A climate of inquiry plus advocacy; team members focused on exploring ideas and learning from each other rather than pushing their own agenda.
- Team members promoting inter-team cooperation and modelling organizational loyalty.
- All team members positively valuing diversity – whether of demographic background, functional specialties, opinion or experience.
- Practising reflexivity in order to learn from errors, identify problems, innovate and grow.

SUMMARY

In response to increasing complexity and change, many organizations have made the team the functional unit of the organization. Instead of individuals being responsible for separate pieces of work, groups of individuals come together to combine their efforts, knowledge and skills to achieve shared goals. Teamworking is one solution adopted by modern organizations for responding to the challenging environments in which they find themselves.

In this chapter we explored theory, research and application to understand how to create effective teamwork within organizations. We defined a work team in terms of its tasks, working relationships between team members and the embedding of teams within organizations. The chapter distinguished between the rhetoric of teamwork in organizations and the reality by characterizing the difference between real teams and pseudo teams. The former have clear objectives, members work interdependently, and the team meets regularly to review performance and how it can be improved.

Several broad categories of teams are strategy and policy teams; production teams; service teams; project and development teams; and action and performing teams. Key dimensions of teamwork include degree of permanence; emphasis on skill/competence development; genuine autonomy and influence; level of task from routine through to strategic. Tasks best performed by teams have high levels of the following characteristics: completeness, varied demands, requirements for interdependence, task significance, opportunities for learning; developmental possibilities for the task; and autonomy.

Teamwork is associated with organizational effectiveness, team member well-being and high levels of organizational responsiveness, adaptability, innovation and creativity. The chapter also presented evidence on the value of teamworking in healthcare settings for patient benefits and staff well-being, including relationships with patient mortality.

Which factors contribute to team effectiveness was considered, using the input–process–output framework. Inputs included task design, team member effort and skills, organizational support and resources. Team member characteristics included size, diversity (which we considered from two theoretical perspectives), personality and ability, teamwork skills, and team member KSAs. In terms of organizational supports, we reviewed organizational structure, organizational culture and climate, and appraisal and reward systems.

Team processes include objectives (clarity, challenge, specificity); participation (information sharing, influence over decision-making and interaction frequency); task focus (constructive controversy, error management); team conflicts (task related and interpersonal); support for creativity and innovation (espoused and enacted); and reflexivity (reflection, planning and action). We considered the dimensions of team effectiveness, including task performance, team innovation, inter-team relationships, team member satisfaction and team attachment. And the literature on team training showed how team-building, team-coaching and team reflexivity and debriefs can dramatically improve team performance.

The chapter has shown how, with effective management of team inputs and processes within organizations, teams can be outstandingly effective not just in achieving organizational aims but in meeting the human needs for growth, belonging and a sense of effectiveness, for those people who make up the team.

DISCUSSION QUESTIONS

1. In practice, how would you know whether a team in an organization was a real team or just given that name for the sake of convenience?

2. How can diversity in teams be best used as a source of creativity and effectiveness?

3. What team inputs should organizations pay most attention to when designing work teams?

4. What three or four team processes are most important in determining the performance of teams?

5. To what extent would the knowledge accumulated through research into teams be of use in developing, leading and coaching a sports team to success?

6. Given the detailed examination of inputs and processes in this chapter, how would you go about forming and leading a team?

7. How would you measure and then go about improving team performance?

FURTHER READING

Lau, D. C., & Liden, R. (2008). Antecedents of co-worker trust: Leaders' blessings. *Journal of Applied Psychology, 93*(5), 1130–1138.

Lau, D. C., & Murnighan, J. K. (1998). Demographic diversity and faultlines: The compositional dynamics of organisational groups. *Academy of Management Review, 23*(2), 325–340.

Lau, D. C., & Murnighan, J. K. (2005). Interactions within groups and subgroups: The dynamic effects of demographic faultlines. *Academy of Management Journal, 48*(4), 645–659.

Mathieu, J. E., Hollenbeck, J. R., van Knippenberg, D., & Ilgen, D. R. (2017). A century of work teams in the Journal of Applied Psychology. *Journal of Applied Psychology, 102*(3), 452–467.

McDaniel, S. H., Salas, E., & Kazak, A. E. (Eds.). (2018). The science of teamwork. *American Psychologist, 73* (4), 305–600.

Salas, E., Rico, R., & Passmore, J. (Eds.). (2017). *The Wiley Blackwell handbook of the psychology of team working and collaborative processes.* Chichester, England: Wiley Blackwell.

Salas, E., Tannenbaum, S., Cohen, D., & Latham, G. (Eds.). (2013). *Developing and enhancing teamwork in organizations: Evidence-based best practices and guidelines* (Vol. 33). Hoboken, NJ: John Wiley & Sons.

West, M. A. (2012). *Effective teamwork: Practical lessons from organizational research* (3rd ed.). Oxford: Blackwell. For tools and methods for developing team based working visit www.affinaod.com

REFERENCES

Ainsworth, M. (1989). Attachments beyond infancy. *American Psychologist, 44,* 709–716.

Allen, J. A., Reiter-Palmon, R., Crowe, J., & Scott, C. (2018). Debriefs: Teams learning from doing in context. *American Psychologist, 73*(4), 504–516.

Anderson, N., & Sleap, S. (2004). An evaluation of gender differences on the Belbin Team Role Self-Perception Inventory. *Journal of Occupational and Organizational Psychology, 77,* 429–437.

Applebaum, E., & Batt, R. (1994). *The new American workplace.* Ithaca, NY: ILR Press.

Bacon, N., & Blyton, P. (2000). High road and low road teamworking: Perceptions of management rationales and organizational and human resource outcomes. *Human Relations, 53,* 1425–1458.

Banker, R. D., Field, J. M., Schroeder, R. G., & Sinha, K. K. (1996). Impact of work teams on manufacturing performance: A longitudinal field study. *Academy of Management Journal, 3,* 867–890.

Barchas, P. (1986). A sociophysiological orientation to small groups. In E. Lawler (Ed.), *Advances in group processes* (Vol. 3, pp. 209–46). Greenwich, CT: JAI Press.

Barrick, M. R., Stewart, G. L., Neubert, M. J., & Mount, M. K. (1998). Relating member ability and personality to work-team processes and team effectiveness. *Journal of Applied Psychology, 83,* 377–91.

Batt, R. (1999). Work organization, technology and performance in customer service and sales. *Industrial and Labour Relations Review, 52,* 539–564.

Baumeister, R. F., & Leary, M. R. (1995). The need to belong: Desire for interpersonal attachments as a fundamental human motivation. *Psychological Bulletin, 117*, 497–529.

Belbin, R. M. (1993). *Team roles at work: A strategy for human resource management.* Oxford, England: Butterworth, Heinemann.

Belbin, R. M., (1981). *Management teams: Why they succeed or fail.* London, England: Butterworth-Heinemann.

Benders, J., & Van Hootegem, G. (1999). Teams and their context: Moving the team discussion beyond existing dichotomies. *Journal of Management Studies, 26*, 609–628.

Boning, B., Ichniowski, C., & Shaw, K. (2001). *Opportunity counts: Teams and the effectiveness of production incentives* (NBER Working Paper No. 8306). Cambridge, MA: National Bureau of Economic Research.

Bradley, B. H., Klotz, A. C., Postlethwaite, B. E., & Brown, K. G. (2013). Ready to rumble: How team personality and task conflict interact to improve performance. *Journal of Applied Psychology, 98*, 385–392.

Brodbeck, F. C. (1996). Criteria for the study of work group functioning. In M. A. West (Ed.), *Handbook of work group psychology* (pp. 285–316). Chichester, England: John Wiley & Sons.

Brown, R. (2000). *Group processes* (2nd ed.). Oxford, England: Blackwell.

Buss, D. M. (1991). Evolutionary personality psychology. *Annual Review of Psychology, 42*, 459–491.

Carter, A. J., & West, M. A. (1999). Sharing the burden – teamwork in health-care settings. In J. Firth-Cozens & R. Payne (Eds.), *Stress in health professionals* (pp. 191–202). Chichester. England: John Wiley & Sons.

Cohen, S. G., & Bailey, D. E. (1997). What makes teams work: Group effectiveness research from the shop floor to the executive suite. *Journal of Management, 23*, 239–290.

Cohen, S. G., Ledford, G. E., & Spreitzer, G. M. (1996). A predictive model of self-managing work team effectiveness. *Human Relations, 49*, 643–676.

Costa, A. C., & Anderson, N. (2017). Team trust. In E. Salas, R. Rico, & J. Passmore (Eds.), *The Wiley Blackwell handbook of the psychology of team working and collaborative processes* (393–416). Hoboken, NJ: John Wiley & Sons.

Dawson, J. F., Yan, X., & West, M. A. (2008). *Positive and negative effects of teamworking in healthcare: Real and pseudo-teams and their impact on health-care safety.* Birmingham, England: Aston University.

de Dreu, C. K. W., & Weingart, L. R. (2003). Task versus relationship conflict, team performance and team member satisfaction: A meta-analysis. *Journal of Applied Psychology, 88*, 741–749.

De Wit, F. R., Greer, L. L., & Jehn, K. A. (2012). The paradox of intragroup conflict: A meta-analysis. *Journal of Applied Psychology, 97*(2), 360–390.

DeChurch, L. A., & Mesmer-Magnus, J. R. (2010). The cognitive underpinnings of effective teamwork: A meta-analysis. *Journal of Applied Psychology, 95*(1), 32–53.

Delarue, A., Van Hootegem, G., Huys, R., & Gryp, S. (2004). *Dossier: Werkt teamwork? De PASO-resultaten rond arbeidsorganisatie doorgelicht.* Leuven: Hoger Instituut voor de Arbeid, Departement TEW, Departement Sociologie (KU Leuven).

Delarue, A., Van Hootegem, G., Procter, S., & Burridge, M. (2008). Teamworking and organizational performance: A review of survey-based research. *International Journal of Management Reviews, 10*, 127–148.

Deutsch, M. (1973). *The resolution of conflict: Constructive and destructive processes.* New Haven, CT: Yale University Press.

DiazGranados, D., Shuffler, M. L., Wingate, J. A., & Salas, E. (2017). In E. Salas, R. Rico, & J. Passmore (Eds.), Team development interventions. In *The Wiley Blackwell handbook of the psychology of team working and collaborative processes* (pp. 555–586). Chichester, England: Wiley Blackwell.

Diehl, M., & Stroebe, W. (1987). Productivity loss in brainstorming groups: Towards the solution of a riddle. *Journal of Personality and Social Psychology, 53*, 497–509.

Dinh, J. V., & Salas, E. (2017). Factors that influence teamwork. In E. Salas, R. Rico, & J. Passmore (Eds.), *The Wiley Blackwell handbook of the psychology of team working and collaborative processes* (pp. 13–41). Chichester, England: Wiley Blackwell.

Dunlop, J. T., & Weil, D. (1996). Diffusion and performance of modular production in the US apparel industry. *Industrial Relations, 35*, 334–355.

Edmondson, A. C. (1996). Learning from mistakes is easier said than done: Group and organizational influences on the detection and correction of human error. *Journal of Applied Behavioural Science, 32*, 5–28.

Edmondson, A. C. (1999). Psychological safety and learning behaviour in work teams. *Administrative Science Quarterly, 44*, 350–383.

Edmondson, A. C., & Roloff, K. S. (2009). Overcoming barriers to collaboration: Psychological safety in diverse teams. In E. Salas, G. F. Goodwin, & C. S. Burke (Eds.), *Team effectiveness in complex organizations: Cross-disciplinary perspectives and approaches* (pp. 183–208). London, England: Routledge.

Elmuti, D. (1997). The perceived impact of team-based management systems on organizational effectiveness. *Team Performance Management, 3*, 179–192.

Furnham, A. Steele, H., & Pendleton, D. (1993). A psychometric assessment of the Belbin Team Role Self-Perception Inventory. *Journal of Occupational and Organizational Psychology, 66*, 245–261.

Glassop, L. I. (2002). The organizational benefits of teams. *Human Relations, 55*, 225–249.

Godard, J. (2001). High performance and the transformation of work? The implications of alternative work practices for the experience and outcomes of work. *Industrial and Labour Relations Review, 54*, 776–805.

Goldberg, L. R. (1990). An alternative "description of personality": The Big-Five factor structure. *Journal of Personality and Social Psychology, 59*(6), 1216–1229. doi:10.1037/0022-3514.59.6.1216

Greer, L. L., & Dannals, J. E. (2017). Conflict in teams. In E. Salas, R. Rico, & J. Passmore (Eds.), *The Wiley Blackwell handbook of team dynamics, teamwork, and collaborative working* (317–344). Chichester, England: Wiley Blackwell.

Grossman, R., Friedman, S. B., & Kalra, S. (2017). Teamwork processes and emergent states. In E. Salas, R. Rico, & J. Passmore (Eds.), *The Wiley Blackwell handbook of the psychology of team working and collaborative processes* (pp. 245–270). Chichester, England: Wiley Blackwell.

Hackman, J. R. (1987). The design of work teams. In J. Lorsch (Ed.), *Handbook of organizational behaviour* (pp. 315–342). Englewood Cliffs, NJ: Prentice-Hall.

Hackman, J. R. (2002). *Leading teams: Setting the stage for great performances*. Boston, MA: Harvard Business School Press.

Hackman, J. R. (2011). *Collaborative intelligence: Using teams to solve hard problems*. Oakland, CA: Berrett-Koehler.

Hertel, G., Geister, S., & Konradt, U. (2005). Managing virtual teams: A review of the current empirical research. *Human Resource Management Review, 15*, 69–95.

Hollenbeck, J. R., Beersma, B., & Shouten, M. E. (2012). Beyond team types and taxonomies: A dimensional scaling conceptualization for team description. *Academy of Management Review, 37*, 82–106.

Ilgen, D. R., Hollenbeck, J. R., Johnson, M., & Jundt, D. (2005). Teams in organizations: From input–process–output models to IMOI models. *Annual Review of Psychology, 56*, 517–543.

Karau, S. J., & Williams, K. D. (1993). Social loafing: A meta-analytic review and theoretical integration. *Journal of Personality and Social Psychology, 65*, 681–706.

Kirkman, B. L., & Mathieu, J. E. (2005). The dimensions and antecedents of team virtuality. *Journal of Management, 31*(5), 700–718.

Korsgaard, M. A., Brodt, S. E., & Sapienza, H. J. (2003). Trust, identity and attachment: Promoting individuals' cooperation in groups. In M. A. West (Ed.), *Handbook of work group psychology*. Chichester, England: John Wiley & Sons.

Kozlowski, S. W. J., & Bell, B. S. (2003). Work groups and teams in organizations. In W. C. Borman, D. R. Ilgen, & R. Klimoski (Eds.), *Industrial/Organizational psychology* (Vol. XII). Chichester, England: John Wiley & Sons.

Kozlowski, S. W. J., & Ilgen, D. R. (2006). Enhancing the effectiveness of work groups and teams. *Psychological Science in the Public Interest, 7*(3), 77–124.

Lacerenza, C. N., Marlow, S. L., Tannenbaum, S. I., & Salas, E. (2018). Team development interventions: Evidence-based approaches for improving teamwork. *American Psychologist, 73*(4), 517–531.

Levine, J. M., & D'Andrea-Tyson, L. (1990). Participation, productivity and the firm's environment. In A. S. Blinder (Ed.), *Paying for productivity* (pp. 183–237). Washington, DC: Brookings Institution.

Locke, E. A., & Latham, G. P. (Eds.). (2013) *New developments in goal setting and performance*. London, England: Routledge.

Lyubovnikova, J., West, M. A., Dawson, J. F., & Carter, M. R. (2015). 24-Karat or fool's gold? Consequences of real team and co-acting group membership in healthcare organizations. *European Journal of Work and Organizational Psychology, 24*(6), 929–950.

Macy, B. A., & Izumi, H. (1993). Organizational change, design and work innovation: A meta-analysis of 131 North American field studies – 1961–1991. In R. W. Woodman & W. A. Pasmore (Eds.), *Research in organizational change and design* (Vol. 7, pp. 235–313). Greenwich, CT: JAI Press.

Marks, M. A., Mathieu, J. E., & Zaccaro, S. J. (2001). A temporally based framework and taxonomy of team processes. *Academy of Management Review, 26*(3), 356–376.

Marks, M. A., Sabella, M. J., Burke, C. S., & Zaccaro, S. J. (2002). The impact of cross-training on team effectiveness. *Journal of Applied Psychology, 87*(1), 3–13.

Mathieu, J., Maynard, M. T., Rapp, T., & Gilson, L. (2008). Team effectiveness 1997–2007: A review of recent advancements and a glimpse into the future. *Journal of Management, 34*(3), 410–476.

Mathieu, J. E., Gilson, L. L., & Ruddy, T. M. (2006). Empowerment and team effectiveness: An empirical test of an integrated model. *Journal of Applied Psychology, 91*, 97–108.

Mathieu, J. E., Hollenbeck, J. R., van Knippenberg, D., & Ilgen, D. R. (2017). A century of work teams in the *Journal of Applied Psychology*. *Journal of Applied Psychology, 102*(3), 452–467.

Mathieu, J. E., & Rapp, T. L. (2009). Laying the foundation for successful team performance trajectories: The roles of team charters and performance strategies. *Journal of Applied Psychology, 94*(1), 90–103.

Mathieu, J. E., Wolfson, M. A., & Park, S. (2018). The evolution of work team research since Hawthorne. *American Psychologist, 73*(4), 308–321.

McDaniel, M. A., Morgeson, F. P., Finnegan, E. B., Campion, M. A., & Braverman, E. P. (2001). Use of situational judgement tests to predict job performance: A clarification of the literature. *Journal of Applied Psychology, 86*, 730–40.

McDaniel, S. H., & Salas, E. (2018). The science of teamwork: Introduction to the special issue. *American Psychologist, 73*(4), 305.

McDowell, W. C., Herdman, A. O., & Aaron, J. (2011). Charting the course: The effects of team charters on emergent behavioral norms. *Organization Development Journal, 29*(1), 79–88.

Meyer, B. (2017). Team diversity: A review of the literature. In E. Salas, R. Rico, & J. Passmore (Eds.), *The Wiley Blackwell handbook of the psychology of teamwork and collaborative processes* (pp. 151–176). Chichester, UK: Wiley-Blackwell.

Mount, M. K., Barrick, M. R., & Stewart, G. L. (1998). Five-factor model of personality and performance in jobs involving interpersonal interactions. *Human Performance, 11*, 145–165.

Nicholson, N. (2013). *The 'I' of leadership*. Chichester, England: Jossey-Bass.

Patterson, M. G., & West, M. A. (1999). Employee attitudes as predictors of organizational performance. Manuscript submitted for publication.

Paul, A. K., & Anantharaman, R. N. (2003). Impact of people management practices on organizational performance: Analysis of a causal model. *International Journal of Human Resource Management, 14*, 1246–1266.

Peterson, N. G., Mumford, M. D., Borman, W. C., & Jeanneret, P. J. (2001). Understanding work using the occupational information network (ONET): Implications for practice and research. *Personnel Psychology, 54*, 451–492.

Procter, S., & Burridge, M. (2004). Extent, intensity and context: Teamworking and performance in the 1998 UK Workplace Employee Relations Survey (WERS 98) (IIRA HRM Study Group Working Papers in Human Resource Management, No. 12).

Rasmussen, T. H., & Jeppesen, H. J. (2006). Teamwork and associated psychological factors: A review. *Work and Stress, 20*, 105–128.

Richter, A. W., Dawson, J. F., & West, M. A. (2011): The effectiveness of teams in organizations: A meta-analysis, *The International Journal of Human Resource Management, 22*(13), 2749–2769.

Richter, A. W., West, M. A., van Dick, R., & Dawson, J. F. (2006). Boundary spanners' identification, intergroup contact and effective intergroup relations. *Academy of Management Journal, 49*, 1252–1269.

Salas, E., DiazGranados, D., Klein, C., Burke, C. S., Stagl, K. C., Goodwin, G. F., & Halpin, S. M. (2008). Does team training improve team performance? A meta-analysis. *Human factors, 50*(6), 903–933.

Salas, E., Rosen, M. A., Burke, C. S., & Goodwin, G. F. (2009). The wisdom of collectives in organizations: An update of competencies. In E. Salas, G. F. Goodwin, & C. S. Burke (Eds.), *Team effectiveness in complex organizations: Cross-disciplinary perspectives and approaches* (pp. 39–79). London, England: Routledge.

Schein, E. H. (1992). *Organizational culture and leadership*. New York, NY: John Wiley.

Schippers, M. C., Den Hartog, D. N., Koopman, P. L., & van Knippenberg, D. (2008). The role of transformational leadership in enhancing team reflexivity. *Human Relations, 61*, 1593–1616.

Schippers, M. C., West, M. A., & Dawson, J. F. (2012). Team reflexivity and innovation: The moderating role of team context. *Journal of Management, 41*(3). doi:10.1177/0149206312441210

Schippers, M. C., West, M. A., & Dawson, J. F. (2015). Team reflexivity and innovation: The moderating role of team context. *Journal of Management, 41*(3), 769–788.

Schippers, M. C., West, M. A., & Edmondson, A. C. (2017). Team reflexivity and innovation. In E. Salas, R. Rico, & J. Passmore (Eds.), *The Wiley Blackwell handbook of the psychology of team working and collaborative processes* (pp. 459–478). Chichester, England: Wiley Blackwell.

Scott, C. P., & Wildman, J. L. (2017). Developing and managing teams. In E. Salas, R. Rico, & J. Passmore (Eds.), *The Wiley Blackwell handbook of the psychology of team working and collaborative processes* (pp. 503–529). Chichester, England: Wiley Blackwell.

Semin, G., & Glendon, A. I. (1973). Polarization and the established group. *British Journal of Social and Clinical Psychology, 12*, 113–21.

Stasser, G., Vaughan, S. I., & Stewart, D. D. (2000). Pooling unshared information: The benefits of knowing how to access information is distributed among group members. *Organizational Behaviour and Human Decision Processes, 82*, 102–116.

Stevens, M. J., & Campion, M. A. (1994). The knowledge, skill, and ability requirements for teamwork: Implications for human resource management. *Journal of Management, 20*(2), 503–530.

Stevens, M. J., & Campion, M. A. (1999). Staffing work teams: Development and validation of a selection test for teamwork settings. *Journal of Management, 25*, 207–28.

Stewart, G. L., & Barrick, M. R. (2000). Team structure and performance: Assessing the mediating role of intra-team process and the moderating role of task type. *Academy of Management Journal, 43*, 135–148.

Tannenbaum, S. I., & Cerasoli, C. P. (2013). Do team and individual debriefs enhance performance? A meta-analysis. *Human factors, 55*(1), 231–245.

Tata, J., & Prasad, S. (2004). Team self-management, organizational structure and judgements of team effectiveness. *Journal of Managerial Issues, 16*, 248–265.

Tjosvold, D. (1991). *Team organisation: An enduring competitive advantage*. Chichester, England: John Wiley & Sons.

Tjosvold, D. (1998). Cooperative and competitive goal approaches to conflict: Accomplishments and challenges. *Applied Psychology: An International Review, 47*, 285–342.

Van Gundy, Jr., A. B. (1988). *Techniques of structured problem solving*. New York, NY: Van Nostrand Reinhold.

van Knippenberg, D. (2017). Team leadership. In E. Salas, R. Rico, & J. Passmore (Eds.), *The Wiley Blackwell handbook of the psychology of team working and collaborative processes* (pp. 345–368). Chichester, England: John Wiley & Sons.

van Knippenberg, D., & Schippers, M. C. (2007). Work group diversity. *Annual Review of Psychology, 58*, 515–41

van Knippenberg, D., & van Ginkel, W. P. (2010). The categorization-elaboration model of work group diversity: Wielding the double-edged sword. In R. J. Crisp (Ed.), *Social issues and interventions: The psychology of social and cultural diversity* (pp. 257–280) Hoboken, NJ: Wiley-Blackwell. Retrieved from dx.doi.org/10.1002/9781444325447.ch11

Vessey, W. B., & Landon, L. B. (2017). Team performance in extreme environments. In E. Salas, R. Rico, & J. Passmore (Eds.), *The Wiley Blackwell handbook of the psychology of team working and collaborative processes* (pp. 531–553). Chichester, England: John Wiley & Sons.

Walker, T. G., & Main, E. C. (1973). Choice shifts in political decision-making: Federal judges and civil liberties cases. *Journal of Applied Social Psychology, 3*, 39–48.

Wang, D., Waldman, D. A., & Zhang, Z. (2014). A meta-analysis of shared leadership and team effectiveness. *Journal of Applied Psychology, 99*(2), 181.

West, M. A. (Ed.). (1996). *Handbook of work group psychology.* Chichester, England: John Wiley & Sons.

West, M. A. (2000). Reflexivity, revolution and innovation in work teams. In M. Beyerlein (Ed.), *Product development teams: Advances in interdisciplinary studies of work teams* (pp. 1–30). Greenwich, CT: JAI.

West, M. A. (2001). The human team. In N. Anderson, D. S. Ones, H. Sinangil, & C. Viswesvaran (Eds.), *Handbook of industrial, work and organizational psychology: Vol. 2. Organizational psychology* (pp. 270–288). London, England: SAGE.

West, M. A. (2002). Sparkling fountains or stagnant ponds: An integrative model of creativity and innovation implementation in work groups. *Applied Psychology: An International Review, 51,* 355–387.

West, M. A. (2004). *The secrets of successful team management: How to lead a team to innovation, creativity and success.* London, England: Duncan Baird.

West, M. A. (2012). *Effective teamwork: Practical lessons from organizational research* (3rd ed.). Oxford, England: Blackwell.

West, M. A., Brodbeck, F. C., & Richter, A. W. (2004). Does the 'romance of teams' exist? The effectiveness of teams in experimental and field settings. *Journal of Occupational and Organizational Psychology, 77,* 467–473.

West, M. A., & Lyubovnikova, J. R. (2012). Real teams or pseudo teams? The changing landscape needs a better map. *Industrial and Organizational Psychology, 5*(1), 25–28.

West, M. A., & Markiewicz, L. (2004). *Building team-based working: A practical guide to organizational transformation.* Oxford, England: Blackwell.

West, M. A., Tjosvold, D., & Smith, K. G. (Eds.) (2003). *The international handbook of organizational teamwork and cooperative working.* Chichester, England: John Wiley & Sons.

Widmer, P. S., Schippers, M. C., & West, M. A. (2009). Recent developments in reflexivity research: A review. *Psychology of Everyday Activity, 2*(2), 2–11.

Wolfson, M. A., & Mathieu, J. E. (2017). Team composition. In E. Salas, R. Rico, & J. Passmore (Eds.), *The Wiley Blackwell handbook of the psychology of team working and collaborative processes* (pp. 129–149). Chichester, England: John Wiley & Sons.

Yu, L., & Zellmer-Bruhn, M. (2018). Introducing team mindfulness and considering its safeguard role against conflict transformation and social undermining. *Academy of Management Journal, 61*(1), 324–347.

Zwick, T. (2004). Employee participation and productivity. *Labour Economics, 11*(6), 715–740.

CHAPTER 13

ORGANIZATIONAL CULTURE, CLIMATE AND CHANGE

LEARNING OBJECTIVES

- Understand the concepts of organizational culture and climate.
- Understand ways of assessing and studying organizational culture and climate.
- Understand how organizational culture and climate relate to organizational outcomes (performance, customer satisfaction, employee engagement).
- Understand what forces cause organizations to change.
- Understand key strategies we can use to achieve or shape organizational change.

In this chapter, we explore what makes organizations different from each other, encapsulated in the concepts of organizational culture and climate. We also explore how culture and climate predict outcomes such as organizational performance and employee satisfaction. We focus on the forces that cause organizations to change and the factors that influence employees' reactions to the changes leaders wish to introduce. The chapter describes methods for successfully introducing change and seeing it through. The overall aim is to help the reader comprehend the different cultures in organizations and to understand how to measure climate and successfully manage change in organizations.

First, what do we mean by organizational culture and climate? Culture is the 'shared values and basic assumptions that explain why organizations do what they do and focus on what they focus on' (Schneider, González-Romá, Ostroff, & West, 2017). Culture research grew from sociological and anthropological traditions and employed mostly qualitative research that required researchers to immerse themselves in the research setting. Culture 'exists at a fundamental, perhaps preconscious, level of awareness, is grounded in history and tradition and is a source of collective identity and commitment' (Schneider et al., 2017). Organizational climate (the shared perceptions of an organization), in contrast, is a composite of multiple observations and experiences that people have in their work – it is a Gestalt (a whole) formed from these. It is a summary perception 'derived from a body of interconnected experiences' (Schneider et al., 2017), including perceptions of organizational policies, practices and procedures. These include how people are managed and the behaviour and actions of leaders in the organization. These observations and perceptions are summarized and shared through employees' day-to-day interactions and conversations with each other to emerge as a Gestalt of climate (Schneider, Erhart, & Macey, 2013). Research into organizational climate was grounded in psychological methods and relied largely on employee survey methods focused on the observable experiences people have in their organizations. Much of the rest of this chapter explores these concepts in more depth before we describe what is known about organizational change.

ORGANIZATIONAL CULTURE

You can be an expert very quickly in understanding organizational culture, just by paying attention. Like an explorer visiting a country for the first time, you need to pay close attention, watch, listen and learn to discover. By paying conscious attention you can discover the cultures and climates of the organizations you encounter every day. Whenever you engage with any organization, whether it is a government employment agency, a primary healthcare team, a voluntary organization or a manufacturing company, you can be a student of culture and climate. But you have to pay attention to discover what is often hidden from those who work within the organization. The goldfish may never know there is water in the bowl, whereas the outsider is likely to see it by paying attention. For an illustration of a large and multi-method study of cultures (in the National Health Service in England), see Dixon-Woods et al. (2013).

For a ten-year period, one of us (MW) led a research programme designed to discover what managerial practices made a difference to company performance (Patterson , West, & Wall, 2004b). This involved the research team visiting over 100 manufacturing organizations, interviewing senior managers, surveying the staff, touring the shop floor and examining the production systems. From the very first phone call our engagement with the organization was a source of information about the culture and climate. How were we dealt with on the phone: put on hold, peremptorily dealt with, welcomed, informed or listened to? When we arrived for our first interviews, what was the reception area like? Clean and bright? Were the plants in reception healthy? Were we offered coffee, kept waiting, smiled at, ignored? Was the mission of the organization on the wall in a smart frame or was there a faded painting, partially hidden by dirty glass? When we entered deeper into the territory of the organization, what did we discover? Did all the staff eat together at lunchtime or were there separate areas for managers and shop floor staff? Did the chief executive claim all the glory or was she full of appreciation for everyone else? How did they talk about customers and suppliers – as partners or as threats? What stories and jokes were we told about the organization and its history and what did they imply about what was valued in the organization? How did it feel overall – warm and welcoming, professional and business-like, creative and exciting, sloppy and drab? Every experience, sight, sound and conversation potentially tells you about the culture and climate of the organization.

Organizations can be described much as we might describe to our friends the experience we had of visiting a foreign country. We might talk about the dress, laws, physical environment, buildings, nightlife, recreational activities, language, humour, food, values and rituals. Similarly, organizations can be described in terms of their cultures – meanings, values, attitudes and beliefs. And they can be described in terms of their climates – what it feels like to work there or to visit the organization.

DISCUSS WITH A COLLEAGUE

Try describing to a fellow student two organizations you have worked in or encountered as if you were describing the experience of visiting a foreign country, and ask him or her to reciprocate. Your conversations will quickly reveal key differences and similarities and also the fundamental dimensions you both use to describe organizations. Then you begin to get a sense of what is meant by organizational culture.

Try giving your descriptions of the same two organizations to each other again, but using just the dimensions described in Table 13.1. This time the descriptions will probably be more disciplined and you will probably discover you need more information to produce a comprehensive description.

Of course, in one sense you are just offering your idiosyncratic descriptions, and those will depend on the lenses through which you view organizations because of your past experience. What psychology can offer is a richer perspective based on theory and research. For example, one model describes culture along the dimensions shown in Table 13.1.

Table 13.1 Surface manifestations of culture

Hierarchy	Such as how many levels from the head of the organization to the lowest-level employee. The greater the number of levels relative to the number of employees, the more bureaucratic and the less innovative the organization will generally be. And the extent to which people from diverse backgrounds are represented at all levels of leadership.
Pay levels	High or low, whether there is performance-related pay, and what the differentials are between people at different grades. Pay matters to people and how it is managed has a big effect on culture.
Job descriptions	How detailed or restrictive they are and what aspects they emphasize, such as safety or productivity, cost saving or quality. How rigid or flexible they seem to be and whether they are regularly reviewed.
Informal practices such as norms	Management and non-management employees sit at separate tables in the dining area; dress is strictly formal, or there are uniforms, or dress is casual and varied. People frequently turn up late to meetings or everyone is always there on time. Customers are spoken about warmly as partners or treated as a target group.
Espoused values and rituals	An emphasis on cooperation and support versus cut-and-thrust competition between teams; cards, gifts and parties for those leaving the organization or such events are not observed. There are always festivities at key points in the calendar (summer barbeque and religious celebrations such as Eid).
Stories, jokes and jargon	Commonly told stories about a particular success or the failings of the chief executive; sarcasm about the HR department, for example; and jargon or acronyms (most large organizations have a lexicon of acronyms and jargon that is often impenetrable to outsiders).
Physical environment	Office space, eating areas, rest rooms; are all spaces clean, tidy and comfortable, or is it only the areas on public display? Are there decorations such as plants and paintings and good facilities such as water fountains? Is the place overrun with paper or cables? Does it feel pleasant, urgent, uncomfortable, overwhelming or exciting to be in?

Organizational culture defined

Culture has been described as the shared meanings, values, attitudes and beliefs that are created and communicated within an organization (for a thorough treatment of this topic, see Ashkanasy, Wilderom, & Peterson, 2000; Schneider et al., 2013, 2017). Schein (1992), a pioneer of research into culture, offered this definition:

> *Organizational culture is the set of shared, taken-for-granted implicit assumptions that members of an organization hold and that determines how they perceive, think about and react to their various environments.*

Models of culture

Schein's model distinguishes between different levels of culture. *Espoused values* are those that are captured in mission statements, visions and company brochures. They are the values the organization wishes to be known for. Then there are enacted values that are expressed in artefacts and in basic underlying assumptions. *Artefacts* include the number of levels in the hierarchy, pay levels, documents, meeting practices (set agendas, for example), ritual celebrations (leaving, long-service awards and performance-excellence awards), etc. Then there are *basic hidden assumptions* that tell a great deal about the organization's true values. These are often invisible to members because they are taken for granted. An example might be that arriving up to ten minutes late for meetings is normal, acceptable and expected. You can imagine that an outsider coming from an organization where punctuality was the norm would notice and be irritated by this. Others, maybe you, never disagree with the chief executive; whatever you ask for will always take much longer than is promised; or people will always drop everything to help a customer who has a problem. A revealing exercise is to ask people you know who work in an organization to write down one unwritten rule in their organization. This is one way of encouraging the discovery of basic hidden assumptions in organizational culture. In effect, Schein suggests that culture is rather like an iceberg with visible artefacts and espoused values above the waterline, but powerful and often unconscious values and behaviours hidden below it. Our task is to reveal and understand culture and how it influences outcomes such as performance and employee well-being.

Goffee and Jones: Sociability versus solidarity

Is there a simpler way of thinking about culture? Goffee and Jones (1998) believe that culture can be represented by two fundamental dimensions. These are the extent to which the organization emphasizes sociability and the strength of commitment to solidarity. They define sociability as sincere friendliness among people (an emphasis on social relations). Solidarity refers to the emphasis on common tasks and shared goals (an emphasis on task performance). Putting these dimensions together into a two-by-two matrix gives four possible configurations.

The *Networked Organization* is characterized by high sociability and low solidarity. Task performance is less highly valued, but what is emphasized is warmth, positive feelings and good social relations. High sociability encourages informal sharing of knowledge, innovative thinking and strong, positive morale. On the other hand, it discourages a full exploration of criticisms and disagreements (for fear of upsetting others). Consequently, poor performance may be tolerated. Family-owned firms may be more likely to develop such networked cultures where social relationships are more important than firm performance.

The *Mercenary Organization* is characterized by low sociability and high solidarity. There is much emphasis on productivity and performance, with little concern for the quality of social relations. It is performance that matters, not how well people get on. This sense of shared purpose, regardless of social relationships, pervades the mercenary organization. Some professional service firms, such as law firms, may be characterized by such a mercenary culture. The downside of such an orientation can be a tournament culture where members question the personal value of decisions and policies and where battles for power and status take up energy and attention.

The *Fragmented Organization* is characterized by low sociability and low solidarity. There is little emphasis on either performance or the quality of social relations. Examples might include a university department where researchers are focused on their own research and writing, and are not concerned with the performance of their department or university overall. Social relationships may not be well developed since the researchers come in to the department only once or twice a week to give their lectures to students and pick up their post, the rest of the time working at home.

Finally, the *Communal Organization* is characterized by both high sociability and high solidarity. There is a strong emphasis on both performance and the quality of social relations. Examples might include an aid agency such as OXFAM operating in an area struck by a disaster. Staff provide each other with strong support since they are all facing huge challenges, but they are also united in their solidarity by a focus on relieving suffering for those affected by the disaster. Goffee and Jones say the communal culture may be inappropriate in some contexts. During periods of change, growth or acquisition, the communal elements of culture may interfere with the need for a hard focus on driving change through and ensuring success. Moreover, there may be an underlying tension between these two cultural elements, which can only be managed by a charismatic and powerful leader.

Which of these four orientations is most appropriate will therefore depend on the environment the organization faces, the tasks it is required to perform and the success of the organization. Where recruitment and retention of staff are vital and there is a shortage of skilled labour, the organization might want to increase sociability. Goffee and Jones say this can be achieved by promoting sharing of ideas and emotions within the organization and by recruiting compatible people – people who will get on with each other. Sociability can also be increased by reducing formality (first names rather than titles) and limiting hierarchical differences. Leaders can also act more like a friend than a boss. Increased solidarity can be achieved by raising employees' awareness of competitors through briefings, newsletters, videos, emails, memos ('we have to focus and work hard to survive given the strength and hunger of our competitors'). By creating a sense of urgency, stimulating the will to win and encouraging commitment to shared corporate goals, the organization will become more mercenary (in the absence of a strong emphasis on sociability).

The obvious critique of this model is that it over-simplifies the complexities of organizational communities into two dimensions and fails to include other possible dimensions (power, diversity, innovation, for example) and offers a somewhat static model that takes insufficient account of the relationship of the organization with its environment.

> **DISCUSS WITH A COLLEAGUE**
>
> Again take your examples and plot descriptions of the same two organizations, but using just the two dimensions described in the Goffee and Jones model. This time the descriptions will be very simple and you will discover you can do this relatively easily.

Competing Values Model

The Competing Values model (Cameron & Quinn, 1997; Quinn & Rohrbaugh, 1981) incorporates two fundamental dimensions of organizational effectiveness into a single model – emphases upon flexibility versus control and a predominantly internal versus external orientation. The framework's four quadrants (see Figure 13.1) present a set of valued outcomes and a managerial strategy for achieving them. It describes how *opposing* values exist in organizations and how they embrace different sets of values that are reflected in their desired ends and in the means to achieve those ends. Such means include their structural designs and mechanisms of coordination and control (Zammuto & O'Connor, 1992, p. 711). Quinn recognizes that organizations generally emphasize all four quadrants but to a greater or lesser extent, with the consequence that they have value emphases in all four but the degree of emphasis or strength in each will vary between organizations (and within organizations over time). Thus, instead of a single point, each organization's overall position will be dependent on its particular emphasis across each of the four quadrants.

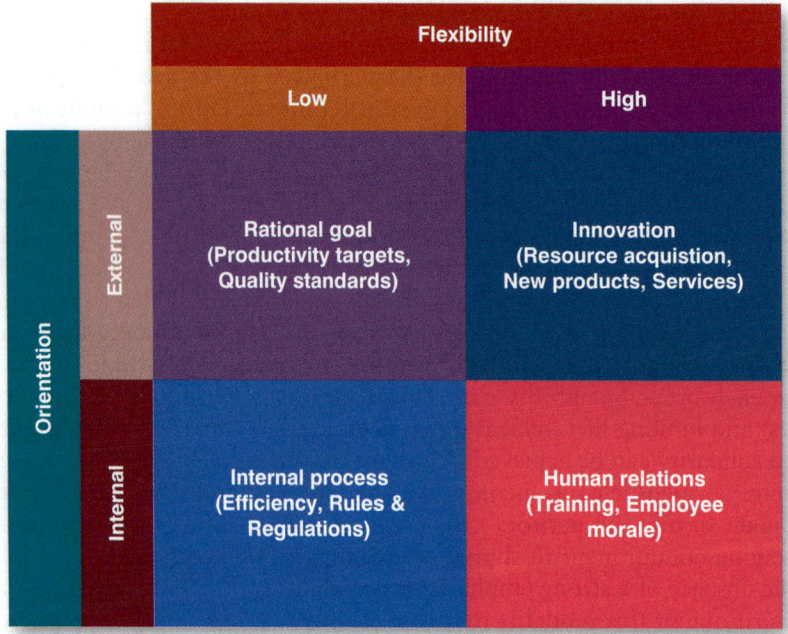

Figure 13.1 The competing values model of organizational effectiveness

> **DISCUSS WITH A COLLEAGUE**
>
> Again take your examples and plot descriptions of the same two organizations, but using just the Competing Values model. Each time you do this work, your understanding of the cultures of the two organizations becomes richer, more valuable and should provide you with a more sophisticated representation than most working in those organizations would be able to achieve. You are already becoming an expert on organizational culture!

A major strength of this model is its derivation from four fundamental orientations to the study of organizational effectiveness. Thus the rational goal approach (external focus but with tight control within the organization) reflects an economic model of organizational functioning in which the emphasis is upon productivity and goal achievement (Hall, 1980; Clinebell, 1984). The open systems approach (external focus and flexibility in response to the environment) emphasizes the interaction and adaptation of the organization in its environment, with managers seeking resources and innovating in response to environmental (or market) demands (Shipper & White, 1983). The internal process approach reflects a Tayloristic concern with formalization and internal control of the organization in order that resources are efficiently used. Finally, the human relations approach reflects the tradition derived from sociotechnical (Emery & Trist, 1965) and human relations schools (e.g. McGregor, 1960), emphasizing the well-being, growth and commitment of those who work in the organization. Quinn (1988) argued that a balance of competing organizational values is required for organizational effectiveness.

Integration, Differentiation and Fragmentation Model

But are organizational cultures so all-encompassing and unitary in their nature? Martin (1992) suggested not, and described three quite different perspectives on culture – integration, differentiation and fragmentation. Adopting all three perspectives, he suggested, we can increase our ability to understand culture quite profoundly:

1 *The integration perspective.* This perspective proposes that a 'strong culture' will lead to more effective organizational performance. A strong culture is one that is shared by those throughout the organization – there is organization-wide consensus and clarity. Senior management set the values and develop a mission statement. When this is effectively communicated and implemented via managerial practices, organization-wide consensus is shaped. So employees know what they are supposed to do and agree on the value of doing it.

   McDonald (1991) described such a culture in the Los Angeles Olympics (1984) Organizing Committee. The employees wore attractive uniforms, developed elaborate rituals, introduced brightly coloured stadium decorations, adopted an intense working pace and told many stories about their charismatic leader, which all reinforced an organization-wide commitment around a shared set of values. However, modern theorists believe that culture is more complicated than the integration perspective alone implies.

2 *The differentiation perspective.* This view recognizes that employees, teams or departments have differing interests, task responsibilities, backgrounds, experiences and expertise, which means that work attitudes and values, as well as pay and working conditions, will vary throughout the organization. Add the differing social identities due to gender, class and ethnic background, and, according to this perspective, the concept of a unifying culture simply overlays an average of widely differing sub-cultures (rather like saying that China – or Russia or the UK – is one culture when in fact there are huge regional and sub-cultural differences within them). Instead, it is proposed that within the organization there are overlapping and nested sub-cultures, which coexist in relationships of harmony, conflict or indifference.

   Van Maanen (1991) found just this differentiation even in the 'strong culture' of Disneyland. Food vendors and street cleaners were at the bottom of the status rankings, whereas, among ride operators, those responsible for 'yellow submarines' and 'jungle boats' had high status. There was evident tension between operators, supervisors and even customers as the different groups interacted. Supervisors were engaged in an endless struggle to catch operators breaking the rules. According to Van Maanen, the conflict or differentiation perspective offers a more realistic account of organizational culture than the integration perspective.

3 *The fragmentation perspective.* Ambiguity is a defining feature of many organizations. According to the fragmentation perspective, this ambiguity occurs because there simply is no consensus about the meanings, attitudes and values of the organization.

Meyerson (1991) demonstrated this approach in a study of a social work organization. Where goals were unclear, there was no consensus about appropriate ways to achieve them, and success was hard to define and to assess. In this organization, ambiguity was the salient feature of working life. One social worker reported: 'It just seems to me like social workers are always a little bit on the fringe; they're part of the institution, but they're not. You know they have to be part of the institution in order to really get what they need for their clients, but basically they're usually at odds with the institution' (p. 140). Clearly this is not a description of every organization, but it is probably accurate for parts of most organizations, particularly with moves to 'outsourcing' of key functions and to the blurring of boundaries (many healthcare organizations employ agency staff and locums who may not feel integrated into the organization).

How do cultures develop?

Leaders in organizations are not simply observers of cultures; they play a powerful role in shaping culture. Indeed, the founder and early leaders of organizations shape the founding culture and at least its initial development. What leaders say, and equally importantly, do, communicates what the organization values. By paying large bonuses to financial traders who take big risks to make and win large profits, employers encourage risk-taking with the public's pension funds and savings. That is why banking and finance sector leaders were blamed for the banking collapse of 2008–2009 in the USA and many European countries. Culture is also affected by the selection practices of organizations – what sorts of people are recruited and selected; with what competencies and values; and are they generally sociable and supportive team workers or hard-driving, successful innovators who are committed to success above all? You can see how selection processes might contribute to increasing sociability or solidarity, using the Goffee and Jones model of culture. Socialization processes will also affect the culture – what employees are told about the organization and its expectations of them will affect what they understand to be the organization's values. US marines are stripped of their prior values and expectations (and even of their hair) and told that their success is based on them obeying orders unquestioningly. A strong set of values is deeply ingrained in them from their very first day until there is no questioning. Then they can be sent into battle in confidence that they will obey orders.

What types of cultures are associated with organizational effectiveness? Evidence from the employees of successful companies tells us which characteristics they associate with their companies' success. These include emphases on customer service, quality of goods and services, involvement of employees in decision-making, training for employees, teamwork and employee satisfaction. An increasingly important factor is the organization's success in nurturing cultures of equality, diversity and inclusion.

KEY THEME

Cultures of inclusion and diversity

Many organizations show signs of progress in relation to BME appointments in shortlisting and in reducing the disproportionate rate of disciplinary action against BME staff. But there is little evidence that the day-to-day discrimination that BME staff experience is changing quickly. In many teams and organizations the evidence suggests that the experience of discrimination at work, including harassment, bullying or abuse, has remained largely static over recent years. What are we to do?

First, we need compassionate leaders who pay attention to those they lead ('listening to them with fascination'). They must seek to understand, through talking with their staff, the challenges they face in their work. They should learn to empathize with all their staff. Their focus must be how they can help those they lead to do the high-quality work they benefit from doing. Organizations must ensure that every leader is trained and practised in implementing compassionate and inclusive leadership in their daily interactions. Such leadership creates the conditions for inclusion and kindness. In contrast, high stress levels and directive, hierarchical leadership create the conditions for discrimination and stereotyping.

Second, it is important that every team has clear, agreed, challenging objectives aligned with the organization's vision and that every individual is clear about their role and what they are required to do in their work. The more work overload, role conflict, role ambiguity and lack of clarity for teams and individuals, the more we create the conditions for anger, hostility, blaming, stereotyping and discrimination.

Third, we must create an environment of enlightened people management, nurturing the engagement and positive emotions that ensure staff thrive and enjoy their workplace interactions. This requires leaders who are authentic, open and honest, who model humility rather than arrogance and narcissism, who are optimistic and compassionate, and who invest constantly in recognizing and appreciating people's efforts. When leaders help to nurture positive emotional environments, they also reduce the likelihood of discrimination. When people feel positive, they perceive less difference between themselves and others who are dissimilar from them on a dimension such as ethnicity.

In addition to every organization agreeing objectives for representation of BME staff in selection panels, disciplinaries, etc., we must implement equality and diversity initiatives that the evidence base demonstrates are most effective in reducing discrimination.

Four UK universities (Sheffield, Lancaster, Liverpool and Liverpool John Moores) have worked together to produce a website providing comprehensive research evidence around making diversity at work effective (see **www.workplaceEDI.com** for extensive evidence and case studies focused on what works). This includes raising awareness of the critical role of allies from non-disadvantaged/discriminated groups who change culture by speaking up when they see BME staff or customers being ignored, treated with incivility, spoken over or otherwise subjected to the weathering micro interactions which corrode the values of compassion and inclusion.

Such transformational processes must also raise awareness of the potential negative messages of some diversity training. The message that all organizations have cultures of discrimination or that all of us are subject to unconscious bias may lead to an acceptance of the status quo because it is the norm. Persistent and consistent messages that focus on the efforts organizations and individuals are making to overcome discrimination and bias are more likely to encourage change.

continued

A focus on setting goals for increasing inclusion and compassion while reducing discrimination at individual, team and organizational levels is likely to achieve culture change. Goal setting is an effective means for changing behaviour – especially when goals are specific, challenging and agreed rather than vague, unambitious (such as 'do your best') and imposed. Changing culture also involves raising awareness among all staff of the subtler aspects of discrimination that are more difficult to identify and change, such as repeated negative but not overtly racist 'humour' directed at BME staff and customers.

Fourth, we must continue to create the conditions for quality improvement and innovation in our organizations. Compassionate leaders who focus on a positive, altruistic vision reinforce the fundamental altruism and intrinsic motivation of their staff, thereby indirectly making discrimination less likely and increasing the likelihood of innovation. These leadership behaviours create a sense of 'psychological safety', enabling staff to speak up about concerns and issues to do with discrimination or incivility and to suggest ideas for new and improved ways of working.

Changing culture also means ensuring that all leaders understand the central role that diversity plays in the efficiency and effectiveness of their organizations. When the diversity of staff members mirrors the diversity of their communities, organizations provide better service and are financially more efficient. Diverse teams with clear objectives, clear roles, good communication and positive attitudes to diversity outperform teams composed of people from similar backgrounds. Such teams are both more productive and significantly more innovative – developing and implementing ideas for new and improved ways of working. Improving equality, diversity and inclusive cultures should be an explicit goal in every organization.

Fifth, building effective teams ensures team members feel a sense of cohesion, optimism and efficacy in their work. Effective teams have dramatically reduced stress levels, which in turn means less aggression, harassment and discrimination. Nurturing effective teams is core to creating positive, non-discriminatory cultures. Such teams are characterized by many specific behaviours, including explicit valuing of people from diverse backgrounds.

These five cultural elements are core to changing organizational cultures to reduce discrimination and ensure inclusion. It also necessary to implement talent management strategies that deliver for all staff, not just a select few.

In the English National Health Service, NHS Improvement, The King's Fund, the Workforce Race Equality Directorate team and the Centre for Creative Leadership have developed a programme for just such a culture change. This is being implemented by more than 80 health care organizations across England. It is a comprehensive evidence-based approach, with free and accessible materials, designed to be implemented by change teams within trusts and to be integrated into the existing workforce, organization development and human resource strategies. It includes a wide variety of tools, with many focused specifically on issues of inclusion. You can read further on the extensive content on this, found at these two websites:

improvement.nhs.uk/resources/culture-and-leadership/

improvement.nhs.uk/resources/culture-and-leadership-programme-phase-2-design/

Globalization and culture

Organizational cultures occur in the context of national cultures, and a major challenge for very large organizations that span many countries is how to ensure that their values are appropriate for and implemented across international boundaries with varied national value emphases. The most influential analysis of national cultures was offered by Geert Hofstede (1980, 1983), a Swedish researcher, who undertook a detailed study of variations in the cultures of outlets of IBM across the world. He concluded that there were four underlying dimensions of national culture.

Individualism–collectivism

This refers to the extent to which people define themselves in relation to individual characteristics (football player, jokey person, someone who reads a particular broadsheet newspaper) versus identity being based on belonging to particular groups (family, profession, political party, social club, work organization). Eastern cultures tend to be high in collectivism, whereas countries such as the UK and USA are high in individualism.

Power distance

Power distance is the extent to which people in a particular culture obey authority figures and are respectful of those in authority. Turkey and many Middle Eastern countries are high in power distance, while Western European countries (for the most part) tend to be low.

Uncertainty avoidance

High uncertainty-avoidant cultures plan carefully ahead, require clarity about tasks, roles, goals and responsibilities and find ambiguity threatening and uncomfortable (Japan, for example). It is sometimes referred to as tolerance of ambiguity.

Masculinity–femininity

This dimension contrasts an emphasis on achievement, winning and recognition with an emphasis on interpersonal relations and support. Countries such as Norway and Sweden tend to have high femininity and it is interesting to note that there is a strong correlation between this dimension at national level and representation of women on boards of companies and in government.

Some years after his initial research, Hofstede agreed that a fifth dimension was useful – *Long-Term Perspective*, typical, for example, of Chinese culture. Subsequent studies have tended to provide broad support for Hofstede's analysis, though controversy persists about the precise number and content of dimensions. The individualism – collectivism dimension has emerged as the most robust description.

These cultural variations have a strong influence on organizational culture since it is difficult for work organizations to develop values that are at variance with the dominant national values of the countries within which they are located.

ORGANIZATIONAL CLIMATE

So far we have explored in depth the concept of organizational culture, and now we turn to the related concept of organizational climate. If culture is what makes the organization distinctive, climate is 'what it feels like to work here'. It is based on employees' perceptions of the work environment (Rousseau, 1988). Climate can include descriptions and perceptions at the individual, group or organizational level of analysis, i.e. what it feels like to me, how the group or team feels, how the whole organization feels.

Individual perceptions of the work environment are usually termed psychological climate, and when shared to a level sufficient for aggregation to the group or organizational level, are labelled group/team or organizational climate. Schneider (1990; Schneider et al., 2013) suggests that organizational climate perceptions reflect the behaviours that are rewarded and supported in an organization. People at work also interpret processes, practices and behaviours in the organizational environment in relation to their own sense of well-being (James, James, & Ashe, 1990), and this contributes to the experience of climate. Where supervisors are authoritarian and demanding, employees' well-being will be negatively affected and thus the organizational climate will be poor.

Individuals can describe the organizational environment in an overall global sense (a great place to work or the opposite), as well as in a more specific, targeted manner. The latter descriptions are sometimes called domain-specific climates and might be focused on the climate for safety (is there a high emphasis on safety in the organization?), climate for service (a strong emphasis on meeting customers' needs), a justice climate or a climate for innovation (much encouragement for employees to develop and implement ideas for new and improved ways of doing things). In relation to the global organizational climate, James and his colleagues (James & James, 1989) describe four dimensions of global organizational climate, which they identified across a number of different work contexts:

a Role stress and lack of harmony (including role ambiguity, conflict and overload, subunit conflict, low organizational identification and low management concern and awareness).

b Job challenge and autonomy (as well as job importance).

c Leadership facilitation and support (including leader trust, support, goal facilitation, promoting positive relationships, psychological versus hierarchical influence).

d Workgroup cooperation, friendliness, and warmth; (James & McIntyre, 1996).

Patterson et al. (2005) developed a measure of overall climate based partly on the Competing Values model and partly on dimensions identified in previous research – called the Organizational Climate Measure. This assesses climate in relation to 17 dimensions, as shown in Figure 13.2.

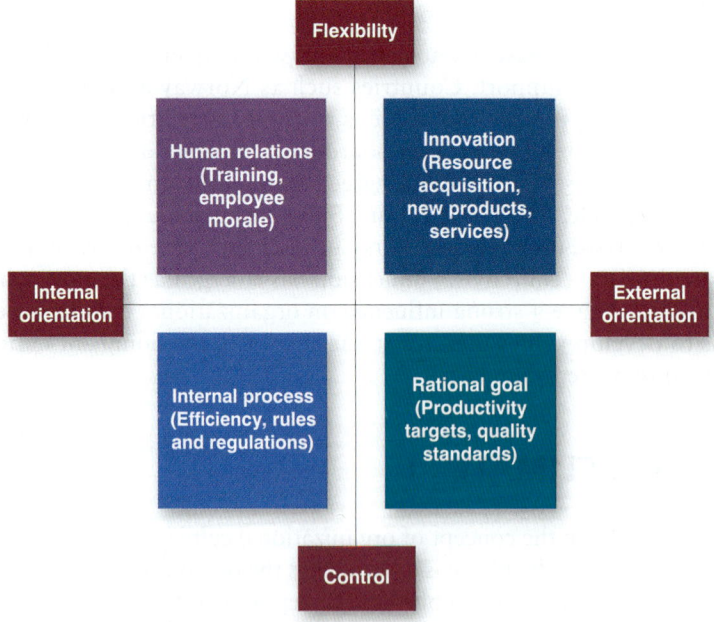

Figure 13.2   The organizational climate measure: dimensions mapped against competing values quadrats

Climate versus culture

Are you clear about the difference between culture and climate so far? Scholars tend to agree that culture is about the shared values and meanings of those within an organization and use an anthropological metaphor to communicate this (imagine being a traveller in a foreign land trying to understand its culture). Climate refers more to how it feels to work in the organization – the experience of it. Climate is a meteorological metaphor so it's about the weather: is it cold, hot, stormy, changeable, warm or mild? For organizational climate this reads across to: is it friendly, competitive, busy, laid-back or authoritarian? There are many attempts to differentiate and contrast the two concepts since they are both used to provide a summative description of the organization. One key difference that writers refer to is the measurement methods associated with each. Some researchers argue that climate is accessible through quantitative survey measures while culture is only accessible using qualitative methods (observation, interview, document analysis, etc.). These are artificial dichotomies, however. It is rather like comparing apples and cars. The key to understanding the two concepts is the metaphorical basis of them. Culture is about traditions, ways of doing things, values, hidden assumptions – the metaphor of understanding national cultures. Climate is a more generalized notion and is derived from the concept of typical weather patterns in an area (cold, wet, stormy, warm, changeable, dark, etc.). Climate is very much infused with the affective reactions of employees to their work environment. It is often described as members' surface experiences and perceptions, while culture shapes (almost unseen) taken-for-granted and even unconscious assumptions about how to behave in the organization and the meaning of events. A recent review of research on climate and culture has called for the concepts to be integrated in theory and research (Schneider et al., 2017), and there is even a new term ('climcult').

Climates for success

Climate perceptions provide the context for understanding employee attitudes and behaviour (Schneider, Bowen, Erhart, & Holcombe, 2000). Research has suggested that climate perceptions are associated with a variety of important outcomes at the individual, group and organizational levels. These include leader behaviour (Rousseau, 1988; Rentsch, 1990), turnover intentions (Rousseau, 1988; Rentsch, 1990), job satisfaction (Mathieu, Hoffmann, & Farr, 1993; James & Tetrick, 1986; James & Jones, 1980), individual job performance (Brown & Leigh, 1996; Pritchard & Karasick, 1973) and organizational performance (Lawler, Hall, & Oldham, 1974; Patterson, Warr, & West, 2004a). The domains of climate and culture that some researchers (Wiley & Brooks, 2000) believe are the key to organizational success are:

- Customer service:
  - Strong emphasis on customer service.
  - Company provides quality service.
  - Customer problems corrected quickly.
  - Delivers products/services in a timely fashion.

- Quality:
  - Senior management committed to quality service and demonstrate that quality is a priority.
  - Supervisors provide guidance for service and set good examples in relation to quality.
  - Quality of work is rated.

- Clear service standards are met.
- Quality is a priority vs meeting deadlines.
- Quality is a priority vs cost containment.
- Continuous improvement.

- Involvement:
  - Front-line staff have the authority to meet customer's needs.
  - Encouragement to be innovative and participate in decisions.
  - Sufficient effort is made to get opinions of staff.
  - Management use employees' good ideas.

- Training:
  - Plans for training and development.
  - Opportunities for staff to attend training and to improve skills.
  - Staff have the right training for them to improve.
  - Staff are satisfied with training opportunities.
  - New employees get necessary training.

- Information/knowledge:
  - Management gives clear vision/direction.
  - Staff understand goals clearly.
  - Staff are informed about issues.
  - Departments keep each other informed.
  - Enough warning about changes.
  - Satisfaction with organizational information.

- Teamwork/organization:
  - Cooperation to get the job done.
  - Management encourages teamwork.
  - Workload fairly divided.
  - Enough people to do the work.
  - Problems in teams corrected quickly.

- Overall satisfaction:
  - High job satisfaction.
  - Jobs use skills and abilities.
  - Work gives a feeling of accomplishment.
  - Satisfaction with organization.
  - Rate the organization as a place to work.
  - Proud to work for the organization.

- Would recommend working for the organization.
- High job security.
- Not seriously considering leaving the organization.

Others argue that there can be no universals and that success depends on the differing contingent relationships between task, environment and cultures that each organization faces. Still others argue that we must look at more specific aspects of climate and culture and relate these to specific outcomes – domain-specific approaches – safety, service, justice and compassion, for example.

Safety climate

When leaders and employees value safety, there are fewer accidents and 'near misses' (Christian, Bradley, Wallace, & Burke, 2009). Safety climate has also been linked with safety behaviours and accidents (Hofmann & Morgeson, 1999), and with safety compliance in the health sector (preventing errors that could harm patients or staff) (Murphy, Gershon, & DeJoy, 1996). Zohar and colleagues have shown in research over several decades that when supervisors model safe behaviour, pay attention to safety issues and reward safe behaviours, a strong safety climate emerges (Zohar, 2010, 2014; Zohar & Polachek, 2014). Understanding how leaders' focus on safety influences the development of safety climate, which in turn impacts on accident frequency, is of course practically relevant in many work settings – construction, military, healthcare, mining, oil and gas, for example. One of us (MW) worked for a year in a coal mine in Wales after completing his PhD and observed that safety was emphasized above all else, both by leaders and by his fellow team members. And the safety focus of the team was critical for ensuring that each team member avoided accidents in what was a hostile environment. In all these settings, psychological research has demonstrated how we can intervene to create safer environments for people at work. Research in the area of innovation also suggests that group climate factors influence levels of innovative behaviour in healthcare that promote high-quality and safer care (West & Anderson, 1996).

Service climate

Researchers in the USA particularly have advanced our knowledge of the concept of a service climate, which refers to a shared orientation within organizations to providing good service to customers and supporting them. Using their model of service climate, Schneider and colleagues demonstrated that service climate is related to customer perceptions of service quality (Schneider, 1980; Schneider, Macey, Lee, & Young, 2009; Schneider, Parkington, & Buxton, 1980; Schneider, White, & Paul, 1998; Salvaggio et al., 2007). Again, leadership behaviours emerge as particularly influential. Other research has explored how aspects of service climate, such as sustaining positive emotional displays (smiling and being enthusiastic with customers), can lead to exhaustion (Lam, Huang, & Janssen, 2010). Research in Europe has shown how employee engagement (vigour, absorption and dedication at work) is associated with higher levels of customer satisfaction (Salanova, Agut, & Peiró, 2005). Service climate also includes the service provided by departments within an organization to the other departments they interact with. When the finance, HR, estates or legal departments are supportive and helpful in their interactions with other departments, this seems to lead to better service towards customers also (Ehrhart, Witt, Schneider, & Perry, 2011). Meta-analysis confirms that service climate within an organization predicts customer satisfaction and that leadership is particularly significant as a determinant of such climates (Hong, Liao, Hu, & Jiang, 2013). What leaders pay attention to, monitor, reward and model in their own behaviour communicates to employees what is valued in the organization. Overall, this research suggests the value of creating psychosocial environments characterized by orientations of altruism, helping, civility and compassion (Worline & Dutton, 2017).

Justice climate

Building on the many individual studies of justice (procedural, distributive, informational, interpersonal), researchers have also studied the extent to which organizations as a whole have a climate of justice. Various measures of justice climate have been used to show that such climates predict higher levels of organizational commitment, lower staff turnover and higher customer satisfaction (Simons & Roberson, 2003). Recent meta-analyses of individual-level justice perceptions (Colquitt et al., 2013) and group-level justice climate (Whitman, Caleo, Carpenter, Horner, & Bernerth, 2012) reveal that justice climates predict group and organizational performance. Of course, it makes sense that the more people perceive their organizations as just, fair and transparent, the more they will be committed, engaged and trusting. This research also shows how important it is for leaders to ensure that people in workplaces perceive their organizations (and leaders) as just and fair.

The research on culture and climate has shown that the shared perceptions of people at work, based on organizational policies, practices and behaviour within teams and across organizations as a whole, are important for safety, justice, discrimination, innovation and (in healthcare) patient mortality (West, Topakas, & Dawson, 2014). And the behaviour of leaders is particularly influential in shaping the climate perceptions of staff. From the work on culture we know that symbols, stories and rituals in organizations do matter, because they communicate to employees what is valued within the organization (not necessarily the same as the statement of values on the organization website).

From the exploration of culture and climate so far, it is clear too that they are dynamic concepts. Culture and climate change as a consequence of many different forces. Indeed, change in organizations is a central concept in work psychology. Below we explore why change occurs, types of change, why employees sometimes resist and sometimes welcome change and the strategies managers can use to achieve change. We also describe different methods of managing the change process.

Climate and culture concepts enable us to understand and articulate the differences between organizations and to begin to understand how we can go about helping them to change for the better. As psychologists we are not only concerned with understanding and describing organizations, but also with making them more nourishing and developmental environments within which people can flourish.

ORGANIZATIONAL CHANGE

Organizations are similar to living organisms in that they must adapt to their environments in order to survive. In 2008, we saw the world plunged into a major financial crisis as banks lost billions of dollars and some collapsed altogether. Credit, which businesses need in order to fund innovation and expansion, was no longer available. Moreover, with changes in bank lending, some existing loans became more expensive. As the confidence felt by consumers fell ('the economy is in bad shape, I might lose my job, so I must spend less'), demand worldwide dropped. Moreover, in some countries (the USA, Japan, the UK, Germany) the property market collapsed and house prices fell by over 20 per cent after years of rapid growth. This led house owners to become even more worried about the drop in the value of their assets. The loss of confidence became a vicious cycle. The effects on employment levels, business bankruptcies and business growth are sudden, dramatic and global.

Faced with these changed circumstances, some businesses dug the trenches within which to weather out the storm, stopped spending, and worked even harder at what had worked well in the past. Others began to look for new markets, or made redundancies to reduce costs. Others decided to spend more on R&D to develop new products and to cut spending in areas such as staff training or travel. Some companies tried to be smart about the decisions to cut R&D spending. They did this by identifying the best bets for new products, cutting out 60 per cent of investment in product development (saving 60 per cent) and increasing by 20 per cent the spend on those they thought were the best bets, thereby saving 40 per cent overall. However, they actually increased the spending on the areas they felt were most important. All these changes occurred because the organizations were trying to survive or even prosper. Economic factors, therefore, cause change. But a wide variety of other factors lead to organizational change, such as:

- *Actions of competitors.* When Apple first produced the new iPhone touch phone, their competitors were left behind and the iPhone sold out in days. Immediately there was a rush to develop and market new touch phones. If the local supermarket cuts prices on its products, the next supermarket down the road is likely to follow suit.
- *Government legislation.* When a government requires organizations to pay for the cost of transport in major cities (such as traffic 'congestion charges'), businesses may decide to relocate in order to reduce costs, moving to a more rural area or another city where such charges do not apply. If a government introduces better maternity benefits (longer paid leave for mothers), some businesses may relocate their activities to other countries with less enlightened policies in order to reduce their wage bills.
- *Environmental factors.* Climate emergency requires businesses to have ever 'greener' policies and practices. Reducing energy costs by changing the way products are made may be a response to higher oil prices and carbon taxes.
- *Demographic factors.* As the European population ages, businesses are finding it tougher to recruit young skilled workers. They are persuading some employees to stay at work longer rather than leaving when they reach 60 or 65, seeking skilled workers from other countries or relocating their operations to countries where the supply of skilled labour is greater (such as India) and the costs of labour are lower.
- *Ethics.* Recognizing the discrimination against women in salary levels which exists internationally, some organizations take action to ensure equality. Concerns with corporate social responsibility may lead some organizations to recognize that exploring every possible loophole in the tax regulations to reduce the amount they pay (including investing assets as much as possible outside the country in 'tax havens') might be considered unethical. They may then reduce the number of accountants and tax lawyers they employ and commit to paying higher tax bills.
- *Leaders.* One insightful Dilbert cartoon describes 'Bungee Bosses' who fly in on a bungee rope, announcing 'I'm your new boss, let's change everything before I am reassigned, whoops, too late – bye', before he or she disappears on the retracting elastic rope. New leaders are very likely to want to demonstrate impact through their interventions and usually initiate change. Barack Obama's first actions as president were to sign an order closing the infamous Guantanamo Bay prison and to set a date for the withdrawal of US troops from Iraq. He also swiftly announced a huge federal budget to stimulate the ailing economy. He struggled to fulfil his commitments, just as Donald Trump struggled to repeal Obamacare and build a wall on the US–Mexico border.

Anything can change in organizations (except perhaps the fact that change is continuous), but the main domains of change are usually:

- Organizational goals and strategies.
- Organizing arrangements: organizational structure, policies and procedures, reward systems, physical setting.

- Social factors: management style.
- Individual attributes: knowledge, skills and abilities (KSAs), motivation, behaviour.
- Work methods: technology, job design, information technology, workflow design.

Change in one area is likely to have an impact in other domains also, so changing reward systems will affect motivation while changes in technology will require changes in KSAs among employees.

Models of change

Episodic and continuous change

Weick and Quinn (1999) believe there are two types of change – episodic and continuous, sometimes respectively referred to as planned and emergent change. Episodic is planned and potentially revolutionary. Its aim is to make a fundamental and lasting change in some aspect of the organization's functioning. Such change tends to be big, noisy and involve lots of major resources in the form of time or money. Making large-scale redundancies, restructuring the organization to reduce the number of layers in the hierarchy, acquiring another organization, opening up a new operation in Malaysia or closing down an existing factory in Ireland – they all involve high-profile, planned and revolutionary change. Weick and Quinn argue that such change is less likely to be successful than continuous change because it is an either/or gamble.

The second type is continuous change. Organizations with a climate of quality improvement change promote continuous reflection and learning. They encourage all staff to take responsibility for learning and change. Their jobs include responsibility for improving task performance, whether it is maintaining the manufacturing equipment or winning new customers. Such a strategy is more likely to be effective where bureaucracy is minimized and there are relatively few hierarchical levels so that employees do not feel they generally have to seek permission to implement new ideas, secure in the knowledge that innovation will generally be supported by managers.

Systems perspective on change

The systems perspective on organizational change views the organization as a dynamic system of interrelated components, epitomized in Senge's (1990) book *Fifth Discipline*. The basic tenet of the systems perspective is that organizations are composed of a multitude of subsystems that vary in their size and scope, and that change within one system will lead to changes in other related systems.

What are these subsystems? Miller (1967) identified four subsystems: organizational goals and values, technical subsystems, psychosocial subsystems and managerial subsystems. Nadler and Tushman (1997) also identified four different systems:

- *The work*. The day-to-day activities carried out by employees. Process design, pressures on the individual and rewards are part of this element.
- *The people*. The knowledge, skills, attitudes, experiences and characteristics of those who work in the organization.
- *The formal organization*. The structure, systems and policies in place.
- *The informal organization*. This consists of all the processes that emerge over time, such as power, influence, values and norms.

The model suggests that in considering change, all four components must be considered as interrelated elements. If you change one element, the other three will need to be attended to. If we change the type of work done, we must also consider how this aligns with individual skills (people), how this fits with the current organization of work in departments and teams (formal organization) and what activities, influences and power relationships will be affected by the change (informal organization). If this alignment is not managed, the organization will not change, but homeostasis will be maintained and change will fizzle out. Systems theories generally extend their perspective to define organizations as 'open' systems. This means that they consider the impact of external or environmental stimuli on organizational systems – organizations are essentially reactive to external change rather than being driven only by internal imperatives.

To help understand systems and their reciprocal effects upon one another, organizational theorists have constructed many guiding models. One example, the Burke–Litwin model, is presented below.

The Burke–Litwin model This model (Burke & Litwin, 1992) is a comprehensive and useful model of organizational performance and change. The model identifies a number of key factors and their relationships with one another. It shows the progression from environmental demands, through macro-level changes to factors such as leadership and strategy, and subsequently through to individual and organizational performance. The key features of the model and approach are:

- The distinction between transformational factors (mission and strategy, leadership, organizational culture) and transactional or operational factors (structure, systems, management, practices and climate). If transformational factors are changed, they have an effect across the whole organization. If transactional factors are changed, they are less likely to have an organization-wide impact.
- The external environment is the most powerful driver of organizational change.
- Changes in the external environment affect transformational factors. These in turn lead to changes in the transactional factors.
- Together, these changes in transformational and transactional factors affect motivation, which in turn affects individual and organizational performance.
- The components of the model interact in particular ways – changes in one will likely lead to specific changes in the others.
- The key factors for major change are the transformational factors.
- Transactional factors are more relevant for optimizing or fine-tuning the organization.

The learning organization

Another perspective on change proposes a proactive approach to change and create cultures within which learning happens continually at all levels to ensure that organizations are shaping as much as being shaped by change. This has led to the development of the notions of action learning and the learning organization. Action learning proposes that organizations should continuously review their functioning, diagnosing gaps between current and desired performance, identifying objectives for change, implementing change, evaluating the outcomes and institutionalizing the whole approach. These steps in action learning are depicted in (Figure 13.3).

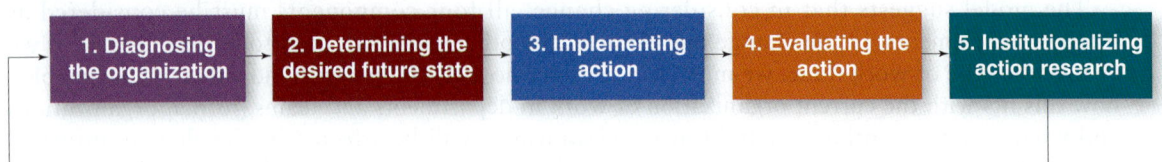

Figure 13.3 The steps in action learning

The *learning organization* works to create, acquire and transfer knowledge in order that the organization adapts itself continually on the basis of new knowledge and insight, as well as to the myriad of powerful external forces that influence its survival. Those who advocate a culture of learning (e.g. Senge, 1990) believe that the rate at which individuals and organizations learn may be the only sustainable competitive advantage in a world characterized by rapid change, highly integrated economies and an increasingly interconnected information world. To produce the conditions for organizational learning and continuous change, managers must put in place mechanisms that encourage employees to take responsibility for learning and for sharing insights with others (Van der Krogt, 1998). These mechanisms include:

- A training and development plan linked to the business strategy (for an organization intent on developing more international markets, training for staff in cross-cultural working might be part of the training and development plan).
- Line managers developing employees, e.g. through coaching them to improve their skills.
- The use of personal development and performance reviews to enable employees to develop objectives to improve their work performance and develop their KSAs.
- Enabling employees to learn about ways of working outside their immediate job role, such as through secondments, visiting external suppliers/customers, work shadowing, job rotations (employees fulfilling a variety of roles on a regular basis rather than staying in one job permanently) (Shipton, Dawson, West, & Patterson, 2002).

How do employees react to change?

Managers are often those who drive change in organizations and they do so (hopefully almost always) because they foresee benefits for the organization, its customers or its employees from the change. Some changes are welcomed by employees, such as schemes to reduce wasteful uses of energy or to improve the speed of information given to customers so that the latter are happier with the service they receive. And some changes are not welcomed or are resisted by employees, especially those that employees believe will make it more difficult for them to do their jobs well.

Managing change involves understanding the reasons why people resist change in organizations and recognizing that resistance to change is not necessarily good or bad. In some instances it is a normal and natural reaction to change. In other instances it is a reasonable reaction to an inappropriate attempt to change the status quo. Not all innovation and change is for the best, nor is it always well thought out. Resistance to change can be an important force for ensuring that change is introduced wisely, or it can be an instinctive and unhelpful reaction to the uncertainty that change heralds.

Why do people sometimes resist change? One reason is the feelings of *uncertainty and insecurity* that reduce people's acceptance of change. When changes to methods of production are proposed with the development of teamworking, employees may feel anxious that their fellow team members will not be up to the job or that they may not get on with them. Another is *selective perception and retention* – when people hear about the change they listen out for and remember better the potentially threatening aspects: 'Team working will mean I won't get credit for the work I do, it will be invisible in the team's efforts. Therefore I won't get my bonus.' A related cause of resistance to change is *misunderstanding* about the nature of the change and its consequences. This often occurs when there is inadequate consultation and information sharing about the changes to be introduced. Consequently, suspicions and misunderstandings grow and people inevitably resist or even sabotage the change. Managing change effectively means informing very fully all those affected by, or who perceive they may be affected by, the change. Then, of course, there is *habit*: 'We have always done it this way and it will just be hard work to change things.' Change is often perceived as posing *threats to status, security, pay, job role or the social environment*. People resist change if they see it threatening their job security, power, status, pay differentials or the variety of their jobs. Working in teams may be seen as 'being forced not to work with the people I have always got on with and working with people I don't know so well and who I may not get on with'. And, as we have already suggested, employees are good judges and may see that *the change is unwise*. Sometimes we simply KNOW that it is not going to help us do our jobs better.

But it is not just individuals who resist change. Sometimes organizations as a whole have powerful means for resisting change – even change that is necessary for the organization to survive and prosper. Argyris (1993) termed the processes by which organizations accomplish this as 'defensive routines'.

As a consequence of their scale and complexity, organizations can be compared with organisms that have a personality and life of their own. Analogous to living organisms, they develop immune systems to fight against attacks that threaten them. These immune systems in one sense are found in the norms and unwritten rules of the organization and can be very difficult to detect. Where they are detrimental to the organization's long-term effectiveness, these organizational defences are referred to as 'defensive routines'. As routines they are set into motion automatically and often without deliberate intent on the part of any one individual. Defensive routines are often designed to reduce difficulty and embarrassment within organizations and so can inhibit learning. Because they are designed to maintain the status quo, they often prevent the organization from dealing with the root causes of problems. They are one of the most important causes of failures in the implementation of change, because anything that threatens to change the status quo is likely to be dealt with as a virus. According to Argyris, who conceived the notion, defensive routines are so closely entwined with organizations' norms that they are undiscussable and their undiscussability is also undiscussable! Defensive routines make the unreasonable seem reasonable and are often disguised as virtues. An example is where people in an organization continually blame market conditions, political changes and economic circumstances for problems the organization is experiencing. Regardless of what goes on within the organization, problems are always explained in terms of what is occurring outside. Consequently, a kind of cohesion is maintained between people within the organization who collude together in not addressing their own performance problems and the need to change.

Another example is denial of the existence of a problem in the first place. The organization might have before it the evidence of a market downturn in sales and orders, but senior managers keep dismissing this simply as a 'blip' in the market, although the blip is clearly, to any outside observer, a major precipice. Another example of this 'faking good' is an immediate reaction of crushing any suggestions for new and improved ways of doing things on the basis that it has been tried and failed elsewhere, or that it will cost too much or that the initiator does not really understand the complexities of the situation. In some organizations, large numbers of people have survived by 'faking good' and marking time in their work. Innovation represents a threat to the cosy system they have created and is habitually resisted. Therefore, the reaction of those within such organizations is always to reject new ideas, but their reaction is undiscussable. Indeed, in such organizations innovation is often promoted verbally, but in practice any attempt to introduce innovation is sharply thwarted. Suggestions for new ideas are tolerated and the innovator is placated by lukewarm words of support, but without the practical follow-through of resources, time and real commitment.

Exposing defensive routines is all the more difficult because they are so hard to detect. People become immensely frustrated at the struggle involved in implementing a clearly sensible innovation, particularly when they are unable to understand why it is proving so difficult and why it arouses so much hostility. Below are some strategies for confronting defensive routines:

- Have arguments well thought out; reasons should be compelling, vigorous and publicly testable.
- Do not promise more than can be delivered; unrealistic promises can be seized upon to reject what is essentially a good idea.
- Be prepared to admit mistakes and then use them as a means of learning (for yourself and the organization).
- Always try to look beneath the surface. Continually ask 'why?' of those who resist the change.
- Surface and bring into the open subjects that seem to be undiscussable, despite the hostility this may generate.
- Learn to be aware of when you are involved in or colluding with defensive routines.
- Try to see through the issues of efficiency (doing things right) to the more important questions of effectiveness (doing the right things).

Forcefield analysis of change

Kurt Lewin, a leading social psychologist of the early 20th century (1890–1947), argued that change occurs when the forces favouring change strengthen, resistance to change lessens or both occur simultaneously. Otherwise organizations remain in equilibrium. This statement (which will probably strike you as self-evident) contains within it a useful means for thinking through how to manage change. Lewin described all situations in which we find ourselves as a 'temporary equilibrium held in place by two sets of forces: driving forces which push change along and restraining forces which pull back against change' (Lewin, 1997). Understanding those forces will help the innovator towards successful implementation. Lewin also suggested that we will often be more successful in implementing change when we reduce the forces against change. The temptation of managers is often just to focus on the forces in favour of change (such as the number of employees who agree with the idea), and they typically do this by trying to increase, via persuasion about the value of the change, the numbers of employees who agree. But forces resisting change are often more powerful (for example, because we resist losses more than we seek potential gains – Kahneman, 2011), and when these are reduced, forces *for* change automatically become more important.

Figure 13.4 describes a strategy for reducing resistance to change based on a combination of stakeholder and forcefield analysis. This exercise enables the development of an overview of how much resistance to change is likely to be present and where major problems may arise within an organization. It enables strategy planning for managing resistance to change and participation processes within an organization.

Step 1 Define the change you wish to implement. **The outcome of the change will be the equilibrium which you are hoping to achieve in the future. It is therefore important that this outcome is clearly defined.**

Step 2 Now identify all those individuals and groups which could have an influence on your ability to introduce the change in your organization. **For each of these 'stakeholders' identify major advantages and disadvantages which may accrue to them with the introduction of the change.**

Stakeholder	Advantages	Disadvantages
_____	_____	_____
_____	_____	_____
_____	_____	_____

Step 3 The forcefield. **Draw a 'forcefield' with an arrow to represent each stakeholder. For each arrow in the forcefield you will need to decide:**

(a) the direction of the arrow, for or against – although it is sometime difficult to know exactly how others are thinking, for the purposes of this exercise you must make a decision based on your current knowledge of the situation. If the arrow represents a group within which there are mixed opinions, you must still decide which side, on balance, the group as a whole will be. You may, however, indicate the situation within the arrow – for example by patchy shading.

(b) the size of the arrow – this will represent the relative power of the individual group or factor to influence the introduction of the change. You may wish to use colour and shading to make the arrows as representative of your view of the situation as possible. The greater their influence, the bigger the arrow and the more you therefore need to concentrate on them.

Restraining Forces

⬇   ⬇   ⬇   ⬇   ⬇

_____ INTRODUCTION OF CHANGE _____

⬆ ⬆   ⬆   ⬆   ⬆   ⬆   ⬆

Driving Forces

Step 4 Action planning. After contemplating the forcefield that you have drawn, you may have some new insights into the situation. Does the environment for the introduction of the change look more positive than you had thought? Alternatively, are the arrows more heavily weighted on the restraining side of the change line? A review of the forcefield will enable you to decide where you need to exert energy in order to:

(a) decrease the power and influence of the restraining forces

(b) increase the power and influence of the driving forces

Based on the analysis, what actions could you take to reduce the influence of the restraining forces and increase the power of the supporting forces? Your action plan should be helpful in determining strategies for moving forward. Try to identify ways in which the balance of the forces can be weighted more strongly in your favour. This may be by finding new helping forces, or by trying to eliminate or lessen the effect of some of the hindering forces. People often find that it tends to be easier to do the latter. To use the car analogy, it is as if one's foot is already down on the floor and there is no way to increase the driving force. The easiest solution may well be to take off the handbrake!

Figure 13.4 Analyzing and managing resistance to change

> **DISCUSS WITH A COLLEAGUE**
>
> Using the forcefield and stakeholder analysis, first identify a change you would like to make in your university or another organization and then develop a plan to bring the change about. Put this plan together, consulting carefully with colleagues, and decide the steps you would need to take to achieve success. Present the plan to your tutor and ask them to provide feedback on what you may have missed in your analysis and get their guidance on whether they feel it is appropriate for you to pursue the idea. Then decide whether you would like to go ahead and try to make the change. Carefully consider the ethical implications of any change you propose to make in any organization.

DESIGNING AND IMPLEMENTING CHANGE AND INNOVATION

Richard Daft (1992) proposed an integrative strategy for implementing change based on seven stages or elements:

1. *Diagnose a true need for change.* Correctly identifying the nature of the problem is fundamental to effective change or innovation. It is therefore important to spend sufficient time diagnosing the true need for change and identifying the nature of the problem.
2. *Find an idea that fits the need.* This means making sure that the correct match is found between the nature of the problem and the idea for change.
3. *Get top management support.* Innovation and change attempts are more successful to the extent that people with power support them.
4. *Design the change for incremental implementation.* Daft argues that the prospects for success for innovations are improved dramatically if each part of the process can be designed and implemented sequentially. Then so-called 'teething problems' can be managed one by one as they appear, rather than trying to deal with a whole jaw-full of problems at the same time.
5. *Develop plans to overcome resistance to change.* Align plans for change with the needs and goals of users. Here it is important to ensure that the innovation meets a real need. If people within the organization do not believe that the change has value, or if top management does not support it, the organization will resist the change. Ways of overcoming resistance include:
   - Communication and education. Clear and persistent communication about the nature of the need, the value of the change and the process of implementation is likely to reduce resistance to change. Daft argues that far more communication and education than managers think is necessary should be undertaken, since typically this is underestimated.
   - Participation and involvement. Extensive and early involvement of those affected by the change will reduce resistance to change. Participation in the design of the change is the single most potent way of reducing resistance.

6 *Create change teams.* Organizational changes are implemented more successfully if teams that carry responsibility for their successful implementation are created.

7 *Foster change champions.* Champions are volunteers who are deeply committed to a particular innovation or change. They have the responsibility of ensuring that all necessary resources and technical supports are available and they persuade people about the value of the implementation.

Even following these prescriptions, many changes are not implemented successfully in organizations. John Kotter (1995) has identified eight core reasons for the failure of organizational changes. They are the failures to:

- Establish a sense of urgency about need for change.
- Form a powerful guiding coalition to drive the change forward.
- Create a vision of the benefits and value of the change.
- Communicate the vision to all affected by the change.
- Empower others to act on the vision, giving employees the opportunity to help make the change happen.
- Plan for and create short-term wins so that people are quickly convinced of the value of the change.
- Consolidate improvements and produce still more change.
- Institutionalize new approaches so that the change is embedded and stable.

Organizational change is constant. The challenge for psychologists and other leaders in organizations is to understand and manage change so that it is shaped to support the fundamental purposes of the organization and to enable the effectiveness and flourishing of those who work within and are served by the organization. That is our challenge, and existing theory and research has taken us some way towards this. One of the biggest challenges is educating leaders in how to manage change effectively in practice.

DISCUSS WITH A COLLEAGUE

What would you identify as the four or five most important principles in managing change, based on the material you have read in this chapter?

PIONEERING WORK PSYCHOLOGISTS

Professor Binna Kandola

Professor Binna Kandola is a Business Psychologist, Senior Partner and co-founder of the company Pearn Kandola, where he has worked for over 30 years on a variety of projects for public and private sector clients both in the UK and overseas. The business is built on a core value of 'embracing the power of difference'. They focus on Diversity and Inclusion, Assessment and Development with a mission of making the modern workplace fair for everyone. Binna Kandola draws on research evidence and much practical experience working with organizations to show that: *'Difference inspires change. It inspires scientists to break new ground. It inspires social media giants to disrupt this new age of communication. It inspires countries to vote for strong female or minority leaders. Most importantly for us, difference inspires business.'*

His work also focuses on gender bias and unconscious bias in organizations. He is the author of three books on these subjects – *The Invention of Difference: The story of gender bias at work*, *The Value of Difference: Eliminating bias in organisations* and *Racism at Work: The danger of indifference*. In 2004, Binna joined the UK Government's National Employment Panel and was appointed Chair of the Minority Ethnic Group. He is currently a visiting professor at Leeds University Business School and at Aston University Business School. In 2012 the University of Aston awarded him an Honorary DSc – Doctor of Science. He is a consulting editor for the *Journal of Occupational and Organisational Psychology*. He is a regular contributor to the media and has appeared on Sky News, BBC Breakfast, Channel 4 News and the Radio 4 Today show. Professor Binna Kandola was awarded an OBE by the Queen in 2008 for his services to disadvantaged people and diversity.

POSITIVE WORK

Climates of compassion

Worline and Dutton (2017) offer the following guidelines for developing climates of compassion in organizations.

Attending

- Noticing suffering at work.
- Inquiring, because this is crucial to awakening compassion.
- Recognizing time pressure, overload and performance demands – these distract us from noticing suffering at work.

- Policies, rules, and norms of conduct can orient us towards blame and punishment rather than curiosity about what is happening with the other person.
- Presence and mindfulness are vital.

Understanding

- Suffering is often masked by missed deadlines, errors or difficult and ambiguous work situations that trigger blame instead of compassion.
- Leaders can learn to be curious about the causes of difficult or ambiguous work situations as a way of cultivating more generous interpretations.
- All leaders can practise cultivating the positive default assumption that others are good, capable and worthy of compassion – offering the benefit of the doubt.
- Leaders can withhold blame by steering conversations about errors towards learning.
- We can imbue others with dignity and worth no matter what their role, position or difference from us.
- We can cultivate presence with suffering as a form of being authentic with others.

Empathizing

- Fostering mindfulness is hugely powerful – an awareness of changing conditions in ourselves and others on a moment-to-moment basis. It helps us to remain calm and steady in the face of suffering – our own as well as others.
- We can cultivate the capacity for attunement, which involves being aware of another person while simultaneously staying in touch with our own somatic senses and experiences. We can heighten the sense of interconnection.
- We can develop empathic listening, the capacity to tune in to feelings of concern as we hear others' perspectives and experiences. This allows us to be present without needing to fix, solve or intervene necessarily.
- Empathy at work helps us to 'feel our way forward' together and motivates compassion.
- Identifying with others leads to empathy and a higher likelihood of compassionate action.
- Feeling similar to the other contributes to identification.
- Physical and psychological presence, conveyed through eye contact, verbal tone, posture and facial expressions, heightens identification.

Helping

- Compassionate acting involves spontaneity and improvisation and is directed by what is most useful for those who are suffering.
- Skilful compassion involves taking actions that address suffering.
- These include creating flexible time to cope with suffering, buffering someone from task overload, monitoring and checking in, generating resources that will alleviate suffering and designing rituals that convey support.
- Compassionate action can be hindered by legalistic approaches that deny human connection.
- Corrosive politics, toxic interactions, consistent underperformance and other forms of conflict at work are sources of suffering that must be addressed. They require 'fierce compassion'.
- Compassion is reduced when people fear that they will be viewed as weak or vulnerable for giving or receiving compassion.
- Importance of integrity and privacy.

SUMMARY

This chapter describes how to study organizational culture by maintaining awareness of all your experiences within organizations. Key dimensions for describing culture include hierarchy, pay differentials, job descriptions, norms (dress formality, for example), espoused values and rituals (award ceremonies, mission statements), stories, jokes and jargon, and the physical environment. Organizational culture is defined as the set of assumptions held by organization members about the organization. Schein's levels of culture are described – artefacts, espoused values and hidden assumptions. Other models of culture are also presented, including Goffee and Jones' Sociability versus Solidarity model, Quinn and Cameron's Competing Values model and Martin's Integration, Differentiation and Fragmentation approach. The development of culture is described and the key roles of leaders and socialization tactics are illustrated. Cross-cultural variations in values are described, including masculinity–femininity, power distance, uncertainty avoidance, individualism versus collectivism and long-term versus short-term time perspective.

Organizational climate is defined as what it feels like to work here and is contrasted with the concept of culture. Dimensions of climate include role stress and lack of harmony, job challenge and autonomy, leadership facilitation and support, and workgroup cooperation, friendliness and warmth. An instrument for measuring climate (Organizational Climate Measure) is described. Climates for success include emphases on customer service, involvement, quality, training, information, teamwork and cooperation, and overall satisfaction.

The chapter identifies the forces leading organizations to change, including economic forces, actions of competitors, government legislation, environmental factors, demographic factors and leaders. Two types of change are described – episodic and continuous. The chapter describes models of change, including Weick and Quinn's episodic and continuous change, and systems models that see change as encompassing multiple elements in the organization. These include Nadler and Tushman's model of interrelated systems and the Burke–Litwin model.

Learning organizations seek to create continuous positive change and use mechanisms such as action learning to promote continuous improvement, learning and development plans for employees, job rotations and secondments to ensure employees continually improve their knowledge skills and abilities.

Employees' reactions to change include selective perception and retention, uncertainty and insecurity, misunderstanding, habitual ways of responding and resistance. Organizational responses to change can include defensive routines designed to protect the organization from change. Strategies for overcoming defensive routines and resistance are described, including the use of forcefield and stakeholder analysis.

The chapter also describes how to diagnose and implement change by diagnosing a true need for change; finding an idea that fits the need; getting top management support; designing the change for incremental implementation; developing plans to overcome resistance to change; creating change teams; and fostering innovation champions. You have been introduced to the complex and exciting topic of organizational change, in order – as Kanter (1983) puts it – that you may become masters rather than victims of change.

DISCUSSION QUESTIONS

1 What is the difference between organizational climate and organizational culture? What is the value of each approach and in what circumstances, as a psychologist, would you focus on one or the other?

2 How is national culture likely to affect organizational culture and climate?

3 How helpful to managers and leaders are notions of culture and climate and how can they use them?

4 Can we change organizational culture and, if so, how?

5 Can you describe an organizational change that you have experienced? Was it successful and, if so, what factors made it successful or unsuccessful? What implications does that have for our understanding of organizational change?

6 Compare the value of the different models of change in describing an organizational change you have experienced.

FURTHER READING

Dixon-Woods, M., Baker, R., Charles, K., Dawson, J., Jerzembek, G., Martin, G., ... & Willars, J. (2014). Culture and behaviour in the English National Health Service: Overview of lessons from a large multimethod study. *BMJ Quality & Safety, 23*(2), 106–115.

Iles, V., & Sutherland, K. I. (2002). *Organisational change: A review for health care managers.* London, England: NCCSDO.

Quinn, R. E. (2004). *Building the bridge as you walk on it: A guide for leading change.* San Francisco, CA: John Wiley.

Schein, E. (2004). *Organizational culture and leadership* (3rd ed.). San Francisco, CA: Jossey-Bass.

Schein, E. H. (2010). *Organizational culture and leadership* (Vol. 2). Hoboken, NJ: John Wiley & Sons.

Schneider, B., & Barbera, K. M. (Eds.). (2014). *Oxford handbook of organizational climate and culture.* New York, NY: Oxford University Press.

Schneider, B., Ehrhart, M. G., & Macey, W. H. (2013). Organizational climate and culture. *Annual Reviews of Psychology, 64,* 361–388.

Schneider, B., González-Romá, V., Ostroff, C., & West, M. (2017). Organizational climate and culture: Reflections on the history of the constructs in the *Journal of Applied Psychology. 102,* 3, 468–482. Retrieved from dx.doi.org/10.1037/apl0000090

REFERENCES

Argyris, C. (1993). *Knowledge for action: A guide to overcoming barriers to organizational change.* San Francisco, CA: Jossey-Bass.

Ashkanasy, N. M., Wilderom, C. P. M., & Peterson, M. F. (2000). *Handbook of organizational culture and climate.* London, England: SAGE.

Brown, S., & Leigh, T. W. (1996). A new look at psychological climate and its relationship to job involvement, effort and performance. *Journal of Applied Psychology, 81,* 358–368.

Burke, W. W., & Litwin, G. H. (1992). A causal model of organizational performance and change. *Journal of Management, 18,* 523–545.

Cameron, K. S., & Quinn, R. E. (1997). *Diagnosing and changing organizational culture.* San Francisco, CA: Jossey-Bass.

Christian, M. S., Bradley, J. C., Wallace, J. C., & Burke, M. J. (2009). Workplace safety: A meta-analysis of the roles of person and situation factors. *Journal of Applied Psychology, 94*(5), 1103–1127. doi:10.1037/a0016172

Clinebell, S. (1984). Organizational effectiveness: An examination of recent empirical studies and the development of a contingency view. In W. D. Terpening & K. R. Thompson (Eds.), *Proceedings of the 27th Annual Conference Midwest Academy* of *Management* (pp. 92–102). University of Notre Dame, IN: Department of Management.

Colquitt, J. A., Scott, B. A., Rodell, J. B., Long, D. M., Zapata, C. P., Conlon, D. E., & Wesson, M. J. (2013). Justice at the millennium, a decade later: A meta-analytic test of social exchange and affect-based perspectives. *Journal of Applied Psychology, 98*(2), 199–236.

Daft, R. L. (1992). *Organizational theory and design* (4th ed.). New York, NY: West Publishing Company.

Dixon-Woods, M., Baker, R., Charles, K., Dawson, J., Jerzembek, G., Martin, G., ...West, M. (2013). Culture and behaviour in the English National Health Service: Overview of lessons from a large multimethod study. *BMJ Quality & Safety, 23*(2), 106–115. doi:10.1136/bmjqs-2013-001947

Ehrhart, K. H., Witt, L. A., Schneider, B., & Perry, S. J. (2011). Service employees give as they get: Internal service as a moderator of the service climate–service outcome relationship. *Journal of Applied Psychology, 96*, 423–431.

Emery, F. E., & Trist, E. L. (1965). The causal texture of organizational environments. *Human Relations, 18*, 21–32.

Goffee, R., & Jones, G. (1998). *The character of a corporation: How your company's culture can make or break your business*. London, England: HarperBusiness.

Hall, R. H. (1980). Effectiveness theory and organizational effectiveness. *Journal of Applied Behavioural Science, 16*, 536–545.

Hofmann, D. A., & Morgeson, F. P. (1999). Safety-related behavior as a social exchange: The role of perceived organizational support and leader–member exchange. *Journal of Applied Psychology, 84*, 286–296. doi:10.1037/0021-9010.84.2.286

Hofstede, G. (1980). *Culture's consequences: International differences in work-related values*. Beverly Hills, CA: SAGE.

Hofstede, G. (1983). The cultural relativity of organizational practices and theories. *Journal of International Business Studies, 14*, 31–46.

Hong, Y., Liao, H., Hu, J., & Jiang, K. (2013). Missing link in the service–profit chain: A meta-analytic review of the antecedents, consequences, and moderators of service climate. *Journal of Applied Psychology, 98*, 237–267.

James, L. A., & James, L. R. (1989). Integrating work environment perceptions: Explorations into the measurement of meaning. *Journal of Applied Psychology, 74*, 739–751.

James, L. R., James, L. A., & Ashe, D. K. (1990). The meaning of organizations: The role of cognition and values. In B. Schneider (Ed.), *Organizational climate and culture* (pp. 40–129). San Francisco, CA: Jossey-Bass.

James, L. R., & Jones, A. P. (1980). Perceived job characteristics and job satisfaction: An examination of reciprocal causation. *Personnel Psychology, 33*, 97–135.

James, L. R., & McIntyre, M. D. (1996). Perceptions of organizational climate. In Kevin R. Murphy (Ed.), *Individual differences and behaviour in organizations*. San Francisco, CA: Jossey-Bass.

James, L. R., & Tetrick, L. E. (1986). Confirmatory analytic tests of three causal models relating job perceptions to job satisfaction. *Journal of Applied Psychology, 71*, 77–82.

Kahneman, D. (2011). *Thinking fast and slow*. New York, NY: Farrar, Straus and Giroux.

Kanter, R. M. (1983). *The change masters: Corporate entrepreneurs at work*. London, England: Allen & Unwin.

Kotter, J. (1995). Leading change: Why transformation efforts fail. *Harvard Business Review, 73*, 59–67.

Lam, C. K., Huang, X., & Janssen, O. (2010). Contextualizing emotional exhaustion and positive emotional display: The signaling effects of supervisors' emotional exhaustion and service climate. *Journal of Applied Psychology, 95*(2), 368–376.

Lawler, E. E., Hall, D. T., & Oldham, G. R. (1974). Organizational climate: Relationship to organizational structure, process and performance. *Organizational Behaviour and Performance, 11*, 139–155.

Lewin, K. (1997). *Resolving social conflicts & Field theory in social science*. New York, NY: Harper & Row. (Reprinted from *Field theory in social science*, by K. Lewin, 1951, New York, NY: Harper & Row.)

Martin, J. (1992). *Cultures in organizations: Three perspectives*. London, England: Oxford University Press.

Mathieu, J. E., Hoffman, D. A., & Farr, J. L. (1993). Job perception–job satisfaction relations: An empirical comparison of three competing theories. *Organizational Behaviour and Human Decision Processes, 56*, 370–387.

McDonald, P. (1991). The Los Angeles Olympic Organizing Committee: Developing organizational culture in the short run. In P. J. Frost, L. Moore, M. Louis, C. Lundberg, & J. Martin (Eds.), *Reframing organizational culture* (pp. 26–38). Beverly Hills, CA: SAGE.

McGregor, D. (1960). *The human side of enterprise.* New York, NY: McGraw-Hill.

Meyerson, D. (1991). Normal ambiguity? A glimpse of an occupational culture. In P. J. Frost, L. Moore, M. Louis, C. Lundberg, & J. Martin (Eds.), *Reframing organizational culture* (pp. 131–144). Beverly Hills, CA: SAGE.

Miller, E. (1967). *Systems of organization.* London, England: Tavistock.

Murphy, L. R., Gershon, R. M., & DeJoy, D. (1996). Stress and occupational exposure to HIV/AIDS. In C. L. Cooper (Ed.), *Handbook of stress, medicine and health* (pp. 176–190). Boca Raton, FL: CRC Press.

Nadler, D. A., & Tushman, M. (1997). *Competing by design: The power of organizational architecture.* Oxford, England: Oxford University Press.

Patterson, M. G., Warr, P. B., & West, M. A. (2004a). Organizational climate and company performance: The role of employee affect and employee level. *Journal of Occupational and Organizational Psychology, 77*, 193–216.

Patterson, M. G., West, M. A., Shackleton, V. J., Dawson, J. F., Lawthom, R., Maitlis, S., & Robinson, D. L. (2005). Validating the organizational climate measure: Links to managerial practices, productivity and innovation. *Journal of Organizational Behaviour, 26*, 379–408.

Patterson, M. G., West, M. A., & Wall, T. D. (2004b). Integrated manufacturing, empowerment, and company performance. *Journal of Organizational Behaviour, 25*, 641–665.

Pritchard, R. D., & Karasick, B. W. (1973). The effects of organizational climate on managerial job performance and satisfaction. *Organizational Behaviour and Human Performance, 9*, 126–146.

Quinn, R. E. (1988). *Beyond rational management: Mastering the paradoxes and competing demands of high performance.* San Francisco, CA: Jossey-Bass.

Quinn, R. E., & Rohrbaugh, J. (1981). A competing values approach to organizational effectiveness. *Public Productivity Review, 5*, 122–140.

Rentsch, J. (1990). Climate and culture: Interaction and qualitative differences in organizational meanings. *Journal of Applied Psychology, 75*, 668–681.

Rousseau, D. M. (1988). The construction of climate in organizational research. In C. L. Cooper & I. T. Robertson (Eds.), *International review of industrial and organizational psychology* (Vol. 3, pp. 139–159). Chichester, England: John Wiley & Sons.

Salanova, M., Agut, S., & Peiró, J. M. (2005). Linking organizational resources and work engagement to employee performance and customer loyalty: The mediation of service climate. *Journal of Applied Psychology, 90*(6), 1217–1227.

Salvaggio, A. N., Schneider, B., Nishii, L. H., Mayer, D. M., Ramesh, A., & Lyon, J. S. (2007). Manager personality, manager service quality orientation, and service climate: Test of a model. *Journal of Applied Psychology, 92*, 1741–1750.

Schein, E. (1992). *Organizational culture and leadership.* San Francisco, CA: Jossey-Bass.

Schneider, B. (1980). The service organization: Climate is crucial. *Organizational Dynamics, 9*(2), 52–65.

Schneider, B. (1990). The climate for service: An application of the climate construct. In B. Schneider (Ed.), *Organizational climate and culture* (pp. 383–412). San Francisco, CA: Jossey-Bass.

Schneider, B., & Barbera, K. M. (Eds.). (2014). (Eds.). *The Oxford handbook of organizational climate and culture.* New York, NY: Oxford University Press.

Schneider, B., Bowen, D. E., Erhart, M. G., & Holcombe, K. M. (2000). The climate for service: Evolution of a construct. In N. M. Ashkanasy, C. P. M. Wilderom, & M. F. Peterson (Eds.), *Handbook of organizational culture and climate* (pp. 21–36). London, England: SAGE.

Schneider, B., Ehrhart, M. G., & Macey, W. H. (2011). Perspectives on organizational climate and culture. In S. Zedeck (Ed.), *APA handbook of industrial and organizational psychology* (pp. 373–414). Washington, DC: American Psychological Association.

Schneider, B., Ehrhart, M. G., & Macey, W. H. (2013). Organizational climate and culture. *Annual Review of Psychology, 64*, 361–388.

Schneider, B., González-Romá, V., Ostroff, C., & West, M. (2017). Organizational climate and culture: Reflections on the history of the constructs in the *Journal of Applied Psychology. Journal of Applied Psychology, 102* (3), 468–482. Retrieved from dx.doi.org/10.1037/apl0000090

Schneider, B., Macey, W. H., Lee, W. C., & Young, S. A. (2009). Organizational service climate drivers of the American Customer Satisfaction Index (ACSI) and financial and market performance. *Journal of Service Research*, 12(1), 3–14.

Schneider, B., Parkington, J. J., & Buxton, V. M. (1980). Employee and customer perceptions of service in banks. *Administrative Science Quarterly*, 25, 252–267.

Schneider, B., White, S. S., & Paul, M. C. (1998). Linking service climate and customer perceptions of service quality: Tests of a causal model. *Journal of Applied Psychology*, 83, 150–163.

Senge, P. (1990). *The fifth discipline*. London, England: Century Business.

Shipper, F., & White, C. S. (1983). Linking organizational effectiveness and environmental change. *Long Range Planning*, 16(3), 99–106.

Shipton, H., Dawson, J., West, M. A., & Patterson, M. (2002). Learning in manufacturing organizations: What factors predict effectiveness? *Human Resource Development International*, 5(1), 55–72.

Simons, T., & Roberson, Q. (2003). Why managers should care about fairness: The effects of aggregate justice perceptions on organizational outcomes. *Journal of Applied Psychology*, 88(3), 432–443.

Van der Krogt, F. (1998). Learning network theory: The tension between learning systems and work systems in organizations. *Human Resource Quarterly*, 9(2), 157–177.

Van Maanen, J. (1991). The smile factory: Work at Disneyland. In P. J. Frost, L. Moore, M. Louis, C. Lundberg, & J. Martin (Eds.), *Reframing organizational culture* (pp. 58–76). Beverly Hills, CA: SAGE.

Weick, K. E., & Quinn, R. E. (1999). Organizational change and development. *Annual Review of Psychology*, 50, 361–388.

West, M. A., & Anderson, N. (1996). Innovation in top management teams. *Journal of Applied Psychology*, 81, 680–693.

West, M. A., Topakas, A., & Dawson, J. F. (2014). Climate and culture for health care. In B. Schneider & K. M. Barbera (Eds.), *The Oxford handbook of organizational climate and culture* (pp. 335–359). New York, NY: Oxford University Press.

Whitman, D. S., Caleo, S., Carpenter, N. C., Horner, M. T., & Bernerth, J. B. (2012). Fairness at the collective level: A meta-analytic examination of the consequences and boundary conditions of organizational justice climate. *Journal of Applied Psychology*, 97(4), 776–791.

Wiley, J. W., & Brooks, S. M. (2000). The high-performance organizational climate: How workers describe top-performing units. In N. M. Ashkanasy, C. P. M. Wilderom, & M. F. Peterson (Eds.), *Handbook of organizational culture and climate* (pp. 177–192). Thousand Oaks, CA: SAGE.

Worline, M. C., & Dutton, J. E. (2017). *Awakening compassion at work: The quiet power that elevates people and organizations*. Oakland, CA: Berrett-Koehler.

Zammuto, R. F., & O'Connor, E. J. (1992). Gaining advanced manufacturing technologies' benefits: The roles of organizational design and culture. *Academy of Management Review*, 17, 701–729.

Zohar, D. (2010). Thirty years of safety climate research: Reflections and future directions. *Accident Analysis & Prevention*, 42(5), 1517–1522.

Zohar, D. (2014). Safety climate: Conceptualization, measurement, and improvement. In B. Schneider & K. M. Barbera (Eds.), *The Oxford handbook of organizational climate and culture* (pp. 317–334). New York, NY: Oxford University Press.

Zohar, D., & Polachek, T. (2014). Discourse-based intervention for modifying supervisory communication as leverage for safety climate and performance improvement: A randomized field study. *Journal of Applied Psychology*, 99(1), 113–124.

CASE STUDIES FOR PART THREE: ORGANIZATIONS

CASE STUDY 3.1

Leadership Development at PETRONAS

PETRONAS is the national oil company of Malaysia. Incorporated in 1974, the organization was established in order to commercialize the huge natural oil resources of Malaysia for the benefit of the nation. It is a multinational oil and gas business in the fullest sense, now ranked in the Fortune Global 500 largest corporations. On their website, PETRONAS give a clear sense of their vision, mission and values (Exhibit 3.1.1).

The oil and gas sector, and energy sector more broadly, are among the most scrutinized in the world. Concern about the use of natural carbon resources to meet global energy needs, and their impact on the world's climate, presents important economic and operating challenges to oil and gas organizations, and more specifically to their leaders.

Vision Statement
To be a Leading Oil and Gas Multinational of Choice

Mission Statement

- We are a business entity
- Petroleum is our core business
- Our primary responsibility is to develop and add value to this national resource
- Our objective is to contribute to the well-being of the people and the nation

Shared Values
Our values are embedded in our culture as the backbone of our business conduct, reflecting our sense of duty and responsibility in upholding our commitment towards contributing to the well-being of peoples and nations wherever we operate.

Loyalty: Loyal to nation and corporation

Integrity: Honest and upright

Professionalism: Committed, innovative and proactive and always striving for excellence

Cohesiveness: United in purpose and fellowship

Exhibit 3.1.1   PETRONAS Vision, Mission, and Shared Values

continued

PETRONAS clearly identified, in the early years of their business, the importance of leadership in achieving their strategic mission. In 1979, an internal training function was established to focus on the development of leaders at the company. That training group grew to become the PETRONAS Leadership Centre (PLC). PLC is now a major provider of leadership development in the oil and gas sector more broadly in Malaysia and beyond. Their objectives are to unleash the potential of programme registrants so that they are able to develop, grow, and lead effectively in their teams.

Programme developers at PLC reflect the dynamic challenges that leaders face at different stages of their careers in a variety of programmes. There are development tracks for new or early career leaders, and for people making the step to general management and to senior management.

One of their 'signature programmes' is the Leadership Excellence at PETRONAS (LEAP) programme. The LEAP programme is a 10-day course, spread across five modules, which, over a three-month period, aims to build the leadership competencies and capabilities of trainees. The programme, focused on development to General Management level, comprises modules on:

- Introduction to Leadership at General Management level
- Leading Self
- Leading Others

The programme is augmented by applied learning modules in which trainees participate in coached applied practice in their teams, to transfer and put their new skills to work. At the end of the programme, a reflective performance review module enables the trainees to reflect on their progress and identify their next learning challenges (see Exhibit 3.1.2).

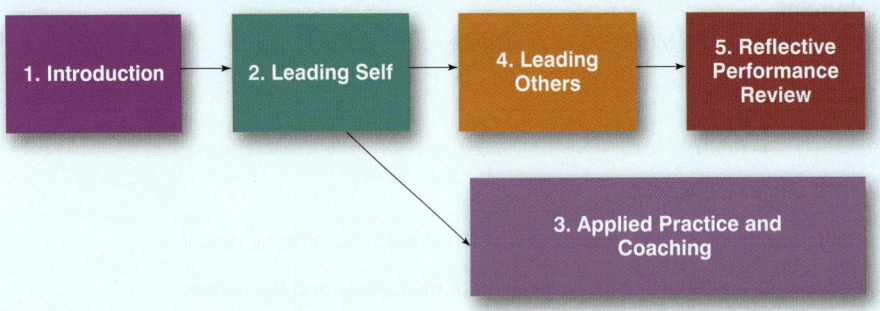

Exhibit 3.1.2   Programme Structure of the PLC Leadership Excellence at PETRONAS programme

Vision Statement

To be a leading oil and gas multinational of choice.

Mission Statement

- We are a business entity.
- Petroleum is our core business.
- Our primary responsibility is to develop and add value to this national resource.
- Our objective is to contribute to the well-being of the people and the nation.

Shared Values

Our values are embedded in our culture as the backbone of our business conduct, reflecting our sense of duty and responsibility in upholding our commitment towards contributing to the well-being of peoples and nations wherever we operate.

Loyalty: Loyal to nation and corporation
Integrity: Honest and upright
Professionalism: Committed, innovative and proactive and always striving for excellence
Cohesiveness: United in purpose and fellowship

Leadership development clearly remains a central concern and interest at PETRONAS as it continues to grow and to work towards realizing its strategic vision and mission.

References and further reading

www.petronas.com.my/
www.petronasleadershipcentre.com.my

Questions

1. What will be the challenges of new leaders at PETRONAS, given the economic, social and environmental context that the oil and gas sector operates in currently?
2. How could research and theory on leadership and other areas of Work and Organizational Psychology be applied in the LEAP programme?
3. What will be the success factors in ensuring that the LEAP programme enables leaders to contribute effectively to the PETRONAS Vision, Mission, and Shared Values?
4. How could research on teams and team effectiveness help leaders undertaking the LEAP programme to manage their teams?
5. Do you have any ideas that could enhance leadership development at PETRONAS further? How and in what ways would these ideas contribute?

CASE STUDY 3.2

European Companies and Their Organizational Structures and Strategies

This case is about the organizational structures and strategies of some European companies.

Organizational Structures

An organizational structure is a mostly hierarchical concept of subordination of entities that collaborate and contribute to serve one common aim. There are various types of organizational structures, some of which include:

- Functional structure: a company organized with a functional structure groups people together into functional departments such as purchasing, accounts, production, sales, marketing. These departments would normally have functional heads who may be called managers or directors depending on whether the function is represented at board level.
- Divisional structure refers to a hierarchical organization wherein each division (focusing on specific products or specific markets) is responsible for all or most of its functional activities.
- Geographical structure refers to an organizational design that focuses on the geographic location of operations. Geographical structures include units that may be responsible for both functional and divisional operations within a geographic region.

In recent times, most companies adopt mixed structures depending on the size of the company and the company strategy. Examples of such companies include the following.

continued

Bayer AG of Germany

Bayer AG is one of the largest and oldest chemical and healthcare products companies in the world. Because of massive sales gains and increased activity overseas in the early 1980s, Bayer announced a reorganization in 1984. Bayer had been successful with a conventional organizational structure that was departmentalized by function. However, in response to new conditions, the company wanted to create a structure that would allow it to achieve three primary goals: 1) shift management control from the then West German parent company to its foreign divisions and subsidiaries; 2) restructure its business divisions to more clearly define their duties; and 3) flatten the organization, or empower lower-level managers to assume more responsibility, so that top executives would have more time to plan strategy.

Bayer selected a relatively diverse matrix management format to pursue its goals. It delineated all of its business activities into six groups under an umbrella company called Bayer World. Within each of the six groups were several subgroups made up of product categories such as dyestuffs, fibres or chemicals. Likewise, each of its administrative and service functions was regrouped under Bayer World into one of several functions, such as human resources, marketing, plant administration or finance. Furthermore, top managers who had formally headed functional groups were given authority over separate geographic regions, which, like the product groups, were supported by and entwined with the functional groups. The net effect of the reorganization was that the original nine functional departments were broken down into 19 multidisciplinary, interconnected business groups. After only one year of operation, Bayer management lauded the new matrix structure as a resounding success. Not only did matrix management allow the company to move towards its primary goals, but it had the added benefits of increasing its responsiveness to change and emerging opportunities, and of helping Bayer to streamline plant administration and service division activities.

DuPont of France

Founded in 1802 in France, DuPont puts science to work by creating sustainable solutions essential to a better, safer, healthier life for people everywhere. Operating in more than 70 countries, DuPont offers a wide range of innovative products and services for markets, including agriculture, nutrition, electronics, communications, safety and protection, home and construction, transportation and apparel.

From 1919 to 1921, DuPont operated a 'functional structure'. This is where a 'president' was responsible for departments with functions of sales, purchasing, treasury, development, production and engineering.

However, as a result of product diversification (strategy) and company expansion, DuPont had to decentralize into separate divisions for each product, hence adopting a product divisional structure. This is where a chairman and CEO were responsible for divisions based on products, e.g. speciality fibres, performance coatings, agriculture and nutrition, polyester, pigments and chemicals, etc. DuPont was the first company in the world to hit upon the structural solution to the problem of diversity.

ABB of Switzerland

ABB is a leader in power and automation technologies that enable utility and industry customers to improve performance while lowering environmental impact. The ABB Group of companies operates in around 100 countries and employs about 120,000 people. ABB was formed in 1988 from the merger of the Swedish ASEA group and the Brown Boveri company of Switzerland. The then CEO, Percy Barnevik, imposed a matrix structure on the company comprising two key dimensions – business segments and geography segments. By the late 1990s, ABB was experiencing considerable frustration with its structure. When a new chief executive took over from Barnevik, one of his first actions was to abolish the regions and restructure the business segments into seven more focused product divisions, apparently taking the company back to a product divisional structure, but within the structural framework of a network multidivisional structure. This multidivisional structure comprised various geographical divisions, each operating individual product divisions with regional functional divisions. This type of structure separates operational responsibility for the individual diversified businesses from strategic responsibility for the make-up and performance of the overall corporate portfolio.

Questions
Consult the websites of the companies concerned to help you deepen your analysis.

1. Compare the choices made by these companies in structuring their activities. What are likely to be the consequences for, and strengths and weaknesses of, the organizations?

2. Which approach, given the nature of each of the businesses, is likely to be most successful?

Organizational Strategies

Unilever of Netherlands *(Unilever's diversification strategy – 'Path to Growth' strategy)*

Unilever is one of the largest packaged consumer goods companies, specializing in hundreds of different brands. Unilever is based in Holland and the UK and is jointly owned by Unilever N.V. and Unilever. Miles and Snow stated that there are four types of organizational strategies pursued by companies: Defenders, Prospectors, Analyzers and Reactors. Unilever is a company that uses the 'Prospectors' organization type. Prospectors are organizations that almost continually search for market opportunities, and they regularly experiment with potential responses to emerging environmental trends.

Unilever was founded on soap and margarine – both products essentially sharing the same raw materials – with diversification into other business areas starting in the mid-1950s, when rapid growth in the Western world resulted in increased competition and lower margins in the company's traditional categories. Unilever's strategy was an active diversification programme through acquisition. The vigour with which this was pursued, while successfully introducing the company into valuable new categories, also brought in a lot of peripheral activities.

Unilever's 13 core business sectors are: ice cream, tea-based beverages, culinary products, hair care, skin care and deodorants (all with superior growth potential); spreads, oral care, laundry care and household care (steady growth); and frozen foods, fragrances and professional cleaning (selective growth).

More recently, Unilever launched its 'Path to Growth Strategy' in 1999, in order to increase competitive advantage and revive the company. A major strength of the company's global environment is the geographic diversification of its major product markets. In 2003, Unilever had sales and marketing efforts in 88 different countries. The key is that it gave decision-making power to its managers in different countries so that they could tailor their products to the market's specific preferences and consumers' local tastes.

Nestlé of Switzerland *(market/product development strategy and horizontal integration strategy)*

Nestlé, with headquarters in Vevey, Switzerland, was founded in 1866 by Henri Nestlé and is today the world's leading nutrition, health and wellness company. Sales for 2008 were CHF 109.9bn, with a net profit of CHF 18.0bn. They employ around 283,000 people and have factories or operations in almost every country in the world. Nestlé adopts a variety of strategies depending on geographical location.

The company's strategy is guided by several fundamental principles. Nestlé's existing products grow through innovation and renovation, while

continued

maintaining a balance in geographic activities and product lines. Long-term potential is never sacrificed for short-term performance. The company's priority is to bring the best and most relevant products to people, wherever they are, whatever their needs, throughout their lives.

Another strategy that has been successful for Nestlé involves striking strategic partnerships with other large companies. In the early 1990s, Nestlé entered into an alliance with Coca-Cola in ready-to-drink teas and coffees in order to benefit from Coca-Cola's worldwide bottling system and expertise in prepared beverages.

In Asia, Nestlé's strategy has been to acquire local companies in order to form a group of autonomous regional managers who know more about the culture of the local markets than Americans or Europeans. Nestlé's strong cash flow and comfortable debt:equity ratio leave it with ample muscle for takeovers. Recently, Nestlé acquired Indofood, Indonesia's largest noodle producer. Their focus will be primarily on expanding sales in the Indonesian market, and in time will look to export Indonesian food products to other countries.

StatoilHydro of Norway (*diversification strategy*)

StatoilHydro is an integrated, technology-based international energy company primarily focused on upstream oil and gas operations. Headquartered in Norway, it has more than 30 years' experience from the Norwegian Continental Shelf, pioneering complex offshore projects under the toughest conditions. The culture is founded on strong values and a high ethical standard.

They aim to deliver long-term growth and continue to develop technologies and manage projects that will meet the world's energy and climate challenges in a sustainable way. StatoilHydro is listed on NYSE and Oslo Stock Exchange.

Following 30 years of growth that gave Norway's national oil company a solid upstream portfolio, Statoil ASA (NYSE: STO) is now pursuing a diversification (growth) strategy that will take it beyond crude oil production on the Norwegian Continental Shelf. This type of diversification strategy is called horizontal diversification, where the company acquires other companies in line with its growth strategy. For example, in 2005, Statoil acquired EnCana's entire Deepwater US Gulf of Mexico portfolio.

Questions

Consult the websites of the companies concerned to help you deepen your analysis.

1. Compare the choices made by these companies in their strategies. What are likely to be the consequences for the organizations in terms of success, culture and management processes?

2. What challenges are they most likely to face and how might the knowledge of work and organizational psychology be of value as they go forward?

Company websites:

Bayer AG of Germany – **www.bayer.com/en/homepage.aspx**
DuPont of France – **www2.dupont.com/DuPont_Home/en_US/index.html**
ABB of Switzerland – **www.abb.com/**
Unilever of Netherlands – **www.unilever.com/**
Nestlé of Switzerland – **www.nestle.com/**
Statoil of Norway – **www.statoil.com/en/Pages/default.aspx**

CHAPTER 14
THE PSYCHOLOGY OF WORK AND ORGANIZATIONS

In the first chapter of this book, we described how large numbers of people around the world spend a significant proportion of their precious lives feeling moderately miserable in their daily work. What the contents of this book have demonstrated is that it doesn't need to be this way. Work and organizations can be domains within which people flourish through growing and developing and feeling a sense of effectiveness; through developing strong, positive connections with others; and through achieving a sense of control and integration in their lives. This final chapter brings together much of the content from the book to explain how we can develop strategies that ensure the experience of organizations and work are like this – fulfilling and enabling rather than depleting and damaging for us.

We begin by reminding you of a topic we covered earlier. This chapter is structured with reference to self-determination theory (SDT) (Stone, Deci, & Ryan, 2009) (more fully described in Chapter 4), which proposes that an understanding of human motivation and well-being requires consideration of our innate psychological needs for competence, autonomy, and relatedness. When these needs are met in the workplace, people will be more intrinsically motivated and will experience better health and well-being. The theory proposes that psychological health requires satisfaction of all three needs; one or two are not enough.

The need for competence reflects a 'deeply structured *effectance*-focused motivation'. We want to be able to have an effect on the environments we find ourselves in as well as to get valued outcomes (be it food, respect, love, power or whatever). Deci and Ryan say that competence or 'effectance' is one of three fundamental psychological needs that motivate human activity and must be satisfied for our long-term psychological health.

The second need, relatedness or belonging, refers to the desire or need to feel and be connected to others – to love and care, and to be loved and cared for (Baumeister & Leary, 1995). The fact that we are more likely to die from loneliness than from the effects of obesity or smoking is a powerful indication of the strength and importance of this need in human behaviour (Holt-Lunstad, Smith, Baker, Harris, & Stephenson, 2015).

Autonomy refers to volition, or having free will, choice and control. The theory describes autonomy as the desire to organize our experiences for ourselves and direct our behaviour in order to be consistent with our sense of self. It is different from the ideas of internal locus of control, independence or individualism because it refers to the experiences of integration (integrating our behaviour and experiences with our sense of self-integrity) and freedom. At the same time, it is not about being independent of others.

In summary the three needs are:
- *Competence*: which drives us to seek to control outcomes and experience mastery or effectiveness.
- *Relatedness*: our need to be connected to, cared for and caring of others around us.
- *Autonomy*: our need to be in control, to be causal agents in our own lives and act consistently with our (relatively) integrated sense of self.

When these needs are met at work, the theory proposes, people's intrinsic motivation and engagement will be high, leading to enhanced performance, persistence and creativity. If any of these three psychological needs is not well met at work or thwarted, it will have a strong negative impact on workplace well-being and on intrinsic motivation. Using the theoretical lens of SDT, the chapter now integrates the contents of the three parts of this book to describe work environments where people can truly flourish.

PART ONE: UNDERSTANDING THE FOUNDATIONS OF WORK AND ORGANIZATIONAL PSYCHOLOGY

In Part One of the book, we examined some of the core foundations of work and organizational psychology focused on understanding people and their behaviour at work. Below we consider how theory and research, examining individual differences, attitudes and behaviour, and motivation at work can help us meet needs for relatedness, competence and autonomy.

Individual differences at work

We began by exploring the differences that define people, and that matter. Much of the research has been based on the idea that personality and intelligence are relatively fixed, and this is an example of how theory can shape human society negatively rather than enable it to develop in positive ways. More recent research and theorizing offers a more positive perspective, suggesting that personality can change as a result of work experience (Woods, Wille, Wu, Lievens, & De Fruyt, 2019). Taking on a leadership role while having supportive coaches and mentors can build confidence and leadership ability. Intelligence can also increase as a result of continuous learning through our lives (Ritchie & Tucker-Drob, 2018). Instead of work psychologists adopting a static approach to recruitment and selection where square pegs are identified and placed in square holes, we can adopt more dynamic perspectives that seek to nurture work environments where people's potential for learning, adaptation and growth can be realized; where their aspirations can determine the jobs they undertake as routes to their goals; and where work environments are designed to ensure continuing growth and development rather than creating a demoralizing feeling of being stuck. Making a positive difference to people's experience of work and organizations requires that we see and promote people's potential for long-term growth and development, rather than suppressing their hopes and aspirations.

Moreover, research (by Li, Fay, Frese, Harms, & Gao, 2014) has demonstrated how people can develop more proactive personalities as a consequence of work environment features, leading them to sculpt and improve their work environments rather than being sculpted by them and cast in stone. When we create work environments with a good balance of job challenge while giving people high levels of support and control, such proactive behaviours are far more likely to develop, resulting in higher levels of engagement. These approaches help people to be confident in addressing the challenges they face at work; excited that new learning and skills will be constant possibilities at work; pleased and proud that they can pursue their long-term career aspirations; and positive about continuing to learn and develop throughout life, which we know is a core element of human well-being. Adopting this orientation is likely to increase the extent to which needs for competence, autonomy and relatedness or belonging are met.

Attitudes and behaviour in organizations

Research over recent decades makes it clear that creating work organizations that lead people to feel more positive (happier) is an effective way to create better-performing organizations. This raises some challenging questions for leaders about their organizational strategies. These are typically formulated to address the means by which the organization can be most productive and profitable (an economic perspective) and people management is engineered to ensure that strategic objectives shape roles and goals for individual staff members and teams. Organization development, training and development, and performance management are also used to ensure that the strategic objectives are being pursued by all staff and that they have the skills to ensure their success. This may be fundamentally misguided.

What the research tells us is that job attitudes (satisfaction and commitment, for example) seem to be critical in determining the extent to which performance management systems relate to productivity and profitability (for example). In the NHS in England, staff attitudes turn out to be the best predictor of hospital performance, predicting not only patient satisfaction but also externally assessed care quality as well as financial performance (West, Dawson, Admasachew, & Topakas, 2011). Yet in many organizations, staff experience is seen as a non-essential by-product rather than a central determinant of good performance. Organizations will be more successful if they focus more on improving staff engagement, well-being and satisfaction than on pursuing productivity and profitability as their primary goals. Two examples of how this might be applied in practice are inclusion and justice in organizations.

Inclusion is, quite simply, about ensuring that management practices are aimed at including rather than excluding people in processes such as recruitment, selection, promotion, training, development, having the opportunity to take on challenging tasks, having voice and influence, and the many other organizational processes we have considered in this book. The benefits of diversity we have described (improved performance and innovation) accrue when there are cultures or climates of inclusion rather than exclusion of people. Inclusive practices ensure that all staff (for example, women and BME staff, LGBT+ staff, staff with disabilities) influence key decisions and processes within their teams and organizations. This results in a richer information pool, more comprehensive decision-making and more positive staff attitudes. Building inclusive teams and organizations will significantly improve job attitudes and performance, creating positive work experiences resulting in higher engagement, trust and a sense of fairness. Contrast this with the deep hurt, anger and rejection felt by people in organizations where discrimination and exclusion are evident (widespread in organizations and teams throughout the world of work). Ensuring inclusion means better meeting the needs of all staff for relatedness, competence and autonomy.

Organizational justice refers to people's perceptions of how fairly they are treated at work, and we saw in Chapter 3 how the concept has been differentiated into perceptions about the distribution of rewards, the means by which they are distributed, the civility with which people are treated and the clarity, openness and honesty of information that is communicated in teams and organizations. The more people perceive their team and organizational environments as just, the more motivated they are to be engaged in their work, loyal to the organization and to go above and beyond what they are strictly required to do. When they perceive injustice, they are more likely to leave the organization, express dissatisfaction and cynicism, harbour silent resentment, spend more time away from work and reduce their commitment and engagement – understandably. Leaders in organizations can help to create positive work environments where people flourish by ensuring that there is a strong commitment to justice in all these domains.

Perceived fairness of procedures in organizations has positive effects on intrinsic motivation, leading to improved job performance. When people feel well treated by their supervisor, this affects their sense of interpersonal treatment at work generally, and leads to more citizenship behaviour and higher organizational commitment. Feeling fairly treated has potentially deeper and longer-standing effects too. Having an inspirational leader who focuses on relationships conveys a greater sense of purpose and makes challenging tasks seem more achievable, enabling team members to grow and develop. And job insecurity has less effect on performance for those with positive perceptions of justice in their teams and organizations (Wang, Lu, & Siu, 2015). Justice is first and foremost a moral issue and it is the role of leaders in any context to create just environments. Justice will impact on people's sense of autonomy and control, relatedness and, to the extent that they respond proactively and positively to taking on challenging tasks, lead to growth development and competence also.

Motivation at work

From the review of motivation at work, we can distil out six important means by which we can increase people's competence, sense of relatedness and autonomy. First, it is important to remove sources of demotivation. Both motivation theory and organizational justice research show how hygiene factors, including pay and rewards, can demotivate people. Systems and procedures in organizations, especially those used to determine reward, have high potential for creating demotivation and dissatisfaction. Second, it is fundamental to agree goals and objectives with teams and individuals. There is overwhelming evidence for the effectiveness of goal setting in ensuring motivation and performance (and role clarity is an important factor in avoiding work stress also). Third, is ensuring that people have a sense of autonomy and control. Achieving this involves listening (with fascination, not passively!) to staff at work, valuing their feedback and ideas, and releasing decision-making control so that people have a choice about how to accomplish work objectives. This means moving away from command and control models of leadership, away from 'individual hero' approaches to leadership, and working towards achieving more collective leadership (see Chapter 11). Collective leadership exists where everyone feels they have leadership responsibility, where there is shared leadership in teams, where there is interdependent leadership (leaders working together across boundaries) and where there are consistent approaches to achieving participative, supportive and compassionate leadership. Fourth, is the importance of feedback – a key motivational process. Feedback on performance allows people to determine whether they are on track to achieving goals, and to better understand the results of their work and thereby to achieve a sense of effectiveness and pride. Of course, it must be timely, accurate and helpful to be effective and it should be predominantly positive and thereby motivating. Fifth, is the importance of ensuring valued outcomes. People are motivated to work on tasks and activities that lead to valued outcomes, so it is important to ensure that such outcomes are available and abundant. For doctors and nurses, for example, it is being able to provide high-quality and compassionate care, not necessarily achieving cost reductions in treatments or increasing the number of patients they are seeing regardless of quality of care provided. And finally, we have to strive to design jobs that make them intrinsically rewarding rather than dull or miserable. The features or characteristics of work are important sources of motivation:

- Task identity – a whole and identifiable piece of work rather than a small component such as on an assembly line.
- Task significance – the extent to which the task is seen as making a significant contribution to the individual, their team, the organization or wider society.
- Skill variety – tasks that require a variety of skills and activities to complete them.
- Autonomy – having the freedom to make choices about how best to do the task.
- Feedback – the amount of helpful information about their task performance the individual receives, either from performing the task or from significant others.

Key to all of this is ensuring that people are involved in the design of their work, rather than having work and tasks imposed. This is why target-driven cultures often demotivate people – they find themselves being forced to aim at targets they think are inappropriate.

By following these prescriptions in organizations we create the conditions where people's needs for relatedness, autonomy and competence are much more likely to be met.

PART TWO: PRACTISING PROFESSIONAL APPLICATIONS OF WORK AND ORGANIZATIONAL PSYCHOLOGY

The second part of this book outlined professional practice areas of work and organizational psychology. Below we consider how approaches to recruitment and selection, learning, training and development, performance management, career management, and safety, stress and health at work can help to transform workplaces to meet our needs for relatedness, competence and autonomy.

Recruitment and selection

Unfair recruitment and selection continue to do damage to people, organizations and our society (e.g. Colella, Hebl, & King, 2017). There remain too few solutions to issues of procedural adverse impact, such as those observed in cognitive testing (Berry, Cullen, & Meyer, 2014). This is despite evidence of potential differential validity for different ethnicity groups and too little contemporary understanding of the problems. Discrimination is too often a consequence of the ways that people are recruited, selected, promoted and developed in our organizations, undermining trust not just in work organizations but in society generally. One reason is that researchers and practitioners have focused on the predictive validity of these procedures as the primary criterion for their use – do they help us select the person who will best perform this role? There has been much less focus on the following question: do the methods we use help us ensure fairness and prevent discrimination?

Another approach would be to prioritize fairness – to make fairness the primary concern. Of course, our methods should still ensure a high level of validity because a method that is not valid as a predictor of performance remains *unfair*. In this approach though, the importance of fairness is raised to at least equivalent status to validity in staff recruitment and selection. And there are methods that have both higher validity and lower adverse impact than, for example, cognitive testing, or no adverse impact at all such as structured interviews (Levashina, Hartwell, Morgeson, & Campion, 2014). Consider the consequences too for effects of people's perceptions of procedural justice, the effects on trust and on their engagement and well-being. In the NHS in England, discrimination against minority groups proves to be the best predictor of staff morale overall. The emotional ripples of discrimination appear to spread out and wash over all staff. Unfair recruitment and selection lead to damaged self-esteem, resentment, and a strong sense of social injustice that affects the whole of society. In order to promote relatedness, competence, and autonomy and control, should we not make fairness our priority?

Performance management

Performance management and feedback can have either very negative or positive impacts on people's experience of work. The aims of performance management should be to ensure that people are clear about what it is they are required to do (aligned around the vision or inspiring purpose of the organization); to provide them with the support, guidance and skills to do their work most effectively; to ensure they feel valued and respected by the organization and its leaders; and to ensure they can influence their work environment to maximize their own effectiveness and that of their team. First and foremost, people need to have a sense of 'psychological safety' rather than perceiving a 'blame culture'. Performance management should focus as much on the future as on the past, with a strong commitment to helping people develop competence, skills and confidence. This mean ensuring that appraisals and performance management are integrated with enabling HR systems such as learning, training and development in high-performance work systems. Performance feedback (whether positive or critical) is considerably more welcome when it includes exploration and discussion of development and learning, whether to close performance gaps or achieve even better performance. And the more staff are involved in the design of performance management and measurement the better. The intervention with by far the largest effects on performance overall is the Productivity Measurement and Enhancement System (ProMES) (Pritchard, Harrell, DiazGranados, & Guzman, 2008), which is based on the involvement of staff in the development of performance indicators (along with goal setting, good performance measurement and innovation). Performance management requires two-way integrity – honest and open communication and a feedback-rich environment where information is seen as credible and trustworthy. Where helpful communication on performance is simply part of a team's regular processes, it is generally accepted and welcome. Think of a good sports team whose members are constantly providing each other with both positive and negative feedback and helpful coaching. That's a positive performance management environment meeting the core needs of those involved, enabling relatedness, competence and autonomy.

Careers and career management

Our work and careers are important to us for helping achieve a stable sense of identity rooted in the fulfilment of the three core needs we are exploring in this chapter. Our careers should offer a means by which we can thrive and flourish in our lives rather than cause us to languish and be depleted. To meet the three needs of relatedness, autonomy and competence, we should not simply get carried along on an inevitable current of career management. Rather we can be proactive and decide how we want to live our lives. How much time do I want to spend at work and how hard do I wish to work? Do I want a full-time (often 50 hours a week) job or do I want to work less – three or four days? Do I want to be self-employed, part of the gig economy or have the security and stability that may come with being part of a large organization? And am I content to do 'bullshit jobs' (Graeber, 2019)? And when should I take a break or leave? Stuck in a work situation that is damaging or depleting or miserable – when vitality is draining away – leaves us with three choices: stick it out, change the situation or leave. The latter two choices (if available) are obviously better. Why spend a large proportion of our lives unhappy at work, unless we have no other choice? We can change the situation by crafting work to be more meaningful, for example by volunteering to take on tasks that are more engaging and fun. And by innovating we meet our needs for autonomy and competence. If there is no alternative, there are opportunities to thrive, learn and develop outside work (Michael West's 92-year-old mother has recently started Welsh lessons). Continuing to learn and contribute are important factors in human well-being throughout our lives. Organizations also bear responsibility for careers, of course, as this chapter makes clear. It is important that they work to minimize incivility and maximize civility, kindness, compassion, humour and respect in the workplace – we return to this shortly. And, as we have repeatedly emphasized, we must promote climates of inclusion that foster trust and respect, enabling thriving at work.

Safety, stress and health

We are discovering a great deal about the importance of positive emotions and relationships at work and the value for business and employees of creating climates with these characteristics. We also know, as a result of research, a great deal about how to prevent work-related illnesses and injuries. A safety climate is key, and there are well-understood steps for creating such a climate. In particular, it requires managerial commitment and control. Given how well developed our knowledge is in this area, there is little excuse for organizations to have poor records of health and safety at work.

Similarly, in relation to stress and strain at work, research has advanced understanding dramatically. We know the causes, processes and consequences of stress at work, from psychological through to biochemical processes. And we know that sustained stress causes heart disease, addictions, gastrointestinal disorders, obesity, cancers, increases in stress hormones and, ultimately, early death. Unfortunately, too much effort in organizations is put into managing the symptoms – encouraging employees to take up relaxation or mindfulness classes (worthy though those these interventions are). Instead, organizations should be focusing on what are now the clearly identified causes of stress, such as role factors, workload, low control, poor or abusive supervision, work pace and emotional labour. Recent work has contrasted burnout with engagement – a positive work-related state of fulfilment characterized by dedication, vigour and absorption. Organizations should be encouraged to adopt enlightened approaches to management that focus on increasing levels of engagement, control and individual growth and development by investing in, rather than neglecting, or worse, exploiting, those who work within organizations. The level of knowledge about stress and health at work is now so well developed that all organizations should make sustained efforts to implement interventions designed to create outstanding work environments for staff, ensuring their needs for relatedness, competence and autonomy are met.

For example, workplace stress may be prevented by job redesign, such as empowering employees and avoiding both work overload and underload; by improving social support; by promoting reasonable reward for effort invested; by adjusting physical settings to workers' abilities, needs and reasonable expectations; and through promoting participative management, flexible work schedules and good career development. Overall, research suggests that efforts to increase employee participation and job control, social support and moderate job demands hold great promise. Good progress has been made nationally in countries such as Denmark, Norway and the Netherlands (by ensuring less job strain, bullying, work–family imbalance, long work hours, job insecurity and effort–reward imbalance). Designing interventions to reduce stress should focus on:

- work tasks and responsibilities
- work timing – shift work, pace, etc.
- work techniques – the methods used to get the job done
- work team – cohesive or conflictual, for example
- work environment (both the physical and social environment)

and should promote:

- employee involvement
- growth and development
- work–life balance
- employee recognition
- health and safety.

Secondary interventions are helpful in general, so encouraging people to take exercise, get enough sleep, practise meditation or mindfulness and take regular breaks is important. Having recovery time aids psychological detachment from work after the working day is over and enables people to recover from job strain. Recovery reduces health complaints, emotional exhaustion, depression, negative mood, fatigue and sleep difficulties (Sonnentag, Mojza, Binnewies, & Scholl, 2008). Frequent short holiday breaks (e.g. monthly respites) are more effective than once-a-year vacations. Organizations can also create physical spaces for work and lunch breaks that allow people to connect with nature. Organizations can also promote psychological detachment from work by restricting email and other forms of communication during evenings and weekends.

Stress kills people, so these recommendations are important. It is the responsibility of employing organizations to ensure they are creating conditions where employees thrive rather than languish or are damaged.

PART THREE: CREATING EFFECTIVE ORGANIZATIONS

Part Three of the book represents a synthesis of the understanding communicated in the first two parts, with the added perspective that comes from considering teams and whole organizations. Now we consider the implications for creating work teams and organizations in which people strive and find their needs for relatedness, competence and autonomy well met in their workplaces. We describe how this can be achieved in relation to organizational strategy and structure, leadership, work teams, and culture and climate.

Strategy and structure

The strategy of an organization – its vision, purposes, objectives and values – plays a powerful role in shaping the organizational process, cultures and climates that affect all those who work within it. For many organizations, strategy has often been limited to a narrow profit-maximizing purpose, neglecting the reality that work organizations are simply a particular form of human community that we have created in order to benefit ourselves. And yet, as we have seen throughout this book, many of them create environments that damage people – limiting their sense of connection, competence and control. By taking a different approach, we suggest, it is possible to change the nature of work organizations. A major international study led by Christopher Peterson and Martin Seligman (2004) reviewed research, philosophies and religions across history and continents to identify the core values or virtues in human societies. They identified six categories of virtues that are valued in every society and enable societal health and well-being.

By conceiving of work organizations as another form of human community, we can ask how these values can be built into the genetic structure of work organizations via their strategies. They are:

1 **Wisdom and knowledge** – the acquisition and use of knowledge within organizations.
  - *Creativity* [originality, ingenuity]: Thinking of novel and productive ways to do things within the organization.
  - *Curiosity* [interest, novelty-seeking, openness to experience]: Inquiring, seeking understanding, challenging assumptions, sensing problems.
  - *Judgement and open-mindedness* [critical thinking]: Thinking issues through and examining them from all sides.
  - *Love of learning*: Mastering new skills, topics, and bodies of knowledge.
  - *Perspective* [**wisdom**]: Valuing wise counsel; having different ways of looking at the challenges of ensuring the organization is contributing to the well-being of staff, the wider society and the environment.

2 **Courage** – emotional strengths that involve the exercise of will to accomplish goals in the face of opposition, external or internal.
  - *Bravery* [valour]: Not shrinking from threat, challenge, difficulty or pain in the fight for what is right; acting on convictions even if they are unpopular in the organization.
  - *Perseverance* [persistence, industriousness]: Finishing what the organization starts; persisting in a course of action focused on maximizing the organization's positive impact on human well-being and the wider environment.
  - *Honesty* [authenticity, integrity]: Speaking the truth, but more broadly, leaders presenting themselves and the organization in a genuine way.
  - *Zest* [vitality, enthusiasm, vigour, energy]: An organization characterized by excitement and energy, that is alive and active in bringing about positive change.

3 **Humanity** – an organizational strength that involves supporting and enabling all.
  - *Caring*: Valuing close relations, in particular those in which sharing and caring are reciprocated; being close to people and the wider community.
  - *Kindness* [generosity, nurturance, care, compassion, 'niceness']: Doing good deeds for others; helping them; building a sense of kindness as a core value.

- *Social intelligence* [emotional intelligence, personal intelligence]: Being aware of the motives and feelings of others as the organization pursues its vision.

4 **Justice** – civic strengths that underlie the commitment to protecting people and a healthy community life.
- *Teamwork* [citizenship, social responsibility, loyalty]: Working well as groups and teams; loyalty to the group in pursuit of the common goal.
- *Fairness*: Treating all people the same according to notions of fairness and justice; everyone being given a fair chance.
- *Leadership*: Encouraging high performance and at the same time good relations within the organization and with the wider community.

5 **Temperance** – Strengths that protect against excess.
- *Forgiveness and mercy*: Forgiving those who have been judged as doing wrong; accepting the shortcomings of others; not being vengeful.
- *Modesty and humility*: Letting accomplishments speak for themselves.
- *Prudence*: Being careful about organizational choices; not taking undue risks.
- *Organizational regulation* [control]: Regulating the organization; being disciplined; controlling organizational appetites and emotions.

6 **Wonder and gratitude** – strengths that forge connections to the larger universe and provide meaning.
- *Appreciation of beauty and excellence* [awe, wonder, elevation]: Noticing and appreciating beauty, excellence in the environment and/or skilled performance in protecting the planet.
- *Gratitude*: Being aware of and thankful for the good things that happen within the organization; taking time to express thanks.
- *Hope* [optimism, future-mindedness, future orientation]: Expecting the best in the future and working to achieve it.
- *Humour* [playfulness]: Laughter and fun within the organization.
- *Religiousness and spirituality* [faith, purpose]: Having coherent beliefs about the higher purpose and meaning of the universe and the contribution of the organization to this in its work.

Imagine the impact of an organization eager to develop such strengths and values in terms of the well-being of its workforce and relationships with the wider community. And there are many good examples internationally of organizations that commit to operating in a way consistent with these values while achieving outstanding business success.

Leadership

There is more discussion, debate, misunderstanding and simplistic thinking about leadership in organizations than any other topic in work and organizational psychology. That is because leadership is archetypal in human affairs and there is a strong need in society to find, appraise and follow leaders.

All of us are called upon at times to be leaders, and having a vision of the difference we want to make; being positive, confident, optimistic; building positive relationships; working across boundaries; taking time to reflect on strategy and processes; and having the courage to make the right decision and acting compassionately, are all skills that can be learned. Critically, so is acting with integrity, humility and honesty.

As in the case of the literature on stress, we have a good understanding of what makes for effective leadership. How then can leaders, in addition to what we have discussed already in this chapter, ensure that they are creating the conditions where the needs for relatedness, competence and autonomy are met? We proposed, as a starting point, the value of adopting a simple model of compassionate leadership (see Chapter 11) that invites us as leaders to model these core compassionate behaviours:

1 *Attending*: paying attention to those we lead and noticing their difficulties, challenges or suffering.
2 *Understanding*: understanding others' challenges or difficulties, ideally through a dialogue with them.
3 *Empathizing*: having an empathic response, a felt relation with their challenges, difficulties or distress.
4 *Helping*: taking intelligent (thoughtful and appropriate) action to work with, serve or help those they lead.

When we deploy such behaviours as leaders, we reinforce in followers a sense of relatedness, autonomy and competence.

And we can also draw on Yukl's sustained scholarship to identify core leadership behaviours that can help us to meet people's needs at work. They include:

- Helping those we lead to interpret the meaning of events. Effective leaders help their followers make sense of change, catastrophes, successes and the future.
- Creating alignment around strategies and objectives. Effective leaders clarify direction, strategy and the priorities for people's efforts.
- Nurturing commitment and optimism.
- Encouraging mutual trust and cooperation: effective leaders help to resolve conflicts quickly and fairly. They continuously build a strong sense of community and supportiveness that ensures people act cooperatively and supportively with colleagues.
- Creating a sense of collective identity: they encourage a strong and positive vision of the value of the team's work and a sense of pride in the efficacy of the group. And they make positive use of rituals, celebrations, humour and stories.
- Organizing and coordinating work efforts: they ensure that people are clear about their roles and contributions and help them work together in a coordinated way towards success. They deal with systems difficulties, resource shortages, work overload and coordination problems so that the team can be successful.
- Enabling collective learning: they ensure that followers engage in collective learning about errors, successes and means of ensuring continually improving quality. They ensure the group regularly takes time out to review objectives, strategies and processes so that they collectively learn and improve.
- Ensuring necessary resources are available: they ensure that the group or organization has the resources (money, staff, IT support, time) necessary for them to get the job done and work actively and tirelessly to ensure these resources are in place.

- Developing and empowering people: Ensuring that followers continue to learn, grow and develop; offering opportunities for challenging tasks; encouraging followers to have a sense of autonomy and control in the workplace; building a sense of shared leadership.
- Promoting social justice and morality: they emphasize fairness and honesty in their dealings with all, challenging unethical practices or social injustices on behalf of all, not only their followers.

Such leadership has a powerful influence on creating conditions within which people's core work needs for relatedness, competence and autonomy are effectively fulfilled.

PIONEERING WORK PSYCHOLOGISTS

Professor Ute Hülsheger

Ute Hülsheger is Professor of Occupational Health Psychology specializing in Work Stress and Individual Resources at the Department of Work and Social Psychology at Maastricht University, The Netherlands. She received her PhD in work and organizational psychology from Bielefeld University in 2006 and worked as a postdoctoral fellow at the Amsterdam Business School, University of Amsterdam, before joining Maastricht University in 2007.

Her research focuses on occupational health-related topics such as emotional labour and the role of mindfulness for employee health and well-being. Furthermore, she is interested in aspects of employee performance such as creativity and innovation and the role of cognitive abilities and personality in job performance. Her work on mindfulness in the workplace, for example, has shown how natural experiences of mindfulness can be promoted in the context of work. One breakthrough she has made is showing how daily fluctuations in workload and recovery experiences (such as psychological detachment and sleep quality) have an influence on subsequent mindfulness. She has shown that the relationship between mindfulness and recovery experiences is reciprocal rather than one way. Her research showed that sleep quality and workload were related to subsequent levels of mindfulness. Fatigue plays a key role in explaining these relationships. She has contributed to the literature on mindfulness and work by identifying what she calls gain spirals associated with recovery experiences and mindfulness. Her research is regularly featured in the top work psychology journals in the world.

Teams and teamworking

Humans have been working in teams for most of our evolutionary history and we now have a good understanding of how important teamwork is, not only for organizations to achieve their purpose, but for the well-being and growth and development of those who work within them. We have seen from the research evidence the importance of teams having a clear, shared understanding of purpose that encapsulates why and how team members need to work together. Ideally, this will be an inspiring vision of the value of the team's work to team members, the organization or the wider society. At the very least the purpose should be seen as significant and valued by team members. And the purpose should be translated into five or six clear, agreed, challenging and measurable objectives.

Teams need to meet regularly and have effective meetings. This means meetings that team members find valuable, energizing and positive. Such meetings are important for a wide variety of reasons, including reviewing progress; checking shared understanding; engaging everyone's knowledge, skills and experience; looking forward; and adjusting team members' ways of working to ensure success for the team. Good practice involves reviewing each meeting at the end to determine its value and how it could be improved.

Great teams have predominantly positive, supportive relationships; they are cohesive with a strong sense of 'psychological safety', enabling them to quickly and constructively work through conflict and to prevent intense or chronic conflicts. This implies that team members are compassionate towards each other – they listen, seek to understand, empathize with and help each other (backing each other up, for example, when the work is too heavy). Psychological safety is encouraged also by more inquiry in team member interactions than advocacy, seeking to understand rather than individuals pushing their own opinions or strategies.

Effective teamwork means ensuring that inter-team cooperation is high, with team members giving collective attention to how they can support the other teams they work with within the organization to ensure their success. And the most effective teams also overtly value diversity, whether diversity in the form of differences of opinion, professional background, demographic background or experience. As we have seen, such a climate leads to better team performance and higher levels of team innovation. And key to effective teamwork is teams regularly taking time out to review their performance and how to improve it. Indeed, meta-analytic evidence suggests that teams that do this are, on average, 38 per cent more productive (McDaniel, Salas, & Kazak, 2018).

Probably the most significant influence on team processes is team leadership. Task- and person-focused leadership both predict team performance, but the research evidence suggests that person-centred leadership has twice the effect of task-centred leadership (Van Knippenberg, 2017; Scott & Wildman, 2017). Leadership team coaching behaviours improve team self-management, team member relationship quality, team climate and team member satisfaction. Team leader displays of positive emotion predict the mood of followers, team cooperation and team performance. Empowering team leadership is also positively related to team performance (Van Knippenberg, 2017), especially relevant given increasing evidence of the effectiveness of shared team leadership, where all team members take responsibility for leadership, even when there is a designated hierarchical leader (Wang, Waldman, & Zhang, 2014). It is easy to see how such leadership promotes a sense of relatedness along with competence and autonomy or control.

Culture and climate

Studying organizations that we encounter every day is fascinating and can be fun. Rather than going in and out of them blind to their vivid colours, we can be alert to their hues, shades and unique pastels. This involves truly becoming a student of organizations – studying them as we experience them. Through maintaining awareness of organizational culture we can become experts at analyzing the nature of organizations, especially when we use the models described earlier in this book. Building such a capacity has an important value for society more generally because the more we understand the culture of organizations, the more we can discern those that promote human and environmental flourishing rather than contributing to degradation and damage. Organizations are part of the societies, communities and ecosystems within which they are located and have a responsibility to contribute to rather than detract from them, to protect the environment and to treat people equally and with dignity and respect. Work and organizational psychology is not and should never be a value-free discipline if we want to make a positive difference in the world. Encouraging cultures of social responsibility and 'outing' cultures of exploitation is part of the legitimate work of change agents in society. Work and organizational psychology should therefore focus on improving cultures and climates in organizations.

A good example is seeking to create cultures of compassion that aim to ensure that people at work flourish rather than languish and, as we have seen, this is also powerfully related to organizational effectiveness. Worline and Dutton (2017) have written extensively about creating cultures of compassion. In such cultures, leaders (and all who work within them) attend to others, noticing when people are having difficulty at work; recognizing time pressure, overload and performance demands that are excessive and seeking to help reduce the pressure; ensuring policies, rules, and norms of conduct are focused on learning in a climate of psychological safety, not oriented towards blame and punishment; seeing missed deadlines, errors or difficulties as most likely symptoms of organizational dysfunction rather than individual dysfunction; leadership with the default assumption that employees, staff and workers are generally good, capable and worthy of compassion; and a culture that values everyone being treated with respect, dignity and worth no matter what their role, position or difference.

To achieve such cultures requires presence and mindfulness among all leaders – indeed all in the organization. Encouraging leadership presence and self-awareness in order to recognize the challenges those in the organization face is a prerequisite. The implication is that all can develop empathic listening, the capacity to emotionally tune in to others' perspectives and experiences. This allows us to be present without necessarily needing to fix, solve or intervene. Such awareness and presence is a precondition to helping and supporting others in the workplace. Organizations must build in flexible time for addressing challenges, buffering people from the task overload endemic in many organizations; monitoring and checking in; and generating resources that will alleviate the stressors that damage so many people in modern work organizations. It also means addressing the corrosive politics, toxic interactions, or chronic underperformance and other forms of conflict at work that are sources of suffering that must be addressed They require 'fierce compassion'. And by constantly seeking to nurture such cultures, of course, the core human needs at work of competence, autonomy and relatedness are met.

An integrated, comprehensive set of tools for creating such cultures is available at improvement.nhs.uk/resources/culture-and-leadership/

SUMMARY AND CONCLUSION

Our reality is our interconnectedness. This has become more apparent over the past century than ever before. We are dependent on each other; on other species; on the ecosystem; and our actions affect others, other species and our planet. We face challenges on a huge scale (many of our making), including the need to reduce and reverse the effects of climate change; to reduce and reverse the effects of our species' role in wiping out so many other species; to prepare for and respond to global pandemics; to support and integrate people forced to migrate because of war, famine or rising sea levels; to foresee and ameliorate the effects of natural disasters; and to contain the potential threats posed by the commercial development of artificial superintelligence (Harari, 2015; Tegmark, 2014). Collaboration, team and inter-team working, and organization effectiveness are key to our ability to respond successfully to these challenges.

The role of compassion or kindness in our interactions with our fellow human beings, fellow workers in organizations, those we lead and those we provide services for (e.g., in healthcare, telecommunications, transport, retail, counselling) is fundamental to sustaining interconnection. And there is much evidence of the beneficial effects of empathy, forgiveness and caring upon well-being and resilience (Batson, Turk, Shaw, & Klein, 1995; Brown, Nesse, Vinokur, & Smith, 2003; Worthington & Scherer, 2004). Neglect, incivility, bullying and harassment have quite opposite effects (Porath & Pearson, 2009). And we have to learn to extend these orientations to the environment we are a part of.

Lawrence and Maitlis (2012) refer to an ethic of care in effective teams and organizations, which is more likely to occur in organizations *"that foster integration, nurture, trust and respect the emotional lives of members, and where members have the opportunity to become competent carers"* (p. 656). Helping leaders to develop compassionate ways of working will equip teams and organizations of the future to deal effectively with the challenges they face. When our focus is on understanding and helping others in service of a shared vision or cause, our collaboration and teamwork will be much more effective than when our focus is on meeting our own goals, regardless of the needs of others (and that applies to other species also).

Humans make up teams and organizations and we must see our species as more collaborative, compassionate and caring than is typically portrayed in management theory and research. Theory creates expectations and shapes behaviour (Ferraro, Pfeffer, & Sutton, 2005; Ghoshal, 2005) and we need theories that take account of our interconnectedness and that confirm the centrality of compassion in human societies, organizations and teams.

Our call to action to you the reader is for each of you to learn the skills of compassion (see, for example, Gilbert, 2010) in the way you work with others in order to create organizations of the future. Where organizations are founded on values and cultures of compassion, they will foster individual, team, inter-organizational, community and ecosystem interconnection characterized by justice, trust, thriving and well-being. Thereby we meet the human needs for relatedness, autonomy and competence at work. That is our challenge and our imperative. And for each of us who works to improve organizations, that is our call to action.

REFERENCES

Batson, C. D., Turk, C. L., Shaw, L. L., & Klein, T. R. (1995). Information function of empathic emotion: Learning that we value the other's welfare. *Journal of Personality and Social Psychology, 68,* 300–313.

Baumeister, R. F., & Leary, M. R. (1995). The need to belong: Desire for interpersonal attachments as a fundamental human motivation. *Psychological Bulletin, 117*(3), 497–529.

Berry, C. M., Cullen, M. J., & Meyer, J. M. (2014). Racial/ethnic subgroup differences in cognitive ability test range restriction: Implications for differential validity. *Journal of Applied Psychology, 99*(1), 21.

Brown, S. L., Nesse, R. M., Vinokur, A. D., & Smith, D. M. (2003). Providing social support may be more beneficial than receiving it results from a prospective study of mortality. *Psychological Science, 14,* 320–327.

Colella, A., Hebl, M., & King, E. (2017). One hundred years of discrimination research in the *Journal of Applied Psychology*: A sobering synopsis. *Journal of Applied Psychology, 102*(3), 500–513.

Ferraro, F., Pfeffer, J., & Sutton, R. I. (2005). Economics language and assumptions: How theories can become self-fulfilling. *Academy of Management Review, 30,* 8–24.

Ghoshal, S. (2005). Bad management theories are destroying good management practices. *Academy of Management Learning & Education, 4,* 75–91.

Gilbert, P. (2010). *The compassionate mind: A new approach to life's challenges.* Oakland CA: New Harbinger.

Graeber, D. (2019). *Bullshit jobs: The rise of pointless work and what we can do about it.* Harmondsworth, England: Penguin Random Books.

Harari, Y. N. (2015). *Sapiens: A brief history of humankind.* New York, NY: Harper.

Holt-Lunstad, J., Smith, T. B., Baker, M., Harris, T., & Stephenson, D. (2015). Loneliness and social isolation as risk factors for mortality: A meta-analytic review. *Perspectives on Psychological Science, 10*(2), 227–237.

Lawrence, T. B., & Maitlis, S. (2012). Care and possibility: Enacting an ethic of care through narrative practice. *Academy of Management Review, 37*(4), 641–663.

Levashina, J., Hartwell, C. J., Morgeson, F. P., & Campion, M. A. (2014). The structured employment interview: Narrative and quantitative review of the research literature. *Personnel Psychology, 67*(1), 241–293.

Li, W. D., Fay, D., Frese, M., Harms, P. D., & Gao, X. Y. (2014). Reciprocal relationship between proactive personality and work characteristics: A latent change score approach. *Journal of Applied Psychology, 99*(5), 948.

McDaniel, S. H., Salas, E., & Kazak, A. E. (Eds.) (2018). The science of teamwork. *American Psychologist, 73*(4), 305–600.

Peterson, C., & Seligman, M. E. (2004). *Character strengths and virtues: A handbook and classification* (Vol. 1). Oxford, England: Oxford University Press.

Porath, C., & Pearson, C. (2009). How toxic colleagues corrode performance. *Harvard Business Review, 32,* 1–135.

Pritchard, R. D., Harrell, M. M., DiazGranados, D., & Guzman, M. J. (2008). The productivity measurement and enhancement system: A meta-analysis. *Journal of Applied Psychology, 93*(3), 540–567.

Ritchie, S. J., & Tucker-Drob, E. M. (2018). How much does education improve intelligence? A meta-analysis. *Psychological science, 29*(8), 1358–1369.

Scott, C. P., & Wildman, J. L. (2017). Developing and managing teams. In E. Salas, R. Rico, & J. Passmore (Eds.), *The Wiley Blackwell handbook of the psychology of team working and collaborative processes* (pp. 503–529). Oxford, England: Wiley Blackwell.

Sonnentag, S., Mojza, E. J., Binnewies, C., & Scholl, A. (2008). Being engaged at work and detached at home: A week-level study on work engagement, psychological detachment, and affect. *Work & Stress, 22*(3), 257–276.

Stone, D. N., Deci, E. L., & Ryan, R. M. (2009). Beyond talk: Creating autonomous motivation through self-determination theory. *Journal of General Management, 34*(3), 75–91.

Tegmark, M. (2014). *Our mathematical universe: My quest for the ultimate nature of reality.* Harmondsworth, England: Penguin.

van Knippenberg, D. (2017). Team leadership. In E. Salas, R. Rico, & J. Passmore (Eds.), *The*

Wiley Blackwell handbook of the psychology of team working and collaborative processes (pp. 345–368). Oxford, England: Wiley Blackwell.

Wang, D., Waldman, D. A., & Zhang, Z. (2014). A meta-analysis of shared leadership and team effectiveness. *Journal of Applied Psychology, 99*(2), 181–198.

Wang, H. J., Lu, C. Q., & Siu, O. L. (2015). Job insecurity and job performance: The moderating role of organizational justice and the mediating role of work engagement. *Journal of Applied Psychology, 100*(4), 1249–1258.

West, M., Dawson, J., Admasachew, L., & Topakas, A. (2011). *NHS staff management and health service quality*. London, England: Department of Health.

Woods, S. A., Wille, B., Wu, C. H., Lievens, F., & De Fruyt, F. (2019). The influence of work on personality trait development: The Demands–Affordances TrAnsactional (DATA) model, an integrative review, and research agenda. *Journal of Vocational Behavior, 110*, 258–271.

Worline, M., & Dutton, J. E. (2017). *Awakening compassion at work: The quiet power that elevates people and organizations*. Oakland, CA: Berrett-Koehler.

Worthington, E. L., & Scherer, M. (2004). Forgiveness is an emotion-focused coping strategy that can reduce health risks and promote health resilience: Theory, review, and hypotheses. *Psychology & Health, 19*, 385–405.

CREDIT PAGES

All figures and boxes *not* listed on this credit page are the authors' own work and so do not require any credit lines, permissions acknowledgements or referencing citations.

Photo Credits

The following photographs have all been reproduced with permission of the copyright holders, and the credit lines are listed below:

p.xiv ©Steve Woods and Michael West
p.14 ©Eden King
p.20 ©iStockphoto.com/blaint
p.31 ©iStockphoto.com/BrianAJackson
p.37 ©iStockphoto.com/RomoloTavani
p.48 ©Sharon Parker
p.74 ©iStockphoto.com/JohnDWilliams
p.91 ©iStockphoto.com/DESKCUBE
p.92 ©iStockphoto.com/vladans
p.117 ©iStockphoto.com/Chainarong Prasertthai
p.122 ©iStockphoto.com/DragonImages
p.123 ©Evangelia Demerouti
p.139 ©iStockphoto.com SeanPavonePhoto
p.155 ©iStockphoto.com/PeopleImages
p.165 ©In-Sue Oh
p.174 ©iStockphoto.com/dorian2013
p.198 ©iStockphoto.com/Rawpixel
p.206 ©iStockphoto.com/monkeybusinessimages
p.209 ©Rebecca Jones
p.244 ©Elaine Pulakos
p.246 ©iStockphoto.com/NicoElNino
p.248 ©iStockphoto.com/EtiAmmos
p.260 ©iStockphoto.com/Daisy-Daisy
p.272 ©Bart Wille
p.281 ©iStockphoto.com/monkeybusinessimages
p.305 ©iStockphoto.com/michaeljung
p.312 ©Cary Cooper
p.334 ©iStockphoto.com RudyBalasko
p.351 ©iStockphoto.com/DaLiu
p.355 ©Yorelis Acosta
p.392 © 2016 GLOBE. All rights reserved.

p.395 ©Koldiana Lanaj
p.423 ©iStockphoto.com/Rawpixel
p.429 ©iStockphoto.com/NicoElNino
p.442 ©Dora C. Lau
p.462 ©iStockphoto.com/benjaminec
p.478 ©Binna Kandola
p.502 ©Ute Hülscheger

Figures, Tables and Boxes Credits

The following third-party figures, tables and boxes have been reproduced from the originals, with the kind permission from the copyright holders and the credit lines are reproduced below:

Figure 3.1 – Ajzen, I., & Fishbein, M. (1977). Attitude–behaviour relations: A theoretical analysis and review of empirical research. *Psychological Bulletin, 84*, 888–918.

Figure 6.6 – Gully, S., & Chen, G. (2009). Individual differences, attribute–treatment interactions, and training outcomes. In S. W. J. Kozlowski & E. Salas (Eds.), *Learning, training, and development in organization*s. New York, NY: Routledge.

BOX 7.1 – Coleman, V. I., & Borman, W. C. (2000). Investigating the underlying structure of the citizenship performance domain. *Human Resource Management Review, 10*, 25–44.

BOX 7.3 – Campion, M. A., Fink, A. A., Ruggeberg, B. J., Carr, L., Phillips, G. M., & Odman, R. B. (2011). Doing competencies well: Best practices in competency modeling. *Personnel Psychology, 64*(1), 225–262.

Figure 8.2 – Holland, J. L. (1973). Holland, J. L. (1994). *Self-directed search: Assessment booklet, a guide to educational and career planning.* Adapted and reproduced by special permission of the Publisher, Psychological Assessment Resources, Inc. (PAR), 16204 North Florida Avenue, Lutz, Florida 33549

Figure 9.1 – Khan, R. L., & Byosiere, P. (1992). Theoretical framework for the study of stress in organizations. In M. D. Dunnette & L. M. Hough (Eds.), *Handbook of industrial and organizational psychology* (2nd ed., pp. 571–650). Palo Alto, CA: Consulting Psychologists Press.

Figure 11.3 – Judge, T. A., Bono, J. E., Ilies, R., & Gerhardt, M. W. (2002). Personality and leadership: A qualitative and quantitative review. *Journal of Applied Psychology, 87*(4), 765–780.

Figure 11.13 – Dorfman, P., Hanges, P. J., & Brodbeck, F. C. (2004). Leadership and cultural variation: The identification of culturally endorsed leadership profiles. In R. J. House, P. J. Hanges, M. Javidan, P. Dorfman, & V. Gupta (Eds.), *Leadership, culture, and organizations: The Globe study of 62 societies* (pp. 669–719). Thousand Oaks, CA: SAGE.

Figure 11.14 – Chhokar, J. S., Brodbeck, F. C., & House, R. J. (2007). *Culture and leadership around the world: The GLOBE book of in-depth studies of 25 societies.* Mahwah, NJ: Lawrence Erlbaum.

Table 12.1 – West, M. A., Markiewicz, L., & Dawson, J. F. (2006). *Aston Team Performance Inventory: Management set*. London, England: ASE.

Table 12.4 – West, M. A., Markiewicz, L., & Dawson, J. F. (2006). *Aston Team Performance Inventory: Management set*. London, England: ASE.

Table 12.5 – West, M. A., Markiewicz, L., & Dawson, J. F. (2006). *Aston Team Performance Inventory: Management set*. London, England: ASE.

Figure 13.2 – © The Organizational Climate Measure (OCM) is copyright Aston Organization Development, 2.

The following figures and tables have all been adapted and changed from the original sources but below are citation references to the research, for referencing purposes:

Box 1.2 Women at Work – References: Adapted from research findings published in *The Economist* (2019). Bartleby – a small step for women, 9 March, p. 62.

Chapter 2 Discuss with a Colleague, Measuring the Five Big Trait – References: Adapted from Woods, S. A., & Hampson, W. E. (2005) Measuring the big five with single items using a bipolar response scale. *European Journal of Personality, 19*(5), 373–390.

Figure 2.3 – Fully adapted from Ackerman, P. L., & Heggestad, E. D. (1997). Intelligence, personality, and interests: Evidence for overlapping traits. *Psychological Bulletin, 121*(2), 219–245.

Figure 3.3 – Fully adapted from Meyer, J. P., & Allen, N. J. (1991). A three-component conceptualization of organizational commitment. *Human Resource Management Review, 1*, 61–89.

Figure 3.4 – Fully adapted from Ashkanasy, N. M., & Daus, C. S. (2002). Emotion in the workplace: The new challenge for managers. *Academy of Management Executive, 16*, 76–86.

Figure 3.6 – Fully adapted from: Guillaume, Y. R., Dawson, J. F., Priola, V., Sacramento, C. A., Woods, S. A., Higson, H. E., Budhwar, P. S., & West, M. A. (2013). Managing diversity in organizations: An integrative model and agenda for future research. *European Journal of Work and Organizational Psychology, 23*(5), 783–802.

Figure 4.3 – Fully adapted from Humphrey, S. E., Nahrgang, J. D., & Morgeson, F. P. (2007). Integrating motivational, social, and contextual work design features: A meta-analytic summary and theoretical extension of the work design literature. *Journal of Applied Psychology, 92*(5), 1332–1356.

Figure 6.4 – Loosely based on Anderson, J. R. (1996). ACT: A simple theory of complex cognition. *American Psychologist, 51*, 355–365.

Figure 7.1 – Fully adapted from Murphy, K. R., & Denisi, A. S. (2008). A model of the appraisal process. In P. S. Budhwar & A. S. Denisi (Eds.), *Performance management systems: A global perspective* (pp. 81–96). London, England: Routledge.

CREDIT PAGES

Figure 7.2 – Adapted from Locke, E. A., & Latham, G. P. (2002). Building a practically useful theory of goal setting and task motivation: A 35-year odyssey. *American Psychologist, 57*(9), 705–717.

Figure 8.1 – Fully adapted from Nicholson, N. (1990). *On the move: The psychology of change and transition*. Chichester, England: John Wiley & Sons.

Figure 8.3 – Adapted from Holland, J. L. (1973). *Making vocational choices: A theory of vocational personalities and environments*. Odessa, FL: Psychological Assessment Resources. Or: Holland, J. L. (1994). *Self-directed search: Assessment booklet, a guide to educational and career planning*. Odessa, FL: Psychological Assessment Resources.

Figure 8.4 – Adapted from Woods, S. A., & Hampson, S. E. (2010). Predicting adult occupational environments from gender and childhood personality traits. *Journal of Applied Psychology, 95*(6), 1045–1057.

Chapter 8 Key Theme Diversity – References: www.theguardian.com/education/2019/feb/04/black-female-professors-report

Chapter 8 Key Theme Digital Economy – References: www.theguardian.com/commentisfree/2019/feb/05/hermes-workers-rights-gig-economy-wages-holiday-pay-uber

Figure 9.2 – References: adapted from Falmer, S., Cooper, C., & Thomas, K. (2004). A model of work stress to underpin the Health & Safety Executive advice for tackling work-related stress and stress risk assessments. *Counselling at Work, Winter*, 2–5.

Figure 10.1 – Fully adapted from Ansoff, I. H. (1965). *Corporate strategy: An analytic approach to business policy for growth and expansion*. New York, NY: McGraw-Hill.

Figure 10.2 – Fully adapted from Porter, M. E. (1990). The competitive advantage of nations. *Harvard Business Review* (offprint). New York, NY: Free Press.

Figure 11.12 – Fully adapted from Judge, T. A., Piccolo, R. F., & Ilies, R. (2004). The forgotten ones? The validity of consideration and initiating structure in leadership research. *Journal of Applied Psychology, 89*, 36–51.

Chapter 12 Key Theme Digital technologies – References: www.inc.com/magazine/19970615/1409.html

Part One Case Study 1.1 – © Cengage Learning EMEA. Taken from Wärnich, S., Carrell, M. R., Elbert, N. F., & Hatfield, R. D. (2018). *Human resource management in South Africa* (6th ed., p. 185).

Part One Case Study 1.2 – References and further reading:

www.unilever.co.uk/about/who-we-are/introduction-to-unilever/

www.unilever.co.uk/about/who-we-are/our-vision/

www.unilever.co.uk/about/who-we-are/purpose-and-principles/

www.unilever.co.uk/about/who-we-are/our-strategy/

www.standard.co.uk/business/unilever-s-new-boss-alan-jope-warns-of-tough-market-ahead-as-sales-disappoint-a4054081.html

www.ft.com/content/95eec1ec-252b-11e9-8ce6-5db4543da632

www.unilever.co.uk/careers/graduates/diversity-and-inclusion.html

www.unilever.co.uk/about/who-we-are/diversity-and-inclusion/

www.unilever.com/sustainable-living/enhancing-livelihoods/opportunities-for-women/advancing-diversity-and-inclusion/

www.unilever.com/Images/unilever-gender-pay-report-2017-final_tcm244-514178_en.pdf

Part One Case Study 1.2 – Exhibit 1.2.1 References: www.unilever.co.uk/about/who-we-are/our-strategy/

Part Two Case Study 2.2 – References and further reading:

www.tesco-careers.com/ – search for graduates
www.marketingweek.com/2010/06/08/sir-terry-leahy-to-retire-in-tesco-board-overhaul/ – 'Sir Terry Leahy to retire in Tesco board overhaul' by Russell Parsons, 2010.

www.telegraph.co.uk/finance/newsbysector/retailandconsumer/9210998/Tesco-the-six-point-turnaround-plan.html – 'Tesco the six point turnaround plan' with Philip Clarke.

www.bbc.co.uk/news/magazine-23988795 – 'Tesco: How one supermarket came to dominate' by Denise Winterman, 2013.

www.managementtoday.co.uk/tesco-boss-philip-clarke-i-feel-bloody-great/article/1182981 – 'Tesco boss Philip Clarke: I feel Bloody Great' by Chris Blackhurst, 2013.

INDEX

ABB 488–9
ability testing 42, 153–4
Acosta, Yorelis 355
ACT (adaptive character of thought) model 192
action learning 402
active learning 211
adaptive character of thought (ACT) model 192
AET (affective events theory) 76–8
affect 75, 76
affective commitment 70, 279
affective component of attitudes 65
affective events theory (AET) 76–8
affective outcomes of learning 195
agreeableness 37, 271
    see also Big Five model of personality traits
AI (artificial intelligence) 11–12, 315–16
Alderfer ERG theory 104
analyzer organizations 363
Ansoff, Igor 338
applicant perspectives 168–70
application forms 152–3
applied psychology 3
appraisals 232–8
    team 431–2
artificial intelligence (AI) 11–12, 315–16
artistic personality type see RIASEC model
ASA (attraction–selection–attrition) model 148
assessment centres 160–3, 175
    leadership 378, 401
attending component of compassion 397, 398, 478–9
attitudes 61
    and behaviour 64–8, 493–4
    of groups and teams 72–3
    work-related 68–72
attraction–selection–attrition (ASA) model 148
attribution theories 80

BAME staff see Black, Asian and Minority Ethnic (BAME) staff/race; diversity and inclusion
Bandura, Albert 26, 27
Bayer AG 488

behaviour, organizational see organizational behaviour (OB)
behavioural consequences of stress 306–7
behavioural indicators of competency 229
behavioural interviews 159, 160
behavioural learning theories 63, 191–2
behavioural scales 235–6
behavioural theories of leadership 380–5
behaviourism 25, 62–4
Belbin's Team Roles Model 424
Big Five model of personality traits 28, 30, 200–1, 424
    criticism 156
    measurement 33–4
    work behaviour, performance and outcomes 35, 36
Binet–Simon intelligence scale 40
biodata 152–3
Black, Asian and Minority Ethnic (BAME) staff/race 12, 275, 493
    see also diversity and inclusion
Blake and Mouton's managerial grid 383–4
boundaryless career 277–8
bounded rationality perspectives on strategy 340–1
'brainstorming groups' 436
bravery 352
British Psychological Society and Division of Occupational Psychology 7
Burke–Litwin model of organizational change 471
burnout 307
    and job engagement 314–15
business process re-engineering 341

career management 279, 496–7
    counselling and advising 279–80
    diversity and inclusion 281
    employee development 280
    facilitating progress 282
    networking 281, 282
    preparation for transition 280
    strategies 282–3

careers
   21st century 256–7
   boundaryless 277–8
   cross-cultural perspective 276
   development stages 257–8
   and employability 278–9
   and gender 273–4
   job transition 261–2
   person–environment fit 263–71
   and racism 275
   retirement 262–3
   work identity 259
caring 353
Categorization Elaboration Model (CEM) 88–9
Centre for Creative Leadership (CCL) 378, 401
change
   organizational *see* organizational change
   orientation of leaders 385, 404
charismatic leadership 389–90
CJAM (combination job analysis method) 146
coaching
   executive 402–3
   team 443
   workplace 206–8
cognition
   metacognition 195, 200
   and motivation 107–14
cognitive ability *see* intelligence/cognitive ability
cognitive dissonance theory 65–6
cognitive learning 192, 195
cognitive perspectives on strategy 348
collective leadership 405
combination job analysis method (CJAM) 146
communal organizations 457
compassionate leadership/climate 397–9, 478–9
competencies
   leadership 377, 379–80
   managerial 231–2
competency analysis 145–6, 189
competency approach to performance measurement 228–32, 238
competency modelling 147
competency-based interviewing 159, 160
Competing Values model of organizational culture 458–9
conditioning and reinforcement 62–4
conflicts in teams 439–40
conformity 84–6

conscientiousness 50, 156, 200
   see also Big Five model of personality traits
conservation of resources model of stress 297–8
constructive controversy in teams 437–8
contingency theories of leadership 385–8
continuous organizational change 470
conventional personality type *see* RIASEC model
Cooper, Cary 312–13
core self-evaluations (CSE) 46–8
counselling and advising on careers 279–80
counterproductive work behaviours (CWB) 228
courage 352
creativity 352, 440
'crew resource management' (CRM) training 443
critical incident interviewing 146
critical scenario exercises 190
critical thinking (judgement) 352
cross-cultural perspectives 463
   careers 276
   leadership 392–5
crystallized ability (gc) 41, 42
CSE (core self-evaluations) 46–8
culture *see* cross-cultural perspectives; organizational culture
curiosity 352
curriculum vitae (CVs) 152–3
CWB (counterproductive work behaviours) 228

DATA (Demands-Affordances Transaction) model 39
debriefs 444
decision-making 81–3
   garbage can model of 340–1
   team-based working 419, 435–6
defender organizations 363
defensive leadership 378
defensive routines 473–4
Demands-Affordances Transaction (DATA) model 39
Demerouti, Evangelia 123
demonstrations 190
derailing of leadership 378
development
   career stages 257–8
   cycle 187–8
   employee 280
   leadership 399–403, 485–7
   teams 443–4
   see also learning, development and training
development centres 190

digital technologies
  attitudes 73–4
  careers 260
  e-learning 191
  internet recruitment 148–9
  motivation 122
  personality traits 30–1
  selection methods 151, 155
  and virtual teams 427–9
disabilities, people with 275, 430, 493
  see also diversity and inclusion
discrimination
  bias and prejudice 144, 170–1
  indirect (adverse impacts) 171–2, 173–5
diversity and inclusion 12–13, 88–90, 92, 493
  career management 281
  model of managing 90
  organizational culture 461–2
  performance management 247–8
  recruitment and selection 173–4
  teams 422–3
  training and development 205–6
  University of South West England (case study) 328–9
Drucker, Peter 340
Dupont 488
dyadic theories of leadership 388–9

e-learning 191
EAPs (employee assistance programmes) 312
EAWOP (European Association of Work and Organizational Psychology) 7
economic perspective on strategy 341–5
effort–reward imbalance model of stress 297–8
EI (emotional intelligence) 43, 299, 353
Eklund, Jonna 13–14
Elaboration Likelihood Model (ELM) 74
emergent organizational strategy 346–8
emotional influences on behaviour 75–8
emotional intelligence (EI) 43, 299, 353
emotional labour 76, 77, 304
emotional stability 201
  leadership 378
  see also Big Five model of personality traits
emotions
  negative 46–8
  positive 290–1
empathizing component of compassion 397, 398–9, 479

employability 278–9
employee assistance programmes (EAPs) 312
employee reactions to change 472–5
employment law and regulations 256
Enron 348–9
enterprising personality type see RIASEC model
environment and sustainability 9–10
  learning and development 198
  motivation 117
  organizational strategy 350–1
  performance management 246
  personality traits 37
  stress 305
episodic organizational change 470
equity theory and equation 114–15
error management 438
ethics 31, 469
ethnicity/race 12, 275, 493
  see also diversity and inclusion
European Association of Work and Organizational Psychology (EAWOP) 7
European companies, organizational structures and strategies (case study) 487–90
European Union (EU): work engagement study 2
executive coaching 402–3
expectancy theory 108–10
extraversion 201
  see also Big Five model of personality traits

fairness see justice
feedback 239–43
  multi-source 241–3, 400–1
'fight or flight' response 294–5
fluid ability (gf) 41, 42
forcefield analysis of change 447
forgiveness and mercy 353
fragmented organizations 457
Freud, Sigmund 24–5

g factor (general intelligence) 40
garbage can model of decision-making 340–1
gc (crystallized ability) 41, 42
gender see diversity and inclusion; women/gender
general adaptation syndrome 295
gf (fluid ability) 41, 42
Gilbreth, Lillian 5
Global Leadership and Organizational Behaviour Effectiveness (GLOBE) programme 392–5

globalization 141, 173, 256
    and national cultures 463
goal-orientation 201–2
goal-setting 110–14, 219–22
goal-striving 112–13
Goffee and Jones 456–7
Gore (W.L.) & Associates, UK 347
gratitude 354
'Great Eight' competencies 231
'group polarization' 436
groups
    attitudes 72–3
    behaviour 83–4
    tasks and discussions 162
'groupthink' 436
growth-oriented organizations 210–11
guided reflection 200

hardiness 299
Hawthorne studies 5–6
health
    occupational health and safety 291–4
    see also stress
helping component of compassion
    397, 399, 479
Herzberg's two-factor theory 104–5
Heuristic/Systemic Model (HSM) 74
high potential selection 166–7
high-performance work systems 246–7
Holland, John see RIASEC model
hope/optimism 299, 354
HSM (Heuristic/Systemic Model) 74
Hülsheger, Ute 502
humanity 353
humility 353
humour 354

inclusion 89–90, 92, 173–4, 493
    see also diversity and inclusion
indirect discrimination (adverse impacts)
    171–2, 173–5
individual differences 21, 492–3
    core self-evaluations (CSE) 46–8
    learning, development and training 199–202
    proactivity 47
    response to stress 298–300
    see also intelligence/cognitive ability;
        personality; personality traits
individualist–collectivist cultures 463

innovation
    and creativity in teams 440
    forms of organizing 364–5
    organizational strategy 336, 342, 344, 345
    see also organizational change
input–process–output (IPO) model see under teams
integration, differentiation and fragmentation model
    of organizational culture 459–60
intelligence/cognitive ability 39–45, 200
    ability testing 42
    definition of 39
    hierarchical model 41–2
    and multiple intelligences 42–3
    and personality 45–6
    Spearman's g factor 40
    structure 40–2
    at work 44–5
inter-team relationships 441–2
International Personality Item Pool (IPIP) 33, 50
internet recruitment 148–9
interpersonal perceptual shortcuts 80
interpersonal processes 438
interpersonal skills 378
interviewing 158–60
intuition 82–3
investigative personality type see RIASEC model
IPIP (International Personality Item Pool) 33, 50
IPO (input–process–output) model see under teams
item response theory (IRT) 52

job analysis 144–7, 188–9
job characteristics 119–21
job demands
    control and support model 296–7
    and resources model 121, 298
job description 145
job design 118–21
job engagement see work engagement
job performance see performance
job rotation 401–2
job satisfaction 68–9, 71–2, 466
job transition 261–2
Jones, Rebecca 209
judgement (critical thinking) 352
justice 115–16, 353, 468

Kandola, Binna 478
kindness 353
King, Eden 14

knowledge, skills, abilities and other characteristics (KSAOs) 145, 146, 152, 189, 190
knowledge, skills and abilities (KSAs) for teamworking 425, 426
knowledge and wisdom 352

laissez-faire leadership 383, 391
Lanaj, Klodiana 395–6
Lau, Dora C. 442
leader-member exchange model 389
leadership 500–2
    assessment centres 378, 401
    behavioural theories 380–5
    charismatic 389–90
    collective 405
    compassionate 397–9, 478–9
    competencies 377, 379–80
    contingency approach 385–8
    cross-cultural perspective 392–5
    definitions of 371–2
    derailing/failure 378
    development 399–403, 485–7
    dyadic theories 388–9
    effective 372–3, 374–6, 404
    and gender 274–5, 396–7
    laissez-faire 391
    and management 380–1
    motivation 376–7
    participative 386–7
    path–goal theory 387–8
    personality traits 168, 374–6, 378–9
    and race 275
    research 373–4
    selection 167–8
    situational 386
    team 441
    transactional 390–1
    transformational 389–92
Lean Manufacturing 341
learning
    action 402
    active 211
    cognitive 192, 195
    cycle 187–8
    e-learning 191
    love of 352
    social 26–7, 63
    theories 26–7, 63, 191–2

learning, development and training
    cycle 187–8
    diversity and inclusion 205–6
    environment and sustainability 198
    individual differences 199–202
    individual outcomes 194–5
    interventions 190–3
    mentoring 210
    needs assessment 188–9
    organizational climate 466
    organizational growth and resilience 210–11
    organizational needs and analysis 188
    organizational outcomes 203–4
    organizational strategy 186–7
    process and implementation 187–98
    success and failure 199–206
    techniques and methods 190–1
    training evaluation 193–7
    training transfer 202–3
    workplace coaching 206–8
    see also development
learning organizations 471–2
lectures 190
LGBT+ staff 275, 493
    see also diversity and inclusion
life events theory 298
locus of control 46, 299
loss aversion in decision-making 82

MBTI (Myers Briggs Type Inventory) 29–30
McClelland's theory of motivation 106, 376–7
management
    by objectives 340
    and leadership 380–1
'management gurus' 348–9
managerial competencies 231–2
managerial grid (Blake and Mouton) 383–4
managerial motivation 376–7
managerial selection 167–8
masculinity-femininity dimension of cultures 463
Maslow's hierarchy of needs 102–3
mentoring 210, 402
mercenary organizations 456–7
metacognition 195, 200
Myers Briggs Type Inventory (MBTI) 29–30
MI (multiple intelligences) 42–3
Michigan leadership studies 382–3
mindfulness 310–11, 381

modesty 353
money 64, 105
motivation 101–28, 494–5
   and cognition 107–14
   definitions of 102
   and goals 111
   and job design 118–21
   justice and equity perspective 114–16
   leadership and management 376–7
   and money 105
   self-determination theory 106–7
   strategies 124–6
   theories 102–5
   as trait 106
motivation-hygiene theory 104
multi trait, multi-method (MTMM) approach 150, 161
multi-source feedback 241–3, 400–1
multiple intelligences (MI) 42–3
Myers Briggs Type Inventory (MBTI) 29–30

Napp Pharmaceutical Holdings 349
National Institute of Industrial Psychology (NIIP) 6
need theories of motivation 102–5
negative emotional style 46–8
Néstle 489–90
networked organizations 456
networking 281, 282
neuroticism 47, 271
   see also Big Five model of personality traits
new technology see digital technologies
NHS
   Black, Asian and Minority Ethnic (BAME) staff 12
   RIASEC model of personality 271
   staff attitudes and performance 493
   strategy and structure 365–6
   stress 307
NIIP (National Institute of Industrial Psychology) 6

OB see organizational behaviour
obedience to authority 86–7
observe, record, classify, evaluate (ORCE) method of assessment 162
OCB see organizational citizenship behaviours
occupational health psychology (OHP) 292
occupational health and safety 291–4
Oh, In-Sue 165
Ohio leadership studies 382
OHP (occupational health psychology) 292
open-mindedness 232, 352

openness to experience 200–1
   see also Big Five model of personality traits
optimism/hope 299, 354
ORCE (observe, record, classify, evaluate) method of assessment 162
organic organizations 361
organization
   definition of 336
   new forms of 364–5
organizational behaviour (OB)
   and attitudes 64–8, 493–4
   change 74–5
   definition of 62
   and emotions 75–8
   modification 62–4
   perception and 79–83
   social influences 83–90
organizational change 468–77
   Burke–Litwin model 471
   designing and implementing 476–7
   domains 469–70
   employee resistance to 472–5
   episodic and continuous 470
   factors causing 468–9
   forcefield analysis of 447
   learning organization 471–2
   systems perspective 470–1
organizational citizenship behaviours (OCB) 226–7
   vs task performance 225–8
organizational climate 463–8
   dimensions 464
   justice 468
   and organizational culture 465, 504
   safety 467, 497
   service 467
   for success 465–7
   for teamwork 431, 466
organizational commitment 69–72
organizational culture 454–63
   competing values model 458–9
   definition of 456
   development 460
   dimensions 455
   diversity and inclusion 461–2
   globalization and national cultures 463
   integration, differentiation and fragmentation model 459–60
   and organizational climate 465, 504

sociability vs solidarity 456–7
    for teamworking 431
organizational needs and analysis 188
organizational regulation 353
organizational restructuring 257
organizational strategy 336–7
    bounded rationality perspectives 340–1
    cognitive perspectives 348
    definition of 337
    economic perspective 341–5
    emergent 346–8
    environment and sustainability 350–1
    history of strategic management 337–9
    integrating values 352–4
    learning, training and development 186–7
    management by objectives 340
    as practice 351
    resource-based view 345–6
    as revolution 348–9
    and structure 362–6, 499–500
organizational structure 356–62
    company examples 487–9
    and strategy 362–6, 499–500
    team-based 361–2, 430
outdoor pursuits programmes 403

Parker, Sharon K. 48
participation in teams 435–6
participative leadership 386–7
path–goal theory of leadership 387–8
Pavlov, Ivan 63
perception and decision-making 79–83
performance
    core self-evaluations (CSE) 46–7
    feedback 239–43
    goal-setting 110–13, 219–22
    improvement 240–1, 242–3
    and job satisfaction 71–2
    proactive personality 47
    and strain relationship 306–7
performance management 218–19, 496
    conditions for positive change 222–3
    critical perspectives 243
    models 245–9
performance measurement 223–38
    appraisal 232–8
    behavioural scales 235–6
    competency approach 228–32, 238

    general models 225
    objectives 224
    rating scales 233–6
    reliability 237–8
    results-based 236
    task performance vs organizational citizenship behaviours (OCB) 225–8
performance review systems 431–2
Periodic Table of Personality Traits (Woods and Anderson) 31–2
perseverance 353
person–environment fit 263–71, 296
personal initiative 47
personality 23
    assessment for selection 155–8
    and intelligence 45–6
    measurement 33–4, 48–52
    in teams 423–4
    theories 23–5
    Type A 299–300
    work influences 38–9, 53
personality traits 25–6
    leadership 168, 374–6, 378–9
    McClelland's theory of motivation 106, 376–7
    and RIASEC model 269–71
    structure and models 27–32
    and wider work criteria 36–7
    work behaviour, performance and outcomes 35
    see also Big Five model of personality traits
PETRONAS, leadership development at (case study) 485–7
physiological consequences of stress 307
planned behaviour theory 66–8
Porter, Michael 341–5
positive emotion 290–1
positive organizational scholarship 7–9
positive work strategies 313–14, 317–18
power distance 463
proactive personality 47
Productivity Measurement and Enhancement System (ProMES) 246
professional associations 7
project management competencies 230
ProMES 246
Prospector organization 362–3
prudence 353
psychoanalysis 24–5
psychological consequences of stress 307

psychological ownership 121
psychometric paradigm 168–9
psychometric tests 48–52, 153, 154, 175, 189
Pulakos, Elaine D. 244

race/BAME staff 12, 275, 493
   see also diversity and inclusion
rating scales 233–6
rational planning model 338
reactor organizations 363
realistic job previews (RJPs) 148
realistic personality type *see* RIASEC model
reasoned action theory 66–8
recruitment and selection 141–5, 165–70, 495–6
   attracting applicants 147–9
   see also selection
reflexivity 434–5
reinforcement 62–4
relations orientation of leaders 382–3, 384, 385, 386, 404
religiousness and spirituality 354
repertory grid 146
research & development (R&D) 338, 360, 468–9
resilient organizations 210–11
resistance to change 472–5
resource-based view (RBV) of strategy 345–6
results-based appraisal 236
retirement 262–3
reward systems 432
RIASEC model 264–70
   and personality traits 269–71
RJPs (realistic job previews) 148
Roberson, Quinetta 91
role stress theory 295–6
role-play 162, 190

safety
   occupational health and 291–4
   organizational climate 467, 497
Schein's career anchors 268–9
scientific management 5
selection 144
   adverse impacts (indirect discrimination) 171–2, 173–5
   assessment centres 160–3, 175
   assessment methods 152–63
   best practice 163–4
   bias and prejudice 144, 170–1
   diversity and inclusion 173–4
   fairness 170–6
   interviewing 158–60
   legal concerns 174–5
   managerial and leadership 167–8
   professional standards 175
   reliability and validity 149–52
   talent and high potential 166–7
   see also recruitment and selection
self-determination theory 106–7
self-efficacy 27, 46, 47
self-esteem 46
self-regulation 78–9, 113–14
self-resources 78–9
service climate 467
shiftwork 318
Simon, Herbert A. 340
Simon, Theodore 40
simulations 190
situational interviews 159, 160
situational judgement tests (SJTs) 158
situational leadership theory 386
sleep and shiftwork 318
sociability vs solidarity 456–7
social desirability in personality testing 157
social identity 87–8
social intelligence *see* emotional intelligence (EI)
social learning 26–7, 63
social loafing 84, 436
social personality type *see* RIASEC model
social support networks 311, 317
Society of Industrial and Organizational Psychology (SIOP) 7
sociotechnical systems approach 119
Spearman's *g* factor 40
StatoilHydro 490
stress 497–8
   consequences of 306–7
   cost of 294
   definition of 294–5
   effort–reward imbalance model 297–8
   emotional intelligence and optimism 299
   environment and sustainability 305
   hardiness 299
   job demands, control and support model 296–7
   locus of control 299
   person–environment fit 296
   role stress theory 295–6
   stressor–strain relationship 300–2, 303–5, 306–7

transactional model 297
Type A personality 299–300
stress reduction and management 498
   artificial intelligence (AI) 315–16
   job engagement 314–15
   positive work strategies 313–14, 317–18
   primary interventions 308–9
   secondary interventions 309–12
   tertiary interventions 312
Super's career development theory 257–8
sustainability *see* environment and sustainability
Switch Appliances (case study) 133–4
systems perspective, organizational change 470–1

talent selection 166–7
task orientation of leaders 232, 383, 384, 385, 386, 404
task performance vs organizational citizenship behaviours (OCB) 225–8
TAT *see* Thematic Apperception Test; Trait Activation Theory
Taylorism 5
team-building 443–4
teams 503
   appraisal 431–2
   attitudes 72–3
   composition 422
   conflicts 439–40
   constructive controversy 437–8
   creativity and innovation 440
   debriefs 444
   decision-making 419, 435–6
   definitions of 414–15
   development 443–4
   digital technologies and virtual teams 427–9
   diversity and inclusion 422–3
   effective 429–30
   error management 438
   input–process–output (IPO) model 419–20
   inputs 421–32
   inter-team relationships 442
   interpersonal processes 438
   leadership 441
   measure for selection 426–7
   objectives 434
   outputs 441–4
   participation 435–6
   performance review systems 431–2
   personality and ability 423–4
   processes 432–41
   'real' vs 'pseudo' 415
   reflexivity 434–5
   reward systems 432
   size 423
   task focus 437
   tasks 417, 421
   top management teams (TMTs) 391–2
   types 416–17
teamwork
   benefits 418–19
   components 415
   organizational climate 431, 466
   organizational culture 431
   organizational structure 361–2, 430
   organizational supports 430–2
   skills 424–6
Tesco Plc (case study) 329–33
Thematic Apperception Test (TAT) 106
360-degree assessment 242–3
top management teams (TMTs) 391–2
Total Quality Management 341
training
   evaluation 193–7
   organizational climate 466
   transfer 202–3
   see also learning, development and training
Trait Activation Theory (TAT) 35, 222
transactional leadership 390–1
transactional memory systems 443
transactional model of stress 297
transformational leadership 389–92
26-facet personality trait model (Woods and Anderson) 32
Type A personality 299–300

uncertainty avoidant cultures 463
understanding component of compassion 397, 398, 479
Unilever (case studies) 134–8, 489
universal leadership concepts 394
University of South West England (case study) 328–9
utility analyses 152

valence, instrumentality and expectancy (VIE) model 108, 109

values
- competing 458–9
- integrating 352–4

virtual teams 427–9

vocational interests *see* RIASEC model

Wechsler Adult Intelligence Scale (WAIS) 42

Wille, Bart 272

wisdom and knowledge 352

women/gender
- and careers 273–4
- dimension of national cultures 463
- equality 12–13
- and leadership 274–5, 396–7

wonder and gratitude 354

Woods and Anderson
- 26-facet personality trait model 32
- 'Periodic Table of Personality Traits' 31–2

word-of-mouth recruitment 149

work adjustment theory 39, 223

work engagement 2, 121
- burnout and 314–15
- W.L. Gore & Associates, UK 347

work identity 259

work and organizational psychology 3
- brief history 5–6
- contemporary themes 9–14
- definition and summary 4
- modern 6–7
- positive organizational scholarship 7–9
- professional associations 7

work stress *see* stress

workplace coaching 206–8

workplace diversity *see* diversity and inclusion

Yukl, Gary 371–2, 378–9, 380, 385, 404, 501–2